WICKED

&

SON
of a
WITCH

Two Complete Novels

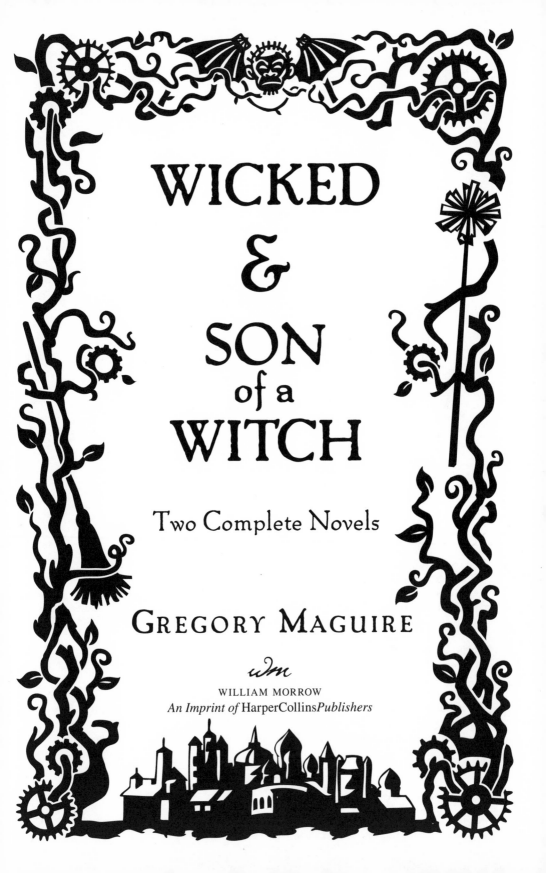

WICKED
&
SON
of a
WITCH

Two Complete Novels

GREGORY MAGUIRE

wm

WILLIAM MORROW
An Imprint of HarperCollins*Publishers*

HarperCollins Publishers
195 Broadway
New York, NY 10007

For information, address HarperCollins Publishers, 195 Broadway, New York, NY 10007.
HarperCollins books may be purchased for educational, business, or sales promotional use.
For information, please e-mail the Special Markets Department at SPsales@harpercollins.com

ISBN-13: 9781435110304

16   17   18   SCP   10   9

GREGORY MAGUIRE is the bestselling author of *Confessions of an Ugly Stepsister,* *Lost, Mirror Mirror,* and the Wicked Years, a series that includes *Wicked, Son of a Witch,* and *A Lion Among Men. Wicked* is the basis for the Tony Award–winning Broadway musical of the same name. Maguire has lectured on art, literature, and culture both at home and abroad. He lives with his family near Boston, Massachusetts.

WICKED

The Life and Times of the Wicked Witch of the West

WICKED

The Life and Times of the Wicked Witch of the West

A NOVEL

GREGORY MAGUIRE

ILLUSTRATIONS BY DOUGLAS SMITH

WILLIAM MORROW
An Imprint of HarperCollins*Publishers*

*This book is for Betty Levin and for all those who
taught me to love and fear goodness.*

✵

*Thanks to those who read this book early:
Moses Cardona, Rafique Keshavjee, Betty Levin, and
William Reiss. Their advice was always helpful.
Any imperfections that remain in the book are mine.*

*I should also like to thank Judith Regan,
Matt Roshkow, David Groff, and Pamela Goddard for
their enthusiastic reception of* Wicked.

*Finally, a word of gratitude to the friends with whom I
nattered on about evil over the past couple of years: They are
too numerous to be named in their entirety, but
they include Linda Cavanagh, Debbie Kirsch, Roger and
Martha Mock, Katie O'Brien, and Maureen Vecchione; the
gang in Edgartown, Massachusetts; and my brother,
Joseph Maguire, a few of whose ideas I have borrowed.
Please don't sue me.*

✵

CONTENTS

I Munchkinlanders

II Gillikin

III City of Emeralds

IV In the Vinkus

V The Murder and Its Afterlife

*'Tis very strange Men should be so fond
of being thought wickeder than they are.*

—DANIEL DEFOE, *A SYSTEM OF MAGICK*

*In historical events great men—so called—are but the
labels that serve to give a name to an event, and like
labels, they have the last possible connection with the
event itself. Every action of theirs, that seems to them
an act of their own free will, is in an historical sense
not free at all, but in bondage to the whole course of
previous history, and predestined from all eternity.*

—LEO NIKOLAEVICH TOLSTOI, *WAR AND PEACE*

*"Well," said the Head, "I will give you my answer.
You have no right to expect me to send you back to
Kansas unless you do something for me in return.
In this country everyone must pay for everything he
gets. If you wish me to use my magic power to send you
home again you must do something for me first.
Help me and I will help you."
"What must I do?" asked the girl.
"Kill the wicked Witch of the West," answered Oz.*

—L. FRANK BAUM, *THE WONDERFUL WIZARD OF OZ*

PROLOGUE

On the Yellow Brick Road

A mile above Oz, the Witch balanced on the wind's forward edge, as if she were a green fleck of the land itself, flung up and sent wheeling away by the turbulent air. White and purple summer thunderheads mounded around her. Below, the Yellow Brick Road looped back on itself, like a relaxed noose. Though winter storms and the crowbars of agitators had torn up the road, still it led, relentlessly, to the Emerald City. The Witch could see the companions trudging along, maneuvering around the buckled sections, skirting trenches, skipping when the way was clear. They seemed oblivious of their fate. But it was not up to the Witch to enlighten them.

She used the broom as a sort of balustrade, stepping down from the sky like one of her flying monkeys. She finished up on the topmost bough of a black willow tree. Beneath, hidden by the fronds, her prey had paused to take their rest. The Witch tucked her broom under her arm. Crablike and quiet, she scuttled down a little at a time, until she was a mere twenty feet above them. Wind moved the dangling tendrils of the tree. The Witch stared and listened.

There were four of them. She could see a huge Cat of some sort—a Lion, was it?—and a shiny woodman. The Tin Woodman was picking nits out of the Lion's mane, and the Lion was muttering and squirming from the aggravation. An animated Scarecrow lolled nearby, blowing dandelion heads into the wind. The girl was out of sight behind shifting curtains of the willow.

"Of course, to hear them tell it, it is the surviving sister who is the crazy one," said the Lion. "What a Witch. Psychologically warped; possessed by demons. Insane. Not a pretty picture."

"She was castrated at birth," replied the Tin Woodman calmly. "She was born hermaphroditic, or maybe entirely male."

"Oh you, you see castration everywhere you look," said the Lion.

"I'm only repeating what folks say," said the Tin Woodman.

"Everyone is entitled to an opinion," said the Lion airily. "She was deprived of a mother's love, is how I've heard it. She was an abused child. She was addicted to medicine for her skin condition."

"She has been unlucky in love," said the Tin Woodman, "like the rest of us." The Tin Woodman paused and placed his hand on the center of his chest, as if in grief.

"She's a woman who prefers the company of other women," said the Scarecrow, sitting up.

"She's the spurned lover of a married man."

"She *is* a married man."

The Witch was so stunned that she nearly lost her grip on the branch. The last thing she ever cared for was gossip. Yet she had been out of touch for so long that she was astonished at the vigorous opinions of these random nobodies.

"She's a despot. A dangerous tyrant," said the Lion with conviction.

The Tin Woodman pulled harder than was necessary on a lock of mane. "Everything's dangerous to you, you craven thing. I hear she's a champion of home rule for the so-called Winkies."

"Whoever she is, she must surely be grieving the death of her sister," said the child, in a somber voice too rich, too sincere for one so young. The Witch's skin crawled.

"Don't go feeling sympathetic now. *I* certainly can't." The Tin Woodman sniffed, a bit cynically.

"But Dorothy's right," said the Scarecrow. "No one is exempt from grief."

The Witch was deeply irked by their patronizing speculations. She moved around the trunk of the tree, stretching to catch a glimpse of the child. The wind was picking up, and the Scarecrow shivered. While the Tin Woodman continued fussing over the Lion's tresses, he leaned against the Lion, who held him tenderly. "Storm on the horizon," said the Scarecrow.

Miles off, thunder echoed. "There—is—a—*Witch* on the horizon," said the Tin Woodman, tickling the Lion. The Lion got spooked and rolled on top of the Scarecrow, whimpering, and the Tin Woodman collapsed on top of them both.

"Good friends, should we be wary of that storm?" said the girl.

The rising winds moved the curtain of greenery at last, and the Witch caught sight of the girl. She was sitting with her feet tucked underneath her and her arms wrapped around her knees. She was not a dainty thing but a good-size farm girl, dressed in blue-and-white checks and a pinafore. In her lap, a vile little dog cowered and whined.

"The storm makes you skittish. It's natural after what you've been through," said the Tin Woodman. "Relax."

The Witch's fingers dug into the bark of the tree. She still could not see the girl's face, just her strong forearms and the crown of her head where her dark hair was pulled back into pigtails. Was she to be taken seriously, or was she merely a blow-away dandelion seed, caught on the wrong side of the wind? If she could see the girl's face, the Witch felt she might know.

But as the Witch craned outward from the trunk, the girl at the same time twisted her face, turning away. "That storm is coming closer, and in a hurry." The feeling in her voice rose as the wind rose. She had a throaty vehemence, like someone arguing through the threat of impending tears. "I know storms, I know how they come upon you!"

"We're safer here," said the Tin Woodman.

"Certainly we are not," answered the girl, "because this tree is the highest point around, and if lightning is to strike, it will strike here." She clutched her dog. "Didn't we see a shed farther up the road? Come, come; Scarecrow, if there's lightning, you'll burn the fastest! Come on!"

She was up and running in an ungainly way, and her companions followed in a mounting panic. As the first hard drops of rain fell, the Witch caught sight, not of the girl's face, but of the shoes. Her sister's shoes. They sparkled even in the darkening afternoon. They sparkled like yellow diamonds, and embers of blood, and thorny stars.

If she had seen the shoes first, the Witch would never have been able to listen to the girl or her friends. But the girl's legs had been tucked beneath her skirt. Now the Witch was reminded of her need. The shoes should be hers!—hadn't she endured enough, hadn't she *earned* them? The Witch would fall on the girl from the sky, and wrestle those shoes off her impertinent feet, if only she could.

But the storm from which the companions raced, farther and faster along the Yellow Brick Road, troubled the Witch more than it did the girl who had gone through rain and the Scarecrow whom lightning could burn. The Witch could not venture out in such a vicious, insinuating wetness. Instead, she had to tuck herself between some exposed roots of the black willow tree, where no water could endanger her, and wait for the storm to pass.

She would emerge. She always had before. The punishing political climate of Oz had beat her down, dried her up, tossed her away—like a seedling she had drifted, apparently too desiccated ever to take root. But surely the curse was on the land of Oz, not on her. Though Oz had given her a twisted life, hadn't it also made her capable?

No matter that the companions had hurried away. The Witch could wait. They would meet again.

I

Munchkinlanders

The Root
of Evil

From the crumpled bed the wife said, "I think today's the day. Look how low I've gone."

"Today? That would be like you, perverse and inconvenient," said her husband, teasing her, standing at the doorway and looking outward, over the lake, the fields, the forested slopes beyond. He could just make out the chimneys of Rush Margins, breakfast fires smoking. "The worst possible moment for my ministry. Naturally."

The wife yawned. "There's not a lot of choice involved. From what I hear. Your body gets this big and it takes over—if you can't accommodate it, sweetheart, you just get out of its way. It's on a track of its own and nothing stops it *now*." She pushed herself up, trying to see over the rise of her belly. "I feel like a hostage to myself. Or to the baby."

"Exert some self-control." He came to her side and helped her sit up. "Think of it as a spiritual exercise. Custody of the senses. Bodily as well as ethical continence."

"Self-control?" She laughed, inching toward the edge of the bed. "I have no *self* left. I'm only a host for the parasite. Where's my *self*, anyway? Where'd I leave that tired old thing?"

"Think of me." His tone had changed; he meant this.

"Frex"—she headed him off—"when the volcano's ready there's no priest in the world can pray it quiet."

"What will my fellow ministers think?"

"They'll get together and say, 'Brother Frexspar, did you allow your wife to deliver your first child when you had a community problem to solve? How inconsiderate of you; it shows a lack of authority. You're fired from the position.'" She was ribbing him now, for there was no one to fire him. The nearest bishop was too distant to pay attention to the particulars of a unionist cleric in the hinterland.

"It's just such terrible *timing*."

"I do think you bear half the blame for the timing," she said. "I mean, after all, Frex."

"That's how the thinking goes, but I wonder."

"You *wonder*?" She laughed, her head going far back. The line from her ear to the hollow below her throat reminded Frex of an elegant silver ladle. Even in morning disarray, with a belly like a scow, she was majestically good-looking. Her hair had the bright lacquered look of wet fallen oak leaves in sunlight. He blamed her for being born to privilege and admired her efforts to overcome it—and all the while he loved her, too.

"You mean you wonder if you're the father"—she grabbed the bedstead; Frex took hold of her other arm and hauled her half-upright—"or do you question the fatherliness of men in general?" She stood, mammoth, an ambulatory island. Moving out the door at a slug's pace, she laughed at such an idea. He could hear her laughing from the outhouse even as he began to dress for the day's battle.

Frex combed his beard and oiled his scalp. He fastened a clasp of bone and rawhide at the nape of his neck, to keep the hair out of his face, because his expressions today had to be readable from a distance: There could be no fuzziness to his meaning. He applied some coal dust to darken his eyebrows, a smear of red wax on his flat cheeks. He shaded his lips. A handsome priest attracted more penitents than a homely one.

In the kitchen yard Melena floated gently, not with the normal gravity of pregnancy but as if inflated, a huge balloon trailing its strings through the dirt. She carried a skillet in one hand and a few eggs and the whiskery tips of autumn chives in the other. She sang to herself, but only in short phrases. Frex wasn't meant to hear her.

His sober gown buttoned tight to the collar, his sandals strapped on over leggings, Frex took from its hiding place—beneath a chest of drawers—the report sent to him from his fellow minister over in the village of Three Dead Trees. He hid the brown pages within his sash. He had been keeping them from his wife, afraid that she would want to come along—to see the fun, if it was amusing, or to suffer the thrill of it if it was terrifying.

As Frex breathed deeply, readying his lungs for a day of oratory, Melena dangled a wooden spoon in the skillet and stirred the eggs. The tinkle of cowbells sounded across the lake. She did not listen; or she listened but to something else, to something inside her. It was sound without melody—like dream music, remembered for its effect but not for its harmonic distresses and recoveries. She imagined it was the child inside her, humming for happiness. She knew he would be a singing child.

Melena heard Frex inside, beginning to extemporize, warming up, calling forth the rolling phrases of his argument, convincing himself again of his righteousness.

How did that proverb go, the one that Nanny singsonged to her, years ago, in the nursery?

> Born in the morning,
> Woe without warning;
> Afternoon child
> Woeful and wild;
> Born in the evening,
> Woe ends in grieving.
> Night baby borning
> Same as the morning.

But she remembered this as a joke, fondly. Woe is the natural end of life, yet we go on having babies.

No, said Nanny, an echo in Melena's mind (and editorializing as usual): No, no, you pretty little pampered hussy. We *don't* go on having babies, that's quite apparent. We only have babies when we're young enough not to know how grim life turns out. Once we really get the full measure of it—we're slow learners, we women—we dry up in disgust and sensibly halt production.

But men don't dry up, Melena objected; they can father to the death.

Ah, we're slow learners, Nanny countered. But *they* can't learn at all.

"Breakfast," said Melena, spooning eggs onto a wooden plate. Her son would not be as dull as most men. She would raise him up to defy the onward progress of woe.

"It is a time of crisis for our society," recited Frex. For a man who condemned worldly pleasures he ate with elegance. She loved to watch the arabesque of fingers and two forks. She suspected that beneath his righteous asceticism he possessed a hidden longing for the easy life.

"Every day is a great crisis for our society." She was being flip, answering him in the terms men use. Dear thick thing, he didn't hear the irony in her voice.

"We stand at a crossroads. Idolatry looms. Traditional values in jeopardy. Truth under siege and virtue abandoned."

He wasn't talking to her so much as practicing his tirade against the coming spectacle of violence and magic. There was a side to Frex that verged on despair; unlike most men, he was able to channel it to benefit his life's work. With some difficulty she set herself down on a bench. Whole choruses were singing wordlessly inside her head! Was this common for every labor and delivery? She would have liked to ask the nosy local women who would come around this afternoon, growling shyly at her condition. But she didn't dare. She couldn't jettison her pretty accent, which they found affected—but she could avoid sounding ignorant about these basic matters.

Frex noticed her silence. "You're not angry I'm leaving you today?"

"Angry?" She raised her eyebrows, as if she had never encountered the concept before.

"History crawls along on the peg legs of small individual lives," said Frex, "and at the same time larger eternal forces converge. You can't attend to both arenas at once."

"Our child may not have a small life."

"Now isn't the time to argue. Do you want to distract me from holy work today? We're facing the presence of real evil in Rush Margins. I couldn't live with myself if I ignored it." He meant this, and for such intensity she had fallen in love with him; but she hated him for it too, of course.

"Threats come—they'll come again." Her last word on the subject. "Your son will only be born once, and if this watery upheaval inside is any indication, I think it's today."

"There will be other children."

She turned away so he could not see the rage in her face.

But she couldn't sustain the fury at him. Perhaps this was her moral failing. (She wasn't much given to worrying about moral failings as a rule; having a minister as a husband seemed to stir enough religious thought for one couple.) She lapsed sullenly into silence. Frex nibbled at his meal.

"It's the devil," said Frex, sighing. "The devil is coming."

"Don't say a thing like that on a day our child is expected!"

"I mean the temptation in Rush Margins! And you know what I mean, Melena!"

"Words are words, and what's said is said!" she answered. "I don't require all your attention, Frex, but I do need some of it!" She dropped the skillet with a crash on the bench that stood against the cottage wall.

"Well, and likewise," he said. "What do you think I'm up against today? How can I convince my flock to turn away from the razzle-dazzle spectacle of idolatry? I will probably come back tonight having lost to a smarter attraction. You might achieve a child today. I look forward to failure." Still, as he said this he looked proud; to fail in the cause of a high moral concern was satisfying to him. How could it compare with the flesh, blood, mess, and noise of having a baby?

He stood at last to leave. A wind came up over the lake now, smudging the topmost reaches of the columns of kitchen smoke. They looked, thought Melena, like funnels of water swirling down drains in narrowing, focusing spirals.

"Be well, my love," said Frex, although he had his stern public expression on, from forehead to toes.

"Yes." Melena sighed. The child punched her, deep down, and she had to hurry to the outhouse again. "Be holy, and I'll be thinking of you—my backbone, my breastplate. And also try not to be killed."

"The will of the Unnamed God," said Frex.

"My will too," she said, blasphemously.

"Apply your will to that which deserves it," he answered. Now he was the minister and she the sinner, an arrangement she did not particularly enjoy.

"Good-bye," she said, and chose the stink and relief of the outhouse over standing to wave him out of sight as he strode along the road to Rush Margins.

The Clock of the Time Dragon

Frex was more concerned for Melena than she knew. He stopped at the first fisherman's hut he saw and spoke with the man at the half-door. Could a woman or two spend the day and if needed the night with Melena? It would be a kindness. Frex nodded with a wince of gratitude, acknowledging without words that Melena was not a great favorite in these parts.

Then, before continuing around the end of Illswater and over to Rush Margins, he stopped at a fallen tree and drew two letters from his sash.

The writer was a distant cousin of Frex's, also a minister. Weeks earlier the cousin had spent time and valuable ink on a description of what was being called the Clock of the Time Dragon. Frex prepared himself for the day's holy campaign by rereading about the idol clock.

I write in haste, Brother Frexspar, to catch my impressions before they fade.

The Clock of the Time Dragon is mounted on a wagon and stands as high as a giraffe. It is nothing more than a tottering, free-standing theatre, punched on all four sides with alcoves and proscenium arches. On the flat roof is a clockwork dragon, an invention of green painted leather, silvery claws, ruby jeweled eyes. Its skin is made of hundreds of overlapping discs of copper, bronze, and iron. Beneath the flexible folds of its scales is an armature controlled by clockwork. The Time Dragon circles on its pedestal, flexes its narrow leathery wings (they make a sound like a bellows), and belches out sulfurous balls of flaming orange stink.

Below, featured in the dozens of doorways, windows, and porches, are puppets, marionettes, figurines. Creatures of folk tale. Caricatures of peasants and royalty alike. Animals and fairies and saints—our unionist saints, Brother Frexspar, stolen out from underneath us! I get *enraged*. The figures move on sprockets. They wheel in and out of doorways. They bend at the waist, they dance and dawdle and dally with each other.

Who had engendered this Time Dragon, this fake oracle, this propaganda tool for wickedness that challenged the power of unionism and of the Unnamed God? The clock's handlers were a dwarf and some narrow-waisted minions who seemed to have only enough brain capacity among them to pass a hat. Who else was benefiting besides the dwarf and his beauty boys?

The cousin's second letter had warned that the clock was making its way next to Rush Margins. It had told a more specific story.

The entertainment began with a thrum of strings and a rattle of bones. The crowd pushed close, oohing. Within the lighted window of a stage, we saw a marriage bed, with a puppet wife and husband. The husband was asleep and the wife sighed. She made a motion with her carved hands to suggest that her husband was disappointingly small. The audience shrieked with laughter. The puppet wife went to sleep herself. When she was snoring, the puppet husband sneaked out of bed.

At this point, up above, the Dragon turned on its base, and pointed its talons into the crowd, indicating—without a doubt—a humble well digger named Grine, who has been a faithful if inattentive husband. Then the dragon reared back and stretched two fingers in a come-hither gesture, isolating a widow named Letta and her snaggle-toothed maiden daughter. The crowd hushed and fell away from Grine, Letta, and the blushing maid, as if they had suddenly been inflicted with running sores.

The Dragon rested again but draped a wing over another archway, which lit up to reveal the puppet husband, wandering out in the night. Along came a puppet widow, with sprigged hair and high color, dragging along a protesting, flinty-toothed daughter. The widow kissed the puppet husband, and pulled off his leather trousers. He was equipped with two full sets of male goods, one in the front and another hanging off the base of his spine. The widow positioned her daughter on the abbreviated prong in the front, and herself took advantage of the more menacing arrangement in the rear. The three puppets bucked and rocked, emitting squeals of glee. When the puppet widow and her daughter were through, they dismounted and kissed the adulterous puppet husband. Then they kneed him, simultaneously, fore and aft. He swung on springs and hinges, trying to hold all his wounded parts.

The audience roared. Grine, the actual well digger, sweated drops as big as grapes. Letta pretended to guffaw, but her daughter had already disappeared from shame. Before the evening was out, Grine was set upon by his agitated neighbors and investigated for the grotesque anomaly. Letta was shunned. Her daughter seems to have vanished entirely. We suspect the worst.

At least Grine wasn't killed. Yet who can say how our souls have been stamped by witnessing such a cruel drama? All souls are hostages to their human envelopes, but souls must decay and suffer at such indignity, don't you agree?

Sometimes it seemed to Frex that every itinerant witch and toothless gibbering seer in Oz who could perform even the most transparent of spells had seized on the outback district of Wend Hardings to scratch out a trade. He knew that folks from Rush Margins were humble. Their lives were hard and their hopes few. As the drought dragged on, their traditional unionist faith was eroding. Frex was aware that the Clock of the Time Dragon combined the appeals of ingenuity and magic—and he would have to call on his deepest reserves of religious conviction to overcome it. If his congregation should prove vulnerable to the so-called pleasure faith, succumbing to spectacle and violence—well, what next?

He would prevail. He was their minister. He had pulled their teeth and buried their babies and blessed their kitchen pots for years now. He had abased himself in their names. He had wandered with an unkempt beard and a begging bowl from hamlet to hamlet, leaving poor Melena alone in the minister's lodge for weeks at a time. He had sacrificed for them. They *couldn't* be swayed by this Time Dragon creature. They *owed* him.

He moved on, shoulders squared, jaw set, stomach in a sour uproar. The sky was brown with flying sand and grit. The wind rushed high over the hills with the sound of a tremulous wail, as if pushing through some fissure of rock, on a ridge beyond any Frex could see.

The Birth of a Witch

It was nearly evening by the time Frex had worked up the courage to enter the ramshackle hamlet of Rush Margins. He was in a deep sweat. He hit his heels to the ground and pumped his clenched fists, and called out in a hoarse, carrying tone. "Hist, oh ye of small confidence! Gather while ye may, for temptation is abroad, to try ye sorely!" The words were archaic, even ridiculous, but they worked. Here came the sullen fishermen, dragging their empty nets up from the dock. Here came the subsistence farmers, whose hardscrabble plots had borne little during this dry year. Before he had even begun, they all looked guilty as sin.

They followed him to the rickety steps of the canoe repair house. Frex knew that everyone expected this evil clock to arrive at any instant; gossip was as contagious as the plague. He yelled at them for their thirsty anticipation. "Ye are dull as toddlers reaching their hands to touch the pretty embers! Ye are as if spawn of dragon womb, ready to suck on teats of fire!" These were time-worn scriptural imprecations and they fell a little flat tonight; he was tired and not at his best.

"Brother Frexspar," said Bfee, the mayor of Rush Margins, "could you perhaps tone down your harangue until we get a chance to see what fresh new form temptation might take?"

"You have no mettle to resist new forms," said Frex, spitting.

"Haven't you been our able teacher these several years?" said Bfee. "We've hardly had such a good chance to prove ourselves against sin! We're looking forward to—to the spiritual test of it all."

The fishermen laughed and jeered, and Frex intensified his glower, but at the sound of unfamiliar wheels in the stony ruts of the road, they all turned their heads and fell silent. He had lost their attention before he had gotten started.

The clock was being drawn by four horses and escorted by the dwarf and his cohort of young thugs. Its broad roof was crowned by the dragon. But what a beast! It looked poised as if ready to spring, as if indeed invested with life. The skin of the house was decorated in carnival colors, burnished with gold leaf. The fishermen gaped as it drew near.

Before the dwarf could announce the time of the performance, before the crowd of youths could draw out their clubs, Frex leaped on the lower step of the thing—a fold-down stage on hinges. "Why is this thing called a clock? The only clock face it has is flat, dull, and lost in all that distracting detail. Furthermore, the hands don't move: Look, see for your-selves! They're painted to remain at one minute before midnight! All you'll see here is mechanics, my friends: I know this for a fact. You'll see mechanical cornfields growing, moons waxing and waning, a volcano to spew a soft red cloth done up with black and red sequins. With all this tiktok-y business, why not have a pair of circulating arms on the clock face? Why not? I ask you, I'm asking you, yes, you, Gawnette, and you, Stoy, and you, Perippa. Why no real clock here?"

They were not listening, Gawnette and Stoy and Perippa, nor were the others. They were too busy staring in anticipation.

"The answer, of course, is that the clock isn't meant to measure earthly time, but the time of the soul. Redemption and condemnation time. For the soul, each instant is always a minute short of judgment.

"One minute short of judgment, my friends! If you died in the next sixty seconds, would you want to spend eternity in the suffocating depths reserved for *idolaters?*"

"Awful lot of noise in the neighborhood tonight," said someone in the shadows—and the spectators laughed. Above Frex—he whirled to see—from a little door had emerged a small, yapping puppet dog, its hair dark and as tightly curled as Frex's own. The dog bounced on a spring, and the pitch of its chatter was annoyingly high. The laughter grew. Evening fell harder, and it was less easy for Frex to tell who was laughing, who now was shouting for him to move aside so they could see.

He wouldn't move, so he was bundled unceremoniously from his perch. The dwarf gave a poetic welcome. "All our lives are activity without meaning; we burrow ratlike into life and we squirm ratlike through it and rat-like we are flung into our graves at the end. Now and then, why shouldn't we hear a voice of prophecy, or see a miracle play? Beneath the apparent sham and indignity of our ratlike lives, a humble pattern and meaning still applies! Come nearer, my good people, and watch what a little extra knowledge augurs for your lives! The Time Dragon sees before and beyond and within the truth of your sorry span of years here! Look at what it shows you!"

The crowd pushed forward. The moon had risen, its light like the eye of an angry, vengeful god. "Give over, let me go," Frex called; it was worse than he had thought. He had never been manhandled by his own congregation.

The clock unfolded a story about a publicly pious man, with lamb's wool beard and dark curly locks, who preached simplicity, poverty, and generosity while keeping a hidden coffer of gold and emeralds—in the double-hinged bosom of a weak-chinned daughter of blue blood society. The scoundrel was run through with a long iron stake in a most indelicate way and served up to his hungry flock as Roast Flank of Minister.

"This panders to your basest instincts!" Frex yelled, his arms folded and his face magenta with fury.

But now that darkness was almost total, someone came up from behind him to silence him. An arm encircled his neck. He twisted to see which damned parishioner took such liberties, but all the faces were cloaked by hoods. He was kneed in the groin and doubled over, his face in the dirt. A foot kicked him square between the buttocks and his bowels released. The rest of the crowd, however, was not watching. They were howling with mirth at some other entertainment put on by the Clock Dragon. A sympathetic woman in a widow's shawl grabbed his arm and led him away—he was too fouled, too much in pain to straighten up and see who it was. "I'll put you down in the root cellar, I will, under a burlap," crooned the goodwife, "for they'll be after you tonight with pitchforks, the way that thing is behaving itself! They'll look for you in your lodge, but they won't look in my keeping room."

"Melena," he croaked, "they'll find her—"

"She'll be seen to," said his neighbor. "We women can manage that much, I guess!"

In the minister's lodge, Melena struggled with consciousness as a pair of midwives went in and out of focus before her. One was a fishwife, the other a palsied crone; they took turns feeling her forehead, peering between her legs, and stealing glances at the few beautiful trinkets and treasures Melena had managed to bring here from Colwen Grounds.

"You chew that paste of pinlobble leaves, duckie, you do that. You'll be unconscious before you know it," said the fishwife. "You'll relax, out will pop the little sweetheart, and all will be well in the morning. Thought you would smell of rosewater and fairy dew, but you stink like the rest of us. Chew on, my duckie, chew on."

At the sound of a knock, the crone looked up guiltily from the chest she was kneeling before and rummaging through. She let the lid close with a bang and affected a position of prayer, eyes closed. "Enter," she called.

A maiden with tender skin and high color came in. "Oh, I hoped someone would be here," she said. "How is she?"

"Nearly out and so is the babe," answered the fishwife. "An hour more, I reckon."

"Well, I'm told to warn you. The men are drunk and on the prowl. They've been riled up by that dragon of the magic clock, you know, and are looking for Frex to kill him. The clock said to. They'll likely stagger out here. We'd better get the wife safely away—can she be moved?"

No, I cannot be moved, thought Melena, and if the peasants find Frex tell them to kill him good and hard for me, for I never knew a pain so extraordinary that it made me see the blood behind my own eyes. Kill him for doing this to me. At this thought, she smiled in a moment of relief and passed out.

"Let's leave her here and run for it!" said the maiden. "The clock said to kill her too, and the little dragon she's going to give birth to. I don't want to get caught."

"We've got our own reputations to uphold," said the fishwife. "We can't abandon the fancy ladything in mid-delivery. I don't care what any clock says."

The crone, her head back in the chest, said, "Anyone for some real lace from Gillikin?"

"There's a hay cart in the lower field, but let's do it now," said the fishwife. "Come, help me fetch it. You, old mother hag, get your face out of the linens and come dampen this pretty pink brow. Right-o, now we go."

A few minutes later the crone, the wife, and the maiden were trundling the hay cart along a rarely used track through the spindles and bracken of the autumn woods. The wind had picked up. It whistled over the treeless foreheads of the Cloth Hills. Melena, sprawled in blankets, heaved and moaned in unconscious pain.

They heard a drunken mob pass, with pitchforks and torches, and the women stood silent and terrified, listening to the slurred curses. Then they pressed on with greater urgency until they came upon a foggy copse—the edge of the graveyard for unconsecrated corpses. Within it they saw the blurred outlines of the clock. It had been left here for safe-keeping by the dwarf—no fool he; he could guess this particular corner of the world was the last place jumpy villagers would seek tonight. "The dwarf and his boykins were drinking in the tavern too," said the maiden breathlessly. "There's no one here to stop us!"

The crone said, "So you've been peering in the tavern windows at the men, you slut?" She pushed open the door in the back of the clock.

She found a crawl space. Pendulums hung ominously in the gloom. Huge toothed wheels looked primed to slice any trespasser into sausage rounds. "Come on, drag her in," said the crone.

The night of torches and fog gave way, at dawn, to broad bluffs of thundercloud, dancing skeletons of lightning. Glimpses of blue sky appeared briefly, though sometimes it rained so hard that it seemed more like mud drops falling than water. The midwives, crawling on hands and knees out of the back of the clock-wagon, had their little discharge at last. They protected the infant from the dripping gutter. "Look, a rainbow," said the senior, bobbing her head. A sickly scarf of colored light hung in the sky.

What they saw, rubbing the caul and blood off the skin—was it just a trick of the light? After all, following the storm the grass did seem to throb with its own color, the roses zinged and hovered with crazy glory on their stems. But even with these effects of light and atmosphere, the midwives couldn't deny what they saw. Beneath the spit of the mother's fluids the infant glistened a scandalous shade of pale emerald.

There was no wail, no bark of newborn outrage. The child opened its mouth, breathed, and then kept its own counsel. "Whine, you fiend," said the crone, "it's your first job." The baby shirked its obligations.

"Another willful boy," said the fishwife, sighing. "Shall we kill it?"

"Don't be so nasty to it," said the crone, "it's a girl."

"Hah," said the bleary-eyed maiden, "look again, there's the weather vane."

For a minute they were in disagreement, even with the child naked before them. Only after a second and third rub was it clear that the child was indeed feminine. Perhaps in labor some bit of organic effluvia had become caught and quickly dried in the cloven place. Once toweled, she was observed to be prettily formed, with a long elegant head, forearms nicely turned out, clever pinching little buttocks, cunning fingers with scratchy little nails.

And an undeniable green cast to the skin. There was a salmon blush in the cheeks and belly, a beige effect around the clenched eyelids, a tawny stripe on the scalp showing the pattern of eventual hair. But the primary effect was vegetable.

"Look what we get for our troubles," said the maiden. "A little green pat of butter. Why don't we kill it? You know what people will say."

"I think it's rotten," said the fishwife, and checked for the root of a tail, counted fingers and toes. "It smells like dung."

"That *is* dung you're smelling, you idiot. You're squatting in a cow pattypie."

"It's sick, it's feeble, that's why the color. Lose it in the puddle, drown the thing. She'll never know. She'll be out for hours in her ladylike faints."

They giggled. They cradled the infant in the crook of their arms, passing it around to test it for weight and balance. To kill it was the kindest course of action. The question was how.

Then the child yawned, and the fishwife absentmindedly gave it a finger to nurse on, and the child bit the finger off at the second knuckle. It almost choked on the gush of blood. The digit dropped out of its mouth into the mud like a bobbin. The women catapulted into action. The fishwife lunged to strangle the girl, and the crone and the maiden flared up in defense. The finger was dug out of the mire and shoved in an apron pocket, possibly to sew back onto the hand that had lost it. "It's a cock, she just realized she didn't have one," screeched the maiden, and fell on the ground laughing. "Oh, beware the stupid boy first tries to please himself with her! She'll snip his young sprout off for a souvenir!"

The midwives crawled back into the clock and dropped the thing at its mother's breast, afraid to consider mercy murder for fear of what else the baby might bite. "Maybe she'll chop the tit next, that'll bring Her Drowsy Frailness around quick enough," the crone chuckled. "Though what a child, that sips blood even before its first suck of mother's milk!" They left a pipkin of water nearby, and under cover of the next squall they went squelching away, to find their sons and husbands and brothers, and berate and beat them if they were available, or bury them if not.

In the shadows, the infant stared overhead at the oiled and regular teeth of time's clock.

Maladies and Remedies

For days Melena couldn't bear to look at the thing. She held it, as a mother must. She waited for the groundwater of maternal affection to rise and overwhelm her. She did not weep. She chewed pinlobble leaves, to float away from the disaster.

It was a she. It was a her. Melena practiced conversions in her thinking when she was alone. The twitching, unhappy bundle was not male; it was not neutered; it was a female. It slept, looking like a heap of cabbage leaves washed and left to drain on the table.

In a panic, Melena wrote to Colwen Grounds to drag Nanny from her retirement. Frex went ahead in a carriage to collect Nanny from the way station at Stonespar End. On the trip back, Nanny asked Frex what was wrong.

"What is wrong." He sighed, and was lost in thought. Nanny realized she had chosen her words poorly; now Frex was distracted. He began to mumble in a general way about the nature of evil. A vacuum set up by the inexplicable absence of the Unnamed God, and into which spiritual poison must rush. A vortex.

"I mean what is the state of the child!" retorted Nanny explosively. "It's not the universe but a single child I need to hear about, if I'm going to be any help! Why does Melena call for me instead of for her mother? Why is there no letter for her grandfather? He's the Eminent Thropp, for goodness sakes! Melena can't have forgotten her duties so thoroughly, or is life out there in the country worse than we thought?"

"It's worse than we thought," said Frex grimly. "The baby—you had better be prepared, Nanny, so you don't scream—the baby is damaged."

"Damaged?" Nanny's grip on her valise tightened and she looked out over the red-leafed pearlfruit trees by the side of the road. "Frex, tell me everything."

"It's a girl," said Frex.

"Damage indeed," said Nanny mockingly, but Frex as usual missed the dig. "Well, at least the family title's preserved for another generation. Has she got all her limbs?"

"Yes."

"Any more than she needs?"

"No."

"Is she sucking?"

"We can't let it. It has extraordinary teeth, Nanny. It has shark's teeth, or something like."

"Well she won't be the first child to grow on a bottle or a rag instead of a tit, don't worry about that."

"It's the wrong color," said Frex.

"What color is the wrong color?"

For a few moments Frex could only shake his head. Nanny did not like him and she *would* not like him, but she softened. "Frex, it can't be that bad. There's always a way out. Tell Nanny."

"It's green," he finally said. "Nanny, it's green as moss."

"She's green, you mean. It's a she, for heaven's sake."

"It's not for heaven's sake." Frex began to weep. "Heaven is not improved by it, Nanny; and heaven does not approve. What are we to do!"

"Hush." Nanny detested weeping men. "It can't be as bad as all that. There isn't a sniff of low blood in Melena's veins. Whatever blight the child has will respond to Nanny's treatment. Trust Nanny."

"I trusted in the Unnamed God," sobbed Frex.

"We don't *always* work at cross purposes, God and Nanny," said Nanny. She knew this was blasphemous, but she couldn't resist a gibe as long as Frex's resistance was down. "But don't worry, I won't breathe a word to Melena's family. We'll sort this all out in a flash, and no one need know. The baby has a name?"

"Elphaba," he said.

"After Saint Aelphaba of the Waterfall?"

"Yes."

"A fine old name. You'll use the common nickname Fabala, I suppose."

"Who even knows if she'll live long enough to grow into a nickname." Frex sounded as if he hoped this would be the case.

"Interesting country, are we in Wend Hardings yet?" Nanny asked, to change the subject. But Frex had folded up inside, barely bothering to guide the horses onto the correct track. The country was filthy, depressed, peasant-ridden; Nanny began to wish she had not set out in her best traveling gown. Roadside robbers might expect to find gold on such a refined-looking older woman, and they would be right, for Nanny sported a golden garter stolen years ago from Her Ladyship's boudoir. What a humiliation, if the garter should turn up these years later on Nanny's well-turned if aging thigh! But Nanny's fears were unfounded, for the carriage arrived, without incident, in the yard of the minister's cottage.

"Let me see the baby first," said Nanny. "It will be easier and fairer on Melena if I know what we're dealing with." And this wasn't hard to arrange, as Melena was out cold thanks to pinlobble leaves, while the baby in a basket on the table wailed softly.

Nanny drew up a chair so she wouldn't hurt herself if she fainted dead away. "Frex, put the basket on the floor where I can look into it." Frex obliged, and then went to return the horses and carriage to Bfee, who rarely needed them for mayoral duties but loaned them out to earn a little political capital.

The infant was wrapped in linens, Nanny saw, and the baby's mouth and ears were strapped with a sling. The nose looked like a knob of bad mushroom, poking up for air, and the eyes were open.

Nanny leaned closer. The child couldn't be, what, three weeks old? Yet as Nanny moved from side to side, looking at the profile of the forehead from this angle and that, so as to judge the shape of the mind, the girl's eyes tracked her back and forth. They were brown and rich, the color of overturned earth, flecked with mica. There was a network of fragile red lines at each soft angle where the eyelids met, as if the girl had been bursting the blood threads from the exertion of watching and understanding.

And the skin, oh yes, the skin was green as sin. Not an ugly color, Nanny thought. Just not a human color.

She reached out and let her finger drift across the baby's cheek. The infant flinched, and her backbone arched, and the wrapping, which was tucked securely around the child from neck to toe, split open like a husk. Nanny gritted her teeth and was determined not to be cowed. The baby had exposed herself, sternum to groin, and the skin on her chest was the same remarkable color. "Have you even touched this child yet, you two?" murmured Nanny. She put her hand palm down on the child's heaving chest, her fingers covering the almost invisible baby nipples, then slid her hand down so she could check the apparatus below. The child was wet and soiled but felt made according to standard design. The skin was the same miracle of pliant smoothness that Melena had possessed as an infant.

"Come to Nanny, you horrid little thing you." Nanny leaned to pick the baby up, mess and all.

The baby swiveled to avoid the touch. Her head beat itself against the rush bottom of the basket.

"You've been dancing in the womb, I see," said Nanny, "I wonder to whose music? Such well-developed muscles! No, you're not getting away from me. Come here, you little demon. Nanny doesn't care. Nanny likes you." She was lying through her teeth, but unlike Frex she believed some lies were sanctioned by heaven.

And she got her hands on Elphaba, and settled her on her lap. There Nanny waited, crooning and every now and then looking away, out the window, to recover herself and keep from vomiting. She rubbed the baby's belly to calm the girl down, but there was no calming her down, not yet anyway.

Melena propped herself up on her elbows in the late afternoon when Nanny brought a tray with tea and bread. "I have made myself at home," said Nanny, "and I've made friends with your tiny darling. Now come to your senses, sweetheart, and let me give you a kiss."

"Oh, Nanny!" Melena allowed herself to be coddled. "Thank you for coming. Have you seen the little monster?"

"She's adorable," said Nanny.

"Don't lie and don't be soft," said Melena. "If you're going to help you must be honest."

"If I'm going to help, *you* must be honest," said Nanny. "We need not go into it now, but I will have to know everything, my sweet. So we can decide what's to be done." They sipped their tea, and because

Elphaba had fallen asleep at last, it seemed for a few moments like the old days at Colwen Grounds, when Melena would come home from afternoon walks with lithesome young gentry on the make, and boast of their masculine beauty to a Nanny who pretended she had not noticed.

In fact, as the weeks went on, Nanny noticed quite a few disturbing things about the baby.

For one thing, Nanny tried to remove the baby's bandages, but Elphaba seemed intent on biting her own hands off, and the teeth inside that pretty, thin-lipped mouth were indeed monstrous. She would bite a hole through the basket if she were left unfettered. She went after her own shoulder and scraped it raw. She looked as if she were strangling.

"Can't a barber be had to pull the teeth out?" Nanny asked. "At least until the baby learns some self-control?"

"You're out of your mind," Melena said. "It will be all over the valley that the little marrow is green. We'll keep the jaw strapped up until we solve the skin problem."

"However in the world did her skin come green?" Nanny wondered, stupidly, for Melena blanched and Frex reddened, and the baby held her breath as if trying to turn blue to please them all. Nanny had to slap her to make her breathe again.

Nanny interviewed Frex out in the yard. After the double blow of the birth and his public embarrassment, he was not yet up to professional engagements and sat whittling praying beads out of oak, scoring and inscribing them with emblems of the Namelessness of God. Nanny set Elphaba down inside—she had an unreasonable fear of being overheard by this infant, and, worse, of being *understood*—and Nanny sat scooping out a pumpkin for supper.

"I don't suppose, Frex, that you have green in your family background," she began, knowing full well that Melena's powerful grandfather would have confirmed such a predisposition before agreeing to let his granddaughter marry a unionist minister—of all the chances she had!

"Our family isn't about money or about earthly power," said Frex, taking no offense for once. "But I'm descended in a direct line from six ministers before me, father to son. We're as well regarded in spiritual circles as Melena's family is in parlors and at the court of Ozma. And no, there is no green, anywhere. I never heard of such a thing before in any family."

Nanny nodded and said, "Well all right, I was only asking. I know you're gooder than goblin martyrs."

"But," Frex said humbly, "Nanny, I think I caused this thing to happen. My tongue slipped on the day of the birthday—I announced that the devil was coming. I *meant* the Clock of the Time Dragon. But suppose those words unlocked room for the devil? . . ."

"The child is no devil!" snapped Nanny. She's no angel either, she thought, but kept it to herself.

"On the other hand," Frex continued, sounding more secure, "she may have been cursed by Melena, accidentally, who took my remark the wrong way and wept about it. Maybe Melena opened up inside herself a window through which an unattached sprite entered and colored the child."

"On the very day she is to be born?" said Nanny. "That's a capable sprite. Is your goodness so exalted you attract the truly high-powered among the Spirits of Aberration?"

Frex shrugged. A few weeks earlier he would have nodded, but his confidence was shattered with his abject failure in Rush Margins. He did not dare suggest what he feared: The child's abnormality was a punishment for his failure to protect his flock from the pleasure faith.

"Well . . ." Nanny asked practically, "if through a curse the goods were damaged, then through what might the ill be overturned?"

"An exorcism," said Frex.

"Are you empowered?"

"If I'm successful at changing her, we'll know that I'm empowered," said Frex. But now that he had a goal, his spirits brightened. He would spend some days in fasting, rehearsing prayers, and collecting supplies for the arcane ritual.

When he was off in the woods, and Elphaba napping, Nanny perched on the side of Melena's hard marriage mattress.

"Frex wonders if his prediction that the devil was coming caused a window in you to open, letting an imp pass through to spoil the baby," said Nanny. She was crocheting an edge of lace, clumsily; she had never excelled at piecework, but she liked handling the polished ivory crochet hook. "I wonder if you opened another window?"

Melena, groggy from pinlobble leaves as usual, arched an eyebrow in confusion.

"Did you sleep with someone other than Frex?" Nanny asked.

"Don't be mad!" said Melena.

"I know you, honey," said Nanny. "I'm not saying you're not a good wife. But when you had the boys buzzing around you in your parents' orchard you changed your perfumed undergarments more than once a day. You were lusty and sneaky and good at it. I'm not looking down at you. But don't pretend to me that your appetites weren't healthy."

Melena buried her face in the pillow. "Oh for those days!" she wailed. "It's not that I don't love Frex! But I hate being better than the local peasant idiots!"

"Well, now this green child brings you down to their level, you ought to be pleased," said Nanny meanly.

"Nanny, I love Frex. But he leaves me alone so often! I would kill for some tinker to pass by and sell me more than a tin coffeepot! I would pay well for someone less godly and more imaginative!"

"That's a question for the future," said Nanny sensibly. "I'm asking you about the past. The recent past. Since your marriage."

But Melena's face was vague and blurry. She nodded, she shrugged, she rocked her head.

"The obvious theory is an elf," said Nanny.

"I wouldn't have sex with an *elf!*" Melena shrieked.

"No more would I," said Nanny, "but the green does give one pause. Are there elves in the neighborhood?"

"There's a gaggle of them, tree elves, up over the hill someplace, but if possible they are more moronic than the fair citizens of Rush Margins. Really, Nanny, I've never even seen one, or only from a distance. The idea is repulsive. Elves giggle at everything, do you know that? One of them falls out of an oak and smashes his skull like a rotten turnip, and they gather and giggle and then forget about him. It's insulting of you even to bring it up."

"Get used to it, if we don't find a way out of this quagmire."

"Well, the answer is *no.*"

"Then someone else. Someone handsome enough on the outside, but carrying a germ that maybe you caught."

Melena looked shocked. She hadn't thought of her own health since Elphaba was born. Could *she* be at risk?

"The truth," said Nanny. "We must know."

"The truth," said Melena distantly. "Well, it is unknowable."

"What are you trying to say?"

"I don't know the answer to your question." And Melena explained. Yes, the cottage was off the beaten track, and of course she never passed more than the *curtest* greetings with local farmers and fishermen and thickheads. But more travelers took to the hills and woods than you would credit. Often she had sat, listless and lonely, while Frex was off preaching, and she had found comfort in giving passersby a simple meal and a buoyant conversation.

"And more?"

But on those boring days, Melena muttered, she had taken to chewing pinlobble leaves. When she would awake, because the sun was setting or Frex was there frowning or grinning at her, she remembered little.

"You mean you indulged in adultery and you don't even have the benefit of a good saucy memory about it?" Nanny was scandalized.

"I don't know that I did!" said Melena. "I wouldn't choose to, I mean not if I was thinking clearly. But I remember once when a tinker with a funny accent gave me a draft of some heady brew from a green glass bottle. And I had rare expansive dreams, Nanny, of the Other World—cities of glass and smoke—noise and color—I tried to remember."

"So you could *well* have been raped by elves. Won't your grandfather be pleased to learn how Frex is taking care of you."

"Stop!" cried Melena.

"Well, I don't know what's to be done!" Nanny lost her temper at last. "Everyone's being irresponsible! If you can't remember whether your marriage vows have been broken or not, there's not much good in acting like an offended saint."

"We can always drown the baby and start over."

"Just try drowning that thing," muttered Nanny. "I pity the poor lake asked to take her in."

Later, Nanny went through Melena's small collection of medicines—herbs, drops, roots, brandies, leaves. She was wondering, without much hope, if she could invent something that might cause the girl's skin to blanch. In the back of the chest Nanny found the green glass bottle spoken of by Melena. The light was bad and her eyes weren't strong, but she could make out the words MIRACLE ELIXIR on a piece of paper pasted to the front.

Though she had a native skill in healing, Nanny was unable to come up with a skin-changing potion. Bathing the child in cow's milk didn't make the skin white, either. But the child would not allow herself to be lowered into a pail of lake water; she twisted like a cat in panic. Nanny kept on with the cow's milk. It left a horrid sour stink if she did not rub it off thoroughly with a cloth.

Frex organized an exorcism. It involved candles and hymns. Nanny watched from a distance. The man was beady-eyed, perspiring with effort even though the mornings were colder and colder. Elphaba slept in her binding cloth in the middle of the carpet, oblivious to the sacrament.

Nothing happened. Frex fell, exhausted and spent, and cradled his green daughter within the crook of his arm, as if finally embracing the proof of some undisclosed sin. Melena's face hardened.

There was only one thing left to try. Nanny gathered the courage to bring it up on the day she was to leave back for Colwen Grounds.

"We see that peasant treatments don't work," said Nanny, "and spiritual intercession has failed. Do you have the courage to think about sorcery? Is there someone local who could magick the green venom out of the child?"

Frex was up and lashing out at Nanny, swinging his fists. Nanny fell backward off her stool, and Melena bobbed about her, shrieking. "How *dare* you!" cried Frex. "In this household! Isn't this green girl insult enough? Sorcery is the refuge of the amoral; when it isn't out-and-out charlatanism, it is dangerously evil! Contracts with the demons!"

Nanny said, "Oooh, preserve me! You fine, fine man, don't you know enough to fight fire with fire?"

"Nanny, enough," said Melena.

"Hitting a feeble old woman," said Nanny, hurt. "Who only tries to help."

The next morning Nanny packed her valise. There was nothing more that she could do, and she wasn't willing to live the rest of her life with a fanatical hermit and a ruined baby, even for the sake of Melena.

Frex drove Nanny back to the inn at Stonespar End, for the coach-and-four to take her home. Nanny knew Melena might still think about killing the child, but somehow she doubted it. Nanny held her valise to her ample bosom, fearing bandits again. Inside her valise was hidden her gold garter (she could always claim it had been planted there without her knowledge, whereas it would have been hard to claim it had been planted on her leg in the same circumstances). She also had squirreled away the ivory crochet hook, three of Frex's prayer beads because she liked the carvings, and the pretty green glass bottle left behind by some itinerant salesman selling, apparently, dreams and passion and somnolence.

She didn't know what she thought. Was Elphaba devil's spawn? Was she half-elf? Was she punishment for her father's failure as a preacher, or for her mother's sloppy morals and bad memory? Or was she merely a physical ailment, a blight like a misshapen apple or a five-legged calf? Nanny knew her worldview was foggy and chaotic, pestered by demons, faith, and folk science. It didn't escape her attention, however, that both Melena and Frex had believed uncompromisingly that they would have a boy. Frex was the seventh son of a seventh son, and to add to that powerful equation he was descended from six ministers in a row. Whatever child of either (or any) sex could dare follow in so auspicious a line?

Perhaps, thought Nanny, little green Elphaba chose her own sex, and her own color, and to hell with her parents.

The Quadling Glassblower

F or one short, wet month, early in the next year, the drought lifted. Spring tipped in like green well water, frothing at the hedges, bubbling at the roadside, splashing from the cottage roof in garlands of ivy and stringflower. Melena went about the yard in a state of mild undress, so that she could feel the sun on her pale skin and the deep warmth she had missed all winter. Strapped in her chair in the doorway, Elphaba, now a year and a half old, hit her breakfast minnow with the bowl of her spoon. "Oh, eat the thing, don't mash it," said Melena, but mildly. Since the child's chin-sling had been removed, mother and daughter had begun to pay some attention to each other. To her surprise, Melena sometimes found Elphaba endearing, the way a baby should be.

This view was the only thing she had seen since leaving the elegant mansion of her family, the only thing she would ever gaze upon again— the windswept surface of Illswater, the distant dark stone cottages and chimneys of Rush Margins on the other side, the hills lying in a torpor beyond. She would go mad; the world was nothing but water and want. If a frolic of elves scampered through the yard she would leap on them for company, for sex, for murder.

"You father is a fraud," she said to Elphaba. "Off finding himself all winter, leaving me with only you for company. Eat that breakfast, for you'll get no more if you throw it on the ground."

Elphaba picked up the fish and threw it on the ground.

"Your father is a charlatan," continued Melena. "He used to be very good in bed for a religious man, and this is how I know his secret. Holy men are supposed to be above earthly pleasures, but your father enjoyed his midnight wrestling. Once upon a time! We must never tell him we know he's a humbug, it would break his heart. We don't want to break his heart, do we?" And then Melena burst into a high peal of laughter.

Elphaba's face was unsmiling, unchanging. She pointed to the fish.

"Breakfast. Breakfast in the dirt. Breakfast for the bugs," Melena said. She dropped the collar of her spring robe a little lower and the pink yoke of her bare shoulders gyrated. "Shall we go walk by the edge of the lake today and maybe you'll drown?"

But Elphaba would never drown, never, because she would not go near the lake.

"Maybe we'll go out in a boat and *tip over!*" Melena shrieked.

Elphaba cocked her head to one side as if listening for some part of her mother not intoxicated with leaves and wine.

The sun swept out from behind a cloud. Elphaba scowled. Melena's robe dropped lower. Her breasts worked their way out from between the dirty ruffles of the collar.

Look at me, thought Melena, showing my breasts to the child I couldn't give milk to for fear of amputation. I who was the rose of Nest Hardings, I who was the beauty of my generation! And now I am reduced to company I don't even want, my own squirming thorny little girl. She is more grasshopper than girl, with those angular little thighs, those arching eyebrows, those poking fingers. She's about the business of learning like any child, but she takes no delight in the world: She pushes and breaks and nibbles on things without any pleasure. As if she has a mission to taste and measure all the disappointments of life. In which Rush Margins is amply supplied. Mercy from the Unnamed God, she's a creep, she is. She *is*.

"Or we might take a walk in the woods today and pick the last of the winter berries." Melena was full of guilt at her lack of motherly feeling. "We can put them in a pie. Can we put them in a pie? Shall we, honey?"

Elphaba didn't speak yet, but she nodded, and began to wiggle to get down. Melena started a clapping game Elphaba took no notice of. The child grunted and pointed to the ground, and arched her long elegant legs to illustrate her desire. Then she gestured to the gate leading from the kitchen garden and the hen yard.

There was a man at the uprights of the gate, leaning, shy and hungry-looking, with skin the color of roses at twilight: a dusky, shadowy red. He had a couple of leathern satchels on his shoulders and back, and a walking staff, and a dangerously handsome, hollow-looking face. Melena screeched and caught herself, directed her voice to a lower register. It had been so long since she had spoken to anyone but a whining toddler. "Good glory, you startled us!" she cried. "Are you searching for some breakfast?" She had lost the social touch. For instance, her breasts should not be staring at him so. Yet she did not clasp her gown.

"Please to forgive a sudden appearance by a strange foreigner at Lady's gate," said the man.

"Forgiven, of course," she said impatiently. "Come in where I can see you—come in, come in!"

Elphaba had seen so few other people in her life that she hid one eye behind her spoon, and peeked with the other eye.

The man approached. His movements showed the clumsiness of exhaustion. He was large of ankle and thick of foot, slender about the waist and shoulders, and thick again in the neck—as if he had been made on a lathe, and worked too briefly at the extremities. His hands, letting down the satchels, seemed like beasts with minds of their own. They were outsized and splendid.

"Traveler not to know where he is," said the man. "Two nights to cross the hills from Downhill Cornings. To look for the inn at Three Dead Trees. To rest."

"You're lost, you've veered," said Melena, deciding not to be perplexed at his scrambled words. "No matter. Let me fix you a meal and you can tell me your story." Her hands were at her hair, which once used to be thought precious as spun brass. At least it was clean.

The man was sleek and fit. When he removed his cap his hair fell out in greasy hanks, sunset red. He washed at the pump, stripping off his shirt, and Melena noticed it was nice to see a waist on a man again (Frex, bless him, had run to plumpness in the year-and-some since Elphaba's birth). Were all Quadlings this delicious dusty rose color? The man's name, Melena learned, was Turtle Heart, and he was a glassblower from Ovvels, in little-known Quadling Country.

She bundled up her breasts at last, reluctantly. Elphaba squawked to be let loose, and without so much as flinching the visitor unbuckled her and swept her in the air and caught her again. The child crowed with surprise, even delight, and Turtle Heart repeated the trick. Melena took advantage of his concentration on the brat to scoop up the uneaten minnow from the dirt and rinse it off. She plopped it among the eggs and mashed tar root, hoping that Elphaba would not suddenly learn to speak and embarrass her. It would be just like the child to do that.

But Elphaba was too charmed by this man to fuss or complain. She didn't even whine when Turtle Heart finally came to the bench and sat to eat. She crawled between his sleek, hairless calves (for he had shucked off his leggings) and she moaned some private tune with a satisfied smirk on her face. Melena found herself jealous of a female not yet two years old. *She* wouldn't have minded sitting on the ground between Turtle Heart's legs.

"I've never met a Quadling before," she said, too loudly, too brightly. The months of solitude had made her forget her manners. "My family would never have Quadlings in to dine—not that there were many, or even *any* for all I know, in the farmlands around my family's estate. The stories make out that Quadlings were sneaky and incapable of telling the truth."

"How can a Quadling to answer such a charge if a Quadling is given always to lie?" He smiled at her.

She melted like butter on warm bread. "I'll believe anything you say."

He told her of the life in the outreaches of Ovvels, the houses rotting gently into the swamp, the harvest of snails and murkweed, the customs of communal living and ancestor worship. "So you believe your ancestors are with you?" she prodded. "I don't mean to be nosy but I've become interested in religion despite myself."

"Does Lady to believe ancestors are with her?"

She could hardly focus on the question, so bright were his eyes, and so wonderful it was to be called *Lady*. Her shoulders straightened. "My immediate ancestors couldn't be farther away," she admitted. "I mean my parents—they're still living, but so uninteresting to me they might as well be dead."

"When dead they may to visit Lady often."

"They are not welcome. Go away." She laughed, shooing. "You mean ghosts? They'd *better* not. That's what I'd call the worst of both worlds—if there is an Other Land."

"There is an otherworld," he said with certainty.

She felt chilled. She scooped Elphaba up and hugged her tightly. Elphaba sagged as if boneless in her arms, neither fussing nor returning the hug, just falling limp from the novelty of being touched. "Are you a seer?" said Melena.

"Turtle Heart to blow glass," he said. He seemed to mean that as an answer.

Melena was suddenly reminded of the dreams she used to have, of exotic places she knew she was too dull to invent. "Married to a minister, and I don't know that I believe in an otherworld," she admitted. She hadn't meant to say that she was married, although she supposed the child implicated her.

But Turtle Heart had finished talking. He put down his plate (he had left the minnow) and he took from his satchels a small pot, a pipe, and some sacks of sand and soda ash and lime and other minerals. "Might Turtle Heart to thank Lady for her welcome?" he asked; she nodded.

He built up the kitchen fire and sorted and mixed his ingredients, and arranged utensils, and cleaned the bowl of his pipe with a special rag folded in its own pouch. Elphaba sat clumplike, her green hands on her green toes, curiosity on her sharp pinched face.

Melena had never seen glass blown, just as she had never seen paper made, cloth woven, or logs hewn from tree trunks. It seemed as marvelous to her as the local stories of the traveling clock that had hexed her husband into the professional paralysis from which he still hadn't quite escaped—though he tried.

Turtle Heart hummed a note through his nose or the pipe as he blew an irregular bulb of hot greenish ice. It steamed and hissed in the air. He knew what to do with it; he was a wizard of glass; Melena had to hold Elphaba back to keep her from burning her hands as she reached for it.

In what seemed like no time at all, in what felt like magic, the glass had gone from being semiliquid and abstract to a hardening, cooling reality.

It was a smooth, impure circle, like a slightly oblong plate. All the while Turtle Heart worked with it, Melena thought of her own character, going from youthful ether to hardening shell, transparently empty. Breakable, too. But before she could lose herself in remorse, Turtle Heart took her two hands and passed them near, but not touching, the flat surface of the glass.

"Lady to talk with ancestors," he said. But she would not struggle to connect with old boring dead people in the Other Land, not when his huge hands covered hers. She breathed through her nose to suppress the smell of breakfast in an unwashed mouth (fruit and one glass of wine, or was it two?). She thought she might well faint.

"Look in glass," he urged her. She could only look at his neck and his raspberry-honey-colored chin.

He looked for her. Elphaba came and steadied herself with a small hand on his knee and peered in, too.

"Husband is near," said Turtle Heart. Was this prophecy through a glass dish or was he asking her a question? But he went on: "Husband is traveling on a donkey and to bring elderly woman to visit you. Is ancestor to visit?"

"Is old nursemaid, probably," Melena said. She was sloping downward into his crippled syntax, in unabashed sympathy. "Can you really to see that in there?"

He nodded. Elphaba nodded too, but at what?

"How much time do we have before he gets here?" she asked.

"Till this evening."

They did not speak another word until sunset. They banked the fire and hooked Elphaba to a harness, and sat her down in front of the cooling glass, which they hung on a string like a lens or a mirror. It seemed to mesmerize and calm her; she did not even gnaw absent-mindedly at her wrists or toes. They left the door to the cottage open so that, from time to time, they could peer out from the bed to check on the child who, in the glare of a sunny day, would not be able to focus her eyes to see in the house shadows, and who anyway never turned to look. Turtle Heart was unbearably beautiful. Melena dragon-snaked with him, covered him with her mouth, poured him in her hands, heated and cooled and shaped his luminosity. He filled her emptiness.

They were washed, and dressed, with supper mostly made, when the donkey brayed a half mile down the lake. Melena blushed. Turtle Heart was back at the pipe, blowing again. Elphaba turned and looked in the direction of the donkey's serrated statement. Her lips, which always looked almost black against the new-apple color of her skin, twisted tight, chewed against each other. She bit her lower lip as if thinking, but she did not bleed; she had learned to manage the teeth somewhat, through trial and error. She put her hand on the shining disc. The glass circlet caught the last blue of the sky, until it looked like a magic mirror showing nothing but silver-cold water within.

Geographies of the Seen and the Unseen

All the way from Stonespar End, where Frex met her coach, Nanny complained. Lumbago, weak kidneys, fallen arches, aching gums, sore haunches. Frex wanted to say, And how about your swollen ego? Though he had been out of circulation for a while, he knew such a remark would be rude. Nanny flounced and petted herself, clinging determinedly to her seat until they arrived at the lodge near Rush Margins.

Melena greeted Frex with affecting shyness. "My breastplate, my backbone," she murmured. She was slender after a hard winter, her cheekbones more prominent. Her skin looked scoured as if by an artist's scratch brush—but she had always had the look of an etching-in-the-flesh. She was usually bold with her kisses and he found her reticence alarming until he realized there was a stranger in the shadows. Then, after introductions, Nanny and Melena fussed to get a meal on the table, and Frex put out some oats for the sorry nag who had to pull the carriage. When this was done he went to sit in the spring evening light and to meet his daughter again.

Elphaba was cautious around him. He found in his pouch a trinket he'd whittled for her, a little sparrow with a cunning beak and upraised wings. "Look, Fabala," he whispered (Melena hated the derivative, so he used it: it was his and Elphaba's private bond, the father-daughter pact against the world). "Look what I found in the forest. A little maplewood bird."

The child took the thing in her hands. She touched it softly, and put its head in her mouth. Frex steeled himself to hear the inevitable splintering, and to hold back his sigh of disappointment. But Elphaba did not bite. She sucked the head and looked at it again. Wet, it had greater life.

"You like it," Frex said.

She nodded, and began to feel its wings. Now that she was distracted, Frex could draw her between his knees. He nuzzled his crinkly-bearded chin into her hair—she smelled like soap and wood smoke, and the char on toast, a good healthy smell—and he closed his eyes. It was good to be home.

He had spent the winter in an abandoned shepherd's hut on the windward slope of Griffon's Head. Praying and fasting, moving deeper inside and then further outside himself. And why not? At home, he had felt the scorn of the people of the whole claustrophobic valley of Illswater; they had connected the Time Dragon's slanderous story of a corrupt minister with the arrival of a deformed child. They had drawn their own conclusions. They avoided his chapel services. So a sort of hermit's life, at least in small intervals, had seemed both penance and preparation for something *else*, something *next*—but what?

He knew this life wasn't what Melena had originally expected, marrying him. With his bloodlines, Frex had looked primed for an elevation to proctor or even, eventually, bishop. He had imagined the happiness Melena would have as a society dame, presiding over feast day dinners and charity balls and episcopal teas. Instead—he could see her in the firelight, grating a last, limp winter carrot onto a pan of fish—here she wasted away, a partner in a difficult marriage on a cold, shadowy lakeshore. Frex had a notion that she wasn't sorry to see him go off from time to time, so that she could be glad to see him come back.

As he ruminated, his beard tickled Elphaba's neck, and she snapped the wings off her wooden sparrow. She sucked on it like a whistle. Twisting away from him, she ran to a glass lens hanging from the projecting eave, and swatted at it.

"Don't, you'll break that!" said her father.

"She cannot to break that." The traveler, the Quadling, came from the sink where he had been washing up.

"She just turned her toy into a cripple," Frex said, pointing at the ruined birdling.

"She is herself pleased at the half things," Turtle Heart said. "I think. The little girl to play with the broken pieces better."

Frex didn't quite get it, but nodded. He knew that months away from the human voice made him clumsy at first. The boy from the inn, who had climbed Griffon's Head to deliver Nanny's request to be picked up at Stonespar End, had obviously thought Frex a wild man, grunting and unkempt. Frex had had to quote a little of the *Oziad* to indicate some sort of humanity—"Land of green abandon, land of endless leaf"—it was all that would come to him.

"Why can't she break it?" asked Frex.

"Because I do not to make it to be broken," answered Turtle Heart. But he smiled at Frex, not aggressively. And Elphaba wandered around with the shiny glass as if it were a toy, catching shadows, reflections, lights on its imperfect surface, almost as if she were playing.

"Where are you going?" asked Frex, just as Turtle Heart was saying, "Where are you from?"

"I'm a Munchkinlander," said Frex.

"I to think all Munchkins to be shorter than I or you."

"The peasants, the farmers, yes," Frex said, "but anyone with bloodlines worth tracing married into height somewhere along the way. And you? You're from Quadling Country."

"Yes," said the Quadling. His reddish hair had been washed and was drying into an airy nimbus. Frex was glad to see Melena so generous as to offer a passerby water to bathe in. Perhaps she was adjusting to country life after all. Because, mercy, a Quadling ranked about as low on the social ladder as it was possible to get and still be human.

"But I to understand," said the Quadling. "Ovvels is a small world. Until I to leave, I am not to know of hills, one beyond the other and from the spiny backbones a world so wide around. The blurry far away to hurt my eyes, for I cannot to make it seen. Please sir to describe the world you know."

Frex picked up a stick. In the soil he drew an egg on its side. "What they taught me in lessons," he said. "Inside the circle is Oz. Make an *X*"—he did so, through the oval—"and roughly speaking, you have a pie in four sections. The top is Gillikin. Full of cities and universities and theatres, civilized life, they say. And industry." He moved clockwise. "East, is Munchkinland, where we are now. Farmland, the bread basket of Oz, except down in the mountainous south—these strokes, in the district of Wend Hardings, are the hills you're climbing." He bumped and squiggled. "Directly south of the center of Oz is Quadling Country. Badlands, I'm told—marshy, useless, infested with bugs and feverish airs." Turtle Heart looked puzzled at this, but nodded. "Then west, what they call Winkie Country. Don't know much about that except it's dry and unpopulated."

"And around?" said Turtle Heart.

"Sandstone deserts north and west, fleckstone desert east and south. They used to say the desert sands were deadly poison; that's just standard propaganda. Keeps invaders from Ev and Quox from trying to get in. Munchkinland is rich and desirable farming territory, and Gillikin's not bad either. In the Glikkus, up here"—he scratched lines in the northeast, on the border between Gillikin and Munchkinland—"are the emerald mines and the famous Glikkus canals. I gather there's a dispute whether the Glikkus is Munchkinlander or Gillikinese, but I have no opinion on that."

Turtle Heart moved his hands over the drawing in the dirt, flexing his palms, as if he were reading the map from above. "But here?" he said. "What is here?"

Frex wondered if he meant the air above Oz. "The realm of the Unnamed God?" he said. "The Other Land? Are you a unionist?"

"Turtle Heart is glassblower," said Turtle Heart.

"I mean religiously."

Turtle Heart bowed his head and didn't meet Frex's eye. "Turtle Heart is not to know what name to call this."

"I don't know about Quadlings," said Frex, warming to a possible convert. "But Gillikinese and Munchkinlanders are largely unionist. Since Lurlinist paganism went out. For centuries, there have been unionist shrines and chapels all over Oz. Are there none in Quadling Country?"

"Turtle Heart does not to recognize what is this," he said.

"And now respectable unionists are going in droves over to the pleasure faith," said Frex, snorting, "or even tiktokism, which hardly even qualifies as a religion. To the ignorant everything is spectacle these days. The ancient unionist monks and maunts knew their place in the universe—acknowledging the life source too sublime to be named—and now we sniff up the skirts of every musty magician who comes along. Hedonists, anarchists, solipsists! Individual freedom and amusement is all! As if sorcery had any moral component! Charms, alley magic, industrial-strength sound and light displays, fake shape-changers! Charlatans, nabobs of necromancy, chemical and herbal wisdoms, humbug hedonists!

Selling their bog recipes and crone aphorisms and schoolboy spells! It makes me sick."

Turtle Heart said, "Shall Turtle Heart to bring you water, shall Turtle Heart to lie you down?" He put fingers soft as calfskin on the side of Frex's neck. Frex shivered and realized he had been shouting. Nanny and Melena were standing in the doorway with the pan of fish, silent.

"It's a figure of speech, I'm not sick," he said, but he was touched at the concern the foreigner had shown. "I think we'll eat."

And they did. Elphaba ignored her food except to prod the eyes out of the baked fish and to try to fit them onto her wingless bird. Nanny grumbled good-naturedly about the wind off the lake, her chills, her backbone, her digestion. Her gas was apparent from more than a few feet away and Frex moved, as discreetly as possible, to be upwind. He found himself sitting next to the Quadling on the bench.

"So is all that clear to you?" Frex pointed a fork at the map of Oz.

"Is Emerald City to be where?" said the Quadling, fish bones poking out from between his lips.

"Dead center," Frex said.

"And there is Ozma," said Turtle Heart.

"Ozma, the ordained Queen of Oz, or so they say," Frex said, "though the Unnamed God must be ruler of all, in our hearts."

"How can unnamed creature to rule—" began Turtle Heart.

"No theology at dinner," sang out Melena, "that's a house rule dating from the start of our marriage, Turtle Heart, and we obey it."

"Besides, *I* still harbor a devotion to Lurline." Nanny made a face in Frex's direction. "Old folks like me are allowed to. Do you know about Lurline, stranger?"

Turtle Heart shook his head.

"If we have no theology then we surely have no arrant pagan nonsense—" began Frex, but Nanny, being a guest and invoking a touch of deafness when it suited her, plowed on.

"Lurline is the Fairy Queen who flew over the sandy wastes, and spotted the green and lovely land of Oz below. She left her daughter Ozma to rule the country in her absence and she promised to return to Oz in its darkest hour."

"Hah!" said Frex.

"No *habs* at me." Nanny sniffed. "I'm as entitled to my beliefs as you are, Frexspar the Godly. At least they don't get me into trouble as yours do."

"Nanny, govern your temper," said Melena, enjoying this.

"It's rubbish," said Frex. "Ozma rules in the Emerald City, and anyone who's seen her, or paintings of her, knows that she's from Gillikinese stock. She's got the same broad band of forehead, the slightly gapped front teeth, the frenzy of curling blond hair, the quick shifts of mood—usually into anger. All characteristic of Gillikinese peoples. You've seen her, Melena, tell him."

"Oh, she is elegant in her way," Melena admitted.

"The daughter of a Fairy Queen?" said Turtle Heart.

"More nonsense," said Frex.

"Not nonsense!" snapped Nanny.

"They think she bears herself again and again like a pfenix," said Frex. "Hah and double hah. There've been three hundred years of very different Ozmas. Ozma the Mendacious was a dedicated maunt, who lowered rulings in a bucket down from the topmost chamber in a cloister tower. She was as mad as a bung beetle. Ozma the Warrior conquered the Glikkus, at least for a time, and commandeered the emeralds with which to decorate the Emerald City. Ozma the Librarian did nothing but read genealogies for her whole life long. Then there was Ozma the Scarcely Beloved, who kept pet ermines. She overtaxed the farmers to begin the road system of yellow brick that they're still struggling to complete, and much luck to them, I say."

"Who is Ozma now?" asked Turtle Heart.

"Actually," said Melena, "I had the pleasure to meet the last Ozma at a social season in the Emerald City—my grandfather the Eminent Thropp had a town house. The winter I was fifteen I was brought out into society there. She was Ozma the Bilious, because of a bad stomach. She was the size of a lake narwhal, but she dressed beautifully. I saw her with her husband, Pastorius, at the Oz Festival of Song and Sentiment."

"She is no longer the Queen?" asked Turtle Heart, confused.

"She died in an unfortunate accident involving some rat poison," said Frex.

"Died," said Nanny, "or her spirit moved next into her child, Ozma Tippetarius."

"The current Ozma is just about the age of Elphaba," said Melena, "so her father, Pastorius, is the Ozma Regent. The good man will rule until Ozma Tippetarius is old enough to take the throne."

Turtle Heart shook his head. Frex was annoyed because they had spent so much time talking about the worldly ruler and ignored the eternal realm, and Nanny lapsed into a bout of indigestion for which they all were very sorry, olfactorily speaking.

Anyway, even being irritated, Frex was glad to be home. Because of the beauty of Melena—she was almost glowing tonight as the sun left the sky—and because of the surprise of Turtle Heart, smiling and un-self-conscious next to him. Maybe because of Turtle Heart's religious emptiness, which Frex found challenging and appealing, almost tempting.

"Then there's the dragon beneath Oz, in a hidden cavern," Nanny was saying to Turtle Heart. "The dragon who has dreamt the world, and who will burn it in flames when he awakes—"

"Shut up that superstitious codswallop!" shouted Frex.

Elphaba, on all fours, advanced on the uneven planks of the flooring. She bared her teeth—as if she knew what a dragon was, as if she were pretending—and roared. Her green skin made her more persuasive, as if she were a dragon child. She roared again—"Oh sweetheart, don't," said Frex—and she peed on the floor, and sniffed her urine with satisfaction and disgust.

Child's Play

One afternoon toward the end of summer, Nanny said, "There's a beast abroad. I've seen it at dusk several times, lurking about in the ferns. What sorts of creatures are native to these hills anyway?"

"You don't find anything larger than a gopher," said Melena. They were at the side of the brook, working at laundry. The small spring wetness had long since ceased, and the drought had clamped its hand down again. The stream was only a thin trickle. Elphaba, who would not come near the water, was stripping a wild pear tree of its stunted crop. She clung to the trunk with her hands and out-turned feet, and threw her head around, catching the sour fruit with her teeth and then spitting seeds and stem on the ground.

"This is larger than a gopher," said Nanny. "Trust me. Have you bears? It could have been a bear cub, though it moved mighty fast."

"No bears. There's the rumor of rock tigers on the felltop, but they tell me not a single one has been sighted in ages. And rock tigers are notoriously skittish and shy. They don't come near human dwellings."

"A wolf then? Are there wolves?" Nanny let the sheet droop in the water. "It could have been a wolf."

"Nanny, you think you're in the desert. Wend Hardings is desolate, I agree, but it's a tame barrenness for all that. You're alarming me with your wolf and your tiger talk."

Elphaba, who would not speak yet, made a low growl in the pocket of her throat.

"I don't like it," said Nanny. "Let's finish up and dry these things back at the house. Enough is enough. Besides, I have other things I want to say to you. Let's give the child to Turtle Heart and let's go off somewhere." She shuddered. "Somewhere safe."

"What you have to say you can say within earshot of Elphaba," said Melena. "You know she doesn't understand a word."

"You confuse not speaking with not listening," said Nanny. "I think she understands plenty."

"Look, she's smearing fruit on her neck, like a cologne—"

"Like a war paint, you mean."

"Oh, dour Nanny, stop being such a goose and scrub those sheets harder. They're filthy."

"I need hardly ask whose sweat and leakage this is . . ."

"Oh you, no you needn't ask, but don't start moralizing at me—"

"But you know Frex is bound to notice sooner or later. These energetic afternoon naps you take—well, you always had an eye for the fellow with a decent helping of sausage and hard-boiled eggs—"

"Nanny, come, this is none of your affair."

"More's the pity," said Nanny, sighing. "Isn't aging a cruel hoax? I'd trade my hard-won pearls of wisdom for a good romp with Uncle Flagpole any day."

Melena flipped a handful of water in Nanny's face to shut her up. The older woman blinked and she said, "Well, it's your garden, plant there what you choose and reap what you may. What I want to talk about is the child, anyway."

The girl was now squatting behind the pear tree, eyes narrowed at something in the distance. She looked, thought Melena, like a sphinx, like a stone beast. A fly even landed on her face and walked across the bridge of her nose, and the child didn't flinch or squirm. Then, suddenly, she leaped and pounced, a naked green kitten after an invisible butterfly.

"What about her?"

"Melena, she needs to get used to other children. She'll start talking a little bit if she sees that other chicks are talking."

"Talking among children is an overrated concept."

"Don't be glib. You know she needs to get used to people other than us. She's not going to have an easy time of it anyhow, unless she sheds her greeny skin as she grows up. She needs the habits of conversation. Look, I give her chores to do, I warble nursery rhymes at her. Melena, why doesn't she respond like other children?"

"She's boring. Some children just are."

"She ought to have other pups to play with. They would infect her with a sense of fun."

"Frankly, Frex doesn't expect a child of his to be interested in fun," said Melena. "Fun is counted for overmuch in this world, Nanny. I agree with him on that."

"So your dragon-snaking with Turtle Heart is what—devotional exercises?"

"I said don't be catty, please!" Melena focused on the toweling, beating it with annoyance. Nanny would go on about this; she was up to something. And Nanny had hit the nail on the head. There crept Turtle Heart into the cool shadows of the cottage, when Melena was tired from a morning's work in the vegetable garden. He covered her with a sense of holiness, and it was more than her undergarments that would drop away from her when they tumbled panting onto the bedclothes. She would lose her sense of shame.

She knew this did not follow conventional reason. Nevertheless, should a tribunal of unionist ministers call her to court for adultery, she would tell the truth. Somehow Turtle Heart had saved her and restored her sense of grace, of hope in the world. Her belief in the goodness of things had been dashed into bits when little green Elphaba crawled into being. The child was extravagant punishment for a sin so minor she didn't even know if she had committed it.

It was not the sex that saved her, though the sex was mighty vigorous, even frightening. It was that Turtle Heart didn't blush when Frex showed up, that he didn't shrink from beastly little Elphaba. He set up shop in the side yard, blowing glass and grinding it, as if life had brought him here just to redeem Melena. Wherever else he might have been heading had been forgotten.

"Very well, you old interfering cow," said Melena. "For the sake of argument, what do you propose?"

"We must take Elphie to Rush Margins and find some small children for her to play with."

Melena sat back on her haunches. "But you have to be jesting!" she cried. "Slow and deliberate as Elphaba is, at least she's unharmed here! I may not be able to summon much maternal warmth, but I feed her, Nanny, and I keep her from hurting herself! How cruel, to inflict the outside world on her! A green child will be an open invitation for scorn and abuse. And children are wickeder than adults, they have no sense of restraint. We might as well go throw her in the lake she's so terrified of."

"No no no," said Nanny, putting her fat hands on her own knees; her voice was thick with determination. "Now I am going to argue with you about this, Melena, until you give in. Time in its wisdom will bring you around to my way of thinking. Listen to me. *Listen* to me. You are only a pampered little rich girl who flitted about from music lessons to dance lessons with neighborhood children equally rich and stupid as you. Of *course* there's cruelty. But Elphaba must learn who she is and she must face down cruelty early. And there will be less of it than you expect."

"Don't play Nanny Goddess with me. I won't have it."

"Nanny is not giving up," said Nanny, just as fiercely. "I have a long-range view of your happiness as well as hers, and believe me, if you don't give her the weapons and armor with which she can defend herself against scorn, she'll make your life miserable as hers will be miserable."

"And the weapons and armor she'll learn from the dirty urchins of Rush Margins?"

"Laughter. Fun. Teasing. Smiling."

"Oh, *please*."

"I'm not above blackmailing you about this, Melena," said Nanny. "I can wander into Rush Margins this afternoon and find where Frex is trying to hold his revival meeting and whisper a few words to him. While Frex is busy cranking up the religious ardor of Rush Margins sluggards, would he be interested in knowing what his wife is up to with Turtle Heart?"

"You are a miserable old fiend! You are a foul, unethical bully!" cried Melena.

Nanny grinned with pride. "No later than tomorrow," she said, "we'll go in tomorrow and get her life started."

In the morning a stiff, unforgiving wind galloped from the heights. It picked up old leaves and the remains of failed crops and kitchen gardens. Nanny pulled a shawl across her rounded shoulders and tugged a bonnet over her brow. Her eyes were full of marginal beasts; she kept turning to see a slinking cat-thing or a vixen dissolve into clots of skeleton leaves and debris.

Nanny found a blackthorn staff as if to aid her over stones and ruts, but she hoped to be ready to wield it against some hungry beast. "The land is dry and cold," she observed, almost to herself. "And so little rain! Of course the big beasts would be driven from the hills. Let's walk together, no running ahead, little green."

They made their way in silence: Nanny fearful, Melena angry at having to miss her afternoon dalliance, and Elphaba like a windup toy, one foot solidly in front of the other. The margins of the lake had receded, and some of the crude docks were now walkways over pebble and drying greenrot, with the water pulled back beyond their reach.

Gawnette's was a dark stone cottage with a roof of moldering thatch. Because of a bad hip, Gawnette was no good at hauling the fishing nets or at kneeling over the wasting vegetable gardens. She had a mess of small children in various stages of undress, squawling and sulking and trotting around the dirty yard in a little pack. She looked up as the minister's family approached.

"Good day, and you must be Gawnette," said Nanny brightly. She was pleased to open the gate and be safely inside the garden, even of this hovel. "Brother Frexspar told us we would find you here."

"Sweet Lurline, what they say is true!" said Gawnette, making a holy sign against Elphaba. "I thought it vicious lies, and here she is!"

The children had slowed to a walk. They were boys and girls, brown-faced and white, all of them filthy, all of them keen on something new. Though they kept walking, playing some game of endurance or make-believe, their eyes never left Elphaba.

"You know this is Melena—of course you do—and I am their Nanny," said Nanny. "We're pleased to meet you, Gawnette." She slid a glance at Melena and bit her upper lip and nodded.

"Very pleased, I'm sure," said Melena stonily.

"And we need some advice, for you come well recommended," said Nanny. "The little girl has problems, and the best of our thinking just doesn't seem to bring forth any good ideas."

Gawnette leaned forward, suspicious.

"The child is green," whispered Nanny confidentially. "You may not have noticed, being attracted by her charm and warmth. Of course, we know the good people of Rush Margins wouldn't let a thing like that bother them. But because she is green, she is shy. Look at her. Little frightened spring turtle. We need to draw her out, make her happier, and we don't know how."

"She's green all right," said Gawnette. "No wonder useless Brother Frexspar retired from his preaching for so long!" She threw back her head and laughed raucously, unkindly. "And he's only now had the nerve to take it up again! Well, that's balls if ever I heard it!"

"Brother Frexspar," interrupted Melena coldly, "reminds us of the scriptures—'No one knows the color of a soul.' Gawnette, he suggested I remind you of that very text."

"Did he now," mumbled Gawnette, chastised. "Well then, what do you want with me?"

"Let her play, let her learn, let her come here and be minded by you. You know more than we do," said Nanny.

The cunning old cow, thought Melena. She is trying that rarest of strategies, telling the truth, and making it sound plausible. They sat down.

"I don't know if they'd take to her," said Gawnette, holding out a while. "And you know my hip doesn't let me hop up and stop them when they get going."

"Let's see. And of course there'd be some payment, some cash, Melena fully agrees," said Nanny. The barren vegetable plot had caught her attention. This was *poverty*. Nanny gave Elphaba a push. "Well, go on in, child, and see what's what."

The girl didn't budge, didn't blink. The children came near to her. There were five boys and two girls. "What an ugly pug," said one of the older boys. He touched Elphaba on the shoulder.

"Play nicely now," said Melena, about to leap up, but Nanny kept her hand out to say, Stay down.

"Tag, let's tag," said the boy, "who's the greenfly?"

"Not it, not it!" The other children shrieked, and rushed in to brush Elphaba with their hands, and then raced away. She stood for a minute, unsure, her own hands down and clenched, and then she ran a few steps, and stopped.

"That's the way, healthful exercise," said Nanny, nodding. "Gawnette, you're a genius."

"I know my chicks," said Gawnette. "Don't say I don't."

Herdlike, the children rushed in again, tapping and darting away, but the girl would not chase them. So they neared her once more.

"Is it true you got a Quadling muckfrog staying with you too?" said Gawnette. "Is it true he only eats grass and dung?"

"I beg your pardon!" cried Melena.

"That's what they say, is it true?" said Gawnette.

"He's a fine man."

"But he's a Quadling?"

"Well—yes."

"Don't bring him around here then, they spread the plague," said Gawnette.

"They spread no such thing," snapped Melena.

"No throwing, Elphie dear," called Nanny.

"I'm only saying what I hear. They say at night that Quadlings fall asleep and their souls climb out through their mouths and go abroad."

"Stupid people say a lot of stupid things." Melena was curt and too loud. "I have never seen his soul climb out of his mouth while he was sleeping, and I've had plenty of opportu—"

"Darling, no rocks," shrilled Nanny. "None of the other children have rocks."

"Now they do," observed Gawnette.

"He is the most sensitive person I've ever met," said Melena.

"Sensitive isn't much use to a fishwife," said Gawnette. "How about to a minister and a minister's wife?"

"Now there's blood, how vexing," said Nanny. "Children, let Elphie up so I can wipe that cut. And I didn't bring a rag. Gawnette?"

"Bleeding is good for them, makes them less hungry," said Gawnette.

"I rate *sensitive* a good sight higher than *stupid*," said Melena, seething.

"No biting," said Gawnette to one of the little boys, and then, seeing Elphaba open her mouth to retaliate, raised herself to her feet, bad hip or no, and screamed, "*no biting, for the love of mercy!*"

"Aren't children divine?" said Nanny.

Darkness
Abroad

Every second or third day Nanny took Elphaba by the hand and wad-dled the shadowy road to Rush Margins. There Elphaba mingled with the greasy children under the eyes of sullen Gawnette. Frex had moved out again (was it confidence or desperation?)—he was scaring miserable hamlets with his frenzied beard and his collected opinions on faith. Gone for eight, ten days at a time. Melena practiced piano arpeggios on a tuneless mock keyboard Frex had carved for her, to perfect scale.

Turtle Heart seemed to wilt and parch as autumn came on. Their afternoons of dalliance began to lose the heat of urgency, and developed in warmth. Melena had always appreciated the attentions of Frex, and been attentive to him, but somehow his body had not been as supple as Turtle Heart's. She drifted off to sleep with Turtle Heart's mouth on one of her nipples and his hands—his big hands—roaming like sentient pets. She imagined that Turtle Heart divided his body when her eyes were closed; his mouth roamed, his cock rose and nudged and leaned, his breath was somewhere other than his mouth, hissing elegantly into her ear, word-lessly, his arms were like stirrups.

Still she didn't know him, not the way she knew Frex; she could not see through him as she could most people. She put this down to his majestic bearing, but Nanny, ever watchful, remarked one evening that it was just that his ways were the ways of a Quadling and Melena had never even acknowledged that he came from a different culture than she did.

"Culture, what's culture," Melena said lazily. "People are people."

"Don't you remember your nursery rhymes?" Nanny put aside her sewing (with relief) and recited.

"Boys study, girls know,
That's the way that lessons go.
Boys learn, girls forget,
That's the way of lessons yet.
Gillikinese are sharp as knives,
Munchkinlanders lead corny lives,
Glikkuns beat their ugly wives,
Winkies swarm in sticky hives.
But the Quadlings, Oh the Quadlings,
Slimy stupid curse-at-godlings,
Eat their young and bury their old
A day before their bodies get cold.
Give me an apple and I'll say it again.

"What do you know of him?" Nanny asked. "Is he married? Why did he leave Lower Slimepit or wherever he comes from? Naturally, it's not my place to ask such personal questions—"

"Since when did you ever know your place or keep it, either?"

"When Nanny leaves her place, believe me, you'll know," said Nanny.

One evening in early autumn, for fun they built up a fire in the yard. Frex was home and good-humored, and Nanny was thinking of heading back to Colwen Grounds, which made Melena good-humored too. Turtle Heart put together a supper, a distasteful goulash of small sour new apples and cheese and bacon.

Frex was feeling expansive. The effect of that blasted tiktok contrivance, the Clock of the Time Dragon, had been wearing off at last—thank the Unnamed God—and the graceless poor had been turning out to hear Frex harangue them. A two-week mission at Three Dead Trees had been a success. Frex had been rewarded with a small wallet of brass coins and barter tokens, and the glow of devotion or even lust on the face of more than one penitent.

"Perhaps our time here is limited," said Frex, sighing with contentment and clasping his arms behind his head—the typical male response to happiness, thought Melena: to predict its demise. Her husband went on. "Perhaps the road from Rush Margins leads us on to higher things, Melena. Grander stations in life."

"Oh please," she said. "My family rose from humble beginnings for nine generations, to produce me with my ankles in the mud out here in the middle of nowhere. I don't believe in higher things."

"I mean the lofty ambitions of the spirit. I don't mean to storm the Emerald City and become personal confessor to the Ozma Regent."

"Why not put yourself forward to be confessor to Ozma Tippetarius?" Nanny asked. She could see herself rising in courtly Emerald City society if Frex had such a position. "So what if the royal baby is only, what, two years old? Three? So we have government by a male regent again. It's only for a limited engagement—like most male encounters. You're young still—she'll grow up—you'll be well-placed to influence policy . . ."

"I don't care about ministering to anyone in court, not even an Ozma the Fanatically Devout." Frex lit a sallowwood pipe. "My mission is to the downtrodden and humble."

"Goodness should to travel to Quadling Country," said Turtle Heart. "Downtrodden there."

Turtle Heart didn't often speak of his past, and Melena remembered Nanny's gibe about her lack of curiosity. She waved the pipe smoke away and said, "Why did you leave Ovvels anyway?"

"Horrors," he said.

Elphaba, who had been hoping for ants to crawl across the grinding stone so she could mash them with a rock, looked up across the shallow basin of the stone. The others waited for Turtle Heart to go on. Melena's heart lifted uneasily—she had a sudden premonition of things changing right here, this very evening, this most splendid gentle night, things going awry just when they had managed to settle down.

"What sort of horrors?" said Frex.

"I feel a chill. I'll get a shawl," said Melena.

"Or minister to Pastorius! The Ozma Regent! Why not, Frex?" Nanny said. "I'm sure with Melena's family connections you could twist an invitation—"

"Horrors," said Elphaba.

It was her first word, and it was greeted with silence. Even the moon, a lambent bowl among the trees, seemed to pause.

"Horrors?" Elphaba said again, looking around. Though her mouth was serious, her eyes glowed; she had realized her own accomplishment. She was nearly two years old. The big sharp teeth in her mouth could not keep her words locked inside her anymore. "Horrors," she tried in a whisper. "Horrors."

"Come to Nanny, darling. Come sit on my lap and hush for a while."

She obeyed, but sat forward, apart from Nanny's cushiony bosom, allowing Nanny's arms to ring around her waist but no contact more than that. She stared at Turtle Heart and waited.

And Turtle Heart said in an awed voice, "Turtle Heart is thinking the child to speak for the first time."

"Yes," said Frex, exhaling a ring of smoke, "and she's asking about the horrors. Unless you don't care to tell us? . . ."

"Turtle Heart to say little. Turtle Heart to work in glass, and to leave words for the Goodness and the Lady and the Nanny. And now for the Girl."

"Say a little, though. Since you brought it up."

Melena shivered; she hadn't gone for the shawl. She could not move. She was heavy as stone.

"Workers from the Emerald City and other places, they to come to Quadling Country. They to look and taste and sample the air, the water, the soil. They to plan the highway. Quadlings to know this is wasted time and wasted effort. They do not to listen to Quadling voices."

"Quadlings aren't road engineers, I suspect," said Frex evenly.

"The country is delicate," said Turtle Heart. "In Ovvels the houses to float between trees. Crops to grow on small platforms hooked by ropes. Boys to dive in shallow water for vegetable pearls. Too many trees and there is not enough light for crops and health. Too few trees and the water rises and roots of plants floating on top cannot to stretch to soil. Quadling Country is poor country but beauty rich. It only to support life by careful planning and cooperation."

"So resistance to the Yellow Brick Road—"

"Is only part of the story. Quadlings cannot to convince road builders, who want to build up dikes of mud and stone and to cut Quadling Country in pieces. Quadlings to argue, and to pray, and to testify, and cannot to win with words."

Frex held his pipe in his two hands and watched Turtle Heart speak. Frex was drawn to him; Frex was always drawn to intensity.

"Quadlings consider to fight," said Turtle Heart. "Because they think this is only the start. When the builders to test soil and to sift water, they to learn of things Quadlings are smart for ever, but Quadlings to keep still."

"Things you know?"

"Turtle Heart to speak of rubies," he said with a great sigh. "Rubies under the water. Red as pigeon blood. Engineers to say: Red corundum in bands of crystalline limestone under swamp. Quadlings to say: The blood of Oz."

"Like the red glass you make?" said Melena.

"Ruby glass to come by adding gold chloride," said Turtle Heart. "But Quadling Country to sit atop real deposits of real rubies. And the news is sure to go to the Emerald City with the builders. What to follow is horror upon horror."

"How do you know?" snapped Melena.

"To look in glass," said Turtle Heart, pointing to the roundel he had made as a toy for Elphaba, "is to see the future, in blood and rubies."

"I don't believe in seeing the future. That smacks of the pleasure faith," said Frex fiercely. "The fatalism of the Time Dragon. Pfaah. No, the Unnamed God has an unnamed history for us, and prophecy is merely guesswork and fear."

"Fear and guesswork is enough to make Turtle Heart to leave Quadling Country, then," said the Quadling glassblower without apology. "Quadlings do not to call their religion a pleasure faith, but they to listen to signs and to watch for messages. As the water to run red with rubies it will to run with the blood of Quadlings."

"Nonsense!" Frex fussed, red himself. "They need a good talking-to."

"Besides, isn't Pastorius a simpleton?" said Melena, who alone of them could claim an informed opinion on the royal house. "What will he do until Ozma is of age but ride the hunt, and eat Munchkinlander pastries, and fuck the odd housemaid on the side?"

"The danger is a foreigner," said Turtle Heart, "not a home-grown king or queen. The old women, and the shamans, and the dying: They to see a stranger king, cruel and mighty."

"What is the Ozma Regent doing, planning roadworks into that godforsaken mire anyway?" Melena asked.

"Progress," said Frex, "same as the Yellow Brick Road through Munchkinland. Progress and control. The movement of troops. The regularization of taxes. Military protection."

"Protection from whom?" said Melena.

"Ahh," said Frex, "always the important question."

"Ahh," said Turtle Heart, almost in a whisper.

"So where are you going?" said Frex. "Not that you need leave here, of course. Melena loves having you around. We all do."

"Horrors," said Elphaba.

"Hush now," said Nanny.

"Lady is kind and Goodness is kind to Turtle Heart. Who did not mean to stay more than a day. Turtle Heart was on his way to the Emerald City and to get lost. Turtle Heart to hope to beg audience with Ozma—"

"Ozma Regent, now," interjected Frex.

"—and to plead mercy for Quadling Country. And to warn of brutal stranger—"

"Horrors," said Elphaba, clapping her hands together in delight.

"The child to remind Turtle Heart of his duties," he said. "To talk of it brings duties back out of the pain of the past. Turtle Heart to forget. But when words are to speak in the air, actions must to follow."

Melena glared hatefully at Nanny, who had dropped the girl on the ground and begun to busy herself with collecting the supper dishes. See what comes of prying and nosiness, Nanny? See? Just the dissolution of my only earthly happiness, that's all. Melena turned her face from her horrid child, who seemed to be smiling, or was that wincing? She looked at her husband with despair. Do something, Frex!

"Perhaps this is the higher ambition we seek," he was murmuring. "We should travel to Quadling Country, Melena. We should leave the luxury of Munchkinland and try ourselves in the fire of a truly needy situation."

"The luxury of Munchkinland?" Melena's voice was screechy.

"When the Unnamed God speaks through a lowly vessel," began Frex, gesturing at Turtle Heart, who was looking desperate again, "we can choose to hear or we can choose to harden our hearts—"

"Well, hear this, then," said Melena, "I'm pregnant, Frex. I can't travel. I can't move. And with a new infant to watch as well as Elphaba to raise, it's too much to suggest tramping around Mudland."

After the stillness had lost some of its steam, she continued, "Well, I didn't intend to tell you like this."

"Congratulations," said Frex coldly.

"Horrors," said Elphaba to her mother. "Horrors, horrors, horrors."

"That's enough thoughtless chatter for one night," said Nanny, taking charge. "Melena, you will catch a chill sitting out here. Summer nights are turning colder again. Come inside and let's let that be that."

But Frex got himself up and went to kiss his wife. It was not clear to anyone whether he suspected that Turtle Heart was the father, nor was it clear to Melena which one, her husband or her lover, was the father. She didn't actually care. She just didn't want Turtle Heart to leave, and she hated him fiercely for being so suddenly riven with moral feeling for his miserable people.

Frex and Turtle Heart conversed in low voices that Melena could not make out. They sat by the fire with their heads low together, and Frex had his arm on Turtle Heart's shaking shoulders. Nanny readied Elphaba for bed, left her outside with the men, and came to sit on Melena's bed with a glass of hot milk on a tray and a small bowl of medicinal capsules.

"Well, I knew this was coming," said Nanny calmly. "Drink the milk, dear, and stop sniveling. You're behaving like a child again. How long have you known?"

"Oh, six weeks," said Melena. "I don't want milk, Nanny, I want my wine."

"You'll drink milk. No more wine till the baby's born. You want another disaster?"

"Drinking wine doesn't change the skin color of embryos," said Melena. "I may be a dolt but I know that much about biology."

"It's bad for your frame of mind, nothing more and nothing less. Drink the milk and swallow one of these capsules."

"What for?"

"I did what I told you I'd do," said Nanny in a conspiratorial voice. "Last fall I poked around the Lower Quarter of our fair capital on your behalf—"

The young woman was suddenly engaged. "Nanny you didn't! How clever! Weren't you terrified?"

"Of course I was. But Nanny loves you, however stupid you are. I found a store marked with the secret insignia of the alchemist's trade." She wrinkled her nose in recollection of the smell of rotting ginger and cat piss. "I sat down with a saucy-looking old biddy from Shiz, a crone named Yackle, and drank the tea and upended the cup so she could read the leaves. Yackle could barely see her own hand, much less read the future."

"A real professional," Melena said dryly.

"Your husband doesn't believe in predictions, so keep your voice down. Anyway, I explained about the greenness of your first child, and the difficulty of knowing exactly why it had happened. We don't want a recurrence, I said. So Yackle ground up some herbs and minerals, and roasted it with oil of gomba, and said some pagan prayers and for all I know she spit in it, I didn't watch too closely. But I paid for a nine months' supply, to be begun as soon as you're sure you've conceived. We're a month late maybe, but this'll be better than nothing. I have supreme confidence in this woman, Melena, and you should too."

"Why should I?" said Melena, swallowing the first of nine capsules. It tasted like boiled marrow.

"Because Yackle predicted greatness for your children," said Nanny. "She said Elphaba will be more than you credit, and your second will follow suit. She said not to give up on your life. She said history waits to be written, and this family has a part in it."

"What does she say about my lover?"

"You are a pest," said Nanny. "She said to rest and not to worry. She gives her blessing. She is a filthy whore but she knows what she's talking about." Nanny didn't mention that Yackle was certain the next child would be a girl too. There was too much chance Melena would try to abort her, and Yackle sounded quite sure that history belonged to two sisters, not a single girl.

"And you got home safely? Did anyone suspect?"

"Who would suspect innocent old Nanny of trading in illegal substances in the Lower Quarter?" laughed Nanny. "I do my knitting and mind my own business. Now go to sleep, my love. Nix to the wine for the next few months, and stay the course with this medicine, and we'll have for you and Frex a decent, healthy child, which will provide no end of recovery for your marriage."

"My marriage is perfectly fine," said Melena, snuggling down under the covers—the capsule had a kick, but she didn't want Nanny to know—"as long as we don't go wading off into the muddy sunset."

"The sun sets in the west, not in the south," said Nanny soothingly. "It was a masterly stroke to bring up the pregnancy tonight, my dear. I wouldn't come to visit you if you went paddling off into Quadling Country, by the way. I'm fifty years old this year, you know. There are some things Nanny is really too old to do."

"Well nobody better go anywhere," said Melena, and began to fall asleep.

Nanny, pleased with herself, glanced out the window again as she prepared to retire. Frex and Turtle Heart were still deep in conversation. Nanny was sharper than she let on; she had seen Turtle Heart's face when he was remembering the threat to his people. It had opened like a hen's egg, and the truth had fluttered and wobbled out of it just as naive as a yellow chick. And as fragile. No wonder Frex was sitting nearer to the beleaguered Quadling than Nanny thought was altogether decent. But there seemed no end of oddity to this family.

"Send the girl in so I can put her down," she called from the window, partly to interrupt their intimacy.

Frex looked around. "She's in, isn't she?"

Nanny glanced. The child was not given to hiding games, neither here nor with the brats in the village. "No, isn't she with you?"

The men turned and looked. Nanny thought she saw a blur of movement in the blue shadows of the wild yew. She stood up and held on to the window ledge. "Well, find her. It's the prowling hour."

"There's nothing here, Nanny, it's your overactive imagination," drawled Frex, but the men were up quickly, and looking around.

"Melena, dear, don't sleep yet; do you know where Elphaba is? Did you see her wander off?" said Nanny.

Melena struggled to lift herself to one elbow. She stared through her hair and her inebriation. "What are you on about?" she asked in a slur, "who is wandering off?"

"Elphaba," Nanny said. "Come on, you better get up. Where could she be. Where could she be." She started to help Melena up, but it was happening too slowly, and Nanny's heart was beginning to beat fast. She fixed Melena's hands to the bedposts, saying, "Now come on, Melena, this is not good," and she reached for her blackthorn staff.

"Who?" said Melena. "Who's lost?"

The men were calling in the purple gloaming. "Fabala! Elphaba! Elphie! Little frog!" They circled out away from the yard, away from the dying embers of the dinner fire, peering and hitting at the lower branches of bushes. "Little snake! Lizard girl! Where are you?"

"It's the thing, the thing has come down from the hills, whatever it is!" cried Nanny.

"There's no thing, you old fool," said Frex, but he leaped more and more vigorously from rock to rock behind the lodge, smacking branches aside. Turtle Heart stood still, his hands out to the sky, as if trying to receive the faint light of the first stars into his palms.

"Is it Elphaba," called Melena from the door, finally focusing, and stepping forward in her nightgown. "Is the child gone?"

"She's wandered off, she's been taken," said Nanny fiercely, "these two idiots were flirting like schoolgirls, and the beast from the hills is abroad!"

Melena called, her words mounting in pitch and terror, "Elphaba! Elphaba, you listen to me! Come here this instant! Elphaba!"

The wind alone answered.

"She is not far," said Turtle Heart after a moment. In the deepening dark he was almost invisible while Melena in her white poplin glowed like an angel, as if lit from within. "She is not far, she just is not here."

"What the devil do you mean," Nanny said, weeping, "with your riddles and your games?"

Turtle Heart turned. Frex had come back to him, to throw an arm around him and hold him up, and Melena came forward to his other side.

He sagged for a minute, as if fainting; Melena cried out in fright. But Turtle Heart straightened up, and began to move forward, and they headed toward the lake.

"Not the lake, not that girl, she can't abide water, you know that," called Nanny, but she was rushing forward now, using her staff to feel the ground ahead of her so she wouldn't stumble.

This is the end, thought Melena. Her brain was too foggy to think anything else, and she said it again and again, as if to prevent it from being true.

This is the beginning, thought Frex, but of what?

"She is not far, she is not here," said Turtle Heart again.

"Punishment for your wicked ways, you two-faced hedonists," Nanny said.

The ground sloped toward the still, receded margin of the lake. First at their feet, then at their waists and higher, the beached dock rose, like a bridge to nowhere, ending in air.

Beneath the dock in the dry shadows there were eyes.

"Oh, sweet Lurline," whispered Nanny.

Elphaba was sitting under the dock with the looking glass that Turtle Heart had made. She held it in two hands, and stared at it with one eye closed. She peered, she squinted; her open eye was distant and hollow.

Reflection from the starlight off the water, thought Frex, hoped Frex, but he knew the bright vacant eye was not lit by starlight.

"Horrors," murmured Elphaba.

Turtle Heart tumbled to his knees. "She sees him coming," he said thickly, "she sees him to come; he is to come from the air; is arriving. A balloon from the sky, the color of a bubble of blood: a huge crimson globe, a ruby globe: he falls from the sky. The Regent is fallen. The House of Ozma is fallen. The Clock was right. A minute to judgment."

He fell over, almost into Elphaba's small lap. She didn't seem to notice him. Behind her was a low growl. There was a beast, a felltop tiger, or some strange hybrid of tiger and dragon, with glowing orangey eyes. Elphaba was sitting in its folded forearms as if on a throne.

"Horrors," she said again, looking without binocular vision, staring at the glass in which her parents and Nanny could make out nothing but darkness. "Horrors."

II

Gillikin

Galinda

I

"Wittica, Settica, Wiccasand Turning, Red Sand, Dixxi House, change at Dixxi House for Shiz; stay aboard this coach for all points East; Tenniken, Brox Hall, and all destinations to Traum"—the conductor paused to catch his breath—"next stop Wittica, Wittica next!"

Galinda clutched her parcel of clothes to her breast. The old goat who sprawled on the seat across from her was missing the Wittica stop. She was glad that trains made passengers sleepy. She didn't want to keep avoiding his eye. At the last minute before she was to board the train, her minder, Ama Clutch, had stepped on a rusty nail and, terrified of the frozen-face syndrome, had begged permission to go to the nearest surgery for medicines and calming spells. "I can surely get myself to Shiz alone," Galinda had said coldly, "don't bother with *me*, Ama Clutch." And Ama Clutch hadn't. Galinda hoped that Ama Clutch would suffer a *little* frozenness of jaw before being well enough to show up in Shiz and chaperone Galinda through whatever was to come.

Her own chin was set, she believed, to imply a worldly boredom with train travel. In fact she had never been more than a day's carriage ride away from her family home in the little market town of Frottica. The railway line, laid down a decade ago, had meant that old dairy farms were being cut up for country estates for the merchants and manufacturers of Shiz. But Galinda's family continued to prefer rural Gillikin, with its fox haunts, its dripping dells, its secluded ancient pagan temples to Lurline. To them, Shiz was a distant urban threat, and even the convenience of rail transportation hadn't tempted them to risk all its complications, curiosities, and evil ways.

Galinda didn't see the verdant world through the glass of the carriage; she saw her own reflection instead. She had the nearsightedness of youth. She reasoned that because she was beautiful she was significant, though what she signified, and to whom, was not clear to her yet. The sway of her head made her creamy ringlets swing, catching the light, like so many jostling stacks of coins. Her lips were perfect, as pouted as an opening maya flower, and colored as brilliantly red. Her green traveling gown with its inset panels of ochre musset suggested wealth, while the black shawl draping just so about the shoulders was a nod to her academic inclinations. She was, after all, on her way to Shiz because she was *smart*.

But there was more than one way to be smart.

She was seventeen. The whole town of Frottica had seen her off. The first girl from the Pertha Hills to be accepted at Shiz! She had written well in the entrance exams, a meditation on Learning Ethics from the Natural World. ("Do Flowers Regret Being Plucked for a Bouquet? Do the Rains Practice Abstinence? Can Animals Really Choose to Be Good? Or: A Moral Philosophy of Springtime.") She had quoted excessively from the *Oziad*, and her rapturous prose had captivated the board of examiners. A three-year fellowship to Crage Hall. It wasn't one of the better colleges—those were still closed to female students. But it *was* Shiz University.

Her companion in the compartment, waking up when the conductor came back through, stretched his heels as he yawned. "Would you be so kind as to reach my ticket, it's in the overhead," he said. Galinda stood and found the ticket, aware that the bearded old thing was eyeing her comely figure. "Here you are," she said, and he answered, "Not to me, dearie, to the conductor. Without opposable thumbs, I have no hope of managing such a tiny piece of cardboard."

The conductor punched the ticket, and said, "You're the rare beast that can afford to travel first class."

"Oh," said the goat, "I object to the term *beast*. But the laws still allow my traveling in first class, I presume?"

"Money's money," said the conductor, without ill will, punching Galinda's ticket and returning it to her.

"No, money's *not* money," said the goat, "not when my ticket cost double what the young lady's did. In this case, money is a visa. I happen to have it."

"Going up to Shiz, are you?" said the conductor to Galinda, ignoring the goat's remark. "I can tell by that academic shawl."

"Oh well, it's something to do," said Galinda. She didn't care to talk to conductors. But when he continued along down the carriage, Galinda found that she liked even less the baleful look that the goat was giving her.

"Do you expect to learn anything at Shiz?" he asked.

"I have already learned not to speak to strangers."

"Then I will introduce myself and we will be strangers no longer. I am Dillamond."

"I am disinclined to know you."

"I am a Fellow of Shiz University, on the Faculty of Biological Arts."

You are a shabby dresser, even for a goat, Galinda thought. Money isn't everything. "Then I must overcome my natural shyness. My name is Galinda. I am of the Arduenna Clan on my mother's side."

"Let me be the first to welcome you to Shiz, Glinda. This is your first year?"

"Please, it is Galinda. The proper old Gillikinese pronunciation, if you don't mind." She could not bring herself to call him *sir*. Not with that horrid goatee and the tatty waistcoat that looked cut from some public house carpet.

"I wonder what you think of the Wizard's proposed Banns on travel?" The goat's eyes were buttery and warm, and frightening. Galinda had never heard of any Banns. She said as much. Dillamond—was it Doctor Dillamond?—explained in a conversational tone that the Wizard had thoughts of restricting Animal travel on public conveyances except in designated transports. Galinda replied that animals had always enjoyed separate services. "No, I am speaking of Animals," said Dillamond. "Those with a spirit."

"Oh, *those*," said Galinda crudely. "Well, I don't see the problem."

"My, my," said Dillamond. "Don't you indeed?" The goatee quivered; he was irritated. He began to hector her about Animal Rights. As things now stood, his own ancient mother couldn't afford to travel first class, and would have to ride in a pen when she wanted to visit him in Shiz. If the Wizard's Banns went through the Hall of Approval, as they were likely to do, the goat himself would be required by law to give up the privileges he had earned through years of study, training, and saving. "Is that right for a creature with a spirit?" he said. "From here to there, there to here, in a *pen?*"

"I quite agree, travel is *so* broadening," said Galinda. They endured the rest of the trip, including the change across the platform at Dixxi House, in a frosty silence.

Seeing her fright at the size and bustle of the terminus at Shiz, Dillamond took pity and offered to engage a carriage to take her to Crage Hall. She followed him, looking as unmortified as she could manage. Her luggage came behind, on the backs of a couple of porters.

Shiz! She tried not to gawp. Everyone hustling on business, laughing and hurrying and kissing, dodging carriages, while the buildings of Railway Square, brownstone and bluestone and covered with vine and moss, steamed softly in the sunlight. The animals—and the Animals! She had scarcely ever come across even the odd chicken squawking philosophically in Frottica—but here was a quartet of tsebras at an outdoor café, dressed flashily in black-and-white satin stripes on the bias to their inborn design; and an elephant on its hind legs directing traffic; and a tiger dressed up in some sort of exotic religious garb, a kind of monk or maunt or nun or something. Yes, yes, it was Tsebras, and Elephant, and Tiger, and she supposed Goat. She would have to get used to enunciating the capital letters or else she would show off her country origins.

Mercifully, Dillamond found her a carriage with a human driver, and directed him to Crage Hall and paid him in advance, for which Galinda had to come up with a weak smile of appreciation. "Our paths will cross again," said Dillamond, gallantly if curtly, as if putting forth a prophecy, and he disappeared as the carriage jolted forward. Galinda sank back into the cushions. She began to be sorry that Ama Clutch had punctured her foot with a nail.

Crage Hall was only twenty minutes from Railway Square. Behind its own bluestone walls, the complex was set with large watery-glass windows in lancet formation. A tessellation of quatrefoils and blind multifoils ran riot at the roofline. The appreciation of architecture was Galinda's private passion, and she pored over the features she could identify, although the vines and flatmoss fudged many of the finer details of the buildings. Too soon she was whisked inside.

The Headmistress of Crage Hall, a fish-faced upper-class Gillikinese woman wearing a lot of cloisonné bangles, was greeting new arrivals in the atrium. The Head eschewed the drabness of professional women's dress that Galinda had expected. Instead the imposing woman was bedecked in a currant-colored gown with patterns of black jet swirling over the bodice like dynamic markings on sheet music. "I am Madame Morrible," she said to Galinda. Her voice was basso profundo, her grip crippling, her posture military, her earrings like holiday tree ornaments. "Flourishes all around, and a quick cup of tea in the parlor. Then we'll assemble in the Main Hall and sort you out as to roomies."

The parlor was filled with pretty young women, all wearing green or blue and trailing black shawls like exhausted shadows behind them. Galinda was glad for the natural advantages of her flaxen hair, and stood by a window so the light could dazzle itself off her curls. She hardly sipped the tea. In a side room, the attendant Amas were serving themselves from a metal urn, and laughing and yakking already as if they were old friends from the same village. It was somewhat grotesque, all those dumpy women smiling at each other, making marketplace noise.

Galinda hadn't read the fine print very closely. She hadn't realized there would be a need for "roomies." Or perhaps had her parents paid extra so she could have a private room? And where would Ama Clutch stay? Looking about her, she could tell that some of these dollies came from families much better off than hers. The pearls and diamonds on them! Galinda was glad she had chosen a simple silver collar with mettanite struts. There was something vulgar about traveling in jewels. As she realized this truth, she codified it into a saying. At the earliest perfect opportunity she would bring it out as proof of her having opinions—and of having traveled. "The overdressed traveler betrays more interest in being seen than in seeing," she murmured, trying it out, "while the *true* traveler knows that the novel world about her serves as the most appropriate accessory." Good, very good.

Madame Morrible counted heads, gripped a cup of tea, and shooed everyone into the Main Hall. There Galinda learned that allowing Ama Clutch to go looking for a surgery had been a colossal mistake. Apparently all that chatter among Amas hadn't been frivolous and social. They had been instructed to sort out among them whose young lady would room with whose. The Amas had been relied upon to get to the nub of the matter more quickly than the students themselves. No one had spoken for Galinda—she had gone unrepresented!

After the forgettable welcome remarks, as couple by couple the students and Amas left to locate their lodgings and settle in, Galinda found herself growing pale with embarrassment. Ama Clutch, the old fool, would have fixed her up nicely with someone just a notch or two above on the social ladder! Near enough that Galinda would suffer no shame, and *above* enough to make it worth the while of socializing. But now, all the better young misses were linked together. Diamond to diamond, emerald to emerald, for all she could tell! As the room began to empty, Galinda wondered if she shouldn't go up and interrupt Madame Morrible and explain the problem. Galinda was, after all, an Arduenna of the Uplands, at least on one side. It was a hideous accident. Her eyes teared up.

But she hadn't the nerve. She stayed perched on the edge of the fragile, stupid chair. Except for her, all the centre of the room had cleared out now, and the shyer, more useless girls were left, around the edges, in the shadows. Surrounded by an obstacle course of empty gilded chairs, Galinda alone sat like an unclaimed valise.

"Now the rest of you are here without Amas, I understand," said Madame Morrible, a bit sniffily. "Since we require chaperonage, I will assign each of you to one of the three dormitories for freshers, which sleep fifteen girls each. There is no social stigma to the dormitory, I might add. None at all." But she was lying, and not even convincingly.

Galinda finally stood up. "Please, Madame Morrible, there is a mistake. I am Galinda of the Arduennas. My Ama took a nail in her foot on the voyage and was detained for a day or two. I am not in the dormitory class, you see."

"How sad for you," said Madame Morrible, smiling. "I'm sure your Ama will be pleased to be a chaperone in, shall we say, the Pink Dormitory? Fourth floor on the right—"

"No, no, she would not," interrupted Galinda, quite bravely. "I am not here to sleep in a dormitory, Pink or otherwise. You have misunderstood."

"I have not misunderstood, Miss Galinda," said Madame Morrible, growing even more fishlike as her eyes began to bulge. "There is accident, there is tardiness, there are decisions to be made. As you were not equipped, through your Ama, to make your own decision, I am empowered to make it for you. Please, we are busy and I must name the other girls who will join you in the Pink Dormitory—"

"I would have a private word with you, Madame," said Galinda in desperation. "For myself, dormitory partners or a single roomie, it is no matter. But I cannot recommend that you ask my Ama to oversee other girls, for reasons I may not say in public." She was lying as fast as she could, and better than Madame Morrible, who seemed at least intrigued.

"You strike me as impertinent, Miss Galinda," she said mildly.

"I have not yet struck you, Madame Morrible." Galinda delivered the daring line with her sweetest smile.

Madame Morrible chose to laugh, thank Lurline! "A spark of spunk! You may come to my chambers this evening and tell me the story of your Ama's shortcomings, as I should know them. But I will compromise with you, Miss Galinda. Unless you object, I will have to ask your Ama to chaperone both you and another girl, one who comes without an Ama. For you see, all the other students with Amas are already paired off, and you are the odd one out."

"I am certain my Ama could manage that, at least."

Madame Morrible scanned the page of names, and said, "Very well. To join Miss Galinda of the Arduennas in a double room—shall I invite the Thropp Third Descending, of Nest Hardings, Elphaba?"

No one stirred. "Elphaba?" said Madame Morrible again, adjusting her bangles and pressing two fingers at the bottom of her throat.

The girl was in the back of the room, a pauper in a red dress with gaudy fretwork, and in clumpy, old-people's boots. At first Galinda thought what she saw was some trick of the light, a reflection off the adjacent buildings covered in vines and flatmoss. But as Elphaba moved forward, lugging her own carpetbags, it became obvious that she was green. A hatchet-faced girl with putrescent green skin and long, foreign-looking black hair. "A Munchkinlander by birth, though with many childhood years spent in Quadling Country," read Madame Morrible from her notes. "How fascinating for us all, Miss Elphaba. We shall look forward to hearing tales of exotic climes and times. Miss Galinda and Miss Elphaba, here are your keys. You may take room twenty-two on the second floor."

She smiled broadly at Galinda as the girls came forward. "Travel is so broadening," she intoned. Galinda started, the curse of her own words lobbed back at her. She curtseyed and fled. Elphaba, eyes on the floor, followed behind.

2

By the time Ama Clutch arrived the next day, her foot bandaged to three times its natural size, Elphaba had already unpacked her few belongings. They hung raglike on hooks in the cupboard: thin, shapeless shifts, shamed into a corner by the fulsome hoops and starched bustles and padded shoulders and cushioned elbows of Galinda's wardrobe. "I am happy as cheese to be your Ama too, don't matter to me," said Ama Clutch, smiling broadly in Elphaba's direction, before Galinda had a chance to get Ama Clutch alone and demand that her minder refuse. "Of course my Papa is paying you to be *my* Ama," said Galinda meaningfully, but Ama Clutch answered, "Not as much as all that, duckie, not as much as all that. I can be making up my own mind."

"Ama," said Galinda when Elphaba had left to use the mildewy facilities, "Ama, are you blind? That Munchkinlander girl is *green*."

"Odd, isn't it? I thought all Munchkinlanders were tiny. She's a proper height, though. I guess they come in a variety of sizes. Oh, are you bothered by the green? Well, it might do you some good, if you let it. If you *let* it. You affect worldly airs, Galinda, but you don't know the world yet. I think it's a lark. Why not? Why ever not?"

"It's not *yours* to organize my education, worldly or otherwise, Ama Clutch!"

"No, my dear," said Ama Clutch, "you've made this mess all by your lonesome. I'm merely being of *service*."

So Galinda was stuck. Last night's brief interview with Madame Morrible had not provided any escape route, either. Galinda had arrived promptly, in a dotted morpheline skirt with lace bodice, a vision, as she'd said to herself, in nocturnal purples and midnight blues. Madame Morrible bade her enter the reception room, in which a small cluster of leather chairs and a settee were drawn up before an unnecessary fire. The Head poured mint tea and offered crystallized ginger wrapped in pearlfruit leaves. She indicated a chair for Galinda, but herself stood by the mantel-piece like a big game hunter.

In the best tradition of the upper-class savoring its luxuries, they sipped and nibbled in silence at first. This gave Galinda the chance to observe that Madame Morrible was fishlike not merely in countenance, but in dress: Her loose-fitting cream foxille flowed like a huge airy bladder from the high frilled neckline to the knees, where it was tightly gathered and dropped straight to the floor, hugging the calves and ankles in neat, anticlimactic pleats. She looked for all the world like a giant carp in a men's club. And a dull, bored carp at that, not even a sentient Carp.

"Now your Ama, my dear. The reason she is incapable of supervising a dormitory. I'm all ears."

Galinda had taken all afternoon to prepare. "You see, Madame Head, I didn't like to say it publicly. But Ama Clutch suffered a terrible fall last summer when we were picnicking in the Pertha Hills. She reached for a handful of wild mountain thyme and went pitching over a cliff. She lay for weeks in a coma, and when she emerged she had no memory of the accident at all. If you asked her about it, she wouldn't even know what you meant. Amnesia by trauma."

"I see. How very tiresome for you. But why does this make her unequal to the job I proposed?"

"She has become addled. Ama Clutch, on occasion, gets confused as to what has Life and what doesn't. She will sit and talk to, oh, say, a chair, and then relate its history back to us. Its aspirations, its reservations—"

"Its joys, its sorrows," said Madame Morrible. "How truly novel. The emotional life of furniture. I never."

"But, silly as this is, and a cause for hours of merriment, the corollary ailment is more alarming. Madame Morrible, I must tell you that Ama Clutch sometimes forgets that *people* are alive. Or animals." Galinda paused, then added, "Or Animals, even."

"Go on, my dear."

"It is all right for me, because Ama has been my Ama all my life, and I know her. I know her ways. But she can sometimes forget a person is there, or needs her, or is a person. Once she cleaned a wardrobe and tipped it over onto the houseboy, breaking his back. She didn't register his screaming right there, right at her feet. She folded the nightclothes and had a conversation with my mother's evening gown, asking it all sorts of impertinent questions."

"What a fascinating condition," said Madame Morrible. "And how vexing for you, really."

"I couldn't have allowed her to accept responsibility for fourteen other girls," Galinda confided. "For me, alone, there is no problem. I love the foolish old woman, in a way."

Madame Morrible had said, "But what of your roomie? Can you jeopardize her well-being?"

"I didn't ask for *her*." Galinda looked the Head in her glazed, unblinking eye. "The poor Munchkinlander appears to be used to a life of distress. Either she will adjust or, I assume, she will petition you to be removed from my room. Unless, of course, you feel it your duty to move her for her own safety."

Madame Morrible said, "I suppose if Miss Elphaba cannot live with what we give her, she will leave Crage Hall on her own accord. Don't you think?"

It was the *we* in *what we give her*: Madame Morrible was binding Galinda into a campaign. They both knew it. Galinda struggled to maintain her autonomy. But she was only seventeen, and she had suffered that same indignity of exclusion in the Main Hall just hours ago. She didn't know what Madame Morrible could have against Elphaba except the looks of her. But there was something, there was clearly something. What was it? She sensed it to be wrong somehow. "Don't you think, dear?" said Madame Morrible, bowing a bit forward like a fish arching in a slow-motion leap.

"Well, of course, we must do what we can," said Galinda, as vaguely as possible. But she seemed the fish, and caught on a most clever hook.

Out of the shadows of the reception room came a small tiktok thing, about three feet high, made of burnished bronze, with an identifying plate screwed into its front. The plate said *Smith and Tinker's Mechanical Man*, in ornate script. The clockwork servant collected the empty teacups and whirred itself away. Galinda didn't know how long it had been there, or what it had heard, but she had never liked tiktok creatures.

Elphaba had a bad case of what Galinda called the reading sulks. Elphaba didn't curl up—she was too bony to curl—but she jackknifed herself nearer to herself, her funny pointed green nose poking in the moldy leaves of a book. She played with her hair while she read, coiling it up and down around fingers so thin and twiglike as to seem almost exoskeletal. Her hair never curled no matter how often Elphaba twined it around her hands. It was beautiful hair, in an odd, awful way, with a shine like the pelt of a healthy giltebeest. Black silk. Coffee spun into threads. Night rain. Galinda, not given to metaphor on the whole, found Elphaba's hair entrancing, the more so because the girl was otherwise so ugly.

They didn't talk much. Galinda was too busy forging alliances with the better girls who had been her rightful roomie prospects. No doubt she could switch rooms at half-term, or at any rate next fall. So Galinda left Elphaba alone, and she flew down the hall to gossip with her new friends. Milla, Pfannee, Shenshen. Just as in children's books about boarding school, each new friend was wealthier than the one before.

At first Galinda didn't mention who her roomie was. And Elphaba showed no sign of expecting Galinda's company, which was a relief. But the gossip had to start sooner or later. The first wave of discussion about Elphaba concerned her wardrobe and her evident poverty, as if her class-mates were above noticing her sickly and sickening color. "Someone told me that Madame Head had said Miss Elphaba was the Thropp Third Descending from Nest Hardings," said Pfannee, who was also a Munch-kinlander, but one of diminutive stock, not full-size like the Thropp fam-ily. "The Thropps are highly regarded in Nest Hardings and even beyond. The Eminent Thropp put together the area's militia and tore up the Yellow Brick Road that the Ozma Regent had been laying in when we all were small—before the Glorious Revolution. There was no callous-ness in the Eminent Thropp or his wife or family, including his grand-daughter Melena, you can be assured." By callousness, of course, Pfannee meant greenness.

"But how the mighty have fallen! She's as ragged as a gypsy," observed Milla. "Have you ever seen such tawdry dresses? Her Ama should be sacked."

"She has no Ama, I think," said Shenshen. Galinda, who knew for sure, said nothing.

"They said she had spent time in Quadling Country," Milla went on. "Perhaps her family had been exiled as criminals?"

"Or they were speculators in rubies," said Shenshen.

"Then where's the wealth?" snapped Milla. "Speculators in rubies did very well, Miss Shenshen. Our Miss Elphaba doesn't have two barter tokens to rub together and call her own."

"Perhaps it's a kind of religious calling? A chosen poverty?" suggested Pfannee, and at this nonsense they all threw back their heads and chortled.

Elphaba, coming into the buttery for a cup of coffee, caused them to escalate into louder roars of laughter. Elphaba did not look over at them, but every other student did glance their way, each girl longing to be included in the jollity, which made the four new friends feel just fine.

Galinda was slow coming to terms with actual learning. She had considered her admission into Shiz University as a sort of testimony to her brilliance, and believed that she would adorn the halls of learning with her beauty and occasional clever sayings. She supposed, glumly, that she had meant to be a sort of living marble bust: This is Youthful Intelligence; admire Her. Isn't She lovely?

It hadn't actually dawned on Galinda that there was more to learn, and furthermore that she was expected to do it. The education all the new girls chiefly wanted, of course, had nothing to do with Madame Morrible or the prattling Animals at lecterns and on daises. What the girls wanted wasn't equations, or quotations, or orations—they wanted Shiz itself. City life. The broad, offensive panoply of life and Life, seamlessly intertwined.

Galinda was relieved that Elphaba never took part in the outings the Amas organized. Since they often stopped at a lunchroom for a modest meal, the weekly brigade became known informally as the Chowder and Marching Society. The university district was aflame with autumn color, not just of dying leaves, but also of fraternity pennants, fluttering from rooftop and spire.

Galinda soaked up the architecture of Shiz. Here and there, mostly in protected College yards and side streets, the oldest surviving domestic architecture still leaned, ancient wattle-and-daub and exposed stud framing held up like paralytic grannies by stronger, newer relatives on either side. Then, in dizzying succession, unparalleled glories: Bloodstone Medieval, Merthic (both Least and the more fantastical Late), Gallantine with its symmetries and restraint, Gallantine Reformed with all those festering ogees and broken pediments, Bluestone Revival, Imperial Bombast, and Industrial Modern, or, as the critics in the liberal press put it, High

Hostile Crudstyle, the form propagated by the modernity-minded Wizard of Oz.

Besides architecture, the excitement was tame, to be sure. On one notable occasion, which no Crage Hall girl present ever forgot, the senior boys from Three Queens College across the canal, for a lark and a dare, had tanked themselves up with beer in the middle of the afternoon, had hired a White Bear violinist, and had gone down to dance together under the willow trees, wearing nothing but their clinging cotton drawers and their school scarves. It was deliciously pagan, as they had set an old chipped statue of Lurline the Fairy Queen on a three-legged stool, and she seemed to smile at their loose-limbed gaiety. The girls and the Amas pretended shock, but poorly; they lingered, watching, until horrified proctors from Three Queens came rushing out to round the revelers up. Near nudity was one thing, but public Lurlinism—even as a joke—bordered on being intolerably retrograde, even royalist. And that *did* not do in the Wizard's reign.

One Saturday evening, when the Amas had a rare night off and had taken themselves in to a pleasure faith meeting in Ticknor Circus, Galinda had a brief and silly squabble with Pfannee and Shenshen, after which she retired early to her bedchamber, complaining of a headache. Elphaba was sitting up in her bed with the commissary brown blanket tucked around her. She was hunched forward over a book, as usual, and her hair hung down like brackets on either side of her face. She looked to Galinda like one of those etchings—the natural history books were full of them—of odd Winkie mountain women who hide their strangeness with a shawl over the head. Elphaba was munching on the pips of an apple, having eaten all the rest of it. "Well, you look cozy enough, Miss Elphaba," said Galinda, challengingly. In three months it was the first social remark she had managed to make to her roomie.

"Looks are only looks," said Elphaba, not looking up.

"Will it break your concentration if I sit in front of the fire?"

"You cast a shadow if you sit just there."

"Oh, *sorry*," said Galinda, and moved. "Mustn't cast shadows, must we, when urgent words are waiting to be read?"

Elphaba was back in her book already, and didn't answer.

"What the dickens are you reading, night and day?"

It seemed as if Elphaba were coming up for air from a still, isolated pool. "While I don't read the same thing every day, you know, tonight I am reading some of the speeches of the early unionist fathers."

"Why ever would anyone want to do that?"

"I don't know. I don't even know if I want to read them. I'm just reading them."

"But why? Miss Elphaba the Delirious, why, why?"

Elphaba looked up at Galinda and smiled. "Elphaba the Delirious. I like it."

Before she had a chance to bite it back, Galinda returned the smile, and at the same time a sweeping wind sent a handful of hail against the glass, and the latch broke. Galinda leaped to swing the casement shut, but Elphaba scuttled to the far corner of the room, away from the wet. "Give me the leather luggage grip, Miss Elphaba, from inside my satchel—there on the shelf, behind the hatboxes—yes—and I'll secure this until we can get the porter to fix it tomorrow." Elphaba found the strap, but in doing so the hat boxes tumbled down, and three colorful hats rolled out onto the cold floor. While Galinda scrabbled up on a chair to organize the window shut again, Elphaba returned the hats to their boxes. "Oh, try it on, try that one on," said Galinda. She meant to have something to laugh at, to tell Misses Pfannee and Shenshen about and so to work her way back into their good graces.

"Oh, I daren't, Miss Galinda," Elphaba said, and went to set the hat away.

"No, do, I insist," Galinda said, "for a lark. I've never seen you in something pretty."

"I don't wear pretty things."

"What's the harm?" said Galinda. "Just here. No one else need see you."

Elphaba stood facing the fire, but turned her head on her shoulders to look long and unblinkingly at Galinda, who had not yet hopped down from the chair. The Munchkinlander was in her nightgown, a drab sack without benefit of lace edging or piping. The green face above the wheat-gray fabric seemed almost to glow, and the glorious long straight black hair fell right over where breasts should be if she would ever reveal any evidence that she possessed them. Elphaba looked like something between an animal and an Animal, like something more than life but not quite Life. There was an expectancy but no intuition, was that it?—like a child who has never remembered having a dream being told to have sweet dreams. You'd almost call it unrefined, but not in a social sense—more in a sense of nature not having done its full job with Elphaba, not quite having managed to make her enough like herself.

"Oh, put the damn hat on, *really*," said Galinda, for whom, where introspection was concerned, enough was enough.

Elphaba obliged. The thing was the lovely roundel bought from the best milliner in the Pertha Hills. It had orangey swags and a yellow lace net that could be draped to achieve varying degrees of disguise. On the wrong head it would look ghastly, and Galinda expected to have to bite the inside of her lip to keep from laughing. It was the kind of super-feminine thing boys in a pantomime wore when they pretended to be girls.

But Elphaba dropped the whole sugary plate onto her strange pointed head, and looked at Galinda again from underneath the broad brim. She seemed like a rare flower, her skin stemlike in its soft pearlescent sheen, the hat a botanical riot. "Oh Miss Elphaba," said Galinda, "you terrible mean thing, you're pretty."

"Oh, and now you have lied, so go confess to the unionist minister," said Elphaba. "Is there a looking glass?"

"Of course there is, down the hall in the lavatory."

"Not there. I'm not going to be seen by those ninnies in this."

"Well then," decided Galinda, "can you find an angle without hiding the firelight, and look at your reflection in the dark window?"

They both gazed at the green and flowery spectre reflected in the watery old glass, surrounded by the blackness, driven through with the wild rain beyond. A maplefruit leaf, shaped like a star with blunted points, or like a heart grown lopsided, suddenly whirled out of the night and plastered itself on the reflection in the glass, gleaming red and reflecting the firelight, just where the heart would be—or so it seemed from the angle at which Galinda stood.

"Entrancing," she said. "There's some strange exotic quality of beauty about you. I never thought."

"Surprise," said Elphaba, and then nearly blushed, if darker green constituted a blush—"I mean, *surprise*, not beauty. It's just surprise. 'Well, what do you know.' It's not beauty."

"Who am I to argue," said Galinda, tossing her curls and striking a pose, and Elphaba actually laughed at that, and Galinda laughed back, partly horrified as she did so. Elphaba tore the hat off then, and returned it to its box, and when she picked up her book again Galinda said, "So what is Beauty reading anyway? I mean really, tell me, why the old sermons?"

"My father is a unionist minister," said Elphaba. "I'm just curious what it's all about, that's all."

"Why don't you just ask him?"

Elphaba didn't answer. Her face took on a solid, waiting look, like that of an owl just about to go for a mouse.

"So what're they on about? Anything interesting?" said Galinda. No sense giving up now, there was nothing else to do and she was too wrought up by the storm to sleep.

"This one is thinking about good and evil," said Elphaba. "Whether they really exist at all."

"Oh, yawn," said Galinda. "Evil exists, I know that, and its name is Boredom, and ministers are the guiltiest crew of all."

"You don't really think that?"

Galinda didn't often stop to consider whether she believed in what she said or not; the whole point of conversation was *flow*. "Well, I didn't mean to insult your father, for all I know he is an entertaining and lively preacher."

"No, I mean do you think evil really exists?"

"Well, how do I know what I think?"

"Well, ask yourself, Miss Galinda. Does evil exist?"

"I don't know. *You* say. Does evil exist?"

"I don't expect to know." The look went slanty and inwards some-how, or was it the hair swinging forward like a veil again?

"Why don't you just ask your father? I don't understand. He should know, that's his job."

"My father taught me a lot," Elphaba said slowly. "He was very well educated indeed. He taught me to read and write and think, and more. But not enough. I just think, like our teachers here, that if ministers are effective, they're good at asking questions to get you to think. I don't think they're supposed to have the answers. Not necessarily."

"Oh, well, tell that to our boring minister at home. He has all the answers, and charges for them, too."

"But maybe there's something to what you say," said Elphaba. "I mean, evil and boredom. Evil and ennui. Evil and the lack of stimulation. Evil and sluggish blood."

"You're writing a poem, it sounds like. Why ever would a girl be interested in evil?"

"I'm not *interested* in it. It's just what the early sermons are all on about. So I'm thinking about what they're thinking about, that's all. Sometimes they talk about diet and not eating Animals, and then I think of that. I just like to think about what I'm reading. Don't you?"

"I don't read very well. So I don't think I think very well either." Galinda smiled. "I dress to kill, though."

There was no response from Elphaba. Galinda, usually pleased that she knew the correct way to steer every conversation into a paean to herself, was flummoxed. She lamely ventured on, annoyed at having to expend the effort. "Well, whatever did those old brutes think about evil, then?"

"It's hard to say exactly. They seemed to be obsessed with locating it somewhere. I mean, an evil spring in the mountains, an evil smoke, evil blood in the veins going from parent to child. They were sort of like the early explorers of Oz, except the maps they made were of invisible stuff, pretty inconsistent one with the other."

"And where *is* evil located?" Galinda asked, flopping onto her bed and closing her eyes.

"Well, they didn't agree, did they? Or else what would they have to write sermons arguing about? Some said the original evil was the vacuum caused by the Fairy Queen Lurline leaving us alone here. When goodness removes itself, the space it occupies corrodes and becomes evil, and maybe splits apart and multiplies. So every evil thing is a sign of the absence of deity."

"Well I wouldn't know an evil thing if it fell on me," said Galinda.

"The early unionists, who were a lot more Lurlinist than unionists are today, argued that some invisible pocket of corruption was floating around the neighborhood, a direct descendent of the pain the world felt when Lurline left. Like a patch of cold air on a warm still night. A perfectly agreeable soul might march through it and become infected, and then go and kill a neighbor. But then was it your *fault* if you walked through a patch of badness? If you couldn't see it? There wasn't ever any council of unionists that decided it one way or the other, and nowadays so many people don't even believe in Lurline."

"But they believe in evil still," said Galinda with a yawn. "Isn't that funny, that deity is passé but the attributes and implications of deity linger—"

"You *are* thinking!" Elphaba cried. Galinda raised herself to her elbows at the enthusiasm in her roomie's voice.

"I am about to sleep, because this is profoundly boring to me," Galinda said, but Elphaba was grinning from ear to ear.

In the morning Ama Clutch regaled them both with tales of the night out. There was a talented young witch in nothing but shocking pink undergarments, adorned with feathers and beads. She sang songs to the audience and collected food tokens in her cleavage from the blushing undergraduate men in the nearer tables. She did a little domestic magic, turning water into orange juice, changing cabbages into carrots, and running knives through a terrified piglet, which spouted champagne instead of blood. They all had a sip. A terrible fat man with a beard came on and chased the witch around as if he would kiss her—oh, it was too funny, too funny! In the end the whole cast and audience together stood and sang "What We Don't Allow in the Public Halls (In Fact Is for Sale in the Cheaper Stalls)." The Amas had a riotous good time, every one of them.

"Really," said Galinda sniffily. "The pleasure faith is so—so common."

"But I see the window broke," said Ama Clutch. "I hope it wasn't boys trying to climb in."

"Are you mad?" said Galinda. "In that storm?"

"What storm?" said Ama Clutch. "That don't make sense. Last night was as calm as moonlight."

"Hah, that was some show," said Galinda. "You were so caught up in pleasure faith you lost your bearings, Ama Clutch." They went down to breakfast together, leaving Elphaba still asleep, or pretending to be asleep maybe. Though as they walked along the corridors, sun through the broad windows making racks of light on the cold slate floors, Galinda did wonder about the capriciousness of weather. Was it even possible for a storm to pitch itself against one part of town and overlook another? There was so much about the world she didn't know.

"She did nothing but chatter about evil," said Galinda to her friends, over buttered brisks with ploughfoot jelly. "Some inside tap was turned on, and prattle just poured out of her. And, girls, when she tried on my hat, I could've died. She looked like somebody's maiden aunt come up out of the grave, I mean as frumpy as a Cow. I endured it only for you, so I could tell you all; otherwise I'd have expired with glee on the spot. It was so very *much!*"

"You poor thing, to have to be our spy and stand the shame of that grasshopper roomie!" said Pfannee devoutly, clasping Galinda's hand. "You're too good!"

3

One evening—the first evening of snow—Madame Morrible held a poetry soiree. Boys from Three Queens and Ozma Towers were invited. Galinda brought out her cerise satin gown with the matching shawl and slippers and an heirloom Gillikinese fan, painted with a pattern of ferns and pfenix. She arrived early to lay claim to the upholstered chair that would best set off her own attire, and she dragged the chair over to the bookshelves so that the light from library tapers would gently fall on her. The rest of the girls—not only the freshers, but the sophisters and seniors—entered in a whispering clot and arranged themselves on sofas and lounges in Crage Hall's nicest parlor. The boys who came were somewhat disappointing; there weren't that many, and they looked terrified, or giggled with one another. Then the professors and doctors arrived, not just the Animals from Crage Hall, but the boys' professors too, who were mostly men. The girls began to be glad they had dressed well, for while the boys were a spotty bunch, the male professors had grave and charming smiles.

Even some of the Amas came, though they sat behind a screen at the back of the room. The sound of their knitting needles going at a rapid rate was soothing to Galinda, somehow. She knew Ama Clutch would be there.

The double doors at the end of the parlor were swept open by that little bronze industrial crab Galinda had met on her first evening at Crage Hall. It had been especially serviced for the occasion; you could still detect the cutting scent of metal polish. Madame Morrible then made an entrance, severe and striking in a coal black cape, which she let drop to the floor (the thingy picked it up and slung it over a sofa back); her gown was a fiery orange, with abalone lake shells stitched all over it. Despite herself Galinda had to admire the effect. In tones even more unctuous than usual, Madame Morrible welcomed the visitors and led polite applause at the notion of Poetry and Its Civilizing Effects.

Then she spoke on the new verse form sweeping the social parlors and poetry dens of Shiz. "It is known as the Quell," said Madame Morrible, in her Headmistress's smile displaying an impressive assembly of teeth. "The Quell is a brief poem, uplifting in nature. It pairs a sequence of thirteen short lines with a concluding, unrhyming apothegm. The reward of the poem is in the revealing contrast between rhyming argument and concluding remark. Sometimes they may contradict each other, but always they illuminate and, like all poetry, sanctify life." She beamed like a beacon in a fog. "Tonight especially, a Quell might serve as an anodyne to the unpleasant disruptions we have been hearing about in our nation's capital." The boy students looked at least alert, and all the professors nodded, though Galinda could tell none of the girl students had a clue as to what "unpleasant disruptions" Madame Morrible was prattling on about.

A third-year girl at the hammer-strung keyboard clattered out a couple of chords, and the guests cleared their throats and looked at their shoes. Galinda saw Elphaba arrive in the back of the room, dressed in her usual casual red shift, two books under her arm and a scarf wound around her head. She sank into the last empty chair, and bit into an apple just as Madame Morrible was drawing in a dramatic breath to begin.

> Sing a hymn to rectitude,
> Ye forward-thinking multitude.
> Advance in humble gratitude
> For strictest rules of attitude.
> To elevate the Common Good
> In Brotherhood and Sisterhood

We celebrate authority.
Fraternity, Sorority,
United, pressing onward, we
Restrict the ills of liberty.
There is no numinosity
Like Power's generosity
In helping curb atrocity.
Bear down on the rod and foil the child.

Madame Morrible lowered her head to signify that she was done. There was a rumbling of indistinct comments. Galinda, who didn't know much about Poetry, thought perhaps this was the accepted way of appreciating it. She grumbled a little bit to Shenshen, who sat in a straightback chair to one side, looking dropsical. Wax from the taper was about to drip onto Shenshen's silk-shouldered white gown with the lemon-chiffon swags, and ruin it, most likely, but Galinda decided Shenshen's family could afford to replace a gown. She kept still.

"Another," said Madame Morrible. "Another Quell."

The room grew silent, but a little uneasily so?

Alas! For impropriety,
The guillotine of piety.
To remedy society
Indulge not to satiety
In mirth and shameless gaiety.
Choose sobering sobriety.
Behave as if the deity
Approaches in its mystery,
And greet it with sonority.
Let your especial history
Be built upon sorority
Whose Virtues do exemplify,
And Social Good thus multiply.
Animals should be seen and not heard.

Again, there was mumbling, but it was of a different nature now, a meaner key. Doctor Dillamond harrumphed and beat a cloven hoof against the floor, and was heard to say, "Well that's not poetry, that's propaganda, and it's not even good propaganda at that."

Elphaba sidled over to Galinda's side with her chair under her arm, and plunked it down between Galinda and Shenshen. She put her bony behind on its slatted seat and leaned to Galinda and asked, "What do you make of this?"

It was the first time Galinda had ever been addressed by Elphaba in public. Mortification bloomed. "I don't know," she said faintly, looking in the other direction.

"It's a cleverness, isn't it?" said Elphaba. "I mean that last line, you couldn't tell by that fancy accent whether it was meant to be Animals or animals. No wonder Dillamond's furious."

And he was. Doctor Dillamond looked around the room as if trying to marshal the opposition. "I'm shocked, shocked," he said. "Deeply shocked," he amended, and he marched out of the room. Professor Lenx, the Boar who taught math, left too, accidentally crushing an antique gilded sideboard through trying to avoid stepping on Miss Milla's yellowlace train. Mister Mikko, the Ape who taught history, sat dolefully in the shadows, too confused and ill at ease to make a move. "Well," said Madame Morrible in a carrying tone, "one expects poetry, if it is Poetry, to offend. It is the Right of Art."

"I think she's bonkers," said Elphaba. Galinda found it too horrible. What if even one of the pimply boys saw Elphaba whispering to her! She'd never hold her head up in society again. Her life was ruined. "Shhh, I'm listening, I *love* poetry," Galinda told her sternly. "Don't talk to me, you're ruining my evening."

Elphaba sat back, and finished her apple, and they both kept listening. The grumbling and murmuring grew louder after each poem, and the boys and girls began to relax and look around at one another.

When the last Quell of the evening had knelled (to the cryptic aphorism "A witch in time saves nine"), Madame Morrible retired to uneven applause. She allowed her bronze servant to administer tea to the guests, and then the girls, and finally the Amas. In a heap of rustling silk and clicking abalone lake shells, she received compliments from the male professors and some of the braver boys, and begged them to sit near her so she could enjoy their criticisms. "Do tell the truth. I was overly dramatic, wasn't I? It is my curse. The stage called, but I chose a life of Service to Girls." She lowered her eyelashes in modesty as her captive audience mumbled a lukewarm protest.

Galinda was still trying to extricate herself from the embarrassing company of Elphaba, who kept on about the Quells and what they meant, and if they were any good. "How do I know, how should I know, we're first-year girls, remember?" said Galinda, yearning to swish over to where Pfannee, Milla, and Shenshen were squeezing lemons into the teacups of a few edgy boys.

"Well, your opinion is as good as hers, I think," said Elphaba. "That's the real power of art, I think. Not to chide but to provoke challenge. Otherwise why bother?"

A boy came up to them. Galinda thought he wasn't much to look at, but anything was better than the green leech at her side. "How do you *do?*" said Galinda, not even waiting for him to get up his nerve. "It's so nice to meet you. You must be from, let's see—"

"Well, I'm from Briscoe Hall, actually," he said. "But I'm a Munchkinlander originally. As you can tell." And she could, for he hardly came up to her shoulder. He wasn't bad looking for all that. A spun-cotton mess of ill-combed golden hair, a toothy smile, a better complexion than some. The evening tunic he wore was a provincial blue, but there were flecks of silver thread running through it. He was trim, nicely so. His boots were polished and he stood a little bandy-legged, feet pointed out.

"This is what I *love,*" said Galinda, "meeting strangers. This is Shiz at its finest. I am Gillikinese." She just managed to keep herself from adding, *of course,* for she believed it evident in her attire. Munchkinlander girls had a habit of quieter dress, so understated that they were often mistaken, in Shiz, for servants.

"Well then, hello to you," said the boy. "My name is Master Boq."

"Miss Galinda of the Arduennas of the Uplands."

"And you?" said Boq, turning to Elphaba. "Who are you?"

"I'm leaving," she said. "Fresh dreams, all."

"No, don't leave," said Boq. "I think I know you."

"You don't know me," said Elphaba, pausing as she turned. "However could you know me?"

"You're Miss Elphie, aren't you?"

"Miss Elphie!" cried Galinda gaily. "How delightful!"

"How do you know who I am?" said Elphaba. "Master Boq from Munchkinland? I don't know you."

"You and I played together when you were tiny," said Boq. "My father was the mayor of the village you were born in. I think. You were born in Rush Margins, in Wend Hardings, weren't you? You're the daughter of the unionist minister, I forget his name."

"Frex," said Elphaba. Her eyes looked slanted and wary.

"Frexspar the Godly!" said Boq. "That's right. You know they still talk about him, and your mama, and the night the Clock of the Time Dragon came to Rush Margins. I was two or three years old and they took me to see it, but I don't remember that. I do remember that you were in a play set with me when I was still in short pants. Do you remember Gawnette? She was the woman who minded us. And Bfee? He is my dad. Do you remember Rush Margins?"

"This is all smoke and guesswork," said Elphaba. "How can I contradict? Let me tell you about what happened in *your* life before *you* can remember it. You were born a frog." (This was unkind, as Boq did have an amphibious look about him.) "You got sacrificed to the Clock of the Time Dragon and were turned into a boy. But on your marriage night when your wife opens her legs you'll turn back into a tadpole and—"

"Miss Elphaba!" cried Galinda, flicking open her fan to wave the flush of shame from her face. "Your tongue!"

"Oh well, I have no childhood," said Elphaba. "So you can say what you like. I grew up in Quadling Country with the marsh people. I squelch when I walk. You don't want to talk to me. Talk to Miss Galinda, she's much better in parlors than I am. I have to go now." Elphaba nodded a good night salute and escaped, almost at a run.

"Why did she say all that?" said Boq, no embarrassment in his voice, just wonder. "Of course I remember her. How many green people *are* there?"

"It's just possible," considered Galinda, "that she didn't like being recognized on account of her skin color. I don't know for sure, but perhaps she's sensitive about it."

"She must know that it's what people would remember."

"Well, as far as I am aware, you are right about who she is," Galinda went on. "They tell me her great-grandfather is the Eminent Thropp of Colwen Grounds in Nest Hardings."

"That's the one," Boq said. "Elphie. I never thought I'd see her again."

"Won't you have some more tea? I'll call the server," Galinda said. "Let us sit here and you can tell me all about Munchkinland. I am aquiver with curiosity." She perched herself back on the chair-in-sympathetic-colors and looked her very best. Boq sat down, and shook his head, as if bewildered by the apparition of Elphaba.

When Galinda retired that evening, Elphaba was already in bed, blankets pulled up over her head, and a patently theatrical snore issuing forth. Galinda huffed herself into bed with a *wump*, annoyed that *she* could feel rejected by the green girl.

In the week that followed much was said about the evening of Quells. Doctor Dillamond interrupted his biology lecture to call for a response from his students. The girls didn't understand what a biological response to poetry might be and sat silent at his leading questions. He finally exploded, "Doesn't anyone make the connection between the expression of those thoughts and what's been going on in the Emerald City?"

Miss Pfannee, who didn't believe she was paying tuition in order to be yelled at, snapped back at him. "We don't have the tiniest notion what's going on in the Emerald City! Stop playing games with us; if you have something to say, say it. Don't bleat so."

Doctor Dillamond stared out the windows and seemed to be trying to control his temper. The students were thrilled with the little drama. Then the Goat turned and in a milder voice than they expected he told them that the Wizard of Oz had proclaimed Banns on Animal Mobility, effective several weeks ago. This meant not only that Animals were restricted in their access to travel conveyances, lodgings, and public services. The Mobility it referred to was also professional. Any Animal coming of age was prohibited from working in the professions or the public sector. They were, effectively, to be herded back to the farmlands and wilds if they wanted to work for wages at all.

"What do you think Madame Morrible was saying when she ended that Quell with the epigram *Animals should be seen and not heard*?" asked the Goat tersely.

"Well, anyone would be upset," said Galinda. "I mean, any Animal. But it's not as if your job is threatened, is it? Here you are, still teaching us."

"What about my children? What about my kids?"

"Do you have kids? I didn't know you were married."

The Goat closed his eyes. "I'm not married, Miss Galinda. But I might be. Or I may. Or perhaps I have nieces and nephews. They have already been banned effectively from studying at Shiz because they can't hold a pencil to write an essay with. How many Animals have you ever seen in this paradise of education?" Well, it was true; there were none.

"Well, I do think it's pretty dreadful," said Galinda. "Why would the Wizard of Oz do such a thing?"

"Why indeed," said the Goat.

"No, really, why. It's a real question. I don't know."

"I don't know either." The Goat turned to his rostrum and shoved some papers this way and that, and was then seen pawing a handkerchief from a lower shelf, and blowing his nose. "My grandmothers were milking-Goats at a farm in Gillikin. Through their lifelong sacrifices and labors they purchased the help of a local schoolteacher to educate me and to take dictation when I went for my exams. Their efforts are about to go to waste."

"But you can still teach!" said Pfannee petulantly.

"The thin edge of the wedge, my dear," said the Goat, and dismissed the class early. Galinda found herself glancing over toward Elphaba, who had a strange, focused look. As Galinda fled the classroom, Elphaba approached the front of the room, where Doctor Dillamond stood shaking in uncontrolled spasms, his horned head bowed.

A few days later, Madame Morrible gave one of her occasional open lectures on Early Hymns and Pagan Paeans. She called for questions, and the entire assembly was startled to see Elphaba unfold herself from her customary fetal position in the back of the room and address the Head.

"Madame Morrible, if you please," said Elphaba, "we never had an opportunity to discuss the Quells that you recited in the parlor last week."

"Discuss," said Madame Morrible with a generous though shooing wave of the bangled hands.

"Well, Doctor Dillamond seemed to think they were in questionable taste, given the Banns on Animal Mobility."

"Doctor Dillamond, alas," said Madame Morrible, "is a doctor. He is not a poet. He is also a Goat, and I might ask you girls if we have ever had a great Goat sonneteer or balladeer? Alas, dear Miss Elphaba, Doctor Dillamond doesn't understand the poetic convention of *irony*. Would you like to define irony for the class, please?"

"I don't believe I can, Madame."

"Irony, some say, is the art of juxtaposing incongruous parts. One needs a knowing *distance*. Irony presupposes detachment, which, alas, in the case of Animal Rights, we may forgive Doctor Dillamond for being without."

"So that phrase that he objected to—*Animals should be seen and not heard*—that was ironic?" continued Elphaba, studying her papers and not looking at Madame Morrible. Galinda and her classmates were enthralled, for it was clear that each of the females at opposite ends of the room would have enjoyed seeing the other crumple in a sudden attack of the spleen.

"One could consider it in an ironic mode if one chose," said Madame Morrible.

"How do you choose?" said Elphaba.

"How impertinent!" said Madame Morrible.

"Well, but I don't mean impertinence. I'm trying to learn. If you— if anyone—thought that statement was true, then it isn't in conflict with the boring bossy bit that preceded it. It's just argument and conclusion, and I don't see the irony."

"You don't see much, Miss Elphaba," said Madame Morrible. "You must learn to put yourself in the shoes of someone wiser than you are, and look from that angle. To be stuck in ignorance, to be circumscribed by the walls of one's own modest acumen, well, it is very sad in one so young and *bright*." She spit out the last word, and it seemed to Galinda, somehow, a low comment on Elphaba's skin color, which today was indeed lustrous with the effort of public speaking.

"But I was trying to put myself in the shoes of Doctor Dillamond," said Elphaba, almost whining, but not giving up.

"In the case of poetic interpretation, I venture to suggest, it may indeed be true. Animals should not be heard," snapped Madame Morrible.

"Do you mean that ironically?" said Elphaba, but she sat down with her hands over her face, and did not look up again for the rest of the session.

4

WHEN the second semester began, and Galinda was still saddled with Elphaba as a roomie, she made a brief protest to Madame Morrible. But the Head would allow no shifting, no rearranging. "Far too upsetting for my other girls," she said. "Unless you'd like to be removed to the Pink Dormitory. Your Ama Clutch seems, to my watchful eye, to be recovering from the ailments you described when first we met. Perhaps now she is up to overseeing fifteen girls?"

"No, no," said Galinda quickly. "There are recurrences from time to time, but I don't mention them. I don't like to be a bother."

"How thoughtful," said Madame Morrible. "Bless you, sweet thing. Now my dear, I wonder if we might take a moment, as long as you've come in for a chat, to discuss your academic plans for next fall? As you know, second year is when girls choose their specialties. Have you given it any thought?"

"Very little," said Galinda. "Frankly, I thought my talents would just emerge and make it clear whether I should try natural science, or the arts, or sorcery, or perhaps even history. I don't think I'm cut out for ministerial work."

"I'm not surprised that one such as you should be in doubt," said Madame Morrible, which wasn't greatly encouraging to Galinda. "But may I suggest sorcery? You could be very good at it. I pride myself on knowing this sort of thing."

"I'll think about it," said Galinda, though her early appetite for sorcery had waned once she'd heard what a grind it was to learn spells and, worse, to *understand* them.

"In the event you choose sorcery, it might—just might—be possible to find for you a new roomie," said Madame Morrible, "given that

Miss Elphaba has already told me her interests lie in the natural sciences."

"Oh well then, I certainly will give it a great deal of thought," said Galinda. She struggled with unnamed conflicts within her. Madame Morrible, for all her upper-class diction and fabulous wardrobe, seemed just a tad—oh—dangerous. As if her big public smile were composed of the light glancing off knives and lances, as if her deep voice masked the rumbling of distant explosions. Galinda always felt as if she couldn't see the whole picture. It was disconcerting, and to her credit at least Galinda felt inside herself the ripping apart of some valuable fabric—was it integrity?—when she sat in Madame Morrible's parlor and drank the perfect tea.

"For the sister, I hear, is eventually coming up to Shiz," concluded Madame Morrible a few minutes later, as if silence had not intervened, and several tasty biscuits, "because there's nothing I can do to stop it. And that, I understand, would be *dreadful*. You would not like it. The sister being as she is. Undoubtedly spending much time in Miss Elphaba's room, being tended to." She smiled wanly. A puff of powdery aroma came forward from the flank of her neck, almost as if Madame Morrible could somehow dispense a pleasant personal odor at will.

"The sister being as she is." Madame Morrible tutted and wagged her head back and forth as she saw Galinda to the door. "Miserable, really, but I suppose we shall all pull together and cope. That is sorority, isn't it?" The Head grasped her shawl and put a gentle hand on Galinda's shoulder. Galinda shivered, and was sure Madame Morrible felt it, knew it, but the Head never registered a sign of it. "But then, my use of sorority—how ironic. Too witty. Given a long enough time, of course, a wide enough frame, there is nothing said or done, ever, that isn't ironic in the end." She squeezed Galinda's shoulder blade as if it were a bicycle handle, almost harder than was proper for a woman to do. "We can only hope— ha ha—that the sister comes with some veils of her own! But that's a year yet. Meanwhile we have time. Think about sorcery, would you? Do. Now good-bye, my pet, and fresh dreams."

Galinda walked back to her room slowly, wondering what Elphaba's sister was like to provoke those catty remarks about veils. She wanted to ask Elphaba. But she couldn't think of how to do it. She didn't have the nerve.

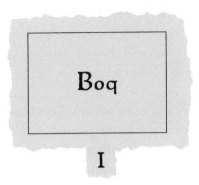

Boq

I

"C ome on out," said the boys. "Come out." They were leaning in the archway to Boq's room, a pell-mell clot of them, backlit by the oil lamp in the study beyond. "We're sick of books. Come with us."

"Can't," said Boq. "I'm behind in irrigation theory."

"Fuck your irrigation theory when the pubs are open," said the strapping Gillikinese bucko named Avaric. "You're not going to improve your grades at this late date, with the exams almost over and the examiners half-crocked themselves."

"It's not the grades," said Boq. "I just don't understand it yet."

"We're off to the *pub*, we're off to the *pub*," chanted some boys who, it seemed, had gotten a head start. "*Fuck* Boq, the ale is waiting, and it's already aged enough!"

"Which pub, then, maybe I'll join you in an hour," Boq said, sitting firmly back in his chair and *not* lifting his feet to the footstool, as he knew that this might incite his classmates to hoist him to their shoulders and carry him off with them for an evening of debauchery. His smallness seemed to inspire such banditry. Feet square on the floor made him look more planted, he figured.

"The Boar and Fennel," said Avaric. "They've got a new witch performing. They say she's hot. She's a Kumbric Witch."

"Hah," said Boq, unconvinced. "Well, go on and get a good view. I'll come along when I can."

The boys rambled away, rattling doors of other friends, knocking aslant the portraits of old boys now grown into august patrons. Avaric stood in the archway and waited a minute longer. "We *might* ditch some of the boors and take a select few of us off to the Philosophy Club," he said enticingly. "Later on, I mean. It's the weekend, after all."

"Oh, Avaric, go take a cold shower," said Boq.

"You admitted you were curious. You *did*. So why not an end-of-semester treat?"

"I'm sorry I ever said I was curious. I'm curious about death, too, but I can wait to find out, thank you. Get lost, Avaric. Better go catch up with your friends. Enjoy the Kumbric antics, which by the way I expect is false advertising. Kumbric Witch talents went out hundreds of years ago. If indeed they ever existed."

Avaric turned up the second collar of his tunic-jacket. The inside was lined with a deep red velvet plush. Against his elegant shaven neck the lining seemed like a single ribbon of privilege. Boq found himself, once again, making mental comparisons between himself and handsome Avaric, and coming up—well, coming up short. "*What*, Avaric," he said, as impatient with himself as he was with his friend.

"Something has happened to you," said Avaric. "I'm not that dull. What's wrong?"

"Nothing's wrong," said Boq.

"Tell me to mind my own business, tell me to go fuck myself, to piss off, go on, say it, but don't tell me *nothing's wrong*. For you're not that good a liar, and I'm not that stupid. Even for a dissipated Gillikinese of decaying nobility." His expression was soft, and Boq, momentarily, was tempted. His mouth opened as he thought of what to say, but at the sound of bells in Ozma Towers, chiming the hour, Avaric's head turned just a fraction. For all his concern, Avaric wasn't *entirely* here. Boq closed his mouth, thought some more, and said, "Call it Munchkinlander stolidity. I won't lie, Avaric, you're too good a friend to lie to. But there's nothing to say now. Now go on and enjoy yourself. But be careful." He was about to add a word of warning against the Philosophy Club, but checked it. If Avaric was annoyed enough, then Boq's nannyish worrying might backfire and goad Avaric into going there.

Avaric came forward and kissed him on both cheeks and on the forehead, an upper-class northern custom that always made Boq profoundly ill at ease. Then with a wink and a dirty gesture, he disappeared.

Boq's room looked out over a cobblestoned alley, down which Avaric and his cronies were swooping and weaving. Boq stood back, in the shadows, but needn't have worried; his friends weren't thinking of him now. They had made it through the halfway point in their exams and had a breather for a couple of days. After the exams, the campus would lie vacant except for the more befuddled of the professors and the poorer of the boys. Boq had lived through this before. He preferred study, however, to scrubbing old manuscripts with a five-haired teck-fur brush, which was what he would be employed to do in the Three Queens library all summer long.

Across the alley ran the bluestone wall of a private stable, attached to some mansion house a few streets away on a fashionable square. Beyond the stable roof you could see the rounded tops of a few fruit trees, in the kitchen garden of Crage Hall, and above them glowed the lancet windows of the dormitories and classrooms. When the girls forgot to draw their drapes—which was astoundingly often—you could see them in various stages of undress. Never the whole body naked, of course; in that case he would have looked away, or told himself sternly that he had *better*. But the pinkness and whiteness of underskirts and camisoles, the frilliness of foundation garments, the rustle about the bustle and the fuss about the bust. It was an education in lingerie if nothing else. Boq, who had no sisters, merely looked.

The Crage Hall dormitory was just far enough away that he couldn't make out the individual girls. And Boq was flushed with desire to see his heartthrob again. Damn! Double damn! He couldn't concentrate. He'd be sent down if he queered his exams! He'd let down his father, old Bfee, and his village, and the other villages.

Hell and hell. Life was hard and barley just wasn't enough. Boq found himself suddenly leaping over the footstool, grabbing his student cape, charging down the corridors, and plummeting around the stone spiral stairs in the corner tower. He couldn't wait any more. He had to do something, and an idea had come to him.

He nodded to the porter on duty, turned left out of the gate, and hurried along the road, in the dusk avoiding as best he could the generous heaps of horse manure. At least with his classmates off gallivanting, he would make no fool of himself in their line of vision. There wasn't a soul left in Briscoe. So he turned left, then left again, and soon was pacing the alley by the stable. A rick of cordwood, the protruding edge of a swollen shutter, the iron bracket of a hoist. Boq was small but he was nimble too, and with hardly a scrape of his knuckles he had swung himself to the tin gutter of the stable, and then was scrabbling like a lake crab up the steeply pitched roof.

Aha! He might have thought of this weeks ago, months ago! But the night that all the boys would be out celebrating, the night he could be sure he himself wouldn't be seen from Briscoe Hall: that was tonight, and maybe only tonight. Some fate had insisted he resist Avaric's invitation out. For now he was mounted on the stable roof, and the wind coursing through the wet leaves of the crawberry and pear trees made a soft fanfare. And there proceeded the girls into their hall—as if they'd been waiting in the corridor until he was properly positioned—as if they'd known he was coming!

Closer up they were not, on the whole, as pretty. . .

But where was the one?

And pretty or not, they were *clear.* The fingers they dove into clumps of satin bow, to untie them, the fingers they peeled gloves off with, and worked cunning rows of forty miniature pearl buttons with, the fingers they loaned to each other, at the inside laces and the private places that college boys knew only by mythology! The unexpected tufts of hair—how tender! How marvelously animallike! His hands clenched and unclenched themselves, of their own accord, but hungry for what he hardly knew—and where was *she?*

"What the *hell* are you doing up there?"

So he slipped, of course, because he was startled, and because fate, having been so kind as to award him this ecstasy, retributively was going to kill him now. He lost his footing and grabbed for the chimney but missed. Head over thighs he rolled out like a child's toy, smashed into the poking branches of the damn pear tree, which probably saved his life, breaking his fall. He landed with a thud on a bed of lettuces, and the wind was loudly knocked out of him, mortifyingly so, through all available orifices.

"Oh, brilliant," said the voice. "The trees are dropping their fruits early this year."

He had a last, lost hope that the person speaking would be his love. He tried to look urbane, though his spectacles had bounced somewhere.

"How do you do," he said uncertainly, sitting up. "This isn't how I intended to arrive."

Barefoot and aproned, she came out from behind an arbor of pink Pertha grapes. It wasn't she, it wasn't the one. It was the other one. He could tell even without his glasses. "Oh, it's you," he said, trying not to sound devastated.

She had a colander with baby grapes in it, the sour ones used in spring salads. "Oh, it's *you*," she said, coming closer. "I know you."

"Master Boq, at your service."

"You mean Master Boq, in my lettuces." She picked up his spectacles from the runner beans, and handed them back.

"How are you, Miss Elphie?"

"I am not as tart as a grape and not as squished as a lettuce," she said. "How are you, Master Boq?"

"I am," he said, "considerably embarrassed. Am I going to get in trouble here?"

"I can arrange it if you like."

"Don't go to the effort. I'll let myself out the way I came in." He looked up at the pear tree. "Poor thing, I've splintered some good-size limbs."

"Pity the poor tree. Why would you do that to it?"

"Well, I was startled," he said, "and I had a choice: either flip myself like a wood nymph through the leaves. Or else just climb quietly down on the other side of the stable, into the street, and go back to my life. Which would you choose?"

"Ah, that's the question," she said, "but I've always learned that the first thing to do is deny the question's validity. Myself, being startled, I would neither climb quietly streetward, nor would I trip noisily treeward and lettucebound. I would turn myself inside out to make myself lighter, I would hover until the air pressure outside me had stabilized. Then I would let the underside of my skin settle, one toe at a time, back on the roof."

"And would you then reverse your skin?" he said, entertained.

"Depends on who was standing there and what they wanted, and whether I minded. Also depends on what color the underside of my skin turns out to be. Never having reversed myself, you know, I can't be sure. I always thought it might be horrid to be pink and white like a piglet."

"It often is," said Boq. "Especially in the shower. You feel like an underdone—" But he stopped. The nonsense was becoming too personal. "I do beg your pardon," he said. "I startled you and I didn't mean to."

"You were looking at the tops of the fruit trees, examining the new growth, I assume?" she said, amused.

"Indeed," he answered coldly.

"Did you see the tree of your dreams?"

"The tree of my dreams is of my dreams, and I don't speak of that to my friends nor to you, whom I hardly know."

"Oh, but you know me. We were in a child play set together, you reminded me when we met last year. Why, we're nearly brother and sister. You can certainly describe your favorite tree to me, and I'll tell you if I know where she grows."

"You mock me, Miss Elphie."

"Well, that I don't mean to do, Boq." She used his name without the honorific in a gentle way, as if to underscore her comment about their being like siblings. "I suspect you want to know about Miss Galinda, the Gillikinese girl you met at Madame Morrible's poetry slaughter last autumn."

"Perhaps you do know me better than I thought." He sighed. "Could I hope she thinks of me?"

"Well, you could *hope*," said Elphaba. "It would be more efficient to ask her and have done with it. At least you'd know."

"But you're a friend of hers, aren't you? Don't you know?"

"You don't want to rely on what *I* know or not," said Elphaba, "or what I say I know. I could be lying. I could be in love with you, and betray my roomie by lying about her—"

"She's *your* roomie?"

"You're very surprised at that?"

"Well—no—just—just pleased."

"The cooks will be wondering what dialogues with the asparagus I'm having now," Elphaba said. "I could arrange to bring Miss Galinda here some evening if you like. Sooner rather than later, so as to kill your joy the more neatly and entirely. If that is what's to happen," she said, "but as I say, how do I know? If I can't predict what we'll have for pudding, how can I predict someone's affections?"

They set a date for three nights hence, and Boq thanked Elphaba fervently, shaking her hand so hard his spectacles jounced on his nose. "You're a dear old friend, Elphie, even if I haven't seen you in fifteen years," he said, giving her back her name without its honorific. She withdrew beneath the boughs of the pear trees and disappeared down the walkway. Boq found his way out of the kitchen garden and back to his room, and reviewed his books again, but the problem wasn't solved, no, not solved. It was exacerbated. He couldn't concentrate. He was still awake to hear the noisy clatterings, the hushings, the crashings, and the muttered balladeerings, when the drunken boys returned to Briscoe Hall.

2

Avaric had left for the summer, once the exams were done, and Boq either had flimflammed his way through or disgraced himself, in which case there was little to lose now. This first rendezvous with Galinda might be the last. Boq bothered with his clothes more than usual, and got an opinion on how to fix his hair from the new look in the cafés (a thin white ribbon around the crown of his head, pulling his hair straight from the nub, so that it burst into curls beneath, like froth exploding from an overturned basin of milk). He cleaned his boots several times over. It was too warm for boots but he had no evening slippers. Make do, make do.

On the appointed evening he retraced his way and, on the stable roof, found that a fruit picker's ladder had been left leaning up against the wall, so he need not descend through the leaves like a vertiginous chimpanzee. He picked his way carefully down the first few rungs, then jumped manfully the rest of the way, avoiding the lettuces this time. On a bench under the wormnut trees sat Elphaba, her knees drawn casually up to her chest and her bare feet flat on the seat of the bench, and Galinda, whose ankles were crossed daintily and who hid behind a satin fan, and who was looking in the other direction anyway.

"Well, my stars and garters, a visitor," said Elphaba. "*Such* a surprise."

"Good evening, ladies," he said.

"Your head looks like a hedgehog in shock, what did you do to your-self?" said Elphaba. At least Galinda turned to see, but then she disappeared behind the fan again. Could she be so nervous? Could her heart be faint?

"Well I am part Hedgehog, didn't I tell you?" said Boq. "On my grandfather's side. He ended up as cutlets for Ozma's retinue one hunt-ing season, and a tasty memory for all. The recipe is handed down in the family, pasted into the picture album. Served with cheese and walnut sauce. Mmmm."

"Are you really?" said Elphaba. She put her chin on her knees. "Really Hedgehog?"

"No, it was a fancy. Good evening, Miss Galinda. It was good of you to agree to meet me again."

"This is highly improper," said Galinda. "For a number of reasons, as you well know, Master Boq. But my roomie would give me no rest until I said yes. I can't say that I am pleased to see you again."

"Oh, say it, say it, maybe it'll make it true," said Elphaba. "Try it out. He's not so bad. For a poor boy."

"I am pleased that you are so taken with me, Master Boq," said Miss Galinda, working at courtesy. "I am flattered." She clearly was not flattered, she was humiliated. "But you must see that there can be no spe-cial friendship between us. Apart from the matter of my feelings, there are too many social impediments for us to proceed. I only agreed to come so that I could tell you this in person. It seemed only fair."

"It seemed only fair and it might be fun, too," said Elphaba. "That's why I'm hanging around."

"There's the issue of different cultures, to start," said Galinda. "I know you are a Munchkinlander. I am a Gillikinese. I will need to marry one of my own. It is the only way, I'm sorry"—she lowered her fan and lifted her hand, palm out, to stop his protest—"and furthermore you are a farmer, from the agricultural school, and I require a statesman or a banker from Ozma Towers. This is just how things are. Besides," said Galinda, "you're too short."

"What about his subversion of custom by coming here this way, what about his silliness?" said Elphaba.

"Enough," said Galinda. "That'll do, Miss Elphaba."

"Please, you're too certain of yourself," said Boq. "If I may be so bold."

"You're not so bold at all," said Elphaba, "you're about as bold as tea made from used leaves. You're embarrassing me with hanging back so. Come on, say something interesting. I'm starting to wish I'd gone to chapel."

"You're interrupting," said Boq. "Miss Elphie, you've done a wonderful thing to encourage Miss Galinda to meet me, but I must ask you to leave us alone to sort things out."

"Neither of you will understand what the other is saying," said Elphaba calmly. "I'm a Munchkinlander by birth anyway, if not by upbringing, and I'm a girl by accident if not by choice. I'm the natural arbiter between you two. I don't believe you can get along without me. In fact if I leave the garden you'll cease to decipher each other's language entirely. She speaks the tongue of Rich, you speak Clotted Poor. Besides, I paid for this show by wheedling Miss Galinda for three days running. I get to watch."

"It would be so good of you to stay, Miss Elphaba," said Galinda, "I require a chaperone when with a boy."

"See what I mean?" Elphaba said to Boq.

"Then if you must stay, at least let me talk," Boq said. "Please let me speak, just for a few minutes. Miss Galinda. What you say is true. You are highborn and I am common. You are Gillikinese and I, Munchkinlander. You have a social pattern to conform to, and so do I. And mine doesn't include marrying a girl too wealthy, too foreign, too expectant. Marriage isn't what I came here to propose."

"See, I'm glad I didn't leave, this is just getting good," said Elphaba, but clamped her lips shut when they both glared at her.

"I came here to propose that we meet from time to time, that's all," said Boq. "That we meet as friends. That, free of expectations, we come to know each other as dear friends. I do not deny that you overwhelm me with your beauty. You are the moon in the season of shadowlight; you are the fruit of the candlewood tree; you are the pfenix in circles of flight—"

"This sounds rehearsed," said Elphaba.

"You are the mythical sea," he concluded, all his eggs in one basket.

"I'm not much for poetry," said Galinda. "But you're very kind." She had seemed to perk up a little at the compliments. Anyway the fan was moving faster. "I don't really understand the point of *friendship*, as

you call it, Master Boq, between unmarried people of our age. It seems—
distracting. I can see it might lead to complications, especially as you confess to an infatuation I cannot hope to return. Not in a million years."

"It's the age of daring," said Boq. "It's the only time we have. We
must live in the present. We are young and alive."

"I don't know if *alive* quite covers it," said Elphaba. "This sounds
scripted to me."

Galinda rapped Elphaba on the head with her fan, which folded
smartly up and opened just as neatly again, an elegant practiced gesture
that impressed all of them. "You're being tiresome, Miss *Elphie.* I appreciate your company but I didn't request a running commentary. I'm perfectly capable of deciding the merits of Master Boq's recital myself. Let me
consider his stupid idea. Lurline above, I can hardly hear myself think!"

Losing her temper, Galinda was prettier than ever. So that old saw
was true, too. Boq was learning so *much* about girls! Her fan was dropping. Was that a good sign? If she hadn't had some affection for him,
would she have worn a dress with a neckline that dipped just a tad lower
than he had dared hope? And there was the essence of rose water on her.
He felt a surge of possibility, an inclination to rub his lips on the place
where her shoulder became her neck.

"Your merits," she was saying. "Well, you're brave, I suppose, and
clever, to have figured this out. If Madame Morrible ever found you here
we'd be in severe trouble. Of course you might not know that, so scratch
the bravery part. Just clever. You're clever and you're sort of, oh, well, I
mean to look at—"

"Handsome?" suggested Elphaba. "Dashing?"

"You're *fun* to look at," decided Galinda.

Boq's face fell. "Fun?" he said.

"I'd give a *lot* to achieve *fun,*" Elphaba said. "The best I usually
hope for is *stirring,* and when people say that they're usually referring to
digestion—"

"Well, I might be all or none of the things you say," said Boq
staunchly, "but you will learn that I am persistent. I will not let you say
no to our friendship, Galinda. It means too much to me."

"Behold the male beast roaring in the jungle for his mate," said
Elphaba. "See how the female beast giggles behind a shrub while she

organizes her face to say, Pardon dear, did you say something?"

"Elphaba!" they both cried at her.

"My word, duckie!" said a voice behind them, and all three turned. It was some middle-aged minder in a striped apron, her thinning gray hair twisted in a knot on her head. "What are you getting yourself up to?"

"Ama Clutch!" Galinda said. "How did you think to look for me here?"

"That Tsebra cook told me some yacky-yacky was going on out here. You think they're blind in there? Now who is this? This don't look good at all, not to me."

Boq stood. "I am Master Boq of Rush Margins, Munchkinland. I am nearly a third-year fellow at Briscoe Hall."

Elphaba yawned. "Is this show over?"

"Well, I am shocked! A guest don't get shown into the vegetable garden, so I guess you arrived uninvited! Sir, get yourself gone from here before I be calling the porters to remove you!"

"Oh, Ama Clutch, don't make a scene," said Galinda, sighing.

"He's hardly developed enough to worry about," pointed out Elphaba. "Look, he's still beardless. And from that we can deduce—"

Boq said in a rush, "Perhaps this is all wrong. I did not come here to be abused. Forgive me, Miss Galinda, if I have failed even to amuse you. As for you, Miss Elphaba"—his voice was as cold as he could make it, and that was colder than he'd ever heard it himself—"I was wrong to have trusted in your compassion."

"Wait and see," said Elphaba. "Wrong takes an awful long time to be proven, in my experience. Meanwhile, why don't you come back sometime?"

"There is no second time to this," said Ama Clutch, tugging at Galinda, who was proving as sedentary as set cement. "Miss Elphaba, shame on you for encouraging this scandal."

"Nothing here has been perpetrated but badinage, and bad badinage at that," said Elphaba. "Miss Galinda, you're mighty stubborn there. You're planting yourself in the vegetable garden for good in the hopes that this Boy Visitation might occur again? Have we misread your interest?"

Galinda stood at last with some dignity. "My dear Master Boq," she said, as if dictating, "it was ever my intention to dissuade you from pursuing me, in romantic attachment or even in *friendship*, as you put it. I had not meant to bruise you. It is not in my nature." At this Elphaba rolled her eyes, but for once kept her mouth shut, perhaps because Ama Clutch had dug her fingernails into Elphaba's elbow. "I will not deign to arrange another meeting like this. As Ama Clutch reminds me, it is beneath me." Ama Clutch hadn't exactly said that, but even so, she nodded grimly. "But if our paths cross in a legitimate way, Master Boq, I will do you the courtesy at least of not ignoring you. I trust you will be satisfied with that."

"Never," said Boq with a smile, "but it's a start."

"And now good evening," said Ama Clutch on behalf of them all, and steered the girls away. "Fresh dreams, Master Boq, and don't come back!"

"Miss Elphie, you were *horrible*," he heard Galinda say, while Elphaba twisted around and waved good-bye with a grin he could not clearly read.

3

So the summer began. Since he passed the exams, Boq was free to plan one last year at Briscoe Hall. Daily he hied himself over to the library at Three Queens, where under the watchful eye of a titanic Rhinoceros, the head archival librarian, he sat cleaning old manuscripts that clearly weren't looked at more than once a century. When the Rhino was out of the room, he had flighty conversations with the two boys on either side of him, classic Queens boys, full of gibbering gossip and arcane references, teasing and loyal. He enjoyed them when they were in good spirits, and he detested their sulks. Crope and Tibbett. Tibbett and Crope. Boq pretended confusion when they got too arch or suggestive, which seemed to happen about once a week, but they backed off quickly. In the afternoons they would all take their cheese sandwiches by the banks of the Suicide Canal and watch the swans. The strong boys at crew, coursing up and down the canal for summer practice, made Crope and Tibbett swoon and fall on their faces in the grass. Boq laughed at them, not unkindly, and waited for fate to deliver Galinda back into his path.

It wasn't too long a wait. About three weeks after their vegetable garden liaison, on a windy summer morning, a small earthquake caused some minor damage in the Three Queens library, and the building had to be closed for some patching. Tibbett, Crope, and Boq took their sandwiches, with some beakers of tea from the buttery, and they flopped down at their favorite place on the grassy banks of the canal. Fifteen minutes later, along came Ama Clutch with Galinda and two other girls.

"I do believe we know you," said Ama Clutch as Galinda stood demurely a step behind. In cases such as these it was the servant's duty to elicit names from the strangers in the group, so that they might greet each other personally. Ama Clutch registered out loud that they were Masters Boq, Crope, and Tibbett, meeting Misses Galinda, Shenshen, and Pfannee. Then Ama Clutch moved a few feet away to allow the young people to address one another.

Boq leaped up and gave a small bow, and Galinda said, "As in line with my promise, Master Boq, may I enquire how you're keeping?"

"Very well, thank you," said Boq.

"He's ripe as a peach," said Tibbett.

"He's downright luscious, from this angle," said Crope, sitting a few steps behind, but Boq turned and glared so fiercely that Crope and Tibbett were chastened, and fell into a mock sulk.

"And you, Miss Galinda?" continued Boq, searching her well-composed face. "You are well? How thrilling to see you in Shiz for the summer." But that wasn't the right thing to say. The better girls went home for the summer, and Galinda as a Gillikinese must feel it deeply that she was stuck here, like a Munchkinlander or a commoner! The fan came up. The eyes went down. The Misses Shenshen and Pfannee touched her shoulders in mute sympathy. But Galinda sallied on.

"My dear friends the Misses Pfannee and Shenshen are taking a house for the month of Highsummer on the shores of Lake Chorge. A little fantasy house near the village of Neverdale. I've decided to make my holiday there instead of taking that tiresome trek back to the Pertha Hills."

"How refreshing." He saw the beveled edges of her lacquered fingernails, the moth-colored eyelashes, the glazed and buffed softness of cheek, the sensitive tuck of skin just at the cleft of her upper lip. In the summer morning light, she was dangerously, inebriatingly magnified.

"Steady," said Crope, and he and Tibbett jumped up and they each caught Boq by an elbow. He then remembered to breathe. He couldn't think of anything else to say though, and Ama Clutch was turning her handbag around and around in her hands.

"So we've got jobs," said Tibbett, to the rescue. "The Three Queens library. We're housekeeping the literature. We're the cleaning maids of culture. Are you working, Miss Galinda?"

"I should think *not*," said Galinda. "I need a rest from my studies. It has been a harrowing year, harrowing. My eyes are still tired from reading."

"How about you girls?" said Crope, outrageously casual. But they only giggled and demurred and inched away. This was their friend's encounter, not theirs. Boq, regaining his composure, could feel the group beginning to shift itself into motion again. "And Miss Elphie?" he enquired, to hold them there. "How is your roomie?"

"Headstrong and difficult," said Galinda severely, for the first time speaking in a normal voice, not the faint social whisper. "But, thank Lurline, *she's* got a job, so I get some relief. She's working in the lab and the library under our Doctor Dillamond. Do you know of him?"

"Doctor Dillamond? Do I *know* of him?" said Boq. "He's the most impressive biology tutor in Shiz."

"By the by," said Galinda, "he's a Goat."

"Yes, yes. I wish he would teach *us*. Even our professors acknowledge his prominence. Apparently, years ago, back in the reign of the Regent, and before, he used to be invited annually to lecture at Briscoe Hall. But the restrictions changed even that, so I've never really met him. Just to see him at that poetry evening, last year, so briefly, was a treat—"

"Well he does go *on*," said Galinda. "Brilliant he may be, but he has no sense of when he's become tedious. Anyway, Miss Elphie's hard at work, doing something or other. She will go *on* about it, too. I think it's contagious!"

"Well, a lab, it breeds things," said Crope.

"Yes," said Tibbett, "and incidentally may I add that you're every bit as lovely as Boq gushes you are. We'd put it down to an overactive imagination born of affectional and physical frustration—"

"You know," said Boq, "between your Miss Elphie and my erstwhile friends here, we have no real hope of friendship at all. Shall we organize a duel and kill each other instead? Count off ten paces, turn and shoot? It would save so much bother."

But Galinda didn't approve of such joking. She nodded in a dismissive way, and the group of females moved out along the graveled path, following the curve of the canal. Miss Shenshen was heard to say in a deep, breathy voice, "Oh, my dear, he *is* sweet, in a toylike way."

The voice faded out, Boq turned to rail at Crope and Tibbett, but they fell to tickling him and they all collapsed in a heap on the remains of their lunch. And since there was no hope in changing them, Boq abandoned the impulse to correct his friends. Really, what difference did their callow banter make if Miss Galinda found him so impossible?

A week or two later, on his afternoon off, Boq took himself in to Railway Square. He lingered at a kiosk, staring. Cigarettes, ersatz love charms, naughty drawings of women undressing, and scrolls painted with lurid sunsets, overladen with one-line inspirational slogans. "Lurline Lives on Within Each Heart." "Safe Keep the Wizard's Laws, and the Wizard's Laws Will Keep You Safe." "I Pray to the Unnamed God That Justice Will Walk Abroad in Oz." Boq noted the variety: the pagan, the authoritarian, and the old-fashioned unionist impulses.

But nothing directly sympathetic to the royalists, who had gone underground in the sixteen harsh years since the Wizard had first wrested power from the Ozma Regent. The Ozma line had been Gillikinese originally, and surely there were active pockets of resistance to the Wizard? But Gillikin had, in fact, thrived under the Wizard, so the royalists kept mum. Besides, everyone had heard the rumors of strict court action against turncoats and peristrophists.

Boq bought a broadsheet published out of the Emerald City—several weeks old, but it was the first he'd seen in some time—and he settled down at a café. He read about the Emerald City Home Guard suppressing some Animal dissenters, who were making a nuisance of themselves in the palace gardens. He looked for news of the provinces, and found a filler about Munchkinland, which continued experiencing near-drought conditions; occasional thunderbursts would drench the ground, but the water would run off or sink uselessly into the clay. They said that hidden subterranean lakes underlay the Vinkus region, that water resources there could serve the whole of Oz. But the idea of a canal system across the entire country made everyone laugh. The expense! There was great disagreement between the Eminences and the Emerald City as to what was to be done.

Secession, thought Boq seditiously, and looked up to see Elphaba, alone, without even a nanny or Ama, standing over him.

"What a delicious expression you have on your face, Boq," she said. "It's much more interesting than love."

"It *is* love, in a way," said Boq, then remembered himself, and leaped to his feet. "Won't you join me? Please, take a seat. Unless you're worried about being unchaperoned."

She sat down, looking a bit etiolated, and allowed him to call for a cup of mineral tea. She had a parcel in brown paper and string under her arm. "A few trinkets for my sister," she said. "She's like Miss Galinda, she loves the fancy outside of things. I found a Vinkus shawl in the bazaar, red roses on a black background, with black and green fringe. I'm sending it to her, and a pair of striped stockings that Ama Clutch knitted for me."

"I didn't know you had a sister," he said. "Was she in the play group we were in together?"

"She's three years younger," Elphaba said. "She'll come to Crage Hall before long."

"Is she as difficult as you are?"

"She's difficult in a different way. She's crippled, pretty severely, is my Nessarose, so she's a handful. Even Madame Morrible doesn't quite know the extent of it. But by then I'll be a third-year girl and will have the nerve to stand up to the Head, I guess. If anything gives me nerve, it's people making life hard for Nessarose. Life is already hard enough for her."

"Is your mama raising her?"

"My mother is dead. My father is in charge, nominally."

"Nominally?"

"He's *religious*," said Elphaba, and made the circling palms gesture that indicated you could grind millstone against millstone all you liked, but there wasn't any quern in the land that could produce flour if there was no grain to grind.

"It sounds very hard for you all. How did your mama die?"

"She died in childbirth, and this is the end of the personal interview."

"Tell me about Doctor Dillamond. I hear you're working for him."

"Tell me about your amusing campaign for the heart of Galinda the Ice Queen."

Boq really wanted to hear about Doctor Dillamond, but was derailed by Elphaba's remark. "I *will* keep on, Elphie, I will! When I see her I'm so smitten with longing, it's like fire in my veins. I can't speak, and the things I think about are like visions. It's like dreaming. It's like floating in your dreams."

"I don't dream."

"Tell me, is there any hope? What does she say? Does she ever even *imagine* that her feelings for me might change?"

Elphaba sat with her two elbows on the table, her hands clasped in front of her face, her two forefingers leaning against each other and against her thin, grayish lips. "You know, Boq," she said, "the thing is I have become fond of Galinda myself. Behind her starry-eyed love of herself there *is* a mind struggling to work. She *does* think about things. When her mind is really working, she could, if led, think on you—even, I suspect, somewhat fondly. I *suspect*. I don't know. But when she slides back into herself, I mean into the girl who spends two hours a day curling that beautiful hair, it's as if the thinking Galinda goes into some internal closet and shuts the door. Or as if she's in hysterical retreat from things that are too big for her. I love her both ways, but I find it odd. I wouldn't mind leaving myself behind if I could, but I don't know the way out."

"I propose you're being hard on her, and you're certainly too forward," said Boq sternly. "Were she sitting here I think she'd be astounded to hear you speak so freely."

"I'm just trying to behave as I think a friend should behave. Granted, I haven't had much practice."

"Well, I question your friendship with me, if you consider Miss Galinda your friend too, and if that's how you tear a friend apart in her absence."

Though Boq was irritated, he found that this was a more lively discussion than the conventional patter he and Galinda had so far exchanged. He didn't want to burn Elphaba off with criticism. "I'm ordering you another mineral tea," he said, in an authoritative voice, his father's voice in fact, "and then you can tell me about Doctor Dillamond."

"Skip the tea, I'm still nursing this one and you have no more money than I do, I bet," said Elphaba, "but I'll tell you about Doctor Dillamond. Unless you are too affronted at the slice and angle of my opinions."

"Please, perhaps I am wrong," said Boq. "Look, it's a nice day, we're both off the campus. How do you come to be out alone, by the way? Is your escape sanctioned by Madame Morrible?"

"Take a guess about that," she said, grinning. "Once it was clear that *you* could come and go from Crage Hall by way of the vegetable garden and the roof of the adjacent stable, I decided I could too. I'm never missed."

"That's hard for me to believe," said he, daringly, "for you're not the kind who blends into the woodwork. Now tell me about Doctor Dillamond. He's my idol."

She sighed, and set the package down on the table at last, and settled in for a long chat. She told him about Doctor Dillamond's work in natural essences, trying to determine by scientific method what the real differences were between animal and Animal tissue, and between Animal and human tissue. The literature on the matter, she had learned from doing the leg-work herself, was all couched in unionist terms, and pagan terms before that, and they didn't hold up to scientific scrutiny. "Don't forget Shiz University was originally a unionist monastery," said Elphaba, "so despite the anything-goes attitude among the educated elite, there are still bedrocks of unionist bias."

"But I'm a unionist," said Boq, "and I don't see the conflict. The Unnamed God is accommodating to many ranges of being, not just human. Are you talking about a subtle bias against Animals, interwoven into early unionist tracts, and still in operation today?"

"That's certainly what Doctor Dillamond thinks. *And* he's a union-ist himself. Explain that paradox and I'd be glad to convert. I admire the Goat intensely. But the real interest of it to me is the political slant. If he can isolate some bit of the biological architecture to prove that there *isn't any difference*, deep down in the invisible pockets of human and Animal flesh—that there's no difference between us—or even among us, if you take in animal flesh too—well, you see the implications."

"No," said Boq, "I don't think I do."

"How can the Banns on Animal Mobility be upheld if Doctor Dillamond can prove, scientifically, that there isn't any inherent difference between humans and Animals?"

"Oh, now that's a blueprint for an impossibly rosy future," said Boq.

"*Think* about it," said Elphaba. "Think, Boq. On what grounds could the Wizard possibly continue to publish those Banns?"

"How could he be persuaded not to? The Wizard has dissolved the Hall of Approval indefinitely. I don't believe, Elphie, that the Wizard is open to entertaining arguments, even by as august an Animal as Doctor Dillamond."

"But of course he must be. He's a man in power, it's his job to consider changes in knowledge. When Doctor Dillamond has his proof, he'll write to the Wizard and begin to lobby for change. No doubt he'll do his best to let Animals the land over know what he's intending, too. He isn't a fool."

"Well I didn't say he was a fool," said Boq. "But how close do you think he is to getting firm evidence?"

"I am a student handmaid," said Elphaba. "I don't even understand what he means. I'm only a secretary, an amanuensis—you know he can't write things himself, he can't manage a pen with his hoofs. I take dictation and I file and I dash to the Crage Hall library and look things up."

"Briscoe Hall library would be a better place to hunt for that kind of material," said Boq. "Even Three Queens, where I work this summer, has stacks of documents from the monks' observations of animal and vegetable life."

"I know I am not traditionally presented," said Elphaba, "but I believe on the grounds of being a girl I am excluded from the Briscoe Hall library. And on the grounds of being an Animal so too, now at least, is Doctor Dillamond. So those valuable resources are off limits to us."

"Well," said Boq carelessly, "if you knew exactly what you wanted . . . I have access to the stacks in both collections."

"And when the good Doctor is finished ferreting out the difference between Animals and people, I will propose he apply the same arguments to the differences between the sexes," said Elphaba. Then she registered what Boq had said, and stretched out her hand, almost as if to touch him. "Oh Boq. Boq. On behalf of Doctor Dillamond, I accept your generous offer of help. I'll get the first list of sources to you within the week. Just leave my name out of it. I don't care so much about incurring Horrible Morrible's wrath against myself, but I don't want her taking out her annoyance on my sister, Nessarose."

She downed the last of her tea, gathered her parcel, and had sprung up almost before Boq could pull himself to his feet. Various customers, lingering over their elevenses with their own broadsheets or novellas, looked up at the ungainly girl pushing out the doors. As Boq settled back down, hardly yet registering what he had gotten himself into, he realized, slowly but thoroughly, that this morning there were no Animals taking their morning tea in here. No Animals at all.

4

In years to come—and Boq would live a long life—he would remember the rest of the summer as scented with the must of old books, when ancient script swam before his eyes. He sleuthed alone in the musty stacks, he hovered over the mahogany drawers lined with vellum manuscripts. All season long, it seemed, the lozenge-paned windows between bluestone mullions and transoms misted over again and again with flecks of small but steady rain, almost as brittle and pesky as sand. Apparently the rain never made it as far as Munchkinland—but Boq tried not to think about that.

Crope and Tibbett were coerced into researching for Doctor Dillamond, too. At first they had to be dissuaded from going about their forays in costumes of disguise—fake pince-nez, powdered wigs, cloaks with high collars, all to be found in the well-stocked locker of the Three Queens Student Theatrical and Terpsichorean Society. But when convinced of the seriousness of the mission, they fell to with gusto. Once a week they met Boq and Elphaba in the café in Railway Square. Elphaba showed up, during these misty weeks, entirely swathed in a brown cloak with a hood and veil that hid all but her eyes. She wore long, frayed gray gloves that she boasted buying secondhand from a local undertaker, cheap for having been used in funeral services. She sheathed her bamboo-pole legs in a double thickness of cotton stocking. The first time Boq saw Elphaba like this, he said, "I just barely manage to convince Crope and Tibbett to lose the espionage drag, and you come in looking like the original Kumbric Witch."

"I don't dress for your approval, boys," she said, shucking her cloak and folding it inside out so that the wet wool never touched her. On the occasion when another café patron would come through, shaking water off an umbrella, Elphaba always recoiled, flinching if she was caught by even a scattering of drops.

"Is that religious conviction, Elphie, that you keep yourself so dry?" said Boq.

"I've told you before, I don't comprehend religion, although *conviction* is a concept I'm beginning to get. In any case, someone with a real religious conviction is, I propose, a religious *convict*, and deserves locking up."

"Hence," observed Crope, "your aversion to all water. Without your knowing it, it might be a baptismal splash, and then your liberty as a free-range agnostic would be curtailed."

"I thought you were too self-absorbed to notice my spiritual pathology," said Elphaba. "Now, boys, what've we got today?"

Every time, Boq thought: Would that Galinda were here. For the casual camaraderie that grew up among them during these weeks was so refreshing—a model of ease and even wit. Against convention they had dropped the honorifics. They interrupted one another and laughed and felt bold and important because of the secrecy of their mission. Crope and Tibbett cared little about Animals or the Banns—they were both Emerald City boys, sons, respectively, of a tax collector and of a palace security advisor—but Elphaba's passionate belief in the work enlivened them. Boq himself grew more involved, too. He imagined Galinda drawing her chair up with them, losing her upper-crust reserve, allowing her eyes to glow with a shared and secret purpose.

"I thought I knew all the shapes of passion," Elphaba said one bright afternoon. "I mean, growing up with a unionist minister for a father. You come to expect that theology is the fundament on which all other thought and belief is based. But boys!—this week, Doctor Dillamond made some sort of a scientific breakthrough. I'm not sure what it was, but it involved manipulating lenses, a pair of them, so he could peer at bits of tissue that he had laid on a transparent glass and backlit by candlelight. He began to dictate, and he was so excited that he sang his findings; he composed arias out of what he was seeing! Recitatives about structure, about color, about the basic shapes of organic life. He has a horrible sandpapery voice, as you might imagine for a Goat;

but how he warbled! Tremolo on the annotations, vibrato on the inter-
pretations, and sostenuto on the implications: long, triumphant open
vowels of discovery! I was sure someone would hear. I sang with him, I
read his notes back to him like a student of musical composition."

The good Doctor was emboldened by his findings, and he required
that their digging become more and more focused. He did not want to
announce any breakthroughs until he had figured out the most politically
advantageous way to present them. Toward the end of the summer the
push was on to find Lurlinist and early unionist disquisitions on how the
Animals and the animals had been created and differentiated. "It's not a
matter of uncovering a scientific theory by a prescientific company of
unionist monks or pagan priests and priestesses," explained Elphaba. "But
Doctor Dillamond wants to authenticate the way our ancestors *thought*
about this. The Wizard's right to impose unjust laws may be better challenged if we know how the old codgers explained it to themselves."

It was an interesting exercise.

"In one form or another, we all know some of the origin myths that
predate the *Oziad*," said Tibbett, throwing his blond bangs back with a
theatrical flourish. "The most coherent one has our dear putative Fairy
Queen Lurline on a voyage. She was tired of travel in the air. She stopped
and called from the desert sands a font of water hidden deep beneath the
earth's dry dunes. The water obeyed, in such abundance that the land of
Oz in all its febrile variety sprang up almost instantly. Lurline drank herself into a stupor and went for a long rest on the top of Mount Runcible.
When she awoke, she relieved herself copiously, and this became the
Gillikin River, running around the vast tracts of the Great Gillikin Forest
and skirting through the eastern edges of the Vinkus, and coming to a
stop at Restwater. The animals were *terricolous* and thus of a lower order
than Lurline and her retinue. Don't look at me like that, I know what that
word means—I looked it up. It means living on or near the ground.

"The animals had come into their being as rolled clots of earth dislodged from the exuberant plant growth. When Lurline let loose, the animals thought the raging stream was a flood, sent to drown their fresh
new world, and they despaired of their existence. In a panic they flung
themselves into the torrent and attempted to swim through Lurline's
urine. Those who became intimidated and turned back remained animals,

beasts of burden, slaughtered for flesh, hunted for fun, counted as profit, admired as innocent. Those who swam on and made it to the farther shore were given the gifts of consciousness and language."

"What a gift, to be able to imagine your own death," muttered Crope.

"Thus, Animals. Convention, as long ago as history can remember, divides the animals and Animals."

"Baptism by piss," said Elphaba. "Is that a subtle way both to explain the talents of Animals and to denigrate them at the same time?"

"And what of the animals who drowned?" asked Boq. "They must have been the real losers."

"Or the martyrs."

"Or the ghosts who live underground now and stop up the water supply so the fields of Munchkinland dry up today."

They all laughed and had more tea brought to the table.

"I've found some later scriptures with a more unionist slant," Boq said. "They tell a story that I guess would be derived from the pagan narra-tive, but it has been cleaned up some. The flood, occurring sometime after creation and before the advent of humankind, wasn't a massive piss by Lurline, but the sea of tears wept by the Unnamed God on the god's only visit to Oz. The Unnamed God perceived the sorrow that would overwhelm the land throughout time, and bawled in pain. The whole of Oz was a mile deep in saltwater tides. The animals kept afloat by means of the odd log, the uprooted tree. Those who swallowed enough of the tears of the Unnamed God were imbued with a fulsome sympathy for their kin, and they began to construct rafts from the flotsam. They saved their kind out of mercy, and from their kindness they became a new, sentient lot: the Animals."

"Another kind of baptism, from within," said Tibbett. "Ingestion. I like it."

"But what of the pleasure faith?" said Crope. "Can a witch or a sor-cerer take an animal and, through a spell, create an Animal?"

"Well, that's the thing I've been looking into," said Elphaba. "The pleasure faithers—the pfaithers—say that if *anything*—Lurline or the Unnamed God—could have done it once, magic could do it again. They even hint that the original distinction between Animals and animals was a Kumbric Witch spell, so strong and enduring it has never worn off. This is dangerous propaganda, malice incarnate. No one knows if there is such a thing as a Kumbric Witch, let alone if there ever was. Myself, I think it's a part of the Lurlinist cycle that's gotten detached and developed independently. Arrant nonsense. We have no proof that magic is so strong—"

"We have no proof that *god* is so strong," interrupted Tibbett.

"Which strikes me as being as good an argument against god as it is against magic," said Elphaba, "but never mind that. The point is, if it *is* an enduring Kumbric spell, centuries old, it may be reversible. Or it may be *perceived* to be reversible, which is just as bad. In the interim, while sorcerers are at work experimenting with charms and spells, the Animals lose their rights, one by one. Just slowly enough so that it's hard to see as a coherent political campaign. It's a dicey scenario, and one that Doctor Dillamond hasn't figured out—"

At this point Elphaba hitched the burnoose part of her cloak up over her head, and disappeared into the shadows of its folds. "What?" said Boq, but she put a finger to her lips. Crope and Tibbett, as if on cue, launched into some silly banter about their professional goals of being abducted by pirates of the desert and made to dance the fandango dressed only in slave shackles. Boq saw nothing amiss: A couple of clerks reading the racing forms, some genteel ladies with their lemonades and novellas, a tiktok creature buying coffee beans by the pound, a parody of an old professor figuring out some theorem by arranging and rearranging some sugar cubes along the edge of his butter knife.

A few minutes later, Elphaba relaxed. "That tiktok thing works at Crage Hall. I think it's called Grommetik. Usually it shadows Madame Morrible like a lovesick puppy. I don't think it saw me."

But she was too jittery to continue the conversation, and after she made sure their next assignments were clear, the crew disbanded into the misty streets.

5

Two weeks before Briscoe Hall reconvened for the new semester, Avaric returned from his home, the seat of the Margreave of Tenmeadows. He was bronzed with summer leisure and eager for fun. He mocked Boq for having struck up friendships with boys from Three

Queens, and under other circumstances Boq would probably have let his new alliance with Crope and Tibbett lapse. But they were all engaged in Doctor Dillamond's research now, and Boq just put up with Avaric's taunting.

Elphaba remarked one day that she had had a letter from Galinda, away with her friends on Lake Chorge. "Can you believe it, she proposed I take a coach and come visit for a weekend," said Elphaba. "She must really be bored out of her mind with those society girls."

"But she's society herself, how could she be bored?" asked Boq.

"Don't ask me to explain the nuances of that circle," said Elphaba, "but I suspect that our Miss Galinda isn't quite as society as she makes out."

"Well, Elphie, when are you going?" asked Boq.

"Never," said Elphaba. "This work is too important."

"Let me see the letter."

"I don't have it."

"Bring it to me."

"What are you on about?"

"Maybe she needs you. She always seems to need you."

"She needs *me?*" Elphaba laughed, coarsely, loudly. "Well I know you're besotted and I feel somewhat responsible. I'll show you the letter next week. But I'm not going to go just to give you a vicarious thrill, Boq. Friend or no friend."

The next week she unfolded the letter.

My dear Miss Elphaba,

I am bade to write to you by my hostesses the Misses Pfannee of Pfann Hall and Shenshen of the Minkos Clan. We are having a lovely summer at Lake Chorge. The air is calm and sweet and all is as pleasant as anything. If you would like to visit us for three or four days before school begins, we know you have been hard at work all summer and so. A little change. If you would like to come no need to write if you would like to visit. Just arrive by coach at Neverdale and come by foot or hire a hansom cab, it's just a mile or two by the bridge. The house is dear, covered in roses and ivy, it's called the "Caprice-in-the-Pines."
Who wouldn't love it here! I *do* hope you can come! I do very

specially hope so for reasons I dare not write. I cannot advise you
as to chaperones as Ama Clutch is already here and so is Ama
Clipp and Ama Vimp. You can decide. We hope for long
hours of amusing conversation. Ever your loving friend,

Miss Galinda
of the Arduennas of the Upland
33 Highsummer, midday
at "Caprice-in-the-Pines"

"But you must go!" Boq cried. "Look how she writes to you!"

"She writes like someone who doesn't write very often," Elphaba
observed.

"'I do hope you can come!' she says. She needs you, Elphie. I insist
that you go!"

"Oh you do? Why don't *you* go then?" said Elphaba.

"I hardly can go without having been invited."

"Well that's easy enough. I'll write and tell her to invite you."
Elphaba reached for a pencil in her pocket.

"Don't patronize me, Miss Elphaba," said Boq sternly. "This must
be taken seriously."

"You are lovesick and deluded," said Elphaba. "And I don't like your
retreating back to 'Miss Elphaba' to punish me for disagreeing with you.
Besides, I can't go. I have no chaperone."

"I'll be your chaperone."

"Hah! As if Madame Morrible would allow that!"

"Well—how about"—Boq tossed it around—"how about my
friend Avaric? He's the son of a margreave. He's spotless by virtue of his
station. Even Madame Morrible would quail before a margreave's son."

"Madame Morrible wouldn't quail before a hurricane. Besides, have
you no concern for me? I don't feel like traveling with this Avaric."

"Elphie," said Boq, "you owe me. I've been helping you out all summer, and I've had Crope and Tibbett helping too. Now you have to pay
me back. You ask Doctor Dillamond for a few days off, and I'll ask Avaric,
who is bursting to do something. The three of us will go to Lake Chorge.
Avaric and I will rent a room in an inn, and we'll stay a very short time.
Just long enough to make sure that Miss Galinda is all right."

"It's you I'm worried about, not her," said Elphaba, and Boq could see that he had won.

Madame Morrible would not release Elphaba in the care of Avaric. "Your dear father would never forgive me," she said. "But I am not the Horrible Morrible you think of me. Oh yes, I know your little pet names for me, Miss Elphaba. Amusing and juvenile! I am concerned for your welfare. And with all your hard work all summer, I see that you have grown, oh, shall we say, verdigrisian? So I shall make a compromise proposal. Provided that you can convince Master Avaric and Master Boq to travel with you and my own little Grommetik, whom I will loan in your care and to care for you, I shall permit your little summer fun."

Elphaba, Boq, and Avaric rode in the coach, and Grommetik was made to ride on top with the luggage. Elphaba met Boq's eyes from time to time, grimacing, but she ignored Avaric, to whom she had taken an instant dis-like.

When he had finished with the pages of his racing form, Avaric teased Boq about this trip. "I should have known when I left for the sum-mer that you were mooning about in the throes of love! You developed this serious set of chin, it misled me. I thought it was consumption at least. You *should* have come out with me that night before I left! A visit to the Philosophy Club would have been just what the doctor ordered."

Boq was mortified to have such a dive mentioned in the presence of a female. But Elphaba seemed to take no offense. Perhaps she didn't know what it was. He tried to steer Avaric away from the subject.

"You don't know Miss Galinda, but you will find her charming," he said. "I guarantee that." And she will probably find *you* charming, he thought, a bit late in the day. But he was even willing to live with that, if it was the price of helping Galinda out of a tricky situation.

Avaric was regarding Elphaba with contempt. "Miss Elphaba," he said formally, "does your name imply any elf blood in your background?"

"What a novel idea," said Elphaba. "If there were, I suppose my limbs would be as brittle as uncooked pasta, and come apart with the slight-est of pressure. Would you care to apply some force?" She proffered a fore-arm, green as a spring limeberry. "Do, I beg you, so we can settle this question for once, for all. We shall conclude that the relative force you need to break my arm—as opposed to other arms you have broken—is proportionate to the relative amount of human versus elfin blood in my veins."

"I certainly will not touch you," said Avaric, managing to say many things at once.

"The elf in the self regrets," said Elphaba. "Were you to have dismembered me, I might have been posted back to Shiz in small pieces and been spared the tedium of this forced holiday. And this company."

"Oh, Elphie." Boq sighed. "This isn't a good start, you know."

"I think it's swell," said Avaric, glaring.

"I didn't think friendship required this much," snapped Elphaba to Boq. "I was better off before."

It was late afternoon by the time they arrived in Neverdale and settled at the inn, and made their way by foot along the lake to Caprice-in-the-Pines.

Two older women were in the sunlight by the portico, shelling string beans and wristwrenchers. The one Boq recognized was Ama Clutch, Galinda's chaperone; the other must be the minder of Miss Shenshen or Miss Pfannee. They started at the sight of the procession coming up the drive, and Ama Clutch leaned forward, the string beans spilling out of her lap. "Well, I never," she said as they drew near, "it's Miss Elphie herself. My uncle's whiskers. I never did." She pulled herself to her feet and clasped Elphaba into her arms. Elphaba stood as stiff as a plaster figure.

"Give us a minute to be catching our breath, duckies," said Ama Clutch. "Whatever in the blameless heaven are you doing here, Miss Elphaba? It don't seem possible."

"I have been invited by Miss Galinda," said Elphaba, "and my fellow travelers here insisted they wanted to accompany me. So I find myself compelled to accept."

"I know nothing of this," said Ama Clutch. "Miss Elphaba, let me take that heavy reticule and find you something clean to put on. You must be frayed from the voyage. You gentlemen will be staying in the village, of *course.* But for now, the girls are in the summerhouse at the edge of the lake."

The travelers made their way along a path interrupted with stone steps at the steeper parts. Grommetik took longer at steps and was left behind, and no one was inclined to stay and lend a hand to a figure with such a hard skin and clockwork thoughts. Skirting the final growth of hollyflight bushes, they came upon the gazebo.

It was a skeleton house of unstripped logs, six sides open to the breezes, with a fretwork of arabesquing twigs, and Lake Chorge a mighty field of blue beyond. The girls were sitting on steps and in wicker chairs, and Ama Clipp was lost in some smallwork involving three needles and many colors of thread.

"Miss Galinda!" broke out Boq, needing his to be the first voice heard.

The girls raised their heads. In evanescent summer frocks, free of hoops and bustles, they looked like birds about to scatter.

"Holy terror!" said Galinda, her jaw dropping. "What're you doing here!"

"I'm not decent!" shrieked Shenshen, drawing attention to her unshod feet and pale exposed ankles.

Pfannee bit one corner of her lip and tried to revise her smirk into a smile of welcome.

"I am not staying for long," said Elphaba. "By the way, girls, this is Master Avaric, the Margreave Descending from Tenmeadows, Gillikin. And this is Master Boq from Munchkinland. They're both at Briscoe Hall. Master Avaric, as if you can't tell by the lovesick expression in Boq's face, this is Miss Galinda of the Arduennas, and Miss Shenshen and Miss Pfannee, who can outline their own pedigrees perfectly well."

"But how enchanting, and how naughty," said Miss Shenshen. "Miss Elphaba who-never-gives-us-the-time-of-day, you have redeemed yourself for *all* time by this pleasant surprise. How do you do, gentlemen."

"But," stammered Galinda, "but why are you here? What's wrong?"

"I am here because I stupidly mentioned your invitation to Master Boq, who saw it as a sign from the Unnamed God that we should visit."

But at this Miss Pfannee could control herself no longer, and fell on the floor of the gazebo, writhing in laughter. "What," said Shenshen, "*what?*"

"But what invitation are you talking about?" asked Galinda.

"I don't need to show you," said Elphaba. For the first time since Boq had known her, she looked confused. "Surely I don't need to bring it out—"

"I believe I have been set up to be *mortified*," said Galinda, glaring at the helpless Pfannee. "I am being humiliated for *sport*. This is not funny, Miss Pfannee! I have half a mind to—to kick you!"

Just then Grommetik made it around the edge of the hollyflight bush. The sight of the stupid copper thing teetering on the edge of a stone step made Shenshen collapse against a column and join Pfannee in uncontrollable laughter. Even Ama Clipp smiled to herself as she began to put away her materials.

"But what is going on?" said Elphaba.

"Were you *born* to plague me?" Galinda said tearfully to her roomie. "Did I ask for your association?"

"Don't," said Boq. "Don't, Miss Galinda, please don't say another word. You're upset."

"I—wrote—the—letter," heaved Pfannee between her gales of laughter. Avaric began to chuckle, and Elphaba's eyes went wide and a little unfocused.

"You mean you didn't write to invite me to visit here?" said Elphaba to Galinda.

"Oh, dear no, I did *not*," said Galinda. In her anger she was beginning to regain some control, even though, Boq guessed, damage had been done for good. "My darling Miss Elphaba, I wouldn't have dreamed of exposing you to such thoughtless cruelties as these girls perpetrate on each other and on me for sheer amusement. Besides, you have no place in a setting like this."

"But I've been invited," said Elphaba. "Miss Pfannee, *you* wrote that letter instead of Miss Galinda?"

"You ate it up!" chortled Pfannee.

"Well this is your home and I accept your invitation even if it was written under false pretenses," Elphaba said, her voice evenly matter-of-fact as she stared into Miss Pfannee's narrowed eyes. "I'll go up and unpack my bags."

She strode away. Only Grommetik followed. The air went stale with things unsaid. By and by Pfannee's hysteria grew quieter, and she merely snorted and wheezed, and then grew still, lying vaporishly and unkempt on the flagstone floor of the gazebo.

"Well you all needn't pierce me with your sniffy attitudes," she said at last. "It was a joke."

Elphaba stayed in her room for a day. Galinda came and went with a dinner. On occasion she would stay for a few minutes. So the boys took to swimming and rowing on the lake with the girls. Boq tried to fan in himself an interest in Shenshen or Pfannee, who certainly were coquettish enough. But they both seemed besotted with Avaric.

At last Boq cornered Galinda on the porch and pleaded with her to talk with him. She agreed, a measure of her demure demeanor returning, and they sat a short distance apart on a swing. "I suppose I'm to blame for not seeing through that ruse," said Boq. "Elphie wasn't inclined to accept that invitation. I made her."

"What is this *Elphie*?" said Galinda. "Where has propriety gone this summer, I ask you?"

"We've become friends."

"Well, I can promise to have gathered that. Why did you make her accept an invitation? Didn't you know I'd never write such a thing?"

"How should I know that? You're her roomie."

"By executive order of Madame Morrible, not by choice! I care to have that remembered!"

"I didn't know. You seem to get along."

She sniffed, and curled a lip, but it seemed to be a remark to herself.

Boq continued, "If you've been woefully humiliated, why don't you leave?"

"Perhaps I shall," she said. "I'm considering. Elphaba says that to leave is to admit defeat. Yet if she comes out of her hiding and begins to trip along with the rest of you—and me—the joke will be unbearable. *They don't like her*," she explained.

"Well neither do you, I'd say!" said Boq, in an explosive whisper.

"It's different, I have a right and a reason," she retorted. "I am forced to put up with her! And all because my stupid Ama stepped on a rusty nail in the railway station in Frottica and missed the orientation! My whole academic career up in smoke because of my Ama's carelessness! When I'm a sorcerer I'll have my revenge on her for that!"

"You could say that Elphaba brought us together," said Boq softly. "I'm closer to her and so I'm closer to you."

Galinda seemed to give up. She leaned her head back on the velvet cushions of the swing and said, "Boq, you know despite myself I think you're a little sweet. You're a little sweet and you're a little charming and you're a little maddening and you're a little habit-forming."

Boq held his breath.

"But you're *little!*" she concluded. "You're a *Munchkin,* for god's sake!"

He kissed her, he kissed her, he kissed her, little by little by little.

The next day Elphaba, Galinda, Boq, and Grommetik—and of course Ama Clutch—made the six-hour trip back to Shiz with fewer than a dozen remarks among them. Avaric stayed behind to disport himself with Pfannee and Shenshen. The pestering rain took up at the outskirts of Shiz, and the august facades of Crage Hall and Briscoe Hall were nearly obliterated with mist by the time they were, at last, home.

6

Boq didn't have time or inclination to remark on his romance when he saw Crope and Tibbett. The Rhino librarian, having paid scant attention to the boys or their progress all summer, had suddenly cottoned on to how little had been achieved, and was all rheumatic huffs and watchful eyes. The boys chattered little, they brushed and cleaned vellum and rubbed finfoot oil on leather bindings and polished brass clasps. Only a few days left of this tedium.

One afternoon Boq let his eye drift down the codex he was handling. Usually he worked without attention to the subject matter of the materials, but his eye was drawn to the bright red paint applied in the illustration. It was a picture—maybe four, five hundred years old?—of a Kumbric Witch. Some monk's visionary zeal or anxiety about magic had inspired his brush. The Witch stood on an isthmus connecting two rocky lands, and on either side of her stretched patches of cerulean blue sea, with white-lipped waves of astonishing vigor and particularity. The Witch held in her hands a beast of unrecognizable species, though it was clearly drowned, or nearly drowned. She cradled it in an arm that, without attention to actual skeletal flexibility, lovingly encircled the beast's wet, spiky-furred back. With her other hand she was freeing a breast from her robe, offering suck to the creature. Her expression was hard to read, or had the monk's hand smudged, or age and grime bestowed a sfumato sympathy? She was nearly motherly, with miserable child. Her look was inward, or sad, or something. But her feet didn't match her expression, for they were planted on the narrow strand with prehensile grip, apparent even through the silver-colored shoes, whose coin-of-the-realm brilliance had first caught Boq's eye. Furthermore, the feet were turned out at ninety-degree angles to the shins. They showed in profile as mirror images, heels clicked together and toes pointing in opposite directions, like a stance in ballet. The gown was a hazy dawn blue. He guessed by the jeweled tones of the work that the document hadn't been opened in centuries.

Dramatically, or teleologically, this image seemed some sort of a hybrid of the creation myths of the Animals. Here were the flood waters, whether they derived from legends of Lurline or the Unnamed God, whether they were rising or sinking. Was the Kumbric Witch interfering with or accomplishing the ordained fate of the beasts? Though in a script too crabbed and archaic for Boq to decipher, perhaps this document supported the fable of a Kumbric Witch spell that gave the Animals the gifts of speech, memory, and remorse. Perhaps it merely refuted it, but glowingly. Any way you looked at it there was the syncretism of myth, myth's happy appetite to engorge on narrative strains. Maybe this painting was the suggestion of some alarmed monk that the Animals received their strengths through yet another sort of baptism, by nursing at the teat of the Kumbric Witch? Inducted through the milk of the Witch?

Such analysis wasn't his strong point. He had a hard enough time with the nutrients and common pests of barley. He should do the unthinkable and deliver this actual scroll to Doctor Dillamond. It would be valuable to know about.

Or maybe, he thought as he hurried to meet Elphaba, the thing safely smuggled into the deep pocket of his cape and out of the Three Queens library, maybe the Witch wasn't feeding the drenched animal, but killing it? Sacrificing it to stay the floods?

Art was *way* beyond him.

He had run into Ama Clutch in the bazaar and begged her to deliver a note to Elphaba. The good woman seemed more sympathetic than usual to him; was Galinda singing his praises in the privacy of her room?

It was his first time to see the funny green jumping bean since arriving back in Shiz. And there she was, on time, arriving at the café as requested, in a gray ghost of a dress, with a knitted overpull fraying at the sleeves, and a man's umbrella, big and black and lancelike when rolled up. Elphaba sat down with a graceless *fromp*, and examined the scroll. She looked at it more closely than she would bring herself to look at Boq. But she listened to his exegesis, and thought it feeble. "What prevents this from being the Fairy Queen Lurline?" she asked.

"Well, the accoutrements of glamour are missing. I mean the golden nimbus of hair. The elegance. The transparent *wings*. The wand."

"Those silver shoes are pretty gaudy." She munched on a dry biscuit.

"It doesn't look like a portrait of determination or—what do I mean—genesis. It looks reactive rather than proactive. That figure is at the very least confused, don't you think?"

"You've been hanging around Crope and Tibbett too long, go back to your barley," she said, pocketing the thing. "You're getting vague and artsy. But I'll give it to Doctor Dillamond. I'll tell you, he keeps making breakthroughs. This business of opposing lenses has opened up a whole new world of corpuscular architecture. He let me look once, but I couldn't make out much except for stress and bias, color and pulse. He's very excited. The problem I see now is getting him to stop—I think he's on the verge of founding a whole new branch of knowledge, and every day's findings provoke a hundred new questions. Clinical, theoretical, hypothetical, empirical, even ontological, I guess. He's been staying up late at night in the labs. We can see his lights on when we pull the drapes at night."

"Well, does he need anything more from us? I only have two days left in that library, and then school starts."

"I can't get him to focus. I think he's just putting together what he's got."

"How about Galinda, then," he said, "if we're done with academic espionage for the time being? How is she? Does she ask for me?"

Elphaba allowed herself to look at Boq. "No. Galinda really hasn't said anything about you. To give you hope you don't deserve, I should add she's hardly said anything to me at all, either. She's in a heavy sulk."

"When will I see her again?"

"Does it mean that much to you?" She smiled wanly. "Boq, does she really mean that much to you?"

"She is my world," he answered.

"Your world is too small if she is it."

"You can't criticize the size of a world. I can't help it and I can't stop it and I can't deny it."

"I should say you look silly," she said, draining the last drops of lukewarm tea from her cup. "I should say you'll look back on this summer and cringe. She may be lovely, Boq—no, she is lovely, I agree—but you're worth a dozen of her." At his shocked expression she threw up her hands. "Not to me! I don't mean me! Please, that stricken look! Spare me!"

But he wasn't sure if he believed her. She gathered her things in a hurry and rushed out, knocking the spitoon over in a clatter, slicing her big umbrella right through someone's newspaper. She didn't look both ways as she lunged across Railway Square and was nearly mowed down by an old Ox on a cumbersome tricycle.

7

The next time Boq saw Elphaba and Galinda, all thoughts of romance fled. It was in the small triangular park outside the gate of Crage Hall. He had been just happening by, once again, this time with Avaric in tow. The gates had opened and Ama Vimp had come flouncing out, face white and nose dripping, and a flurry of girls poured out after her. Among them were Elphaba and Galinda and Shenshen and Pfannee and Milla. Free of their walls, the girls huddled in chattering circles, or stood beneath the trees in shock, or hugged each other, and wailed, and wiped each other's eyes.

Boq and Avaric hurried up to their friends. Elphaba had her shoulders high, like a cat's bony yoke, and hers was the only dry face. She stayed arm's length away from Galinda and the others. Boq longed to take Galinda in his arms, but she didn't look at him more than once before diving her face into Milla's teck-fur collar.

"What is it? What has happened?" said Avaric. "Miss Shenshen, Miss Pfannee?"

"It's too horrible," they cried, and Galinda nodded, and her nose ran messily along the shoulder seam of Milla's blouse. "The police are there, and a doctor, but it seems to be—"

"What," said Boq, and turned to Elphaba. "Elphie what is it, what?"

"They found out," she said. Her eyes were glazed like old Shizian porcelain. "Somehow the bastards found out."

The gate creaked open again, and petals of early autumn vineflowers, blue and purple, came dancing over the college wall. They hung, and stepped like butterflies, and fell slowly, as three caped policemen and a doctor in a dark cap emerged carrying a stretcher. A red blanket had covered the patient, but the wind that tossed the petals caught a corner of the blanket and pulled it back in a triangular fold. The girls all shrieked and Ama Vimp ran forward to tuck the blanket down, but in the sunlight all had looked down and seen the twisted shoulders and back-thrown head of Doctor Dillamond. His throat was still knotted with congealed ropes of black blood, where it had been slit as thoroughly as if he had wandered into an abattoir.

Boq sat down, disgusted and alarmed, hoping he had not seen death, just a horrible treatable wound. But the police and doctor weren't hurrying, there was no reason to hurry now. Boq fell back against the wall, and Avaric, who had never seen the Goat before, held Boq's hands tightly with one hand and covered his own face with the other.

Before long Galinda and Elphaba sank down beside him, and there was some weeping, some long weeping, before words could be spoken. At last Galinda told the story.

"We went to bed last night—and Ama Clutch got up to pull the drapes closed. As she does. And she looks down and says almost to herself, 'Well there's the lights on, Doctor Goat is at it again.' Then she peers a little closer, down the yard, and says, 'Well now isn't that funny?' And I don't pay any attention, I'm just sitting there staring, but Elphaba says, 'What's funny, Ama Clutch?' And Ama Clutch just pulls the drape very tightly and says in a funny voice, 'Oh, nothing, my ducks. I'll just step down to check and make sure everything's all right. As long as you girls are abed.' She says good night and she leaves, and I don't know if she goes down there or what, but we both fall asleep and in the morning she isn't there with the tea. She *always* gets the tea! She always does!"

Galinda gave herself to tears, sinking and then raising herself to her knees and trying to tear her black silk gown with the white epaulets and the white bobbing. Elphaba, dry-eyed as a desert stone, continued.

"We waited until after breakfast, but then we went to Madame Morrible's," said Elphaba, "and told her that we didn't know where Ama Clutch was. And Madame Morrible said that Ama Clutch had had a relapse during the night and was recovering in the infirmary. She wouldn't let us in to see her at first, but then when Doctor Dillamond didn't show up for our first lecture of the semester, we wandered over there and just pushed our way in. Ama Clutch was in a hospital bed. Her face looked funny, like the last pancake of the batch, the way it goes all wrong. We said, 'Ama Clutch, Ama Clutch, what has happened to you?' She didn't say anything even though her eyes were open. She didn't seem to hear us. We thought maybe she was asleep or in shock, but her breathing was regular and her color was good even though her face seemed awry. Then as we were leaving she turned and she looked at the bedside table.

"Next to a medicine bottle and a cup of lemon water there was a long rusty nail on a silver tray. She reached a shaky hand out to the nail and picked it up and held it in her palm, tenderly, and she talked to it. She said something like, 'Oh well then, I know you didn't mean to stab my foot last year. You were only trying to get my attention. That's what mis-behavior is all about, just a little extra loving being asked for. Well, don't you worry Nail, because I'm going to love you just as much as you need. And after I have a little nap you can tell me how you came to be holding up the platform of the railway station at Frottica, for it seems quite a leap from your early years as a common hook for a CLOSED FOR THE SEASON sign in that dingy hotel you were talking about.'"

But Boq could not listen to this blather. He could not take in the story of a live Nail while a dead Goat was being prayed over by hysterical faculty members. Boq could not listen to the sounds of the prayers for the repose of the Animal's spirit. He could not watch the departure of the corpse, when they trundled it away. For it had been clear, with a glimpse of the Goat's still face, that whatever had given the doctor his enlivening character had already disappeared.

The Charmed Circle

I

There was no doubt in the minds of anyone who had seen the corpse that the word, the correct word, was murder. The way the pelt about the neck had bunched up, caked together like an improperly cleaned worker's paintbrush; the raw amber hollow in the eye. The official story was that the doctor had broken a magnifying lens and stumbled against it, cutting an artery in the process—but nobody believed it.

The only one they could think of to ask, Ama Clutch, merely smiled when they came to visit, with handfuls of pretty yellowing leaves or a plate of late Pertha grapes. She devoured the grapes and chatted with the leaves. It was an ailment no one had ever seen before.

Glinda—for out of some belated apology for her initial rudeness to the martyred Goat, she now called herself as he had once called her— Glinda seemed to be stricken dumb before the fact of Ama Clutch. Glinda wouldn't visit, nor discuss the poor woman's condition, so Elphaba sneaked in once or twice a day. Boq assumed that Ama Clutch suffered a passing malady. But after three weeks Madame Morrible began to make sounds of concern that Elphaba and Glinda—still roomies—had no chaperone. She suggested the common dormitory for them both. Glinda, who would no longer go to see Madame Morrible on her own, nodded and accepted the demotion. It was Elphaba who came up with a solution, mostly to salvage some shred of Glinda's dignity.

Thus it was that ten days later Boq found himself in the beer garden of the Cock and Pumpkins, waiting for the midweek coach from the Emerald City. Madame Morrible didn't allow Elphaba and Glinda to join him, so he had to decide for himself which two of the seven passengers alighting were Nanny and Nessarose. The deformities of Elphaba's sister were well concealed, Elphaba had warned him; Nessarose could even descend from a carriage with grace, providing the step was secure and the ground flat.

He met them, said hello. Nanny was a stewed plum of a woman, red and loose, her old skin looking ready to trail off but for the tucks at the corners of the mouth, the fleshy rivets by the edges of the eyes. More than a score of years in the badlands of Quadling Country had made her lethargic, careless, and saturated with resentment. At her age she ought to have been allowed to nod off in some warm chimney nook. "Good to see a little Munchkinlander," she murmured to Boq. "It's like the old times." Then she turned and said into the shadows, "Come, my poppet."

Had he not been warned, Boq wouldn't have taken Nessarose as Elphaba's sister. She was by no means green, or even blue-white like a genteel person with bad circulation. Nessarose stepped from the carriage elegantly, gingerly, strangely, sinking her heel to touch the iron step at the same time as her toe. Walking as oddly as she did, she drew attention to her feet, which kept eyes away from the torso, at least at first.

The feet landed on the ground, driven there with a ferocious intention to balance, and Nessarose stood before him. She was as Elphaba had said: gorgeous, pink, slender as a wheat stalk, and armless. The academic shawl over her shoulders was cunningly folded to soften the shock.

"Hello, good sir," she said, nodding her head very slightly. "The valises are on top. Can you manage?" Her voice was as smooth and oiled as Elphaba's was serrated. Nanny propelled Nessarose gently toward the hansom cab that Boq had engaged. He saw that Nessarose did not move well without being able to lean backward against a steadying hand.

"So now Nanny has to see the girls through their schooling," said Nanny to Boq as they rode along. "What with their sainted mother in her waterlogged grave these long years, and their father off his head. Well, the family always was bright, and brightness, as you know, decays brilliantly. Madness is the most shining way. The elderly man, the Eminent Thropp, he's *still* alive, and sensible as an old ploughshare. Survived his daughter *and* his granddaughter. Elphaba is the Thropp Third Descending. She'll be the Eminence one day. As a Munchkinlander, you know about such things."

"Nanny don't gossip, it hurts my soul," Nessarose said.

"Oh my pretty, don't you fret. This Boq is an old friend, or as good as," said Nanny. "Out in the swamps of Quadling hell, my friend, we've lost the art of conversation. We croak in chorus with what's left of the froggie folk."

"I intend to have a headache from shame," said Nessarose, charmingly.

"But I knew Elphie when she was a small thing," said Boq. "I'm from Rush Margins in Wend Hardings. I must've met you too."

"Primarily I preferred to reside at Colwen Grounds," said Nanny. "I was a mortal comfort to the Lady Partra, the Thropp Second Descending. But occasionally I visited Rush Margins. So I may have met you when you were young enough to run around without trousers."

"How do you do," said Nessarose.

"The name is Boq," said Boq.

"This is Nessarose," said Nanny, as if it were too painful for the girl to introduce herself. "She was to come up to Shiz next year, but we have learned there's a problem with some Gillikinese minder going loopy. So Nanny is called to step in, and can Nanny leave her sweet? You see why not."

"A sad mystery, we hope for improvement," said Boq.

At Crage Hall, Boq witnessed the reunion of the sisters, which was warm and gratifying. Madame Morrible had her Grommetik thing wheel out tea and brisks for the Thropp females, and for Nanny, Boq, and Glinda. Boq, who had begun to worry about Glinda's retreat into silence, was relieved to see Glinda cast a hard, appraising eye over the elegant dress of Nessarose. How could it be, he wondered if Glinda was wondering, that two sisters should each be disfigured, and should clothe themselves so unlike? Elphaba wore the humblest of dark frocks; today she was in a deep purple, almost a black. Nessarose, balanced on a sofa next to Nanny, who assisted by lifting teacups and crumpling buttery bits of crumpet, was in green silks, the colors of moss, emerald, and yellow-green roses. Green Elphaba, sitting on her other side and lending her support between the shoulders as she tilted her head back to sip her tea, looked like a fashion accessory.

"The whole arrangement is highly unusual," Madame Morrible was saying, "but we don't have unlimited room to accommodate peculiarities, alas. We'll leave Miss Elphaba and Miss Galinda—Glinda is it now, dear? How novel—we'll leave those two old pals as they are, and we'll set you up, Miss Nessarose, with your Nanny in the adjoining room that poor old Ama Clutch had. It's small but you must think of it as *cozy*."

"But when Ama Clutch recovers?" asked Glinda.

"Oh, but my dear," said Madame Morrible, "such confidence the young have! Touching, really." She continued in a more steely voice. "You have already told me of the long-standing recurrence of this unusual medical condition. I can only assume this has deteriorated into a permanent relapse." She munched a biscuit in her slow, fishy way, her cheeks going in and out like the leather flaps of a bellows. "Of course we can all hope. Not much more than that, I'm afraid."

"And we can pray," Nessarose said.

"Oh well yes, *that*," said the Head. "That goes without saying among people of good breeding, Miss Nessarose."

Boq watched Nessarose and Elphaba both blush. Glinda excused herself and went away. The usual pang of panic Boq felt at her departure was softened by knowing he would see her again in life sciences next week, for, with the new prohibitions on Animal hiring, the colleges had decided to give assembly lectures to all the students from all the colleges, at once. Boq would see Glinda at the first coeducation lecture ever held at Shiz. He couldn't wait.

Though she had changed. She had surely changed.

2

Glinda *was* changed. She knew it herself. She had come to Shiz a vain, silly thing, and she now found herself in a coven of vipers. Maybe it was her own fault. She had invented a nonsense disease for Ama Clutch, and Ama Clutch had come down with it. Was this proof of an inherent talent of sorcery? Glinda opted to specialize in sorcery this year, and accepted it as her punishment that Madame Morrible didn't change her roomie as promised. Glinda no longer cared. Beside Doctor Dillamond's death, a lot of other matters now seemed insignificant.

But she didn't trust Madame Morrible either. Glinda had told nobody else that stupid and extravagant lie. So now she would no longer allow Madame Morrible so much as a fingerhold into her life. And Glinda still didn't have the nerve to confess her unintentional crime to anyone. While she fretted, Boq, that pesky little flea, kept zizzing around her looking for attention. She was sorry she had let him kiss her. What a mistake! Well, all that was behind her now, that trembling on the edges of social disaster. She had seen the Misses Pfannee et cetera for what they were—shallow, self-serving snobs—and she would have no more to do with them.

So Elphaba, no longer a social liability, had all the potential of becoming an actual friend. If being saddled with this broken doll of a baby sister didn't interfere too much. It was only with prodding that Glinda had gotten Elphaba to talk at all about her sister, so that Glinda might be prepared for Nessarose's arrival and the enlargement of their social circle.

"She was born at Colwen Grounds, when I was about three," Elphaba had told her. "My family had gone back to Colwen Grounds for a short stay. It was one of those times of intense drought. Our father told us later, after our mother had died, that Nessarose's birth had coincided with a temporary resurgence of well water in the vicinity. They'd been doing pagan dances and there was a human sacrifice."

Glinda had stared at Elphaba, who sounded at once unwilling and offhand.

"A friend of theirs, a Quadling glassblower. The crowd, incited by some rabble-rousing pfaithers and a prophetic clock, fell on him and killed him. A man named Turtle Heart." Elphaba had pressed the palms of her hands over the high uppers of her stiff black secondhand shoes, and kept her eyes trained on the floor. "I think that was why my parents became missionaries to the Quadling people, why they never went back to Colwen Grounds or Munchkinland."

"But your mother died in childbirth?" said Glinda. "How could she have been a missionary?"

"She didn't die for five years," said Elphaba, looking at the folds of her dress, as if the story were an embarrassment. "She died when our younger brother was born. My father named him Shell, after Turtle Heart, I think. So Shell and Nessarose and I lived the lives of gypsy children, slopping around from Quadling settlement to settlement with Nanny and our father, Frex. He preached, and Nanny taught us and raised us up and kept house such as we ever had, which wasn't much. Meanwhile the Wizard's men began draining the badlands to get at the ruby deposits. It never worked, of course. They managed to chase the Quadlings out and kill them, round them up in settlement camps for their own protection and starve them. They despoiled the badlands, raked up the rubies, and left. My father went barmy over it. There never *were* enough rubies to make it worth the effort; we still have no canal system to run that legendary water from the Vinkus all the way cross-country to Munchkinland. And the drought, after a few promising reprieves, continues unabated. The Animals are recalled to the lands of their ancestors, a ploy to give the farmers a sense of control over *something* anyway. It's a systematic marginalizing of populations, Glinda, that's what the Wizard's all about."

"We were talking about your childhood," said Glinda.

"Well that's it, that's all part of it. You can't divorce your particulars from politics," Elphaba said. "You want to know what we ate? How we played?"

"I want to know what Nessarose is like, and Shell," said Glinda.

"Nessarose is a strong-willed semi-invalid," said Elphaba. "She's very smart, and thinks she is holy. She has inherited my father's taste for religion. She isn't good at taking care of other people because she has never learned how to take care of herself. She can't. My father required me to baby-sit her through most of my childhood. What she will do when Nanny dies I don't know. I suppose I'll have to take care of her again."

"Oh, what a hideous prospect for a life," said Glinda, before she could stop herself.

But Elphaba only nodded grimly. "I can't agree with you more," she said.

"As for Shell—" continued Glinda, wondering what fresh pain she might tread upon.

"Male, and white, and whole," she said. "He's now about ten, I guess. He'll stay at home and take care of our father. He is a boy, just as boys are. A little dull, maybe, but he hasn't had the advantages we've had."

"Which are?" prompted Glinda.

"Even for a short time," said Elphaba, "we had a mother. Giddy, alcoholic, imaginative, uncertain, desperate, brave, stubborn, supportive woman. We had her. Melena. Shell had no mother but Nanny, who did her best."

"And who was your mother's favorite?" said Glinda.

"Can't tell *that*," said Elphaba casually, "don't know. Would have been Shell, probably, since he's a boy. But she died without seeing him so she didn't even get that small consolation."

"Your father's favorite?"

"Oh, that's easy," said Elphaba, jumping up and finding her books on her shelf, and getting ready to run out and stop the conversation in its tracks. "That's Nessarose. You'll see why when you meet her. She'd be anyone's favorite." She skidded out of the room with no more than a brief flurry of green fingers, a good-bye.

Glinda wasn't so sure she favored Elphaba's sister. Nessarose seemed so demanding. Nanny was overly attentive, and Elphaba kept suggesting adjustments in their living arrangements to make things perfect. Hitch the drapes to this angle instead of that, to keep the touch of the sun off Nessarose's pretty skin. Can we have the oil lamp turned up high so Nessarose can read? Shhh, no chatting after hours; Nessarose has retired and she is such a light sleeper.

Glinda was a bit awed by Nessarose's freaky beauty. Nessarose dressed well (if not extravagantly). She deflected attention from herself, though, by a system of little social tics—the head lowered in a sudden onslaught of devotion, the eyes batting. It was especially moving—and irritating—to have to wipe away a trickle of tears brought on by some epiphany in Nessarose's rich inner spiritual life of which bystanders could have no inkling. What did one *say?*

Glinda began to retreat into her studies. Sorcery was being taught by a louche new instructor named Miss Greyling. She had a gushing respect for the subject but, it soon became apparent, little natural ability. "At its most elemental, a spell is no more than a recipe for change," she would flute at them. But when the chicken she tried to turn into a piece of toast became instead a mess of used coffee grounds cupped in a lettuce leaf, the students all made a mental note never to accept an invitation to dine with her.

In the back of the room, creeping with pretend invisibility so that she might observe, Madame Morrible shook her head and clucked. Once or twice she could not stop herself from interfering. "No dab hand in the sorcerer's parlor I," she would protest, "yet surely Miss Greyling you've omitted the steps to bind and convince? I'm merely asking. Let me try. You know I take a special pleasure in our training of sorceresses." Inevitably Miss Greyling sat on what was left of a previous demonstration, or dropped her purse, collapsing into a heap of shame and mortification. The girls giggled, and didn't feel that they were learning much.

Or were they? The benefit of Miss Greyling's clumsiness was that they were not afraid to try for themselves. And she didn't stint at enthusiasm if a student managed to accomplish the day's task. The first time Glinda was able to mask a spool of thread with a spell of invisibility, even for a few seconds, Miss Greyling clapped her hands and jumped up and down and broke a heel off her shoe. It was gratifying, and encouraging.

"Not that I have any objection," said Elphaba one day, when she and Glinda and Nessarose (and, inevitably, Nanny) sat under a pearlfruit tree by the Suicide Canal. "But I have to wonder. How does the university get away with teaching sorcery when its original charter was so strictly unionist?"

"Well, there isn't anything inherently either religious or nonreligious about sorcery," said Glinda. "Is there? There isn't anything inherently pleasure faithist about it either."

"Spells, changings, apparitions? It's all entertainment," said Elphaba. "It's theatre."

"Well, it can look like theatre, and in the hands of Miss Greyling it often looks like bad theatre," admitted Glinda. "But the gist of it isn't concerned with application. It's a practical skill, like—like reading and writing. It's not that you can, it's *what* you read or write. Or, if you'll excuse the play on words, *what* you spell."

"Father disapproved mightily," Nessarose said, in the dulcet tones of the unflappably faithful. "Father always said that magic was the sleight of hand of the devil. He said pleasure faith was no more than an exercise to distract the masses from the true object of their devotion."

"That's a unionist talking," said Glinda, not taking offense. "A sensible opinion, if what you're up against is charlatans or street performers. But sorcery doesn't *have* to be that. What about the common witches up in the Glikkus? They say that they magick the cows they've imported from Munchkinland so they don't go mooing over the edge of some precipice. Who could ever afford to put a fence on every ledge there? The magic is a local skill, a contribution to community well-being. It doesn't have to supplant religion."

"It may not have to," said Nessarose, "but if it tends to, then have we a duty to be wary of it?"

"Oh, wary, well, I'm wary of the water I drink, it might be poisoned," said Glinda. "That doesn't mean I stop drinking water."

"Well, *I* don't even think it's so big an issue," said Elphaba. "I think sorcery is trivial. It's concerned with itself mostly, it doesn't lead outward."

Glinda concentrated very hard and tried to make Elphaba's leftover sandwich elevate outward over the canal. She only succeeded in exploding the thing in a small combustion of mayonnaise and shredded carrot and chopped olives. Nessarose lost her balance laughing, and Nanny had to prop her up again. Elphaba was covered in bits of food, which she picked off herself and ate, to the disgust and laughter of everyone else. "It's all effects, Glinda," she said. "There's nothing ontologically interesting about magic. Not that I believe in unionism either," she protested. "I'm an atheist and an aspiritualist."

"You say that to shock and scandalize," said Nessarose primly. "Glinda, don't listen to a word of her. She always does this, usually to make Father irate."

"Father's not around," Elphaba reminded her sister.

"I stand in for him and I am offended," said Nessarose. "It's all very well to turn your nose up at unionism when you have been *given* a nose by the Unnamed God. It's quite funny, isn't it, Glinda? Childish." She looked spitting angry.

"Father's not around," said Elphaba again, in a tone that verged on the apologetic. "You needn't rush to public defense of his obsessions."

"What you term his obsessions are my articles of faith," she said with a chilly clarity.

"Well you're not a bad sorceress, for a beginner," said Elphaba, turning to Glinda. "That was a pretty good mess you made of my lunch."

"Thank you," Glinda said. "I didn't mean to pelt you with it. But I am getting better, aren't I? And out in public."

"A shocking display," Nessarose said. "That's exactly what Father would have deplored about sorcery. The allure is all in the surface."

"I agree, it still tastes like olives," Elphaba said, finding a clump of black olive in her sleeve and holding it out on the tip of her finger to her sister's mouth. "Taste, Nessa?"

But Nessarose turned her face away and lost herself in silent prayer.

3

A few days later Boq managed to catch Elphaba's eye at the break of their life sciences class, and they met up in an alcove off the main corridor. "What do you think of this new Doctor Nikidik?" he asked.

"I find it hard to listen," she said, "but that's because I still want to hear Doctor Dillamond and I can't believe he's gone." On her face was a look of gray submission to impossible reality.

"Well that's one of the things I'm curious about," he said. "You told me all about Doctor Dillamond's breakthrough. Do you know if his lab has been cleared out yet? Maybe there's something there worth finding. You took the notes for him, couldn't they be the basis of some proposal, or at least some further study?"

She looked at him with a wiry, strong expression. "Do you think I'm not way ahead of you?" she asked. "Of course I went tramping through there the day his body was found. Before anyone could lace up the door with padlocks and binding spells. Boq, do you take me for a fool?"

"No, I don't take you for a fool, so tell me what you found," he said.

"His findings are well hidden away," she said, "and though there are colossal holes in my training, I am studying it on my own."

"You mean you're not going to show me?" He was shocked.

"It was never your particular interest," she said. "Besides, until there's something to prove, what's the point? I don't think Doctor Dillamond was there yet."

"I am a Munchkinlander," he answered proudly. "Look, Elphie, you've more or less convinced me what the Wizard is up to. The confining of Animals back onto farms—to give the dissatisfied Munchkinlander farmers the impression he's doing something for them—and also to provide forced labor for the sinking of useless new wells. It's vile. But this affects Wend Hardings and the towns that sent me here. I have a right to know what you know. Maybe we can figure it out together, work to make a change."

"You have too much to lose," she said. "I'm going to take this on myself."

"Take what on?"

She only shook her head. "The less you know the better, and I mean for your sake. Whoever killed Doctor Dillamond doesn't want his findings made public. What kind of a friend would I be to you if I put you at risk too?"

"What kind of friend would I be to you if I didn't insist?" he retorted.

But she wouldn't tell him. When he sat next to her during the rest of the class and passed her little notes, she ignored them all. Later he thought that they might have developed a genuine impasse in their friendship had the odd attack on the newcomer not occurred during that very session.

Doctor Nikidik had been lecturing on the Life Force. Entwining around each wrist the two separate tendrils of his long straggly beard, he spoke in falling tones so that only the first half of each sentence made it to the back of the room. Hardly a single student was following. When Doctor Nikidik took a small bottle from his vest pocket and mumbled something about "Extract of Biological Intention," only the students in the front row sat up and opened their eyes. For Boq and Elphaba, and everyone else, the patter ran—"A little sauce for the soup mumble mumble, as if creation were an unconcluded mumble mumble mumble, notwithstanding the obligations of all sentient mumble mumble mumble, and so as a little exercise to make those nodding off in the back of the mumble mumble mumble, behold a little mundane miracle, courtesy of mumble mumble mumble."

A frisson of excitement had woken everyone up. The Doctor uncorked the smoky bottle and made a jerky movement. They could all see a small puff of dust, like an effervescence of talcum powder, jostle itself in a swimming plume in the air above the neck of the bottle. The Doctor rowed his hands a couple of times, to start the air currents eddying upward. Keeping some rare sort of spatial coherence, the plume began to migrate upward and over. The *ooohs* that the students were inclined to make were all postponed. Doctor Nikidik held a finger out to them to shush them, and they could tell why. A vast intake of breath would change the pattern of air currents and divert the floating musk of powder. But the students began to smile, despite themselves. Above the stage, amid the standard ceremonial stags' horns and brass trumpets on braid, hung four oil portraits of the founding fathers of Ozma Towers. In their ancient garb and serious expressions they looked down on today's students. If this "biological intention" were to be applied to one of the founding fathers, what would he say, seeing men and women students together in the great hall? What would he have to say about anything? It was a grand moment of anticipation.

But when a door to the side of the stage opened, the mechanics of the air currents were disturbed. A student looked in, puzzled. A new student, oddly dressed in suede leggings and a white cotton shirt, with a pattern of blue diamonds tattooed on the dark skin of his face and hands. No one had seen him before, or anyone like him. Boq clutched Elphaba's hand tightly and whispered, "Look! A Winkie!"

And so it seemed, a student from the Vinkus, in strange ceremonial garb, coming late for class, opening the wrong door, confused and apologetic, but the door had shut behind him and locked from this side, and there were no nearby seats available in the front rows. So he dropped where he was and sat with his back against the door, hoping, no doubt, to look inconspicuous.

"Drat and damn, the thing's been shabbed off course," said Doctor Nikidik. "You fool, why don't you come to class on time?"

The shining mist, about the size of a bouquet of flowers, had veered upward in a draft, and it bypassed the ranks of long-dead dignitaries waiting an unexpected chance to speak again. Instead it cloaked one of the racks of antlers, seeming for a few moments to hang itself on the twisting prongs. "Well, I can scarcely hope to hear a word of wisdom from *them*, and I refuse to waste any more of this precious commodity on classroom demonstrations," said Doctor Nikidik. "The research is still incomplete and I had thought that mumble mumble mumble. Let you discover for yourselves if mumble mumble mumble. I should hardly wish to prejudice your mumble."

The antlers suddenly took a convulsive twist on the wall, and wrenched themselves out of the oaken paneling. They tumbled and clattered to the floor, to the shrieking and laughing of the students, especially because for a minute Doctor Nikidik didn't know what the uproar was about. He turned around in time to see the antlers right themselves and wait, quivering, twitching, on the dais, like a fighting cock all nastied up and ready to go into the ring.

"Oh well, don't look at me," said Doctor Nikidik, collecting his books, "I didn't ask for anything from *you*. Blame that one if you must." And he casually pointed at the Vinkus student, who was cowering so wide-eyed that the more cynical of the older students began to suspect this was all a setup.

The antlers stood on their points and skittered, crablike, across the stage. As the students rose in a common scream, the antlers scrabbled up the body of the Vinkus boy and pinned him against the locked door. One wing of the rack caught him by the neck, shackling him in its V yoke, and the other reared back in the air to stab him in the face.

Doctor Nikidik tried to move fast, and fell to his arthritic knees, but before he could right himself two boys were up on the stage, out of the front row, grabbing the antlers and wrestling them to the ground. The Vinkus boy shrieked in a foreign tongue. "That's Crope and Tibbett!" said Boq, jouncing Elphaba in the shoulder, "look!" The sorcery students were all jumping on their seats and trying to lob spells at the murderous antlers, and Crope and Tibbett found their grips and lost them and found them again, until at last they succeeded in breaking off one driving tine, then another, and the pieces, still twitching, fell to the stage floor without further momentum.

"Oh the poor guy," said Boq, for the Vinkus student had slumped down and was volubly weeping behind his blue-diamonded hands. "I never saw a student from the Vinkus before. What an awful welcome to Shiz."

The attack on the Vinkus student provoked gossip and speculation. In sorcery the next day Glinda asked Miss Greyling to explain something. "How could Doctor Nikidik's Extract of Biological Intention or whatever it was, how could it fall under the heading of life sciences when it behaved like a master spell? What really is the difference between science and sorcery?"

"Ah," said Miss Greyling, choosing this moment to apply herself to the care of her hair. "Science, my dears, is the systematic dissection of nature, to reduce it to working parts that more or less obey universal laws. Sorcery moves in the opposite direction. It doesn't rend, it repairs. It is synthesis rather than analysis. It builds anew rather than revealing the old. In the hands of someone truly skilled"—at this she jabbed herself with a hair pin and yelped—"it is Art. One might in fact call it the Superior, or the Finest, Art. It bypasses the Fine Arts of painting and drama and recitation. It doesn't pose or represent the world. It *becomes*. A very noble calling." She began to weep softly with the force of her own rhetoric. "Can there be a higher desire than to change the world? Not to draw Utopian blueprints, but really to order change? To revise the misshapen, reshape the mistaken, to justify the margins of this ragged error of a universe? Through sorcery to survive?"

At teatime, still awed and amused, Glinda reported Miss Greyling's little heartfelt speech to the two Thropp sisters. Nessarose said, "Only the Unnamed God *creates*, Glinda. If Miss Greyling confuses sorcery with creation she is in grave danger of corrupting your morals."

"Well," said Glinda, thinking of Ama Clutch on the bed of mental pain Glinda had once imagined for her, "my morals aren't in the greatest shape to start out with, Nessa."

"Then if sorcery is to be helpful at all, it must be in reconstructing your character," said Nessarose firmly. "If you apply yourself in that direction, I suspect it will be all right in the end. *Use* your talent at sorcery, don't be used by it."

Glinda suspected that Nessarose might develop a knack for being witheringly superior. She winced in advance, even while taking Nessarose's suggestion to heart.

But Elphaba said, "Glinda, that was a good question. I wish Miss Greyling had answered it. That little nightmare with the antlers looked more like magic than science to me, too. The poor Vinkus fellow! Suppose we ask Doctor Nikidik next week?"

"Who ever would have the courage to do that?" cried Glinda. "Miss Greyling is at least ridiculous. Doctor Nikidik, with that lovable bumbling mumbling incoherent way he has—he's so distinguished."

At the life sciences lecture the following week, all eyes were on the new Vinkus boy. He arrived early and settled himself in the balcony, about as far from the lectern as he could get. Boq had the suspicion of nomads all settled farmers possessed. But Boq had to admit that the expression in the new boy's eyes was intelligent. Avaric, sliding into the seat next to Boq, said, "He's a prince, they say. A prince without a purse or a throne. A pauper noble. In his particular tribe, I mean. He stays at Ozma Towers and his name is Fiyero. He's a real Winkie, full-blood. Wonder what he makes of civilization?"

"If that was civilization, last week, he must long for his own barbaric kind," said Elphaba from the seat on the other side of Boq.

"What's he wearing such silly paint for?" said Avaric. "He only draws attention to himself. And that skin. I wouldn't want to have skin the color of shit."

"What a thing to say," said Elphaba. "If you ask me, that's a shitty opinion."

"Oh *please*," said Boq. "Let's just shut up."

"I forgot, Elphie, skin is your issue too," said Avaric.

"Leave me out of this," she said. "We just had lunch, and you give me dyspepsia, Avaric. You and the beans we had at lunch."

"I'm changing my seat," warned Boq, but Doctor Nikidik came in just then, and the class rose to its feet in routine respect, then settled back noisily, chummily, chattering.

For a few minutes Elphaba waved her hand to get the Doctor's attention, but she was sitting too far back and he was burbling on about something else. She finally leaned over to Boq and said, "At the recess I'll change my seat and go forward so he can see me." Then the class watched as Doctor Nikidik finished his inaudible preamble and beckoned a student to open the same door at the side of the stage that Fiyero had stumbled through the previous week.

In came a boy from Three Queens rolling a table like a tea tray. On it, crouched as if to make itself as small as possible, was a lion cub. Even from the balcony they could sense the terror of the beast. Its tail, a little whip the color of mashed peanuts, lashed back and forth, and its shoulders hunched. It had no mane to speak of yet, it was too tiny. But the tawny head twisted this way and that, as if counting the threats. It opened its mouth in a little terrified *yawp*, the infant form of an adult roar. All over the room hearts melted and people said "Awwwwww."

"Hardly more than a kitten," said Doctor Nikidik. "I had thought to call it Prrr, but it shivers more often than it purrs, so I call it Brrr instead."

The creature looked at Doctor Nikidik, and removed itself to the far edge of the trolley.

"Now the question of the morning is this," said Doctor Nikidik. "Picking up from the somewhat skewed interests of Doctor Dillamond, who mumble mumble. Who can tell me if this is an Animal or an animal?"

Elphaba didn't wait to be called on. She stood up in the balcony and launched her answer out in a clear, strong voice. "Doctor Nikidik, the question you asked was who can tell if this is an Animal or an animal. It seems to me the answer is that its mother can. Where is its mother?"

A buzz of amusement. "Caught in the swamp of syntactical semantics, I see," said the Doctor merrily. He spoke louder, as if having only now realized that there was a balcony in the hall. "Well done, Miss. Let me rephrase the question. Will someone here venture a hypothesis as to the nature of this specimen? And give a reason for such an assessment? We see before us a beast at a tender age, long before any such beast could command language if language were part of its makeup. Before language—assuming language—is this still an Animal?"

"I repeat my question, Doctor," sang out Elphaba. "This is a very young cub. Where is its mother? Why is it taken from its mother at such an early age? How even can it feed?"

"Those are impertinent questions to the academic issue at hand," said the Doctor. "Still, the youthful heart bleeds easily. The mother, shall we say, died in a sadly timed explosion. Let us presume for the sake of argument that there was no way of telling whether the mother was a Lioness or a lioness. After all, as you may have heard, some Animals are going back to the wild to escape the implications of the current laws."

Elphaba sat down, nonplused. "It doesn't seem right to me," she said to Boq and Avaric. "For the sake of a science lesson to drag a cub in here without its mother. Look how terrified it is. It *is* shivering. And it can't be cold."

Other students began to venture opinions, but the Doctor shot them down one by one. The point being, apparently, that without language or contextual clues, at its infant stages a beast was not clearly Animal or animal.

"This has a political implication," said Elphaba loudly. "I thought this was life sciences, not current events."

Boq and Avaric shushed her. She was getting a terrible reputation as a loudmouth.

The Doctor dragged the episode out long after everyone had digested the point. But finally he turned and said, "Now do you think that if we could cauterize that part of the brain that develops language, we could eliminate the notion of pain and thus its existence? Early tests on this little tom lion show interesting results." He had picked up a small hammer with a rubber head, and a syringe. The beast drew itself up and hissed, and then backed up and fell on the floor, and streaked toward the door, which had closed and locked from this side as it had the previous week.

But it wasn't only Elphaba who was on her feet yelling. Half a dozen students were shouting at the Doctor. "Pain? Eliminate pain? Look at the thing, it's terrified! It already *gets* pain! Don't do that, what are you, crazy?"

The Doctor paused, visibly tightening his grip on the mallet. "I will not preside over such shocking refusal to learn!" he said, affronted. "You are leaping to harebrained conclusions based on sentiment and no obser-vation. Bring the beast here. Bring it back. Young lady, I insist. I shall be quite cross."

But two girls from Briscoe Hall disobeyed and ran out of the room carrying the clawing lion club in an apron between them. The room col-lapsed in an uproar and Doctor Nikidik stalked off the stage. Elphaba turned to Boq and said, "Well, I guess I don't get to ask Glinda's good question about the difference between science and sorcery, do I? We were definitely headed down a different path today." But her voice was shaking.

"You felt for that beast, didn't you?" Boq was touched. "Elphie, you're trembling. I don't mean this in an insulting way, but you've nearly gone white with passion. Come on, let's sneak out and get a tea at the café at Railway Square, for old times' sake."

4

Perhaps every accidental cluster of people has a short period of grace, in between the initial shyness and prejudice on the one hand and eventual repugnance and betrayal on the other. For Boq it seemed that his summer obsession with the-then-Galinda made sense if only to usher in this following, more mature comfort with a circle of friends who had begun to feel inevitably and permanently connected.

The boys still weren't allowed access to Crage Hall, nor the girls to the boys' schools, but the city centre area of Shiz became an extension of the parlors and lecture halls in which they were allowed to mingle. On a midweek afternoon, on a weekend morning, they would meet by the canal with a bottle of wine, or in a café or student watering hole, or they would walk about and discuss the fine points of Shiz architecture, or they would laugh about the excesses of their teachers. Boq and Avaric, Elphaba and Nessarose (with Nanny), Glinda, and sometimes Pfannee and Shenshen and Milla, and sometimes Crope and Tibbett. And Crope brought Fiyero along and introduced him, which frosted Tibbett for a week or so until the evening that Fiyero said, in his shy formal way, "Of course—I have been married for some time. We marry young in the Vinkus." The others were agog at the notion, and felt juvenile.

To be sure, Elphaba and Avaric needled each other mercilessly. Nessarose tried everyone's patience with her religious rantings. Crope's and Tibbett's stream of saucy remarks got them dumped in the canal more than once. But Boq was relieved to find that his crush on Glinda was lifting somewhat. She sat on the edge of the picnic blanket with a look of self-reliance, and she diverted conversation away from herself. He had loved the girl who had loved the glamour in herself, and that girl seemed to have disappeared. But he was happy to have Glinda as a friend. Well, in a nutshell: he had loved *Galinda* and this now was *Glinda*. Someone he could no longer quite figure out. Case closed.

It was a charmed circle.

All the girls steered clear of Madame Morrible while they could. One cold evening, however, Grommetik came hunting for the Thropp sisters. Nanny huffed and wound the strings of a fresh apron around her waist, and prodded Nessarose and Elphaba downstairs toward the parlor of the Head.

"I hate that Grommetik thing," said Nessarose. "However does it work, anyway? Is it clockwork or is it magicked, or some combination of the two?"

"I always imagined a bit of nonsense—that there was a dwarf inside, or an acrobatic family of elves each working a limb," said Elphaba.

"Whenever Grommetik comes around, my hand gets a strange hunger for a hammer."

"I can't imagine," Nessarose said. "Hand hunger, I mean."

"Hush, you two, the thing has ears," Nanny said.

Madame Morrible was glancing through the financial papers, making a few marks in the margin before she deigned to acknowledge her students. "This won't take but a moment," she said. "I've had a letter from your dear father, and a package for you. I thought it kindest to deliver the news myself."

"News?" said Nessarose, blanching.

"He could have written to us as well as to you," said Elphaba.

Madame Morrible ignored her. "He writes to ask of Nessarose's health and progress, and to tell you both that he is going to undertake a fast and penance for the return of Ozma Tippetarius."

"Oh, the blessed little girl," said Nanny, warming to one of her favorite subjects. "When the Wizard took over the Palace all those years ago and he had the Ozma Regent jailed, we all thought that the sainted Ozma child would call down disaster upon the Wizard's head. But they say she's been spirited away and frozen in a cave, like Lurlina. Has Frexspar got the mettle to melt her—is now her time to return?"

"Please," said Madame Morrible to the sisters, with a sour glance at Nanny, "I haven't asked you here so that your Nanny could discuss this contemporary apocrypha, nor to slander our glorious Wizard. It was a peaceful transition of power. That the Ozma Regent's health failed while under house arrest was a mere coincidence, nothing more. As to the power of your father to raise the missing royal child from some unsubstantiated state of somnolence—well, you've as much as admitted to me that your father is erratic, if not mad. I can only wish him health in his endeavors. But I feel it my duty to point out to you girls that we do not smile on seditious attitudes at Crage Hall. I hope you have not imported your father's royalist yearnings into the dormitories here."

"We assign ourselves to the Unnamed God, not to the Wizard nor to any possible remnant of the Royal Family," Nessarose said proudly.

"I have no feeling on the matter at all," muttered Elphaba, "except that Father loves lost causes."

"Very well," said the Head. "As it should be. Now I have had a package for you." She handed it to Elphaba, but added, "It is for Nessarose, I think."

"Open it, Elphie, please," said Nessarose. Nanny leaned forward to look.

Elphaba undid the cord and opened the wooden box. From a pile of ash shavings she withdrew a shoe, and then another. Were they silver?—or blue?—or now red?—lacquered with a candy shell brilliance of polish? It was hard to tell and it didn't matter; the effect was dazzling. Even Madame Morrible gasped at their splendor. The surface of the shoes seemed to pulse with hundreds of reflections and refractions. In the firelight, it was like looking at boiling corpuscles of blood under a magnifying glass.

"He writes that he bought them for you from some toothless tinker woman outside Ovvels," said Madame Morrible, "and that he dressed them up with silver glass beads that he made himself—that someone had taught him to make?—"

"Turtle Heart," said Nanny darkly.

"—and"— Madame Morrible flipped the letter over, squinting—"he says he had hoped to give you something special before you left for university, but in the sudden circumstances of Ama Clutch's sickness . . . blah blah . . . he was unprepared. So now he sends them to his Nessarose to keep her beautiful feet warm and dry and beautiful, and he sends them with his love."

Elphaba drove her fingers through the curlicues of shavings. There was nothing else in the box, nothing for her.

"Aren't they gorgeous!" Nessarose exclaimed. "Elphie, fix them on my feet, would you please? Oh, how they sparkle!"

Elphaba went on her knees before her sister. Nessarose sat as regal as any Ozma, spine erect and face glowing. Elphaba lifted her sister's feet and slipped off the common house slippers, and replaced them with the dazzling shoes.

"How thoughtful he is!" said Nessarose.

"Good thing you can stand on your own two feet, you," muttered Nanny to Elphaba, and put her old hand patronizingly on Elphaba's shoulder blades, but Elphaba shrugged it away.

"They're just gorgeous," said Elphaba thickly. "Nessarose, they're made for you. They fit like a dream."

"Oh, Elphie, don't be cross," Nessarose said, looking down at her feet. "Don't ruin my small happiness with resentment, will you? He knows you don't need this kind of thing . . ."

"Of course not," said Elphaba. "Of course I don't."

That evening the friends risked breaking curfew by ordering another bottle of wine. Nanny tutted and fretted, but as she kept downing her portion as neatly as anyone else, she was overruled. Fiyero told the story of how he had been married at the age of seven to a girl from a neighboring tribe. They all gawped at his apparent lack of shame. He had only seen his bride once, by accident, when they were both about nine. "I won't really take up with her until we are twenty, and I'm now only eighteen," he added. With the relief of imagining he might still be as virginal as the rest of them, they ordered yet another bottle of wine.

The candles guttered, a small autumnal rain fell. Though the room was dry, Elphaba drew her cloak about her as if anticipating the walk home. She had gotten over the sting of being overlooked by Frex. She and Nessarose began to tell funny stories about their father, as if to prove to themselves and to everyone else that nothing was amiss. Nessarose, who wasn't much of a drinker, allowed herself to laugh. "Despite my appearance, or maybe because of it, he always called me his beautiful pet," she said, alluding to her lack of arms for the first time in public. "He would say, 'Come here, my pet, and let me give you a piece of apple.' And I would walk over as best I could, tilting and tottering if Nanny or Elphie or Mother wasn't around to support me, and fall into his lap, and lean up smiling, and he'd drop small pieces of fruit into my mouth."

"What did he call you, Elphie?" asked Glinda.

"He called her Fabala," interrupted Nessarose.

"At home, at home *only*," Elphaba said.

"True, you are your father's little Fabala," crooned Nanny, almost to herself, just outside the circle of smiling faces. "Little Fabala, little Elphaba, little Elphie."

"He never called *me* pet,'" said Elphaba, raising her glass to her sister. "But we all know he told the truth, as Nessarose is the pet in the family. Hence those splendid shoes."

Nessarose blushed and accepted a toast. "Ah, but while I had his attention because of my condition, you captured his heart when you sang," she said.

"Captured his heart? Hah. You mean I performed a necessary function."

But the others said to Elphaba, "Oh, do you sing? Well then! Sing, sing, you must! Another bottle, another glass, push back the chair, and before we leave for the night, you must sing! Go on!"

"Only if the others will," said Elphaba, bossily. "Boq? Some Munchkinlander spinniel? Avaric, a Gillikinese ballad? Glinda? Nanny, a lullaby?"

"We know a dirty round, we'll go next if you go," said Crope and Tibbett.

"And I will sing a Vinkus hunting chant," said Fiyero. Everyone chortled with pleasure and clapped him on the back. So then Elphaba had to stand, push her chair aside, clear her throat and sound a note into her cupped hands, and start. As if she were singing for her father, again, after all this time.

The bar mother slapped her rag at some noisy older men to shush them, and the dart players dropped their hands to their sides. The room quieted down. Elphaba made up a little song on the spot, a song of longing and otherness, of far aways and future days. Strangers closed their eyes to listen.

Boq did too. Elphaba had an okay voice. He saw the imaginary place she conjured up, a land where injustice and common cruelty and despotic rule and the beggaring fist of drought didn't work together to hold everyone by the neck. No, he wasn't giving her credit: Elphaba had a *good* voice. It was controlled and feeling and not histrionic. He listened through to the end, and the song faded into the hush of a respectful pub. Later, he thought: The melody faded like a rainbow after a storm, or like winds calming down at last; and what was left was calm, and possibility, and relief.

"You next, you promised," cried Elphaba, pointing at Fiyero, but nobody would sing again, because she had done so well. Nessarose nodded to Nanny to wipe a tear from the corner of her eye.

"Elphaba *says* she's not religious but see how feelingly she sings of the afterlife," said Nessarose, and for once no one was inclined to argue.

5

Early one morning, when the world was hoary with rimefrost, Grommetik arrived with a note for Glinda. Ama Clutch, it seemed, was on her way out. Glinda and her roommates hurried to the infirmary.

The Head met them there, and led them to a windowless alcove. Ama Clutch was thrashing about in the bed and talking to the pillowcase. "Don't put *up* with me," she was saying wildly, "for what will I ever do for you? I will abuse your good nature, duckie, and rest my oily locks upon your fine close weave and I will be picking with my teeth at your lacy appliquéd edge! You are a stupid nuisance to allow it, I say! I don't *care* about notions of service! It's all bunk, I tell you, bunk!"

"Ama Clutch, Ama Clutch, it's me," said Glinda. "Listen, dear, it's me! It's your little Galinda."

Ama Clutch turned her head from side to side. "Your protest is insulting to your forebears!" she went on, rolling her eyes toward the pillowcase again. "Those cotton plants on the banks of Restwater didn't allow themselves to be harvested so you could lie down like a mat and let any filthy person slobber all over you with night drool! It don't make a lick of sense!"

"Ama!" Glinda wept. "Please! You're raving!"

"Aha, I see you have nothing to say to *that*," said Ama Clutch with satisfaction.

"Come back, Ama, come back, one more time before you go!"

"Oh sweet Lurline, this is dreadful," Nanny said. "Darlings, if I ever get like this, poison me, will you?"

"She's going, I can see it," Elphaba said. "I saw it enough in Quadling Country, I know the signs. Glinda, say what you need to say, quickly."

"Madame Morrible, may I have privacy?" Glinda said.

"I will stay by your side and support you. It's my duty to my girls," said the Head, settling her hamlike hands determinedly on her waist. But Elphaba and Nanny got up and elbowed her out of the alcove, down the hall, and through the door and closed it and locked it. Nanny clucked all the while, saying, "Now, isn't that nice of you, Madame Head, but no need. No need at all."

Glinda gripped Ama Clutch's hand. Beads of white sweat were forming like potato water on the servant's forehead. She struggled to pull her hand away but her strength was going. "Ama Clutch, you're dying," Glinda said, "and it's my fault."

"Oh stop," Elphaba said.

"It is," Glinda said fiercely, "it *is*."

"I'm not arguing that," said Elphaba, "I just mean cut yourself out of the conversation; this is *her* death, not your interview with the Unnamed God. Come *on*. Do something!"

Glinda grabbed the hands, both hands, even tighter. "I am going to magick you back," she said between gritted teeth. "Ama Clutch, you do as I say! I'm still your employer and your better, and you have to obey me! Now listen to this spell and behave yourself!"

The Ama's teeth gnashed, the eyes rolled, and the chin twisted knobbily, as if trying to impale some invisible demon in the air above her bed. Glinda's eyes shut and her jaw worked, and a thread of sound, sylla-bles incoherent even to herself, came spooling out from her blanched lips. "Hope you don't explode her like a sandwich," muttered Elphaba.

Glinda ignored this. She hummed and worked, she rocked and panted. Ama Clutch's eyelids moved so frantically over the closed eyes that it looked as if her eye sockets were chewing her own eyes. "Magicordium senssus ovinda clenx," Glinda concluded out loud, "and if that doesn't do it, I give up; even the smells and bells of a full kit wouldn't help, I think."

On the straw pallet Ama Clutch fell back. A little blood ran from the outer edge of each eye. But the wild turning motion of the focus had shuttered itself down. "Oh my dear," she murmured, "so you're all right then, or am I dead now?"

"Not yet," said Glinda. "Yes, dear Ama, yes, I'm fine. But sweet-heart, I think you're going."

"Of course I am, the Wind is here, can't you hear it?" Ama Clutch said. "No matter. Oh there's Elphie, too. Good-bye, my ducks. Stay out of the Wind until the time is right or you'll be blown in the wrong direction."

Glinda said, "Ama Clutch, I have something to say to you—I have to make my apology—"

But Elphaba leaned forward, cutting Glinda off from Ama Clutch's line of sight, and said, "Ama Clutch, before you go, tell us who killed Doctor Dillamond."

"Surely you know that," Ama Clutch said.

"Make us sure," Elphaba said.

"Well, I saw it, I mean nearly. It had just happened and the knife was still there"—Ama Clutch worked for breath—"smeared with blood that hadn't had a chance to dry."

"What did you see? This is important."

"I saw the knife in the air, I saw the Wind come to take Doctor Dillamond away, I saw the clockwork turn and the Goat's time stop."

"It was Grommetik, wasn't it," Elphaba murmured, trying to get the old woman to speak the words.

"Well, that's what I'm *saying*, duckie," said Ama Clutch.

"And did it see you, did it turn on you?" cried Glinda. "Did that make you ill, Ama Clutch?"

"It was my time to be ill," said Ama Clutch gently, "so I couldn't complain. And it is my time to die, so leave me be. Just hold my hand, dear."

"But the fault is mine—" began Glinda.

"You would do me more good if you hushed, sweet Galinda, my duck," said Ama Clutch gently, and patted Glinda's hand. Then she closed her eyes and breathed in and out a couple of times. They sat there in a silence that seemed peculiarly servant-class-Gillikinese, though it was hard, later on, to explain why. Outside, Madame Morrible moved up and down the floorboards, pacing. Then they imagined they heard a Wind, or an echo of a Wind, and Ama Clutch was gone, and the overly subordinate pillowcase took a small spill of human juice from the edge of her slackened mouth.

6

The funeral was modest, a love-her-and-shove-her affair. Glinda's close friends attended, filling two pews, and in the second tier of the chapel a flock of Amas made a professional coterie. The rest of the chapel was empty.

After the corpse in its winding sheet slid along the oiled chute to the furnace, the mourners and colleagues retired to Madame Morrible's private parlor, where she proved to have sanctioned no expense in the refreshments. The tea was ancient stock, stale as sawdust, the biscuits were hard, and there was no saffron cream or tamorna marmalade. Glinda said reprovingly to the Head, "Not even a small bowl of cream?" and Madame Morrible answered, "My girl, I try to protect my charges from the worst of the food shortages by judicious shopping and by going without myself, but I am not wholly responsible for your *ignorance*. If only people would obey the Wizard absolutely, there would be abundance. Don't you realize that conditions verge on famine and cows are dying of starvation two hundred miles from here? This makes saffron cream very dear in the market." Glinda began to move away, but Madame Morrible reached out a raft of cushiony, bulbous, bejeweled fingers. The touch made Glinda's blood run cold. "I should like to see you, and Miss Nessarose, and Miss Elphaba," said the Head. "After the guests leave. Please wait behind."

"We're nabbed for a lecture," whispered Glinda to the Thropp sisters. "We have to be yelled at."

"Not a word about what Ama Clutch said—or that she came back," said Elphaba urgently. "Got that, Nessa? Nanny?"

They all nodded. Boq and Avaric, making their good-byes, said that the group was reconvening at the pub in the Regent's Parade. The girls agreed to meet them there after their interview with the Head. They would manage a more honest memorial service for Ama Clutch at the Peach and Kidneys.

When the small crowd had dispersed, only Grommetik clearing away the cups and crumbs, Madame Morrible herself banked up the fire—a gesture of chumminess lost on no one—and sent Grommetik away. "Later, thingy," she said, "later. Go lubricate yourself in some closet somewhere." Grommetik wheeled away with, if it was possible, an offended air. Elphaba had to repress an urge to kick it with the tip of her stout black walking boot.

"You too, Nanny," Madame Morrible said. "A little break from your labors."

"Oh no," Nanny said. "Nanny doesn't leave her Nessa."

"Yes Nanny does. Her sister is perfectly capable of caring for her," said the Head. "Aren't you, Miss Elphaba? The very soul of charity."

Elphaba opened her mouth—the word *soul* always provoked her, Glinda knew—but closed it again. She made a wincing nod toward the door. Without a word, Nanny got up to leave, but before the door closed behind her Nanny said, "It's not my place to complain, but really: *no cream?* At a funeral?"

"Help," said Madame Morrible when the door closed, but Glinda wasn't sure if this was a criticism of servants or a bid for sympathy. The Head rallied herself by arranging her skirts and the vents and braids of her smart parlor jacket. In orangey copper sequins she looked like a huge, upholstered, upended goldfish goddess. How ever did she get to be Head? Glinda wondered.

"Now that Ama Clutch has gone to ash, we shall, nay, we *must* move bravely on," Madame Morrible began. "My girls, may I first ask you to recount the sad story of her last words. It is essential therapy in your recovery from grief."

The girls didn't look at one another. Glinda, in this situation the spokesperson, took a breath and said, "Oh, she spewed nonsense to the last."

"No surprise, the dotty old thing," said Madame Morrible, "but what nonsense?"

"We couldn't make it out," said Glinda.

"I had wondered if she talked about the death of the Goat."

Glinda said, "Oh the Goat? Well I could hardly tell—"

"I suspected that, in her deranged condition, she might return to that critical moment. The dying often try to make sense, at the last possible moment, of the puzzles of their lives. Useless effort, of course. No doubt Ama Clutch was puzzled by what she came across, the Goat's body, the blood. And Grommetik."

"Oh?" said Glinda faintly. The sisters beside her were careful not to stir.

"That terrible morning I was up early—at my spiritual meditations—and I noticed the light in Doctor Dillamond's lab. So I sent Grommetik over with a cheering pot of tea for the old Goat. Grommetik found the Animal slumped over a broken lens; he'd apparently stumbled and severed his own jugular vein. *Such* a sad accident, born of academic zeal (not to say hubris) and a pitiful lack of common sense. Rest, we all need rest, the brightest of us need our rest. Grommetik in its confusion felt for a pulse—none to be found—and I surmise that is just when Ama Clutch arrived. To see dear Grommetik splashed with the spurts of a strong circulatory pulse. Ama Clutch arrived out of nowhere and none of her business, I might add, but let's not malign the dead, shall we?"

Glinda gulped back new tears, and did not mention that Ama Clutch had mentioned seeing something unusual *the evening before*, and had wandered out to check.

"I did always think that the shock of all that blood might have been the final straw that sent Ama Clutch pitching back into her ailment. Incidentally, you see why I dismissed Grommetik just now. It's still very sensitive and suspects, I believe, that Ama Clutch thought *it* responsible for the Goat's slaughter."

Glinda said waveringly, "Madame Morrible, you should know that Ama Clutch had never suffered such a disease as I described to you. I invented it. But I didn't assign it. I didn't commit it to her, or her to it."

Elphaba looked at Madame Morrible steadily, keeping her interest modest. Nessarose's eyelashes fluttered. If Madame Morrible knew Glinda's news already, her face didn't give her away. She looked as placid as a tethered rowboat. "Well, this only lends weight to my observations," she allowed. "There is an imaginative, even a prophetic power in your pointed little society skull, Miss Glinda."

The Head stood, her skirts rustling, wind through a field of wheat. "What I say now I say in strictest confidence. I expect my girls to obey my command. Are we agreed?" She seemed to take their stunned silence as assent. She looked down on them. That's why she seems so like a fish, Glinda suddenly thought. She hardly ever blinks.

"By an authority vested in me that is too high to be named, I have been charged with a crucial task," said the Head. "A task essential to the internal security of Oz. I have been working to fulfill this task for some years, and the time is right, and the goods are at my disposal." She scrutinized them. They were the goods.

"You will not repeat what you hear in this room," she said. "You will not want to, you will not choose to, and you will not be able to. I am wrapping each one of you in a binding cocoon as regards this very sensitive material. No"—she held up a hand at Elphaba's protest—"no you have no right to object. The deed is already done and you must listen and be open to what I say."

Glinda tried to examine herself to see if she felt wrapped, or bound, or spell-chilled. But she only felt frightened and young, which may be close to the same thing. She glanced at the sisters. Nessarose in her dazzling shoes was back in her chair, nostrils dilating in fright or excitement. Elphaba on the other hand looked as stolid and cross as usual.

"You live in a little womb here, a tight little nest, girl with girl. Oh I know you have your silly boys on the edge, forgettable things. Good for one thing only and not even reliable at that. But I digress. I must say that you know little or nothing of the state of the nation today. You have no sense of the pitch of unrest to which things have mounted. Setting communities on edge, ethnic groups against one another, bankers against farmers and factories against shopkeepers. Oz is a seething volcano threatening to erupt and burn us in its own poisonous pus.

"Our Wizard seems strong enough. Ah, but is he? Is he really? He has a grasp of internal politics. He's no slouch at negotiating rates of exchange with the bloodsuckers of Ev or Jemmicoe or Fliaan. He rules the Emerald City with an industry and an ability that the decaying knob-jawed Ozma line never dreamed of. Without him we'd have been swept away in firestorm, years ago. We can but be grateful. A strong fist does wonders in a rotten situation. Walk softly but carry a bit stick. I see I offend. Well, a man is always good for the public face of power, no?

"Yes. But things are not always as they seem. And it has been clear for some time that the Wizard's bag of tricks would not do forever. There are bound to be popular uprisings—the stupid, senseless kind, in which strong dumb people enjoy getting killed for the sake of political changes that'll be rolled back within the decade. Adds such meaning to meaningless lives, don't you think? One can't imagine any other reason for it. At any rate, the Wizard needs some agents. He requires a few generals. In the long run. Some people with managing skills. Some people with gumption.

"In a word, women.

"I have called you three girls in here. You are not women yet, but the moment is closing in on you, faster than you might think. Despite my opinion as to your behavior, I have had to single you out. There is more in each one of you than meets the eye. Miss Nessarose, being the newest, you are the most hidden to me, but once you outgrow that fetching habit of faith you will display a ferocious authority. Your bodily disorder is of no significance here. Miss Elphaba, you are an isolate, and even in my binding spell you sit there stewing in scorn of every word I say. This is evidence of great internal power and force of will, something I deeply respect even when marshaled against me. You have shown no sign of interest in sorcery and I don't claim you have any natural aptitude. But your splendid lone-wolf spit and spirit can be harnessed, oh yes it can, and you needn't live a life of unfulfilled rage. And Miss Glinda: You have surprised yourself with the talents at sorcery you possess. I knew you would. I had hoped your inclinations might rub off on Miss Elphaba, but that they haven't is only firmer proof of Miss Elphaba's iron character.

"I see in your eyes you all question my methods. You think, somewhat wildly: Did Horrible Morrible cause that nail to pierce my Ama Clutch's foot, making me have to room with Elphaba? Did she cause Ama Clutch to come downstairs and find the dead Goat, the better to get her out of the way and require Nanny and thus Nessarose to show up on the scene? How flattering that you even imagine I have such power."

The Head paused and came near to blushing, which in her was something like the separating of cream on a flame set too high. "I am a handmaiden at the service of superiors," she continued, "and my special talent is to encourage talent. In my own small way I have been called to a vocation of education, and here I make my little contributions to history.

"Now to be specific. I want you to consider your futures. I would like to name you, to baptize you as it were, as a trio of Adepts. In the long run I would like to assign you behind-the-scenes ministerial duties in different parts of the country. I am empowered to do this, remember, by those whose boot straps I am not worthy to lick." But she looked smug, as if she thought herself quite worthy enough, indeed, of attention from these mysterious forces. "Let us say you will be secret partners of the highest level of government. You will be anonymous ambassadors of peace, helping to restrain the unruly element among our less civilized populations. Nothing is decided yet, of course, and you do have a say in the matter—a say to me, and not to each other nor anyone else, as the spell goes—but I would like you to think about it. I need—eventually—to place an Adept in Gillikin somewhere. Miss Glinda, with your middle-range social position and your transparent ambitions, you can slime your way into ballrooms of margreaves and still be at home in the pigsties. Oh, don't *squirm* so, your good blood is only on one side and it's not a terribly refined strain anyway. The Adept of Gillikin, Miss Glinda? Does it appeal?"

Glinda could only listen. "Miss Elphaba," said Madame Morrible, "full of the teenage scorn of inherited position, you are nonetheless the Thropp Third Descending, and your great-grandfather, the Eminent Thropp, is in his dotage. One day you will inherit what is left of Colwen Grounds, that pretentious pile in Nest Hardings, and you could manage to be the Adept of Munchkinland. Your unfortunate skin condition notwithstanding—indeed, perhaps because of it—you have developed a feistiness and an iconoclasm that is just faintly appealing when it doesn't nauseate. It will come in service. Believe me.

"And Miss Nessarose," she went on, "having grown up in Quadling Country, you will want to return there with Nanny. The social situation in Quadling Country is such a mess, what with the decimation of the squelchy froglet population, but it may come back, in small measure, and there should be someone to oversee the ruby mines. We need someone to look after things in the South. Once you recover from your religious mania, it'll be a perfect setting. You don't expect a life of high society anyway, not without arms. After all, how can one dance without arms?

"As for the Vinkus, we don't imagine we'll need an Adept stationed there, at least not in your lifetimes. The master plans eradicate any appreciable population in that godforsaken place."

Here the Head paused and looked around. "Oh, girls. I know you are young. I know this grieves you. You mustn't think of it as a prison sentence, though, but an opportunity. You ask yourselves: How will I grow in a position, albeit a silent one, of prominence and responsibility? How may my talents flourish? How, my dears, how may I help my Oz?"

Elphaba's foot twisted, caught the edge of a side table, and a cup and saucer fell to the floor and smashed.

"You're so predictable," said Madame Morrible, sighing. "That's what makes my job so easy. Now girls, bound as you are to an oath of silence, I bid you to go away and think on what I have said. Please don't even try to discuss it together as it'll just give you a headache and cramps. You won't be able to manage it. Sometime in the next semester I will call each of you in here and you can give me your answer. And if you should choose not to help your country in its hour of need . . ." She clasped her hands in a parody of despair. "Well, you are not the only fish in the sea, are you?"

The afternoon had turned glowery, with heaps of plum-colored clouds in the north, beyond the bluestone spires and steeples. The temperature had dropped twenty degrees since the morning, and the girls kept their shawls pulled close as they walked to the pub. Nanny, shivering in the dirty wind, cried, "And what did the old busybody have to say that I couldn't be allowed to hear?"

But there was nothing they could say. Glinda couldn't even meet the others' eyes. "We'll lift a glass of champagne for Ama Clutch," said Elphaba finally, "when we get to the Peach and Kidneys."

"I'd settle for a spoonful of real cream," said Nanny. "How pinching that old sow is. No respect for the dead."

But Glinda found that the binding spell was deeper, cut closer than she had even understood. It wasn't merely that they couldn't talk about it. Already she had begun—to lose the words about it, to falter in her thinking, to fail to commit the interview to memory. There was the proposal. It was a proposal, wasn't it? Of some questionable proposition in (was it) the civil service? Doing some—some ballroom dancing, which didn't make sense. Some laughing, a glass of champagne, a handsome man taking off his cummerbund and pressing his starched cuffs against her neck, nibbling the teardrop-shaped rubies at her ears . . . Talk softly but carry a bit stick. Or was it not a proposal but a prophecy? A little friendly encouragement about the future? And she had been alone, the others hadn't been listening. Madame Morrible had spoken directly to her. A lovely testimony to Glinda's . . . potential. The chance to rise. Walk softly but marry a big prick. A man draping his evening tie on a bedstead and rolling his diamond studs, nudging them with his nose, down the declivity of her superior neck . . . It was a dream, Madame Morrible couldn't have said that! She must be dazed with grief. Poor Ama Clutch. It had only been a quiet word of condolence from the dear and self-effacing Head, who found it hard to speak in public. But a man's tongue between her legs, a spoonful of saffron cream . . .

Nessarose said, "Catch her, I can't, I'm—" and she sagged against Nanny's bosom, and Glinda swooned at the same moment. Elphaba thrust out strong arms and scooped Glinda in mid-collapse. Glinda didn't really lose consciousness, but the uncomfortable physical nearness of hawk-faced Elphaba after that undesired act of desire made her want to shiver with revulsion and to purr at the same time. "Steady on, girl, not here," said Elphaba, "resist, come on!" Resist was just what Glinda didn't want to do. But after all, in the shadow of an apple cart, on the edge of the market where merchants were selling the last fish of the day, cheap, well, this was hardly the place. "Tough, tough skin," said Elphaba, appearing to pull words from the back of her throat. "Come on, Glinda—you've got better brains—come on! I love you too much, snap out of it, you idiot!"

"Well, really," she said as Elphaba dumped her on a heap of moldy packing straw. "No need to be so romantic about it!" But she felt better, as if a wave of illness had just passed.

"You girls, I tell you, the faints, it comes from those tight shoes," said Nanny, huffing and loosening Nessarose's glamorous footwear. "Sensible folk wear leather or wood." She massaged Nessarose's insteps for a minute, and Nessarose moaned and arched her back, but began in a few moments to breathe more normally.

"Welcome back to Oz," said Nanny after a while. "What goodies were you all snacking on, in there with the Head?"

"Come on, they're waiting," said Elphaba. "No sense dawdling. Anyway, I'm afraid it might rain."

At the Peach and Kidneys, the rest of the gang had commandeered a table in an alcove several steps above the main floor. They were well into their cups by that point in the afternoon, and it was clear tears had been shed. Avaric sat slouched against the brick wall of the student den, one arm slung around Fiyero and his legs stretched out in Shenshen's lap. Boq and Crope were arguing about something, anything, and Tibbett was singing an interminable song to Pfannee, who looked as if she wanted to drive a dart into the thick of his thigh. "Ahh, the ladies," slurred Avaric, and made as if to rise.

They sang, and chattered, and ordered sandwiches, and Avaric plunked down an embarrassment of coins to demand a salver of saffron cream, in Ama Clutch's memory. Money did wonders and the cream was found in the larder, which gave Glinda an uneasy feeling, though she didn't know why. They spooned the airy mounds into one another's mouths, sculpted with it, mixed it in their champagne, threw it in small gobbets at one another until the manager came over and told them to get the hell out. They complied, grumbling. They didn't know it was the last time they would all be together, or they might have lingered.

A brisk rain had come and gone, but the streets were still noisy with runoff, and the lamplight glistened and danced in the silvery black curvetts of water caught among the cobbles. Imagining the possible brigand in the shadows, or the hungry wanderer lurking nearby, they stood close together. "I've got an idea," said Avaric, putting one foot this way and the other that, as if he were as flexible as a man of straw. "Who's man enough for the Philosophy Club tonight?"

"Oh, no you don't," said Nanny, who hadn't had that much to drink.

"I want to go," whined Nessarose, swaying more than usual.

"You don't even know what it is," said Boq, giggling and hiccuping.

"I don't care, I don't want to leave tonight," Nessarose said. "We only have one another and I don't want to be left out, and I don't want to go home!"

"Hush Nessa, hush hush, my pretty," said Elphaba. "That's not the place for you, or me either. Come on, we're going home. Glinda, come on."

"I have no Ama now," said wide-eyed Glinda, stabbing a finger toward Elphaba. "I am my own agent. I want to go to the Philosophy Club and see if it's true."

"The rest can do what they want but we're going home," said Elphaba.

Glinda veered over toward Elphaba, who was homing in on a very uncertain-looking Boq. "Now Boq, you don't want to go to that disgusting place, do you?" Elphaba was saying. "Come on, don't let the boys make you do something you don't want."

"You don't know me," he said, appearing to address the hitching post. "Elphie, how do you know what I want? Unless I find out? Hmmm?"

"Come with us," said Fiyero to Elphaba. "Please, if we ask you politely?"

"I want to go too," whined Glinda.

"Oh, come, Glinny-dinny," said Boq, "maybe they'll pick us. For old times' sake, as never was."

The others had awakened a slumbering cab driver and hired his services. "Boq, Glinda, Elphie, come on," Avaric called from the window. "Where's your nerve?"

"Boq, think about this," Elphaba urged.

"I always think, I never feel, I never live," he moaned. "Can't I live once in a while? Just once? Just because I'm short I'm not an infant, Elphie!"

"Not till now," said Elphaba. Rather smarmy tonight, thought Glinda, and wrenched herself away to climb into the cab. But Elphaba grabbed her by the elbow and pivoted her around. "You can't," she whispered. "We're going to the Emerald City."

"I'm going to the Philosophy Club with my friends—"

"Tonight," hissed Elphaba. "You little idiot, we have no time to waste on sex!"

Nanny had led Nessarose away already, and the cabbie clucked his reins and the equipage lumbered away. Glinda stumbled and said, "What did you think you were just about to say? To say?"

"I already said it and I'm not saying it again," said Elphaba. "My dear, you and I are going back to Crage Hall tonight only to pack a valise. Then we're away."

"But the gates'll be locked—"

"It's over the garden wall," said Elphaba, "and we're going to see the Wizard, come what may and hell to pay."

7

Boq could not believe he was heading to the Philosophy Club at last. He hoped he wouldn't vomit at a crucial moment. He hoped he would remember the whole thing tomorrow, or at least some kernel of it, despite the headache forming vengefully in the hollows at his temples.

The place was discreet, though it was the best known dive in Shiz. It hid behind a facade of paneled-up windows. A couple of Apes roamed the street in front, bouncing troublemakers ahead of time. Avaric counted the party carefully as they fell from the cab. "Shenshen, Crope, me, Boq, Tibbett, Fiyero, and Pfannee. Seven. Boy how'd we all fit in the cab, could hardly fit us I'd think." He paid the cabbie and tipped him, in some obscure homage still to Ama Clutch, and then pushed to the front of the silent knot of companions. "Come on, we're the right age and the right drunk," he said, and to the shadowed face at the window, "Seven. Seven of us, good sir."

The face came forward to the glass and leered at him. "The name is Yackle, and I'm not a sir nor am I good. What kind are you up to tonight, Master Fellow?" Speaking through the pane was a crone, with random teeth and a shiny white-pink wig slipping westwards off her pearly scalp.

"Kind?" said Avaric, then more bravely, "Any kind."

"I mean the tickets, sweetbread. Strutting and strumming on the sprung floor, or strumpeting in the old wine cellars?"

"The works," said Avaric.

"You understand house rules? The locked doors, the if-you-pay-you-play policy?"

"Give us seven, and hurry up about it. We're not fools."

"You never are fools," said the beastly woman. "Well, here you are then, and come what may. Or who may." She affected a stance of virtue, like a painting of a unionist virgin saint. "Enter and be saved."

The door swung open, and they went down a flight of uneven brick steps. At the bottom of the flight was a dwarf in a purple burnoose. He looked at their tickets, and said, "Where are you soft things from? Out of town?"

"We're all at the university," said Avaric.

"A motley crew. Well, you've seven-of-diamond tickets. See here, the seven red diamonds printed here, and here." He said, "Have a drink on the house, watch the girlie show, and dance a little if you want. Every hour or so I close this street door and open the next." He pointed to a huge oak door, barred with two monstrous timbers in iron hasps. "You all go in together or you don't go in at all. That's the rule of the house."

There was a chanteuse singing a send-up of "What Is Oz Without Ozma," and teasing herself with a parrot-colored feather boa. A small band of elves—real elves!—tootled and rattled out a tinny accompaniment. Boq had never seen an elf, even though he knew there was a colony of them not far from Rush Margins. "How weird," he said, inching forward. They looked like hairless monkeys, naked but for little red caps, and without any appreciable sex characteristics. They were as green as sin. Boq turned to say, Look, Elphie, it's like you had a passel of babies, but he didn't see her and remembered then that she hadn't come. Nor had Glinda, apparently. Damn.

They danced. The crowd was the most mixed Boq had seen in some time. There were Animals, humans, dwarfs, elves, and several tik-tok things of incomplete or experimental gender. A squadron of well-built blond boys circulated with tumblers of rotgut squash wine, which the friends drank because it was free.

"I don't know if I want to go any more daring than this," said Pfannee to Boq at one point. "I mean, look, that hussy of a Baboon is almost out of her dress. Perhaps we should call it a night."

"Do you think?" said Boq. "I mean, I'm game, but if you're feeling uneasy." Oh hurrah, a way out. He was feeling uneasy himself. "Well let's get Avaric. He's over there nosing up to Shenshen."

But before they could make their way across the crowded dance floor, the elves began to let out a banshee screech, and the singer thrust out her hip and said, "That's the mating call, dollies! Ladies and gentle-friends! We're doing, and I do mean *doing*"—she glanced at a note in her hand—"five black clubs, three black clubs, six red hearts, seven red diamonds, and—on their honeymoon, isn't it *sweet*"—she simulated gagging—"two black spades. Up to the mouth of everlasting bliss, fraidies and gentlehens."

"Avaric, no," said Boq.

But the crone from the front, who called herself Yackle, came knocking through the hall—having apparently locked up the front door for the time being—and she remembered the holders of the designated cards, and brought them forward with a smile. "All rides, all riders, on the ready," she said, "here we be, at the shank end of the evening! Lighten up, lads, it's not a funeral, it's an entertainment!" It *had* been a funeral, Boq remembered, trying to invoke the warm, self-effacing spirit of Ama Clutch. But the time to back out, if such a time existed, had passed.

They were swept through the oak doors and along a slightly sloping passage whose walls were padded in red and blue velvet. A merry tune was playing farther on, a dancing ragged melody. A smell of roasting timm leaves—sweet and softening, you could almost feel them turning up their purplish edges. Yackle led the way, and the twenty-three revelers processed, in a confused state of apprehension, elation, and randiness. The dwarf followed behind. Boq took stock, as best his stumbling mind could manage. An erect Tiger in hip boots and a cape. A couple of bankers and their evening consorts, all wearing black masques: as a protection against blackmail or as an aphrodisiac? A party of merchants from Ev and Fliaan, in town on business. A couple of women rather long in the tooth, bedecked in costume jewelry. The honeymoon couple were Glikkuns. Boq hoped that his crowd wasn't gawping as much as the Glikkuns were. As he glanced around, only Avaric and Shenshen looked eager—and Fiyero, possibly because he hadn't yet grasped what this was all about. The others looked more than a little squeamish.

They entered a small dark theatre-in-the-round, with the space for the public divided into six stalls. Above, the ceiling was lost in a stony blackness. Tapers fluttered, and a hollow music issued through fissures in the wall, increasing an unearthly air of dislocation and otherness. The stalls circled and faced the central stage, which was enshrouded in black drapes. The stalls were separated from one another by vertical strips of latticed wood and slats of mirror. All the parties were being mixed up, all friends and partners separated. Was there incense in the air too? It seemed to make Boq's mind split in half, like a husk, and allow a tenderer, complacent mind to emerge. The softer, more bruisable aspect, the private intention, the surrendering self.

He felt he was knowing less and less, and it was more and more beautiful to do so. Why had he been alarmed? He was sitting on a stool, and around him in the stall sat, almost preternaturally near, a man in a black masque, an Asp he hadn't noticed before, the Tiger whose breath ran hot and meaty on his neck, a beautiful schoolgirl, or was that the bride on her honeymoon? Did the whole stall then tilt forward, like a gently swung bucket? Anyway, they leaned together toward the central dais, an altar of veils and sacrifices. Boq loosened his collar and then his belt, felt the gingery appetite between heart and stomach and the resulting stiffening apparatus below that. The music of pipes and whistles was slowing, or was it that as he watched and waited and breathed so, so slowly, that the secret area inside himself uncloaked itself, where nothing mattered?

The dwarf, in a darker hood now, appeared on the stage. He could see from his vantage point into all the stalls but the revelers in separate stalls couldn't see one another. The dwarf leaned and reached a hand here, there, welcoming, beckoning. He encouraged from one stall the fig- ure of a woman, from another a man (was it Tibbett?), and from the stall where Boq sat he gestured to the Tiger. Boq felt only faintly sorry not to be chosen himself as he watched the dwarf pass a smoking vial beneath the nostrils of the three acolytes, and help them to remove their clothes. There were shackles, and a tray of scented oils and emollients, and a chest whose contents were still in shadow. The dwarf bound black blind- folds around the heads of the scholars.

The Tiger was pacing on all fours and growling softly, tossing his head back and forth in distress or excitement. Tibbett—for it was he, though nearly out of consciousness—was made to lie on his back on the floor of the stage. The Tiger strode over him and stood still while the dwarf and his assistants lifted Tibbett and tied his wrists together, around the Tiger's chest, and his ankles around the Tiger's pelvis, so Tibbett hung beneath the Tiger's belly, like a trussed pig, his face lost in the Tiger's chest hair.

The woman was set on a sloping stool, almost like a huge tilting bowl, and the dwarf tucked something aromatic and runny up in the shadowy regions. Then the dwarf pointed to Tibbett, who was beginning to twist and moan into the Tiger's chest. "Let X be the Unknown God," said the dwarf, poking Tibbett in the ribs. The dwarf then slapped the Tiger on his flank with a riding crop, and the Tiger strained forward, posi- tioning his head between the woman's legs. "Let Y be the Dragon of Time in its cave," said the dwarf, hitting the Tiger again.

As he laced the woman into the half-shell, stroking her nipples with a glowing salve, he handed her a riding crop with which she could lash at the Tiger's flanks and face. "And let Z be the Kumbric Witch, and let us see if she exists tonight . . ." The crowd drew nearer, almost participants themselves, and the musky sense of adventure made them tear at their own buttons and nibble their own lips, leaning in, in, in.

"Such are the variables in our equation," said the dwarf as the room darkened even further. "So now, let the true, clandestine study of knowledge begin."

8

The industrialists of Shiz, from an early stage wary of the growing power of the Wizard, had elected not to lay down the rail line from Shiz to the Emerald City as originally planned. Therefore, it was a good three days' journey from Shiz to the Emerald City—and this was in the best of weather, for the wealthy who could pay for a constant change of horses. For Glinda and Elphaba it took more than a week. A bleak, cold-scoured week, as the winds of autumn ripped the leaves off trees with a dry screech and a rattle of brittle, protesting limbs.

They rested, like other third-class travelers, in the back rooms above inn kitchens. In a single lumpy bed, they huddled together for warmth and encouragement and, Glinda told herself, protection. The ostlers cooed and shrieked in the stableyard below, the kitchen maids came and went noisily, at odd hours. Glinda would start as if from a frightful dream, and nestle in nearer to Elphaba, who seemed at night never to sleep. Daytimes, the long hours spent in poorly sprung carriages, Elphaba would nod off against Glinda's shoulder. The land outside grew less succulent and varied. Trees were crabbed, as if conserving their strength.

And then the sandy scrubland was domesticated by farm life. Overgrazed fields were dotted with cows, their withers shriveled and papery, their lowing desperate. An emptiness settled in the farmyards. Once Glinda saw a farm woman standing on her doorstep, hands sunk deep in apron pockets, face lined with grief and rage at the useless sky. The woman watched the carriage pass, and her face showed a yearning to be on it, to be dead, to be anywhere else other than on this carcass of a property.

The farms gave way to deserted mills and abandoned granges. Then, abrupt and decisive, the Emerald City rose before them. A city of insistence, of blanket declaration. It made no sense, clotting up the horizon, sprouting like a mirage on the characterless plains of central Oz. Glinda hated it from the moment she saw it. Brash upstart of a city. She supposed it was her Gillikinese superiority asserting itself. She was glad of it.

The carriage passed through one of the northern gates, and the scramble of life aroused itself again, but in an urban key, less restrained and self-forgiving than that of Shiz. The Emerald City was not amused by itself, nor did it consider amusement a proper attitude for a city. Its high self-regard sprang up in public spaces, ceremonial squares, parks and facades and reflecting pools. "How juvenile, how devoid of irony," murmured Glinda. "The pomp, the pretension!"

But Elphaba, who had passed through the Emerald City only once before, on her way up to Shiz, had no interest in architecture. She had her eyes glued on the people. "No Animals," she said, "not so you can see, anyway. Maybe they have all gone underground."

"Underground?" said Glinda, thinking of legendary menaces like the Nome King and his subterranean colony, or dwarves in their mines in Glikkus, or the Time Dragon of the old myths, dreaming the world of Oz from his airless tomb.

"In hiding," said Elphaba. "Look, the poor—I mean are they the poor? The hungry of Oz? From the failed farms? Or is it just the—the surplus? The expendable human selvage? Look at them, Glinda, this is a real question. The Quadlings, having nothing, looked—more—than these—"

Off the boulevard on which they rode branched alleys, where shelves of tin and cardboard served as roofs for the flood of indigents. Many of them were children, though some were the diminutive Munchkinlanders, and some were dwarves, and some were Gillikinese bowed with hunger and strain. The carriage moved slowly, and faces stood out. A Glikkun youth with no teeth and no feet or calves, on his stumpy knees in a box, begging. A Quadling—"Look, a Quadling!" said Elphaba, grabbing Glinda's wrist. Glinda caught a glimpse of a ruddy brown woman in a shawl, lifting a small apple to the child in a sling around her neck. Three Gillikinese girls dressed like women for hire. More children in a pack, running and squealing like piglets, pressing up against a merchant, to pick his pockets. Rag merchants with pushcarts. Kiosk keepers whose goods lay locked beneath safety grilles. And a sort of civil army, if you could call it that, strolling in foursomes on every second or third street, brandishing clubs, angular with swords.

They paid the carriage master and walked with their parcels of clothes toward the Palace. It rose, in stepped-back fashion, a growth of domes and minarets, high flared buttresses in green marble, blue agate screens in the recessed windows. Central and most prominent, the broad, gentle-browed canopies of the pagoda lifted over the Throne Room, covered with hammered scales of virgin gold, brilliant in the late afternoon gloom.

Five days later they had made it past the gatekeeper, the receptionists, and the social secretary. They had sat for hours awaiting a three-minute interview with the Commander-General of Audiences. Elphaba, a hard, twisted look on her face, had managed to eject the words "Madame Morrible" from between her clamping lips. "Tomorrow at eleven," said the Commander-General. "You will have four minutes between the Ambassador to Ix and the Matron of the Ladies' Home Guard Social Nourishment Brigade. Dress code is formal." He handed them a card of regulations that, being unequipped with courtly dress, they were obliged to ignore.

At three the following afternoon (everything running late), the Ambassador to Ix left the Throne Room looking agitated and splenetic. Glinda fluffed the bedraggled feathers in her traveling hat for the eightieth time, and sighed, "Now you're the one who says what should be said." Elphaba nodded. To Glinda she looked tired, terrified, but strong, as if her form were knit with iron and whiskey instead of bones and blood. The Commander-General of Audiences appeared in the doorway of the waiting salon.

"You have four minutes," he said. "Do not approach until you are bade to do so. Do not speak until you are addressed. Do not venture a remark unless it is to answer a comment or question. You may refer to the Wizard as 'Your Highness.'"

"That sounds pretty regal to me. I thought that royalty had been—" But here Glinda elbowed Elphaba to make her shut up. Really, Elphaba had no common sense sometimes. They hadn't come so far just to be turned away because of adolescent radicalism.

The Commander-General took no notice. As they approached a set of tall double doors, carved with sigils and other occult hieroglyphs, the Commander-General mentioned, "The Wizard is not in a good humor today due to the reports of a riot in the Ugabu district in the north of

Winkie Country. I should be prepared for what I find, were I you." Two stoical doormen opened the doors then, and they passed through.

But the throne did not lie before them. Instead, the antechamber led left, and through an archway there was another, but on a shifting axis to the right, and another beyond that, and another. It was like looking through a reflection of a corridor in mirrors set opposite each other; it veered inward. Or, thought Glinda, like processing through the narrowing, deviating chambers of a nautilus. They made a circuit through eight or ten salons, each slightly smaller than the other, each steeped in a curdled light that fell from leaded panes above. At last the antechambers concluded at an archway into a cavernous circular hall, higher than it was wide, and dark as a chapel. Antique wrought-iron stands held ziggurats of molded beeswax burning with a multitude of wicks, and the air was close and slightly floury. The Wizard was absent, though they saw the throne on a circular dais, inset emeralds gleaming dully in the candlelight.

"He stepped out to use the toilet," said Elphaba. "Well, we'll wait."

They stood at the archway, not daring to venture farther without invitation.

"If we only have four minutes, I hope this doesn't count," said Glinda. "I mean, it took us two minutes just to get from there to here."

"At this point—" said Elphaba, and then, "Shhhhh."

Glinda shhhhhhed. She didn't think she heard anything, then she wasn't sure. There was no change that she could identify in the gloom, but Elphaba looked like a pointer on alert. Her chin was out, her nose high and nostrils flared, her dark eyes squinting and widening.

"What," said Glinda, "what?"

"The sound of—"

Glinda heard no sounds, unless it was the hot air lifting from the flames into the chilly shadows between dark rafters. Or was it the rustle of silk robes? Was the Wizard approaching? She looked this way and that. No—there was a rustle, a sort of hiss, as of bacon rashers in a skillet. The candle flames suddenly all genuflected, obeisant to a sour wind that beat from the area of the throne.

Then the dais was pelted with thick drops of rain, and a shudder of homegrown thunder blatted out, more dropped kitchen kettles than timpani. On the throne was a skeleton of dancing lights; at first Glinda thought lightning, but then she realized it was luminescent bones hitched together to suggest something vaguely human, or at least mammalian. The rib cage flexed open like two fretted hands, and a voice spoke in the storm, not from the skull but from the dark eye of the storm where the heart of the lightning creature should be, in the tabernacle of the rib cage.

"I am Oz, the Great and Terrible," it said, and shook the room with its related weather. "Who are you?"

Glinda glanced at Elphaba. "Go on, Elphie," she said, nudging her. But Elphaba looked terrified. Well, of course, the rain. She had that thing about rainstorms.

"Whooo arrrre youuuu?" bellowed the thing, the Wizard of Oz, whatever.

"Elphie," hissed Glinda. Then, "Oh, you useless thing, all talk and no—I'm Glinda from Frottica, if you please, Your Highness, descended matrilineally from the Arduennas of the Upland, and this if you please is Elphaba, the Thropp Third Descending from Nest Hardings. If you please."

"And if I don't please?" said the Wizard.

"Oh really, how like a child," said Glinda under her breath. "Elphie, come on, I can't say why we're here!"

But the banal comment of the Wizard's seemed to snap Elphaba out of her terror. Staying where she was at the edge of the room, gripping Glinda's hand for support, Elphaba said, "We're students of Madame Morrible at Crage Hall in Shiz, Your Highness, and we're in possession of some vital information."

"We are?" said Glinda. "Thanks for telling me."

The small rain seemed to let up a bit, though the room stayed dark as an eclipse. "Madame Morrible, that paragon of paradoxes," said the Wizard. "Vital information of her, I wonder?"

"No," said Elphaba. "That is, it is not for us to interpret what we hear. Gossip is unreliable. But—"

"Gossip is instructive," said the Wizard. "It tells which way the wind is blowing." The wind then blew in the direction of the girls, and Elphaba danced back to avoid being spattered. "Go ahead, girls, gossip."

"No," said Elphaba. "We're here on more important business."

"Elphie!" said Glinda. "Do you want to get us thrown in prison?"

"Who are you to decide what is important business?" roared the Wizard.

"I keep my eyes open," said Elphaba. "You didn't call us here to ask for our gossip; we came with our own agenda."

"How do you know I didn't call you here?"

Well, they didn't know, especially after whatever it was had happened to them at tea with Madame Morrible. "Scale down, Elphie," whispered Glinda, "you're making him mad."

"So what?" Elphaba said. "I'm mad." She spoke up again. "I have news of the murder of a great scientist and a great thinker, Your Highness. I have news of important discoveries that he was making, and their suppression. I have every interest in the pursuit of justice and I know you do too, so that the amazing revelations of Doctor Dillamond will help you to reverse your recent judgments on the rights of Animals—"

"Doctor Dillamond?" said the Wizard. "Is that all this is about?"

"It is about an entire population of Animals systematically deprived of their—"

"I know of Doctor Dillamond and I know of his work," said the glowing bones of the Wizard, snorting. "Derivative, unauthenticated, specious garbage. What you'd expect of an academic Animal. Predicated on shaky political notions. Empiricism, quackery, tomfoolery. Cant, rant, and rhetoric. Were you taken in perhaps by his enthusiasm? His Animal passion?" The skeleton danced a jig, or perhaps it was a twitch of disgust. "I know of his interests and his findings. I know little of what you call his murder and I care less."

"I am not a slave to emotions," Elphaba said sternly. She was pulling papers from her sleeve, where she had apparently rolled them up around her arm. "This is not propaganda, Your Highness. This is a well-argued Theory of Consciousness Inclination, is what he calls it. And you will be amazed to learn of his discoveries! No right-thinking ruler can afford to ignore the implica—"

"That you presume me to be right-thinking is touching," said the Wizard. "You may drop the things where you stand. Unless you prefer to approach?" The lightning-marionette grinned and stretched out its arms. "My pet?"

Elphaba dropped the papers. "Good, my Lord," she said in a piercing, pretentious voice, "I shall take you to be right-thinking, for did I not, I should be obliged to join an army against you."

"Oh hell, Elphie," said Glinda, then more loudly, "she doesn't speak for the both of us, Your Highness, I'm an independent person here."

"Please," said Elphaba, at once hard and soft, proud and pleading. Glinda realized she had never before witnessed Elphaba wanting anything. "Please, sir. The hardship on the Animals is more than can be borne. It isn't just the murder of Doctor Dillamond. It's this forced repatriation, this—this chattelizing of free Beasts. You must get out and see the sorrow. There is talk of—there is worry that the next step will be slaughter and cannibalism. This isn't merely youthful outrage. Please, sir. This is not untrammeled emotion. What's happening is immoral—"

"I do not listen when anyone uses the word *immoral*," said the Wizard. "In the young it is ridiculous, in the old it is sententious and reactionary and an early warning sign of apoplexy. In the middle-aged, who love and fear the idea of moral life the most, it is hypocritical."

"If not *immoral*, then what word can I use to imply *wrong?*" said Elphaba.

"Try *mysterious* and then relax a little. The thing is, my green girlie, it is not for a girl, or a student, or a citizen to assess what is wrong. This is the job of leaders, and why we exist."

"But then nothing would keep me from assassinating you, did I not know what wrong was."

"I don't believe in assassination, I don't even know what it *means,*" Glinda called. "*Yoo hoo.* I'm going to take my leave now while I'm still alive."

"Wait," said the Wizard. "I have something to ask you."

They stood still. They stood for minutes. The skeleton fingered its ribs, played them like the brittle strings of a harp. Music like stones turning over in a streambed. The skeleton collected its lighted teeth from its jaws and juggled them. Then it tossed them at the seat of the throne, where they exploded in candy-colored flashes. The rain was running down a drain in the floor, Glinda noticed.

"Madame Morrible," said the Wizard. "Agent provocateur and gossip, crony and companion, teacher and minister. Tell me why she sent you here."

"She didn't," said Elphaba.

"Do you even know the meaning of the word pawn?" shrieked the Wizard.

"Do you know what resistance means?" Elphaba shot back.

But the Wizard only laughed instead of killing them on the spot. "What does she want of you?"

Glinda spoke up; it was about time. "A decent education. For all her bombastic ways she's a capable administrator. It can't be easy." Elphaba was staring at her with a queer, slanted look.

"Has she brought you in—?"

Glinda didn't quite understand. "We're only sophisters. We have only begun to specialize. I in sorcery, Elphaba in life sciences."

"I see." The Wizard seemed to consider. "And after you graduate next year?"

"I suppose I'll go back to Frottica and get married."

"And you?"

Elphaba didn't answer.

The Wizard turned itself around, broke off its femurs, and pounded the seat of the throne as if it were a kettledrum. "Really, this is getting ridiculous, it's all pleasure faith showbiz," said Elphaba. She took a step or two forward. "Excuse me, Your Highness? Before our time is up?"

The Wizard turned back. Its skull was on fire, a fire not quenched by the thickening curtain of rain. "I shall say one last thing," the Wizard ventured, in a voice like a groan, a voice of one in pain. "I shall quote from the *Oziad*, the hero tale of ancient Oz."

The girls waited.

The Wizard of Oz recited:

> "Then hobbling like a glacier, old Kumbricia
> Rubs the naked sky till it rains with blood.
> She tears the skin off the sun and eats it hot.
> She tucks the sickle moon in her patient purse.
> She bears it out, a full-grown changeling stone.
> Shard by shard she rearranges the world.
> It looks the same, she says, but it is not.
> It looks as they expect, but it is not.

"Beware whom you serve," said the Wizard of Oz. Then he was gone, and the gutters in the floor gurgled, and the candles went instantly out. There was nothing for them to do but retrace their steps.

At the carriage, Glinda had settled in and made a little nest for them in the desirable forward-facing seat, guarding Elphaba's place against three other passengers. "My sister," she lied, "I am saving this seat for my sister." And how I have changed, she thought, in a year and some. From despising the colored girl to claiming we are blood! So university life does change you in ways you cannot guess. I may be the only person in all the Pertha Hills ever to meet our Wizard. Not on my own steam, not of my initiative—still, I was there. I did it. And we're not dead.

But we didn't accomplish much.

Then, there was Elphie, at last, barreling along the paving stones with her elbows jutting and her thin bony torso swathed against the elements, as usual, in a cape. She came up through the crowd, batting at more refined passengers to get past, and Glinda shoved open the door. "Thank heavens, I thought you'd be late," she said. "The driver is eager to leave. Did you get a lunch for us?"

Elphaba tossed in her lap a couple of oranges, a hunk of unrepentant cheese, and a loaf of bread that filled the compartment with pungent staleness. "This'll have to do you till your stop this evening," she said.

"Me, me?" said Glinda. "What do you mean, me? Have you got something better to eat for yourself?"

"Something worse, I expect," said Elphaba, "but needs to be done. I've come to say good-bye. I'm not going back with you to Crage Hall. I'll find a place to study on my own. I'll not be part of—Madame Morrible's—school—again—"

"No, no," cried Glinda, "I can't let you! Nanny will eat me alive! Nessarose will die! Madame Morrible will—Elphie, no. No!"

"Tell them I kidnapped you and made you come here, they'll believe that of me," said Elphaba. She stood on the mounting tread. A fat Glikkun female dwarf, having caught the gist of the drama, shifted to the more comfortable seat next to Glinda. "They needn't look for me, Glinda, for I'm not going to be findable. I'm going down."

"Down where? Back to Quadling Country?"

"That would be telling," Elphaba said. "But I won't lie to you, my dear. No need to lie. I don't know yet where I'm going. I haven't decided so I wouldn't have to lie."

"Elphie, get in this cab, don't be a fool," Glinda cried. The driver was adjusting the reins and yelling at Elphaba to sod off.

"You'll be all right," Elphaba said, "now you're a seasoned traveler. This is just the return leg of a voyage you already know." She put her face against Glinda's and kissed her. "Hold out, if you can," she murmured, and kissed her again. "Hold out, my sweet."

The driver clucked the reins, and pitched a cry to leave. Glinda craned her head to see Elphaba drift back into the crowds. For all her singularity of complexion, it was astounding how quickly she became camouflaged in the ragamuffin variety of street life in the Emerald City. Or maybe it was foolish tears blurring Glinda's vision. Elphaba hadn't cried, of course. Her head had turned away quickly as she stepped down, not to hide her tears but to soften the fact of their absence. But the sting, to Glinda, was real.

III

City of Emeralds

On a clammy late summer evening about three years after graduating from Shiz University, Fiyero stopped at the unionist chapel in Saint Glinda's Square, to pass some time before meeting a fellow countryman at the opera.

Fiyero hadn't taken to unionism as a student, but he had developed an eye for frescoes that often adorned the cubbyholes of older chapels. He was hoping to find a portrait of Saint Glinda. He had not seen Glinda of the Arduennas of the Uplands since her graduation—she had finished a year before he did. But he hoped it wouldn't be sacrilegious to light a charmwax candle in front of Saint Glinda's likeness, and to think of her namesake.

A service was ending, and the congregation of sensitive adolescent boys and black-scarved grandmothers drifted slowly out. Fiyero waited until the lyre player in the nave had finished fingering a tricky *diminuet*, then he approached her. "Do forgive me—I'm a visitor from the west." Well obviously, with his rich ochre skin color and tribal markings. "I don't see a sexton—a verger—a sacristan, whatever the word is—nor can I find a pamphlet to tell me—I was looking to find an ikon of Saint Glinda?"

Her face remained grave. "You'll be lucky if it hasn't been papered over with a poster of Our Glorious Wizard. I'm an itinerant musician, only through this way once in a while. But I think you might look in the last aisle; there's an oratory to Saint Glinda, or used to be. Good luck."

Locating it—a tomblike space with an archer's slit instead of a true window—Fiyero saw, lit by a pinkish sanctuary light, a smoky image of the Saint, leaning a bit to the right. The portrait was merely sentimental and not robustly primitive, a disappointment. Water damage had made great white stains like laundry soap mistakes on the Saint's holy garments. He couldn't remember her particular legend, nor the uplifting way that she had gagged on death for the sake of her soul and for the edification of her admirers.

But then he saw, in the underwatery shadows, that the oratory was inhabited by a penitent. The head was bowed in prayer, and he was about to move away when it struck him that he knew who it was.

"Elphaba!" he said.

She turned her head slowly; a lace shawl dropped to her shoulders. Her hair was looped on her head and skewered with ivory hair corkscrews. Her eyes batted once or twice slowly, as if she were moving toward him from a great distance away. He had interrupted her at prayer—he hadn't remembered her to be religious—maybe she didn't recognize him.

"Elphaba, it's Fiyero," he said, moving into the doorway, blocking her exit, and also the light—suddenly he couldn't see her face, and wondered if he heard correctly when she said, "I beg your pardon, sir?"

"Elphie—I'm Fiyero—we were at Shiz," he said. "My splendid Elphie—how are you?"

"Sir, I believe you are mistaking me for someone else," she said, in Elphaba's voice.

"Elphaba, the Thropp Third Descending, if I remember the nomenclature," he said, laughing stoutly, "I'm not mistaken at all. I'm Fiyero of the Arjikis—you know me, you *remember* me! From Doctor Nikidik's lectures in the life sciences!"

"You have confused yourself," she said, "*sir*." That last word sounded a bit shirty, absolutely Elphaba. "Now you don't mind if I am about my devotions in peace?" She drew her shawl up above her head, and arranged it to fall about her temples. The chin in profile could slice a salami, and even in the low light he knew he *wasn't* wrong.

"What is it?" he said. "Elphie—well, Miss Elphaba, if you require—don't shab me off like this. Of course it's you. There's no disguising you. What game are you about?"

She didn't answer him in words, but by telling her beads ostentatiously she was telling him to get lost.

"I'm not going," he said.

"You're interrupting my meditation, sir," she said softly. "Do I have to call the verger and have you removed?"

"I'll meet you outside," he said. "How long do you need to pray? Half an hour? An hour? I'll wait."

"In an hour, then, across the street; there's a small public fountain with some benches. I'll talk with you for five minutes, five minutes only, and show you that you've made a mistake. Not a serious one, but increasingly annoying to me."

"Forgive the intrusion. In an hour then—*Elphaba*." He wasn't going to let her get away with whatever game she was playing. He withdrew, however, and went to the musician at the back of the nave. "Is there another exit to this building besides the main doors?" he asked, over her spurts of arpeggio. When it was convenient to answer him, she tucked her head and moved her eyes. "Side door through to the cloister of the maunts, it's not open to the public, but you can get out to a servants' delivery alley through there."

He lingered in the shadow of a pillar. In about forty minutes, a cloaked figure entered the chapel and moved, hobbling with a cane, directly to the oratory Elphie occupied. He was too far away to hear if words were exchanged, or anything else. (Perhaps the newcomer was merely another disciple of Saint Glinda, and wanted solitude to pray.) The figure didn't linger; it left again as quickly as its stiff joints would allow.

Fiyero dropped an offering in the poor box—a note, so to avoid the clink of coin. In a quarter of the city so infested with the urban poor, his situation of comparative wealth required the penitential gift, though his motivation was characterized more by guilt than charity. Then he slipped out through the side door, into an overgrown cloister garden. Some ancient women in wheeled chairs were chortling at the far end and didn't notice him. He wondered if Elphaba belonged to this community of monastic nuns—maunts, they were called. He now remembered that they were females living in that most paradoxical of institutions: a community of hermits. Apparently, however, their vows of silence were revoked in the decay of old age. He decided that Elphaba couldn't have changed *that* much in five years. So he let himself out the servants' entrance, into an alleyway.

Three minutes passed, and Elphaba emerged from the same servants' entrance, as he had suspected she would. She was *intent* on avoiding him! Why, why? The last he had seen of her—he remembered it well!—was the day of Ama Clutch's funeral, and the drunken party at the pub. She had fled to the Emerald City on some obscure mission, never to return, while he had been dragged off to the eye-opening joys and terrors of the Philosophy Club. Rumor held that the great-grandfather, the Eminent Thropp, had engaged agents to look for her in Shiz, in the Emerald City. From Elphaba herself there was never a postcard, never a message, never a clue. Nessarose had been inconsolable at first, and then grew to resent her sister's putting her through this pain of separation. Nessa had lost herself deeper in religion, to the point where her friends had begun to avoid her.

Tomorrow Fiyero would make his apologies for missing the opera and standing up his business colleague. Tonight he would not lose Elphaba. As she hurried through the streets, checking over her shoulder more than once, he thought: If you *were* trying to lose someone, if you *did* think someone was on your trail, this is the time of day to do it—not because of shadows, but because of light. Elphaba kept turning corners into the summer sun that, setting, was bowling blinding shafts of light along side streets, through arcades, over the walls of gardens.

But he had had many years of practice at stalking animals under similar conditions—nowhere in Oz was the sun as much an adversary as in the Thousand Year Grasslands. He knew to squint his eyes and follow the persistence of motion, and forget about identifying by shape. He also knew how to duck sideways without tipping over or losing his balance, how to crouch suddenly, how to look for other clues that the prey had begun to move again—the startled birds, the change in sound, the disrupted wind. She could not lose him, and she could not know he was on her trail.

So he wound halfway across the city, from the elegant city centre to the low-rent warehouse district, in whose shadowy doorways the destitute made their malodorous homes. Within spitting distance of an army barracks, Elphaba stopped before a boarded-up corn exchange, ferreted a key from some inner pocket, and opened the door.

He called from a short distance, in an ordinary voice—"Fabala!" Even in the act of turning she caught herself and tried to rearrange her expression. But it was too late. She had shown that she recognized him, and she realized it. His foot was blocking the way before she could slam the heavy door shut.

"Are you in trouble?" he asked.

"Leave me alone," she said, "please. *Please.*"

"You're in trouble, let me in."

"*You're* trouble. Stay out." Pure Elphaba. His last doubts fled. He cracked the door open with his shoulder.

"You're making me into a monster," he said, grunting with the effort—she was strong. "I'm not going to rob you or rape you. I just—won't—be ignored like that. Why?"

She gave up then, and he fell stupidly against the unplastered brick wall of the stairwell, like a pratfalling twit in a vaudeville hour. "I remembered you as full of delicacy and grace," she said. "Did you catch something by accident, or did you study awkwardness?"

"Come on," he said, "you force someone to behave like a clumping boor, you give them no choice. Don't be so surprised. I can still manage grace. I can do delicacy. Half a minute."

"Shiz got to you," she said, eyebrows up, but mockingly; she wasn't really surprised. "Listen to those graduate school affectations. Where's the native boy reeking that appealing naiveté like a well-chosen musk?"

"You're looking well too," he said, a bit hurt. "Do you live in this stairwell or are we going someplace even a little bit homey?"

She cursed and mounted the stairs; they were covered with mouse turds and scraps of packing straw. A soupy evening light seeped in the grimy gray glass windows. At a bend in the stairs a white cat was waiting, haughty and disaffected like all its kin. "Malky, Malky, miaow miaow," said Elphaba as she passed it, and it deigned to follow her up to the pointy arched doorway at the top of the stairs.

"Your familiar?" said Fiyero.

"Oh, that's rich," said Elphaba. "Well, I'd as soon be thought a witch as anything else. Why not. Here Malky, some milk."

The room was large and seemed only casually arranged for dwelling. Originally a storeroom, it had barricaded double doors that could be swung outward, to receive or dispense sacks of grain hauled up by a winch from the street. The only natural light fell in through a couple of cracked panes of glass in a skylight open four or five inches. Pigeon feathers and white-and-bloody flux on the floor below. Eight or ten crates in a circle, as if for sitting. A bedroll. Clothes folded on a trunk. Some odd feathers, bits of bones, strung teeth, and a wizened dodo claw, brown and twisted like beef jerky: These were hung on nails pounded into the wall, and arranged for art or for a spell. A sallowwood table—a nice piece of furniture, that!—whose three arching legs tapered down into elegantly carved doe's hooves. A few tin plates, red with white speckles, some food wrapped in cloth and cord. A pile of books at the bedside. A cat toy tied to a string. Most effectively, and gruesomely, the skull of an elephant hung on a rafter, and a bouquet of dried creamy pink roses emerged from the central hole in the hull of its cranium—like the exploding brains of a dying animal, he couldn't help thinking, remembering Elphaba's youthful concerns. Or maybe an homage to the putative magical talents of elephants?

Below it hung a crude glass oval, scratched and chipped, used as a looking glass, perhaps, though its reflective qualities appeared unreliable.

"So this is home," said Fiyero as Elphaba brought out some food for the cat and ignored Fiyero some more.

"Ask me no questions and I'll spell you no lies," she said.

"May I sit down?"

"That's a question"—but she was grinning—"oh, well then, sit for ten minutes and tell me about yourself. How did you of all people turn into a sophisticate?"

"Appearances are deceiving," he said. "I can afford the garb and affect the language, but I'm still an Arjiki tribal boy underneath."

"What is your life like?"

"Is there something to drink? Not alcohol—I'm just thirsty."

"I don't have running water. I don't use it. There's some questionable milk—at least Malky will still drink it—or perhaps there's a bottle of ale up there on the shelf—help yourself."

She took a little ale in a pipkin, left the rest for him.

He told her the barest outline of things. His wife, Sarima, the childhood bride grown up and grown fecund—their three children. The old Office of Public Works waterworks headquarters at Kiamo Ko, which by ambush and occupation his father had converted to a chieftain's seat and a tribal stronghold back in the time of the Ozma Regent. The dizzying schizoid life of moving every year from the Thousand Year Grasslands in the spring and summer, where the clan hunted and feasted, to a more settled autumn and winter at Kiamo Ko. "An Arjiki prince has business interests here in the Emerald City?" said Elphaba. "If it were banking you'd be in Shiz. The business of *this* city is military, my old friend. What are you up to?"

"You've heard enough from me," he said. "I can play coy and deceptive too, even if it's all pretend and no dark secrets to speak of." He guessed the quiet business of trade agreements would not impress his old friend; he was embarrassed his affairs weren't more audacious or thrilling. "But I've gone on. What of you, Elphie?"

She wouldn't say anything for a few minutes. She unrolled some dried sausage and some graying bread, and found a couple of oranges and a lemon, and put them unceremoniously on the table. In the mothy atmosphere she looked more like a shadow than a person; her green skin seemed oddly soft, like spring leaves at their tenderest, and beaten, like copper. He had an unprecedented urge to grab her wrist and make her stop moving about—if not to make her talk, at least to keep her still, so he could look at her.

"Eat this stuff," she said at last. "I'm not hungry. You eat it, go on."

"Tell me something," he begged. "You left us at Shiz—you disappeared like the morning fog. Why, where to, and what then?"

"How poetic you are," she said. "I've a notion that poetry is the highest form of self-deception."

"Don't change the subject."

But she was agitated. Her fingers twitched; she called for the cat, and then irritated it and sent it flying off her lap. Finally she said, "Oh well, this much then. But you're *never* to come here again. I don't want to have to find a new place, this is too good for me. Do you promise?"

"I will agree to consider promising, that's all. How can I promise any more than that? I don't know a thing yet."

She said, hurriedly, "Well, I was fed up with Shiz. The death of Doctor Dillamond vexed me, and everybody grieved and nobody cared. Not really. It wasn't the right place for me anyway, all those silly girls. Although I liked Glinda well enough. How is she anyway?"

"I'm not in touch. I keep expecting to run into her at some Palace reception or other. I hear through the grapevine that she married a Paltos baronet."

Elphaba looked annoyed and her back stiffened. "Only a baronet? Not a baron or a viscount at least? What a disappointment. Her early promise was never to pan out, then." Meant as a joke, her remark was stiff and unfunny. "Is she a mother?"

"I don't know. I'm asking the questions now, remember?"

"Yes, but Palace receptions?" she said. "Are you in cahoots with Our Glorious Wizard?"

"I hear he's mostly gone reclusive. I've never met him," Fiyero said. "He shows up at the opera and listens behind a portable screen. At his own formal dinners he dines apart, in an adjoining chamber behind a carved marble grill. I've seen a profile of a stately man walking along a promenade. If that's even the Wizard, that's all I've met of him. But you, you: *you*. Why did you cut us all off?"

"I loved you too much to keep in touch."

"What does *that* mean?"

"Don't *ask* me," she said, thrashing a bit, her arms like oars rowing in the blue summer evening lightlessness.

"Yes, I am asking. Have you lived here ever since? For five years? Do you study? Do you work?" He rubbed his bare forearms as he tried to guess about her: What *would* she be up to? "Are you associated with the Animal Relief League, or one of those defiant little humanitarian organizations?"

"I never use the words *humanist* or *humanitarian*, as it seems to me that to be human is to be capable of the most heinous crimes in nature."

"You're evading again."

"That's my job," she said. "There, that's a clue for you, dear Fiyero."

"Amplify."

"I went underground," she said softly, "and I am still underground. You're the first one to crack my anonymity since I said good-bye to Glinda five years ago. So you now know why I can't say any more, or why you can't see me again. For all I know you will turn me in to the Gale Force."

"Hah! Those martinets! You think very little of me if you think I—"

"How do I know, how *could* I know?" She twisted her fingers together, a puzzle of green sticks. "They march in those boots all over the poor and the weak. They terrify households at three in the morning and drag away dissenters—and break up printing presses with their axes—and hold mock trials for treason at midnight and executions at dawn. They rake over every quarter of this beautiful, false city. They harvest a crop of victims on a monthly basis. It's government by terror. They could be massing on the street right now. Never having yet followed me, they may have followed you."

"You're not as hard to follow as you think," he told her. "You're good but not that good. I could teach you a few things."

"I bet you could," she said, "but you won't, for we won't meet again. It's too dangerous, for you as well as for me. That's what I mean when I say I loved you all too much to keep in touch. Do you think the

Gale Force is above torturing friends and family to get at sensitive information? You've got a wife and children, and I'm merely an old college
friend you ran into once. Clever you to have followed me. Never again, do
you hear? I *will* move if I find you're trailing me. I can pick up right now,
and be away in thirty seconds. It's my training."

"Don't do this to me," he said.

"We're old friends," she said, "but we're not even especially good
friends. Don't turn this into a sentimental rendezvous. It's nice to see you
but I don't ever want to see you again. Take care of yourself and beware
high connections with bastards, because when the revolution comes
there won't be mercy for toadying ass-lickers."

"At what—twenty three years old?—you're playing the Lady
Rebel?" he said. "It's not becoming."

"It's unbecoming," she agreed. "A perfect word for my new life.
Unbecoming. I who have always been unbecoming am becoming un.
Though I point out you are the same age as I, and prancing about as a
prince. But have you eaten enough? We have to say good-bye now."

"We don't," he said, firmly. He wanted to take her hands in his—
he didn't remember that he'd ever touched her before. He corrected himself—he *knew* he never had.

It was almost as if she could read his mind. "You know who you
are," she said, "but you don't know who I am. You can't—I mean you
can't and you *can't*—it's not allowed, for one, and you're not capable for
the other. Godspeed, if they use that phrase in the Vinkus—if it's not a
curse. Godspeed, Fiyero."

She handed him his opera cape, and held out her hand to shake his.
He grabbed her hand, and looked up into her face, which just for a second had fallen open. What he saw there made him chill and hot flash, in
dizzying simultaneity, with the shape and scale of its need.

"What do you hear of Boq?" she asked, the next time they met.

"You just won't answer me anything about yourself, will you?" he
said. He was lounging with his feet up on her table. "Why did you finally
agree to let me come back if you keep yourself locked up like a prisoner?"

"I rather liked Boq, that's all." She grinned. "I let you come back so
I could pump you for news of him, and of the others."

He told her what he knew. Boq had married Miss Milla, of all surprising turns. She had been dragged out to Nest Hardings, and she hated
it. She kept trying suicide. "His letters sent at Lurlinemas every year are
hysterical; they annotate her failed attempts at killing herself like a sort of
annual family report."

"It makes me wonder, in the same circumstances, what *my* mother
must have gone through," said Elphaba. "The privileged childhood in the
big home of the ascendancy, then the rude shock of a hard life out there in
nowhere-land. In Mama's case, from Colwen Grounds to Rush Margins,
then the Quadling lowlands. It's actually a penance of the most severe sort."

"Like mother like daughter," said Fiyero. "Haven't you left a certain
amount of privilege yourself, to live here like a snail? Hidden and private?"

"I remember the first time I saw you," she said, shaking drops of
vinegar over the roots and vegetables she was preparing for a supper. "It
was in that lecture hall of what's-his-name—Doctor . . ."

"Doctor Nikidik," said Fiyero. He blushed.

"You had those beautiful markings on your face—I'd never seen
such before. Did you plan that entrance, to win your way into our
hearts?"

"On my honor, could I have done *anything* else, I would have. I was
both mortified and terrified. Do you know, I thought those enchanted
antlers were going to kill me? And it was prancing Crope and flibberty
Tibbett who saved me."

"Crope and Tibbett! Tibbett and Crope! I'd forgotten all about *them*.
How are they?"

"Tibbett was never the same after that escapade at the Philosophy
Club. Crope, I think, entered an arts auction house, and still flits around
with the theatrical set. I see him from time to time at occasions. We don't
speak."

"My, you're disapproving!" She laughed. "Of course being as pruri-
ent as the next creature I always wondered what the Philosophy Club had
turned out to be like. You know, in another life I'd like to see them all
again. And Glinda, dear Glinda. And even nasty Avaric. What of him?"

"Avaric I *do* speak to. He's most of the year installed in the
Margreavate, but he has a house in Shiz. And when in the Emerald City
we stay at the same club."

"Is he still a smug boor?"

"My, *you're* disapproving now."

"I suppose I am." They ate their dinner. Fiyero waited for her to ask more about his family. But it was their respective families they were keeping from each other, apparently: his Vinkus wife and children, her circle of agitators and insurrectionists.

The next time he came, he thought, he must wear a shirt open at the neck, so she could see that the pattern of blue diamonds on his face continued unbroken down his chest . . . Since she seemed to like that.

"Surely you don't spend the entire autumn season in the Emerald City?" she asked one evening when the cold was drawing in.

"I've send word to Sarima that business is keeping me here indefinitely. She doesn't care. How could she care? Plucked out of a filthy caravansary and married as a small child to an Arjiki prince? Her family wasn't stupid. She's got food, servants, and the solid stone walls of Kiamo Ko for defense against the other tribes. She's going a little fat after her third child. She doesn't really notice whether I'm home or not—well, she has five sisters, and they all moved in. I married a harem."

"No!" Elphaba sounded intrigued and a little embarrassed at the idea.

"You're right, no, not really. Sarima has proposed once or twice that her younger sisters could and would happily occupy my energies at nighttime. Once you pass over the Great Kells, the taboo against such an exercise isn't as strong as it seems to be in the rest of Oz, so stop looking so shocked."

"I can't help it. Did you do it?"

"Did I 'do it'?" He was teasing her.

"Did you sleep with your sisters-in-law?"

"No," he said. "Not out of lofty moral standards, or a lack of interest, either. It's just that Sarima is a shrewd wife, and everything in marriage is a campaign. I would have been in her thrall even more than I am."

"Such a bad thing?"

"You're not married, you don't know: Yes, a bad thing."

"I am married," she said, "just not to a man."

He raised his eyebrows. She put her hands to her face. He'd never seen her look like that—her words had shocked herself. She had to turn her head away for an instant, clear her throat, blow her nose. "Oh damn, *tears*, they burn like fire," she cried, suddenly in a fury, and ran for an old blanket to dab her eyes before the salty wetness could run down her cheeks.

She stood bent over like an old woman, one arm on the counter, the blanket falling from her face to the floor. "Elphie, Elphie," he said, horrified, and lurched after her, and put his arms around her. The blanket hung between them, chin to ankles, but seemed about to burst into flame itself, or roses, or a fountain of champagne and incense. Odd how the richest images bloomed in the mind when the body itself was most alert . . .

"No," she cried, "no, no, I'm not a harem, I'm not a woman, I'm not a person, no." But her arms wheeled of their own accord, like windmill sails, like those magicked antlers, not to kill him, but to pin him with love, to mount him against the wall.

Malky, with a rare display of discretion, climbed to the windowsill and looked away from them.

They conducted their love affair in the room above the abandoned corn exchange as the autumn weather came lop-leggedly in from the east: now a warm day, now a sunny one, now four days of cold winds and thin rain.

There were long days in a row when they couldn't meet. "I have business, I have work, trust me or I shall disappear on you," she said. "I shall write to Glinda and ask her to share the spell on how to go up in a puff of smoke. I am teasing, but I mean it, Fiyero."

Fiyero + Fae he wrote, in the flour that spilled when she rolled out a piecrust. Fae, she had whispered, as if even to keep it from the cat, was her code name. No one in the cell could know one another's real names.

She would not let him see her naked in the light, but since he also was not allowed to visit during the day this was hardly a problem. She waited for him on the appointed evenings, sitting naked under the blanket, reading essays on political theory or moral philosophy. "I don't know that I understand them, I read them as poetry," she once admitted. "I like the sound of the words, but I don't ever really expect my slow, slanted impression of the world to change by what I read."

"Is it changing by how you live?" he asked, turning down the light and slipping out of his clothes.

"You think all this is new to me," she said, sighing. "You think I am such a virgin."

"You didn't bleed the first time," he observed. "So what's to think about?"

"I know what you think," she said. "But how experienced are *you*, Lord Sir Fiyero, Arjiki Prince of Kiamo Ko, Mightiest Stalker of the Thousand Year Grasslands, Chiefest Chieftain in the Great Kells?"

"I am putty in your hands," he said, truthfully. "I married a child bride and to preserve my power I haven't been unfaithful. Until now. You are not like her," he said. "You don't feel like her, it doesn't feel the same. You're more secret."

"I don't exist," she said, "so you're still not being unfaithful, either."

"Let's not be unfaithful right now then," he said, "I can't wait," running his hands along her ribs, down the tight plane of her stomach. She always brought his hands to her thin, expressive breasts; she would not be touched below the waist by hands. They moved together, blue diamonds on a green field.

He didn't have enough to do during the days. Being the chieftain of the Arjiki people, he knew it was in their political interest to be tied ineluctably to the commercial hub of the Emerald City. Yet Arjiki business concerns only required Fiyero to show his face at social engagements, in board meetings and financial parlors. The rest of the time he wandered about, seeking frescoes of Saint Glinda and other saints. Elphaba-Fabala-Elphie-Fae would never tell him what she had been doing in the chapel of Saint Glinda attached to the mauntery in Saint Glinda's Square.

One day he looked up Avaric and they had lunch. Avaric suggested a girlie show afterward, and Fiyero begged off. Avaric was opinionated, cynical, corrupt, and as good-looking as ever. There wasn't much gossip to bring back to Elphaba.

The wind tore the leaves from the trees. The Gale Force continued to frog-march Animals and collaborators out of town. Interest rates in the Gillikin banks went soaring up—good for investors, bad for those who had adjustable rate loans. Foreclosures on a lot of valuable city-centre properties. Too early, businesses began stringing the green and gold lights of Lurlinemas, trying to woo cautious and depressed citizens into the shops.

More than anything else he wanted to walk the streets of the Emerald City with Elphaba—there was no more beautiful place to be in love, especially at dusk as the shop lights went on, golden against the blue-purple evening sky. He had never been in love before, he now saw. It humbled him. It scared him. He couldn't bear it when their forced absence went four or five days.

"Kisses to Irji, Manek, and Nor," he wrote on the bottom of his weekly letter to Sarima, who couldn't write back because, among other things, she had never learned either alphabet. Somehow her silence seemed a tacit approval of this vow-shattering interlude. He didn't write *kisses* to her, too. He hoped the chocolates would do.

He rolled over, tugging the blanket with him; she tugged it back. The air in the room was so cold it seemed clammy. Malky endured their thrashing legs in order to stay near them, to receive warmth, and to give whatever passes for affection in cats.

"My darling Fae," said Fiyero. "You probably know this, and I'm not about to become a co-conspirator at whatever it is you're working for—reducing library fines or revoking the need for cat collars or whatever. But I do keep my ears open. The Quadlings are under the thumb of the marching militia again. At least that's what they're saying in the lounge of the club, over newspapers and pipes. Apparently an army division has gone down into Quadling Country as far as Qhoyre, on some sort of a slash-and-burn mission. Your father, your brother, and Nessarose—are they still there?"

Elphaba didn't answer for a while. She seemed to be working out not only what she wanted to say, but perhaps even what she could remember. Her expression was of puzzlement, even testiness. She said, "We lived in Qhoyre for a time, when I was about ten. It's a funny little low town, built on boggy ground. Half the streets are canals. The roofs are low, the windows are grilled or louvred to provide privacy and ventilation, the air is steamy and the flora excessive—huge roundels of palmy leaf, almost like shallow quilted pillows, making a sound as they beat against each other in the wind—tirrr tirrr, tirrr tirrr."

"I don't know that there's much of Qhoyre left," said Fiyero carefully. "If the gossip I picked up is accurate."

"No, Papa isn't there now, thank—thank whoever, whatever, thank nothing," continued Elphaba. "Unless things have changed. The good people of Qhoyre weren't very responsive to missionary efforts. They'd invite Papa and me in, serve us little damp cakelets and lukewarm red mint tea. We'd all sit on low, mildewing cushions, scaring geckos and spiders into the deeper shadows. Papa would drone on about the generous nature of the Unnamed God, doing his basic xenophiliac slant. He pointed to me as proof. I would grin with horrible sweetness and sing a hymn—the only music Papa approved of. I was miserably shy and ashamed of my color, but Papa had convinced me of the value of this work. Invariably the gentle citizens of Qhoyre would capitulate out of hospitality. They'd allow themselves to be led in prayers to the Unnamed God, but you couldn't say their hearts were in it. I think I sensed a great deal more—more *dishearteningly* than Papa did—how ineffectual we really were."

"So where are they now? Papa, Nessarose, and the boy—your brother, what's his name?"

"Shell, that's his name. Well, Papa felt his work was farther south in Quadling Country, in the real outback. We had a series of small cramped homes around Ovvels–the Hovels in Ovvels, we called them—that dreary, beastly countryside, full of a bloody beauty."

At his questioning expression she continued. "I mean, fifteen, twenty years ago, Fiyero, the Emerald City speculators discovered the ruby deposits there. First under the Ozma Regent, then after the coup, under the Wizard: same ugly business practices. Though under the Ozma Regent the exploitation did not require murder and brutality. Using elephants, the engineers hauled in gravel, they dammed up springs, they perfected a complicated system of strip mining under three feet of brackish groundwater. Papa thought this disarray in their little moist society was a situation ready-made for mission work. And he was right. The Quadlings struggled against the Wizard with ill-argued proclamations, they resorted to totems, but their only military weapons were slingshots. So they rallied around my father. He converted them, they went into the struggle with the zeal of the newly chastised. They were dispossessed and disappeared. All with the benefit of unionist grace."

"My, you're bitter."

"I was a *tool*. My dear father used me—and Nessarose less so, because of her trouble moving about—he *used* me as an object lesson. Looking as I did, even singing as I can—they trusted him partly as a response to the freakiness of me. If the Unnamed God could love *me*, how much more responsible it'd be to the unadulterated *them*."

"So, my dear, you don't care where he is, or what happens to him now?"

"How can you *say* that?" She sat up, steaming. "I love the mad old tunnel-visioned bastard. He really believed in what he preached. He even thought that a Quadling corpse found floating faceup in a brackwater pond—provided it had a tattoo of conversion on it somewhere—was better off than a survivor. He felt he'd written a single ticket to the Other Land assembly of the Unnamed God. I think he considered it work well done."

"And you don't?" Fiyero had a fairly anemic spiritual life; he felt unqualified to voice an opinion about her father's vocation.

"Maybe it *was* work well done," she said sadly. "How do I know? But not for me. Settlement by settlement we reaped converts. Settlement by settlement the civil engineering corps came in, to detonate the village life. There was no *outcry* throughout Oz proper. Nobody was listening. Who cared about the Quadlings?"

"But what brought him there in the first place?"

"He and Mama had had a friend, a Quadling, who died in my family home—a Quadling itinerant, a glassblower." Elphaba frowned and closed her eyes, and would say no more. Fiyero kissed her fingernails. He kissed the V between her thumb and forefinger, he sucked on it as if it were a lemon rind. She slipped backward to allow him greater purchase.

A while later he said, "But Elphie-Fabala-Fae—are you really not worried about your father and Nessarose, and little himmy-who?"

"My father chases hopeless causes. It gives his failure at life some legitimacy. For a while he proclaimed himself a prophet of the return of the last, lost tadpole of the Ozma line. *That's* over now. And my brother Shell—he is probably fifteen by now. Look Fiyero, how can I be worried about them and be worried about the campaign of the season too? I can't course around Oz—on that broomstick there, like a storybook witch!—

I've chosen to go underground so that I *can't* worry. Besides, I know what will happen to Nessarose at least. Sooner or later."

"What?"

"When my great-grandfather finally pops off, she'll be the next Eminent Thropp."

"You're in line, I thought. Aren't you older?"

"I'm gone, dearie, I'm magicked away in a puff of smoke. Forget it. And you know, that'll be good for Nessarose. She'll be a sort of local queen out there in Nest Hardings."

"She apparently did a course in sorcery, did you know? In Shiz?"

"No, I didn't. Well, bully for her. If she ever comes down off that plinth—the one that has words written on it along the edges in gold, reading MOST SUPERIOR IN MORAL RECTITUDE—if she ever allows herself to be the bitch she really is, she'll be the Bitch of the East. Nanny and the devoted staff at Colwen Grounds will prop her up."

"I thought you were fond of her!"

"Don't you know affection when you see it?" scoffed Elphaba. "I love Nessie. She's a pain in the neck, she's intolerably righteous, she's a nasty piece of work. I'm *devoted* to her."

"She'll be the Eminent Thropp."

"Better she than I," said Elphaba dryly. "For one thing, she has great taste in shoes."

One evening through the skylight the full moon fell heavily on Elphaba sleeping. Fiyero had awakened and gone to take a leak into the chamber pot. Malky was stalking mice on the stairs. Coming back, Fiyero looked at the form of his lover, more pearly than green tonight. He had brought her a traditional Vinkus fringed silk scarf—roses on a black background—and he had tied it around her waist, and from then on it was a costume for lovemaking. Tonight in sleeping she had nudged it up, and he admired the curve of her flank, the tender fragility of her knee, the bony ankle. There was a smell of perfume still in the air, and the resiny, animal smell, and the smell of the mystical sea, and the sweet cloaking smell of hair all riled up by sex. He sat by the side of the bed and looked at her. Her pubic hair grew, almost more purple than black, in small spangled curls, a different pattern than Sarima's. There was an odd shadow near the groin—for a sleepy moment he wondered if some of his blue diamonds had, in the heat of sex, been steamed onto her own skin—or was it a scar?

But she woke up just then, and in the moonlight covered herself with a blanket. She smiled at him drowsily and called him "Yero, my hero," and that melted his heart.

She could get so angry, though!

"I wouldn't be surprised if the pork roll you're devouring, in such perfect mindless affluence, is cut from a Pig," she snapped at him once.

"Just because you've already eaten, you don't need to ruin my appetite," he protested mildly. Free-living Animals were not much in evidence in his home territory, and the few sentient creatures he'd known at Shiz had, except at the Philosophy Club that night, made little impression. The plight of the Animals had not much touched him.

"This is why you shouldn't fall in love, it blinds you. Love is wicked distraction."

"Now you have put me off my lunch." He fed the rest of the pork roll to Malky. "What in the world do you know about wickedness? You're a bit player in this network of renegades, aren't you? You're a novice."

"I know this: The wickedness of men is that their power breeds stupidity and blindness," she said.

"And of women?"

"Women are weaker, but their weakness is full of cunning and an equally rigid moral certainty. Since their arena is smaller, their capacity for real damage is less alarming. Though being more intimate they are the more treacherous."

"And my capacity for evil?" said Fiyero, feeling implicated and uncomfortable. "And yours?"

"Fiyero's capacity for evil is in believing too strenuously in a capacity for good."

"And yours?"

"Mine is in thinking in epigrams."

"You let yourself off lightly," he said, suddenly a little annoyed. "Is that what you're engaged by your secret network to do? Generate witty epigrams?"

"Oh, there's big doings afoot," she said, uncharacteristically. "I won't be at the center of it, but I'll be on the fringes helping out, believe me."

"What are you talking about? A coup?"

"Never you mind, and you'll stay blameless. Just as you want to be." This was nastiness on her part.

"An assassination? And so what if you do kill some General Butcher? What does that make you? A saint? A saint of the revolution? Or a martyr if you're killed in the campaign?"

She wouldn't answer. She shook her narrow head in irritation, then flung the rosy shawl across the room as if it infuriated her.

"What if some innocent bystander is killed as you aim for General Pig Butcher?"

"I don't know or care much about martyrs," she said. "All that smacks of a higher plan, a cosmology—something I don't believe in. If we can't comprehend the plan at hand, how could a higher plan make any more sense? But were I to believe in martyrdom, I suppose I'd say you can only be a martyr if you know what you are dying for, and *choose* it."

"Ah, so then there *are* innocent victims in this trade. Those who don't choose to die but are in the line of fire."

"There are . . . there will be . . . accidents, I guess."

"Can there be grief, regret, in your exalted circle? Is there any such thing as a mistake? Is there a concept of tragedy?"

"Fiyero, you disaffected fool, the tragedy is *all around us*. Worrying about anything smaller is a distraction. Any casualty of the struggle is their fault, not ours. We don't embrace violence but we don't deny its existence—how can we deny it when its effects are all around us? That kind of denial is a sin, if anything is—"

"Ah—now I've heard the word I never expected to hear you say."

"Denial? Sin?"

"No. *We*."

"I don't know why—"

"The lone dissenter at Crage Hall turns institutional? A company gal? A team player? Our former Miss Queen of Solitaire?"

"You misunderstand. There is a campaign but no agents, there is a game but no players. I have no *colleagues*. I have no *self*. I never did, in fact, but that's beside the point. I am just a muscular twitch in the larger organism."

"Hah! You the *most* individual, the *most* separate, the *most* real . . ."

"Like everyone else you refer to my looks. And you make fun of them."

"I *adore* your looks and I acknowledge them. Fae!"

They parted that day without speaking, and he spent the evening at the betting parlor, losing money.

The next time he saw her, he brought three green candles and three gold candles and decorated her flat for Lurlinemas. "I don't believe in religious feast days," she said, but relented to admit, "they are pretty, though."

"You have no soul," he teased her.

"You're right," she answered soberly. "I didn't think it showed."

"You're only playing word games now."

"No," she said, "what proof have I of a soul?"

"How can you have a conscience if you don't have a soul?" he asked despite himself—he wanted to keep things light, to get back onto a better footing after their last episode of moral wrestling and estrangement.

"How can a bird feed its young if it has no consciousness of before and after? A conscience, Yero my hero, is only consciousness in another dimension, the dimension of time. What you call conscience I prefer to call instinct. Birds feed their young without understanding why, without weeping about how all that is born must die, sob sob. I do my work with a similar motivation: the movement in the gut toward food, fairness, and safety. I am a pack animal wheeling with the herd, that's all. I'm a forgettable leaf on a tree."

"Since your work is terrorism, that's the most extreme argument for crime I've ever heard. You're eschewing all personal responsibility. It's as bad as those who sacrifice their personal will into the gloomy morasses of the unknowable will of some unnameable god. If you suppress the idea of personhood then you suppress the notion of individual culpability."

"What is worse, Fiyero? Suppressing the *idea* of personhood or suppressing, through torture and incarceration and starvation, *real living* persons? Look: Would you worry about saving one precious sentimental portrait in a museum of fine arts when the city around you is on fire and real people are burning to death? Keep some proportion in all this!"

"But even some innocent bystander—say an annoying society dame—is a real *person*, not a portrait. Your metaphor is distracting and belittling, it's a blind excuse for crime."

"A society dame has *chosen* to parade herself as a living portrait. She must be treated as such. It's her due. That denial of it, that's *your* evil, to go back to the other day. I say you save the innocent bystander if you can, even if she's a society dame, or he's a captain of industry thriving mightily on all these repressive moves—but not, not, *not* at the expense of other, realer people. And if you can't save them, you can't. Everything costs."

"I don't believe in this concept of 'real' or 'realer' people."

"You don't?" She smiled, not nicely. "When I do disappear again, dearie, I'll surely be less real than I am now." She made to simulate sex against him; he turned his head, surprised at the vigor of his aversion.

Later that night, when they had made up, she suffered a racking paroxysm and painful sweats. She would not let him touch her. "You should go away, I'm not worthy of you," she moaned, and some time later, when she was calmer, she murmured before sleeping again, "I love you so much, Fiyero, you just don't understand: Being born with a talent or an inclination for goodness *is the aberration.*"

She was right. He didn't understand. He wiped her brow with a dry towel and kept close to her. There was frost on the skylight, and they slept beneath their winter coats to keep warm.

One brisk afternoon he sent off a propitiatory package of bright wooden toys for the children and a jeweled torque for Sarima. The pack train was going around the Great Kells via the northern route. It wouldn't deliver Lurlinemas presents to Kiamo Ko until well into the spring, but he could pretend to have sent them earlier. If the snows held off, he would be home by then, restless and chafing in the tall narrow rooms of the mountain stronghold, but maybe he would get the credit for thoughtfulness. And perhaps deserved, why not? To be sure, Sarima would be in her winter doldrums (as distinct from her spring moods, her summer ennui, and her congenital autumn condition). A torque eventually would cheer her up, at least a little.

He stopped for a coffee in a café in a neighborhood just enough off the beaten track to be both bohemian and pricey. The management apologized: The winter garden, usually heated with braziers and brazen with expensive forced flowers, had been the site of an explosion the night before. "The neighborhood is troubled; who'd have thought it?" said the manager, touching Fiyero on the elbow. "Our Glorious Wizard was to have eradicated civil unrest: wasn't that the whole point of curfews and containment laws?"

Fiyero was not inclined to comment, and the manager took his silence for agreement. "I've moved a few tables into my private parlor up the stairs, if you don't mind roughing it amidst my family memorabilia," he said, leading the way. "Finding good Munchkinlander help to repair the damage is getting harder, too. The Munchkinlander tiktok touch, there's nothing like it. But a lot of our friends in the service sector have gone back to their eastern farms. Scared of violence against them—well, so many of them are so *small*, don't you think they seem to provoke it?—they're all cowards." He interrupted himself to say, "I can tell you have no Munchkinlander relatives or I wouldn't comment this way."

"My wife is from Nest Hardings," said Fiyero, lying unconvincingly, but the point was made.

"I recommend the cherry chocolate frappe today, fresh and delicious," said the manager, retreating into repentant formality, and pulling out a chair at a table near high old windows. Fiyero sat and looked out. One fretted shutter had warped and couldn't fold back against the outer wall as designed, but there was still enough of a view. Rooflines, ornamental chimney pots, the odd high window box stuffed with dark winter pansies, and pigeons swooping and scissoring like lords of the sky.

The manager was of that peculiar stock; after so many generations in the Emerald City, it seemed a separate ethnic strand. The paintings of his family showed the bright gimlet hazel eyes, and refined receding hairlines on men and women alike (and plucked into the scalps of children, too, in the fashion of the Emerald City upwardly yearning middle class). At the sight of simpering boys in pink satin with frizzy-headed lapdogs, and girlettes in womanish dark rouge and plunging necklines (revealing their innocent lack of breasts), Fiyero felt the sudden longing, again, for his own cold and distant children. Though bruised by their particular family life—and who wasn't?—in his memory Irji, Manek, and Nor managed more integrity than these hothouse scions of a family on the make.

But that was cruel, and he was responding to artistic convention, not to the actual children. He turned his gaze out the window when the order came, to avoid hideous art, to avoid the other people in the salon.

Having coffee in the winter garden below usually provided a view of vine-covered brick walls, shrubs, and the occasional marble statue of some improbably beautiful and vulnerably naked stripling. However, from a flight up, one could see over the wall, into an interior mews area. One part was a stables, another a neighborhood toilet, apparently; and just within the range of his vision was the wall broken by the explosion. Some sort of twisted, thorny wire netting had been erected across the opening, which led into a schoolyard.

As he watched, one of the doors of the adjacent school was pushed open, and a small crowd emerged, shaking and stretching into the sunlight. There seemed to be—Fiyero peered—a couple of elderly Quadling women and some adolescent male Quadlings, straplings with early mustaches making a bluish-colored shadow against their fine rose-rust skin. Five, six, seven Quadlings—and a couple of stout men who might have been part Gillikinese, it was hard to tell—and a family of bears. No— Bears. Smallish Red Bears, a mother and father and a toddler.

The little Bear went unerringly to some balls and hoops under the stairs. The Quadlings made a circle and began to sing and dance. The old ones, with arthritic steps, joined their hands with the teenagers and moved in a widdershins pattern, in and out, as if making a clock face that reversed the clockwise movement of time. The stocky Gillikinese men shared a cigarette and gazed out the wiry barrier across the break in the wall. The Red Bears were more dispirited. The male sat on the wooden edge of a sandlot, rubbing his eyes and combing the fur below his chin. The female moved back and forth, kicking at the ball just often enough to keep the cub occupied, then stroking the bowed head of her mate.

Fiyero sipped his drink and inched forward. If there were, what, twelve prisoners, and only a wire fence between them and freedom, why didn't they rush it? Why were they separated into their racial and species groups?

After ten minutes the doors opened again and a Gale Forcer came out, trim and—yes, Fiyero had to admit it at last—terrifying. Terrifying in the brick red uniform with the green boots, and the emerald cross that quartered the breast of the shirt, one vertical strap from groin to high starched collar, the other strap from armpit to armpit across the pectorals. He was only a youth whose curly hair was so blond as to look nearly white in the winter sun. He stood with legs apart on the step of the school's verandah.

Though Fiyero couldn't hear a thing through the closed window, the soldier apparently gave a command. The Bears stiffened and the cub began to wail and clutch the ball to itself. The Gillikinese men came and stood quiescently ready. The Quadlings ignored the order and kept on with their dance. They swung their hips, and they held their arms at shoulder height, moving their hands in a semaphoric message, though what it meant Fiyero could only guess. He had never seen a Quadling before.

The Gale Forcer raised his voice. He had a truncheon in a thong loop at his waist. The cub hid behind the father, and the mother could be seen to growl.

Work together, Fiyero found himself thinking, hardly aware he could have such a thought. Work as a team—there are twelve of you and only one of him. Is it your differences from one another that keep you docile? Or are there relatives inside who will be tortured if you make a break for freedom?

It was all speculation; Fiyero couldn't tell the dynamics of the situation, but he was riveted. He realized his hand was open, palm up against the glass of the window. Below, because the Bears had not stood to join the lineup, the soldier raised his cudgel and it came down on the skull of the cub. Fiyero's body jerked, he spilled his drink and the cup broke, porcelain shards on the buttery herringbone-laid oak flooring.

The manager appeared from behind a green baize door and tutted, and twitched the drapes closed, but not before Fiyero had seen one last thing. Recoiling as if he had never hunted and killed in the Thousand Year Grasslands, he averted his eyes and they wheeled upward, where he glimpsed the pale blond coins of faces—two or three dozen schoolchildren in the upper windows of the school, staring down with fascination and open mouths at the scene in their playing field.

"They have no *concern* for neighbors who have a business to run, bills to pay, and loved ones to feed," snapped the manager. "You don't need to see those antics as you enjoy your coffee, sir."

"The disruption in your winter garden," said Fiyero. "That was some-one trying to break down your wall into that yard, and get them out alive."

"Don't even *suggest* it," shot the manager in a low voice. "There are more ears in this room than yours and mine. How do I know who was up to what, or why? I'm a private citizen and I mind my own business."

Fiyero didn't take a replacement cup of cherry chocolate. There were racking cries from the mother Bear, and then a silence in the world outside the heavy damask drapes. Was it an accident I saw that, Fiyero wondered, looking at the manager with new eyes. Or is it just that the world unwraps itself to you, again and again, as soon as you are ready to see it anew?

He wanted to tell Elphie what he had seen, but he held back for reasons he couldn't name. In some way, in the balance of their affections, he sensed she needed an identity separate from his. Were he to become a convert to her cause, she might drift away. He did not dare to risk it. But the vision of the battered Bear cub haunted him. He held Elphie the tighter, trying to communicate a deeper passion without speaking it.

He noticed, too, that when she was agitated she was the more lib-eral in her lovemaking. He began to be able to tell when she was going to say "Not till next week." She seemed more abandoned, more salacious, perhaps as a cleansing exercise before disappearing for a few days. One morning, as he was stealing some of the cat's milk for his coffee, she rubbed some oil on her skin, wincing with sensitivity, and said over her shoulder of soft green marble, "A fortnight, my dear. My pet, as my father used to say. I need a fortnight of privacy now."

He had a sudden pang, a premonition, that she was going to leave him. It was a way for her to get two weeks' head start. "No!" he said. "That's not on, Fae-Fae. It's *not* all right, it's too long."

"We need it." She expanded: "Not you and I, I mean the other *we*. Obviously I can't tell you what we're about, but the last plans for the autumn campaign are falling into place. There's going to be an episode— I can't say more—and I must be available to the network at all times."

"A coup?" he said. "An assassination? A bomb? A kidnapping? What? Just the nature of it, not the specifics, *what?*"

"Not only can I not tell you," she said, "I don't even know. I'll be told only my small part, and I'll do it. I only know it's a complicated maneuver with a lot of interlocking pieces."

"Are you the dart?" he said. "Are you the knife? The fuse?"

She said (though he wasn't convinced): "My dearie, my poppet, I am too green to walk into a public place and do something bad. It's all too expected. Security guards watch me like owls on a mouse. My very presence provokes alarm and heightened vigilance. No, no, the part I'll play will be a handmaiden's part, a little assistance in the shadows."

"Don't do it," he said.

"You're selfish," she said, "and you're a coward. I love you, my sweet, but your protests about this are wrongheaded. You just want to preserve *my* insignificant life, you don't even have a moral feeling about whether I'm doing right or wrong. Not that I want you to, not that I care what you think about it. But I only observe, your objections are of the weakest sort. Now this isn't something to be argued. Two weeks from tonight, come back."

"Will the—the *action*—be completed by then? Who decides?"

"I don't know what it is yet, and I don't even know who decides, so don't ask me."

"Fae—" Suddenly he didn't like her code name anymore. "*Elphaba.* Do you really not know who is pulling the strings that make you move? How do you know you're not being manipulated by the *Wizard?*"

"You are a novice at this, for all your status as a tribal prince!" she said. "Why shouldn't I know if I was being a pawn of the Wizard? I could tell when I was being manipulated by that harridan, Madame Morrible. I learned something about prevarication and straight talking back at Crage Hall. Give me the credit for having spent some *years* at this, Fiyero."

"You can't tell me for sure who is or isn't the boss."

"Papa didn't know the name of his Unnamed God," she said, rising and rubbing oil on her stomach and between her legs, but modestly turning her back to him. "It never is the *who,* is it? It's always the *why.*"

"How do you hear? How do they tell you what to do?"

"Look, you know I can't say."

"I know you *can.*"

She turned. "Oil my breasts, will you."

"I'm not that *stupidly* male, Elphaba."

"Yes you are"—she laughed, but lovingly—"come on."

It was daylight, the wind roared and even shook the floorboards. The cold sky above the glass was a rare pinkish blue. She dropped her shyness like a nightgown, and in the liquid glare of sunlight on old boards she held up her hands—as if, in the terror of the upcoming skir-mish, she had at last understood that she was beautiful. In her way.

The collapse of her reticence frightened him more than anything else.

He took some coconut oil and warmed it between his palms, and slid his hands like leathery velvet animals on her small, responding breasts. The nipples stood, the color flushed. He was already fully dressed, but recklessly he pressed himself against her mildly resisting form. One hand slid down her back; she arched against him, moaning. But perhaps, this time, not from need?

Still his hand moved down onto her buttocks, felt between her cheeks, beyond, felt the place one muscle pulled in crookedly, endear-ingly, felt the very faintest etching of hair beginning its crosshatch shad-ows, its swirl toward vortex. He worked his intelligent hand, reading the signs of her resistance.

"I have four companions," she said suddenly, wrenching away in a motion soft enough not to disengage but to discourage. "Oh heart, I have four comrades; they don't know who our cell leader is, it's all done in the dark, with a masking spell to shadow the voice and distort the features. If I knew more, the Gale Force could catch me and torture it out of me, don't you see?"

"What is your object?" he breathed, kissing her, loosening his trousers again, as if this were the first time, his tongue tracing the twist-ing funnel of her ear.

"Kill the Wizard," she answered, looping her legs around him. "I am not the arrowhead, I am not the dart, I am just the shaft, the quiver—" She cupped more oil in her hand and as they slid and fell into the light, she made him bright and anguished with oil, took him deeper in than ever before.

"Even after all this time, you could be an agent for the Palace," she said later.

"I'm not," he said. "I'm *good*."

⚒   ⚒   ⚒

A little snow fell one week, then some more the next. The feast of Lurlinemas drew nearer. The unionist chapels, having appropriated and transformed the most visible parts of the old pagan beliefs, hung themselves shamelessly in green and gold, set out green candles and golden gongs and greenberry wreaths and gilded fruit. Along Merchant Row, shops outdid themselves (and the churches) in decor, with displays of fashionable clothes, and useless and expensive trinkets. In display windows, papier-mâché figures evoked the good Fairy Queen Lurline in her winged chariot, and her assistant, the minor fairy Preenella, who strewed gift-wrapped delights from her capacious magic basket.

He asked himself, again and again, if he was in love with Elphaba.

He also asked himself why he was so late coming to this question, after two months of a passionate affair; and if he knew what the words even meant; and if it mattered.

He chose more gifts for the kids and for sulky Sarima, that well-fed malcontent, that monster. He missed her a little; his feelings for Elphaba seemed not to vie with those for Sarima, but to complement them. No two women could be more unlike. Elphaba demonstrated the proud independence of Arjiki mountain women that Sarima, married so young, had never developed. And Elphie wasn't just a different (not to say novel) provincial type—she seemed an advance on the gender, she seemed a different *species* sometimes. He caught himself with a mammoth erection just remembering that last time, and he had to hide himself behind some ladies' scarves in a shop until it subsided.

He bought three, four, six scarves for Sarima, who didn't wear scarves. He bought six scarves for Elphaba, who did.

The shop girl, a dull Munchkinlander midget who had to stand on a chair to reach the till, said over his shoulder, "Just in a minute, ma'am." He turned to make room at the counter for the other customer.

"But Master Fiyero!" cried Glinda.

"Miss Glinda," he said, flabbergasted. "What a surprise."

"A dozen scarves," she said. "Look, Crope, look who's here!"

And there was Crope, a little jowly though he couldn't be twenty-five yet, could he?—looking guiltily up from a display of feathery, plumy things.

"We must have tea," said Glinda, "we must. Come now. Pay the nice little lady and off we fly." In her voluminous skirts she rustled like a corps of ballerinas.

He hadn't remembered her quite so giddy; maybe this was married life. He slid a glance at Crope, who was rolling his eyes behind her back.

"Just you put this on Sir Chuffrey's account, and this, and *this*," Glinda said, mounding things on the counter, "and have them sent along to our rooms in the Florinthwaite Club. I'll need them for dining so have someone run over with them right now if you would. How dear. So kind. Ta ta. Boys, come along."

She gripped Fiyero with a pinching hand and steered him away; Crope followed like a lapdog. The Florinthwaite Club was only a street or two over and they could easily have carried the purchases back themselves. Glinda capered and clattered down the grand staircase into the Oak Parlor, making enough noise so that every female resident looked up in a rewarding sort of disapproval.

"Now, you, Crope, *there*, so you can be Mother and pour when we've ordered, and dear Fiyero, you *here*, right next to me, that is if you're not *too* married."

They ordered tea; Glinda got used to him a bit and began to calm down.

"But really, who would have thought it?" she said, picking up a biscuit and putting it down again, about eight times in a row. "We were the great and the good at Shiz, really. Look at you, Fiyero—you're a prince, aren't you? Do we call you Your Highness? I never could. And you're still married to that little child?"

"She's grown up now, and we have a family," Fiyero told her warily. "Three children."

"And she's here. I must meet her."

"No, she's back at our winter home in the Great Kells."

"Then you're having an affair," said Glinda, "because you look so happy. Who with? Anyone I know?"

"I'm just happy to see you," he said; and in fact he was. She looked wonderful. She had filled out some. That wraithlike beauty had bloomed but not coarsened. She was more woman than waif, and more wife than woman. Her hair was cut short in a boyish style, very becoming, and there was a tiaralike thing in her curls. "And now you're a sorceress."

"Oh *hardly*," she said. "Can I even get that damned serving girl to *hurry up* with the scones and jam? I can *not*. Yes, I can sign a hundred greeting cards for the holiday season at one go. But it's a very *minor* talent, I tell you. Sorcery is vastly overrated in the popular press. Otherwise, why wouldn't the Wizard just magick the hell out of his adversaries? No, I'm content to try to be a good partner for my Chuffrey. He's at the exchange today, doing financial thingies. Oh do you know who else is in town? It's too rich, Crope tell him."

Crope, surprised to be given an opening, choked on his mouthful of tea. Glinda rushed in. "Nessarose! Can you believe it? She's at the family home over there in Lower Mennipin Street—an address that's come up quite a lot in the past decade, I might add. We saw her where, Crope, where? It was the Coffee Emporium—"

"It was the Ice Garden—"

"No, I remember, it was the Spangletown Cabaret! Fiyero do you know, we went to see that old Sillipede, do you remember? No you don't, I can see it in your face. She was the singer who was performing at the Oz Festival of Song and Sentiment the day our Glorious Wizard arrived out of the sky in a balloon and orchestrated that coup! She's making yet another of her innumerable comeback tours. She's a bit camp now but so what, it was gales of fun. And there at a better table than *we* had, I might tell you, was Nessie! She was with her grandfather, or is it the great-grandfather? The Eminent Thropp? He must be eleventy-hundredy years old by now. I was shocked to see her until I realized she went merely to provide him an escort. She didn't think much of the music—she scowled and prayed all through the entr'acte. And the Nanny was there too. Who would've imagined it, Fiyero—you're a prince, and Nessarose just about installed as the next Eminent Thropp, and Avaric, of course, the Margreave of Tenmeadows, and humble little me-eee married to Sir Chuffrey, holder of the most useless title and the biggest stock portfolio in the Pertha Hills?" Glinda almost stopped for breath, but lunged on kindly, "And Crope, of course, dear Crope. Crope, tell Fiyero all about yourself, he's dying to know, I can see it."

Actually Fiyero was interested, if only for a rest from the staccato chatter.

"He's shy," Glinda pushed on, "shy shy shy, always was." Fiyero and Crope exchanged glances and tried to keep their mouths from twitch-ing. "He's got this so avant-garde little *palace* of a loft apartment on the top floor of a doctor's surgery, could you imagine? Stunning views, the best views in the Emerald City, and at this time of year! He dabbles a bit in painting, don't you dear? Painting, a little musical operetta set design here and there. When we were young we thought the world revolved around Shiz. You know there's real theatre here now, the Wizard has made this a much more *cosmopolitan* city, don't you think?"

"It's good to see you, Fiyero," said Crope, "say something about yourself, fast, before it's too late."

"You cad, you kid me *mercilessly*," sang Glinda. "I'll tell him about your little affair with—well never mind. I'm not that mean."

"There's nothing to say," Fiyero said, feeling even more taciturn and Vinkus than he had when he first arrived in Shiz. "I like my life, I lead my clan when they need it, which isn't often. My children are healthy. My wife is—well, I don't know . . ."

"Fertile," supplied Glinda.

"Yes." He grinned. "She's fertile and I love her, and I'm not going to stay much longer as I'm meeting someone for a business conference across town."

"We *must* meet," said Glinda, suddenly plaintive, suddenly looking lonely. "Oh Fiyero, we're not old yet, but we're old enough to be old friends already, aren't we? Look, I've gushed on like a debutante who for-got to splash on her Eau d'Demure. I'm sorry. It's just that that was such a wonderful time, even in its strangeness and sadness—and life isn't the same now. It's wonderful, but it isn't the same."

"I know," he said, "but I don't think I can meet you again. There's so little time, and I have to go back to Kiamo Ko. I've been away since the late summer."

"Look, we're all here, me and Chuffrey, Crope, Nessarose, you—is Avaric around, we could get him? We could get together, we could have a quiet dinner together in our rooms upstairs. I promise not to be so giddy. Please, Fiyero, please, Your Highness. It would do me *such* an honor." She cocked her head and put a single finger to her chin, elegantly, and he could tell she was struggling through the language of her class to say something real.

"If I think I can, I'll let you know, but please, you mustn't count on it," he said. "There'll be other times. I'm not usually in town so late in the season—this is an anomaly. My children are waiting—have you children, Glinda?"

"Chuffrey is dry as two baked walnuts," said Glinda, making Crope choke on his tea again. "Before you go—I can see you're getting ready to dash—dear, dear Fiyero—what do you hear from Elphaba?"

But he was prepared for this, and had readied his face to be blank, and he only said, "Now that's a name I don't hear every day. Did she ever turn up? Surely Nessarose must have said."

"Nessarose says if her sister ever *does* turn up she'll spit in her face," Glinda remarked, "so we must all pray that Nessarose never loses her faith, for that would mean the evaporation of such tolerance and kindness. I think she would *kill* Elphaba. Nessa was abandoned, rejected, left to look after her crazy father, her grandfather-thingy, that brother, that nurse, that house, the staff—and you can't even say single-handedly, as she doesn't have any hands!"

"I thought I saw Elphaba once," said Crope.

"Oh?" said Fiyero and Glinda together, and Glinda continued, "You never told me that, Crope."

"I wasn't sure," he said. "I was on the trolley that runs along the reflecting pool by the Palace. It was raining—some years ago now—and I saw a figure struggling with a big umbrella. I thought she was about to be blown away. A gust of wind blew the umbrella inside out and the face, a greenish face which is why I noticed, ducked down to avoid the splash of rainwater—you remember how Elphaba hated getting wet."

"She was *allergic* to water," Glinda opined. "I never knew how she kept herself so clean, and I her roommate."

"Oil, I think," said Fiyero. They both looked at him. "That is, in the Vinkus," he stammered, "the elderly rub oil into their skin instead of water—I've always assumed that's what Elphie did. I don't know. Glinda, if I were to meet up with you again, what's a good day?"

She rooted in her reticule for a diary. Crope took the opportunity to lean forward and say to Fiyero, "It really is good to see you, you know."

"You too," said Fiyero, surprised that he meant it. "If you ever get out into the central Kells, come stay at Kiamo Ko with us. Just send word ahead, as we're only there for half a year at a time."

"That's just your speed, Crope, the wild beasts of the untamed Vinkus," said Glinda. "I think the fashion possibilities, all those leather thongs and fringe and such, they might interest you, but I can't see you as Mister Mountain Boy."

"No, probably not," agreed Crope. "Unless it affords fabulous cafés every four or five blocks, I don't think a landscape quite developed enough for human habitation."

Fiyero shook hands with Crope and then, remembering the rumors about poor Tibbett's deterioration, kissed him; he threw his arms around Glinda and hugged her hard. She laced her arm through his and walked him to the door.

"Do let me shake off Crope and have you back, all to myself," she said in a low voice, her patter evaporating into seriousness. "I can't tell you, dear Fiyero. The past seems both more mysterious and more understandable with you right here before me. I feel there are things I could yet learn. I don't want to wallow, dear boy, never that! But we go way back." She held his hand between hers. "Something's going on in your life. I'm not as dumb as I act. Something good and bad at the same time. Maybe I can help."

"You were always sweet," he said, and motioned to the doorman to hail a hansom cab. "How I regret that I won't meet Sir Chuffrey."

He moved out the doorway, across the marble entrance pavement, and turned to tip his hat at her. In the doors (the doormen held them open to enhance his parting view) she was a calm, resigned woman, neither transparent nor ineffectual—even, it might have been said, a woman full of grace. "If you should see her," said Glinda lightly, "tell her I miss her still."

He didn't see Glinda again. He didn't call at the Florinthwaite Club. He didn't stroll past the Thropp family house in Lower Mennipin Street (though he was sorely tempted). He didn't stop a scalper to try to get one of the tickets to Sillipede's triumphant fourth annual comeback tour. He found himself in the Chapel of Saint Glinda in Saint Glinda Square, from which he could sometimes hear the cloistered maunts next door chanting and susurrating like a swarm of bees.

When the two weeks had passed at last, and the city was worked up to a froth over Lurlinemas, he went to see Elphaba, half-expecting she would have vanished.

But there she was, stern and loving and in the midst of making a vegetable pie for him. Her precious Malky was putting his feet in the flour and making paw prints all over the room. They talked awkwardly until Malky upset the bowl of vegetable stock, and that made them both laugh.

He didn't tell her about Glinda. How could he? Elphaba had worked so hard to keep them all at bay, and now she was engaged in the major campaign of her life, the thing she had been working toward for five years. He did not approve of anarchy (well, he knew he was in lazy doubt about *everything*; doubt was much more energy efficient than conviction). But even after seeing the Bear cub struck down, he had to keep an even, cautious relationship with the Power on the throne—for the sake of his tribe.

Also, Fiyero didn't want to make Elphie's life harder than it was. And his selfish need to be comfortable with her surmounted his need to gossip. So he didn't tell her Nessarose and Nanny were in town either, or had been. (For all he knew, he rationalized silently, they had already moved on.)

"I wonder," she said that night, as the stars peered through the crazy frost pattern on the skylight, "I wonder if you should get out of town before Lurlinemas Eve."

"Is all hell going to break loose?"

"I told you, I don't know the whole picture; I can't know; I *shouldn't* know. But maybe *some* hell will break loose. Maybe it would be best for you to go."

"I'm not going and you can't make me."

"I've been taking correspondence courses in sorcery on the side, I'll go *puff* and turn you into stone."

"You mean you'll make me hard? I'm already hard."

"Stop. *Stop.*"

"Oh you wicked woman, you have bewitched me again, look, it has a mind of its own—"

"Fiyero stop. *Stop.* Now look, I mean it. I want to know where you're going to be on Lurlinemas Eve. Just so I can be sure you're not going to get hurt. Tell me."

"You mean we won't be together?"

"It's a work night for me," she said grimly. "I'll see you the next day."

"I'll wait here for you."

"No you won't. I think we've covered our tracks pretty well, but there's still a chance even at this late date that somebody could come here to intercept me. No—you stay in your club and take a bath. Take a nice long *cold bath*. Got it? Don't even go out. They say it might be snowy by then anyway."

"It's Lurlinemas Eve! I'm not going to spend the holiday in a bathtub *all alone*."

"Well, hire some company, see if I care."

"As if you don't."

"Just stay away from anything social, I mean theatre or crowds, or even restaurants, please, will you promise me that?"

"If you could be more specific I could be more careful."

"You could be *most* careful if you left town completely."

"You could be most careful if you told me—"

"Give over with that, cut it out. I don't think I even want to know where you are, come to think of it. I just want you to be safe. Will you be safe? Will you stay inside, away from drunken pagan celebrations?"

"Can I go to chapel and pray for you?"

"*No.*" She looked so fierce that he didn't even tease her about it again.

"Why should I keep myself so safe?" he asked her, but he was almost asking himself. What is there in my life worth preserving? With a good wife back there in the mountains, serviceable as an old spoon, dry in the heart from having been scared of marriage since she was six? With three children so shy of their father, the Prince of the Arjikis, that they will hardly come near him? With a careworn clan moving here, moving there, going through the same disputes, herding the same herds, praying the same prayers, as they have done for five hundred years? And me, with a shallow and undirected mind, no artfulness in word or habit, no especial kindness toward the world? What is there that makes my life worth preserving?

"I love you," said Elphaba.

"So that's that then, and that's it," he answered her, and himself. "And I love you. So I promise to be careful."

Careful of us both, he thought.

❈   ❈   ❈

So he stalked her again. Love makes hunters of us all. She had swathed herself in long dark skirts, like some sort of a religious woman, and tucked up her hair inside a tall wide-brimmed hat with a crown like a cone. There was a dark scarf, purple and gold, wound around her neck, and pulled over her mouth, though she would need more than a scarf to mask that lovely prow of a nose. She wore elegant, tight-fitting gloves, a nicer type of accessory than she usually went in for, though he feared it was to allow for nimbler control of her hands. Her feet were lost in big, steel-toed boots like the kind worn by miners in the Glikkus.

If you didn't *know* she was green, it would be hard to tell—in this dark afternoon, in this raking skittle of snow.

She didn't look behind her; perhaps she didn't care if she was being followed. Her circuit took her around some of the major squares of the city. She ducked in for a minute to the chapel of Saint Glinda next to the mauntery, the one where he had first seen her. Perhaps she was getting last-minute instructions, but she didn't try to give him (or anyone else) the slip. She emerged in a minute or two.

Or perhaps—perish the thought—she was actually praying for guidance and strength?

She crossed the Law Courts Bridge, she wandered along the Ozma Embankment and cut diagonally through the abandoned rose gardens of the Royal Mall. The snow pestered her; she kept twining her cape the more tightly around; the silhouette of her thin, dark-stockinged legs in those huge comical boots showed up against the snowy blankness of the Oz Deer Park (now of course bereft of Deer and deer). She marched, head tucked down, past the cenotaphs and obelisks and memorial tablets to the Magnificent Dead of this escapade or that. The decades—Fiyero thought, in love with her or at least so frightened for her that he could mistake it for love—the decades looked on and didn't notice her passing. They stared from their fixed mounts across at each other and didn't see revolution striding between them, on her way to destiny.

But the Wizard must not be her aim. She must have told the truth in saying that she was too untried, and too obvious, to be selected as the Wizard's assassin. She must be involved in a diversionary tactic, or in taking out a possible successor or high-level ally. For tonight the Wizard would be opening the antiroyalist, revisionist Exhibit of Struggle and Virtue at the People's Academy of Art and Mechanics near the Palace. Yet at the top of the Shiz Road Elphaba struck out sideways, away from the Palace district, cutting through the small, fashionable district of Goldhaven. The homes of the filthy rich were guarded by mercenaries, and she clopped past them on the pavements, past the stableboys out sweeping the snow off the pavement with their brooms. She did not look up or down or back over her shoulder. Fiyero guessed he was the more ostentatious figure, striding in his opera cape in the snow a hundred paces behind.

At the edge of Goldhaven was perched a small bluestone jewel of a theatre, the Lady's Mystique. In the shallow but elegant square before it, white lights and gold and green spangles hung in profusion, looped from streetlight to streetlight. Some holiday oratorio or other was scheduled—he could only read SOLD OUT on the board in front—and the doors weren't yet opened. The crowd was gathering, some vendors sold hot chocolate in tall ceramic glasses, and a crowd of self-approving youngsters amused themselves and bothered some elderly people by singing a parody of an old unionist hymn of the season. The snow came down on all, on the lights, the theatre, the crowds; it landed in the hot chocolate, it was churned to mush and ice on the bricks.

Bravely, foolishly—without decision or choice, it felt like—Fiyero climbed the steps of a nearby private library, to keep an eye on Elphaba, who lost herself in the crowd. Was there to be a murder in the theatre? Was there to be arson, the innocent sybarites roasted like chestnuts? Was it a single mark, an appointed victim, or was it mayhem and disaster, the more, the worse, the better?

He didn't know if he was there to prevent what she was about to do, or to save whomever he could from the catastrophe, or to tend anyone hurt accidentally, or even maybe just to witness it, so he could know more about her. And love her or not love her, but know which of the two it was.

She was circulating through the crowd, as if trying to locate someone. He believed, incredibly, that she didn't know he was there—was she so intent on finding the right victim, and he didn't fill the bill? Could she not *feel* her lover in the same open-air square with her as the wind moved the curtains of snow?

A phalanx of Gale Forcers appeared from an alley between the the-atre and a school next door. They took up their places before the bank of glass doors in front. Elphaba mounted the steps of an ancient wool mar-ket, a kind of stone gazebo. Fiyero saw that she had something under her cloak. Explosives? Some magic implement?

Did she have colleagues in the square? Were they lining themselves up one with another? The crowd kept getting thicker, as the hour for the oratorio drew near. Inside the glass doors, house management was busy lining up stanchions and stringing velvet ropes to promote a genteel entry into the hall. Nobody pushed and shoved into a public space like the very rich, Fiyero knew.

A carriage came around the corner of a building on the far side of the square. It couldn't come right up to the doors of the theatre, as the crowds were too dense, but it proceeded as far as it was able. Sensing the presence of someone with authority, the crowd drew a little still. Could this be the elusive Wizard, on an unannounced visit? A coachman in a teck-fur headpiece flung the door open, and reached his hand in to assist the passenger in alighting.

Fiyero held his breath; Elphaba stiffened into petrified wood. This was the target.

Out into the snowy street, in a tidal wave of black silk and silver spangles, swept a huge woman; she was magisterial and august, she was Madame Morrible, no other; even Fiyero recognized her, having met her only once.

He saw that Elphaba knew that this was the one she must kill; she had known this; in an instant all was dead clear. If she was caught and captured and tried, her motivation couldn't be more wonderful—she was merely a mad student from Madame Morrible's own Crage Hall, she car-ried a grudge, she never forgot. It was too perfect.

But could Madame Morrible be involved in intrigue with the Wizard? Or was this just a diversion, to take the mind of the authorities away from some more urgent target?

Elphaba's cape twitched; her hand went up and down inside it, as if priming something. Madame Morrible was growling a greeting to the crowd, which, while not necessarily knowing who she was, appreciated the spectacle if not the bulk of her arrival.

The Head of Crage Hall walked four steps toward the theatre, on the arm of a tiktok minion, and Elphaba leaned a little forward from under the wool market. Her chin was now sharply jutting out from the scarf, her nose aiming forward; she looked as if she could snip Madame Morrible into shreds, just using the serrated blades of her natural features. Her hands continued to figure out things beneath the cape.

But then were thrown open the front doors of the building Madame Morrible was walking past—not the theatre, but the adjacent school, Madame Teastane's Female Seminary. Out the doors swarmed a cluster, a little upper-class mob of schoolgirls. What were they doing in school on a Lurlinemas Eve? Fiyero caught Elphaba looking wildly surprised. The girls were six or seven, small creamy lumps of uncurdled femininity, spooned into furry muffs and tucked into furry scarves and tipped into boots with furry edges. They were laughing and singing, raucous and rough as the elite adults they would become, and in their midst was a pantomime player, someone being the Fairy Preenella. It was a man, as the convention had it, a man done up in silly clownlike makeup, and mock bouncing bosom, and a wig and extravagant skirts, and a straw hat, and a huge basket with trinkets and treasures spilling out. "Oh la, socie-tee," he fluted at Madame Morrible, "even Fairy Preenella can have a present for the Lucky Pedestrian."

For a moment Fiyero thought the man in drag was going to pull out a knife and kill Madame Morrible right in front of the children. But no, espionage was organized but not that organized—this was a real accident, a disruption. They hadn't figured on there being a school occasion this evening, nor on a screaming flock of schoolgirls greedily tugging at an actor in skirts and falsetto.

Fiyero turned back to look at Elphaba. Her face struggled with disbelief. The children were in the way of whatever she was supposed to do. They were a small unruly mob, chasing around the Head, teasing Preenella, leaping up at him/her, grabbing for presents. The children were the accidental context—noisy, innocent daughters of tycoons, despots, and butcher generals.

He could see Elphaba working, he could see her hands fighting with each other, to do it anyway, to keep from doing it—whatever *it* was.

Madame Morrible pushed on, like a huge float in a Remembrance

Day parade, and the doors of the theatre opened for her. She passed grandly into safety. Outside, the children danced and sang in the snow, the crowd surged this way and that. Elphaba crumpled and sank back against a pillar, shivering with self-loathing so violently that Fiyero could see it from fifty yards away. He began to push toward her, devil come what may, but by the time he reached the steps she had, for the first and only time, managed to lose him.

The audience filed into the theatre. The children shrieked their song in the street, awash with greed and joy. The carriage that had brought Madame Morrible around was able to draw up in front of the theatre and start its long wait for her to come out again. Fiyero paused, unsure, in case there was a backup plan, in case Elphaba had something else up her sleeve, in case the theatre exploded.

Then he began to worry that, in the few minutes of losing sight of her, Elphaba had been rounded up by the Gale Force. Could they have whisked her out of sight that fast? What should he do if she became one of the disappeared?

At a clip, he headed back across town. Mercifully he found a waiting cab, and he had the cab drive him directly to the street of warehouses adjacent to the military garrison in the city's ninth district.

In a state of profound agitation he arrived back at Elphaba's little eyrie atop the corn exchange. As he climbed the stairs, his bowels turned suddenly to water, and it was only with effort he managed to make it to the chamber pot. His insides slopped noisily, wetly out, and he held his perspiring face in his hands. The cat was perched atop the wardrobe, glaring down at him. Voided, washed down, and at least loosely done up again, he tried to coax Malky with a bowl of milk. She would have none of it.

He found a couple of dried crackers, and ate them miserably, and then pulled on the chain to open the skylight, to help air the room. A couple of plops of snow fell in and sat there not melting, it was that cold in the damn place. He went to build up a fire, pulled open the iron door of the stove.

The fire caught, then flared, and the shadows detached themselves and moved as shadows will, but these shadows moved fast, across the room, at him before he could register what they were. Except that there were three, or four, or five, and they were wearing black clothes, and black char on their faces, and their heads were wrapped in colored scarves like the ones he had bought for Elphaba, for Sarima. On the shoulder of one he saw the glint of a gilded epaulet: a senior member of the Gale Force. There was a club and it beat down on him, like the kick of a horse, like the falling limb of a tree hit by lightning. There must be pain, but he was too surprised to notice. That must be his blood, squirting a ruby stain on the white cat, making it flinch. He saw its eyes open, twin golden green moons, befitting of the season, and the cat then scarpered through the open skylight and was lost in the snowy night.

The youngest maunt was obliged to answer the convent door if the bell sounded during mealtime. In fact she was clearing away the remains of pumpkin soup and rye brisks, the other maunts already wafting, in a cerebral mood, toward their cloister chapel upstairs. She hesitated before deciding to answer the bell—in another three minutes she too would have been losing herself in devotions, and the bell would have gone unheeded. She had rather get the dishes to soak, frankly. But the seasonal cheer bullied her into charity.

She opened the huge door to find a figure crouched like a monkey in the dark corner of the stone porch. Beyond, snow was wrinkling the facade of the adjacent Church of Saint Glinda, making it look like a reflection in water, only right way up. The streets were empty and a noise of choirs came filtering out of the candle-lit church.

"What is it?" said the novice, remembering then to add, "Good Lurlinemas, my friend."

She decided, once she saw the blood on the odd green wrists, and the darting look in the eyes, that holiday decency required her to drag the creature inside. But she could hear her sister maunts assembling in their private chapel, and the mother maunt beginning to sing a prelude in her silvery contralto. This was the novice's first big liturgical event as a member of this community, and she didn't want to miss a moment of it.

"Come with me, dolly," she said, and the creature—a young woman a year or two older than she was—managed to straighten up enough to walk, or hobble, like a cripple, like a person so malnourished that their extensors cannot flex and their limbs look as if they are about to snap.

The novice stopped in a washroom to rinse the blood off the wrists, and to make certain that it was indeed splattered mess from the behead-ing of some hen for a holiday supper, and not a sad attempt at suicide. But the stranger recoiled from the sight of water, and looked so deranged and unhappy that the novice stopped. She used a dry towel instead.

The maunts were beginning antiphonal chants upstairs! How mad-dening! The novice took the path of least resistance. She dragged the for-lorn thing down toward the winter salon, where the old retired biddies lived out their lives in a haze of amnesia and the discreetly placed clumps of marginium plants, whose sweet miasma helped mask the odors of the old and incontinent. The crones lived in a time of their own, they couldn't be carted upstairs to the sacred chapel anyway.

"Look, I'll sit you down here," she said to the woman. "I don't know if you need sanctuary or food or a bath or forgiveness, whatever. But you can stop here, warm and dry and safe and quiet. I'll come back to you after midnight. It's the feast day, you see. It's the vigil service. Watch and wait, and hope."

She pushed the hunted, haunted woman into a soft chair, and found a blanket. Most of the crones were snoring away, their heads nodding on their breastbones, dribbling softly onto bibs ornamented with green and gold berries and leaves. A few were telling their beads. The courtyard, open in summer, was now welled in with glass panels for the winter, so it looked like a square fish tank in an aquarium; snow falling in it always made them peaceful.

"Look, you can see the snow, white as the grace of the Unnamed God," said the novice, remembering her pastoral requirements. "Think on that, and rest, and sleep. Here's a pillow. Here's a stool for your feet. Upstairs we'll be singing and praising the Unnamed God. I'll pray for you."

"Don't—" said the green ghostly guest, then slumped her head against the pillow.

"It's my *pleasure* to," said the novice, a bit aggressively, and fled, just in time to catch the processional hymn.

For a while the winter salon was still. It was like a fishbowl into which a new acquisition has been dropped. The snow moved as if done by a machine, gently and mesmerizingly, with a soft *churr*. The blossoms of the marginium plants closed a bit in the strengthening cold of the room. Oil lamps issued their funereal crepe ribbons into the air. On the other side of the garden—hardly visible through the snow and the two windows—a decrepit maunt, with a more precise grasp of the calendar than her sisters, began to hum a saucy old pagan hymn to Lurline.

Up to the shivering figure of the newcomer came one of the elders, inching forward in a wheeled chair. She leaned forward and sniffed. From a cloak of plaid blanket, blue and ivory, she pawed her old hands along the armrests. She reached out and touched Elphaba's hand.

"Well, the poor dolly is sick, the poor dolly is tired," said the ancient thing. Her hands felt, as the novice's had done, for open wounds on the wrists. Nothing. "Though intact, the poor dolly is in pain," she said, as if approving. A dome of near-balding scalp came into view under the hood of the blanket. "The poor dolly is faint, the poor dolly is faltering," she went on. She rocked a bit and pressed Elphaba's hands between her own, as if to warm them, but it was doubtful that her anemic and incompetent old circulatory system could heat a stranger when it could scarcely heat herself. Still she kept on. "The poor poppet is failure itself," she murmured. "Happy holidays to one and all. Come my dear, lay your breast on old Mother's bosom. Old Mother Maunt will set things right." She couldn't quite pull Elphaba out of her position of dreamless, sleepless grief. She could only keep Elphaba's hands tightly clutched within her own, as a sepal sockets the furls of young petal. "Come, my precious and all will be well. Rest in the bosom of mad Mother Yackle. Mother Yackle will see you home."

IV

In the Vinkus

The Voyage Out

I

On the day the seven-year maunt was to leave, Sister Bursar took the huge iron key from her bosom and unlocked the store chamber, and said, "Come in." She pulled from the press three black shifts, six camisoles, gloves, and a shawl. She also handed over the broom. Finally, for emergencies, a basket of simples—herbs and roots, tinctures, rues, salves and balms.

There was paper, too, though not much: a dozen pages or so, in different shapes and thicknesses. Paper was in ever shorter supply in all of Oz. "Make it last, make it important," advised Sister Bursar. "You're a bright one, for all your sulks and silences." She found a pen. A pfenix feather, known for the endurance and strength of the quill. Three pots of black ink, sealed under knobby wristholds of wax.

Oatsie Manglehand was waiting in the ambulatory with the old Superior Maunt. The convent was paying a decent penny for this service, and Oatsie needed the fees. But she didn't like the look of the sullen maunt that Sister Bursar ushered in. "This is your passenger," said the Superior Maunt. "Her name is Sister Saint Aelphaba. She's spent many years in solitary life and in nursing. The habit of gossip is lost. But it's time for her to move on, and move on she will. You'll find her no trouble."

Oatsie looked the passenger over and said, "The Grasstrail Train doesn't promise the survival of its party, Mother. I've led two dozen trips these past ten years or so, and there have been more casualties than I like to admit."

"She leaves of her own free will," said the Superior Maunt. "Should she wish to return at any point, we would take her in. She is one of us."

She didn't look one of anything to Oatsie, neither flesh nor fowl, neither idiot nor intellectual. Sister Saint Aelphaba just stared at the floor. Though she seemed to be about thirty, she had a sallow, adolescent look about her.

"And there's the luggage—you can manage it?" The Superior Maunt pointed to the small heap of supplies in the immaculate forecourt in front of the mauntery. Then she turned to the departing maunt. "Sweet child of the Unnamed God," said the Superior Maunt, "you go from us to conduct an exercise in expiation. You feel there is a penalty to pay before you may find peace. The unquestioning silence of the cloister is no longer what you need. You are returning to yourself. So we send you from us with our love and with our expectations of your success. Godspeed, my good sister."

The passenger kept her eyes trained on the ground and did not answer.

The Superior Maunt sighed. "We must be off to our devotions." She peeled a few notes from a roll of money kept in the recesses of her veils, and handed them over to Oatsie Manglehand. "This should see you through, and more besides."

It was a healthy amount. Oatsie stood to earn a lot from escorting this taciturn woman through the Kells—more than from the whole rest of her party combined. "You are too good, Mother Maunt," she said. She took the cash with her strong hand, and made a gesture of deference with her limp one.

"No one is too good," said the Superior Maunt, but nicely, and retired with surprising speed behind the cloister doors. Sister Bursar said, "You're on your own now, Sister Elphie, and may all the stars smile you on your way!" and she disappeared as well. Oatsie went to load the luggage and supplies in the wagon. There was a small, chunky ragamuffin boy asleep behind the trunk. "Off with you," said Oatsie, but the boy muttered, "I'm to go too, that's what they told me." When Sister Saint Aelphaba neither confirmed nor denied this plan, Oatsie began to understand why the payment to take the green maunt away had been more than generous.

The Cloister of Saint Glinda was located in the Shale Shallows, twelve miles southwest of the Emerald City. It was an outpost mauntery, under the aegis of the one in town. Sister Saint Aelphaba had spent two years in town and five years here, according to the Mother Maunt. "You want to be called Sister still, now that you're sprung from that holy prison?" asked Oatsie as she clucked the reins and urged the packhorses on.

"Elphie is fine," said the passenger.

"And the boy, what's he called?"

Elphie shrugged.

The coach met the rest of the caravan a few miles on. There were four wagons in all, and fifteen travelers. Elphie and the boy were the last to join. Oatsie Manglehand outlined the proposed route: south along the edge of Kellswater, west through Kumbricia's Pass, northwest through the Thousand Year Grasslands, stopping at Kiamo Ko, and then wintering a bit farther northwest. The Vinkus was uncivilized land, Oatsie told them, and there were tribal groups to be wary of: the Yunamata, the Scrow, the Arjiki. And there were animals. And spirits. They would need to stick together. They would need to trust one another.

Elphie showed no sign of listening. She fiddled with the pfenix feather and drew patterns in the soil between her feet, coiling shapes like dragons writhing or smoke rising. The boy squatted eight or ten feet away, wary and shuttered. He seemed to be her page, for he managed her bags and attended her needs, but they did not look at each other, or speak. Oatsie found it strange in the extreme, and hoped it didn't augur ill.

The Grasstrail Train set off at sunset, and made only a few miles before its first camp at a streambed. The party—mostly Gillikinese—chattered in nervous amazement at their courage, to go so far afield from the safety of central Oz! All for different reasons: for business, for family needs, to pay a debt, to kill an enemy. The Vinkus was a frontier, and the Winkies a beknighted, bloodthirsty folk who knew little about indoor plumbing or the rules of etiquette so the party regaled itself in song. Oatsie took part for a short time, but she knew there was hardly one among them who wouldn't prefer to stay where they were and avoid the depths of the Vinkus altogether. Except perhaps that Elphie, who was keeping pretty much to herself.

They left the rich edge of Gillikin behind. The Vinkus began with a mesh of pebbles spread on brown wet soil. At night the Lizard Star pointed the

direction: south, south along the edge of the Great Kells, to the dangerous gap of Kumbricia's Pass. Pines and black starsaps stood up like teeth
on every embankment. By day they were welcoming, sometimes giving
shade. By night they towered, and harbored snatchowls and bats.

Elphie was often awake at night. Thought was returning to her, perhaps expanding under the fierce openness, where the birds cried in falling
voices, and the meteors stitched omens into the sky. Sometimes she tried
to write with her pfenix feather; sometimes she sat and thought words
out, and didn't commit them to paper.

Life outside the cloister seemed to cloud up with such particularity—the shape of her seven years past was already being crowded out. All
that undifferentiated time, washing terra-cotta floors without dipping her
hands in the bucket—it took hours to do a single room, but no floor was
ever cleaner. Making wine, taking in the sick, working in the infirmary
wing, which had reminded her briefly of Crage Hall. The benefit of a uniform was that one need not struggle to be unique—how many unique-
nesses could the Unnamed God or nature create? One could sink self-
lessly into the daily pattern, one could find one's way without groping.
The little changes—the red bird landing on the windowsill, and that was
spring—the leaves to rake from the terrace, and that was fall—they were
enough. Three years of absolute silence, two years of whisper, and then,
moved up (and outward) by the decision of the Superior Maunt, two
years on the ward for incurables.

There, for nine months—thought Elphie under the stars, picturing
it to herself as if telling someone else—she tended the dying, and those
too clumsy to die. She grew to see dying as a pattern, beautiful in its way.
A human form is like a leaf, it dies in a set piece unless something interferes: first this, then that, then this. She might have gone on as a nurse
forever, arranging wrists in a pleasing pattern above starched bedsheets,
reading the nonsense words of scripture that seemed to help so. She
could manage the dying.

Then, a year ago, pale invalid Tibbett was carted to the Home for
the Incurables. He wasn't too far gone to recognize her even behind her
veil and silences. Weak, unable to shit or piss without help, his skin
falling in rags and parchment, he was better at life than she was. He self-
ishly required that she be an individual, and he addressed her by her

name. He joked, he remembered stories, he criticized old friends for aban-
doning him, he noticed the differences in how she moved from day to day,
how she thought. He reminded her that she *did* think. Under the
scrutiny of his tired frame she was re-created, against her will, as an individual. Or nearly.

At last he died, and the Superior Maunt had said that it was time for
her to go and atone for her mistakes, though not even the Superior
Maunt knew what they were. When that was done?—well, she was still a
young woman, she could raise a family. Take her broom and remember:
obedience and mystery.

"You can't sleep," said Oatsie one night as Elphie sat under the
stars.

But though her thoughts were rich and complicated, her words
were poor, and she merely grunted. Oatsie made a few jokes at which
Elphie tried to smile, but Oatsie laughed enough for both of them. Big,
full laughs. It made Elphie tired.

"Isn't that cook a piece of work?" said Oatsie, and told some
episode that seemed pointless, and she chortled at her own story. Elphie
tried to enjoy, tried to grin, but above her the stars grew thicker, more
like glittering fishspawn than salt; they turned on their stalks with a cursing, grinding sound, if only she could hear it. She couldn't hear it; Oatsie
was too coarse and loud.

There was much to hate in this world, and too much to love.

Before long they came to the edge of Kellswater, a murderous slice
of water lying as if cleft from the side of a thundercloud. It was all gray, no
lights on it. "That," said Oatsie, "is why the horses don't drink from it,
nor travelers; that's why it was never tapped in aqueducts and run to the
Emerald City. It's dead water. And you thought you'd seen it all." Still,
the travelers were impressed. A lavender heaviness arose on its western
edge—the first hint of the Great Kells, the mountains that separated the
Vinkus from the rest of Oz. From here the mountains appeared as thin as
gas.

Oatsie demonstrated the use of the fog charm in the event of an
attack by a band of Yunamata hunters. "Are we going to be attacked?"
asked the boy who seemed to be Elphie's page. "I'll get 'em dead before
no one knows what's on." The fear rose up from him and caught on in

the others. "We usually do well," said Oatsie, "we just need to be pre-pared. They can be friends. If we are friends."

The caravan straggled by day, four wagons keeping their distance, accom-panied by nine horses, two cows, a bull, a heifer, and various chickens without much personality. The cook had a dog named Killyjoy who seemed to Elphie a Makejoy instead, a panting, sniffy thing. Some people thought for a time he might actually be a Dog, in hiding, but they gave up that idea. "Hah," Elphie said to the others, "have you spoken to Animals so seldom that you can't remember the difference anymore?" No, he was just a dog, but a most glorious doggy dog, full of rages and exaggerated devotions. Killyjoy was a mountain breed, part Linster collie, part Lenx terrier, and maybe part wolf. His nose went up like a butter curl, in gray-black ridges and ribs. He could not be kept from hunting but he did not catch much either. By night, when the wagons squared off together, the cooking fire within, the animals just nearby, without, and the singing began at last, Killyjoy hid under the wagon.

Oatsie heard the boy tell the dog his name. "I'm Liir," said the boy. "You can be my dog, sort of." She had to smile. The fat child was not good at making friends, and a lonely child should have a dog.

Kellswater slipped back, out of sight. Some felt safer away from it. Almost hourly the Great Kells rose and thickened, the color now like the brown rind of a butterdew melon. Still the track meandered along the valley, the Vinkus River on its right, the mountains beyond it. Oatsie knew several places to ford, but they weren't clearly marked. While they searched, Killyjoy caught a valley grite at last. He bled and whined, and was treated for poison. Liir let him ride in his arms, which made Elphie faintly jealous. She was almost amused to note in herself such a turgid, old-fashioned feel-ing as jealousy.

The cook was angry that Killyjoy preferred someone else's company more than his—he shook his ladle overhead as if summoning the wrath of angel chefs among the stars. Elphie thought of him as a butcher cook, as he seemed to have no scruples about shooting rabbits and eating them. "How do you know they're not Rabbits?" she said, and she wouldn't touch a bite.

"Quiet, you, or I'll cook that little boy instead," he answered.

She tried to raise with Oatsie the notion of firing the cook, but Oatsie would not listen. "We're coming in to Kumbricia's Pass," she said, "my mind is on other matters."

They couldn't help but feel the unsettling eroticism of the landscape. From the eastern approach, the Kumbricia Pass looked like a woman lying on her back, her legs spread apart, welcoming them.

Up in the slopes, the pine boughs shaded the sun, the wild pears tangled their twisted branches together as if wrestling. A sudden dampness, a new private climate—the bark ran wet, the air sank heavily against the skin like half-laundered toweling. Once inside the forest, the travelers could not see the hills. Everything smelled of ferns and fiddlegreens. And on the shores of a small lake stood a dead tree. It harbored a community of bees, at their work of chamber music and honey.

"I want to take them with us," said Elphie. "I'll talk to them and see if they'll come."

There had been bees in the kitchen garden at Crage Hall, and again at the Cloister of Saint Glinda in the Shale Shallows. Elphie was entranced by them. But Liir was terrified, and the cook threatened to disappear and leave the group traumatized by an inability to do a really topnotch bechamel sauce in the wilderness. Discussion was waged. An old man in the party, heading westward to die because of some midnight vision, ventured as to how a little honey would improve the tasteless sparrowleaf tea. A Glikkun mail-order bride agreed. Oatsie, of sentimental enthusiasms when least expected, voted for honey. So Elphie climbed the tree and talked to the bees, and they came along in a swarm, but most travelers stayed in the other wagons, suddenly scared of every fleck of dust that flitted against the skin.

They sent out a request, using drums and mist, to attract the attention of a hired rafiqi, for caravans were not allowed to move through the lands of different Vinkus tribes without a guide to negotiate permissions and fees. Bored one evening, and responding to the gloom, the travelers fell to discussing the legend of the Kumbric Witch. Who comes first, the Fairy Queen Lurline or the Kumbric Witch?

Igo, the sick old man, quoted the *Oziad*, and reminded them all of how creation worked: the Dragon of Time created the sun and the moon, and Lurline cursed them and said that their children wouldn't know their own parents, and then the Kumbric Witch came along and the flood, the battle, the spilling of evil in the world.

Oatsie Manglehand disagreed. She said, "You old fools, the *Oziad* is just a frilly, romantic poem of older, harsher legends. What lives in folk memory is truer than how some artsy poet says it. In folk memory evil always predates good."

"Can this be true?" asked Igo, with interest.

"Surely there is the handful of nursery *märchen* that start, 'Once in the middle of a forest lived an old witch' or 'The devil was out walking one day and met a child,'" said Oatsie, who was showing that she had some education as well as grit. "To the grim poor there need be no *pour quoi* tale about where evil arises; it just arises; it always is. One never learns how the witch became wicked, or whether that was the right choice for her—is it ever the right choice? Does the devil ever struggle to be good again, or if so is he not a devil? It is at the very least a question of definitions."

"It certainly is true that tales of the Kumbric Witch abound," agreed Igo. "Every other witch is just a shadow, a daughter, a sister, a decadent descendant; the Kumbric Witch is the model further back than which it seems impossible to go."

Elphie remembered the ambiguous scroll painting of the Kumbric Witch—was it she?—found in the library of Three Queens, that summer long ago: standing in shiny shoes, straddling a continent, nursing or choking a beast.

"I don't believe in the Kumbric Witch, even in Kumbricia's Pass," boasted the cook.

"You don't believe in Rabbits either," snarled Elphie, suddenly annoyed. "The question is, does the Kumbric Witch believe in you?"

"Temper," sang out Oatsie, and turned it into a singalong song. Elphie stamped away. This was too much like her childhood, discussions with her father and Nessarose about where evil begins. As if one could ever know! Her father used to orchestrate proofs about evil as a way of persuading his flock to convert. Elphie had come to think, back in Shiz, that as women wore cologne, men wore proofs: to secure their own sense of themselves, and thus to be attractive. But surely evil was beyond proof, just as the Kumbric Witch was beyond the grasp of knowable history?

2

The rafiqi arrived, a thin, balding man with battle scars. There might be trouble from the Yunamata this year, he told them. "The caravan comes after a season of dirty forays by cavalry from the Emerald City. Winkie roundup," he complained. It wasn't clear if he was talking about a local argument over a drunken slight to a Vinkus maiden or about a slave trade and resettlement camps.

The camp was broken, the lake left behind, and the silent forest continued for a half a day. Sunlight speared through the canopy from time to time, but it was a thin, egg yolk light, and seemed always to be off to the side, never spotlighting down on the path ahead. It was eerie, as if Kumbricia herself were moving along beside them, hidden, unbidden, passing from tree to tree, sliding behind rocks, waiting in shadowy depths, watching and listening. The ailing old man wailed nasally, and prayed to emerge from this mystery wood before he died, or his spirit might never find its way out. The boy wept like a girl. The cook wrung the neck of a chicken.

Even the bees stopped humming.

In the middle of the night the cook disappeared. There was consternation among all except Elphie, who didn't care. Was it a kidnapping, or a sleepwalking episode, or a suicide? Were the angry Yunamata near, and watching? Was it Kumbricia herself taking revenge on them for discussing her so glibly? There were many opinions, and the breakfast eggs were runny and inedible.

Killyjoy did not notice the cook's disappearance. He snuggled, grinning in his coma-sleep, closer to Liir.

The bees went into some sort of mysterious hibernation inside the joint of tree trunk brought along to make them happy. Killyjoy, still smarting from grite poison, slept twenty-two hours a day. The travelers, afraid of being overheard, stopped talking altogether.

Toward the evening the pines at last began to thin, and the forest to shift to stag-head oak, which with its broader branches let in more of the sky—a pasty yellow sky, but at last a sky—and then there was a cliff edge. They had climbed higher than anyone had quite realized; beneath and beyond stretched the rest of Kumbricia's Pass, a journey of four or five days. Beyond *that* was the beginning of the Thousand Year Grasslands.

No one was sorry for the light and room that the sky afforded. Even Elphie felt her heart lift, unexpectedly.

In the middle of the night the Yunamata arrived. They brought gifts of dried fruit and sang tribal songs, and made those who would dance get up and dance. The travelers were more terrified of their hospitality than of the attack that they had expected.

As Elphie thought about it, the Yunamata seemed soft, compliant folk, only as fearful and fearless as schoolgirls—at least that was all they showed. They were cavorting, opinionated; they reminded her of the Quadlings with whom she had grown up. Perhaps ethnically they were distant cousins. Long lashes. Narrow elbows. Babylike supple wrists. Oblong heads and thin concentrated lips—even with their foreign tongue they made her feel at home.

The Yunamata left in the morning, complaining rudely about the runniness of the breakfast eggs. The rafiqi said that the Yunamata would make no further trouble. Even he seemed disappointed, as if his employ-ment hadn't been required.

There was no word about the cook. The Yunamata didn't seem to know anything about him.

As the caravan continued its descent, the sky opened up again, brisk and autumnal, wide as remorse. From *there* to *there!*—the eye could hardly take it in. The plain below, compared to the mountains, seemed level as a lake. The wind made strokes across it, as if spelling things in a language of curls and stripes. No wildlife was visible from this distance, though there were tribal fires here and there. Kumbricia's Pass was left behind, or nearly.

Then a Yunamata messenger came on swift leathery feet, arriving from the Pass behind them, to share the news that a body had been found at the base of a cliff. Perhaps it was the cook; it was thought to be a man, but the surface of the corpse was so swollen with lesions that the particu-lars were lost. "It was the bees," said someone, full of rage.

"Oh, was it?" came Elphie's calm voice. "They've been asleep for so long. Wouldn't there have been screams if they'd attacked a man in the middle of the night? Did the bees sting his throat first, to swell his vocal cords shut? Very talented bees, those."

"It was the bees," was the mutter, and the implication was clear. *You too.*

"Oh, I forgot the size of the human imagination," Elphie said meanly. "How very large it is, after all."

But she wasn't upset, not really. For Killyjoy was back to himself, at last, and the bees woke up too. Perhaps the high altitudes at the top of the Kumbricia Pass had given them such sleep. Elphie began to prefer their company to the rest of the travelers. As they woke up, coming down from the heights, she felt herself more and more awake, too.

The rafiqi pointed out on the horizon several mounding coils of smoke. At first the travelers guessed they were windstorms, but Oatsie soothed them and alarmed them: It was evening fires for a large encampment. *Scrow.* It was autumn hunting season, though nothing had been seen of any game bigger than a hare or a grass fox (its brush a wild swipe of bronze on melting golden meadow, its feet in black stockings like a serving maid's). Killyjoy was ecstatic with the possibilities of encounter; he could hardly bear to rest at night. Even in his dreams he twitched with the hunt.

The travelers feared the Scrow more than they had the Yunamata. The rafiqi did not say much to allay their fears. He was more tentative than it had first seemed; perhaps the job of negotiating among suspicious peoples required caution. Liir idolized him hopelessly, after only a few days of travel. Elphie thought: Such silly things, children—and so embarrassing—because they keep changing themselves out of shame, out of a need to be loved or something. While animals are born who they are, accept it, and that is that. They live with greater peace than people do.

She felt in herself a jolt of pleasurable expectation over the thought of approaching the Scrow. Along with so much else, she had forgotten what pleasurable expectation was. As night fell, everyone seemed more alert, out of fear and excitement. The skies throbbed with turquoise, even at midnight. Starlight and comet tails burned the tips of endless grass below into a hammered silver. Like thousands of tapers in the chapel, just blown out but still glowing.

If one could drown in the grass, thought Elphie, it might be the best way to die.

3

It was noon when the caravan pulled up to the edge of the Scrow camp. A committee of Scrow had ridden to their domestic margin, where the sand-colored tents petered out into untrampled grass—men and women alike sat on horseback, about seven or eight of them, in blue ribbons and ivory bangles. Also, obviously senior, was a huge slab of an old woman carried in a palanquin of some sort, its frame all hung round with tambours and clinking amulets and gauzy veils. She let the rafiqi and the tribal paladins trade compliments or insults. After a while she grunted a direction and her curtains were withdrawn so she could see. She had an overhung lip, so large that it doubled back on itself like an upside-down spout on a pitcher. Her eyes were ringed with kohl. On her shoulders sat two dyspeptic-looking crows. Their feet were shackled in gold links and attached to loops in her ornamental collar, into which the old woman had dribbled traces of the fruit she had been eating as she waited. Her shoulders were speckled with crow droppings.

"The Princess Nastoya," said the rafiqi at last.

She was the filthiest, least-educated princess anyone had ever seen, yet she had some dignity; even the most ardent democrat among the travelers genuflected. She laughed raucously. Then she bade her bearers lug her away to someplace less tedious.

The Scrow camp was arranged in concentric circles, with the Princess's tent in the middle, prettied up with extensions of faded striped baldaquins on all sides. It was a little airy palace in silks and cotton muslin. Her advisors and concubine-husbands seemed to live in the nearest circle (and a scrawny lot the husbands were, thought Elphie, but perhaps they were chosen for timidity and scrawniness, to make her seem ever the larger). Beyond the Princess's settlement ranged four hundred tents, which meant maybe a thousand people altogether. A thousand humans, with their poached-salmon skin, their moistly protruding eyes (but sensitive, in lowered gazes, to avoid being met), their handsome generous noses, and big buttocks, and wide rolling hips, men and women alike.

Most of the caravan travelers stayed glued to the doors of their wagons, imagining crime just beyond the nearest tent. But Elphie found it impossible to keep still, with all this newness beckoning. When Elphie walked, there were gasps, and the adults shyly retreated out of her path. But only ten minutes had passed before there were sixty children in a noisy crowd, following behind, running ahead, like a cloud of midges.

The rafiqi advised caution, advised return to the camp; but childhood in the Quadling badlands had made Elphaba not only bold, but curious. There were more ways to live than the ones given by one's superiors.

After the evening meal, a delegation of erect old Scrow dignitaries approached the Grasstrail Train and entered into a lengthy palaver with the rafiqi. In the end, the rafiqi translated the message: a small band was invited—requested—(ordered?)—to the Scrow shrine. It would take an hour by camel. For her sin of skin color, presumably, or possibly for having had the nerve to take a solitary stroll through the Scrow tent city, Elphie was told to join Oatsie, the rafiqi, Igo for his venerable age, and one of the financial adventurers—named Pinchweed, or maybe that was just a nasty nickname.

By the light of sallowwood torches, the camels, in glittering caparisons, lurched and lumbered on a worn track. It was like going up and down a staircase at the same time. Elphie sat above the grass, a vantage point over the great flickering surface. Although the ocean was only an idea sprung out of mythology, she could almost see where it came from—there were small grasshawks launching themselves like fish leaping out of the spume, nipping at the fireflies, pocketing them, then falling back in a dry splash. Bats passed, making a guttering, sputtering sound that ended in an extinguishing *swoop*. The plain itself seemed to bring forth night color: now a heliotrope, now a bronzy green, now a dun color skeined through with red and silver. The moon rose, an opalescent goddess tipping light from her harsh maternal scimitar. Nothing more need have happened; it seemed enough to Elphaba to find herself capable of such a weird ecstatic response to soft color and safe space. But no, on—on.

Eventually Elphie noticed a plantation of trees, carefully tended in this devastating openness. First a stand of scrub spruce, contorted by the winds into gnarled figures of split bark and hissing needles—and the pagan odor of sap. Beyond, a rise of higher hedges, then, yet higher trees.

It was the circular pattern of the Scrow encampment again. The party passed into it in silence, as through a maze, along curving corridors of whispering brush, moving from outer to inner circles lit by oil lamps hammered to carven posts.

Within, at the center, was the Princess Nastoya girded in a native costume of leather and grass made all the more effective by a length of striped purple and white toweling she must have bargained from some traveler or other. She stood, distracted and breathing heavily, leaning on stout walking sticks; around her, sarsen stones like gapped teeth resembled a stone cage through which she could hardly pass, given her bulk.

The guests joined the hosts in eating, drinking, and smoking on a pipe with a bowl carved like a crow's head. Crows ranged all around on the tops of the sarsens, twenty, thirty, forty? Elphie's head spun, the moon rose, the plain at night, invisible from the secret garden of the green maze, wheeled about like a child's top. She could almost hear the spinning. The Scrow elders chanted in a drone.

When the drone died out, the Princess Nastoya raised her head.

The huge wattles of old flesh beneath her small chin wobbled. Her toweling fell to the ground. She was naked and old and strong; what had seemed like boredom was revealed as patience, memory, control. She shook the very hair off her head and it uncoiled down her back and disappeared. Her feet moved massively, as if seeking the best purchase, like columns, like pillars of stone. She dropped her arms forward and her back was a dome; still her head was up, her eyes the brighter, her nose working mightily; she was an Elephant.

An Elephant goddess, Elphie thought, her mind recoiling in terror and delight, but the Princess Nastoya said, "No." She spoke through the rafiqi still; he had obviously seen this before, though with the alcohol he stuttered and had to search for words.

One by one she asked the intentions of the travelers.

"Money and commerce," said Pinchweed, shocked into honesty: money and commerce and pillage and plunder at whatever cost.

"A place to die where I can rest, and my spirit go abroad," ventured Igo.

"Safety and movement, out of harm's way," said Oatsie spunkily, by which it was clear she meant: out of men's way.

The rafiqi indicated that Elphie's own answer was still needed.

In the presence of such an Animal, Elphie could not stay aloof. So she spoke it as best as she could. "To retire from the world after making sure of the safety of the survivors of my lover. To face his widow, Sarima, in guilt and responsibility, and then to remove myself from the darkening world."

The Elephant told the others, except the rafiqi, to leave.

The Elephant raised her trunk and sniffed the wind. Her rheumy old eyes blinked slowly and her ears moved back and forth, raking the air for nuance. She pissed hugely in a steaming flow, with dignity and non-chalance, eyes firmly latched on Elphaba.

Through the rafiqi, the Elephant then said, "Daughter of the dragon, I too am under a spell. I know how it may be broken—but I choose to live as a changeling. An Elephant is a hunted thing in these times. The Scrow approve of me. They have worshipped elephants from the time before language, the time before history began. They know I am not a goddess. They know I am a beast who chooses magical incarcera-tion as a human over the dangerous liberty of my own powerful form.

"When the times are a crucible, when the air is full of crisis," she said, "those who are the most themselves are the victims."

Elphie could only look, she could not speak.

"But the choice to save yourself can itself be deadly," said the Princess Nastoya.

Elphie nodded, looked away, looked back.

"I will give you three crows as your familiars," said the Princess. "You are in hiding as a witch now. That is your guise." She spoke a word to the crows, and three mangy, evil-looking things came and waited nearby.

"A witch?" Elphaba said. What her father would think! "Hiding from what?"

"We have the same enemy," replied the Princess. "We are both at risk. If you need help send the crows. If I am still alive, as an old matri-arch monarch, or as a free Elephant, I'll come to your aid."

"Why?" asked Elphie.

"Because no retreat from the world can mask what is in your face," she answered.

The Princess said more. It had been years—more than a decade—since Elphie had been able to talk to an Animal. Who, Elphie asked the Princess, had enchanted her? But the Princess Nastoya wouldn't say—in part as self-protection, for the death of the enchanter could sometimes mean the revocation of binding spells, and her curse was her safety.

"But is life worth living in the wrong form?" said Elphie.

"The interior doesn't change," she answered, "except by self-involvement. Of which be not afraid, and also beware."

"I have no interior," said Elphaba.

"*Something* told those bees to kill the cook," said the Princess Nastoya, with a glitter in her eye. Elphaba felt herself go pale.

"I didn't!" she said. "No, it couldn't have been me! And how did you know?"

"You did, on some level. You are a strong woman. And I can hear bees, you know. My ears are keen."

"I would like to stay here with you," said Elphaba. "Life has been very hard. If you can hear me when I cannot hear myself—something the Superior Maunt could never do—you could help me do no harm in this world. That's all I want—to do no harm."

"By your own admission, you have a job to do," said the Princess. She curled her trunk around Elphaba's face, feeling its contours and truths. "Go and do it."

"May I return to you?" asked Elphie.

But the Princess wouldn't answer. She was tiring—she was an old old thing even for an Elephant. Her trunk went back and forth like a pendulum on a clock. Then the great nose-hand came forward and set itself with wonderful weight and precision on Elphaba's shoulders, and curled a bit around her neck. "Listen to me, sister," she said. "Remember this: Nothing is written in the stars. Not these stars, nor any others. No one controls your destiny."

Elphaba could not answer, so shocked was she at the touch. She backed away when dismissed, her mind all but out of her.

Then the return on camels across the shuddering colors of night grass: hypnotic, vague, and distressing.

Yet there was blessing in this night. Elphaba had forgotten blessing, too—like so much else.

4

They left the Scrow encampment and the Princess Nastoya behind. The Grasstrail Train moved in a circle north, now, a wide arch.

Igo died, and was buried in a sandy mound. "Give his spirit movement and flight," said Elphie at the ceremony.

The rafiqi admitted later that he had thought one of the guests of the command meeting with the Princess Nastoya was to be sacrificed in a ritual slaughter. It had happened before. The Princess, though coping with her dilemma, was not above a sense of revenge. It was the honesty of Pinchweed that saved him, as he was the obvious choice. Or perhaps Igo wore the prospect of his death closer to the surface than humans could see, and the Elephant took pity.

The crows were annoying; they pestered the bees, shat all over the wagon, teased Killyjoy. The Glikkun, Raraynee, stopped at a well, met her isolated widower husband-to-be, and left the Grasstrail Train. The toothless new husband already had six motherless children, and they took to Raraynee like orphaned ducklings behind a farm dog. There were only ten travelers left.

"Now we're entering Arjiki tribal lands," said the rafiqi.

The first Arjiki band approached a few days later. They wore nothing so splendid as what Fiyero had worn, in the way of blue markings—these were nomads, shepherds, rounding up the sheep from the western foothills of the Great Kells for their annual counting and, it seemed, sale to the East. Still, just the handsome look of them ripped Elphie's heart into pieces. Their wildness. Their otherness. This may be a punishment to the hour of my death, she thought.

The Grasstrail Train by now was down to only two wagons: in one, the rafiqi, Oatsie, Liir the boy, Pinchweed the entrepreneur, and a Gillikinese mechanic named Kowpp. In the other, Elphie herself, and the bees, the crows, and Killyjoy. Already she had, it seemed, been accepted as a witch. It was not an entirely unlikable disguise.

Kiamo Ko was just a week away.

The Grasstrail Train turned eastward, into the steel gray passes of the steep Great Kells. Winter was almost here, and the last travelers were grateful that the snows had held off. Oatsie intended to stop the winter in an Arjiki camp some twenty miles on. In the spring she would head back to the Emerald City, making the northern route through Ugabu, and the Pertha Hills of Gillikin. Elphie thought of sending a note to Glinda, if after all these years she was still there—but, being unable to decide yes, she decided no.

"Tomorrow," said Oatsie, "we'll see Kiamo Ko. The mountain strong-hold of the ruling clan of the Arjikis. Are you ready, Sister Elphie?"

She was teasing, and Elphie didn't like it. "I am no longer a sister, I am a witch," she said, and tried to think poisonous thoughts at Oatsie. But Oatsie was a stronger person than the cook, apparently, for she just laughed and went on her way.

The Grasstrail Train stopped on the side of a small tarn. The oth-ers said its water was refreshing, though icy cold; Elphie didn't know or care about that. But in the middle was an island—a tiny thing, the size of a mattress, sprouting one leafless tree like an umbrella that has lost its fabric.

Before Elphaba could quite make it out—the evening light came early at this time of year, and even earlier in the mountains—Killyjoy had plunged feverishly into the water, and splashed and swum his way to the island, intent on some small movement or interesting scent he had picked up. He ferreted in the sedge, and then clamped his teeth—the most wolflike of his features—gently around the skull of a small beast in the grass.

Elphie couldn't see but it looked like a baby.

Oatsie screamed, Liir quivered like a blob of jelly, Killyjoy released his grip, but only to get a further hold; he was drooling over the scalp of the thing he had caught.

There was no way to go through the water—that would be death—

But her feet *went out anyway*—

They hit the water hard, the water hit hard back—

The water turned to ice as she ran—foot by foot of ice under foot by foot of hurry. A silvering plate formed instantly, cantilevering forward, making a cold safe bridge to the island—

Where Killyjoy could be scolded, and the baby saved, though she hadn't dared hope she could be in time. She pried Killyjoy's jaws apart, and scooped up the thing. It shivered in terror and the cold. Its bright black eyes were alert and watching, ready to upbraid or condemn or love, same as any capable adult thing.

The others were surprised to see it, as surprised as they'd been to see the ice form, perhaps by some magic spell left on the tarn from some passing wizard or witch. It was a small monkey—of the variety called the snow monkey. A baby abandoned by its mother and its tribe, or maybe separated by accident?

It didn't think much of Killyjoy but it liked the warmth of the wagon.

They pitched their camp halfway up the perilous slope to Kiamo Ko. The castle rose in steep black angles out of black rock. Elphie could see it perched above them like an eagle with folded wings; its conical-roofed towers, its battlements and bartizans, its portcullis and arrow-slit windows—they all belied its original intention as the head of a waterworks. Below it wound a powerful tributary of the Vinkus River on which the Ozma Regent once had meant to build a dam and channel water into the center of Oz—back when the droughts were their most threatening. Fiyero's father had taken this stronghold by siege and storm and made it the seat of the Arjiki princes, before dying and leaving the clan leadership to his only son, if Elphaba remembered rightly.

The small luggage was packed, the bees hummed (their melodies ever more amusing as she listened, week by week), Killyjoy was still sulking over being denied the kill, the crows sensed that a change was coming and wouldn't eat dinner. The monkey, who was called Chistery because of the sound he made, chittered and chattered now that he was warm and safe.

Around the campfire good-byes were spoken, a few toasts, even a few regrets. The sky was blacker than it had been before: perhaps it was the contrast of the whiteness of snowy peaks all around. Liir showed up with a parcel of clothing and some sort of musical instrument, and said good-byes too.

"Oh, so you're stopping here, are you?" said Elphie.

"Yes," he said, "with you."

"With the crows, with the monkey, with the bees, with the dog, and with the Witch?" she said. "With me?"

"Where else can I go?" he asked.

"I'm sure I don't know," she answered.

"I can take care of the dog," he said calmly. "I can collect the honey for you."

"It makes no difference to me," she said.

"All right," he said, and so Liir prepared to enter his father's house.

The Jasper Gates of Kiamo Ko

I

Sarima," said her youngest sister, "wake up. Naptime's over. We have a houseguest at supper, and I need to know if we have to kill a hen. There are so few left, and what we give the traveler we miss all winter in eggs . . . What do you think?"

The Dowager Princess of the Arjikis groaned. "Details, details," she said, "can't I train you to figure out anything for yourself?"

"Very well," snapped the sister, "I shall decide, and then *you* can go without your morning egg when we're one short."

"Oh Six, don't mind me," said Sarima, "it's just that I'm scarcely awake. Who is it? Some patriarch with bad breath, who plans to bore us with tales of the hunting he did fifty years ago? Why do we allow it?"

"It's a woman—more or less," said Six.

"Now *that's* uncalled for," said Sarima, sitting up. "We are none of us the blushing nymphs we once were, Six." From across the room she saw herself reflected in the wardrobe glass: pale as milk pudding, her still pretty face nestled in the puddles of fat that fell according to the laws of gravity. "Just because you're the youngest, Six, and can still locate your waist, there's no need to be unkind."

Six pouted. "Well, it's just a woman, then: so chicken or no? Tell me now so Four can hack off its head and get to plucking, or we won't eat before midnight."

"We'll have fruit and cheese and bread and fish. Is there fish in the fishwell, I suppose?" Yes, there was. Six turned to go, but remembered to say, "I brought you a glass of sweet tea, it's there on your vanity."

"Bless you. Now tell me, without sarcasm if you please, what's our guest like, really?"

"Green as sin, thin and crooked, older than any of us. Dressed in black like an old maunt—but not all *that* old. I'd guess about, oh, thirty, thirty-two? She won't give her name."

"Green? How divine," said Sarima.

"Divine isn't the word that comes to mind," said Six.

"You don't mean green with jealousy—you mean actually *green?*"

"Maybe it's from jealousy, I could not say, but she is surely *green.* Genuine grass green."

"Oh la. Well, I'll wear white tonight so as not to clash. Is she alone?"

"She came in with the caravan we saw down in the valley yesterday. She stopped here with a little company of beasts—a wolfdog, a hive of bees, a youth, some crows, and a baby monkey."

"What'll she do with all of *them* in the mountains in winter?"

"Ask her yourself." Six wrinkled her nose. "She made me shudder."

"Half-set gelatin makes *you* shudder. When's dinner tonight?"

"Seven chimes and a half. She turns my stomach."

Six left, having run out of expressions of disgust, and Sarima had her tea in bed until her bladder complained. Six had banked up the fire and drawn the curtains, but Sarima pulled them back to look down into the courtyard. Kiamo Ko boasted corner turrets and towers, built on massive circular salients thrusting upward from the stone of the mountain itself. After the Arjiki clan had wrested the building from the waterworks commission, they had added toothy crenellations for defense. Despite the reworkings, the plan of the house was still simple. It was built in the general shape of a U, a central hall with two long narrow wings thrusting forward around a steeply pitched yard. When it rained, the water churned over the cobbles, and slipped out under the carved gates of iron oak and jasper panels, past the sickly cluster of village houses nestled up against the castle's outside walls. At this hour the courtyard was charcoal gray. Cold and filthy with scraps of hay and bits of leaf flying in the wind. There was a light in the old cobbler's shed, and smoke spinning from the chimney that badly wanted repointing—like everything else in this decaying manse. Sarima was glad the guest hadn't been shown into the house proper. As Dowager Princess of the Arjikis, she enjoyed the privilege of welcoming a traveler into the private chambers of Kiamo Ko.

After bathing, she dressed in a white shift with white piping, and put on the beautiful torque that had arrived, like a message from the Other Land, from her dear departed husband several months after the Incident. Out of habit Sarima shed a few tears admiring herself within the flat embrace of its jeweled, segmented collar. If it was too dressy for this itinerant, Sarima could always drape a napkin over it. But she would still know it was there. Even before her tears had dried she was humming, looking forward to the novelty of a guest.

She peeped in on the children before going down. They were jumpy; strangers always did that to them. Irji and Manek, twelve and eleven, were almost old enough to want to bust out of this nest of venomous doves. Irji was soft and cried a lot, but Manek was a little bantam, always had been. If she let them go off to the Grasslands with the clan, in the summer migration, they both might have their throats slit—there were too many clansmen to claim leadership for themselves or their sons. So Sarima had kept her boys near.

Her daughter, Nor, long-legged and thumb-sucking at nine years old, still needed a lap to crawl into before going to sleep. Dressed for the meal, Sarima was inclined to forbid it, but relented. Nor had a delicate lisp and she said *wunning in the wain* for *running in the rain*. She befriended stones and candles and blades of grass that grew against all logic in the cracks of the coping stones around the windows. She sighed and rubbed her face against the torque and said, "There's a boy too, Mama. We played with him in the mill yard."

"What's he like? Is he green too?"

"Nah. He's all right. He's a big baby—fat and strong, and Manek was throwing stones at him to see how far they would bounce off him. He *let* him do it. Maybe if you're so fat it doesn't hurt?"

"I doubt it. What's his name?"

"Liir. Isn't that a queer name?"

"It sounds foreign. And his mother?"

"I don't know her name and I don't think she's his *mother*. He wouldn't say when we asked. Irji said he must be a bastard. Liir said he didn't care. He's nice." She moved her right thumb to her mouth, and with her left hand felt the cloth of Sarima's gown just below the torque, until she found a nipple, and she ran her thumb over it lovingly as if it were a small pet. "Manek made him pull down his trousers so we could make sure his thing wasn't green."

Sarima disapproved—on the grounds of hospitality if nothing else—but was compelled to ask, "And what did you see?"

"Oh well *you* know." Nor turned her head into her mother's neck, and then sneezed from the powder with which Sarima kept her chins from chafing. "Stupid-looking boy's thing. Smaller than Manek and Irji. But not green. I was so *bored* I didn't look much."

"Neither would I. That was very rude."

"*I* didn't make him do it. Manek did!"

"Well, no more of that. Now let's have a story before sleeping. I've got to go down soon, so a short one. What do you want to hear, my little one?"

"I want to hear the story of the Witch and the fox babies."

With less drama than usual Sarima rattled through the tale of how the three fox babies were kidnapped and caged and fed to fatness, in preparation for a cheese-and-foxling casserole, and how the Witch went to get fire from the sun to cook them. But when the Witch came back to her cave, exhausted and in possession of father flame, the foxlings outwitted her by singing a lullaby to make her sleep. When the Witch's arm fell, the flame from the sun burned the door off the cage, and out the foxlings ran. Then they howled down old mother moon to come and stand as an unmovable door in the entrance of the cave. Sarima ended with the traditional back-and-forth. "And there the wicked old Witch stayed, for a good long time."

"Did she ever come out?" asked Nor, doing her line from an almost hypnagogic state.

"*Not yet*," said Sarima, kissing and biting her daughter on the wrist, which made them both giggle, and then lights out.

The stairs from Sarima's private apartment ran without railings down into the castle keep, hugging first one wall and then, after the corner, another. She descended the first flight full of grace and self-possession, her white skirts billowing, her torque a yoke of soft colors and precious metals, her face a careful composition of welcome.

At the landing she saw the traveler, sitting on a bench in an alcove, looking up at her.

She made it down the second flight to the flagstoned level, aware of the cynicism that seethed beneath her loyal remembrance of Fiyero, aware of her overbite; of her lost prettiness; of her weight; of the silliness of being the doyenne over nothing but irritating children and backbiting younger sisters; of the thin pretense of authority that scarcely masked her fear of the present, the future, and even the past.

"How do you do," she managed.

"You are Sarima," said the woman, standing, her stalactite of chin thrust forward like a rotted swede.

"Likely to be!" she said, glad of the torque; it seemed like a shield now, to protect her heart from being punctured by that chin. "Greetings to you, my friend. Yes, I am Sarima, mistress of Kiamo Ko. Where do you come from, and how are you called?"

"I come from the back of the wind," said the woman, "and I have given up my name so often I don't like to bring it out again for you."

"Well, you are welcome here," said Sarima as smoothly as she could, "but if we have nothing else to call you by, you will have to be Auntie. Will you come in to dine? We'll be serving out soon."

"I won't eat until we speak," said the guest. "Not under your roof in false pretenses for one night; I'd rather lie at the bottom of a lake. Sarima, I know who you are. I went to school with your husband. I've known about you for a dozen years or so."

"Of course," said Sarima then, things clicking. The old, treasured details of her husband's life came rushing up. "Of course Fiyero talked of you—and of your sister, Nessie, right? *Nessarose*. And of the glamorous Glinda, with whom I think he was a little in love, and the playful inverted boys, and Avaric, and solid old Boq! I had wondered if that happy time of his life was always to be self-contained, always his and never mine—you are good to have come to call. I should have liked a season or two at Shiz, but I didn't have the brains, I fear, nor my family the money. I would have remembered you in a minute, well, the color of your skin, there's nothing like it, is there? Or am I too provincial?"

"No, it's unique," said the guest. "Before we say ten sentences of polite nonsense to each other, I have to tell you something, Sarima. I think I was the cause of Fiyero's death—"

"Well, you're not the only one," interrupted Sarima, "it's a national pastime out here, blaming oneself for the death of a prince. An opportunity for public grieving and atonement, which I secretly believe people enjoy just a little bit."

The guest twisted her fingers, as if to pry open a space for herself in Sarima's opinions. "I can tell you how, I want to tell you—"

"Not unless I want to hear it, which is my prerogative. This is my house and I choose to hear what I want."

"You must hear it, so that I can be forgiven," said the woman, turning her shoulders this way and that, almost as if she were a beast of burden with an invisible yoke on her.

Sarima did not like to be ambushed in her own home. Time enough to consider these sudden implications. When she felt up to it. And not until. She reminded herself that *she was in charge.* And thus she could afford to be kind.

"If I remember rightly," said Sarima—her mind was racing with memory—"you're the one, Fiyero talked of you, of course—Elphaba, that's it—you're the one who didn't believe in the soul. I remember that much, so what's to forgive, dearie? I know you're travel weary—it's impossible to get here *without* being travel weary—and you need a good hot meal and a few nights of sleep, and we'll chat some morning next week?"

Sarima linked her arm with Elphaba's. "But I'll preserve your name from them, if you like," said Sarima. She walked Elphaba through the tall warped oak doors into the dining hall and called, "Look who's here, Auntie Guest." The sisters were standing beside their chairs, hungry and curious and impatient. Four had the ladle in the tureen, stirring; Six had dressed in a hostile puce; Two and Three, the twins, looked piously at their prayer cards; Five was smoking and blowing concentric rings toward the platter of yellow eyeless fish they had dragged up from the underground lake. "Sisters, rejoice, an old friend of Fiyero's has come to share fond memories and enliven our lives. Welcome her as you do me." Perhaps an unfortunate choice of words, as the sisters all resented and despised Sarima. *Why* had she married someone who would die so early and condemn them not just to spinsterhood but to deprivation and denial?

Elphaba didn't speak through the entire meal or look up from her plate. She devoured the fish, though, and the cheese and the fruit. Sarima deduced from her eating habits that she had lived under a rule of silence at meals, and wasn't surprised, later, to hear about the mauntery.

They took a glass of precious sherry in the music room, and Six entertained them with a wobbling nocturne. The guest looked miserable, which made the sisters happy. Sarima sighed. The one thing that could be said about the guest was this: She was *older* than Sarima. Perhaps, for the short while of her stay, Elphaba would come out of that sulk and lend an ear to hear how troubling and trying Sarima's life was. It would be nice to chat with someone not in the family.

2

A week passed before Sarima said to Three, "Please tell our Auntie Guest that I'd like to see her tomorrow for elevenses in the Solar." Sarima thought that Elphaba had had enough time now to get the measure of things. The suffering green woman was in some sort of slow-motion thrall, or fit. She moved jerkily, stalking about the courtyard, or stamping in to meals as if trying to poke holes in the flooring with her heels. Her elbows were always bent at right angles, and her hands clenched and unclenched themselves.

Sarima felt stronger than ever, which wasn't very. It did her some good to have a contemporary around, however thwarted she might be. The sisters disapproved of Sarima's cordiality, but the higher mountain passes were already closed for the winter, and you just couldn't send a stranger packing into the treacherous valleys. The sisters conferred in their parlor, as they busied themselves knitting hateful gray potholders for the undeserving poor at Lurlinemas. She's sick, they said; she's inert, unfinished (even more than they were, was the unspoken corollary, an *immensely* gratifying notion); she's damned. And is that fat balloon of a boy her son, or a child slave, or is he one of her familiars? Behind Sarima's back they called the woman living in the cobbleshed Auntie Witch, echoing the old legends of Kumbricia, which were viler—and more persistent—in the Kells than elsewhere in Oz.

It was Manek, Sarima's middle child, who was the most curious. One morning, as the boys all stood on a battlement pissing over the side (a game poor Nor had to pretend no interest in), Manek said, "What if we peed on Auntie? Would she scream?"

"She'd turn you into a toad," said Liir.

"No, I mean would it hurt her? She looks like water gives her the aches and shakes. Does she even drink it? Or does it make her insides hurt?"

Liir, not an especially observant child, said, "I think she doesn't drink it. Sometimes she washes things, but she uses sticks and brushes. We better not pee on her."

"And what does she do with all those bees and the monkey? Are they magic?"

"Yeah," said Liir.

"What kind of magic?"

"I don't know." They stepped away from the dizzying drop and Nor came running up. "I have a magic straw," she said, holding up a brown bristle. "From the Witch's broom."

"Is the broom magic?" said Manek to Liir.

"Yes. It can sweep the floor real fast."

"Can it talk? Is it enchanted? What does it say?"

They got more interested, and Liir bloomed and blushed under their curiosity. "I can't tell. It's a secret."

"Is it still a secret if we push you off the tower?"

Liir considered. "What do you mean?"

"Will you tell us or we'll do it."

"Don't push me off the tower, you oafs."

"If the broom is magic it'll come flying by and save you. Besides, you're so fat you'd probably bounce."

Irji and Nor laughed at that, despite themselves. It made a very funny picture in their minds.

"We only want to know what secrets the broom says to you," said Manek with a big smile. "So tell us. Or we'll push you off."

"You're not being nice, he's *company*," said Nor. "Come on, let's go find some mice in the pantry and make friends."

"In a minute. Let's push Liir off the roof first."

"No," said Nor, beginning to cry. "You boys are *so mean*. Are you sure that broom is magic, Liir?"

But Liir by now didn't want to say any more.

Manek tossed a pebble off the roof and it seemed a very long time before the *ping* of impact.

Liir's face had, in a matter of moments, developed deep black pockets under the eyes. He held his hands down by his sides like a traitor at a court martial. "The Witch'll be so mad at you that she will hate you," Liir said.

"I don't think so," said Manek, taking a step forward. "She won't care. She likes the monkey more than she likes you. She won't even notice if you're dead."

Liir gasped for air. Although he had just peed, the front of his baggy trousers turned dark with wet. "Look, Irji," said Manek, and his older brother looked. "He's not even very good at being alive is he? It's not like it would be much of a loss. Come on, Liir, *tell* me. What did the damned broom say to you?"

Liir's upper torso was going in and out like a bellows. He whispered, "The broom told me—that—that—you're all going to die!"

"Oh, is that all," said Manek. "We already knew that. Everybody dies. We knew that already."

"You did?" said Liir, who hadn't.

"Come on," Irji said, "come on, let's catch some mice in the pantry and we can cut off their tails and use Nor's magic straw to prick their eyes."

"No!" said Nor, but Irji had swiped the straw from her. Manek and Irji went clattering, loose-limbed as marionettes, along the parapet and down the stairs. With a huge, aggrieved sigh, Liir composed himself and adjusted his clothes, and followed them like a condemned dwarf laborer in the emerald mines. Nor stayed behind, her arms folded defiantly, her chin working with frustration. Then she spit over the edge and felt better, and chased after the boys.

At midmorning, Six showed the guest into the Solar. With a smirk behind Auntie's back, she deposited a tray of cruel little biscuits, hard as slate, on a table covered with a carpet gone brown and patternless. Sarima, having made her way through what she could of her daily spiritual ablutions, felt ready.

"You've been here a week and it's likely to be longer," said Sarima, allowing Six to pour out some gallroot coffee before dismissing her. "The trail north is snowed in by now, and there's not a safe haven between here and the plains. The winters are hard in the mountains, and while we can make do with our stores and our own company, we treasure a change.

Milk? I do not know exactly what you had—intended. Once you had vis-ited us sufficiently, I mean."

"There are rumors of caves in these Kells," Elphaba said, almost more to herself than to Sarima. "I lived for some years at the Cloister of Saint Glinda in the Shale Shallows, outside of the Emerald City. Dignitaries would visit, and while we were often under a vow of silence, nonetheless people would talk of what they knew. Monastic cells. I had thought, when I was done here, that I might take myself to a cave and—and—"

"And set up housekeeping," said Sarima, as if this were as usual as marrying and bearing babies. "Some do it, I know. There's an old hermit on the western slope of Broken Bottle—that's a peak nearby—they say he's been there for some years, and has reverted to a more primitive moment of nature. Of *his* nature, I mean."

"A life without words," Elphie said, looking in her coffee and not drinking it.

"They say this hermit has forgotten about personal hygiene," said Sarima, "which, given how the boys smell when they go unwashed for a couple of weeks, strikes me as nature's defense against marauding beasts."

"I didn't expect to be here for a long time," Elphie said, twisting her head on her neck like a parrot and looking at Sarima in an odd way. Oh, beware, thought Sarima carefully, though she tended to like this guest: Beware, she's taking the direction of the discussion into her own hands. This won't do. But the guest went on: "I had thought that I would have a night or two, maybe three, and could find myself a hidey-hole before win-ter set in. I was working on the wrong calendar, I was thinking of how, and when, winter came to Shiz and the Emerald City. But you're six weeks ahead here."

"Ahead in the autumn and behind in the spring, alas," said Sarima. She took her feet off her hassock and placed them on the floor, flatly, to indicate seriousness. "Now, my new friend, there are some things I need to say to you."

"I have things too," Elphie said, but Sarima went on this time.

"You will think me an unpolished person, and you are right of course. Oh, when I was selected to be a child bride, a good governess was hired from Gillikin to teach me and my sisters how to use verbs and pronouns and salad forks. And lately I have begun to master reading. But most of what I picked up about polite behavior was from what Fiyero was good enough to instruct me in when he returned from his education. No doubt I make social mistakes. You have every right to snigger behind my back."

"I am not given to sniggering," snapped Elphaba.

"As it may be. But I still have opinions, and I'm observant even if unschooled. Despite my sheltered life, married at the age of seven as you may know, raised and reared behind castle curtain walls. I trust my own sense of things and won't be dissuaded. So let me continue," she said, as Elphaba tried to interrupt. "There is plenty of time and the sun is nice in here, isn't it? *My* little hideaway.

"It seems to me that you have come here to—shall we say—relieve yourself of some sad business or other. You have the look about you. Don't be startled, my dear, if there's a look I do recognize, it's the look of someone carrying a burden. Remember, I listen to my sisters, year in and year out, as they graciously share with me all the ways they hate me, and why." She smiled, amused at her own wit. "You want to throw down your burden, throw it down at my feet, or across my shoulders. You want per-haps to weep a little, to say good-bye, and then to leave. And when you leave here you will walk right out of the world."

"I will do no such thing," said Elphie.

"You will indeed, even if you don't know it. You will have nothing left to tie you to the world. But I know my own limits, Auntie Guest, and I know what you're here for. You told me. You told me in the hall, you said you felt you were responsible for Fiyero's death—"

"I—"

"*Don't.* Just don't. This is my home, I am a nominal Dowager Princess of Duckshit, but I have a right to hear and I have a right not to hear. Even to make a traveler feel better."

"I—"

"Don't."

"But I don't want to burden you, Sarima, I want to unburden you with the truth—if you permit me, you are the larger, the lighter; forgive-ness blesses the donor as well as the receiver."

"I'll overlook that remark about my being the larger," said Sarima. "But I still have the right to choose. And I think you wish me ill. You wish me ill and you don't even know it. You want to punish me for something. Maybe for not being a good enough wife to Fiyero. You wish me ill and you fool yourself to think it's some therapeutic course of tablets."

"Do you know how he died, at least?" said Elphaba.

"I know it was a violent action, I know his body was never found, I know it was in a little love nest," said Sarima, for a minute losing her resolve. "I don't care to know who it was exactly, but I have heard enough about that vile Sir Chuffrey to have my strong opin—"

"Sir *Chuffrey!*"

"I said *no*. I said *no more.* Now I have an offer to make of you, Auntie, if you will have it. You and the boy may move into the southeast tower if you like. There are a couple of big round rooms with high ceilings, and good light, and you'll be out of that drafty cobbleshed, and warmer. You'll have your own staircase to come and go into the main hall, and you won't bother the girls and they won't trouble you. You can't stay in that cobbleshed all winter. The boy has been looking pale and blubbery, I think he's always cold. You're there on the condition, I'm afraid, that you accept my firmest word on these matters. I don't care to discuss my husband or the affairs of his death with you."

Elphaba looked horror-struck, and beaten. "I have no choice but to accept," she said, "at least for the time being. But I warn you, I intend to befriend you so thoroughly that you will change your mind. And I do think you need to hear things, you need to talk about them, as I do—and I can't leave into the wilderness until I have your solemn promise of—"

"Enough!" said Sarima. "Call the porter from the gatehouse and have him bring your luggage to the tower. Come, I'll show you. You haven't touched your coffee." She stood. For an awkward moment there was respect and suspicion, in equal measure, simmering on the carpet like the dust in the sunbeams. "Come," Sarima said, more softly, "at the very least you need to be warm. You must be able to say that much of us country mice here at Kiamo Ko."

3

As far as Elphaba was concerned, it was a witch's room, and she reveled in it. Like all good witch's rooms in children's stories, it was a room with bowed walls, following the essential form of a tower. It had one broad window that, since it faced east, away from the wind, could be unbarred and opened without blowing everyone and everything out into the snowy valleys. Beyond, the Great Kells were a rank of sentinels, pur-ple-black when the winter sun rose over them, draining into blue-white screens as the sun moved overhead, and going golden and ruddy in the late afternoon. There were sometimes rumbling collapses of ice and scree.

The winter gripped the house. Elphaba learned soon enough to stay put unless she was sure another room had a warmer fire. And except for Sarima, she didn't care for the other human company the house afforded. Sarima lived in the west wing, with the children: the boys Irji and Manek, the girl Nor. Sarima's five sisters lived in the east wing—they were called numbers Two through Six, and if they had ever had other names they had withered away from disuse. By right of their unmarriageability, the sisters claimed the best rooms in the place, although Sarima had the Solar. Where Liir curled up to sleep Elphaba did not know, but he reappeared every morning to change the rags at the bottom of the crows' perch. He brought her cocoa, too.

Lurlinemas drew near, and out came some tired decorations from which the gilt had all but vanished. The children spent a whole day tying baubles and toys to the archways, making the grown-ups bump their heads and curse. Manek and Irji took a saw and without permission went beyond the castle walls to claim some boughs of spruce and sprigs of holly. Nor stayed behind and painted scenes of happy life in the castle on sheets of paper that she and Liir had found in Auntie Witch's room. Liir said he couldn't draw, so he wandered off and disappeared, perhaps to stay clear of Manek and Irji. The house fell still until there was a flurry of copper pans thrown about the kitchen. Nor went running to see, and Liir arrived from some hiding cubby to look too.

It was Chistery. The monkey was having a fit, and all the sisters, baking gingerbread, were throwing gobbets of batter at him, trying to knock him off the wheel that hung, noisy with swinging utensils, above the worktable.

"How'd he get in here?" said Nor.

"Get him out, Liir, call him!" said Two. But Liir had no more authority over Chistery than they did. The monkey flew to the top of a wardrobe, then to a huge dried goods canister, and he pulled open a drawer and found a precious store of raisins, which he stuffed in his mouth. Six said, "Go get the ladder from the hall, you two, and bring it here," but when they had, Chistery was back on the wheel, making it whirl and clatter like a roundabout at a carnival.

Four put a lump of mashed melon in a bowl. Five and Three took off their aprons, ready to rush him when he came down. Chistery was still eyeing the fruit when the door smacked open against the wall and Elphaba came lolloping in. "All this commotion, how can you hear yourselves think?" she cried, and then took in the sight of Chistery, suddenly abject and remorseful, and of the sisters, poised to ensnare him in their floury aprons.

"What the *hell* is this?" she said.

"No need to yell," said Two sulkily, quietly, but they put down their aprons.

"I mean, what is this? What is *really going on here?* You all look like Killyjoy, with blood lust in your faces! You're white with rage at this poor beast!"

"I think it's not rage, it's flour," said Five, which made them giggle.

"You filthy savages," said Elphie. "Chistery come here, come down here. Right now. You women *deserve* to be unmarried, so you don't bring any little savage creepy children into the world. Don't you ever lay a hand on this monkey, do you hear me? And how did he get out of my room anyway? I was in the Solar with your sister."

"Oh," said Nor, remembering, "oh, Auntie, I'm sorry. It was us."

"You?" She turned and looked at Nor as if for the first time, and Nor didn't like it much. She shrank back against the door of the cold cellar. "What were you skulking about in my room for?" said Elphie.

"Some paper," said Nor faintly, and in a desperate, all-or-nothing gamble, said, "I made some paintings for *everybody*, do you want to see, come here."

Chistery in her arms, Elphaba followed them into the drafty hall, where the wind under the front door was making the papers flutter against the carved stone. The sisters came too, a safe distance behind.

Elphie got very quiet. "This is my paper," she said. "I didn't say you could use it. Look, it has words on the back. Do you know what words are?"

"Of course I do, do you think I am slow?" responded Nor sassily.

"You leave my papers alone," said Elphaba. She and Chistery then flew up the steps, and the door to the tower slammed behind them.

"Who wants to help roll out the gingerbread?" said Two, relieved that skulls hadn't been knocked together. "And this hall looks very pretty, chickadees, I'm sure Preenella and Lurline will be impressed tonight." The children went back into the kitchen and made gingerbread people, and crows, and monkeys, and dogs, but they couldn't do bees, they were too small. When Irji and Manek came in, dumping snowy greens on the slate floor, they helped at the gingerbread shapes too, but they made naughty shapes that they wouldn't show the younger children, and they kept gobbling up the raw dough and laughing hysterically at it, which made everyone else testy.

In the morning the children awoke and ran downstairs to see if Lurline and Preenella had been there. Sure enough, there was a brown wicker basket with a green and gold ribbon on it (a basket and a ribbon that Sarima's children had seen many years in a row), and in it were three small colored boxes, each one with an orange, a puppet, a small sack of marbles, and a gingerbread mouse.

"Where's mine?" said Liir.

"Don't see one with your name on it," said Irji. "Look: *Irji. Manek. Nor.* Guess Preenella left it for you at your old house. Where did you used to live?"

"I don't know," said Liir, and started to cry.

"Here, you can have the tail of my mouse, *just* the tail," said Nor kindly. "First you have to say, May I please have the tail of your mouse?"

"May I please have the tail of your mouse," said Liir, though his words were almost unintelligible.

"And I promise to obey you."

Liir mumbled on. The exchange was eventually completed. From shame, Liir didn't mention the oversight. Sarima and the sisters never took it in.

Elphaba didn't show her face all day, but she sent down a message that Lurlinemas Eve and Lurlinemas always made her ill, and she was taking a few days in solitary comfort, and she wanted to be disturbed neither with meals, nor visitors, nor noise of any kind.

So while Sarima took herself off to her private chapel to remember her dear husband on this holy day, the sisters and the children all sang carols as loudly as they could.

4

A few weeks later, when the children were having snowball battles, and Sarima was concocting some medicinal toddy in the kitchen, Elphie left her room at last and skulked down the stairs and knocked on the door of the sisters' parlor.

They didn't like it, but they felt obliged to welcome her. The silver tray with bottles of hard liquor, the precious crystal carried on donkey all the way from Dixxi House in Gillikin, the prettiest and red-richest of native carpets on the floor, the luxury of fireplaces at both sides of the room, each blazing merrily—well, they would have toned it down some had they had any warning. As it was, Four hid in the sofa cushions the leather volume from which she had been reading aloud, a racy history of a poor young woman beset by an abundance of handsome suitors. It had been a gift from Fiyero once, the best gift he had ever sent the sisters—also the only one.

"Would you like some lemon barley water?" said Six, ever the servant until the day she died, unless by luck everyone else died sooner.

"Yes, all right," Elphaba said.

"Do take a seat—this seat here, you'll find it most comfy."

Elphie didn't look as if she wanted to be comfy, but she sat there anyway, stiff and uneasy in that quilted cocoon of a room.

She took the tiniest sip possible from her drink, as if suspecting hellebore.

"I suppose I need to apologize for that flurry over Chistery," she said. "I know I am your guest here at Kiamo Ko. I just flew off the handle."

"Well, you did just that," started Five, but the others said, "Oh, think nothing of it, we all have days like that, in fact for us it usually happens on the same day, it's been that way for years . . ."

"It's very taxing," Elphie said with some effort. "I spent many years under a vow of silence, and I haven't always learned how—loud—it is permissible to get. Besides that, this is a foreign culture, in a way."

"We Arjikis have always been proud of being able to speak to any other citizen in Oz," said Two. "We are as equally at home with the ragged vagabond Scrow to our south as with the elite in the Emerald City to our east." Not that they'd ever been out of the Vinkus.

"A little nibble?" said Three, bringing out a tin of marzipan fruits.

"No," Elphie said, "but I wonder what you could tell me of your sister's particular sadness."

They sat poised, tempted, and suspicious.

"I enjoy my chats with her in the Solar," said Elphie, "but whenever the talk gets around to her departed husband—whom as you may realize I myself knew—she is unwilling to discuss a thing."

"Oh, well, it was so sad," said Two.

"A tragedy," said Three.

"For her," said Four.

"For *us*," said Five.

"Auntie Guest, take a little orange liqueur in your lemon barley," said Six, "it comes from the balmy slopes of the Lesser Kells and is *quite* a luxury."

"Well, just a drop," said Elphie, but didn't sip it. She put her elbows on her knees and leaned forward and said, "Please tell me how she learned of Fiyero's death."

There was a silence. The sisters avoided casting glances at one another, busying themselves with the pleats of their skirts. After a pause, it was Two who said, "That sad day. It stings in the memory still."

The others adjusted themselves in their seats, turning slightly toward her. Elphaba blinked twice, looking like one of her own crows.

Two told the tale, without sentiment or drama. One of Fiyero's business colleagues, an Arjiki trader, had come through the mountain pass at the first spring thaw, on the back of a mountain skark. He asked to meet with Sarima and insisted her sisters be around to support her at his woeful news. He told them how, on Lurlinemas, he had received at his club an anonymous message that Fiyero had been murdered. There was an address in a disreputable area—not even a residential neighborhood. The clansman hired a couple of brutes and broke down the door of the warehouse. Inside was a small apartment hidden upstairs, a place of assignation, obviously. (The clansman reported this without flinching, perhaps as a power-mongering maneuver.) There was evidence of struggle and massive quantities of blood, so thick in places that it was still tacky. The body had been removed, and it was never recovered.

Elphaba only nodded, grimly, at this recounting.

"For a year," continued Two, "our dear distraught Sarima refused to believe he was really dead. We would not have been surprised at a ransom note. But by the following Lurlinemas, when no further word about it had arrived, we had to accept the inevitable. Besides, the clan had gone on as long as it could with an ad hoc collaborative leadership; they demanded a single chief, and one was put forward, and he's served well. When Irji comes of age he may claim the rights of progenitorship, if he's bold enough; he is not yet bold at all. Manek is the more obvious candidate, but he's only second in line."

"And what does Sarima believe happened?" said Elphie. "And you? All of you?"

Now that the grimmest part of the story had been told, the other sisters felt they could chime in. It emerged that Sarima had for some years suspected Fiyero of having an affair with an old college chum named Glinda, a Gillikinese girl of legendary beauty.

"Legendary?" Elphie said.

"He told us all how charming she was, how self-effacing, what grace and sparkle—"

"Is it all that likely he'd gush on and on about a woman he was committing adultery with?"

"Men," said Two, "are, as we all know, both cruel and cunning. What better ruse than to admit fervently and often that he admired her? Sarima had no grounds on which to accuse him of slyness and deception. He never stopped being attentive to her—"

"In his cold, morose, withdrawn, embittered fashion," interjected Three.

"Hardly the thing one reads about in novels," said Four.

"If one read novels," said Five.

"Which we don't," said Six, closing her lips over a marzipan pear.

"And so Sarima believes her husband was carrying on with this— this—"

"This dazzler," said Two. "You must have known her, didn't you go to Shiz?"

"I knew her a bit," Elphie said, her mouth forgetting to shut itself. She was having a hard time keeping up with the multiple narrators. "I haven't seen her in years."

"And it is clear in Sarima's mind what happened," said Two. "Glinda was—for all I know still is—married to a wealthy older gentleman named Sir Chuffrey. He must have suspected something, and had her followed, and found out what was going on. Then he had some thugs kill the bastard. I mean poor Fiyero. Doesn't that make sense?"

"It's entirely plausible," Elphie said slowly. "But is there any proof?"

"No proof at all," said Four. "If there were, family honor would have required a retributive murder of Sir Chuffrey. But he may still be in robust good health. No, it's only a theory, but it's what Sarima believes."

"Clings to," said Six.

"And why not," said Five.

"It's her prerogative," said Three.

"Everything's her prerogative," said Two sadly. "Besides, think of it. If your husband were murdered, wouldn't it be easier to bear if you thought he deserved it, even just a little?"

"No," Elphie said, "I don't think it would."

"Neither do we," admitted Two, "but we think that's what *she* thinks."

"And you?" Elphie asked, studying the pattern in the carpet, the blood red lozenges, the thorny margins, the beasts and acanthus leaves and rose medallions. "What do you think?"

"We hardly can be expected to subscribe to a unanimous opinion," said Two, but she barreled ahead anyway. "It seems reasonable to suppose that unbeknownst to us, Fiyero had gotten involved in some political enterprise in the Emerald City."

"A stay that was to be a month became four," said Four.

"Had he political—sensibilities?" said Elphaba.

"He was the Prince of the Arjikis," Five reminded them all. "He had connections—responsibilities—allegiances—who of us could guess at them? It was his duty to have opinions on things we shouldn't need to know about."

"Was he sympathetic to the Wizard?" said Elphie.

"Are you saying was he involved in any of those campaigns? Those—pogroms? First the Quadlings, then the Animals?" said Three. "You look surprised that we should know about these things. Do you think we're so very removed from the rest of Oz?"

"We are removed," said Two. "But we listen to talk. We like to feed travelers when they come to stop. We know life can be rotten out there."

"The Wizard is a despot," said Four.

"Our home is our castle," said Five at the same time. "Some removal from all this is healthy. We retain our moral fiber, unsullied."

They all smirked, simultaneously.

"But do you think Fiyero had an opinion about the Wizard?" Elphaba asked again, pressing with some urgency.

"He kept his own counsel," snapped Two. "For the sake of sweet Lurline, dear Auntie, he was a prince and a man!—and we were nothing but his younger, dependent sisters-in-law! Do you think he would confide in us? He could have been a high-level crony of the Wizard for all we know! He surely would've had liaisons with the Palace, he was a prince. Even if only of our small tribe. What he did with those liaisons—how are we to say? But we *don't* think he died as the victim of a jealous husband. Maybe we're sheltered, but we don't. We think he got caught in the crossfire of some fringe struggle. Or he was found out in the act of betrayal of one excitable group or other. He was a handsome man," said Two, "and none of us would deny it, then or now. But he was intense and private and we doubt he'd have loosened up enough to have an affair." By the smallest gesture—a sucking in of her abdomen and a squaring of her shoulders—Two betrayed the foundation of her position: How could he have succumbed to this Glinda's charms if he had been able to resist his own sisters-in-law?

"But," Elphie asked in a small voice, "do you really think he was a spy for someone?"

"Why was his body never found?" said Two. "If it had been a jealous rage, his body needn't have been removed. Perhaps he hadn't died yet. Perhaps he was taken to be tortured. No, in our limited experience, we think that this smacks of treachery of a political stripe, not a romantic one."

"I—" said Elphaba.

"You're pale, dear. Six, please, a beaker of water—"

"No," said Elphaba. "It's just so—one never thought at the time—I never. Shall I tell you what little I know of it? And perhaps you can mention it to Sarima." She began to pace. "I saw Fiyero—"

But, at the oddest possible moment, family solidarity kicked in. "Dear Auntie Guest," said Two, in a responsible tone, "we are under the strictest orders from our sister not to allow you to tire yourself by chatting about Fiyero and the sad circumstances of his death." Clearly Two had to work to get this out, as the appetite to hear what Elphaba had to say was huge. Stomachs were rumbling for the meat of it. But propriety won out, or fear of Sarima's wrath if she were to find out. "No," said Two again, "no, I'm afraid we mustn't express undue interest. We may not listen and we will not tell Sarima what we hear."

In the end, Elphaba left them, drooping. "Another time," she kept saying, "when you're ready, when she's ready. You see it's essential; there's so much grief she could be released from—and that she herself could lift, too—"

"Good-bye for now," they said, and the door closed behind her. The fires in the twin fireplaces mirrored back and forth across the room, and they took up positions of frustrated worthiness, at having to obey their older sister—curse her to hell.

5

Ice crusted the roofs, dislodged tiles, and dripped dirtily into the private chambers, the music room, the towers. Elphaba took to wearing her hat indoors to avoid the random icy dart on her scalp. The crows were mildewy around the beak and had algae between the claws. The sisters finished their novel, and collectively sighed—for life, for life!—and began to read it again, as they had done for eight years. In the fierce updraft from the valley, the snow seemed as often to be rising as falling. The children adored it.

One glum afternoon Sarima bedecked herself in red woolen wraps and, out of boredom, went wandering through musty, disused rooms. She located a staircase in a trapezoidal, slanting shaft—perhaps this high alcove leaned against the side of the gable you couldn't see, she wasn't good at imagining architecture in three dimensions. She mounted the stairs anyway. At the top, through a crude grillwork, she saw a figure in the white gloom. Sarima coughed so as not to startle her.

Elphaba was bent almost double over a huge folio laid out on a carpenter's work bench. She turned, surprised but not very, and said, "We've had the same inclination, how curious."

"You've found some books, I'd completely forgotten," said Sarima. She could read now, but not well, and books made her feel inferior. "I couldn't tell you what they're all about. So many words, you'd hardly think the world deserved such scrutiny."

"Over here is an archaic geography," said Elphie, "and some records of usufruct pacts among various families of the Arjiki—I bet there are leaders who would be very happy to see these. Unless they're outdated. Some texts that Fiyero had in Shiz—I recognize them too, the life sciences course of studies."

"And this big thing—purple pages and silver ink, how grand."

"I found it on the floor of this wardrobe. It seems to be a Grimmerie," Elphie said, running her hand down a page only softly buckled with moisture. It made a pretty contrast, her hand on the vellum.

"What is that, besides beautiful?"

"As I understand it," Elphie said, "a sort of encyclopedia of things numinous. Magic; and of the spirit world; and of things seen and unseen; and of things once and future. I can only make out a line here or there. Look how it scrambles itself as you watch." She pointed to a paragraph of hand-lettered text. Sarima peered. Though her skill at reading was minimal, she gaped at what she saw. The letters floated and rearranged themselves on the page, as if enlivened. The page was changing its mind as they watched it. The letters clotted together in a big black snarl, like a mound of ants. Then Elphaba turned a page. "Here, this section is a book of beasts." There were elegant, attenuated drawings in blood red and gold leaf, on the front and rear elevations of (it seemed) an angel, with notes in a fine hand on the aerodynamic aspects of holiness. The wings flexed up and down and the angel smiled with a saucy sort of sanctity. "And a recipe on this page. It says 'Of apples with black skin and white flesh: to fill the stomach with greed unto Death.'"

"I remember this book now," Sarima said. "I do remember how it came to be here, I even put it up here myself; I had forgotten. Well, books are so easy to set aside, aren't they?"

Elphie looked up, her eyes leveling out under her smooth, rocklike brow. "Tell me, Sarima, please."

The Dowager Princess of Kiamo Ko was flustered. She went to a small window and tried to open it, but encrustations of ice prevented her. So she sat down in a flump on a packing crate and told Elphaba the story. She couldn't remember exactly when, but it was a long time ago, when everyone was young and slim. Beloved Fiyero was still alive but he was off in the Grasslands with the tribe. Complaining of a headache, she was home in the castle all alone. The bell at the drawbridge sounded and she went to see who it was.

"Madame Morrible," Elphaba said. "Some Kumbric Witch or other."

"No, it was no madame. It was an elderly man in a tunic and leggings, with a cloak badly in need of attention by a seamstress. He said he was a sorcerer, but perhaps he was just mad. He asked for a meal and a bath, which he got, and then he said he wanted to pay by giving me this book. I told him with a castle to run I didn't have much time for frivolity, reading and such. He said never mind."

Sarima drew her robes about her, and traced a pattern in the cold dust on a nearby stack of codexes. "He told me a fabulous tale and persuaded me to take this thing from him. He said that it was a book of knowledge, and that it belonged in another world, but it wasn't safe there. So he had brought it here—where it could be hidden and out of harm's way."

"What a load of tripe," said Elphie. "If it came from another world I shouldn't be able to read any of it. And I can make out a little."

"Even if it's as magic as he says?" said Sarima. "But you know, I believed him. He said there was more congress between worlds than anyone would credit, that our world has attributes of his, and his of ours, a kind of leakage effect, or an infection maybe. He had a long fringy white-and-gray beard, and a very kind and abstracted manner, and he smelled of garlic and sour cream."

"Indisputable proof of other-worldliness—"

"Don't mock me," said Sarima blandly, "you've asked me, so I'm telling you. He said it was too powerful to be destroyed, but too threatening—to that other place—to be preserved. So he made a magic trip or something and came here."

"Kiamo Ko called to him and he couldn't resist her attractions—"

"He said we were isolated, and a stronghold," said Sarima, "and I couldn't disagree! And what did it mean to me to take another book? We just lugged it up here, and put it with the rest. I don't even know if I told anyone about it. Then he blessed me and left. He walked with an oak-thorn staff over the Locklimb Trail."

"Can you really say you thought the man who brought this here was a sorcerer?" said Elphie. "And that this book comes from—another world? Do you even believe in other worlds?"

"I find it a great effort to believe in this one," said Sarima, "yet it seems to be here, so why should I trust my skepticism about other worlds? Don't you believe?"

"I tried to, as a child," said Elphie. "I made an effort. The mothy, gormless, indistinct sunrise of salvation world—the Other Land—I couldn't get it, I couldn't focus. Now I just think it's our own lives that are hidden from us. The mystery—who is that person in the mirror—that's shocking and unfathomable enough for me."

"Well he was a very nice sorcerer, or madman, or whatever."

"Maybe it was some agent loyal to the Ozma Regent," said Elphie. "Secreting some ancient Lurlinist tract here. Anticipating a revival of royalism, a Palace coup, worried about the kidnapped, sleep-charmed Ozma Tippetarius, coming in disguise to hide this document far away, but still retrievable. . . ."

"You are full of conspiracy theories," said Sarima. "I've noticed that about you. This was an elderly gentleman, very elderly. And he spoke with an accent. He surely was a wandering magician from some other place. And hasn't he been right? The thing has sat here, forgotten, for what, ten years or more already."

"May I take it and look at it?"

"I don't care. He never said not to read it," said Sarima. "At the time I perhaps couldn't read at all—I forget. But look at that beautiful angel there! Do you really mean to say you don't believe in the Other Land? In an afterlife?"

"Just what we need." Elphaba snorted as she picked up the tome. "A post Vale-of-Tears Vale-of-Tears."

6

One morning, after Six had tried and given up once again at some sort of lessons for the children, Irji suggested an indoor game of hide-and-seek. They drew straws and Nor lost, so she hid her eyes and counted. When she got bored with waiting she called out "One hundred!" and looked about.

She tagged Liir first. Though he liked to disappear alone for hours at a time, he was bad at hiding when it was required of him. So they hunted together for the older boys, and found Irji in Sarima's Solar, crouching behind the velvet ruffles suspended from the perch of a stuffed gryphon.

But Manek, the best at hiding, couldn't be found. Not in the kitchen, the music room, the towers. Running out of ideas, the children even dared to go down into the musty basement.

"There's tunnels from here all the way to hell," said Irji.

"Where? Why?" said Nor, and Liir echoed.

"They're hidden. I don't know where. But everybody says so. Ask Six. I think because this used to be a waterworks headquarters—it did. Hell burns so hot they need water, and the devils tunneled up to here."

Nor said, "Look, Liir, here's the fishwell."

In the center of a low-vaulted room, damp with moisture beaded up on its stone walls, stood a low well with a wooden lid. There was a simple device with a chain and a stone for shifting the lid sideways. It was child's play to uncover the shaft.

"Down there," said Irji, "is where we get the fish we eat. Nobody knows if there's a whole lake down there or if it's bottomless, or if you can go down right to hell." He moved the rushlight about, and there was a round of black water shining back a reflection, in chips and circles of chilly white light.

"Six says there's a gold carp in there," said Nor. "She saw it once. Biggest old thing, she thought it was a floating brass kettle bobbing to the surface, and then it turned and looked at her."

"Maybe it *was* a brass kettle," said Liir.

"Kettles don't have eyes," said Nor.

"Anyway, Manek's not here," said Irji. "Is he?" He called, "Hello, Manek," and the echo rolled and dissolved in the wet dark.

"Maybe Manek went down to hell in one of those tunnels," said Liir.

Irji swung the lid back on the fishwell. "But you're *it*, Nor, I'm not going to look down here anymore."

They gave themselves the creeps, and raced back upstairs. Four yelled at them for making too much noise.

Nor found Manek at last on the stairs outside the door to Auntie Guest's rooms. "Shhh," he said as they came near, and Nor tapped him anyway, saying, "You're out."

"Shhh," he said again, more urgently.

They took turns looking through the crack in the weathered grain of the door.

Auntie had her finger in a book, and she was mumbling things to herself, sounding them out this way and that. On the dresser next to her squatted Chistery, in an uneasy, obedient silence.

"What's happening?" said Nor.

"She's trying to teach him to talk," said Manek.

"Let me look," said Liir.

"Say *spirit*," said Auntie in a kind voice. "Say *spirit. Spirit. Spirit.*"

Chistery twisted his mouth to one side, as if considering it.

"There is no difference," said Auntie to herself, or maybe to Chistery. "The strands are the same, the skeins are the same; the rock remembers; the water has memory; the air has a past for which it can be held accountable; the flame renews itself like a pfenix. What is an animal, but made of rock and water and fire and ether! Remember how to speak, Chistery. You are animal, but Animal is your cousin, damn you. Say *spirit*."

Chistery picked a nit off his chest and ate it.

"Spirit," sang Auntie, "there is spirit, I know it. Spirit!"

"Spit," said Chistery, or something like it.

Irji shoved Manek aside and the children almost fell through the door trying to see Auntie laugh and dance and sing. She picked up Chistery and hugged him, and said, "Spirit, oh spirit, Chistery! There is spirit! Say spirit!"

"Spit, spit, spit," said Chistery, unimpressed with himself. "Spite."

But Killyjoy woke from a nap at the sound of a new voice.

"Spirit," said Auntie.

"Speared," said Chistery patiently. "Spared. Spored. Sput sput sput. Spat spate spit, speed spurt spot."

"Spirit," said Auntie, "oh, my Chistery, we'll find ourselves a link with Doctor Dillamond's old work yet! There is a universal design among us all, could we get in deeply enough to see! Everything is not in vain! Spirit, my friend, spirit!"

"Sport," said Chistery.

The children couldn't stop laughing. They clattered down the stairs and fell into the dormitory, and giggled into the bedclothes.

They didn't mention what they saw to Sarima or the sisters. They were afraid Auntie would be stopped, and they all wanted Chistery to learn enough language so that he could play with them.

One windless day, when it seemed they must get out of Kiamo Ko or expire of boredom, Sarima had the idea that they go skating on a nearby pond. The sisters agreed, and dug out the rusting skates Fiyero had brought back from the Emerald City. The sisters baked caramel sweets and prepared flasks of cocoa, and even decorated themselves with green and gold ribbons, as if it were a second Lurlinemas. Sarima adorned herself in a brown velvet robe with fur tippets, the children put on extra trousers and tunics, and even Elphaba came along, in a thick cloak of purple brocade and heavy Arjiki goatskin boots, and mittens, carrying her broom. Chistery lugged along a basket of dried apricots. The sisters in sensible men's tribal overcoats, belted and latched, drew up the rear.

The villagers had cleared the snow off the center of the pond. It was a ballroom dance floor of silver plate, engraved with the flourishes of a thousand arabesques, mounded round with pillows and bolsters of snow to provide a safe repose for skaters who forget how to brake or turn. In the fierce sunlight, the mountains looked razor sharp against the blue; great snowy egrets and ice griffons wheeled high above. The ice rink was already noisy with screaming urchins and lurching adolescents (taking every opportunity to tumble and heap each other cozily in suggestive positions). Their elders moved more slowly, processionally around the ice. The crowd fell silent as the household of Kiamo Ko approached, but, children being children, the silence didn't last for long.

Sarima ventured out onto the ice, her sisters in a knot around her with linked arms. Being largish, Sarima was nervous of falling, nor were her ankles strong. But before long she had remembered how things went—this foot, then that, long languorous strides—and the uneasy meeting of social classes was accomplished. Elphaba looked like one of her crows: knees out, elbows flailing, rags flapping, gloved hands raking for balance.

After the adults had had enough excitement (but the children were only still warming up) Sarima and the sisters and Elphie collapsed on some bearskins that the citizenry had spread out for them.

"In the summer," said Sarima, "we have a huge bonfire and slaughter some pigs, before the men descend to the plains, or the boys ascend to the slopes to guard the sheep and the goats. They all come into the castle for a chew of pork and a few tankards of ale. And of course, any time there's a mountain lion or a particularly nasty bear, we let them into the keep until the beast is killed or wanders away." She smiled with noblesse oblige in an abbreviated way, off into the middle distance, though the locals were ignoring the castle folk by now. "Auntie dear, you looked quite the sight in that robe, and poking along with that broom."

"Liir says it's a magic broom," said Nor, who had run up to throw a handful of granular snowflakes into her mother's face. Elphaba turned her head quickly and tugged her collar up to avoid ricocheting snow spray. Nor laughed unkindly in a beautiful phrase like a woodwind, and scampered away.

"So tell us how your broom came to be magic," said Sarima.

"I never said it was magic. I got it from an elderly maunt named Mother Yackle. She took me under her wing, when she was alert enough, and gave me—well, guidance, I suppose you'd call it."

"Guidance," said Sarima.

"The old maunt said the broom would be my link to my destiny," said Elphie. "I assume she meant that my destiny was domestic. Not magic."

"Join the sisterhood." Sarima yawned.

"I never knew if Mother Yackle was completely mad or a wise, prophetic old hen," said Elphie, but the others weren't listening, so she lapsed into silence.

After a while Nor came flinging herself into her mother's lap again. "Tell me a story, Mama," she said. "Those boys are nasty."

"Boys are vexing creatures," agreed her mother. "Sometimes. Shall I tell you the story of when you were born?"

"No, not that," said Nor, yawning. "A real story. Tell me about the Witch and the fox babies again."

Sarima protested, knowing full well that the children considered Auntie Guest a witch. But Nor was stubborn and Sarima relented, and told the tale. Elphaba listened. Her father had taught her moral precepts, had lectured her about responsibility; Nanny had gossiped; Nessarose had whined. But no one had told stories to her when she was young. She pulled herself forward a little so she could hear over the noise of the crowd.

Sarima recited the tale with little dramatic involvement, but even so, Elphaba felt a twinge when she heard the conclusion. "And there the wicked old Witch stayed, for a good long time."

"Did she ever come out?" recited Nor, eyes gleaming with the fun of the ritual.

"*Not yet*," answered Sarima, and leaned forward, pretending to bite Nor on the neck. Nor squealed and jiggled herself away, and ran to rejoin the boys.

"I think that's shameful, even if it's just a story, to propose an after-life for evil," said Elphaba. "*Any* afterlife notion is a manipulation and a sop. It's shameful the way the unionists and the pagans both keep talking up hell for intimidation and the airy Other Land for reward."

"Don't," Sarima said. "For one thing, that's where Fiyero is waiting for me. And you know it."

Elphaba's jaw dropped. When she least expected it, Sarima always seemed ready to rush in with a surprise attack. "In the *afterlife?*" said Elphie.

"Oh, what you *do* take against," said Sarima. "I pity the community of the afterlife when they're asked to welcome *you* in. What a sour apple you always are."

7

She's crazy," said Manek knowledgeably. "Everyone knows that you can't teach an animal to talk."

They were in the abandoned summer stable, jumping off a loft, making puffs of hay and snow billow in the patchy light.

"Well, what is she doing with Chistery then?" asked Irji. "If you're so sure of it?"

"She's teaching him to mimic, like a parrot," said Manek.

"I think she's magic," said Nor.

"You, you think everything's magic," Manek said. "Stupid girl."

"Well, everything is," said Nor, launching herself away from the boys as a further editorial comment on their skepticism.

"Do you really think she's magic?" said Manek to Liir. "You know her better than any of us. She's your mother."

"She's my Auntie, isn't she?" Liir said.

"She's *our* Auntie, she's *your* mother."

"*I* know," said Irji, pretending full immersion in the topic to avoid another jump. "Liir is Chistery's brother. Liir is what Chistery was like before she taught him how to talk. You're a monkey, Liir."

"I'm not a monkey," said Liir, "and I'm not magicked."

"Well, let's go ask Chistery," said Manek. "Is this the day that Auntie has her coffee with Mama? Let's go see if Chistery has learned enough words to answer some questions."

They scampered up the stone spiral staircase to Auntie Witch's apartment.

True, she was gone, and there was Chistery nibbling on some nut-shells, and Killyjoy dozing by the fire, growling in his sleep, and the bees doing their ceaseless chorus. The children didn't like bees much, nor did they care for Killyjoy. Even Liir had lost interest in the dog once he had children to play with. But Chistery was a favorite. "Sweet thing, oh the little baby," said Nor. "Here, you little beast, come to Auntie Nor." The monkey looked doubtful, but then on knuckles and capable feet he swung across the floor and vaulted into her arms. He inspected her ears for treats, peered over her shoulders at the boys.

"You tell us, Chistery boy, is Auntie Witch really magic?" said Nor. "Tell us all about Auntie Witch."

"Watch Witch," said Chistery, playing with his fingers. "Which wretch which?" They could have sworn it was a question, the way his forehead wrinkled like eyebrows.

"Are you under a spell?" said Manek.

"Spell ill. Spoil spell," answered Chistery. "Spill all."

"How do we spoil the spell? How do we turn you back to a boy?" asked Irji, the oldest but just as caught up as the others. "Is there a special way?"

"Why way?" said Chistery. "We woo, we weigh woe. Why?"

"Tell us what to do," said Nor, petting him.

"Do, die," said Chistery.

"Great," said Irji. "So we can't break the spell you're under?"

"Oh, he's only babbling," Elphaba said from the doorway. "Look, I have visitors I didn't even invite."

"Oh hello, Auntie," they said. They knew they shouldn't be there. "He's talking, sort of. He's magicked."

"He mostly just repeats what you say," said Elphaba, moving closer. "So leave him alone. You're not allowed here."

They said, "Sorry," and left. Back in the boys' room, they fell on the mattress and roared until they wept, and couldn't say what was so funny. Maybe it was the relief of having escaped without harm from the Witch's rooms, even though they had no business there. The children decided they were no longer scared of Auntie Witch.

8

They were tired of being housebound, but finally it was raining out instead of snowing. They played hide-and-seek a lot, waiting for the rain to lift so they could go outside.

One morning, Nor was it. She kept finding Manek easily, because Liir always hid near him and gave him away. Manek lost his patience. "I always get caught, because you're so hopeless. Why can't you hide well?"

"I *can't* hide in the well," Liir said, misunderstanding.

"Oh yes you can," Manek said, delighted.

The next round began, and Manek led Liir right down the basement steps. The basement was even damper than usual, with the groundwater seeping through the foundation stones. When they swiveled the lid off the fishwell, they could see the water level had risen. But it was still a good twelve or fourteen feet down.

"This'll just be fine," Manek said, "look, if we loop the rope over this hook, the bucket will hold steady enough for you to climb in it. Then when I let the crank out, the bucket will slowly slide down the side of the well. I'll stop it before it gets to the water, don't worry. Then I'll put the lid on and Nor will look and look! She'll never find you."

Liir peered into the clammy shaft. "What if there are spiders?"

"Spiders hate water," said Manek authoritatively. "Don't worry about spiders."

"Why don't you do it?" said Liir.

"You're not strong enough to lower me, that's why," said Manek patiently.

"Don't hide far away," said Liir. "Don't let me down too far. Don't push the cover on all the way, I don't like the dark."

"You're always complaining," Manek said, giving him a hand. "That's why we don't like you, you know."

"Well, everybody's mean to me," Liir said.

"Crouch down now. Hold on to the ropes with both hands. If the bucket scrapes against the wall a little bit just push yourself away. I'll let it down slowly."

"Where are you going to hide?" Liir said. "There isn't anyplace else in this room."

"I'll hide under the stairs. She'll never find me in the shadows, she hates spiders."

"I thought you said there weren't any spiders!"

"She thinks there are," Manek said. "One two three. This is really a good idea, Liir. You're so brave." He grunted with the effort. Liir was heavier in the bucket than he had figured, and the rope spooled too quickly. It jammed in the joint between the windlass and the struts, and the bucket stopped and smashed against the wall with an echoing thud.

"That was too *fast*," came Liir's voice, ghostly in the gloom.

"Oh, don't be a sissy," Manek said. "Now shhh, I'm going to pivot the cover back on partway, so she won't guess. Don't make any noise."

"I think there's fish down here."

"Of course there are, it's a fishwell."

"Well, I'm awfully near the water. Do they jump?"

"Yes they jump, and they have sharp teeth, you ninny, and they like fat little boys," said Manek. "*Of course they don't jump.* Would I put you in danger like that if they did? Honestly, you don't trust me at all, do you?" He sighed, as if disappointed beyond words, and when the cover slid all the way on instead of part way, he noted without surprise that Liir was too hurt to complain.

Manek hid under the stairs for a little while. When Nor didn't come down he decided that behind the altar skirts of the old musty chapel would be an even better hiding place. "Be right back, Liir," he hissed, but since Liir didn't answer Manek guessed he was still nursing his grievances.

Sarima was taking a rare turn in the kitchen, concocting a stew out of limp vegetables from the keeping room. The sisters were having a dance recital amongst themselves in the music room overhead. "Sounds like a herd of elephants," Sarima said, when Auntie Guest came wandering through, looking for something to snack on.

"I didn't expect to see you here," said Elphaba. "You know, I have a complaint to lodge against your children."

"The sweet little vandals, what now," Sarima said, stirring. "Have they been putting spiders in your bedsheets again?"

"I wouldn't mind spiders. At least the crows could eat them. No, Sarima, the children rifle through my belongings, they tease Chistery unmercifully, and they will not listen when I talk to them. Can't you do anything with them?"

"What's to be done?" said Sarima. "Here, taste this rutabaga, is it gone to the dogs?"

"Even Killyjoy wouldn't touch this," decided Elphie. "You better stick with the carrots. I think those children are ungovernable, Sarima. Oughtn't they be off to school?"

"Oh yes, in a better life they would be, but how can they?" said their mother placidly. "I've already told you that they're sitting targets for ambitious Arjiki tribesmen. It's bad enough even to let them run around on the slopes near Kiamo Ko in the summer, I never know when they're going to be found, trussed, and bled like a pig, and brought home for burying. It's the cost of widowhood, Auntie; we must do the best we can."

"I was a good child," Elphie said stoutly. "I took care of my little sister, who was horribly disfigured from birth. I obeyed my father, and my mother until she died. I tramped around as a missionary child and gave testimonials to the Unnamed God even though I was essentially faithless. I believed in obedience, and I don't believe it hurt me."

"Then what did hurt you?" asked Sarima wittily.

"You won't listen," said Elphie, "so I won't even say. But for whatever reasons, your children are ungovernable. I disapprove of your lax ways."

"Oh, children are good at heart," Sarima said, intent on scraping carrots. "They are so innocent and gay. It cheers me up to see them dashing about the house in this game or that. All too soon these precious days will be past, dear Auntie, and then we will look back on when this house was filled with peals of childish laughter."

"Fiendish laughter."

"There is something inherently good about children," said Sarima decidedly, warming to the subject. "You know that little Ozma, who all those years ago was deposed by the Wizard? They say that she is off someplace, frozen in a cave—perhaps even in the Kells, for all I know. She's preserved in her childhood innocence because the Wizard hasn't the courage to kill her. One day she'll come back to rule Oz, and she'll be the best and wisest sovereign we ever had, because of the wisdom of youth."

"I've never believed in child saviors," Elphaba said. "As far as I'm concerned, children are the ones who need saving."

"You're just cross because the children have such high spirits."

"Your children are evil sprites," Elphie said, in a snit.

"My children aren't evil, nor were my sisters and I evil children."

"Your children aren't *good*," said Elphie.

"Well, how do you judge Liir in this regard, then?"

"Oh, Liir," Elphie said, and made an expression, and said *pfaaaah*, with her tongue and hands. Sarima was about to pursue this—a matter she had long been curious about—when Three came rushing into the kitchen.

"The passes below us must have melted sooner than usual," she said, "for we have sighted a caravan struggling its way over the Locklimb Trail, coming from the north! It'll be here by tomorrow!"

"Oh, rapture," Sarima said, "and the castle such a mess! This always happens. Why don't we learn? Quick, call the children and we'll have to organize a scrub and polish. You never know, Auntie, it could be an honored guest. You have to be prepared."

Manek and Nor and Irji came running from their game. Three told them the news, and they immediately had to dash up the highest tower to see what they could see through the slackening rain, and to wave aprons and handkerchiefs. Yes, there was a caravan, five or six skarks and a small wagon, pulling through the snow and the mud, having trouble fording this stream, stopping to mend a split wheel, stopping to feed the skarks! It was a wonderful treat, and all through the dinner meal of vegetable soup the children chattered away at the surprises they might find among the passengers in the caravan. "They've never stopped thinking their father is going to come back," said Sarima under her breath to Elphaba. "This excitement is a hope for him, though they don't remember it."

"Where is Liir?" asked Four, "it's a perfect waste of good soup when he doesn't show up on time. He shan't get any if he comes whining to me afterward. Children, where is Liir?"

"He was playing with us earlier. Maybe he fell asleep," said Irji.

"Let's go set a bonfire and smoke the travelers a hello," said Manek, leaping from the table.

9

It was lunchtime when the skarks and the wagon began the final, difficult ascent up the slope to the castle portcullis and the gates of jasper and oak. The townspeople came out from their hovels and leaned their weight against the carriage, helping it through the ruts of mud and ice, until at last it turned in and crossed the open drawbridge. Elphaba, her curiosity as piqued as anyone else's, stood with the Dowager Princess of the Arjikis and her sisters on a parapet above the crudely carved front doorway. The children waited in the cobblestoned yard below, all but Liir.

The leader, a grizzled young man, made the faintest mountain obeisance to Sarima. The skarks defecated sloppily on the cobbles, to the delight of the children, who had never seen skark fewmets before. Then the leader went to the cabin and opened the door, and climbed inside. They could hear his voice, raised loudly as if talking to someone hard of hearing.

They waited. The sky was a piercing blue, really almost a spring blue, and the icicles hung from the eaves in dangerous daggers, melting like mad. The sisters all sucked in their stomachs, cursing the extra piece of gingerbread, the honeyed cream in the coffee, vowing to do better. Please, sweet Lurlina, let it be a *man*.

The leader came out again, and proffered a hand, and he helped a figure alight from the cabin: an old, creaky-limbed figure, in sad dark skirts and a hideously out-fashioned bonnet, even from the provincial point of view.

But Elphaba was leaning forward, cleaving the air with her sharp chin and hatchet nose, and sniffing like a beast. The visitor turned and the sun struck her face.

"Good glory," breathed Elphie. "It's my old Nanny!" And she left the parapet to run and gather the old woman in her arms.

"Human feeling, will you look at that," said Four, sniffily. "I wouldn't have guessed her capable." For Auntie Guest was all but sobbing with pleasure.

The caravan leader wouldn't stay for a meal, but Nanny with her valises and trunks clearly did not intend to go any farther. She settled in a small musty room just below Elphaba's, and took the endless time it takes the elderly to make her toilet. By the time she was ready to be sociable, dinner was served. A gamey old hen, more rope than flesh, lay in a thin pepper sauce on one of the good salvers. The children were dressed in their best, and allowed this once to dine in the formal hall. Nanny came in on the arm of Elphaba, and sat at her right hand. Because this was a visitor to Elphie, the sisters had kindly put Elphie's napkin ring at the foot of the table, opposite Sarima—a place by custom left vacant, in honor of poor dead Fiyero. It was a big mistake, and they would recognize it almost immediately, as Elphaba never relinquished her advancement. But for now all was smiles and savory hospitality. The only small annoyance (besides that Nanny wasn't a young eligible princeling looking for a bride) was that Liir still conducted his campaign of sullen disappearance. The children didn't know where he was.

Nanny was a tired and fruity old woman, skin cracked like dried soap, hair thin and yellowy white, hands with veins as prominent as the cords around a good Arjiki goat cheese. She communicated wheezily, with lots of pauses to breathe and think, that she had heard through someone named Crope, in the Emerald City, that her old charge Elphaba had attended Tibbett in his last days at the Cloister of Saint Glinda outside the Emerald City. No one in the family had heard from Elphaba in years and years, and Nanny had decided to take it upon herself to find her. The maunts were reluctant at first, but Nanny had persisted, and then she had waited until a new caravan was ready to leave. The maunts had told her about Elphaba's mission in Kiamo Ko, and Nanny had booked passage the following spring. And here she was.

"And of the outside world?" asked Two eagerly. Let them catch up on family gossip on their own time.

"What do you mean?" said Nanny.

"Politics, science, fashion, the arts, the driving edge!" said Two.

"Well, our redoubtable Wizard has crowned himself Emperor," said Nanny. "Did you know that?"

They hadn't heard. "By whose authority?" asked Five, scoffing, "And furthermore, Emperor over *what*?"

"There isn't anyone who has any *more* authority, he said," said Nanny calmly, "and who could argue with that? He's in the business of handing out honors annually as it is. He just tacked on an extra one for himself. As for Emperor over what, I couldn't say. Some people whisper that this implies expansionist aims. But where he could expand to—I couldn't say, I just couldn't. Into the desert? Beyond, to Quox, or Ix, or Fliaan?"

"Or does he mean to have a more tight-fisted hold on terrain he's only loosely governed," asked Elphaba, "like the Vinkus?" She felt a chill, like an old wound deep beneath her breastbone.

"No one is particularly happy," said Nanny. "There is an enforced conscription now, and the Gale Force threatens to outnumber the Royal Army. One doesn't know if there could be an internal struggle for power, and the Wizard is preparing against an eventual takeover attempt. How can one have an opinion about such things? Old and female as we are?" She smiled to include them all. The sisters and Sarima glared as youthfully as they could back at her.

10

The next day hardly dawned at all, so gloomy with rain, so glowery with featureless clouds.

In the parlor, waiting for Nanny to emerge and continue her obligation of entertaining them, the sisters and Sarima discussed what new facts they had learned about their Auntie Guest. "Elphaba," mused Two. "It's a pretty enough name. Where does it come from?"

"I remember," said Five, who had once gone through a faintly religious phase when she realized marriage possibilities were growing dim. "I had a *Lives of the Saints* once. Saint Aelphaba of the Waterfall—she was a Munchkinlander mystic, six or seven centuries ago. Don't you remember? She wanted to pray, but she was of such beauty that the local men kept pestering her for—attention."

They all sighed, in chorus.

"To preserve her sanctity, she went into the wilderness with her holy scriptures and a single bunch of grapes. Wild beasts threatened her, and wild men hunted after her, and she was sore distressed. Then she came upon a huge waterfall coursing off a cliff. She said, 'This is my cave,' and took off all her clothes, and she walked right through the screen of pounding water. Beyond was a cavern hollowed out by the splashing water. She sat down there, and in the light that came through the wall of water she read her holy book and pondered on spiritual matters. She ate a grape every now and then. When at last she had finished her grapes, she emerged from the cave. Hundreds of years had passed. There was a village built on the banks of the stream, and even a milldam nearby. The villagers shrank in horror, for as children they had all played in the cavern behind the waterfall—lovers had trysted there—murders and foul deeds had taken place there—treasure had been buried there—and never had anyone ever seen Saint Aelphaba in her naked beauty. But all Saint Aelphaba had to do was open her mouth and speak the old speech, and they all knew that it must be she, and they built a chapel in her honor. She blessed the children and the elderly, and heard the confessions of the middle-aged, and healed some sick and fed some hungry, that sort of stuff, and then disappeared behind the waterfall again with another bunch of grapes. I think a bigger bunch this time. And that's the last anyone has seen of her."

"So you *can* disappear and not be dead," said Sarima, looking out the window a little dreamily, past the rain.

"If you're a saint," said Two pointedly.

"If you even believe it," said Elphaba, who had come into the parlor during the end of the recitation. "The reemerging Saint Aelphaba might have been some hussy from the next town over who wanted to give gullible peasants a good going over."

"That's doubt for you, it scours hope out of everything," Sarima said dismissively. "Auntie, you kill me sometimes, you really do."

"I think it would be charming to call you Elphaba," said Six, "because that is a charming story. And it's nice to hear your real name on Nanny's lips."

"Don't you try it," said Elphie. "If Nanny can't help herself, so be it; she's ancient and it's hard to change. But not you."

Six pursed her lips as if to make an argument, but just then there was a clattering of feet from downstairs, and Nor and Irji burst into the room.

"We found Liir!" they said. "Come on, we think he's dead! He's fallen in the fishwell!"

They all pounded down the stairs to the basement. Chistery had been the one to find him. The snow monkey's nose had wrinkled when he and the boys passed the fishwell, and he had whined, and whimpered, and tugged at the weighted cover. Nor and Irji had had an idea to lower him down in the bucket then, but when they swiveled the cover off, the lurid gleam of light on pale human flesh had terrified them.

Manek came running when he heard the noise of his mother and the others exclaiming before the well. They pulled Liir up. The water had risen, what with continued melting and the further rain. Liir was like a corpse left in a stream, bloated. "Oh, is that where he was," said Manek in a funny voice. "You know he said he wanted to go down in that fishwell once."

"Get away, children, you shouldn't see this, go upstairs," Sarima said, scolding. "Come on now, behave, upstairs for you." They didn't know what they were looking at and they were afraid to look too closely.

"I cannot believe it, this is so terrible," said Manek excitedly, and Elphaba gave him a sharp, hateful look.

"Obey your mother," she snapped, and Manek made a nasty face, but he and Irji and Nor clomped upstairs, and huddled around the open doorway at the top to listen, and peer.

"Oh, who has the art of medicine in their hands, have you, Auntie?" asked Sarima. "Quick now, there may be time. You have the arts, don't you, you studied the life sciences! What can you do?"

"Irji, go get Nanny, tell her it's an emergency," shouted Elphie. "We'll bring him up to the kitchen, gently now. No, Sarima, I don't know enough."

"Use your spells, use your magic!" exclaimed Five.

"Bring him back," urged Six, and Three added, "You can do it, don't be hidden and shy about it now!"

"I can't bring him back," said Elphaba, "I can't! I have no aptitude for sorcery! I never did! That was all a foolish campaign of Madame Morrible's, which I rejected!" The six sisters looked at her askance.

Irji escorted Nanny to the kitchen, Nor brought the broom, Manek brought the Grimmerie, and the sisters and Sarima brought the body of Liir, dripping and bloated, and laid him on the butcher's block. "Oh, now who's this one," mused Nanny, but got to work pumping the legs and the arms, and set Sarima to pressing in at the abdomen.

Elphaba flipped through the Grimmerie, she screwed up her face and hit herself on the temple with her fists, and wailed, "But I have no personal experience with a soul—how can I find his if I don't know what one looks like?"

"He's even fatter than usual," said Irji.

"If you prick his eyes out with a magic straw from the magic broom, his soul will come back," said Manek.

"I wonder why he went in the fishwell?" said Nor. "I never would."

"Holy Lurlina, mercy on us, mercy!" said Sarima, weeping, and the sisters began to mumble the service of the dead, honoring the Unnamed God for the life departed.

"Nanny can't do everything," snapped Nanny, "Elphaba, be some help! You're just like your mother in a crisis! Put your mouth on his and push air into his lungs! Go on!"

Elphaba wiped the wet off Liir's pasty face with the edge of her sleeve. The face stayed where it was pushed. She grimaced, and nearly vomited, and spit something into a bucket, and then she sank her mouth down on the child's, and breathed out, pushing into the sour passage her own sour breath. Her fingers tensed at the sides of the butcher's block, gouging splinters, as if in an ecstasy of sexual tension. Chistery breathed along with her, breath for breath.

"He smells like fish," Nor said under her breath.

"If that's what you look like when you drown, I'd rather burn to death," said Irji.

"I'm just not going to die," Manek said, "and nobody can make me."

The body of Liir began to choke. They thought at first it was an involuntary reaction, air from Elphaba's mouth pocketing and blurting out again, and then there was a small stream of yellowish yuck. Then Liir's eyelids moved, and his hand twitched of its own accord.

"Oh mercy," Sarima murmured. "It's a miracle. Thank you Lurlina! Bless you!"

"We're not out of the woods yet," said Nanny. "He may still die of exposure. Quick now, off with his clothes."

The children watched the silly indignity of grown-up women tearing stupid Liir's trousers and tunic off. They rubbed him all over with lard. This gave the children a case of the giggles, and made Irji feel very funny in his trousers, for the first time in his life. Then they wrapped Liir in a woolen blanket, which made *quite* a mess, and prepared to put him to bed.

"Where does he sleep?" said Sarima.

They all looked at one another. The sisters looked at Elphaba, and Elphaba looked at the children.

"Oh, sometimes on the floor in our room, sometimes on the floor in Nor's," said Manek.

"He wants to sleep in my bed too but I push him out," said Nor. "He's too fat, there'd be no room for me and my dollies."

"He doesn't even have a bed?" Sarima coldly asked Elphie.

"Well, don't ask me, this is your house," said Elphie.

And Liir stirred somewhat, and said, "The fish talked to me. I talked to the fish. The goldfish talked to me. She said she was. . . ."

"Hush, little one," said Nanny, "time for that later." She glared around at the women and children in the kitchen. "Well, it shouldn't take Nanny to have to find him a proper bed, but if there's none other for him he can come up to my room, and *I'll* sleep on the floor!"

"Of course not, the very idea," began Sarima, bustling ahead.

"Barbarians, the lot of you!" snapped Nanny.

For which no one in Kiamo Ko ever forgave her.

Sarima lectured Auntie Guest severely for what had happened to Liir. Elphaba tried to say that it was not her doing, it was not her fault. "It was some boys' trick, some game, some dare," she said. Their accusations spent, they fell to talking about the differences between boys and girls.

Sarima told Auntie Guest what she knew of the boys' initiation rite in the tribe. "They are taken out in the grasslands, and left with nothing but a loincloth and a musical instrument. They are required to call forth spirits and animals out of the night, to converse with them, to learn from them, to soothe them if they need soothing, to fight them if they need fighting. The child who dies at night clearly lacks the discretion to decide if its company needs fighting, or soothing. So it is correct that he should die young and not burden the tribe with his foolishness."

"What do the boys say of spirits who approach them?" asked Auntie Guest.

"Boys say very little, especially about the spirit world," she answered. "Nonetheless, you pick up what you pick up. And I think some of the spirits are very patient, very wearing, very obdurate. The lore supposes there should be conflict, hostility, battle, but I wonder, in contact with spirits, if what the boy needs is a good helping of cold anger."

"Cold anger?"

"Oh yes, don't you know that distinction? Tribal mothers always tell their children that there are two kinds of anger: hot and cold. Boys and girls experience both, but as they grow up the angers separate according to the sex. Boys need hot anger to survive. They need the inclination to fight, the drive to sink the knife into the flesh, the energy and initiative of fury. It's a requirement of hunting, of defense, of pride. Maybe of sex, too."

"Yes, I know," said Elphaba, remembering.

Sarima blushed and looked unhappy, and continued. "And girls need cold anger. They need the cold simmer, the ceaseless grudge, the talent to avoid forgiveness, the sidestepping of compromise. They need to know when they say something that they will never back down, ever, ever. It's the compensation for a more limited scope in the world. Cross a man and you struggle, one of you wins, you adjust and go on—or you lie there dead. Cross a woman and the universe is changed, once again, for cold anger requires an eternal vigilance in all matters of slight and offense." She glared at Elphaba, pinning her with unspoken accusations about Fiyero, about Liir.

Elphaba thought about this. She thought about hot anger and cold anger, and if it divided by the sexes, and which she felt, if either, if ever. She thought about her mother dying young, and her father with his obsessions. She thought about the anger that Doctor Dillamond had had—an anger that drove him to study and research. She thought about the anger that Madame Morrible could barely disguise, as she tried to seduce the college girls into the secret service of government.

She sat and thought about it the following morning as she watched the strengthening sun beat down on the mounds of snow on the sloping tiled roofs below. She watched the sun bleed ice water out of the icicle. Warm and cold working together to make an icicle. Warm and cold anger working together to make a fury, a fury worthy enough to use as a weapon against the old things that still needed fighting.

In a fashion—without any way to confirm it, of course—she had always felt as capable of hot anger as any man. But to be successful, one would need access to both sorts . . .

Liir survived, but Manek did not. The icicle that Elphaba trained her gaze on, thinking on the weapons one needed to fight such abuse—it broke like a lance from the eaves, and drove whistling downward, and caught him in the skull as he went out to find some new way of belea-guering Liir.

Uprisings

I

"They're calling you a witch, do you know that?" said Nanny. "Now why ever is that?"

"Silliness and stupidity," said Elphaba. "When I arrived I was distanced from my name, after my years at the mauntery, where I was called Sister Saint Aelphaba. *Elphaba* seemed like the name of someone long ago. I told them to call me Auntie. Though I never felt like anyone's Auntie, nor would I know what it felt like. I never had any aunts or uncles."

"Hmmm," said Nanny, "I don't think you're much of a witch. Your mother would be scandalized, bless her soul. Your father too."

They were walking in the apple orchard. A cloud of blossoms thickened the air with scent. The Witch's bees were having a field day, humming throatily. Killyjoy sat wagging his tail in the shadow of Manek's tombstone, placed near the wall. The crows had relay races overhead, scaring away all other birds except the eagles. Irji and Nor and Liir, at Nanny's insistence, had been taken into the schoolroom of the village. Kiamo Ko was blissfully quiet until midday.

Nanny was seventy-eight. She walked with a cane. She hadn't given up on her little efforts toward beauty, though now they seemed to coarsen rather than dignify her. Her powder was on too thick, her lip rouge smeared and off center, and the flimsy lace shawl was useless in the updraft from the valley. For her part, Nanny thought that Elphaba was looking poorly, as if she were going moldy from the inside out. Pale. A disintegration of sorts. Elphaba didn't seem to care for her beautiful hair at all, keeping it knotted up out of sight underneath that ridiculous hat. And the black gown needed a good washing and airing.

They stopped at a lopsided wall, and leaned against it. The sisters were gathering flowers a few fields away, and Sarima ballooned along. In her dark mourning gown she resembled a huge dangerous cocoon broken loose from its mooring. It was good to hear her laugh again, even if falsely; light had that strange, ameliorative effect on everybody, even Elphaba.

Nanny had told Elphie about her family. The Eminent Thropp had died at last. In Elphaba's absence and presumed death, the mantle of Eminence had fallen to Nessarose. So the younger sister was now ensconced in Colwen Grounds, issuing dogmatic statements about faith and blame. Frex was there with her too, his career of ministry almost at an end. As he gave up the effort his mind was returning to balance. Shell? He came and went. Rumors abounded that he was an agitator for Munchkinland's secession from Oz. He had grown up handsome and fine, in Nanny's biased opinion: straight of limb, clear of skin, direct of speech, bold of heart. He was now in his early twenties.

"And what does Nessarose think of secession?" Elphie had asked. "Her opinion about it will be important if she's the Eminent Thropp now."

Nanny reported that Nessarose had grown to be far cleverer than anyone anticipated. She kept her cards close to her chest and issued vague statements about the revolutionary cause, statements that could be read several ways, depending on the audience. Nanny assumed Nessarose intended to set up some sort of theocracy, incorporating into the governing laws of Munchkinland her own restrictive interpretation of unionism. "Your sainted father Frex himself doesn't know if this would be a good or bad thing, and keeps silent on the matter. He's not much for politics, he prefers the mystical realm." There was, Nanny observed, even some local support for Nessarose's plans. But since Nessarose governed her remarks well, the Wizard's armed forces garrisoned in the area could find no excuse to arrest her. "She's adept at this," Nanny admitted. "Shiz taught her well. She stands on her own two feet now."

The word *adept* sent chills down Elphie's spine. Was Nessarose even now responding to some sort of spell that Madame Morrible had placed on her, those foggy years ago in the parlor at Crage Hall? Was she in fact a pawn, an Adept of the Wizard, or of Madame Morrible? Did she know *why* she did what she did? For that matter, was Elphaba herself merely a playing piece of a higher, evil power?

The recollection of Madame Morrible's proposals for their careers—hers, and Nessarose's, and Glinda's—had come back to Elphie with a shock following the recovery of Liir from his saturation and near drowning last winter. When he finally came around enough to answer questions about how he had come to be in the fishwell, he could only say "The fish talked to me, she told me to come down." Elphie knew in her heart that it was Manek, horrible evil Manek, who had tortured the boy unmercifully and openly all winter. She didn't care that Manek died, even if Manek was the precious son of Fiyero. Any torturer was fair game for javelin icicles. But she had to pause, gulping, at what Liir had said next. He said, "The fish told me she was magic. She said that Fiyero was my father, and that Irji and Manek and Nor are my brothers and my sister."

"Goldfish don't talk, sweetheart!" Sarima said. "You're imagining things. You were down there too long and your brain got waterlogged."

Elphaba had yearned toward Liir, a strange, unhappy compulsion. Who was this boy who lived in her life? Oh, she knew more or less where he came from, but who he *was*—it seemed to make a difference, for the first time in her life. She had reached out and put her hand on his shoulder. He had twitched it off; he was not used to such a gesture. And she had felt rebuffed.

"Want to see my pet mouse, Liir?" said Nor, who had been warm to the boy during his convalescence. Liir always chose the company of his peers over questioning by the grown-ups, and it was impossible to pry further information out of him about his ordeal. He didn't seem much changed, except that with Manek dead, Liir charged around Kiamo Ko with greater zest and liberty.

And Sarima had looked at Elphaba, and Elphaba thought the hour of her liberation was at hand at last. "How silly of the boy, he's delusional," Sarima had said at last. "The idea of Fiyero being his father. Fiyero didn't have an ounce of fat on his body, and look at the boy."

Under the terms of her welcome, Elphaba could not prod Sarima to change her mind, but she stared at her hostess, willing her to accept the facts. But she wouldn't. "And whoever might the mother be?" said Sarima blandly, touching the hem of her skirt softly. "It's preposterous beyond words."

For the first time, Elphie wished that Liir had at least an undertone of green in his skin.

Sarima had swept away, to weep in her chapel for her husband, for her second son.

And the terms of Elphie's imprisonment—as an unwilling traitor, as an exiled maunt, as a hapless mother, as a failed insurrectionist, as a Witch in disguise—remained unchanged.

Though the idea of a Goldfish or a Carp in the fishwell telling such things to Liir—was there any possibility in that? Or had Madame Morrible the ability to change her shape, to live in cold darkness, to slip in and observe what Elphie was up to? Liir had no imagination to speak of, he couldn't have come up with that by himself. Could he?

When she went to look in the fishwell, many times at all hours of the day or night, the old carp—or Carp—stayed out of sight.

"I'm glad to hear Nessarose is on her two feet," said Elphaba at last, coming back to the orchard from her musings. Nanny was gnawing at a piece of sugar candy.

"I mean that literally, you know," said Nanny through her spittle. "She doesn't need to be propped up anymore. Not figuratively or literally. She can stand on her own, stand and sit."

"Without benefit of arms? I don't believe it," said the Witch.

"You'll have to. Do you remember that pair of shoes that Frex had decorated for her?"

Of course Elphaba remembered! The beautiful shoes! Her father's sign of devotion to his second daughter, his desire to accentuate her beauty and draw attention away from her deformity.

"Well, old Glinda of the Arduennas, remember her? Married to Sir Chuffrey, and gone a bit to seed, in my humble opinion. She came to Colwen Grounds a couple of years ago. She and Nessarose had a wild old time, remembering college days. And she put those very same shoes through something of an enchantment. Don't ask me. Magic was never my cup of tea. The shoes allowed Nessarose to sit and stand and walk without support. She is never without them. She claims they give her moral virtue too, but then she has buckets more of *that* than she needs. You'd be surprised how superstitious Munchkinlanders have become these days." Nanny sighed. "That's why I was free to look you up, dearie.

The magic shoes made me redundant. Nanny is out of a job."

"You're too old to work, you sit and enjoy the sun," said Elphaba. "You can stay here as long as you like."

"You talk as if this is your house," said Nanny. "As if you have the right to issue such invitations."

"Until I'm allowed to leave, this is my house," said Elphie. "I can't help it."

Nanny shaded her eyes and looked out over the mountains, which in the midday light looked like polished horn. "It's too rich, to think of you being a Witch, after a fashion anyway, and your sister trying out as resident Saint. Who would have thought, back in those muddy years in the Quadling badlands? I don't think you're a Witch, whatever you say. But one thing I do want to know. Is Liir your son?"

Elphaba shivered, though her heart, deep inside its pocket of cold, roiled in hot energy. "It is not a question I can answer," she said sadly.

"You needn't keep anything from me, dearie. Remember, Nanny was nursemaid to your mother too, and a more outgoing, sensual woman I have yet to meet. Convention didn't bind her, not in youth nor in married life."

"I don't think I want to hear about this," said Elphie.

"Then let's talk about Liir. What in blazes can you mean, you can't answer a simple question like that? Either you conceived him and bore him, or you didn't. As far as I know in this world there are no other stories."

"What I mean," said Elphaba "and the only remark about it I will ever make is this. When I first went to the mauntery, under the kind offices of Mother Yackle, I was in no state to know what was happening to me, and I spent about a year in a deathly sleep. It's just possible I brought a child to term and delivered it. I was another full year recovering. When I was first assigned duties, I worked with the sick and the dying, and also with abandoned children. I had no more congress with Liir than with any other of several dozen brats. When I left the mauntery to come here, it was under the condition that I would take Liir with me. I didn't question the instruction—one doesn't question the instructions of superiors. I have no motherly warmth toward the boy"—she gulped, in case this was no longer true—"and I don't feel as if I've ever gone through the experience of bearing a child. I don't quite believe myself capable, in fact, although I'm willing to concede that this may be simply ignorance and blindness. But that's all there is to say about it. I'll say no more, and no more will you."

"Have you an obligation to be motherly to him then, despite the mystery?"

"The only other obligations I'm under are the ones I assign to myself. And that, Nanny, is that."

"You are too tart, this situation makes you unhappy. But if you think I came here to raise yet another generation of Thropps, forget it. Nanny is in her senility now, remember, and happily so."

But Elphaba couldn't help noting that in the weeks that followed, Nanny began to attend to Liir's needs more lovingly than she did the needs of Nor and Irji. Elphaba registered it with shame, for she also saw how willingly Liir responded to Nanny's attention.

In telling tales of Shell's derring-do—her racy old heart pitter-pattering almost visibly beneath her breastbone—Nanny revealed details of the Wizard's campaigns. It made Elphaba furious, for she had kept hoping to lose interest in the ways of evil men.

Nanny buzzed on about the Wizard's having mounted a new kind of youth camp, the Emperor's Garden—a pretty, euphemistic name. All Munchkinlander children from four to ten were required to attend, in month-long summer residencies. The children were sworn to secrecy—a great game for them, no doubt. Nanny told a long-winded tale, more suited to toothless cronies in a fireside inglenook than to a dinner table with upright and repressed Arjiki spinsters, of how Shell, dear stranger brother Shell, disguised himself as a potato man doing deliveries. And got in the gates. Oh la, the many amusing adventures of a rake! The Camp General's nubile daughter in deshabille, Shell's inventive alibis, his dalliances, his narrow escapes! Almost being discovered at his liaisons—by *children!* What a lark! Nanny remained a mouthy old peasant at heart despite her airs. Elphaba thought: She hardly comprehends she is talking about indoctrination, betrayal, forced conscription of children into low-level warfare. With Elphie's newfound awareness of Liir hovering at the edges of her life, bumbling gently through her days, she found these tales of indoctrinated children horrifying and repugnant.

She went to the Grimmerie and hauled open its massive cover—leather ornamented with golden hasps and pins, and tooled with silver leaf—and pored through the tome to find what makes people thirst for such authority and muscle. Is it the sheer nature of the beast within, the human animal inside the Human Being?

She looked for a recipe for the overthrow of a regime. She found much on power, and damage, but little on strategy.

The Grimmerie described poisoning the lips of goblets, charming the steps of a staircase to buckle, agitating a monarch's favorite lapdog to make a fatal bite in an unwelcome direction. It suggested the nocturnal insertion, through any convenient orifice, of a fiendish invention, a thread like a piano wire, part tapeworm and part burning fuse, for a particularly painful demise. All of this seemed carnival sleight of hand to Elphaba. What was more interesting, in her reading, was a small drawing she saw next to a section marked Evil Particulars. The drawing—done, if you would believe gullible Sarima, in some world other than theirs—was a clever sketch of a broad-faced woman-fiend. Written in an angular, bronchiating script with elegant tapering serifs, all around the illustration, were the words YAKAL SNARLING. Elphaba looked again. She saw a creature part woman, part grassland jackal, its jaws open, its hand-paw lifted to rip the heart out of a spiderweb. And the creature reminded her of old Mother Yackle from the mauntery.

Conspiracy theories, as Sarima had said, seemed to bedevil her thinking. She turned the page.

Nothing in the Grimmerie on how to depose a tyrant—nothing useful. Armies of holy angels were not answerable to her. Nothing there that described why men and women could turn out so horrible. Or so wonderful—if that ever happened anymore.

2

In truth, the family was devastated over Manek's death. There was an unspoken feeling, that somehow Liir's life had been saved at the expense of Manek's. The sisters suffered from that most dreadful of losses: the theft of the *adult* Manek from their lives. Their sad lot had been bearable all these years because Manek was going to be the man

Fiyero had been, and maybe more. They realized in retrospect that they had expected Manek to restore the fallen fortunes of Kiamo Ko.

Feckless Irji had no more sense of destiny than a prairie dog. And Nor was a girl, more flighty and distractible than usual. So Sarima, behind her gestures of ecstatic acceptance of life (its joys, its sorrows, its mysteries, as she was fond of elaborating), became more aloof. Never close to her sisters, she began to take her meals alone in the Solar.

Irji and Nor, who had enjoyed a sort of allegiance from time to time against the headstrong malice of Manek, had less to bind them together now. Irji began to moon about in the old unionist chapel, teaching himself to read better by scrutinizing moldy hymnals and breviaries. Nor didn't like the chapel—she thought the ghost of Manek lingered there, as that was the last place she had seen his body in the unwrapped shroud—so she tried to ingratiate herself with Auntie Witch—but to no avail. "You are out to make mischief with Chistery," snapped Elphie, "and I've work to do. Go bother someone else." She aimed a kick at Nor, who, whimpering and screaming as if it had hit home, left in a funk.

Nor took to wandering—now that the summer was coming in—down the high valley, the one with the stream at its bottom—and up the other side, where the sheep were nibbling on the best grass they would get all year. In previous years she would either have been with her brothers, or she would have been forbidden to go climbing alone. This year no one was paying enough attention to her to forbid it. She wouldn't have minded being forbidden, she wouldn't have minded the strap even. She was lonely.

One day she wandered particularly far down the valley, luxuriating in the strength and endurance of her strong legs. She was only ten, but a strapping, mature ten. She had hiked her green skirt up into her belt, and because the sun was high and strong, she had shucked off her blouse and tied it like a bandanna around her head. She hardly had a swelling here or there on her chest with which to startle any sheep, and anyway she expected to be able to spot a shepherd from miles away.

How in the world did I come to be here, of all places in Oz, she asked herself, freshly treading upon the terrain of reflection. Here I am, a girl on a mountain, nothing but wind and sheep and grass like an emerald brushfire, green and golden as Lurlinemas decorations, silky in the updraft, coarse in the downdraft. Just me and the sun and the wind. And that group of soldiers coming out from behind the rock.

She slid down onto her back in the grass, fixed up her blouse, and raised herself to her elbows, hiding.

They were not soldiers such as she had seen before. They were not Arjiki men in their ceremonial brasses and helmets, with their spears and shields. These were men in brown uniforms and caps, with muskets or something slung over their shoulders. They were wearing a kind of boot rather high and inappropriate for hill walking, and when one of them had stopped and was fiddling with a nail or a stone in his boot, his arm disappeared inside it right up to his elbow.

There was a green stripe down the front of their uniforms, and a bar across it, and Nor felt cold with an unfamiliar sense of anticipation. At the same time she wanted to be seen. What would Manek have done? she asked herself. Irji would run, Liir would puzzle and dither, but Manek? Manek would have marched right up to them and found out what was going on.

And so would she. She checked once again to make sure her buttons were done up, and then she strode down the slope toward them. By the time she had got all their attention, and the man with the boot off had slipped it back on, she was beginning to rethink the wisdom of the plan. But it was too late to run away now.

"Hail," she said in a formal way, using the language of the east, not her own Arjiki vernacular. "Hail, and halt. I am the Princess Daughter of the Arjikis, and this is *my* valley you are marching your big black boots along."

It was broad noon when she delivered them into the castle keep of Kiamo Ko. The sisters were in their summer laundry yard, beating carpets themselves because they didn't trust the local scrubwives to treat them respectfully enough. The sound of boots on cobbles brought the sisters running through an archway, all flushed and dusty, hair wrapped in cotton scarves. Elphaba heard the noise, too, and threw her window open and stared. "Not an inch farther until I come down," she called, "or I'll turn you all to rodents. Nor, come away from them. All of you, come away."

"I shall fetch the Dowager Princess," said Two, "if it please you gentlemen."

But by the time Sarima arrived, drowsy from a nap, Elphaba had descended, her broom over her shoulder, her eyebrows up to her scalp. "You have no invitation here," said Elphie, looking more like a Witch than ever in her mauntish skirts, "so just how welcome would you like to be made? Who is in charge here? You? Who's the senior one leads this mission? You?"

"If you please, Madame," said someone, a strapping Gillikinese man of about thirty. "I am the Commander—the name is Cherrystone—and I'm under the Emperor's orders to requisition a house large enough to shelter our party while we are in this district of the Kells. We are doing a survey of the passes to the Thousand Year Grasslands." He produced a sweat-stained document from inside his shirt.

"I found them, Auntie Witch," said Nor proudly.

"Go away. Go inside," said Elphaba to the girl. "You men aren't welcome here and the girl has no right to invite you. Turn around and march yourself out over that drawbridge at once." Nor's face fell.

"This is not a request, it is an order," said Commander Cherrystone in an apologetic tone.

"This isn't a suggestion, it's a warning," said Elphaba. "Go, or suffer the consequences."

Sarima by now had taken in enough to step forward, her sisters buzzing in a thrill around her. "Auntie Guest," she said, "you forget the code of the mountains, the same code by which you came to lodge here, and your old Nanny after you. We do not turn visitors away. Please, sirs, excuse our excitable friend. And excuse us. It has been some time since we saw soldiers in uniform."

The sisters were primping away as best they could at such short notice.

"I won't have it, Sarima," Elphaba said, "you've never been out of here, you don't know who these men are or what they will do! I won't have it, do you hear?"

"It's the high spirits, the determination, it makes her so much fun to have around," said Sarima a trifle meanly, as in general she really did enjoy Elphaba's company. But she did not like having her authority usurped. "Gentlemen, this way. I'll show you where you can wash up."

Irji wasn't sure what to make of military men, and wouldn't go very near. Whether he was afraid of being conscripted or enchanted he couldn't say.

He dragged a sleeping roll down into the chapel and slept there, now that it was warm enough. It was Nanny's opinion he was going weird. "Believe me, after a life looking after your dear mother's devout husband, Frex, and your sister after that, I know a religious lunatic when I see one," she said to Elphaba. "That boy ought to be taking some lessons from these men in manliness, whatever else is going on here."

On the other hand, Liir was in heaven. He followed Commander Cherrystone around unless he was turned back, and he fetched water for the men and polished their boots, in a surfeit of ill-concealed romance. The tramping they did, reconnoitering about the local valleys, mapping the places to ford the river, pinpointing spots for beacons, gave Liir more exercise and fresh air than he had ever had before. His spine, which had threatened to become curved like the arc of a mountain harp, seemed to straighten out. The soldiers were indifferent to him, but they were not manifestly unkind, and Liir took this as approval and fondness.

The sisters regained some sense when they stopped to consider what class of men would go into the army. But it wasn't easy.

Sarima alone seemed unperturbed by the disturbance to their routine. She cast about among the villagers and called in favors to help her feed the host of soldiers, and in mixed resentment and fear her neighbors came up with milk, eggs, cheese, and vegetables. There was stouch or garmot from the fishwell almost every evening. And the summer game, of course—quail, hill pfenix, baby roc—which the men proved a dab hand at bringing in themselves. Nanny suspected that the reconnaissance team was helping Sarima over her grief, bringing her back to the family table at least.

But Elphaba was furious at them all. She and the Commander had words every day. Elphie forbade him to allow Liir to tag along—and she forbade Liir himself—to absolutely no effect. Her first true motherly feelings were of incompetence and of being blithely ignored as inconsequential. She could not understand how the human race had ever managed to develop past a single generation. She continually wanted to strangle Liir, as a means of saving him from smooth-talking father figures.

As Elphie tried harder to ferret out the nature of his mission, with every sidestepping pleasantry Commander Cherrystone grew more icy and polite. The one thing Elphaba had never been able to manage was a parlor manner, and this soldier—of all people—was a master at it. It made her feel as she had felt among the society girls at Crage Hall. "Pay those soldiers no mind, they'll go away eventually," said Nanny, who was at the time of her life when everything was either the final fatal crisis or a dismissible matter indeed.

"Sarima says that she has rarely *seen* any of the Wizard's forces in the Vinkus. This was always arid, lifeless, of little interest to the farmers and merchants of northern and eastern Oz. The tribes have lived here for decades, centuries I suppose, with nothing but the occasional cartographer passing through and beating a quick retreat. Don't you think this suggests some sort of campaign in these parts? What else *can* it suggest?"

"Look at how long it has taken these young men to recuperate from their overland trek," said Nanny. "This is surely just a reconnaissance mission, as they say. They'll get their information and then leave. Besides, everyone is always telling me, the whole damn place is swamped in snow or mud for two thirds of the year. You're a worrier, you always were. The way you gripped the Quadlings we used to proselytize, as if they were your own private dolls! How you went on when they were relocated or whatever! It used to trouble your mother no end, believe me."

"It's been well documented that the Quadlings were being exterminated, and *we were witnesses*," said Elphaba strictly. "You too, Nanny."

"I look after my young, I can't look after the world," said Nanny, quaffing a cup of tea and scratching Killyjoy's nose. "I look after Liir, which is more than you do."

Elphaba didn't think it worth her while to lambaste the old biddy. She flipped through the Grimmerie again, trying to find some small spell of binding with which she could close the castle gates against the men. She wished she had at least sat in on Miss Greyling's class in magic at school.

"Of course your mother was worried about you, she always was," said Nanny. "You were such an odd little thing. And the trials that poor woman had! You remind me of her now, only you're more rigid than she was. She could really let her hair down. Do you know, she was so upset with having you be a girl—she was so convinced you'd be a boy—she sent me to the Emerald City to find an elixir to ensure . . ." But Nanny stopped, muddled. "Or was that elixir to prevent her next child from being born green? Yes, that was it."

"Why did she want me to be a boy?" said Elphaba. "I would have obliged her if I'd had a say in the matter. Not to be simplistic, but it always made me feel horrible, to know how I'd disappointed her so early on. Not to mention the looks."

"Oh, don't credit her with nasty motives," said Nanny. She eased her shoes off and rubbed the backs of her feet with her cane. "Melena had hated her life at Colwen Grounds, you know. That's why she contrived to fall in love with Frex and get out of there. Her grandfather the Eminent Thropp had made it all too clear that she would inherit the title. The Munchkinlander title descends through the female line unless there are no daughters. The family seat, and all its attendant responsibilities, would go from him, to Lady Partra, to Melena, and then to the first daughter Melena had. She was hoping to have only sons, to keep them out of that place."

"She always talked about it so lovingly!" said Elphaba, astounded.

"Oh, everything is gorgeous once it's gone. But for a young person, trained up in all that wealth and responsibility—well, she hated it. She revolted by having sex early and often, with anyone who would oblige, and she as good as ran off with Frex, who was the first suitor she had who loved her for herself and not her position and inheritance. She thought a daughter of hers would find it equally deadly, so she wanted sons."

"But that makes no sense. If she had sons and no daughters, then her oldest son would inherit. If I'd been a boy without sisters, I'd still have been stuck in the same mess."

"Not necessarily," said Nanny. "Your mother had one older sister, who was born with a permanent case of overwrought nerves, maybe also lacking in the brains department. She was housed off-grounds. But she was old enough to breed, and healthy enough, and was just as likely to bear a daughter. If she had borne a daughter first, her daughter would have inherited the title of Eminence, and the estate and fortunes with it."

"So I have a mad aunt," said the Witch. "Maybe madness runs in the family. Where is she now?"

"Died of the flu when you were still a small child, and left no issue. So Melena's hopes were dashed. But that was her thinking, back in those brash, brave days of youthful blunder."

Elphaba had few memories of her mother, and they were warm, sometimes searing. "But what's this about her taking medicine to prevent Nessarose from being born green?"

"I got her some tablets in the Emerald City, from some gypsy woman," said Nanny. "I explained to the beastly creature what had happened—I mean that you'd been born an unfortunate color, and those *teeth*—thank Lurline your second set were more human!—and the gypsy woman made some silly prophecy about two sisters being instrumental in the history of Oz. She gave me some powerful pills. I've always wondered if the pills were the *cause* of Nessarose's affliction. I wouldn't mess with gypsy potions anymore, believe me. Not with what we know these days." She smiled, having long ago forgiven herself of any culpability in the whole affair.

"Nessarose's affliction," mused Elphaba. "Our mother took some gypsy remedy, and bore a second daughter without arms. It was either green or armless. Mama didn't have very good luck at girls, did she."

"Shell, however, is a sight for sore eyes," said Nanny rosily. "Then, who is to say it was all your mother's fault? First there was the confusion about who was really Nessarose's father, and then the pills from that old Yackle person, and your father's moodiness—"

"Yackle person? What do you mean?" asked Elphaba, starting. "And who the hell was Nessarose's father if it wasn't Papa?"

"Oh la," said Nanny, "pour me another cup of tea and I'll tell you all. You're old enough now, and Melena's long dead." She meandered through a story about the Quadling glassblower named Turtle Heart, and Melena's uncertainty whether Nessarose was his child or Frex's, and the visit to Yackle, about whom she could remember nothing else but the name, the pills, and the prophecy, can't pull teeth from a hen so stop trying. She didn't mention (and she never had) how depressed Melena became when Elphaba was born. There was no point.

Elphie listened to all this, impatient and annoyed. On the one hand she wanted to throw it out the window: The past was immaterial. On the other, things fell into a slightly different order now. And that Yackle! Was the name just a coincidence? She was tempted to show Nanny the picture of *Yakal Snarling* in the Grimmerie, but resisted. No sense alarming the old woman, or giving her the nighttime frights.

So the two women poured each other tea and restrained themselves from painful observations about the past. But Elphaba began to fret about Nessarose. Perhaps Nessie didn't want the position of Eminence, and was just as incarcerated there as her older sister was here. Perhaps Elphaba owed her the chance of liberty. Yet how much really could you owe other people? Was it endless?

3

Nor was beside herself. In a short time her whole life had changed, so utterly. The world was more magic than ever, but it seemed lodged inside her now, not outside. Her body was waiting to flame, to blossom, and no one seemed to care or to notice.

Liir had become a water boy for the expeditionary soldiers. Irji spent his time composing long devotional libretti in honor of Lurlina. In a state of uncertainty over the men in residence, the sisters remained confined to their chambers by their own inclination, yet quivering with readiness should things change. Nothing *could* change, as convention dictated, unless Sarima married again, and then they would be free to court. Their domestic campaigns to throw Commander Cherrystone and Sarima together, however, met with no success. They redoubled their efforts. Three even approached Auntie Witch for a love potion from that magic encyclopedia. "Hah," said Elphaba, "that'll be the day," and that was that about that.

Nor, bereft of companionship, took to hanging around the men's dormitory, trying to pitch in with chores that Liir wasn't asked to do, that men didn't much care about. She hung out their cloaks in the sun. She polished their buttons. She brought them flowers from the hills. She prepared a tray of summer fruits and cheeses that seemed to please them, especially when she served them herself. One young, dark, balding soldier with a captivating smile liked her to pop the orange segments right in his lips, and he sucked the juice from her fingers, to the mingled enjoyment and envy of the others. "Sit on my lap," he said, "and let me feed you." He offered her a strawberry, but she wouldn't sit on his lap—and she loved refusing.

One day she decided to treat them to a full-scale chamber cleaning. They were out doing an inventory of the vineyards on the lower slopes and would be gone all day. Nor arrayed herself with rags, yoked herself with buckets, and since Auntie Witch was deep in conversation with Nanny about, it seemed, Sarima, Nor swiped the Witch's broom, for its thicker brush and longer handle. She headed to the barracks.

She couldn't read much, so she ignored the letters and maps that spilled from the leathern satchels left carelessly slung over the back of a chair. She tidied the trunks, and swept, and in the effort raised a lot of dust, and felt warm.

She took off her blouse, and slung one of the men's rough capes over her sun-browned shoulders. It gave off such a heady aroma of maleness, even after its airing, that she nearly swooned. She lay down on someone's pallet with the cape just slightly falling open, so that she could imagine falling asleep and having the men return and see the beautiful line of flat skin that ran between her fresh new breasts. She considered pretending to fall asleep. But she knew she wouldn't do this. She sat up, dissatisfied with the possibilities, and reached out to grab the nearest thing—it happened to be the broom—so she could whack something in frustration.

The broom was out of reach, but it lunged a little toward her. It came across the floor of its own accord. She saw it. The broom was magic.

She touched it, almost fearfully, as if she guessed it had intentions. It felt no different from an ordinary broom. It merely moved, as if guided by the hand of an invisible spirit. "What tree are you whittled from, what field are you mown from?" she asked it, almost tenderly, but she expected no answer and she got none. The broom quivered, and elevated itself a lit-tle off the floor, as if waiting.

The cape had a hood on it, and she drew this up over her face. Then she hiked her summer skirt to her knees, and threw one leg over the broom, to ride it as a child rides a hobby horse.

The thing rose, tentatively, so she could keep her balance by trail-ing her toes on the floor, correcting, correcting—the center of gravity was high, and the span was so narrow. The top of the handle tilted farther up, and she slid down the shaft until she was caught against the brush top, as if it were a saddle of sorts. She held on tightly; her legs, especially in the upper thigh, felt as if they were swelling, the better to clench the handle between them. The large window at the end of the room hung open, for air and light, and the broom moved a couple of feet across the floor, until it had reached the sill.

Then the broom rose a few feet, and carried her out the window. Nor's stomach pitched, and her heels beat against the underside of the brush. Mercifully she had emerged not in the castle courtyard, where she would likely be seen, but on the other side, where the land did not fall away quite so far and fast. Nor wailed softly in the strangeness and ecstasy of the adventure. The cape flared out, exposing her chest, and how could she *ever* have imagined she wanted to be seen without a blouse? "Oh oh," she cried, but whether to the broom or to some guardian spirit, she did not know. She shuddered with exposure and shock, and the broom rose higher and higher, until it had come to a level with the uppermost window, which was in the Witch's tower.

The Witch and her nanny were watching, open-mouthed, with cups of tea halfway to their lips.

"You come down from there at once," ordered the Witch. Nor didn't know if it was she who was being addressed, or the broom. She had no reins to tug, no words of magic to wield. However the broom, apparently chastened, turned back, descended, and made a somewhat clumsy landing on the floor of the men's barracks. Nor flung herself off, weeping and shivering, and reclothed herself properly. She didn't want to touch the broom again, but when she picked it up the life had gone out of it, and she carried it up to the Witch's apartments expecting a severe reprimand.

"What were you doing with my broom?" barked the Witch.

"I was cleaning the soldiers' quarters," gabbled Nor. "It's such a mess, their papers all over, their clothes, their maps . . ."

"Keep your hands off my things, you," said the Witch. "What kinds of papers?"

"Plans, maps, letters, I don't know," said Nor, regaining her spunk, "go look for yourself. I didn't pay attention."

The Witch took the broom and appeared to consider hitting Nor with it. "Don't be a fool, Nor. Stay away from those men," she said coldly. "Stay away from them!" She raised the broom like a truncheon. "They'll hurt you as soon as spit at you. Stay away from them, I say. And stay away from me!"

Elphaba remembered that the broom was given her by Mother Yackle. The young woman had seen the old maunt as crippled, senile, a bother, but now Elphaba looked back and wondered if there was more to her than met the eye. Was that broom magicked by Mother Yackle, with a vestige of some Kumbricial instinct? Or did Nor have a power developing in her, and did she bring it out in the senseless broom? Nor apparently was a fervid believer in magic; maybe the broom was waiting to be believed in. Would it fly for Elphaba, too?

One night when everyone else had retired, Elphaba brought the broom out to the courtyard. She felt a little foolish, crouching down on the broom like a child on a hobbyhorse. "Come on, fly, you fool thing," she muttered. The broom twitched back and forth in a naughty way, enough to raise welts in her inner thighs. "I'm not a blushing schoolgirl, stop that nonsense," said Elphaba. The broom rose a foot and a half and then dumped Elphie on her rear end.

"I'll set you afire and that'll be the end of you," said Elphaba. "I'm too old for this sort of indignity."

It took five or six nights of trying before she managed even to hover six feet off the ground. She had been useless in sorcery. Was she doomed to be useless at everything? It was a pleasure, finally, to scare the barn owls and bats senseless. And it was good to be abroad. When she had more confidence, she wobbled far down the valley to the remains of the Ozma Regent's attempt at a dam; she rested and hoped that she wouldn't have to walk back. She didn't. The broom was resistant to her intention, but she could always threaten it with fire.

She felt like a night angel.

In midsummer, an Arjiki trader came along with pots and spoons and spools of thread, and he carried with him some letters left at an outpost far-ther north. Among them was a note from Frex—apparently Nanny had told him of her intentions to hunt Elphaba down, and he wrote to the mauntery, which had forwarded the letter on to Kiamo Ko in the Vinkus. Frex wrote that Nessarose had orchestrated a revolt, and that Munchkinland—or most of it anyway—had seceded from Oz, and set itself up as an independent state.

Nessarose as the Eminent Thropp had become the political head of state. Frex apparently thought this was Elphaba's birthright, and that she should come to Colwen Grounds and challenge her sister for it. "It may be she isn't the right woman for the job," he wrote, though Elphaba found his apprehension surprising. Wasn't Nessarose the warmly spiritual daughter that Elphie could never be?

Elphaba had no thirst for leadership, and did not want to challenge Nessarose in any way. But now that the broom seemed able to carry her for long distances, she wondered if she could fly by night to Colwen Grounds, and spend a few days seeing Papa, Nessie, and Shell once again. It had been a dozen years since she left Nessie in Shiz, drunk and sobbing following the death of Ama Clutch.

For Munchkinland to be free of the Wizard's iron grip!—that alone would be worth the trip. It made Elphie grin a bit at herself, to feel her old contempt for the Wizard flare up. Perhaps this was what healing meant, after all.

To be safe, one afternoon Elphaba went through the soldiers' empty barracks. She pawed through their papers. All the documents related to issues of mapping and geological survey. Nothing else. There seemed to be no hidden agenda of threat to the Arjikis or the other Vinkus tribes.

The earlier she went, the sooner she would return. And it would be better if no one know. So she told everyone she was taking a period of isolation in her tower, and she wanted neither food nor visitors for some days. When midnight struck, she set out for Colwen Grounds, now the home of her powerful sister.

4

She slept by daylight in the shadows of barns, the overhang of eaves, the lee of chimneys. She traveled by night. In the gloom, Oz spread out below—she hovered above it at about eighty feet, near as she could reckon—and the countryside made its geographical transformations with the ease of a vaudeville backdrop on rollers. The hardest passage was down the steep flanks of the Great Kells. Once free of the mountains, however, she saw Oz level out into the rich alluvial plain of the Gillikin River.

She flew along the waterway, above trading vessels and islands, until it fed at last into Restwater, Oz's largest lake. She kept to its southern edge, and took a whole night to traverse it, as it endlessly lapped in black oily silk waves, into sedge and swamp. She had trouble finding the mouth of the Munchkin River, which drained into Restwater from the eastern direction. Once she did, though, it was easy to locate the Yellow Brick Road. The farmland beyond grew even more lush. The effects of the drought, so drastic in her childhood, had been eradicated, and dairy farms and small villages seemed to prosper, happy as a child's toy town set, cunning and cozy in the wrinkled, nappy land of arable soil and accommodating climate.

The farther east she went, however, the more torn up the highway became. Crowbars had pried out bricks, trees had been felled and brush walls erected. It looked as if a few of the smaller bridges had been dynamited. A safeguard against retaliation by the Wizard's army?

Seven days after leaving her chambers at Kiamo Ko, Elphaba flew into the hamlet of Colwen Grounds, and slept under a green bay tree. When she awoke, she asked a merchant for the great house, and he tremblingly pointed her the way, as if she were a demon. So a green skin still gives Munchkinlanders the creeps, she observed, and walked the last couple of miles, and arrived at the front gates of Colwen Grounds a little after breakfast.

She had heard her mother speak of Colwen Grounds, wistfully and angrily, as they had slopped in waterproof boots through six inches of Quadling Country water. Elphie's years in the smug antiquity of Shiz, and the pomp of the Emerald City, ought to have prepared her for an imposing mansion. But she was startled, even shocked, at the grandeur of Colwen Grounds.

The gate was gilded, the forecourt swept clean of every scrap of grass and dung, and a bank of topiary saints in terra-cotta pots lined the balcony above the massive front door. Dignitaries with ribbons denoting new rank and prestige in the Free State of Munchkinland, she guessed, stood in small groups to one side. Coffee cups in hand, the officials had apparently just finished an early morning privy council meeting. Inside the gate, swordsmen stepped neatly up and barred her way. She began to protest—instantly branded a menace and a loon, she could see—and she was about to be ejected when a figure wandered into view from around the corner of a folly, and called for them to stop.

"Fabala!" he said.

"Yes, Papa, I'm here," she answered, with a child's politeness.

She turned. The dignitaries paused in their discussions, and then resumed, as if realizing that overhearing this reunion would be the height of rudeness. The guards withdrew their barrier when Frex approached. His hair was thin and long and caught up by a rawhide implement, as it always had been. His beard was the color of cream and reached his waist when he took his hands away from it.

"This is the sister of the Eminence of the East," said Frex, staring at Elphaba, "and my oldest daughter. Let her pass through, dear men, now and every time she approaches." He reached and caught her hand, and turned his head as a bird might to see her through one capable eye. The other eye, she realized, was dead.

"Come, we will greet each other in private, away from this attention," said Frex. "My word, Fabala, you have become your mother in these long years!" He linked his arm into hers, and they went into the building through a side door and found a small salon done up in saffron silks and plum velvet cushions. The door closed behind them. Frex lowered himself cautiously to the sofa and patted the upholstery next to him. She sat down, wary, tired, astonished at the wealth of her own feeling for him. She was full of need. But, she reminded herself, you're a grown woman.

"I knew you would come if I wrote," he said. "Fabala, I always knew that." He wrapped her in his arms, stiffly. "I may cry for a minute." When he was through, he asked her where she had gone, and what she had done, and why she had never come back.

"I was not sure there was a *back* to come to," she answered, realizing the truth of it as she spoke. "When you finished converting a town, Papa, you moved on to new fields. Your home was in the pasture of souls; mine never was. Besides, I had my own work to do." She added, a moment later, in a low voice, "Or I thought I did."

She mentioned her years in the Emerald City, but did not say why.

"And was Nanny right? Were you a maunt? I didn't raise you for such submission," he said. "I'm surprised. Such conformity and obedience—"

"I was no more a maunt than I ever was a unionist," she chided him gently, "but I lived with the maunts. They did good work, whatever the error or inspiration of their beliefs. It was a time of recuperation from a difficult passage. And then, last year, I went to the Vinkus, and I guess I've made my home there, although for how long I cannot say."

"And what do you do?" he said. "Are you married?"

"I'm a witch," she answered. He recoiled, peered through the working eye to see if she spoke in jest.

"Tell me about Nessie before I see her, and Shell," she said. "Your letter sounded as if you thought she needed help. I'll do what I can in the short while I can be here."

He told her about her sister's rise to Eminence, and the secession in the late spring. "Yes, yes, I know of it but not why," she said, prodding. So he described the burning of a grange where opposition meetings had been gathering, the reported rape of a couple of Munchkinlander maidens following a cotillion of the Wizard's army garrisoned near Dragon Cupboard. He mentioned the Massacre at Far Applerue and the heavy taxation on farm crops. "The last straw," he said, "as far as Nessie was concerned, anyway, was the callow despoiling by the Wizard's soldiers of simple country meetinghouses."

"Unlikely last straw," said Elphaba. "Isn't the back room of a colliery as holy a place to pray as a meetinghouse? I mean, according to teaching?"

"Well, teaching," said Frex. He shrugged; such distinctions were beyond him now. "Nessie was incensed, and communicated her outrage, and before she knew it the spark had been thrown out and the tinder caught. Within a week of her firing off a furious letter to the Emperor Wizard himself—a dangerous and seditious act—the revolutionary fever had coalesced around her. It happened right here in the forecourt of Colwen Grounds. It was magnificent, and you'd have guessed Nessie was groomed for treason. She addressed the senior men among the farming communities both near and far, and kept her religious agenda in check, sensibly, I think. So her appeal for their support was overwhelmingly answered. There was a unanimous approval for secession."

Papa's gone pragmatic in his old age, Elphaba observed with some surprise.

"But how did you slip through the border patrols?" he asked. "Things being what they are—hotting up, as they say."

"I just flew right through, a little black bird at nighttime," she answered, smiling at him, and touching his hand. It was glazed and mottled pink, like a lake lobster on the boil. "But what I don't know, Papa, is why you called me here. What do you expect me to do?"

"I had thought you might join your sister in her seat of authority," he said, with the simple-minded hope of one whose family has been too long apart. "I know who you are, Fabala. I doubt you have much changed over the years. I know your cunning and your conviction. I also know that Nessie is at the mercy of her religious voices, and she could slip and undo the terrible good she is helping to create right now by being a focal figure for resistance. If that happens, it will not go well for her."

So I am to be a whipping girl, thought Elphaba, I am to be a first line of defense. Her pleasure evaporated.

"And it will not go well for them, the eager supporters," Frex said, waving a hand to indicate most of Munchkinland. His face sagged—his smile was an effort too, she thought coolly—and his shoulders fell. "They have had more than a generation of gentle dictatorship from our Glorious Wizard scoundrel—oh, even I forget, we're now in the Free State of Munchkinland—these farmers surely underestimate the size of the eventual retaliation. In fact, Shell has found from reliable sources that the stockpiles of grain in the Emerald City are massive, and we can be left for some time without needing to be overrun. Short of routing some divisions of soldiers across the border, and jailing some drunken hooligans, this has been a most genteel disengagement so far. We are deluded into believing we are safe. I mean Nessie is deluded too, I think. You, I have always felt, had a clearer mind about you. You can help her prepare, you can provide the balance and the support."

"I always did that, Papa," she said. "In childhood and at college. Now I am told she can stand up for herself."

"You've heard of my precious shoes," he said. "I bought them from a decrepit crone, and then I retooled them for Nessa with my own hands, using skills in glass and metal that I had once learned from Turtle Heart. I made them to give her a sense of beauty, but I didn't expect them to be enchanted by someone else. I am not *sorry* they are. But Nessa now thinks she needs no one, to help her stand or help her govern. She listens less than ever. In some ways I think those shoes are dangerous."

"I wish you had made them for me, Papa," she said in a quiet voice.

"You didn't need them. You had your voice, your intensity, even your cruelty as your armor."

"My cruelty!" She reared back.

"Oh, you were a fiendish little thing," said Frex, "but so what, children grow into and out of themselves. You were a terror when you first were around other children. You only calmed down when we began to travel and you got to hold the baby. It was Nessarose who tamed you, you know. You have her to thank; she was holy and blessed even from the day she was born. Even as an infant, she soothed your wildness with her obvious need. You don't remember that, I suppose."

Elphie wasn't able to remember, she wasn't able to think about all that. Even the idea of being cruel was slipping from her. Instead, she was trying to feel fondness toward her father, despite the exhaustion of being commandeered to be a second lieutenant once again, in service of dear needy Nessarose. She concentrated on her father's concern for the citizens of Munchkinland. Ever a pastoral sensibility, his. Though rejecting his theology, she adored him for his commitment.

"I must hear more about Turtle Heart one day," she said in a light voice, "but now, I suppose I should go greet my sister. And I *will* think about what you say, Papa. I can't imagine being part of a governmental troika, with you and Nessarose—or a committee, should Shell be involved too. But I'll suspend judgment for a while. And Shell, Papa, how is he?"

"Behind enemy lines, so they say," Frex answered as she got up to leave. "He is a foolhardy boy and will be among the first casualties, once this really gets going. He resembles you in some ways."

"He's gone green?" she asked, amused.

"He's stubborn as sin stains," he answered.

Nessarose was secluded in an upstairs parlor, conducting her morning meditation. Frex saw that Elphaba was given license to wander about the house and demesne. After all, in another configuration of events, Elphaba could have been (or could yet become) the Eminent Thropp, the Eminence of the East, the nominated head of the Free State of Munchkinland. Frex watched his green daughter amble down marble corridors, dragging her broom like a charwoman, gazing at the ormolu, the damask, the fresh flowers, the servants in livery, the portraits. He felt, as always, a twinge of pain deep in his breast, for the hidden and unknowable things that he had done wrong in raising her. But he was glad that she was here at last.

Elphaba found her way into a private chapel at the end of a hall of polished mahogany. It was baroque rather than ancient, and it was in the midst of being redecorated. Nessarose must have ordered the frescoes to be whitewashed; perhaps the succulent images would distract people from their meditative tasks. Elphie sat on a bench on the side, amidst buckets of limestone wash and paintbrushes and ladders. She did not pretend to pray, though she felt very uneasy about this whole thing. She trained her gaze, to focus her mind, on a huge section still boasting its images. It featured several rotund angels levitating with the aid of sizable wings. Their garments had been cut to accommodate the anatomical irregularity, she saw. They were rather full-bodied dames, but the wings weren't bulging with straining arteries nor snapping at the tip. The artist had considered the optimal length and breadth of wing required to hoist ample ladies aloft. The formula looked to be about three times wing length to the length of arm, corrected perhaps to account for the portliness. If you could sweep your way to the Other Land on wings, what about on a broom? she wondered. And realized she must be very tired; usually she'd cut off senseless speculation about unionist nonsense like an afterlife, a Beyond, an Other Land.

I should remember my lessons from that life sciences course, she thought. All the devastating borders of knowledge Doctor Dillamond was about to cross. I almost understood some of it. I could stitch wings onto Chistery. He could join me in flight. What a lark.

She rose and went to find her sister.

Nessarose was less surprised to see Elphaba than Elphie would have guessed. Perhaps, Elphie considered, it was because Nessa had become used to being the center of attention. Then again, she had *always* been the center of attention. "Darling Elphie," she said, looking up from a pair of identical books some attendant had laid out, next to each other, so she could read four pages without calling for someone to turn the page. "Give us a kiss."

"Oh there, then," Elphie said, obliging. "How are you, Nessie? You look fine."

Nessarose stood, in her beautiful shoes, and smiled brilliantly. "The grace of the Unnamed God gives me strength, as ever," she said.

But Elphaba could not be annoyed. "You have risen, and I don't just mean to your feet," she said. "History has chosen you for a role, and you've accepted it. I'm proud of you."

"You needn't be proud," said Nessarose. "But thank you, dear. I thought you'd probably come. Did Father drag you here to take care of me?"

"No one dragged me here, but Papa did write."

"So all those years in solitude, and political turmoil brings you out at last. Where were you?"

"Here and there."

"You know we thought you'd died," said Nessarose. "Drape that shawl around my shoulders and fix it with a pin, will you, so I needn't call a maid? I mean that awful, awful time when you left me alone in Shiz. I am still furious with you about it, I just remembered." She curled her lip, prettily; Elphaba was glad to see she possessed at least a residual sense of humor.

"We were all young then, and perhaps I was wrong," said Elphie. "It didn't do you any lasting harm, anyway. At least not so I can see."

"I had to put up with Madame Morrible all by myself, for two more years. Glinda was a help for a while, then she graduated and went on. Nanny was my salvation, but she was old even then. She's gone on to you lately, hasn't she? Well, back then I felt horribly alone. Only my faith saw me through."

"Well, faith will do that," said Elphie, "if you've got it."

"You speak as one still living in the shadowland of doubt."

"In fact I think we have more important things to discuss than the state of my soul or lack thereof. You have a revolution on your hands— sorry, I guess I've gotten out of the habit!—and you're the resident com- mander general. Congratulations."

"Oh, tiresome events of the distracting world, yes yes," said Nessa- rose. "Look, it's just beautiful out there in the gardens. Let's go walk for a bit and get some air. You look green about the gills—"

"All right, I deserved that—"

"—and there's plenty of time to go into diplomatic matters. I have a meeting in a little while, but there's time for a stroll. You should get to know this place. Let me show it to you."

5

Elphaba could only get Nessarose's attention for small snatches of time. However dismissive of the demands of leadership, Nessarose was clearheaded about her schedule, and spent hours preparing for meetings.

And at first the discussion was frivolous—family memories, school days. Elphie was impatient to get around to the meat of the matter here. But Nessarose wouldn't be rushed. Sometimes she let Elphie sit in when she held audiences with citizens. Elphie wasn't entirely pleased with what she saw.

One afternoon an old woman from some hamlet in the Corn Basket came in. She made obeisance in a most disgusting and obsequious manner, and Nessarose seemed to shine back at her with glory. The woman complained that she had a maid who, having fallen in love with a wood-cutter, wanted to leave her service to get married. But the old woman had already given three sons to the new local militia for defense, and she and the maid were all the labor available to bring in the crops. If the maid ran off with her woodcutter, the crops would spoil and she would be ruined. "And all for the sake of liberty," she concluded bitterly.

"Well, what do you want me to do about it?" said the Eminence of the East.

"I can give you two Sheep and a Cow," said the woman.

"I have livestock—" said Nessarose, but Elphaba interrupted and said, "Did you say Sheep? A Cow? You mean Animals?"

"My very own Animals," the woman replied proudly.

"How do you come to own Animals?" Elphaba asked, her teeth clenched. "Are Animals no more than chattel now in Munchkinland?"

"Elphie, please," said Nessarose quietly.

"What will you take to release them?" demanded Elphie, in a passion.

"I already said. Do something about this woodcutter."

"What do you have in mind?" interrupted Nessarose, displeased that her sister was usurping her role as arbiter of justice.

"I brought you his axe. I thought you might bewitch it and cause it to kill him."

"Fie," said Elphaba, but Nessarose said, "Oh well, that wouldn't be very nice."

"Very *nice?*" Elphie said. "No indeed it wouldn't be very *nice*, Nessie."

"Well, you're the legal answer around here," said the old woman stoutly. "What do you suggest?"

"I might bewitch his axe and let it slip," said Nessarose thoughtfully, "just enough perhaps to cut off his arm. I know from experience that a person without an arm isn't as desirable to the opposite sex as one fully armed."

"Fair enough," said the woman, "but if it doesn't work I'll come back and you'll do more, for the same price. Sheep and a Cow don't come cheap around here, you know."

"Nessarose, you're not a witch, no, I don't believe it," said Elphie. "*You* don't do spells, of all things!"

"The righteous person can work miracles in the honor of the Unnamed God," said Nessarose calmly. "Show me that axe, if you've brought it."

The old woman held forward a woodcutter's axe, and Nessarose knelt down near it, as if she were praying. It was an odd, even a frightening thing, to see that narrow armless body able to lean forward, unaided and off balance, and then, when the spell was through, able to right itself. Those are some shoes, thought Elphie soberly, bitterly. Glinda has got some power in her, for all her social dazzle, or maybe the power comes from the love of our father for his Nessie. Or some combination. And if Nessarose isn't pulling the wool over this old biddy's eyes, she's become a sorceress too, by whatever name she chooses to call it.

"You *are* a witch," said Elphaba again; she couldn't help it. This perhaps was a mistake, as the old woman was just thanking Nessarose for her efforts. "I'll bring the Animals by the barn out back," she said. "They're tethered in town."

"Animals! Tethered!" exclaimed Elphie, seething.

"Thank you, Miss Eminence," said the old woman. "The Eminence of the East. Or should I call you the Witch of the East?" She grinned toothily, having gotten her way, and went out the door carrying the enchanted axe over her shoulder the way a strapping young lumberjack would do.

They weren't to be alone again for a while. Elphaba went prowling around the stable and sheds until she found an attendant who could point her toward the two Sheep and the Cow. They were in a pen with clean straw, each one facing a different corner, chewing in abstraction.

"You're the new Animals, brought here by that old vengeful fiend," said Elphaba. The Cow looked over as if unaccustomed to being addressed. The Sheep made no sign of having understood.

"What's your beef?" said the Cow, in a dark humor.

"I've been living in the Vinkus," said Elphie. "There aren't many Animals there. At one time I was an agitator in the Animal Rights grass-roots sweep—I don't really know how things stand for Munchkinlander Animals now. What can you tell me?"

"I can tell you to mind your own business," said the Cow.

"And the Sheep?"

"These Sheep can tell you nothing, they've gone dumb."

"Are they—sheep? Does that happen?"

"They talk about humans becoming vegetables—or nuts—or even fruits," said the Cow, "but they don't mean it literally. Sheep don't become sheep, they become mute Sheep. They don't really need to be discussed here as if they're not listening, by the way."

"Of course. My apologies," she said to the Sheep, one of whom blinked balefully. To the Cow she added, "I'd rather call you by your name."

"I've given up using my name in public," said the Cow. "It's not afforded me any individual rights to have an individual name. I reserve it for my private use."

"I understand that," said Elphaba. "I feel the same. I'm just the Witch now."

"Her Eminence herself?" A gummy rope of spittle dropped from the Cow's jaw. "I'm flattered. I didn't know you called yourself Witch, I thought that was just a nasty backfield nickname. The Witch of the East."

"Well no. I'm her sister. I suppose I'm the Witch of the West, if you will." She grinned. "In fact I didn't know she was so disliked."

The Cow had blundered. "Surely I meant no disregard to your family," she said. "I should just keep my mouth closed and concentrate on my cud. The thing is, I'm in shock—to be sold in exchange for a witch's spell! There's nothing wrong with that woodcutter—oh I've got ears, I have, though they forget—and the thought of a warmhearted simpleton like Nick Chopper coming to harm through a witch's spell—and I part of the barter cost—well, it's hard to imagine how much lower one could sink in life."

"I've come to free you," Elphie said.

"By whose authority?" The Cow snorted suspiciously.

"I told you, I'm the sister of the Eminent Thropp—the Eminence of the East." She amended herself: "The Witch of the East. It's my prerogative here."

"And free to go where? To do what?" said the Cow. "We'd get from here to Lower Muckslop and be roped in again. Subjected to slavery under the Wizard, and catechisms under the Eminent Thropp! We don't exactly blend in with those creepy little Munchkinlander humans."

"You're gone a bit dour," said Elphaba.

"Haven't you ever heard of a mad Cow?" she answered. "Sweetheart, my udder is sore from their daily yanking. I am tapped for milk morning and night. I won't even go into what it's like to be mounted by a—well, just never mind. But worst, my children have been fattened on milk and slaughtered for veal. I could hear their cries from the abattoir, they didn't even bother to move me out of hearing range!" Here she turned her head to the wall, and the Sheep came up on either side of her, pressing like a living pair of warm bookends against her lower sides and underbelly.

Elphaba said, "I can't be sorrier or more ashamed. Look, I was working with Doctor Dillamond—have you heard of him?—in Shiz, years ago. I went to the Wizard himself to protest what was happening . . ."

"Oh, the Wizard doesn't show himself to the likes of us," said the Cow, after she had regained her composure. "I don't feel like talking anymore. Everybody's on your side until they want something from you. The Eminent Nessarose has probably brought us in order to impress us into some religious ceremonial procession. My silken flanks tarted up with garlands or the like. And we all know what happens *next*."

"Now you *must* be wrong in that," said the Witch. "I *do* object. Nessarose is a strict unionist. They don't go in for—blood sacrifice—"

"Times change," said the Cow. "And she's got a population of ill-educated, nervous subjects to pacify. What, pray tell, works better than ritual slaughter?"

"But however could it come to this?" said the Witch. "Assuming you're telling the truth? This is farming country. You ought to be well established here."

"Animals in pens have lots of time to develop theories," said the Cow. "I've heard more than one clever creature draw a connection between the rise of tiktokism and the erosion of traditional Animal labor. We weren't beasts of burden, but we were good reliable laborers. If we were made redundant in the workforce, it was only a matter of time before we'd be socially redundant too. Anyway, that's one theory. My own feeling is that there is real evil abroad in the land. The Wizard sets the standard for it, and the society follows suit like a bunch of sheep. Forgive the slanderous reference," she said, nodding to her companions in the pen. "It was a slip."

Elphaba threw open the gate of the pen. "Come on, you're free," she said. "What you make of it is your own affair. If you turn it down, it's on your own heads."

"It's on our own heads if we walk out, too. Do you think a Witch who would charm an axe to dismember a human being would pause over a couple of Sheep and an annoying old Cow?"

"But this might be your only chance!" Elphaba cried.

The Cow moved out, and the Sheep followed. "We'll be back," she said. "This is an exercise in your education, not ours. Mark my words, my rump'll be served up rare on your finest Dixxi House porcelain dinner plates before the year is out." She mooed a last remark—"I hope you choke"—and, tail swishing the flies, she meandered away.

6

An ambassador from the Glikkus, darling," Nessarose said, when Elphaba demanded a meeting. "Really, I *can't* turn her away. She's come to discuss mutual defense pacts in the event that the Glikkus secedes next. She thinks there are agents trailing her family, and she needs to leave on her return journey tonight. But we'll dine together, just like old times? You, me, and my server?"

Elphaba had no choice but to while away another afternoon. She located Frex and persuaded him to go for a stroll out beyond the ornamental ponds and pristine lawns, where the woods came up to the back edge of Colwen Grounds. He walked so stiffly, so slowly, it was torture; she was a strider. But she kept herself in check.

"How do you find your sister?" he asked her. "After all these years? Much changed?"

"She was always confident, in her way," Elphie said reservedly.

"I never thought so, and I don't now," Frex said. "But I think it was a good act, and it's gotten better."

"What really did you ask me to come here for, Papa?" Elphaba said. "I haven't much time, you know. You must be frank."

"You would make a smarter Eminence than Nessie," he said. "And it's your birthright. Yes, I know the strict rules of title inheritance weren't important to your mother. I just think that the people of Munch-kinland would do better with you at the helm. Nessa is—too devout, if such a thing exists. Too devout to be a central figure in public life, anyway."

"This may be the only respect in which I take after my mother," Elphaba said, "but an inherited position is of no interest to me, and it carries no weight at all that I'm the rightful Eminence. I've long ago abdicated my position in the family in that respect. Nessarose has every right to abdicate hers, and then Shell can be located to stand in. Or better yet, the foolish custom can be abolished, and let the Munchkinlanders govern themselves to death."

"Nobody ever suggested a leader isn't just as much a scapegoat as a lowly peon," said Frex. "Anyway, it's possible. But I'm talking about *leadership*, not about rank and privilege. I'm talking about the nature of the times we live in, and the job that needs to be done. Fabala, you were always the more capable sibling. Shell is a madcap cutup, currently playing secret agent, and Nessie is a bruised little girl—"

"Oh please," she said in disgust. "Isn't it time to get over that?"

"*She* hasn't," he said, hurt. "Do you see her wrapped in some lover's arms? Do you see her bearing her own children, engaging in life in a way that makes sense? She hides behind her devotion the way a terrorist hides behind his ideals—" He saw her flinch at this, and paused.

"I have known terrorists capable of love," she said evenly, "and I have known good maunts, unmarried and childless, doing charity for stricken people."

"Have you known Nessa to have an adult bond with anyone other than the Unnamed God?"

"You're one to talk," she said. "You had your wife and your children, but they came lower on the order of priorities than Quadlings waiting to be converted."

"I did what had to be done," he said rigidly. "I won't be lectured by my daughter."

"Well, I won't be lectured by you about my everlasting duties to Nessie. I gave her my childhood, I got her going at Shiz. She's made her life the way she wants it, and she still has choice and free will even now. And so do her subjects, who can depose her and cut off her head if her prayers get in their way."

"She is a rather powerful woman," Frex said sadly. Elphie glanced sideways at him, and for the first time she saw him as feckless—the kind of old man that Irji, if he survived, would grow to be. Constantly pawing at the edge of events, reacting instead of acting, mourning the past and praying for the future instead of stirring up the present.

"How did she get so powerful?" she asked, trying to be kind. "She had two good parents."

He didn't answer this.

They walked on and came out of the woods along the edge of a cornfield. A couple of farmhands were repairing a fence and erecting a scarecrow. "Afternoon, Brother Frexspar," they said, doffing their caps. They looked a little askance at Elphaba. When she and her father had continued out of earshot, she said, "They were wearing a little talisman or something on their tunics, did you see it? It looked like a small straw dolly or something."

"Oh yes, the straw man." He sighed. "Another pagan custom that had almost gone underground, and then was revived during the Great Drought. Ignorant field-workers wear a straw man as a charm against the pests of crops: drought, crows, insects, rot. Once upon a time there was a tradition of human sacrifice about it." He paused to catch his breath and wipe his face. "Our family friend, Turtle Heart, the Quadling—he was butchered right here in Colwen Grounds, on the day that Nessarose was born. An itinerant dwarf and a huge tiktok entertaining clock were making the circuit that year, and providing a conduit for the ugliest of human inclinations. We arrived here just in time for Turtle Heart to be nabbed. I've never forgiven myself for not seeing what was about to happen—but your mother was in her labor, and we'd been run out of town. I wasn't thinking clearly enough all the way around things."

Elphaba had heard all this before—even so. "You were in love with him," she said, to make it easier.

"We both were, we shared him," said Frex. "Your mother and I did. It was a lifetime ago and I don't know why anymore; I don't think I knew why then. I haven't loved anyone else since your mother died, except of course my children."

"What a brutal history of sacrifices," she said. "I was just talking to a Cow who expects to be a blood victim. Is that possible?"

"The more civilized we become, the more horrendous our entertainments," said Frex.

"And it'll never change, or will it? I remember the etymology of the word *Oz*, at least as proposed at a lecture by our Head, Madame Morrible. She said that academics were inclined to locate the root of the term in the Gillikinese cognate *oos*, which carries freights of meaning about growth, development, power, generation. Even *ooze*, with its distant companion noun *virus*, is thought to belong to the same general family. The older I get, the more accurate this derivation seems to be."

"And yet the poet of the *Oziad* calls it 'Land of green abandon, land in endless leaf.'"

"Poets are just as responsible for empire building as any other professional hacks."

"Sometimes I would give anything to get away from here, but I dread the thought of a trip across the deadly sands."

"That's only a legend," said Elphie. "Papa, *you* taught me that the sands are no more deadly than these fields. That reminds me of the other theory, that Oz is related to the word *oasis*. What the nomadic peoples of the north thought of Gillikin, time beyond thinking, when Oz was first discovered and settled. Now look, Papa, you needn't go so far. The Vinkus is nearly another country. Why don't you come back with me?"

"I would love to, honey," he said. "But how could I leave Nessarose? I never could."

"Even if she's Turtle Heart's daughter and not yours?" she said, stingingly because stung.

"Especially if that," he answered.

And Elphaba saw that by not knowing for sure if Nesssarose had been fathered by himself or by Turtle Heart, Frex had decided in some subrational way that she was the daughter of them both. Nessarose was the proof of their brief union—theirs, and, obviously, Melena's as well. It didn't matter how crippled Nessarose was; she would always be more than Elphaba, always. She would always *mean* more.

Elphaba and Nessarose sat in Nessa's bedchamber. A handmaid served some soup made of cow's stomach. Elphie, not normally squeamish, couldn't eat it. The maid neatly spooned tiny portions into Nessie's mouth.

"I'm not going to beat around the bush," Nessarose said. "I would like you to join me here as a sister-at-arms, to lead my circle of advisors and to manage in my absence if I should travel."

"I have no love of Munchkinland, from what I've seen so far," said Elphaba. "The people are cruel and impressed by charades, the pomp of this place is oppressive, and I do believe you're sitting on a powder keg."

"All the more reason you should stay and help me," said Nessarose. "Weren't we raised up to expect a life of service?"

"Your shoes have made you strong," said Elphie. "I didn't know shoes could do that. I don't think you need me. Don't lose those shoes, though." She thought: Your shoes give you an unnatural balance. You look like a serpent standing on its tail.

"Surely you remember them from before?"

"Yes, but I hear Glinda amplified them with a magic spell, or something."

"Oh, that Glinda! What a card." Nessie swallowed and smiled. "Well, you can have the shoes, my dear—over my dead body. I'll rewrite my will and leave them to you. Though what they would do for you, I can hardly imagine. They didn't grow me new arms. Perhaps enchanted shoes won't change the color of your skin but will make you enticing enough so that it won't matter."

"I'm already too old to be that enticing."

"Why you're still in the prime of life, and so am I!" said Nessarose, laughing. "Tell me you've got some romancing man in a Vinkus yurt or tent or teepee or whatever it is they call home there. Come on."

"I have been wondering something, ever since I saw you do that spell this morning," Elphie said. "The spell over the axe."

"Oh right. Small potatoes, that one."

"Do you by any chance remember that time in Shiz, when Madame Morrible said she was putting us under a spell? And that we couldn't talk to each other about it?"

"Go on. Sounds familiar. She was so creepy, wasn't she? A master of tyranny."

"She said she had chosen us—me, you, and Glinda—to be Adepts. To be agents of someone quite high up. To be sorceresses and, I don't know, secret accomplices. She promised we'd be highly placed and effectual. She made us think we couldn't ever discuss it with one another."

"Oh yes, that. I do remember. What a witch she was."

"Well, do you think there's any truth to that? Do you think she had the power to bind us into silence? To make us powerful sorceresses?"

"She had the power to scare us out of our wits, but we were young and *very* stupid, as I remember."

"I had the feeling at the time that she was in collusion with the Wizard, and that she ordered her tiktok thing—Grommetik, the name's just come back to me, isn't memory odd like that—to kill Doctor Dillamond."

"You saw fiends with knives behind every chair, you always did," Nessarose said. "I don't think that Madame Morrible had any real power. She was a manipulative woman, but her power was very limited, and in our naiveté we saw her as a villain. She was merely full of self-importance."

"I wonder. I tried to say something about it afterward. Didn't we all faint?"

"We were innocent and *horribly* suggestible, Elphie."

"And Glinda's gone on to marry money, as Madame Morrible said. Is Sir Chuffrey still alive?"

"If you can call it that, yes. And Glinda is a sorceress, there's no questioning that. But Madame Morrible was merely predicting things to us; she saw our talents, as an educator could be expected to do, and she advised us on how to make the most of them. What's so surprising about that?"

"She tried to seduce us into a secret service for an unknown master. I'm not inventing this, Nessie."

"She knew how to get to *you*, obviously, by appealing to your sense of conspiracy. I don't remember such alluring nonsense."

Elphaba fell silent. Perhaps Nessie was right. And yet here they were, a dozen years later: two Witches, in a manner of speaking. And Glinda a sorceress for the public good. It was enough to make Elphie go back to Kiamo Ko and burn that Grimmerie, and burn the broom too, for that matter.

"She always reminded Glinda of a carp," said Nessarose. "Can you really be scared of a fish, after all these years?"

"I saw in a book once a drawing of a lake monster, or a sea monster if you believe in oceans," said Elphie. "I may not be sure if monsters exist, but I'd rather live my life in doubt than be persuaded by a real experience of one."

"You said much the same thing about the Unnamed God once," said Nessarose quietly.

"Oh, now please don't start on that."

"A soul is too valuable to ignore, Elphie."

"Well, isn't it good I don't have one then, so there's no muss, no fuss."

"You have a soul. Everyone does."

"How about the Cow you bartered for today, and the Sheep?"

"I'm not talking about lower orders."

"That sort of talk offends me, Nessie. I freed those Animals today, you know."

Nessarose shrugged. "You have some rights in Colwen Grounds. I'm not going to walk around prohibiting your little pet missions."

"They said some pretty horrible things about how Animals are being treated here. I thought it was the Emerald City and Gillikin only; I somehow guessed Munchkinland, being more rural, would have more common sense."

"You know," said Nessie, indicating that the maid should wipe her mouth with a napkin, "once at a prayer service I met a soldier. He had lost a limb in a campaign against some restless Quadlings. He said every morning he slapped the stump where his arm used to be. He got the blood ringing, and after a few minutes there was a tingling sensation, and he developed a kind of phantom limb. Not all at once, and not in physical form: What he regained was a sense of what it had *felt like*. It would grow to the elbow, and then his memory, his bodily memory, of limbs in three-dimensional space, would extend, eventually, all the way down to his fingers. Once his phantom limb was in place, mentally, that is, he could face the day as a crippled man. Furthermore, he had better physical balance."

Elphaba, feeling more and more like a real Witch, looked at her sister, waiting for the punch.

"I tried it for a while. For months in fact. I had Nanny massage my little knobs there. After much hard work on poor Nanny's part, I began to develop just the beginning of a sense of what it would be like to have arms. It never went very far, until Glinda dazzled up these shoes. Now— I don't know why, maybe they're too tight and my circulation is complaining—after an hour on my feet, I have phantom arms. First time in my life. I can't quite get the feel of fingers."

"Phantom limbs," said Elphie. "Well, I'm pleased for you."

"You know, if you slapped yourself around, spiritually speaking," said Nessarose, "you might develop a phantom soul, or something that felt like one. It's a good internal guide, a soul. I suspect you might even recognize that it's not a phantom at all—it's a real one."

"That'll do, Nessie," said Elphaba. "I don't care to discuss my spiritual trials with you."

"Why don't you stay here with me, join my staff, and we can have you baptized," said Nessarose warmly.

"Water is profoundly painful to me, as you well know, and I won't discuss it again. I can't pledge allegiance to anything Unnamed. It's a sham."

"You're condemning yourself to a life of sadness," Nessarose said.

"Well, that I'm already familiar with, so at least there's nothing to jump out and surprise me." Elphie threw down her napkin. "I can't stay here, Nessie. I can't help you out. I have responsibilities of my own back in the Vinkus, which you have shown precious little interest in finding out about. Oh, all right, I know, a revolution has occurred and you're a new prime minister or something, you surely have a right to be distracted if anyone does. Either accept the burden of leadership or turn it down, but either way make sure it's your choice in the matter, and not an accident of history, a martyrdom by default. I worry about you, but I can't stay and be your dogsbody."

"I've just been clumsy and outspoken. Don't expect me to remember how to be sisterly in such a short while—"

"You've had Shell to practice on all these years," Elphaba said sternly.

"Just like that, you're getting up and going?" Nessarose stood too, in that sinuous, unsettling way she had. "After twelve years of separation, we have three, four days of reunion and that's that?"

"Keep yourself well," Elphie said, and kissed her sister on both cheeks. "I know you'll be a good Eminence for as long as you want to be."

"I shall pray for your soul," promised Nessarose.

"I shall wait for your shoes," Elphie answered.

On her way out, Elphie thought about going to say good-bye to her father, and then decided against it. She had said to him everything that she could bring herself to say. They had ganged up on her, in the claustrophobic, loving way of families, and she wanted no more of it.

7

Taking the northern route over the Madeleines, she realized she would pass Lake Chorge. She decided to pause there, about halfway home, interested to note that she was actually glad to be heading back. She paced the edge of the lake, looking for Caprice-in-the-Pines, but she could not pick it out of the many resort villas that had sprung up since that visit in her youth.

But it wasn't the visible terrain she was really seeing. It was the world at large. The character it seemed to have, how it seemed to refer to itself. How could Nessarose believe in the Unnamed God? Behind every aspect of the world is another aspect of the world. In a sense, wasn't that what Doctor Dillamond had been on about? He had imagined another true foundation of the world, defensible by proofs and experiments; he had figured out how to locate it. But she was not a visionary. Behind the blue and white marbleized paper of the lake, beyond the watered silk of the sky, Elphaba couldn't see any deeper in.

Not about the raw material of life: the muscle structure of angels' wings, the capillary action involved in focusing a gimlet gaze. Nor about the gooey subjects of the empyrean: not about good, if the Unnamed God was good. Not about evil, either.

For who was in thrall to whom, really? And could it ever be known? Each agent working in collusion and antagonism—like the cold and the sun alike creating a deadly spear of ice . . . Was the Wizard a charlatan, a fraud, a despot of merely human power and failure? Did he control the Adepts—Nessarose and Glinda, and an unnamed third, for it surely wasn't Elphie—or was it only *put* to him by Madame Morrible that he did, to assuage his obvious ego, his appetite for the semblance of power?

And Madame Morrible? And Yackle? Was there any connection? Were they the same person, were they harsh divinities, avatars of a power of darkness, were they poisonous flitches struck from the evil body of the Kumbric Witch? Or were they—singly, or together—old Kumbricia herself, or such as could be presumed to have survived from the heroic age of mythology into these crabbed, cramped, modern days? Did they govern the Wizard, jerk him about like a marionette?

Who is in thrall to whom?

And while you wait to learn, the deadly icicle, formed by all opposing forces, falls and drives its cold nail into penetrable flesh.

She left the pine-needled shores of Lake Chorge in a state of high frustration and energy. Having no confidence to decide about matters of political or theological hierarchy, she felt driven to dig up those old notes she had collected from Doctor Dillamond's study the day after he was murdered. Something concrete under her fingertips. A magnifying lens, a surgical knife, a sterilized probe. Perhaps now she was old enough to understand what he had been getting at. He had been a unionist essentialist; she was a novice atheist. But she still might profit from his work, after all this time.

The winds were with her as far as the lower slopes of the Great Kells. Thereafter she had a harder time, both finding her way and keeping her seat. A number of times she had to dismount and walk. Fortunately it wasn't very cold, and she came upon small clusters of nomads in the protected vales, who kept her heading in the right direction. Still, she was two weeks returning, even with the help of a broom.

Late in the afternoon, with the sun still hot and high compared to its winter habits, she toiled her way up the last slopes, Kiamo Ko raising its narrow dark profile above her. She felt like a child looking up at the top hat of a very tall gentleman. Eager to avoid ceremony and fuss, she skirted the village. Without the broom this approach would be nearly impossible; as it was, even the broom seemed to be feeling the effort. She came to a halt in the orchard, made her way to the back door, and found it open, which meant the sisters were out flower picking or some such nonsense.

The place was quiet. She grabbed a browning apple from the sideboard and trudged up the steps of her tower without running into anyone. When she passed Nanny's room, she rattled the doorknob and said, "Nanny?"

"Oh," came a little shriek, "you startled me!"

"May I come in?"

"Just a minute." There was the sound of furniture being dragged away from the door. "Well, this is a fine mess, Miss Elphaba! Going off and leaving us to be murdered in our beds, or just as likely!"

"What are you talking about? Let me in."

"And not saying a word. You had us frantic with worry—" The last piece scraped across the floor, and Nanny flung open the door. "You hideous ungrateful woman!" She fell heavily into her arms and burst into tears.

"Please, I've had enough drama to last me the rest of my life," said Elphaba. "What are you going on about?"

Nanny took some while to calm down. She rummaged through her bag for some smelling salts, pulling out enough little bottles and satchels to set up her own apothecary business. There were blue glass vials, clear pillboxes, snakeskin envelopes of powders and pills, and a beautiful green glass bottle that had an old torn label on it, MIRACLE ELI·.

She administered calming agents to herself, and when she could breathe again, she said, "Well, you know—my dear—you saw I suppose, that everyone has disappeared?"

Elphaba scowled in confusion. And rising, sudden fear.

Nanny took a deep breath. "Now don't be angry at Nanny. It's not Nanny's fault. Those soldiers suddenly decided that their exercises were finished. I don't know how, maybe Nor told them you were gone? She told us; she'd been sneaking around looking for your broom, and she said you weren't here. So maybe she mentioned it to them. You know how nice they were to her, how they adored her. The soldiers came to the front door and said that they needed to escort the entire family, Sarima and her sisters and Nor and Irji, back to their base camp, wherever it is. They didn't require me, they said, which was very insulting indeed, and I let them know as much. Sarima asked why, and that nice Commander Cherrystone said that it was for their own protection. In case a fighting battalion comes through, he said, it won't do to have any members of the ruling family still here, or there might be a bloody incident."

"Coming through, a battalion? When?" Elphie hit the windowsill with her open palm.

"I'm trying to tell you. No time soon, he said; this is just advance planning. They became insistent. Those soldiers scattered the peasants in the village—I don't think there was any killing, it all seemed quite humane, except for the chains—and only I was left behind, being too old to march down a mountain, and no relation besides. Also, they left Liir, since he was no threat and I think they'd become fond of him. But a few days later Liir disappeared, too. I'm sure he was desperately lonely for them, and he must have followed them to their camp."

"And nobody protested?" shrieked Elphie.

"Don't yell at me. Of course they protested. Well, Sarima fell in a heap, fainting dead away, and Irji and Nor looked after her. But the sisters, that mealy-mouthed lot, they barricaded the dining room and set fire to the chapel wing, trying to draw attention, and Three slammed a sharpening stone on the hand of Commander Cherrystone and broke every bone in his wrist, I bet. Five and Six rang the bell, but the shepherds are too far away, and it all happened too fast. Two wrote messages and tried to tie them to the feet of your crows, but they wouldn't be liberated, they just kept roosting on the windowsills again, useless old things. Four had a great idea about boiling oil, but they couldn't get the flame high enough.

Oh, it was a merry chase here for a day or two, but of course the soldiers won. Men always win."

Nanny continued petulantly, "And we all thought they'd ambushed you earlier, to get you out of the way. You're the only effective one here, everyone knows that. They all think you're a Witch. The townspeople told me that if you come back you're to be in touch with the hamlet of Red Windmill down below the dam, you know the one. They seem to think you can rescue their royal family, such as they are. I told them it was misplaced trust, that you wouldn't be interested, but I promised to give you the message, so there it is."

Elphaba strode back and forth. She pulled her hair from its custom-ary knot and shook it out, as if trying to shake away what she was hear-ing. "And Chistery?" she said at last.

"Cowering behind the piano in the music room, no doubt."

"Well, this is a fine kettle of fish."

She strode, she sat, she stroked her chin, she kicked Nanny's cham-ber pot and broke it. "What have I got," she mumbled. "There's the broom. There's the bees. There's the monkey. There's Killyjoy—did they hurt Killyjoy? There's Killyjoy. There's the crows. There's Nanny. There's the villagers, if they're unharmed. There's the questionable Grimmerie. It's not a lot."

"No, it's not," said Nanny, sighing. "Doom, doom, I say."

"We can get them back," said Elphie. "We will."

"Count Nanny in," said Nanny, "though I never did like those sis-ters, I'll tell you."

Elphie clenched her fists and tried to keep from striking herself. "Liir gone too," she said. "I came here to make my apologies to Sarima, and I lost Liir in the bargain. Am I good for nothing in this life?"

Kiamo Ko was deathly still, except for old Nanny's labored breath-ing as she took a catnap in her rocking chair. Killyjoy thumped his tail on the floor, happy to see his mistress. The sky was broad and hopeless beyond the windows. Elphaba was tired herself, but she couldn't sleep. For, from time to time, she imagined she could hear the sound of water lapping against the sides of the fishwell, as if the legendary underground lake were rising to drown them all.

V

The Murder and Its Afterlife

I

Afterward, there was a lot of discussion about what people had thought it was. The noise had seemed to come from all corners of the sky at once.

Journalists, armed with the thesaurus and apocalyptic scriptures, fumbled and were defeated by it. "A gulfy deliquescence of deranged and harnessed air" . . . "A volcano of the invisible, darkly construed" . . .

To the pleasure faithers with tiktok affections, it was the sound of clockworks uncoiling their springs and running down at a terrible speed. It was the release of vengeful energy.

To the essentialists, it seemed as if the world had suddenly found itself too crammed with life, with cells splitting by the billions, molecules uncoupling to annihilation, atoms shuddering and juggernauting in their casings.

To the superstitious it was the collapsing of time. It was the oozing of the ills of the world into one crepuscular muscle, intent on stabbing the world to its core for once and for all.

To the more traditionally religious it was the blitzkrieg of vengeful angel armies, the awful name of the Unnamed God sounding itself at last—*surprise*—and the evaporation of all hopes for mercy.

One or two pretended to think it was squadrons of flying dragons overhead, trained for attack, breaking the sky from its moorings by the thrash of tripartite wings.

In the wake of the destruction it caused, no one had the hubris or courage (or the prior experience) to lie and claim to have known the act of terror for what it was: a wind twisted up in a vortical braid.

In short: a tornado.

The lives of many Munchkinlanders were lost—along with square miles of topsoil from hundred of years of cultivation. The shifting margins of sand in the eastern desert covered several villages without a trace, and no survivors were left to tell the tale of their suffering. Whirling like something from a nightmare, the wind funnel drove into Oz thirty miles north of Stonespar End, and delicately maneuvered around Colwen Grounds, leaving every rose petal attached and every thorn in place. The tornado sliced through the Corn Basket, devastating the basis of the economy of the renegade nation, and petered out, as if by design, not only at the eastern terminus of the largely defunct Yellow Brick Road, but also at the precise spot—the hamlet of Center Munch—where, outside a local chapel, Nessarose was awarding prizes for perfect attendance at religious education classes. The storm dropped a house on her head.

All the children survived to pray for Nessarose's soul at the memorial service. Perfect attendance was never more perfect.

There were a great many jokes about the disaster, naturally. "You can't hide from destiny," some said, "that house had her *name* on it." "That Nessarose, she was giving such a good speech about religious lessons, she really brought down the house!" "Everybody needs to grow up and leave home sometimes, but sometimes HOME DOESN'T LIKE IT." "What's the difference between a shooting star and a falling house?" "One which is propitious grants delicious wishes, the other which is vicious squishes witches." "What's big, thick, makes the earth move, and wants to have its way with you?" "I don't know, but can you introduce me?"

Such a maelstrom had not been known in Oz before. Various terrorist groups claimed credit, especially when news got around that the Wicked Witch of the East—also known as the Eminent Thropp, depending on your political stripe—had been snuffed out. It was not widely understood at first that the house carried passengers. The mere presence of a house of exotic design, set down almost intact upon the platform rigged up for the visiting dignitaries, was stretching credulity enough. That creatures might have survived such a fall was either patently unbelievable or a clear indication of the hand of the Unnamed God in the affair. Predictably, there were a few blind people who suddenly cried "I can see!" a lame Pig that stood and danced a jig, only to be led away—that sort of thing. The alien girl—she called herself Dorothy—was by virtue of her survival elevated to living sainthood. The dog was merely annoying.

2

When the news of Nessarose's premature death arrived at Kiamo Ko by carrier pigeon, the Witch was deep in an operation of sorts, stitching the wings of a white-crested male roc into the back muscles of one of her current crop of snow monkeys. She had more or less perfected the procedure, after years of botched and hideous failures, when mercy killing seemed the only fair thing to do to the suffering subject. Fiyero's old schoolbooks in the life sciences, from Doctor Nikidik's course, had given some leads. Also the Grimmerie had helped, if she was reading it correctly: She had found spells to convince the axial nerves to think skyward instead of treeward. And once she got it right, the winged monkeys seemed happy enough with their lot. She had yet to see a female monkey in her population produce a winged baby, but she still had hopes.

Certainly they had taken better to flying than they had to language. Chistery, now a patriarch in the castle menagerie, had plateaued at words of one syllable, and still seemed to have no clear idea of what he was saying.

It was Chistery, in fact, who brought the pigeon's letter in to Elphaba's operating salon. The Witch had him hold the fascia-slasher while she unfolded the page. Shell's brief message told of the tornado and informed her of the memorial service, which was scheduled for several weeks later in the hope that she would receive this message in time to come.

She put the message down and went back to work, placing grief and regret away from her. It was a tricky business, wing attachment, and the sedative she had administered to this monkey wouldn't last all morning. "Chistery, it's time to help Nanny down the stairs, and find Liir if you can, and tell him I need to talk to him at lunch," she said, through her gritted teeth, glancing again at her own diagrams to make sure she had the over-lapping of muscle groups in the correct arrangement, front to back.

It was an achievement if Nanny could now make it to the dining room once a day. "That's my job, that and sleeping, and Nanny does both very well," she said every single noontime when she arrived, hungry from her exertions on the stairs. Liir put out the cheese and bread and the occa-sional cold joint, at which the three of them hacked and nibbled, usually in an unsocial mood, before darting off to their afternoon chores.

Liir was fourteen, and insisted he was going to accompany the Witch to Colwen Grounds. "I have never been *anywhere*, except that time with the soldiers," he complained. "You never let me do *anything*."

"Someone has to stay and take care of Nanny," said the Witch. "Now there isn't any point in arguing about it."

"Chistery can do it."

"Chistery can't. He's getting forgetful, and between him and Nanny they'd burn the place to the ground. No, there's no more discussion about it, Liir; you're not going. Besides, I'm going to have to travel on my broom, I think, to get there in time."

"You never let me do anything."

"You can do the washing up."

"You know what I mean."

"What's he arguing about now, sweet thing?" asked Nanny loudly.

"Nothing," said the Witch.

"What's that you say?"

"*Nothing.*"

"Aren't you going to tell her?" said Liir. "She helped raise Nessarose, didn't she?"

"She's too old, she doesn't need to know. She's eighty-five, it'll only upset her."

"Nanny," said Liir, "Nessie's dead."

"Hush, you useless boy, before I remove your testicles with my foot."

"Nessie did what?" screeched Nanny, looking rheumily out at them.

"Did died dead," intoned Chistery.

"Did what?"

"Nessie DIED," said Liir.

Nanny began to weep at the idea before she had even confirmed it. "Can this be true, Elphie? Is your sister dead?"

"Liir, you'll answer for this," said the Witch. "Yes, Nanny, I cannot lie to you. There was a storm and a building collapsed. She went very peacefully, they say."

"She went straight to the bosom of Lurlina," said Nanny, sobbing. "Lurlina's golden chariot came to take her home." She patted the piece of cheese on her plate, inexplicably. Then she buttered a napkin and took a bite. "When do we leave for the funeral?"

"You're too old to travel, dear. I'm going in a few days. Liir will stay and look after you."

"I will not," said Liir.

"He's a good boy," said Nanny, "but not as good as Nessarose. Oh, sorrowful day! Liir, I'll take my tea in my room, I can't sit and talk to you as if nothing's happened." She hauled herself to her feet, leaning on Chistery's head. (Chistery was devoted to her.) "You know, darling," she said to the Witch, "I don't think the boy is old enough to see to my needs. What if the castle is attacked again? Remember what happened the last time you went away." She made a small, accusatory moue.

"Nanny, the Arjiki militia guard this place day and night. The Wizard's army is well housed in the town of Red Windmill down below. They have no intention of leaving that safe haven and risking decimation in these mountain passes—not after what they did. *That* was their skirmish, *that* was their campaign. Now they're just watchdogs. They staff the outpost to report signs of an invasion or trouble from the mountain clans. You know that. You have nothing to fear."

"I'm too old to be taken in chains like poor Sarima and her family," Nanny said. "And how could you rescue me, if you couldn't get *them* back?"

"I'm still working on that," said the Witch into Nanny's left ear.

"Seven years. You're very stubborn. It's my opinion they're all moldering in a common grave, these seven long years. Liir, you have to thank Lurlina that you weren't among them."

"I tried to rescue them," said Liir stubbornly, who had rewritten the escapade in his own mind to give himself a more heroic role. It was not longing for the companionship of soldiers, he told himself, no, it was a courageous effort to save the family! In fact, Commander Cherrystone out of kindness had had Liir tied up and left him in a sack in someone's barn, to prevent their having to incarcerate him with the others. The Commander had not realized Liir was a bastard son of Fiyero, for Liir himself didn't know it.

"Yes well, that's a good boy." Nanny was now distracted from the sad news, drifting back to the tragedy she remembered more viscerally. "Of course I did everything I could, but Nanny was an old woman even then. Elphie, do you think they're dead?"

"I could find out nothing," said the Witch for the ten thousandth time. "If they were spirited to the Emerald City or if they were murdered, I could not tell. You know this, Nanny. I bribed people. I spied around. I hired agents to follow every lead. I wrote to the Princess Nastoya of the Scrow for advice. I spent a year following every useless clue. You *know* this. Don't torture me with the memory of my failure."

"It was my failure, I'm sure," said Nanny peacefully; they all knew she didn't think so for a minute. "I should have been younger and more vigorous. I'd have given that Commander Cherrystone a piece of my mind! And now Sarima is gone, gone, and her sisters too. I suppose it's none of our fault, really," she concluded disingenuously, scowling at the Witch. "You had someplace to go, so you went; who can criticize you for that?"

But the image of Sarima in chains, Sarima as a decaying corpse, still withholding from the Witch her forgiveness for Fiyero's death—it pained her like water. "Give up, you old harridan," said the Witch, "must my own household whip me so? Go have your tea, you fiend."

The Witch sat down at last and thought of Nessarose, and what might come. The Witch had tried to stay removed from the affairs of the political world, but she knew a change of leadership in Munchkinland could throw things out of balance—maybe to a positive effect. She felt a guilty lightness at the death of her sister.

She made a list of things to bring with her to the memorial service. Foremost was a page of the Grimmerie. In her chamber she pored over the huge musty tome, and finally she ripped out an especially cryptic page. Its letters still continued to contort beneath her eyes, sometimes scrambling and unscrambling as she looked, as if they were formed by a colony of ants. Whenever she gazed at the book, meaning might emerge on a page that a day earlier had been illegible chicken scratches; and meaning sometimes disappeared as she stared. She would ask her father, who with his holy eyes would see the truth better.

3

Colwen Grounds was draped in black swags and purple bunting. When the Witch arrived, she was greeted by a one-man less-than-welcoming committee, a bearded Munchkinlander named Nipp, who seemed to be concierge, janitor, and acting Prime Minister. "Your lineage no longer allows you any particular liberties in Munchkinland," she was told. "With the death of Nessarose, the honorific of Eminence is at last abolished." The Witch didn't much care, but she wasn't inclined to accept a unilateral dictum without a retort. She answered, "It is abolished when I accept that it is abolished." Not that the honorific had been used much in recent years; according to the occasional rambling letter from Frex,

Nessarose had begun to be amused by the slur of "Wicked Witch of the East," and had considered it a public penance worthy of a person with such high moral standing. She even took to referring to herself as such.

Nipp showed her to her room. "I don't need much," said the Wicked Witch of the West (as, in contrast, she allowed herself to be called, at least by these Munchkinlander upstarts). "A bed for a couple of days, and I'd like to see my father and attend the service. I'll collect a few things, and be off soon. Now, do you know if our brother, Shell, will be here?"

"Shell has disappeared again," said Nipp. "He left his regards. There is a mission he is undertaking in the Glikkus, it can't wait. Some of us think he is defecting, worried about a change in government here now that the tyrant is dead. As well he might," he added coldly. "Have you fresh towels?"

"I don't use them," said the Witch, "it's all right. Go away now." She was very tired, and sad.

At sixty-three, Frex was even balder, and his beard whiter, than he had been last time. His shoulders hunched in, as if trying to meet each other, his head sank into a natural cavity made by a deteriorating spine and neck. He sat covered by a blanket on the verandah. "And who is this," he said when the Witch came up and sat next to him. She realized his sight had nearly gone for good.

"It's your other daughter, Papa," she said, "the one that's left."

"Fabala," he said, "what will I do without my pretty Nessarose? How will I live without my pet?"

She held his hand until he fell asleep, and wiped his face though his tears burned her skin.

The liberated Munchkinlanders were destroying the house. The Witch had no use for frippery, but it seemed a shame to waste a property this way. Desecration was so shortsighted; didn't they know that, however they now decided to live, Colwen Grounds could be their parliament building?

She spent time with her father, but they didn't speak much. One morning, when he was more alert and energetic than usual, he asked her if she really was a witch. "Oh well, what's a witch? Who has ever trusted language in this family?" she replied. "Father, will you look at something for me? Will you tell me what you see?" She withdrew from an inner pocket the page from the Grimmerie and she unfolded it like a large napkin on his lap. He ran his hands over it, as if he could pick up meaning through his fingertips, and then held it near, peering and squinting.

"What do you see?" she asked. "Can you tell me the nature of this writing? Is it for good or for ill?"

"The markings are crisp enough, and large. I ought to be able to make it out." He turned it upside down. "But little Fabala, I can't read this alphabet. It is in a foreign tongue. Can you?"

"Well, sometimes I seem to be able to, but the talent is fleeting," said the Witch. "I don't know if it's my eyes or if it's the manuscript that's being tricky."

"You always had strong eyes," said her father. "Even as a toddler you could see things no one else could."

"Hah," she said, "I don't know what you mean."

"You had a looking glass that sweet Turtle Heart made for you, and you looked in it as if you could see other worlds, other times."

"I was probably looking at myself."

But they both knew that wasn't true, and Frex, for once, said so. "You didn't look at yourself," he said, "you hated to. You hated your skin, your sharp features, your strange eyes."

"Where did I learn that hate?" she asked.

"You were born knowing it," he said. "It was a curse. You were born to curse my life." He patted her hand affectionately, as if he didn't mean much by this. "When you lost your weird baby teeth, and your second teeth came in normally, we all relaxed a little. But for the first couple of years—until Nessarose was born—you were a little beast. Only when saintly Nessarose was delivered to us, even more scarred than you, did you settle down like a normal child."

"Why was I cursed to be different?" she said. "You are a holy man, you must know."

"You are my fault," he said. Despite his words he was somehow pinning blame on her instead of himself, though she still wasn't clever enough to see how this was done. "For what I had failed to do, you were born to plague me. But don't worry yourself about it now," he added, "that's all long ago."

"And Nessarose?" she asked. "How do the weights and balances of shame and guilt account for her?"

"She is a portrait of the lax morals of your mother," Frex said calmly.

"And that's why you could love her so much," said the Witch. "Because her human frailty wasn't your fault."

"Don't stew so, you always stewed," Frex said. "And now she is dead, so what does it matter?"

"My life is still running on."

"But mine is running out," he answered, sadly. So she put his hand back on his lap, and kissed him gently, and folded up the page of the Grimmerie and tucked it in her pocket. Then she turned to greet the person approaching them across the lawn. She thought it was someone with tea (Frex was still accorded a measure of service, due to his age and his mildness, and, she supposed, his vocation), but she stood and pressed down the front of her homespun black skirt when she saw who it was.

"Miss Glinda of the Arduennas," she said, her heart churring.

"Oh, you came, I knew you would," said Glinda. "Miss Elphaba, the last true Eminent Thropp, no matter what they say!"

Glinda approached slowly, either through age or shyness, or because her ridiculous gown weighed so much that it was hard for her to get up enough steam to stride. She looked like a huge Glindaberry bush, was all the Witch could think; under that skirt there must be a bustle the size of the dome of Saint Florix. There were sequins and furbelows and a sort of History of Oz, it seemed, stitched in trapunto in six or seven ovoid panels all around the skirting. But her face: beneath the powdered skin, the wrinkles at eyelid and mouth, was the face of the timid schoolgirl from the Pertha Hills.

"You haven't changed a whit," said Glinda. "Is this your father?"

The Witch nodded but shushed her; Frex had dropped off again. "Come, we'll walk in the gardens before they root up the roses out of some beknighted attempt at eradicating injustice." The Witch took Glinda's arm. "Glinda, you look hideous in that getup. I thought you'd have developed some sense by now."

"When in the provinces," she said, "you have to show them a little style. I don't think it's so bad. Or are the satin bells at the shoulder a bit too *too*?"

"Excessive," agreed the Witch. "Someone get the scissors; this is a disaster."

They laughed. "My dear, what they've done to this grand old place," said Glinda. "Look, those pediments are meant to support graven urns, and those revolutionary slogans are painted all over that exquisite belvedere. I hope you'll have something done, Elphie. There isn't a belvedere to match that outside of the capital."

"I never had the love of architecture that you did, Glinda," said the Witch. "I just read the slogans: SHE WALKED ALL OVER US. Why shouldn't they paint all over her belvedere? If she did in fact walk all over them?"

"Tyrants come and go, belvederes are forever," said Glinda. "I can recommend topnotch restorers the moment you ask."

"I hear you were one of the first on the scene," said the Witch, "when Nessarose died. How did that come to be?"

"Sir Chuffrey—my hubby—he has some investments in pork futures, you know, and Munchkinland is trying to diversify its economic base so as not to be at the mercy of Gillikin banks and the Emerald City Corn Exchange. You never know what relationship might develop between Munchkinland and the rest of Oz, and it's best to be prepared. So where Sir Chuffrey does business, I do good. It's a partnership made in heaven. You know I have more money than I can give away?" She giggled and squeezed the Witch's arm. "I never imagined that doing public charity would provide such a rush."

"So you were here in Munchkinland—?"

"Yes, I had been at an orphanage on the shores of Mossmere, and for a lark I thought I'd go to the game park—they have dragons there now, and I'd never seen a dragon—so I was scarcely a dozen miles away when the storm hit. We had terrible winds even there; I cannot imagine how a ceremony could have been in progress in Center Munch. In Mossmere there were whole sections of the park closed to visitors due to the fear of falling trees and escaping Animals—"

"Oh, so they call it a game park, with Animals?" said the Witch.

"You must go, dear, it's a lark. Well, as I was saying, the house came right out of the blue, and I suppose I mean that literally—if they'd sensed a big storm, they'd surely have canceled the event and run for cover. Anyway, the news system is very advanced now in parts of

Munchkinland; Nessarose herself oversaw a system of beacons and tiktok code signals, to warn of invasions from the Wizard and points west. So it was only a matter of minutes before the news was being flashed in all directions. I commandeered a Mature Pfenix and asked her to bring me to Center Munch, and I arrived before most of the locals had quite figured out what had hit them."

"Tell me about it," said the Witch.

"You'll be pleased to hear there was no blood. I venture to guess there were massive internal injuries, but there was no blood. Of course Nessarose's last few devoted followers thought this meant her spirit was taken up intact, and that she suffered little. I don't imagine she suffered *much*, not with that kind of clonk on the noggin. Her more unhappy sub-jects, who were the greater in number, thought it a droll act of Lurlina, releasing them from Nessarose's particular sort of fundamentalist bondage. There was revelry when I arrived, and much feting of the funny girl and the dog who seem to have lived in the house."

"Oh, who's that?" said the Witch, who hadn't heard this part.

"Well, you know how Munchkinlanders bow and scrape no matter what their democratic inclinations. No sooner had I arrived than they deferred to me, introducing me as a witch. I tried to correct them, a sorceress is really much more apt, but never mind. It was no doubt the outfit, it cowed them. I was in a salmon-pink fantasy that day, and really it suited me."

"Go on," said the Witch, who had never liked talking about clothes.

"Well, the child introduced herself: Dorothy from Kansas. I didn't know the place, and said as much. She appeared as much surprised as anyone else about what had happened, and she had a nasty little pooch yapping about her heels. Tata or Toto or something. Toto. So this Dorothy was in some state of shock, I can tell you. A fairly homely little girl with little fashion sense, but I suppose that comes later in life for some than others." She glanced sideways at the Witch. "*Much* later, in some cases." And they both chuckled at that.

"Dorothy supposed she should try to get back to her home, but as she couldn't remember having studied anything about Oz in school, nor could I recall a place named Kansas, we decided that she should look for help elsewhere. The fickle Munchkinlanders seemed ready to nominate her as Nessie's successor, which would have angered Nipp and all those ministers in Colwen Grounds who've spent their careers jockeying for position when and if Nessarose ever saw fit to die. Besides, there may be other developments afoot. Dorothy might have gotten in the way."

"An eye to public affairs, well, somehow I'm not surprised," said the Witch, in fact quite pleased. "I always knew you were in there somewhere, Glinda."

"Well, I thought the better move would be to get Dorothy out of Munchkinland before a civil war tore this place up even worse than it already is. There are factions, you know, who support the re-annexation of Munchkinland by Oz. It would do the girl no good to get caught in the crossfire of opposing interests."

"Oh, so she's not here," said the Witch. "I had thought I'd meet her."

"Dorothy? Now you're not going to take against her, are you?" said Glinda. "She's a child, really. Big by Munchkinlander standards, of course, but a squat little thing nonetheless. She's an innocent, Elphie; I can see by the gleam in your eye that you're up to your old paranoia thing again. She wasn't *piloting* that house, you know, she was trapped in it. This would be one struggle you'd do well just to leave alone."

The Witch sighed. "You may be right. You know, I'm getting used to stiff muscles in the morning. Sometimes I think that vengeance is habit forming too. A stiffness of the attitude. I keep hoping that the Wizard will be toppled in my lifetime, and this aim seems to be at odds with happiness. I suppose I can't take on avenging the death of a sister I didn't get on all that well with anyway."

"Especially if the death is an accident," Glinda said.

"Glinda," said the Witch, "I know you must remember Fiyero, and you have heard of his death. Fifteen years ago."

"Of course," said she. "Well, I *heard* he died, under mysterious circumstances."

"I knew his wife," said the Witch, "and his in-laws. It was suggested to me once that he had been carrying on an affair with you in the Emerald City."

Glinda turned yellow-pink. "My dear," she said, "I was fond of Fiyero and he was a good man and a fine statesman. But among other things, you will remember he was dark-skinned. Even if I took up dalliances—an inclination I believe rarely benefits anyone—you are once again being suspicious and cranky to suspect me and Fiyero! The idea!"

And the Witch realized, sinkingly, that this was of course true; the ugly skill at snobbery had returned to Glinda in her middle years.

But for her part, Glinda had no real inkling that the Witch was implicating herself as Fiyero's adulterous lover. Glinda was too fussed to listen that closely. The Witch in fact alarmed her a little. It was not just the novelty of seeing her again, but the strange charisma Elphaba possessed, which had always put Glinda in the shade. Also there was the thrill, basis indeterminable, which made Glinda shy, and caused her to rush her words, and to speak in a false high voice like an adolescent. How quickly you could be thrown back to the terrible uncertainty of your youth!

For when she chose to remember her youth at all, she could scarcely dredge up an ounce of recollection about that daring meeting with the Wizard. She could recall far more clearly how she and Elphie had shared a bed on the road to the Emerald City. How brave that had made her feel, and how vulnerable too.

They walked for a way in a restless silence.

"Things might begin to improve now," said the Witch after a time. "I mean Munchkinland will be a mess for a while. A tyrant is terrible, but at least he or she imposes order. The anarchy that follows the deposition of a tyrant can be bloodier than before. Still, things may work out all right. Father always said that when left to themselves, the Munchkinlanders had a great deal of common sense. And Nessie was, for all practical purposes, a foreigner. She was raised in Quadling Country, and you know, she may have been half Quadling herself, I've come to realize. She was a foreign queen on this soil, despite her inherited title. With her gone, the Munchkinlanders might just right themselves."

"Bless her soul," said Glinda. "Or do you still not believe in the soul?"

"I can make no comment on the souls of others," said the Witch.

They walked some more. Here and there the Witch saw, as before, the totemic straw men, pinned to tunics, and erected like effigies in the corners of fields. "I find them somewhat creepy," she said to Glinda. "Now one other thing I want to ask you; I asked this of Nessa once. Do you remember Madame Morrible's corralling us into her parlor, and proposing we become three Adepts, three high witches of Oz? Sort of secret local priestesses, shaping public policy behind the scenes, contributing to the stability—or instability—of Oz as required by some unnamed higher authority?"

"Oh, that farce, that melodrama, how could I forget it?" said Glinda.

"I wonder if we were put under a spell then? Do you remember, she said we couldn't talk about it, and it didn't seem that we could?"

"Well we are talking about it, so if there was any truth to it, which I doubt, it's certainly worn off by now."

"But look what's happened to us. Nessarose was the Wicked Witch of the East—you know that's what they called her, don't pretend to be so shocked—and I have a stronghold in the West, and I seem to have rallied the Arjikis around me, by dint of the absence of their ruling family—and there you are, sitting pretty in the North with your bank accounts and your legendary skills at sorcery."

"Legendary nothing; I simply see to it that I am admired in the right circles," said Glinda. "Now, my memory is just as good as yours. And Madame Morrible proposed that I be an Adept of Gillikin, but that you be an Adept of Munchkinland, and Nessa be an Adept of Quadling Country. The Vinkus she didn't think worth bothering about. If she was seeing the future, she got it wrong. She got you and Nessa all wrong."

"Forget the details," said the Witch tartly. "I just mean, Glinda, is it possible we could be living our entire adult lives under someone's spell? How could we tell if we were the pawns of someone's darker game? I know, I know, I can see it in your face: *Elphie, you're sniffing conspiracy theories again.* But *you* were there. You heard what I heard. How do you know your life hasn't been pulled by the strings of some malign magic?"

"Well, I pray a lot," said Glinda, "not terribly genuinely, I admit, but I try. I think the Unnamed God would have mercy on me and give me the benefit of the doubt, and release me from a spell if I had accidentally fallen under one. Don't you? Or are you still so atheistic?"

"I have always felt like a pawn," said the Witch. "My skin color's been a curse, my missionary parents made me sober and intense, my school days brought me up against political crimes against Animals, my love life imploded and my lover died, and if I had any life's work of my own, I haven't found it yet, except in animal husbandry, if you could call it that."

"I'm no pawn," said Glinda. "I take all the credit in the world for my own foolishness. Good gracious, dear, all of life is a spell. You know that. But you do have some choice."

"Well, I wonder," said the Witch.

They walked on. Graffiti was splattered on the sides of the granite plinths of statues. NOW THE SHOE'S ON THE OTHER FOOT. Glinda tchtched. "Animal husbandry?" she said.

They crossed a little bridge. Bluebirds twinkled music above them like a sentimental entertainment.

"I sent this Dorothy, this girl, on to the Emerald City," said Glinda. "I told her I'd never seen the Wizard—well, I had to lie, don't look at me like that; if I told her the truth about him she would never have left here. I told her to ask him to send her home. With his reconnaissance spies all over Oz, and no doubt elsewhere, he has heard of Kansas, I'm sure. Nobody else has."

"That was a cruel thing to do," said the Witch.

"She's such a harmless child, no one should take her seriously," said Glinda carelessly. "If the Munchkinlanders started rallying around her, reunification might be a more bloody affair than we all hope."

"So you hope for reunification?" muttered the Witch, disgusted. "You support it?"

"Besides," Glinda went on blithely, "having some motherly instinct somewhere inside this pushed-up bosom of mine, I gave her Nessa's shoes as a sort of protection."

"You *what?*" The Witch whirled and faced Glinda. For a moment she was dumb with rage, but only for a moment. "Not only does she come whomping out of the sky and stepping her big clumsy house all over my sister, but she gets the shoes too? Glinda, those shoes weren't yours to give away! My father made them for her! And furthermore, Nessa promised I could have them when she died!"

"Oh yes," said Glinda in a false calm, surveying the Witch up and down, "and they would make the perfect accessory for that glass-of-fashion outfit you have on. Come on, Elphie, since when have you cared about shoes, of all things? Look at those army boots you have on!"

"Whether I'd wear them or not is none of your concern. You can't go handing out a person's effects like that, what right had you? Papa reshaped those shoes from skills he learned from Turtle Heart. You've stuck your fancy wand in where it wasn't wanted!"

"I'll remind you," said Glinda, "that those shoes were coming apart until I had them resoled, and I laced them through with a special binding spell of my own. Neither your father nor you did that much for her. Elphie, I stood by her when you abandoned her in Shiz. As you abandoned me. You *did*, don't deny it, stop those lightning bolt looks at me, I won't have it. I became her surrogate sister. And as an old friend I gave her the power to stand upright by herself through those shoes, and if I made a mistake I'm sorry, Elphie, but I still feel they were more mine to give away than yours."

"Well, I want them back," said the Witch.

"Oh, put it behind you, will you, they're only shoes," said Glinda, "you're behaving as if they're holy relics. They were shoes, and a bit out of style, truth be told. Let the girl have them. She has nothing else."

"Look how the people here thought of them," said the Witch; she pointed to a stable on which was scrawled, in broad red letters, WALK ALL OVER YOU YOU OLD WITCH.

"Please, give it a rest," said Glinda, "I have such a headache coming on."

"Where is she?" said the Witch. "If you won't retrieve them, I'll get them myself."

"If I'd known you wanted them," said Glinda, trying to make things all right, "I'd have saved them for you. But you have to see, Elphie, the shoes couldn't stay here. The ignorant pagan Munchkinlanders—Lurlinists all, once you scratch the skin—they had put too much credit in those silly shoes. I mean, a magic sword I could understand, but *shoes?* Please. I had to get them out of Munchkinland."

"You are working in collusion with the Wizard to render Munchkinland ready for annexation," said the Witch. "You have no agenda of charity, Glinda. At least don't fool yourself. Or are you really under some rusty spell of Madame Morrible, after all this time?"

"I won't have you snapping at me," said Glinda. "The girl has left, she's been on the road for a week now, she headed west. I tell you, she's only a timid child, and means no harm. She'd be distressed to know she'd taken something you wanted. There is no power in them for you, Elphie."

The Witch said, "Glinda, if those shoes fall into the hands of the Wizard, he'll use them somehow in a maneuver to reannex Munchkinland. By now they have too much significance to Munchkinlanders. The Wizard mustn't have those shoes!"

Glinda reached out and touched the Witch's elbow. "They won't make your father love you any better," she said.

The Witch pulled back. They stood glaring at each other. They had too much common history to come apart over a pair of shoes, yet the shoes were planted between them, a grotesque icon of their differences. Neither one could retreat, or move forward. It was silly, and they were stuck, and someone needed to break the spell. But all the Witch could do was insist, "I want those *shoes*."

4

At the memorial service, Glinda and Sir Chuffrey perched in the balcony reserved for dignitaries and ambassadors. The Wizard sent a representative, resplendent in his dress reds with the emerald cross marking quadrants on his chest, a crew of bodyguards at attention all around him. The Witch sat below, and did not meet Glinda's eyes. Frex wept until he brought on an attack of asthma, and the Witch helped him out a side door, where he could catch his breath.

After the service, the Wizard's emissary approached the Witch. He said, "You have been invited to an audience with the Wizard. He is traveling by special diplomatic immunity, via a Pfenix, to offer his condolences to the family this evening. You will be prepared to meet him at Colwen Grounds this evening."

"He can't come here!" said the Witch. "He wouldn't dare!"

"Those who now make the decisions think otherwise," said the emissary. "Be that as it may, he comes under cover of darkness, and only to speak to you and your family."

"My father is not up to receiving the Wizard," said the Witch. "I won't have it."

"He will see you, then," said the emissary. "He insists. He has questions of a diplomatic nature to put to you. But you are not to make this visit public, or it could go very hard on your father and your brother.

And on you," he added, as if that were not already evident.

She considered how she might use this command audience to her own advantage: Sarima, the safety of Frex, the fate of Fiyero. "I agree," she concluded. "I will meet him." And, despite herself, she was glad for a moment that Nessarose's magicked shoes *were* safely out of the vicinity.

As the vesper bells rang, the Witch was summoned from her room by a Munchkinlander maid. "You will have to submit to a search," said the Wizard's emissary, meeting her in an antechamber. "You must understand the protocol here."

She concentrated on her fury as she was probed and prodded by the officers who ringed the waiting area. "What is this?" they said when they found the page of the Grimmerie in her pocket.

"Oh that," she said, thinking fast. "His Highness will want to see that."

"You can bring nothing in with you," they told her, and they took the page from her.

"By my bloodlines, I can reinstate the office of the Eminent Thropp tonight and have your leader arrested," she called after them. "Do not tell me what I can and cannot do in this house."

They paid her no mind and ushered her into a small chamber, bare but for a couple of upholstered chairs set upon a flowery carpet. Along the baseboards, dust mice rolled in the draft.

"His Highness, the Emperor Wizard of Oz," said an attendant, and withdrew. For a minute the Witch sat alone. Then the Wizard walked into the room.

He was without disguise, a plain-looking older man wearing a high-collared shirt and a greatcoat, with a watch and fob hanging from a waistcoat pocket. His head was pink and mottled, and tufts of hair stuck out above his ears. He mopped his brow with a handkerchief and sat down, motioning the Witch to sit, too. She did not sit.

"How do you do," he said.

"What do you want with me," she answered.

"There are two things," he said. "There is what I had come here to say to you, and then there is the matter of what you bring to my attention."

"You talk to me," she said, "for I have nothing to say to you."

"There is no point in beating around the bush," he said. "I would like to know your intentions about your position as the last Eminence."

"Had I any intention," she said, "it would be none of your business."

"Ah, alas, it is my business, for reunification is under way," said the Wizard, "even as we speak. I understand that Lady Glinda, bless her well-meaning foolishness, has sensibly evacuated both the unfortunate girl and the totemic shoes from the district, which should make annexation less troublesome. I should like to have those shoes in my possession, to prevent their giving you ideas. So you see, I need to know your intentions in the matter. You were not, I take it, in warm sympathy with your sister's style of religious tyranny, but I hope you do not intend to set up shop here. If you do, we must strike a little bargain—something I was never able to do with your sister."

"There is little for me here," said the Witch, "and I am not suited to govern anyone, not even myself, it seems."

"Besides, there's the small matter of the army at—is it Red Windmill?—the town below Kiamo Ko."

"So that's why they've been there all these years," said the Witch.

"To keep you in check," he said. "An expense, but there you are."

"To spite you, I should reclaim the title of Eminence," said the Witch. "But I care little for these foolish people. What the Munchkinlanders do now is of no interest to me. As long as my father is left unharmed. If that is all—"

"There is the other matter," he said. His manner became more lively. "You brought a page with you. I wonder where you got it?"

"That is mine and your people have no right to it."

"What I want is to know where you got it, and where I can find the rest."

"What will you give me if I tell you?"

"What could you want from me?"

This was why she had agreed to meet him. She drew a deep breath, and said, "To know if Sarima, Dowager Princess of the Arjikis, is still alive. And where I might find her, and how I might negotiate her freedom."

The Wizard smiled. "How all things work together. Now isn't it interesting that I could guess of your concern." He waved a hand.

Unseen attendants outside the open door ushered in a dwarf in clean white trousers and tunic.

No, it wasn't a dwarf, she saw; it was a young woman crouching. Chains sewn into the collar of her tunic ran through her clothes to her ankles, keeping her bent over; the chains were only two or three feet long. The Witch had to peer to see for sure that it was Nor. She would be sixteen by now, or seventeen. The age that Elphie had been when she went up to Crage Hall at Shiz.

"Nor," said the Witch, "Nor, are you there?"

Nor's knees were filthy and her fingers curled around the links of her bondage. Her hair was cut short, and welts were visible beneath the patchy tresses. She tossed her head as if listening to music, but she would not shift her gaze toward Elphaba.

"Nor, it's Auntie Witch. I've come to bargain for your release, at last," said the Witch, improvising.

But the Wizard motioned the unseen attendants to usher Nor out of sight. "I'm afraid that is not possible," he said. "She is my protection from you, you see."

"The others?" said the Witch. "I must know."

"Everything is undocumented," said the Wizard, "but I believe Sarima and her sisters are all dead."

The Witch's breath caught in her chest. The last hopes of forgiveness gone! . . . but the Wizard was continuing. "Perhaps some underling who had no authority in the matter had an appetite for a bloodbath. It's so hard to get reliable help in the armed forces."

"Irji?" said the Witch, gripping her elbows.

"Now he *had* to die," said the Wizard apologetically. "He was the next in line to be Prince, wasn't he?"

"Tell me it was not brutal," said the Witch. "Oh, tell me so!"

"The Paraffin Necklace," admitted the Wizard. "Well, it was a public affair. A statement needed to be made. There now, against my better judgment, I have told you what you wanted to know. Now it is your turn. Where can I find the book that this page is from?" The Wizard took the paper out of his pocket and pressed it out onto his lap. His hands were trembling. He looked at the page. "A spell for the Administration of Dragons," he said, wonderingly.

"Is that what it is?" she said, surprised. "I could not be sure."

"Of course. You must have a hard time making this out," he said. "You see, it does not come from this world. It comes from my world."

He was mad, obsessed with other worlds. Like her father.

"You are not telling the truth," said the Witch, hoping she was right.

"Oh, what care I for the truth," he said, "but I am truthful, as it happens."

"Why would you want that?" said the Witch, trying to buy some time, trying to figure out how she could barter for Nor's life. "I don't even know what it is. I don't believe you do either."

"I do," he said. "This is an ancient manuscript of magic, generated in a world far away from this one. It was long thought to be merely legendary, or else destroyed in the dark onslaughts of the northern invaders. It had been removed from our world for safety by a wizard more capable than I. It is why I came to Oz in the first place," he continued, almost talking to himself, as old men are prone to do. "Madame Blavatsky located it in a crystal ball, and I made the appropriate sacrifices and—*arrangements*—to travel here forty years ago. I was a young man, full of ardor and failure. I had not intended to rule a country here, but just to find this document and return it to its own world, and to study its secrets there."

"What kind of sacrifices?" she said. "You do not stint from murder here."

"*Murder* is a word used by the sanctimonious," he said. "It is an expedient expression with which they condemn any courageous action beyond their ken. What I did, what I do, cannot be murder. For, coming from another world, I cannot be held accountable to the silly conventions of a naive civilization. I am beyond that lisping childish recital of wrongs and rights." His eyes did not burn as he spoke; they were sunk behind veils of cold blue detachment.

"If I give the Grimmerie to you, will you go?" she said. "Give me Nor and take your brand of evil and leave us alone at last?"

"I am too old to travel now," he said, "and why should I give up what I have worked for all these years?"

"Because I will use this book and destroy you with it if you don't," she said.

"You cannot read it," he said. "You are of Oz and you cannot do such a thing."

"I can read more of it than you suspect," she said. "I do not know what it all means. I have seen pages about unleashing the hidden energies of matter. I have seen pages about tampering with the orderly flow of time. I have seen disquisitions about weapons too vile to use, about how to poison water, about how to breed a more docile population. There are diagrams of weapons of torture. Though the drawings and the words seem misty to my eyes, I can continue to learn. *I* am not too old."

"Those are ideas of great interest to our times," he said, though he seemed surprised that she had taken in as much as she had.

"Not to me," she said. "You have done enough already. If I give it to you, will you surrender Nor to me?"

"You should not trust my promise," he said, sighing. "Really, my child." But he continued to stare at the page she had handed over to him. "One might learn how to subjugate a dragon to one's own purposes," he mused, and flipped the page over to read what was on the back.

"Please," she said. "I think I have never begged for anything before in my life. But I beg of you. It is not right that you should be here. Assuming for a moment you can sometimes tell the truth—go back to that other world, go anywhere, just leave the throne. Leave us alone. Take the book with you, do with it what you will. Let me accomplish at least this in my life."

"In exchange for my telling you about the kith and kin of your beloved Fiyero, you are to tell me where this book is," he reminded her.

"Well, I won't," she answered. "I have revised my offer. Give me Nor, and I will get you the Grimmerie. The book is already hidden so deeply that you will never find it. You have not the skill." She hoped she was being persuasive.

He stood and pocketed the page. "I shall not have you executed," he said. "At least, not at this audience. I *will* have that book, for here or for there. You cannot bind me to a promise, I am beyond being bound by words. I will think of what you have said. But meanwhile, I will keep my young slave-girl at my side. For she is my defense against your anger."

"Give her to me!" said the Witch. "Now, now, now: Act like a man, not like a mountebank! Give her to me and I will send you that book!"

"It is for others to bargain," said the Wizard. Rather than sounding offended, he seemed merely depressed, as if he were talking to himself instead of to her. "I do not bargain. But I do think. I will wait and see how the reunification with Munchkinland goes, and if you do not interfere, I may be kindly disposed to think about what you have said. But I do not bargain."

The Witch breathed in deeply. "I have met you before, you know," she said. "You once granted me an interview in the Throne Room, when I was a schoolgirl from Shiz."

"Is that so?" he said. "Oh, of course—you must have been one of the darling girls of Madame Morrible. That wonderful aid and helpmeet. In her dotage now, but in her heyday, what she taught me about breaking the spirits of willful young girls! No doubt, like the rest, you were taken with her?"

"She tried to recruit me to serve some master. Was it you?"

"Who can say. We were always hatching some plot or other. She was good fun. She would never be as crude as that"—he pointed to the open door through which crouching Nor could still be seen, humming to herself—"she could manage girl students with much greater finesse!" He was about to leave the room, but he turned back at the door. "You know, now I remember. It was she who warned me about you. She told me you had betrayed her, you had rejected her offers. She was the one who advised me to have you watched. It is because of her that we found out about your little romance with the diamond-skinned prince."

"No!"

"So you met me before. I had forgotten. In what form did I appear?"

She had to clutch herself to keep from vomiting. "You were a skeleton with lighted bones, dancing in a storm."

"Oh, yes. That was clever, that was. Were you impressed?"

"Sir," she said, "I think you are a very bad wizard."

"And you," he answered, stung, "are only a caricature of a witch."

"Wait," she called as he headed away through the panel, "wait, please. How will I receive your answer?"

"I will send a messenger to you before the year is out," he said. The panel slammed tightly behind him.

She fell to her knees, her forehead dropping almost to the floor. At her sides her fists clenched. She had no intention of surrendering the Grimmerie to such a monster, ever. If need be she would die to keep it out of his hands. But could she arrange a deception so that he would sur-render Nor to her first?

She left a few days later, first making sure that her father was not to be turned out of his room in Colwen Grounds. He did not want to join her in the Vinkus; he was too old to make the journey. Besides, he thought that Shell would come back sooner or later looking for him. The Witch knew that Frex wouldn't live long, grieving so for Nessarose. She tried to put away her anger at him when she said good-bye for what she suspected was the last time.

As she strode through the forecourt of Colwen Grounds, she crossed paths once again with Glinda. But both women averted their eyes and hurried their feet along their opposing ways. For the Witch, the sky was a huge boulder pressing down on her. For Glinda it was much the same. But Glinda wheeled about, and cried out, "Oh Elphie!"

The Witch did not turn. They never saw each other again.

5

She knew that she couldn't afford the time to mount a full-scale chase against this Dorothy. Glinda ought to be hiring accomplices to track those shoes down; it was the least she could do, with her money and her connections. Still, the Witch stopped here and there along the Yellow Brick Road, and asked those taking an afternoon tipple at a roadside pub-lic house if they had seen a foreign girl in blue and white checks, walking with a small dog. There was some animated discussion as the patrons of the pub struggled to decide whether the green Witch intended the child harm—apparently the child had that rare skill of enchanting strangers—but when they had satisfied themselves that no harm was likely, they responded. Dorothy had come through a few days ago, and it was said that she had spent the night with someone a mile or two down the road, before continuing on. "The well-kept house with the yellow domed roof," they said, "and the minaret-chimney. You can't miss it."

The Witch found it, and she found Boq on a bench in the yard, dandling a baby on his knee.

"You!" he said. "I know why you're here! Milla, look, who's here, come quickly! It's Miss Elphaba, from Crage Hall! In the flesh!"

Milla came, a couple of naked children clutching her apron strings. Flushed from laundry, she lifted her straggling hair out of her eyes and said, "Oh my, and we forgot to dress in our finery today. Look who's come to laugh at us in our rustic state."

"Isn't she *something!*" said Boq fondly.

Milla had kept her figure, though there were four or five offspring in evidence, and no doubt more out of sight. Boq had gone barrel-chested, and his fine spiky hair had grown prematurely silver, giving him a dignity he had never had as an undergraduate. "We heard about your sister's death, Elphie," he said, "and we sent our condolences to your father. We didn't know where you were. We heard you had come here following Nessie's ascension to governor of Munchkinland, but we didn't know where you went back to when you left. It's good to see you again."

The sourness that she had felt over Glinda's betrayal was ameliorated by Boq's common courtesy and direct speech. She had always liked him, for his passion and for his sense. "You are a sight, you are," she said.

"Rikla, get up off that stool and let our guest have a seat," said Milla to one of the children. "And Yellowgage, run to Uncle's and borrow some rice and onions and yogurt. Hurry now, so I can start a meal."

"I won't be staying, Milla, I'm in a hurry," said the Witch. "Yellowgage, don't bother. I'd love to spend some time, and catch up on all your news, but I'm trying to locate this girl stranger, who passed by here, someone said, and stayed a night or two."

Boq shoved his hands in his pockets. "Well, she did that, Elphie. What do you want with her?"

"I want my sister's shoes. They belong to me."

Boq seemed as surprised as Glinda had. "You weren't ever into fancy trappings like society shoes," he said.

"Yes, well, perhaps I'm about to make my belated debut in Emerald City society at last, and have a coming-out ball." But she was being tart with Boq, and didn't want that. "It's a personal matter, Boq; I want the shoes. My father made them and they're mine now, and Glinda gave them to this girl without my permission. And woe betide Munchkinland if they fall into the Wizard's hands. What is she like, this Dorothy?"

"We adored her," he said. "Plain and straightforward as mustard seed. She shouldn't have any problems, although it's a long walk for a child, from here to the Emerald City. But all who see her are bound to help her, I'd say. We sat up till the moon rose, chatting about her home, and Oz, and what she might expect on the road. She hasn't traveled widely before this."

"How charming," said the Witch. "How novel for her."

"Are you brewing one of your campaigns?" said Milla suddenly, cannily. "You know, Elphie, when you didn't come back from the Emerald City with Glinda that time, everyone said you'd gone mad, and had become an assassin."

"People always did like to talk, didn't they? That's why I call myself a witch now: the Wicked Witch of the West, if you want the full glory of it. As long as people are going to call you a lunatic anyway, why not get the benefit of it? It liberates you from convention."

"You're not wicked," said Boq.

"How do you know? It's been so long," said the Witch, but she smiled at him.

Boq returned the smile, warmly. "Glinda used her glitter beads, and you used your exotic looks and background, but weren't you just doing the same thing, trying to maximize what you had in order to get what you wanted? People who claim that they're evil are usually no worse than the rest of us." He sighed. "It's people who claim that they're good, or anyway better than the rest of us, that you have to be wary of."

"Like Nessarose," said Milla meanly, but she was telling the truth, too, and they all nodded.

The Witch took one of Boq's children on her knee and clucked at it absentmindedly. She liked children no more than she ever had, but years of dealing with monkeys had given her an insight into the infant mentality she had never grasped before. The baby cooed and wet itself with pleasure. The Witch handed it back quickly before the wet could soak through her skirt.

"Regardless of the shoes," said the Witch, "do you think a child like that should be sent unarmed straight into the jaws of the Wizard? Has she been told what a monster he is?"

Boq looked uncomfortable. "Well, Elphie, I don't like speaking ill of the Wizard. I'm afraid there are too many pitchers with big ears in this community, and you never know who is on what side. Between you and me, I hope Nessa's death will result in some sort of a sensible govern-ment, but if we are overrun with an invading army in two months I wouldn't want it bruited about that I'd been bad-mouthing the invaders. And there are rumors of reunification."

"Oh, don't tell me you're hoping for that," she said, "not you too."

"I'm not hoping for anything, except for peace and quiet," he said. "I have enough trouble getting crops out of these rocky fields. That's what I was in Shiz to learn, do you remember?—agriculture. I've put the best of my efforts into our small holdings, and we only manage to eke out a living."

But he looked rather proud about it, and so did Milla.

"And I guess you have a couple of Cows in your barn," said the Witch.

"Oh, you're testy. Of course we don't. Do you think I could forget what we worked for—you and Crope and Tibbett and I? It was the high point of a very quiet life."

"You didn't have to have a quiet life, Boq," said the Witch.

"Don't be superior. I didn't say I was sorry for it, neither the excite-ment of a righteous campaign nor the relief of a family and a farm. Did we ever do any good back then?"

"If nothing else," said the Witch, "we helped Doctor Dillamond. He was very much alone in his work, you know. And the philosophical basis for the resistance grew out of his pioneering hypotheses. His find-ings outlived him; they still do." She did not mention her own experi-ments with the winged monkeys. Her practical applications were directly derived from Doctor Dillamond's theories.

"We had no idea we were at the end of a golden age," Boq said, sighing. "When's the last time you saw an Animal in the professions?"

"Ah, don't get me started," the Witch said. She couldn't stay seated.

"Do you remember, you hoarded those notes of Dillamond's. You never really let me know what they were all about. Did you make any use of them?"

"I learned enough from his research to keep questioning," said the Witch, but she felt bombastic, and wanted to stop talking. It made her feel too sad, too desperate. Milla saw this, and with a brusque charity declared, "Those times are over and gone, and good riddance to them, too. We were hopelessly high-spirited. Now we're the thick-waisted generation, dragging along our children behind us and carrying our parents on our backs. And we're in charge, while the figures who used to command our respect are wasting away."

"The Wizard doesn't," said the Witch.

"Well, Madame Morrible does," said Milla. "Or so Shenshen told me in her last letter."

"Oh?" said the Witch.

"Yes, that's right," said Boq. "Though from her bed of pain Madame Morrible continues to advise our Emperor Wizard on policy matters about education. I'm surprised that Glinda didn't send Dorothy to Shiz to study with Madame Morrible. Instead she directed her to the Emerald City."

The Witch could not picture Dorothy, but for a moment she saw the stooped figure of Nor. She saw a crowd of girls like Nor, in chains and yokes, drifting around Madame Morrible the way those schoolgirls had, all those years ago.

"Elphie, sit down again, you don't look well," said Boq. "This is a hard time for you. You didn't get along well with Nessarose, I seem to remember."

But the Witch didn't want to think of her sister. "It's a rather ugly name, Dorothy," she said. "Don't you think?" She sat back down heavily, and Boq relaxed on a stool a few feet away.

"I don't know," he said. "Actually we had a chat about it. She said that the King of her homeland was a man named Theodore. Her teacher explained that the name meant Gift of God, and that this was a sign that he was ordained to be King or Prime Minister. Dorothy remarked that *Dorothy* was a sort of backward *Theodore*, but the teacher looked it up and said no, *Dorothy* meant Goddess of Gifts."

"Well, I know what she can give *me*," said the Witch. "She can give me my shoes. Are you trying to say that you think she was a gift of God, or that she is some sort of queen or goddess? Boq, you used not to go in for superstition."

"I'm not saying anything of the sort. I'm having a conversation on word derivations," he answered calmly. "Let others more enlightened

than I ferret out the hidden meanings of life. But I do think it interesting
that her name so resembles the name of her king."

Milla said, "Well, I think she's a holy little girl, ordinary and sancti-
fied just as any child is, no more no less. Yellowgage, get your paws off
that lemon tart, I can see you from here, or I'll whip you from now to
eternity. The Dorothy child reminded me of what Ozma might have been
like, or might yet be like, if she ever comes out of the deep sleep she's
supposed to be enchanted into."

"She sounds like a little fright," said the Witch. "Ozma, Dorothy—
all this talk about savior children. I have always detested it."

"You know what it is?" said Boq, thinking carefully. "Since we're talking about the old days, it comes back to me . . . I wonder if you remember
that medieval painting I once found in the library at Three Queens? The
one with the female figure cradling the beast? There was a sort of tender-
ness and awfulness in that painting. Well, there's something in Dorothy
that reminds me of that unnamed figure. You might even call it the
Unnamed Goddess—is that sacrilegious or what? Dorothy has this sweet
charity toward her dog, a pretty dreadful little beast. And whiffy? You
wouldn't believe how repugnant. Once she swooped the dog up in her arms
and bent over it, crooning to it, in just the same pose as that medieval figure. Dorothy is a child, but she has a heaviness of bearing like an adult, and
a gravity you don't often find in the young. It's very becoming. Elphie, I was
charmed by her, to tell you the truth." He cracked a couple of walnuts and
eastern macarands, and passed them around. "I am sure you will be, too."

"I would like to avoid her at all costs, at the sound of it," said the
Witch. "The last thing I'm in a mood for these days is to be charmed by
juvenile purity. But I insist on recovering my property."

"The shoes are very magic, are they?" said Milla. "Or is it just sym-
bolic?"

"How do I even know?" said the Witch. "I haven't ever put them
on. But if I could get them and they could walk me out of this parlous life,
I wouldn't be sorry."

"Anyway, everyone blamed the shoes for Nessa's tyranny. I think
it's good of Glinda to have gotten them out of Munchkinland. The child
is smuggling them abroad without even knowing it."

"Glinda has sent the girl to the Emerald City," said the Witch pointedly. "If the Wizard gets hold of them, it'll be a license to march into Munchkinland. And you're fools to sit on the fence as if it makes no difference whether he does or not."

"You'll stay for something, at least some tea," said Milla soothingly. "Look, I've had Clarinda make a fresh pot, and we've saffron cream. Remember the saffron cream party after Ama Clutch's funeral?"

The Witch breathed heavily for a moment; there was a pain in her esophagus. She did not like to remember those trying times. And Glinda had known full well that Madame Morrible was behind the death of Ama Clutch. Now as Lady Glinda she was part of the same ruling class. It was hideous. And Dorothy, whatever her origins, was still only a child, and they were using her to help rid Munchkinland of those damned totemic shoes. Or to get the shoes to the Wizard. Just as Madame Morrible had used her students as Adepts.

"I can't stop here chattering like an idiot," she cried, startling them, spilling the bowl of nuts to the ground. "Didn't we waste enough time talking ourselves to death in school?" She grabbed for her broom and her hat.

Boq looked startled and almost fell backward off his seat. "Well, Elphie, why are you taking offense—?"

She was beyond answering. She whirled in a small cyclone of black skirts and scarves, and ran out to the road.

She hurried on foot along the Yellow Brick Road, hardly realizing that a plan was forming in her mind. But she was thinking so hard that for a while she completely forgot she was carrying her broom, and it was only when she paused to rest, and leaned on it, that she remembered it.

Boq, Glinda, even her father, Frex: how disappointing they all seemed now. Had these folks deteriorated in virtue since their youth, or had she been too naive then to see them for what they were? She felt disgusted with people, and longed to be home. She was too out of sorts to seek lodging in an inn or a public house. It was warm enough to stay outside and rest.

She lay awake at the edge of a field of barley. The moon rose, huge as it sometimes is when first breaking over the horizon. It backlit a stake with a crossbar, standing as if awaiting a body to crucify, or a scarecrow to hang.

Why hadn't she joined forces with Nessarose, and raised armies against the Wizard? Old family resentments had gotten in the way.

Nessarose had asked for help in governing Munchkinland, and the Witch had denied her request. Instead the Witch had gone back to Kiamo Ko these seven years. She had squandered the chance to merge forces with her sister.

Virtually every campaign she'd set out for herself had ended in failure.

She squirmed in the light of the moon, and at midnight, tortured by the thoughts of Nessa's death—the physical fact of being squished like a bug finally taking on some imaginative shape in the Witch's fantasies—she arose, and took a new path. Dorothy would no doubt follow the Yellow Brick Road to the Emerald City, and someone as exotic as she could be easily located anywhere along the route. The Witch would go and try to accomplish the task set out for herself fifteen years ago. Madame Morrible still waited to be killed.

6

Shiz was a money factory now. The Colleges, occupying an historic district, remained largely unchanged, but for some contemporary dormitories and flashy athletic buildings. Outside the university district, however, Shiz had thrived in the war-alert economy. A huge monument in brass and marble, *The Spirit of Empire*, dominated what was left of Railway Square, and the air and light around it was cut off by hulking industrial buildings, spewing black columns of filth into the air. The bluestone was now grimestone. The air itself seemed warm and earnest—the ten thousand exhalations of a city panting every second to increase its wealth. The trees were shriveled and gray. And not a single Animal in sight.

Crage Hall looked absurdly older and newer at once. The Witch chose not to bother the porter, and flew herself up over the wall into the kitchen garden, where once Boq had tumbled off an adjoining roof, almost into her lap. The back lawn beyond the orchard was gone, and in its place stood a stone structure, above whose gleaming poxite doors was carved THE SIR CHUFFREY AND LADY GLINDA CONSERVATORY OF MUSIC AND THE THEATRICAL ARTS.

Three girls came hurrying down the path, chattering away, their books clutched close to their bosoms. They gave the Witch a start, as if they were ghosts of Nessarose, Glinda and herself. She had to hold on to her broomstick and steady herself. She had not taken in how far she had come, how much she had aged.

"I need to see the Head," she said, startling them.

But one recovered her youthful aplomb and pointed the way. The Head's office was still in Main Hall. "You'll find her in," they said. "She's always in at this hour of the morning, having tea by herself or with contributors."

Security must be greatly relaxed if none of them questions my being in the kitchen garden, thought the Witch. All the better; I may even escape unstopped.

The Head had a secretary now, a plump older gentleman with a goatee. "She's not expecting you?" he said. "I'll see if she's free." He returned and said, "Madame Head will see you now. Would you like to leave your broom in the umbrella stand?"

"How kind. No thanks," said the Witch, and walked through.

The Head rose from a leather armchair. She wasn't Madame Morrible anymore; she was a small pinky white woman with copper-colored curls and an energetic manner. "I didn't catch your name?" she said politely. "You're an old girl, but I'm a new one"—she laughed at her own witticism, and the Witch did not—"and I'm afraid I haven't yet grasped the truth: dozens of old girls come back every month to relive the pleasant moments of their growing up here. Please, may I have your name, and I'll call for some tea."

With some effort, the Witch said, "I was called Miss Elphaba when I was here, more years ago than I realized could be possible. In fact I won't take tea, I can't stay long. I was misinformed. I was hoping to see Madame Morrible? Do you know of her whereabouts?"

"Well, is this good luck or is it bad?" said the current Head. "Up till very recently she has spent part of every semester in the Emerald City, consulting with His Highness himself, on education policies through Loyal Oz. But she's recently returned to her retirement apartment in the Doddery—I'm sorry, that's a joke of the girls and it slipped out. It is called the Daughter Building, really, as it was financed by the generous daughters of Crage Hall, our alums. You see, her health has deteriorated, and—though I hate to be the bearer of bad tidings—I fear she is very near the end."

"I'd love to pop in and say hello," said the Witch. Playacting had never suited her, and it was only because the new Head was so young, such a fool, such a girl herself, that the Witch could get away with it. "I was a great favorite of hers, you know; it would give her a wonderful surprise."

"I'll call Grommetik to take you there," said the Head. "But I should ask Madame Morrible's nurse first if she's up to a visit."

"Don't call Grommetik, I can find my own way. I will chat with the nurse, and I will only stop in for a moment. And then I'll come back here before I leave, I promise, and perhaps I can see my way clear to making a contribution toward the annual fund, or some little endowment drive you must be mounting at present?"

To the best of her recollection she had never lied before in her life.

The Doddery was a broad round tower, like a squat silo, sitting adjacent to the chapel in which Doctor Dillamond had been eulogized. A scout, passing by with buckets and brooms, told the Witch that Madame Morrible was one flight up, behind the door with the Wizard's standard mounted on it.

A minute later the Witch stood looking at the Wizard's standard. A balloon with a basket beneath it, commemorating his spectacular arrival in the Emerald City, and crossed swords below. From a few feet away it looked like a huge skull, and the basket a leering jaw, and the crossed swords a forbidding X. The doorknob turned under her tug, and she entered the apartments.

There were several rooms, all cluttered with school memorabilia and tokens of esteem from various Emerald City institutions, including the Palace of the Emperor. The Witch passed through a sort of parlor, with a fire burning in it despite the warmth of the season, and a kitchen-scullery area. To one side was a water closet, and the Witch could hear the sound of someone sobbing inside, and the blowing of a nose. The Witch pushed a dresser against the door, and continued on into a sleeping chamber.

Madame Morrible was propped halfway up in a huge bed shaped like a pfenix. A carved gold pfenix neck and head emerged from the head-board, and the sides of the bed simulated the bird's wings. Its feet joined at the footboard. The idea of its tail feathers had apparently defeated the ingenuity of the cabinetmaker, for there weren't any. It was a bird in an awkward position, actually, as if being blown backward through the air by gunshot, or as if laboring in a human way to deliver itself of the great mound of flesh sitting on its stomach and reclining against its breast.

On the floor was a pile of the financial papers, and an old-fashioned pair of spectacles was set on top of them. But the time for reading was past.

Madame Morrible rested in a gray mound, her hands folded upon her belly, and her eyes open and shallow, without motion. She was still like a mammoth Carp, in all but the fishy smell—a candle had been so recently lit that the stink of the match's sulfur still lingered in the room.

The Witch pulled at her broom. From the other room came a pounding on the door of the water closet. "Did you think you would always be safe by hiding behind schoolchildren?" said the Witch, beyond herself, beyond caring, and she raised her broom. But Madame Morrible made a sluggish, indifferent corpse.

The Witch struck Madame Morrible with the flat of the broom, on the side of the head and the face. It made no mark. Then the Witch searched the mantelpiece for the testimonial trophy with the biggest marble base, and she bashed in Madame Morrible's skull with it, with a sound like a splitting of firewood.

She left it in the old woman's arms. Its statement could be read by all, except the carved pfenix who would be looking at it upside down. IN APPRECIATION OF EVERYTHING YOU HAVE DONE, it said.

7

The Witch had waited fifteen years, but her timing was off by five minutes. So the temptation to go back and dismember Grommetik was intense. But the Witch resisted. She didn't care if she was sentenced and executed for the battery of Madame Morrible's corpse, but she didn't want to be caught because of vengeance against a machine.

She took a meal at a café and glanced at the tabloids. Then she wandered in the shopping district. Never one for frippery, she was intensely bored, but she wanted to hear them talking about the death of Madame Morrible. She was waiting for the reviews, as it were. And she would never come back to Shiz, she suspected, nor to any other city. This was her last chance to see Loyal Oz in action.

As the afternoon wore on, however, she began to worry. What if there was a cover-up? What if the current Head, to avoid scandal, hushed up the news of the assault? Especially a crime against one so close to the Emperor? The Witch began to fret that she would be denied the credit for her deed. She racked her brains for someone to confess to, someone who would be sure to rush to the authorities. What about Crope, or Shenshen, or Pfannee? Or, for that matter, the Margreave of Tenmeadows, nasty Avaric?

The town house of the Margreave was set out in the deer park at the edge of Shiz. It was late afternoon by the time she reached the Emperor's Green, as it was now called. Private residences were dotted about the expanse, each protected by its own security force, high walls lined with broken glass bottles, fierce dogs. The Witch had a way with dogs and high walls didn't bother her. She welcomed herself over the wall onto a terrace, where a maid tending a floxflower bed had a conniption and resigned on the spot. The Witch found Avaric in his study, signing some documents with a huge plumed pen, and sipping some honey-colored whiskey in a crystal glass. "I said that I won't come out for cocktails, you're on your own, can't you listen?" he began, but then he saw who it was.

"However did you get in here without being announced?" he said. "I know you. Don't I?"

"Of course you do, Avaric. I'm the green girl of Crage Hall."

"Oh yes. What was your name?"

"My name was Elphaba."

He lit a lamp—the afternoon was darkening, or perhaps clouding over now—and they looked at each other. "Have a seat, then. I suppose if society forces itself in one's study door, one has no further right to deny it. A drink?"

"A wee one."

Alone of them all, he, who had been too handsome to believe, had grown better looking. He wore his hair swept back; it was rich and full, the color of polished nickel, and he clearly had the benefit of a life of exercise and rest, for his figure was strong and slim, his bearing erect, his color good. Those born with advantages know how to capitalize on them, observed the Witch, after her first sip.

"To what do I owe this honor?" he said, seating himself across from her with a freshened drink in his own hands. "Or is the whole world playing reprises today?"

"What do you mean by that?"

"I had a walk at noon," he said, "in the park, with my bodyguards, as usual. And I came across a carnival entertainment set up there. It opens tomorrow, I think, and the park will be mobbed with clever students, household servants and factory workers, and with greasy gabbling families from Little Glikkus. There were the usual cast of children caught up in the allure of a good circus act, mostly teenage boys helping out, no doubt having run away from tiresome families and small provincial towns. But the guy in charge was a bloody little dwarf."

"Bloody, how do you mean?" asked the Witch.

"I mean *offensive*, pardon my slang. We've all seen dwarves before, that's not the point. It's just that I had seen this very dwarf before. I recognized him from years ago."

"Fancy that."

"Well, I wouldn't have thought anything more of it, but then you show up this afternoon from more or less the same zone of memory. Weren't you there, yourself? Didn't you go with us to the Philosophy Club that night, we got so drunk, and they had that charmed-sex thing, and that effeminate Tibbett got so wasted and lost his mind and just about everything else when that Tiger . . . ? You were there, surely."

"I don't think I was."

"Weren't you? Boq was, squiggly little Boq, and Pfannee, and Fiyero, I think, and some others. Don't you remember? There was that hag who called herself Yackle, and the dwarf, and they let us in, and they were so creepy? Anyway, doesn't matter—it's just—"

"Not Yackle," said the Witch. She dropped her drink. "This is insanity, my ears are having delusions. Everyone is right, I'm paranoid. No, Avaric, I refuse to admit you could remember someone's name for twenty years like that."

"She was a balding gypsy woman with a wig, and sort of chestnut-colored eyes, in thick with this dwarf. I don't know what he was called. Why shouldn't I remember it?"

"You didn't remember *my* name."

"You didn't scare me half as much. In fact you never scared me." He laughed. "I was probably pretty nasty to you. I was an asshole back then."

"You still are."

"Well, practice makes perfect, and more than once I've been called a perfect asshole."

"I came by to tell you that I killed Madame Morrible today," said the Witch. She was so proud of the phrase; it seemed less false when said aloud. Maybe it *was* true. "I killed her. I wanted someone who would be believed to know about it."

"Oh, why ever did you do that?"

"You know, the reasons just reassemble themselves in different patterns every time I think about it." She sat up a little straighter. "Because she deserved it."

"The Avenging Angel of Justice is now green?"

"A pretty good disguise, don't you think?" They both grinned.

"So about this Madame Morrible, whom you claim to have killed? Did you know that she gathered your friends and associates together and gave us a little lecture after you'd run away?"

"*You* were never my friend."

"I was too near to be excused. I remember the situation. Nessarose was mortified and shattered by the whole thing. Madame Morrible took out your records and read to us a profile of your character as assessed by your various teachers. We were warned about your spikiness, your fringiness, what were the words they used? I can't remember *that*, they weren't memorable words. But we were told you might try to recruit us in some sort of juvenile attempt to galvanize some sort of student uprising. You were to be avoided at all costs."

"And Nessarose was mortified, well, that figures," said the Witch grimly.

"Glinda too," said Avaric. "She went through another slide, like the one she went into after Doctor Dillamond fell on his magnifying lens—"

"Oh please, is that hoary old lie still in circulation?"

"—oh all right, *was brutally murdered by brigands unknown*, have it your way. Brigands in the form of Madame Morrible, that's what you mean me to suppose. So why really did you do it?"

"Madame Morrible had a *choice*. No one was better placed than she to see that her students got an education and not a brainwashing. By hooking up with the Emerald City, she sold out all her students who believed that a liberal education meant learning to think for themselves.

Besides, she was a vile fiend, and she did conspire to have Doctor Dillamond murdered. No matter what you say."

But the Witch stopped herself short, hearing in her words about Madame Morrible—she had a choice—an echo of what the Elephant Princess Nastoya had once said to her: No one controls your destiny. Even at the very worst—there is always choice.

Avaric was rattling on. "And you've had *her* murdered. Two wrongs don't make a right, as we boys used to chant on the playground, usually when we were on the ground with someone's knee on our groin. Why don't you stay for a meal? We've got guests, a clever bunch."

"So you can call the police? No thanks."

"I won't call the police. You and I, we're above petulant justice like that."

The Witch believed him. "All right," she said. "Who are you married to, by the way? Did you get married to Pfannee, or Shenshen, or someone else? I can't remember."

"Whoever," said Avaric, pouring another finger of whiskey. "I can't keep small details in my mind, never could."

The Margreave's pantry was fulsome, his cook a genius, and his wine cellar unparalleled. The guests tucked into snails and garlic, roast crest of fallowhen with cilantro and clementine chutney, and the Witch allowed herself a sumptuous helping of lime tart with saffron cream. The crystal goblets were never empty. The conversation was exalted and loopy, and by the time the Margreavess led them to the comfortable chairs in the drawing room, the plaster appliqué on the ceiling seemed to swirl like the cigarette smoke.

"Why, you're flushed," said Avaric. "You ought to have been a tippler all along, Elphaba."

"I'm not sure red wine agrees with me," she said.

"You're in no condition to go anywhere. The maid will do up one of the corner rooms. It's lovely, there's a view clear to the pagoda on the island."

"I don't care for prepared views."

"Don't you want to wait for the morning papers, to see if they got it right? If they got it at all?"

"I'll ask you to send me one. No, I must go, I feel the need of some fresh air. Avaric—Madame—friends—it's been a surprise and I suppose a pleasure." But she felt grudging as she said it.

"A pleasure to some," said the Margreavess, who hadn't approved of the conversation. "I think it improper to talk about evil all during a meal. It spoils the digestion."

"Oh, but come," the Witch said, "is it only in youth that we can have the nerve to ask ourselves such serious questions?"

"Well, I stick with my suggestion," said Avaric. "Evil isn't *doing* bad things, it's *feeling* bad about them afterward. There's no absolute value to behavior. First of all—"

"Institutional inertia," claimed the Witch. "But whatever is the great attraction of absolute power anyway?"

"That's why I say it's merely an affliction of the psyche, like vanity or greed," said a copper magnate. "And we all know vanity and greed can produce some pretty astounding results in human affairs, not all of them reprehensible."

"It's an absence of good, that's all," said his paramour, an agony aunt for the *Shiz Informer*. "The nature of the world is to be calm, and enhance and support life, and evil is an absence of the inclination of matter to be at peace."

"Pigspittle," said Avaric. "Evil is an early or primitive stage of moral development. All children are fiends by nature. The criminals among us are only those who didn't progress . . ."

"I think it's a presence, not an absence," said an artist. "Evil's an incarnated character, an incubus or a succubus. It's an other. It's not *us*."

"Not even me?" said the Witch, playing the part more vigorously than she expected. "A self-confessed murderer?"

"Oh go on with you," said the artist, "we all of us show ourselves in our best light. That's just normal vanity."

"Evil isn't a thing, it's not a person, it's an attribute like beauty . . ."

"It's a power, like wind . . ."

"It's an infection . . ."

"It's metaphysical, essentially: the corruptibility of creation—"

"Blame it on the Unnamed God, then."

"But did the Unnamed God create evil intentionally, or was it just a mistake in creation?"

"It's not of air and eternity, evil isn't; it's of earth; it's physical, a disjointedness between our bodies and our souls. Evil is inanely corporeal, humans causing one another pain, no more no less—"

"I *like* pain, if I'm wearing calfskin chaps and have my wrists tied behind me—"

"No, you're all wrong, our childhood religion had it right: Evil is moral at its heart—the selection of vice over virtue; you can pretend not to know, you can rationalize, but you know it in your conscience—"

"Evil is an act, not an appetite. How many haven't wanted to slash the throat of some boor across the dining room table? Present company excepted of *course*. Everyone has the appetite. If you give in to it, it, that *act* is evil. The appetite is normal."

"Oh no, evil is repressing that appetite. I never repress any appetite."

"I won't have this talk in my drawing room," said the Margreavess, near tears. "You've been behaving all night as if an old woman hadn't been slaughtered in her bedclothes. Didn't she have a mother too? Didn't she have a soul?"

Avaric yawned and said, "You're so tender and naive. When it's not embarrassing it's quite appealing."

The Witch stood up, sat down quickly, and stood up again, aided by her broom.

"Why did you do it?" asked the hostess with spirit.

The Witch shrugged. "For fun? Maybe evil is an art form."

But as she wobbled toward the door, she said, "You know, you're all a pack of fools. You ought to have turned me in instead of entertaining me all evening."

"You entertained *us*," said Avaric broadly, gallantly. "This'll end up being the dinner party of the season. Even if you've been lying all evening about killing this old schoolmarm. What a treat." The dinner guests drolly applauded her.

"The real thing about evil," said the Witch at the doorway, "isn't any of what you said. You figure out one side of it—the human side, say— and the eternal side goes into shadow. Or vice versa. It's like the old saw: What does a dragon in its shell look like? Well no one can ever tell, for as soon as you break the shell to see, the dragon is no longer *in* its shell. The real disaster of this inquiry is that it is the nature of evil to be *secret*."

8

The moon was up again, a little less swollen than the night before. The Witch didn't trust herself to ride on the broom, so she meandered in a zigzaggy way across the greensward. She would find a place to nap outside of the claustrophobia of a society den.

She came upon the construction that Avaric had talked about. It was an old, early tiktok thing, a sort of portable stupa made of carved wood and figurines, too variegated and numerous for the Witch to comprehend tonight. Perhaps there was a running board where she could rest underneath, a platform elevated just a couple of inches off the dampish ground. She peered, and moved forward.

"And where do you think you're going?"

A Munchkinlander, no, a dwarf, stood in her way. He had a cudgel in one hand, and was thwacking it into the thick leathery palm of his other hand.

"Going to sleep, when I can," she said. "So you're the dwarf, and this is the thing Avaric talked about."

"The Clock of the Time Dragon," he said, "open for business tomorrow night, and not until."

"I'll be dead and gone by tomorrow night," she said.

"No you won't," he answered.

"Well, gone anyway." She looked at it and straightened up, then something came back to her. "I wonder how you knew Yackle," she said.

"Oh, Yackle," he said. "Who doesn't know Yackle? Not such a surprise."

"Was she killed today?" said the Witch. "By any chance?"

"No chance," he answered.

"Who are you?" She was afraid, suddenly, after all this headiness of sorrow and violence.

"Oh, the least significant little one," he said.

"Who do you work for?"

"Who haven't I worked for?" said the dwarf. "The devil is a very big angel, but a very little man. But I have no name in this world, so don't bother with me."

"I'm drunk and disorderly," she said, "and I cannot take any more riddles. I killed someone today, I can kill you too."

"You didn't kill her, she was already dead," said the dwarf calmly. "And you can't kill me, for I'm immortal. But you try very hard at life, and so I will tell you this. I am the guardian of the book, and I was brought to this dreaded, forsaken land to watch over the book's history, to keep it from getting back to where it comes from. I am not good, I am not bad; but I am locked here, condemned to a deathless life to guard the book. I don't care what happens to you or anyone else, but I protect the book: that is my charge."

"The book?" She was struggling to understand; she felt drunker the more she heard.

"What you call the Grimmerie. It has other names—no matter."

"Then why don't you take it, why don't you have it?"

"I don't work like that. I am the silent partner. I work through events, I live on the sidelines, I dabble in causes and effects, I watch how the misbegotten creatures of this world live their lives. I interfere only to keep the book safe. To some extent I can see what's coming, and to that extent I meddle in the affairs of men and beasts." He jigged like a little fiend. "You see me here, you see me there. Having second sight is a great advantage in the security business."

"You work with Yackle."

"We sometimes have the same intentions, and we sometimes do not. Her interest seems to be different from mine."

"Who is she? What is her interest? Why do you hover at the edges of my life?"

"In the world I come from, there are guardian angels," said the dwarf, "but so far as I can work it out, she is an opposite number, and her concern is you."

"Why do I deserve such a fiend? Why is my life so *plagued*? Who positioned her to influence my life?"

"There are things I don't know, and things I do," said the dwarf. "Who Yackle answers to, if anyone, if anything, is beyond my realm of knowledge or interest. But *why* you? You must know this. For you"—the dwarf spoke in a bright, offhand tone—"are neither this nor that—or shall I say *both* this and that? Both of Oz and of the other world. Your old Frex always was wrong; you were never a punishment for his crimes. You are a half-breed, you are a new breed, you are a grafted limb, you are a dangerous anomaly. Always you were drawn to the composite creatures, the broken and reassembled, for that is what you are. Can you be so dull that you have not figured this out?"

"Show me something," she said. "I do not know what you mean. Show me something the world hasn't shown me yet."

"For you, a pleasure." He disappeared, and there was the sound of mechanical parts being wound up, moving against one another, the grind of lubricated gears, the slap of leather belts, the chuck-chuck of pendulums swinging. "A private audience with the Time Dragon itself."

At the top, a beast prowled, flexing its wings in a dance of gestures, both bidding welcome and holding at bay. The Witch stared.

A small area halfway up was illuminated. "A three-act play," came the voice of the dwarf, from deep within. "Act One: The Birth of Holiness."

Later she could not have said how she knew what it was, but what she saw, in an abbreviated pantomime, was the life of Saint Aelphaba. The good woman, the mystic and recluse, who disappeared to pray behind a waterfall. The Witch flinched to see the saint walk straight through the waterfall (a guttering spout overhead drained real water out into a hidden tray below). She waited for the tiktok saint to come out, but she didn't come, and eventually the lights went out.

"Act Two: The Birth of Evil."

"Wait, the Saint didn't emerge as the tales say she did," said the Witch. "I want my money's worth or not at all, please."

"Act Two: The Birth of Evil."

Lights came up on another little stage. There was a credible likeness of Colwen Grounds painted on a cardboard backdrop beyond. A figurine who was Melena kissed her parents good-bye and went off with Frex, a handsome little puppet with a short black beard and a jaunty step. They stopped in a small hut, and Frex kissed her and continued on to preach. All through the rest of the scene he was off to one side, yammering away to some peasants who were busy screwing each other on the ground before him, hacking each other to pieces and eating their sexual parts, which ran with a real gravy; you could smell the garlic and sauteed mushrooms. Melena, at home, yawned and waited, and teased her pretty hair. Along came a man whom the Witch could not identify at first. He had a small black bag and from it he extracted a green glass bottle. He gave it to Melena to drink, and when she had, she fell into his arms, either stupefied and drunk as the Witch was tonight, or liberated. It wasn't clear. The traveler and Melena made love in the same bouncy rhythm as Frex's parishioners. Frex started to dance to the rhythm himself. Then, when the act of love was done, the traveler pulled himself off Melena. He snapped his fingers, and a balloon with a basket beneath descended from the fly space above. The traveler got in. It was the Wizard.

"Oh, nonsense," said the Witch. "This is pure poppycock."

The lights dimmed. The voice of the dwarf sounded from inside the contraption. "Act Three," he said. "The Marriage of the Sacred and the Wicked."

She waited, but no area was illuminated, no puppet moved.

"Well?" she said.

"Well what?" he answered.

"Where's the end of the play?"

He stuck his head out of a trap door and winked at her. "Who said the end was written yet?" he answered, and slammed the door shut. Another door opened, just by the Witch's hand, and a tray slid out. Lying on it was an oval looking glass, cracked along one side, scratched on its surfaces. It looked like the glass she had had since childhood, the one she used to imagine she could see the Other Land in, back when she believed in such a thing. The last she remembered of the oval glass was in her hideaway digs in the Emerald City. Inside the glass lived reflections of a young and beautiful Fiyero, and a young and impassioned Fae. The Witch took the mirror and hid it in her apron, and wandered away.

There was nothing in the morning papers about the death of Madame Morrible. The Witch, with a treacherous headache, decided that she could wait no longer. Either Avaric and his beastly companions would spread the rumors, or they wouldn't. There was nothing left to be done.

Just let word get to the Wizard, though, said the Witch to herself. I would like to be a fly on the wall of his bunker when *that* happens. Let him think I killed her. Let that be how the news goes.

9

She returned to Munchkinland in a punishing journey, exhausting herself. She had slept so little, and her head still throbbed. But she was proud of herself. She arrived in the front yard of Boq's cottage, and called for the family to come.

Boq was out in the field, and one of his children had to be dispatched to fetch him. When he came running, he had an adze in one hand. "I wasn't expecting you, it took me a minute," he said, panting.

"You'd have run quicker if you'd left your blade behind," she noted.

But he didn't drop it. "Elphie, why have you come back?"

"To tell you what I have done," she said. "I thought you would like to know. I have killed Madame Morrible, and she can no longer harm anyone."

But Boq did not look pleased. "You took against that old woman?" he said. "Surely she was beyond the point of hurting anyone now?"

"You've made the mistake that everyone makes," said the Witch, cruelly disappointed. "Don't you know there is no such point?"

"You had worked to protect the Animals," said Boq. "But you did not intend to sink to the level of those who brutalized them."

"I have fought fire with fire," said the Witch, "and I ought to have done it sooner! Boq, you've become an equivocating fool."

"Children," said Boq, "run inside and find your mother."

He was scared of her.

"You're sitting on the fence," she said. "Here your precious Munchkinland is going to be sucked back into the folds of Royal Oz, under His Highness the Emperor Wizard. And you see what Glinda is up to, and you send that child on her way with the shoes that belong to me. You took a stand when you were young, Boq! How can you have—*spoiled* so!"

"Elphie," said Boq, "look at me. You are beside yourself. Have you been *drinking?* Dorothy is *just a child.* You may not retell this to make her into some sort of fiend!"

Milla, alerted to the tension in the front yard, came out and stood behind Boq. She carried a kitchen knife. Whispering noisily, the children watched from the window.

"You do not need to defend yourselves with knives and adzes," said the Witch coldly. "I had thought you would care to know about Madame Morrible."

"You are shaking," said Boq. "Look, I will put down this thing. Clearly you are upset. Nessa's death has been hard on you. But you must get control of yourself, Elphie. Don't take against Dorothy. She is an innocent creature. She's all alone. I beg of you."

"Oh, don't beg, don't beg," said the Witch, "I could not abide begging, from you, of all people!" She ground her teeth and clenched her fists. "I will promise you nothing, Boq!"

And this time she got on her broom and flew away. Recklessly, she mounted the sides of air currents, until the ground below had lost any detail sharp enough to cause her pain.

She was beginning to feel too long away from Kiamo Ko. Liir was an idiot, headstrong and lily-livered by turns, and Nanny sometimes forgot where she was. The Witch didn't want to think about yesterday, the death of Madame Morrible, the accusations made by the puppet play. She could hardly be more averse to the Wizard than she already was; if there was a shred of possibility to that sick idea of his having fathered her, it only made her hate him the more. She would ask Nanny about it when she got home.

When she got home. She was thirty-eight, and just realizing what it felt like to have a sense of home. For that, Sarima, thank you, she thought. Maybe the definition of home is the place where you are never forgiven, so you may always belong there, bound by guilt. And maybe the cost of belonging is worth it.

But she decided to head toward Kiamo Ko by following the Yellow Brick Road. She would make one last try for the shoes. She had nothing left to lose. If the shoes fell into the hands of the Wizard, he would use them to bolster his claim to Munchkinland. Maybe, if she tried, she could shrug her shoulders and leave Munchkinland to its own fate—but damn it, the shoes were *hers*.

She finally found a peddler who had seen Dorothy. He stopped by the side of his wagon and rubbed the ears of his donkey as he discussed it with her. "She passed here a few hours ago," he said, chewing on a carrot and sharing it with the donkey. "No, she wasn't alone. She had a raga-muffin crew of friends with her. Bodyguards, I suspect."

"Oh, the poor frightened thing," said the Witch. "Who? Munchkinlander beefcake boys, I wonder?"

"Not exactly," said the peddler. "There was a straw man, and a tin woodman, and a big cat who hid in the bushes when I passed—a leopard maybe, or a cougar."

"A man of straw?" said the Witch. "She's awakening the figures of myth, she's charming them to life? This must be some attractive child. Did you notice her shoes?"

"I wanted to buy them from her."

"Yes! Yes, did you?"

"Not for sale. She seemed very attached to them. They were given her by a Good Witch."

"Pigspittle, they were."

"None of my affair either way," said the peddler. "Can I interest you in anything?"

"An umbrella," said the Witch. "I've come out without one, and it looks nasty."

"I remember the good old days of the drought," said the peddler, fishing out a somewhat worn umbrella. "Ah, here's the bumbershoot. Yours for a nickel florin."

"Mine for free," said the Witch. "You wouldn't deny a poor old woman in need, would you, my friend?"

"Not and live to tell about it, I see," he answered, and went on his way uncompensated.

But as the wagon passed, the Witch heard another voice: "Of course, no one asks a beast of burden, but it's my opinion she's Ozma come out of the deep sleep chamber, and marching on Oz to restore herself to the throne."

"I hate royalists," said the peddler, and lashed out with a crop. "I hate Animals with attitude." But the Witch could not stop to intervene. So far she had been unable to save Nor, she had been incompetent at bargaining with the Wizard. She had been a moment too late to murder Madame Morrible—or had she been just in time? Either way, she should not try what was clearly beyond her.

10

The Witch trembled on the lip of an updraft. She had brought the broom higher than ever before; she was in a state of exhilaration and panic. Should she pursue Dorothy, should she snatch those shoes away—and what were her real motives? Was it to keep them out of the hands of the Wizard, just as Glinda had wanted them out of the hands of power-hungry Munchkinlanders? Or was it to snatch back some small shred of Frex's attention, whether she had ever deserved it or not?

Beneath the broom, clouds began to gauze the view of rock-freckled hills and patchwork meadows of melon and corn. The thin twists of vapor looked like the marks of erasure made by a schoolchild's rubber, streaking whitely along a watercolor sketch of a landscape. What if she should just keep on, urging the broom higher, yanking it up? Would it splinter as it beat itself against the heavens?

She could give up these efforts. She could forsake Nor. She could release Liir. She could abandon Nanny. She could surrender Dorothy. She could give up the shoes.

But a wind came up, a shoulder of hard air leaning onto her left side. She could not force the broom against it. She was driven sideways, and down, until the Yellow Brick Road once again etched a golden thread between forests and fields. There was a storm on the horizon, slotting bars of brownish rain between lavender-gray clouds and gray-green fields. She hadn't much time.

Then she thought she caught sight of them below, and dove down to see. Were they stopping to rest beneath a black willow tree? If so, she could finish things up now.

11

By the time the storm lifted—and the Witch awoke from what she now identified as a horrible hangover—she wasn't sure it was the same day. She wasn't even sure she had gotten near them—could she have let them slip through her fingers like that? But whatever the case, delusion or foggy memory, the Witch didn't dare follow them into the

Emerald City. Madame Morrible had many friends in this rotten regime, and the news would have gotten through by now. There might even be search parties out for the Witch. So be it.

Though it galled her, for the time being she had to give up on the idea of reclaiming Nessa's shoes. She scarcely rested during the entire trip back to Kiamo Ko, except to stop and pick some berries, and nibble some nuts and sweet roots, to keep her strength up.

The castle had not been burned down. The Wizard's reconnaissance army was still camped at its outpost near Red Windmill in a state of bored readiness. Nanny was busy crocheting a pretty casket cover for her own funeral, and making guest lists. Most of the guests were already in the Other Land, presuming that for Nanny there *was* an Other Land. "How nice it would be to see Ama Clutch again, I quite agree," shouted the Witch, giving Nanny's shoulders a squeeze. "I always liked her. She had more character than that simpering Glinda."

"You were devoted to Glinda, you were," said Nanny. "Everyone knew it."

"Well, no more," said the Witch. "The traitor."

"You smell of blood, go wash up," said Nanny. "Is it your time?"

"I never wash, you know that. Where's Liir?"

"Who?"

"*Liir.*"

"Oh, around somewhere." She smiled. "Look in the fishwell!" By now an old family joke.

"What new nonsense is this?" said the Witch, finding Liir in the music room.

"They were right all along," he said. "Look what I finally caught, after all these years."

It was the golden carp that had long haunted the fishwell. "Oh, I admit that it was dead and I brought it up with the bucket, not a hook or a net. But even so. Do you think we'll ever be able to tell them we finally caught it?"

All these last months he had begun to talk about Sarima and the family as if they were ghosts, hiding just around the curve of the spiral staircase in the tower, suppressing giggles at this long, long game of hide-and-seek.

"We can only hope so," she said. She wondered, faintly, if it was immoral to raise children in the habit of hope. Was it not, in the end, all the harder for them to adjust to the reality of how the world worked? "Everything else was all right while I was gone?"

"Just fine," he said. "But I'm glad you're back."

She grunted, and went to greet Chistery and the chattering kin.

In her room she hung the old glass with a cord and a nail, and kept from looking at it. She had the horrible feeling that she would see Dorothy, and she didn't want to see her again. The child reminded her of someone. It was that unquestioning directness, that gaze unblinkered by shame. She was as natural as a raccoon—or a fern—or a comet. The Witch thought: Is it Nor? Is it that Dorothy reminds me of how Nor was at this age?

But back then the Witch had not cared for Nor, not really, even though her face had been a small, velvet reworking of Fiyero's. Except for Nessarose, and Shell, the Witch had never warmed to the glowing promise of children. She had always felt more alone in this regard than in her color.

No—and now her glance *did* fall on the tired old looking glass, despite her intentions. She thought: the Witch with her mirror. Who do we ever see but ourselves, and *that's* the curse—Dorothy reminds me of myself, at that age, whatever it is . . .

. . . The time in Ovvels. There is the green girl, shy, gawky, and humiliated. To avoid the pain of damp feet, splashing around in clammy leggings made of swampcalf hide and waterproof boots. Mama, pregnant with Shell, huge as a barge. Mama praying nonstop for months that she might at last bring a healthy child into the world. Mama dumping the bottles of liquor and the pinlobble leaves into the mud.

Nanny tends to little Nessa, papoosing her around in the daily hunt for charfish, needle flowers, and broad bean vines. Nessa can see but she cannot touch: what a curse for a child! (No wonder she believed in things she couldn't see—*nothing* is provable by touch.) For *his* atonement, Papa takes the green girl with him on an expedition to the relatives of Turtle Heart, a many-branched family living in a nest of huts and walkways suspended in a grove of broad, rotting suppletrees. The Quadlings, who are more comfortable on their haunches, duck their heads. The smell of raw fish in their homes, on their skin. They are frightened of the unionist minister, finding them out in their squalid hamlet. I have no firm memory of individuals, but for one old matriarch, toothless and proud.

The Quadlings come up, after a period of shyness, not to the minister but to me, the green girl. She is no longer I, she is too long ago, she is only she, impenetrably mysterious and dense—she stands as Dorothy stood, some inborn courage making her spine straight, her eyes unblinking. Her shoulders back, her hands at her side. Submissive to the stroke of their fingers on her face. Unflinching in the cause of missionary work.

Papa asks forgiveness for the death of Turtle Heart, maybe some five years earlier. He says it is his fault. He and his wife had both fallen in love with the Quadling glassblower. What can I give you to make up for it, he says. Elphaba the girl thinks he is mad, she thinks they are not listening, they are mesmerized by her weirdness. Please forgive me, he says.

The matriarch alone responds to these words; maybe she is the only one who actually remembers Turtle Heart. She has a look of someone caught venturing out from beneath a rock. Well, in a people whose moral code is so lax, so little is *wrong*. For her this encounter is a mysterious, complicated transaction.

She says something like, We don't shrive, we don't shrive, and not for Turtle Heart, no, and she strikes Papa on the face with a reed, cutting him with thin stripes. I was only a witness, I was not really alive then, but I saw: This was when Papa began to lose his way, it dates from this whipping.

I see him shocked: It doesn't occur in his conception of moral life that some sins are unforgivable. He blanches, onion white behind the blood-pearled perforations of her attack. Maybe she has every right to do what she's done, but in Papa's life she's become old Kumbricia.

I see her, willful, proud: *Her* moral system doesn't allow for forgiveness, and she is just as incarcerated as he, but she doesn't know it. She grins, all gums and menace, and rests the reed on her collarbone, where its fletching tip falls like a necklace around her own neck.

He points to me, and says—not to me, but to them all—Isn't this punishment enough?

Elphaba the girl does not know how to see her father as a broken man. All she knows is that he passes his brokenness on to her. Daily his habits of loathing and self-loathing cripple her. Daily she loves him back because she knows no other way.

I see myself there: the girl witness, wide-eyed as Dorothy. Staring at a world too horrible to comprehend, believing—by dint of ignorance and innocence—that beneath this unbreakable contract of guilt and blame there is always an older contract that may bind and release in a more salutary way. A more ancient precedent of ransom, that we may not always be tormented by our shame. Neither Dorothy nor young Elphaba can speak of this, but the belief of it is in both our faces . . .

The Witch had taken the green glass bottle, whose label still read MIRA-CLE ELI-, and placed it on her bedside table. She took a spoonful of the ancient elixir before sleeping, hoping for miracles, seeking some version of the fabulous alibi Dorothy was unwinding, that she had come from a country somehow *other*—not the real states across the desert, but a whole separate geophysical existence. Even metaphysical. The Wizard made such a claim for himself, and if the dwarf was right, the Witch had this ancestry too. At night she tried to train herself to look on the periphery of her dreams, to note the details. It was a little like trying to see around the edges of a mirror, but, she found, more rewarding.

But what did she get? Everything flickered, like a guttering candle but more harshly, more stridently. People moved in short, jerky motions. They were colorless, they were vapid, they were drugged, they were manic. Buildings were high and cruel. Winds were strong. The Wizard stepped in and out of these pictures, a very humble-looking man in this context. In one window, in a shop from which the Wizard was emerging rather dejectedly, she thought, she caught some words once, and willed herself with tremendous effort to wake up so she could write them down. But they didn't make any sense to her. NO IRISH NEED APPLY.

Then one night she had a nightmare. Again the Wizard began it. He walked over some hills of sand, with tall gray grasses blowing in a fierce gale—a thousand thousand grasses like the scratchy sedge with which the old Quadling matriarch had struck Frex—and the Wizard stopped along a broad flat stretch. He stepped out of his clothes, and looked at a timepiece in his hands, as if memorizing an historic instant. Then he walked forward, naked and broken. When the Witch realized what he was approaching, she tried to back out of the dream with a howl, but could not manage to disengage herself. This was the mythical ocean, and the Wizard walked into water up to his knees, his thighs, his waist; he paused and shivered, and slopped water over the rest of himself as a kind of penance. Then he kept walking, and disappeared entirely into the sea, as Saint Aelphaba of the Waterfall had disappeared behind her watery veil. The sea rocked like an earthquake, vomiting against the sandy shore, pounding in a kettledrum commotion. There was no Other Side to it. It threw the Wizard back, again and again, though again and again he forged in, more and more exhausted. The stoicism, the determination: no wonder he had managed to overcome a nation. The dream ended with him washed back on shore one last time, weeping with frustration.

She woke, gagging, terrified beyond telling, salt in her nostrils. Thereafter she avoided the miracle elixir. Instead, she concocted a potion derived both from Nanny's recipe book and the Grimmerie's marginalia, on how to keep awake. If she fell asleep again, she would be prey to that vision of earthly destruction, and she would rather die.

Nanny didn't have very much to say about nightmares. "Your mother had them too," she remarked at last. "She used to say she saw the unknown city of anger in her dreams. She was so enraged over how you turned out, you know—I mean physically, dear, don't look like that at me: a green girl isn't easy for any mother to explain away—that she gulped down those pills like candy when Nessarose was expected. If Nessarose were still around to take up a grudge, she could blame you, in a way, for what happened to her."

"But where did you get that green bottle?" said the Witch into Nanny's good ear. "Look at it, Nanny dear, and try to remember."

"I suspect I bought it at a jumble sale," she said. "I could stretch a penny, believe me."

You could stretch the truth even further, thought the Witch. She suppressed a desire to smash the green glass. How deeply bound by cords of family anger we all are, thought the Witch. None of us breaks free.

12

One afternoon a few weeks later, Liir came back from a ramble all hot and bothered. The Witch hated to hear that he had been hob-nobbing again with the Wizard's soldiers down in Red Windmill.

"They had news, a dispatch from the Emerald City," he said. "A delegation of strangers got in to see the Wizard. And just a girl! Dorothy, they said, a girl from the Other Land. And some friends. The Wizard hasn't allowed an audience with his subjects in years—he works through ministers, they say. A lot of soldiers think he died long ago, and it's a Palace plot to safeguard the peace. But Dorothy and her friends got in, and they saw him, and told everyone what it was like!"

"Well well," said the Witch. "Imagine that. All of Oz, Loyal and Otherwise, is yapping about this Dorothy. What did the fools say next?"

"The dispatch soldier said that the guests asked the Wizard to grant them some wishes. The Scarecrow asked for a brain, Nick Chopper the Tin Woodman asked for a heart, and the Cowardly Lion asked for courage."

"And I suppose Dorothy asked for a shoe horn?"

"Dorothy asked to be sent home."

"I hope she gets her wish. And?"

But Liir got coy.

"Oh come on, I'm too old to be put off my supper by gossip," she snapped.

Liir looked flushed with guilty pleasure. "The soldiers said that the Wizard had rejected the odd requests."

"And you're so very surprised?"

"The Wizard told Dorothy that he would grant them their wishes—when they had—when they had—"

"You haven't stuttered in years. Don't start again, or I'll beat you."

"Dorothy and his friends have to come here and kill you," he finished. "The soldiers said it's because you murdered an old lady in Shiz, a famous old lady, and you're an assassin. Also you're crazy, they said."

"I'm a more likely murderer than those incompetent vagabonds could be," she said. "He was just trying to get rid of them. Probably he's instructed his own Gale Forcers to slit the girl's throat as soon as she's safely out of the limelight." And no doubt the Wizard had confiscated the shoes. It galled her. But how flattered she felt that the news of her attack had gotten out. By now she was sure she *had* killed Madame Morrible. It only made sense that she had.

But Liir shook his head. "The funny thing," he said, "is that Dorothy is called Dorothy *Gale*. The soldiers at Red Windmill said the Gale Forcers wouldn't touch her, they're too superstitious."

"What do these soldiers know of intrigue, stationed here out at the edge of the moon?"

Liir shrugged. "Aren't you impressed that the Wizard of Oz even knows who you are? Are you a murderer?"

"Oh Liir, you'll understand when you're older. Or anyway not understanding will become second nature, and it won't matter. I wouldn't harm *you*, if that's what you mean. But you sound so surprised that I should be known in the Emerald City. Just because you disobey me and treat me like refuse, do you think the whole world does?" Yet she was pleased. "But you know, Liir, if there's even the slightest chance that there's any truth to these rumors, you had better stay away from Red Windmill for a while. They might kidnap you and hold you for ransom until I give myself up to this schoolgirl and her needy companions."

"I want to meet Dorothy," he said.

"You're not that age already, please preserve us," she said. "I always intended to pickle you before you got to puberty."

"Well, I'm not getting kidnapped, so don't worry," he said. "Besides, I want to be here when they get here."

"Worry is the last thing I'd do if you got kidnapped," she answered. "It'd be your own damn fault, and a great relief to me to have one less mouth to feed."

"Oh well, then who'd carry the firewood up all those stairs every winter?"

"I'll hire that Nick Chopper fellow. His axe looks pretty sharp to me."

"You've seen him?" Liir's mouth dropped open. "No, you haven't!"

"I have, as a matter of fact," she said. "Who says I don't travel in the best circles?"

"What's she like?" he said, his face eager and bright. "You must have seen Dorothy too. What's she like, Auntie Witch?"

"Don't you Auntie me, you know that makes me sick."

He pestered without stopping until finally she had to screech at him. "She's a beautiful little dolt who believes everything everybody says to her! And if she gets here and you tell her you love her, she'll probably believe you! Now get out of here, I have work to do!"

He lingered at the door, and said, "The Lion wants courage, the Tin

Man a heart, and the Scarecrow brains. Dorothy wants to go home. What do you want?"

"A little peace and quiet."

"No, really."

She couldn't say *forgiveness*, not to Liir. She started to say "a soldier," to make fun of his mooning affections over the guys in uniform. But realizing even as she said it that he would be hurt, she caught herself halfway, and in the end what came out of her mouth surprised them both. She said, "A soul—"

He blinked at her.

"And you?" she said in a quieter voice. "What do you want Liir, if the Wizard could give you anything?"

"A father," he answered.

13

She wondered, briefly, if she was going insane. That night she sat up in a chair and thought about what she had said.

A person who doesn't believe in the Unnamed God, or anything else, can't believe in a soul.

If you could take the skewers of religion, those that riddle your frame, make you aware every time you move—if you could withdraw the scimitars of religion from your mental and moral systems—could you even stand? Or do you need religion as, say, the hippos in the Grasslands need the poisonous little parasites within them, to help them digest fiber and pulp? The history of peoples who have shucked off religion isn't an especially persuasive argument for living without it. Is religion itself—that tired and ironic phrase—the necessary evil?

The idea of religion worked for Nessarose, it worked for Frex. There may be no real city in the clouds, but dreaming of it can enliven the spirit.

Perhaps in our age's generous attempt at unionism, allowing all devotional urges life and breath under the canopy of the Unnamed God, perhaps we have sealed our own doom. Perhaps it's time to name the Unnamed God, even feebly and in our own wicked image, that we may at least survive under the illusion of an authority that *could* care for us.

For whittle away from the Unnamed God anything approximating character, and what have you got? A big hollow wind. And wind may have gale force but it may not have moral force; and a voice in a whirl-wind is a carnival barker's trick.

More appealing—she now saw, for once—the old-timers' notions of paganism. Lurlina in her fairy chariot, hovering just out of sight in the clouds, ready to swoop down some millennium or other and remember who we are. The Unnamed God, by virtue of its anonymity, can't ever be suspected of a surprise visit.

And would we recognize the Unnamed God if it knocked on our doors?

14

Sometimes she napped, against her will, her chin sagging on her chest, sometimes driving right down to the tabletop, jarring her teeth and rattling her jaw, and startling herself awake.

She had taken to standing at the window, looking down in the val-ley. It would be weeks before Dorothy and her band arrived, if indeed they hadn't already been murdered and their corpses burned, just as Sarima's must have been.

One night Liir came back from a visit to the barracks. He was teary and inarticulate, and she tried not to care about it, but was too curious to let it go. Finally he told her. One of the soldiers had proposed to his fel-lows that when Dorothy and friends arrive, the friends be killed and Dorothy be tied up for a little amusement among the lonely, randy men.

"Oh, men will have their fantasies," said the Witch, but she was troubled.

What had made Liir cry was that his friends had reported the sol-dier's remarks to their superior. The soldier had been stripped and cas-trated, and nailed to the windmill. His body rotated in circles as the vul-tures came and tried to peck at his entrails. He still wasn't even dead.

"It isn't hard to find evil in this world," said the Witch. "Evil is always more easily imagined than good, somehow." But she was struck at the vehemence of the Commander's response against one of his own. So Dorothy might well be alive still, and was apparently under orders of pro-tection from the highest military offices in the land.

Liir held Chistery in his lap and sobbed onto his scalp. Chistery said, "Well, we'll wail while woe'll wheel," and he cried along with Liir.

"Aren't they the sweet pair," observed Nanny. "Wouldn't that make the sweetest painting?"

Under cover of darkness the Witch slipped away on her broom, and saw to it that the suffering soldier died at once.

She thought one afternoon, inexplicably, of the baby lion cub taken from its mother, and pressed into service in Doctor Nikidik's lab back in Shiz. She remembered how it had cowered, she remembered the fuss she had made about it. Or was she only glorifying herself in hindsight?

If it was the same Lion, grown up timid and unnatural, it should have no bone to pick with her. She had saved it when it was young. Hadn't she?

They confused her, this band of Yellow Brick Road Irregulars. The Tin Woodman was hollow, a tiktok cipher, or an eviscerated human under a spell. The Lion was a perversion of its own natural instincts. She could deal with tiktok clockworks, she could handle Animals. But it was the Scarecrow she feared. Was it a spell? Was it a mask? Was there merely some clever dancer inside? All three of them were emasculated in some way or other, deluded under the spell of the girl's innocence.

She could give the Lion a history, and think of him as that abused cub in a Shiz science hall. She suspected that Nick Chopper was the victim of her own sister's spite and magic, casualty of the enchanted axe. But she had no way to place the Scarecrow.

She began to think that behind that painted cornmeal sack of a face, there was a face she would know, a face she had been waiting for.

She lit a candle and said the words aloud, as if she really could do spells. The words blew aside the taper of grayish smoke that rose from the fatty tallow. If they had any other effect in the world than that, she didn't know it yet. "Fiyero didn't die," she said. "He was imprisoned, and he has escaped. He is coming home to Kiamo Ko, he is coming home to me, and he is disguised as a scarecrow because he doesn't yet know what he will find."

It would take brains to think up such a plan.

She took an old tunic of Fiyero's. She called elderly Killyjoy and bade him sniff it well, and sent him down into the valley every day, so that if the travelers showed up, Killyjoy would be able to find them, and lead them home rejoicing.

And though she tried not to sleep, on occasion she could not help it; her dreams brought Fiyero closer and closer to home.

15

There was a day, in the first gusts of autumn, that the banners and standards of the camp below were shifted and bugles blew tinnily up the slopes to the castle. By this the Witch guessed that the troupe had arrived in Red Windmill, and were being given a royal welcome. "They've come so far, they won't wait now," she said. "Go, Killyjoy, go find them and show them the quickest way here."

She loosed the senior dog, and so strong were his exhortations that the entire pack of his kin went racing along with him, howling with joy and frantic to do their duty.

"Nanny," cried the Witch, "put on a clean petticoat and change your apron, we'll have company by nightfall!"

But the dogs didn't come back, all afternoon and into the gloaming, and the Witch could see why. With a telescopic eye in a cylindrical casing—invented by the Witch along the lines of Doctor Dillamond's discovery about opposing lenses—she followed a shock of carnage. Dorothy and the Lion trembled with the Scarecrow beyond while the Tin Woodman struck the heads of her beasts one after the other with his axe. Killyjoy and his wolfy relations lay scattered like dead soldiers on a field of retreat.

The Witch danced with rage, and summoned Liir. "Your dog is dead, look what they did!" she cried. "Look and make sure that I didn't only imagine it!"

"Well, I didn't like that dog very much anymore," said Liir. "He had a good long life, anyway." He concurred, tremblingly, but then trained the glass on the slope again.

"You fool, that Dorothy is not for messing with!" she cried, slapping the instrument out of his hand.

"You're awfully on edge for someone about to have company," he said sullenly.

"They are supposed to be coming to kill me, if you remember," she said, although she had forgotten that, as she had forgotten her desire for the shoes until she saw them again in the glass. The Wizard had *not* demanded them of Dorothy! Why not? What fresh campaign of intrigue was this?

She wheeled about her room, whipping pages of the Grimmerie back and forth. She recited a spell, did it wrong, did it again, and then turned and tried to apply it to the crows. Though the original three crows had long since fallen stiffly from the top of the door frame, there were plenty of others in residence still, rather inbred and silly, but suggestible in a stupid, moblike way.

"Go," she said. "Look with your eyes more closely than I can, pull the mask off the Scarecrow so we can know who he is. Get them for me. Peck out the eyes of Dorothy and the Lion. And three of you, go on ahead to the old Princess Nastoya, out there in the Thousand Year Grasslands, for the time is coming when we will be reunited, all of us. With the help of the Grimmerie, the Wizard may topple at last!"

"I never know what you're talking about anymore," said Liir. "You can't blind them!"

"Oh, watch me," snarled the Witch. The crows blew away in a black cloud and dropped like buckshot through the sky, down the jagged precipices, until they came to the travelers.

"A pretty sunset, is there?" said Nanny, coming up to the Witch's room in one of her rare forays, Chistery as always providing service.

"She's sent the crows out to blind the guests coming for dinner!"

"What?"

"She's BLINDING THE GUESTS COMING FOR DINNER!"

"Well, that's one way to avoid having to dust, I suppose."

"Will you lunatics hush up?" The Witch was twitching as if with a nervous disorder; her elbows flapped, as if she were a crow herself. She gave out a long howl when she found them in the glass.

"What, what, let me see," said Liir, grabbing the thing. He explained to Nanny, because the Witch was almost beyond speech by now. "Well, I guess the Scarecrow knows how to scare crows, all right."

"Why, what's he done?"

"They're not coming back, that's all I'll say," said Liir, glancing at the Witch.

"It still could be him," she said at last, breathing heavily. "You might get your wish yet, Liir."

"My wish?" He didn't remember asking for a father, and she didn't bother to remind him. Nothing had yet suggested to her that the Scarecrow wasn't a man in disguise. She would not need forgiveness if Fiyero had not died!

The light was failing, and the odd band of friends was making good time up the hill. They had come without an escort of soldiers, perhaps because the soldiers really believed that Kiamo Ko was run by a Wicked Witch.

"Come on, bees," said the Witch, "work with me now. All together on this one, honeys. We need a little sting, we need a little zip, we want a little nasty, can you give us a little jab? No, not us, listen when I talk to you, you simpletons! The girl on the hill below. She's after your Queen Bee! And when you're through with your job, I'll go down and collect those shoes."

"What's that old hag blathering about now?" said Nanny to Liir.

The bees were alert to the pitch in the Witch's voice, and they rose to swarm out the window.

"You watch, I can't look," said the Witch.

"The moon is just like a pretty peach rising over the mountains," said Nanny with the telescope to her old cataracted eye. "Why don't we put in some peach trees instead of all those infernal apples in the back?"

"The *bees*, Nanny. Liir, take that from her and tell me what happens."

Liir gave a blow-by-blow recounting. "They're swooping down, they look like a genie or something, all flying in a big clump with a straggly tail. The travelers see them coming. Yes! Yes! The Scarecrow is taking straw out of his chest and leggings, and covering the Lion and Dorothy, and there's a little dog, too. So the bees can't get through the straw, and the Scarecrow is all in pieces on the ground."

It couldn't be. The Witch grabbed the eyepiece. "Liir, you are a filthy liar," she shouted. Her heart roared like a wind.

But it was true. There was nothing but straw and air inside the Scarecrow's clothes. No hidden lover returning, no last hope of salvation.

And the bees, having none left to attack but the Tin Woodman, flung themselves against him, and dropped in black heaps on the ground, like charred shadows, their stingers blunted on his fenders.

"You've got to give our guests credit for ingenuity," said Liir.

"Will you shut up before I tie your tongue in a knot?" said the Witch.

"I suppose I should start down and get some hors d'oeuvres going, they'll be peckish after these ordeals you're setting them," said Nanny. "Have you an opinion as to cheese and crackers or fresh vegetables with pepper sauce?"

"I say cheese," said Liir.

"Elphaba? What's your opinion?"

But she was too busy doing research in the Grimmerie. "It's up to me, as always was the case," said Nanny. "I get to do all the work. I'm supposed to be teary with joy, at my age. You'd think I could rest my feet for once, but no. Always the bridesmaid, never the bride."

"Always the godfather, never the god," said Liir.

"Will you two please have mercy on me! Now go on, Nanny, if you're going!" Nanny headed out the door as fast as her old limbs could take her. The Witch said, "Chistery, let her go under her own steam, I need you here."

"Sure, let me tumble to my death, delighted to be of service," said Nanny. "It's going to be cheese, for that."

The Witch explained to Chistery what she wanted. "This is fool-ish. It'll be dark before long, and they'll tumble over some cliff and die. The poor dears, I'd rather not. I mean the Tin Woodman and the Scarecrow, they can tumble all they want, and not be much hurt, I imag-ine. A good tinsmith could repair a battered torso. But bring me Dorothy and the Lion. Dorothy has my shoes, and I have a rendezvous with the Lion. We're old friends. Can you do this?"

Chistery squinted, nodded, shook his head, shrugged, spat.

"Well try, what good are you if you don't try," she said. "Off with you, and your cronies with you."

She turned to Liir. "There, are you satisfied? I haven't asked them to be killed. They're being escorted here as our guests. I'll get the shoes and let them go on their way. And then I'll walk this Grimmerie into the mountains and live in a cave. You're old enough to take care of yourself. Good riddance to bad rubbish. Who needs forgiveness now? Well?"

"They're coming to kill you," he said.

"Yes, and aren't you just breathless with anticipation for that!"

"I'll protect you," he said, uneasily, and then added, "but not to the extent of harming Dorothy."

"Oh, go set the table, and tell Nanny to forget the cheese and crackers, and go with the vegetables." She shook her broom at him. "Go, I tell you, when I tell you to go!"

When she was alone, she sank in a heap. Either phenomenal luck lay with these travelers, or they had enough courage, brains, and heart among them to do quite well. She was taking the wrong approach, clearly. She should welcome the child, explain the situation nicely, and get the damned shoes while she could. With the shoes, with the help of the Princess Nastoya, maybe there would be vengeance against the Wizard yet. Anyway, the Grimmerie would be hidden. One way or the other. And the shoes removed outside the Wizard's reach.

But the shock of the death of her familiars made her blood run cold inside her. She could feel her thoughts and intentions tumbling over and over one another. And she wasn't really sure what she would do when face-to-face with Dorothy.

16

Liir and Nanny stood on either side of the doorway, smiling, when Chistery and his companions came down with an ill-judged whump, dumping their passengers onto the cobbles of the inner courtyard. The Lion moaned in pain and wept from vertigo. Dorothy sat up, clutching the small dog in her arms, and said, "And where might we be now?"

"Welcome," said Nanny, genuflecting.

"Hello," said Liir, twisting one foot around the other and falling over into a bucket of water.

"You must be tired after your long trip," said Nanny. "Would you like to freshen up some before we have a little light meal? Nothing fancy, you know, we're way off the beaten track."

"This is Kiamo Ko," said Liir, beet red and standing up again. "The stronghold of the Arjiki tribe."

"This *is* still Winkie territory?" said the girl anxiously.

"What'd she say, the little poppins, tell her to speak up," said Nanny.

"It's called the Vinkus," said Liir. "*Winkie* is a kind of insult."

"Oh goodness, I wouldn't want to offend anyone!" she said. "Mercy, no."

"Aren't you a pretty little girl, all your arms and legs in the right place, and such delicate sensible inoffensive skin," said Nanny, smiling.

"I'm Liir," he said, "and I live here. This is my castle."

"I'm Dorothy," she said, "and I'm very worried about my friends—the Tin Woodman and the Scarecrow. Oh, please, can't somebody do something for them? It's dark, and they'll be lost!"

"They can't be hurt. I'll go get them tomorrow in the daylight," said Liir. "Promise. I'd do *anything*. Really, anything."

"You're so sweet, just like everyone else here," said Dorothy. "Oh, Lion, are you all right? Was it terrible?"

"If the Unnamed God had wanted Lions to fly, he'd have given them hot-air balloons," said the Lion. "I'm afraid I lost my lunch somewhere over the ravine."

"Warm welcomes," Nanny chirped. "We've been expecting you. I've worn my fingers to the bone, making a little something. It's not much, but everything we have is yours. That's our motto here in the mountains. The traveler is always welcome. Now let's go find some hot water and soap at the pump, shall we, and then go in."

"You're too kind—but I need to find the Wicked Witch of the West," Dorothy said. "I said THE WICKED WITCH OF THE WEST. I'm so sorry to trouble you. And it looks like a perfectly wonderful castle. Perhaps on the way back, if my travels take me this way."

"Oh, well, she lives here, too," said Liir. "With me. Don't worry, she's here."

Dorothy looked a little pale. "She is?"

The Witch appeared at the doorway. "She is indeed, and here she is," she said, and came down the steps at a clip, her skirts whirling, her broom hurrying to keep up. "Well, Chistery, you did good work! I'm glad to see *all* my efforts haven't been for naught. You, Dorothy, Dorothy Gale, the one whose house had the nerve to make a crash landing on my sister!"

"Well, it wasn't my house, in a legal sense, strictly speaking," said

Dorothy, "and in fact it hardly belonged much to Auntie Em and Uncle Henry, except for maybe a couple of windows and the chimney. I mean the Mechanics and Farmers First State Bank of Wichita holds the mortgage, so they're the responsible parties. I mean if you need to be in touch with someone. They're the bank that cares," she explained.

The Witch felt suddenly, oddly calm. "It's nothing to me who owns the house," she said. "The fact is that my sister was alive before you arrived, and now she's dead."

"Oh, and I'm so very sorry about that," said Dorothy nervously. "Really I am. I'd have done anything to avoid it. I know how terrible I'd feel if a house fell on Auntie Em. Once a board in the porch roof fell on her. She had a big bump on her head and sang hymns all afternoon, but by evening she was her old cranky self."

Dorothy tucked her little dog under her arm and went up and took the Witch's hands in hers. "*Really* I'm sorry," she insisted. "It's a terrible thing to lose someone. I lost my parents when I was small, and I remember."

"Get off me," said the Witch, "I hate false sentiment. It makes my skin crawl."

But the girl held on, with a ragged sort of intensity, and said nothing, just waited.

"Let go, let go," said the Witch.

"Were you close to your sister?" asked Dorothy.

"That's not the point," she snapped.

"Because I was very close to my Mama, and when she and Papa were lost at sea, I could hardly bear it."

"Lost at sea, how do you mean," said the Witch, detaching herself from the clinging child.

"They were on their way to visit my grandmama in the old country, because she was dying, and a storm came up and their ship went over and broke in half and sank to the bottom of the sea. And they drowned, every soul onboard."

"Oh, so they had souls," said the Witch, her mind recoiling at the image of a ship in all that water.

"And still do. That's all they have left, I suspect."

"Please will you not cling so. And come in for something to eat."

"Come on, you too," said the girl to the Lion, and it sulkily rolled onto its big padded paws and followed along.

So now we turn into a restaurant, thought the Witch darkly. What, shall I send a flying monkey down to Red Windmill to engage a violinist, for mood music? What a most peculiar murderer she is turning out to be.

The Witch began to think about how she might disarm the girl. It was hard to tell what her weapons were, except for that sort of inane good sense and emotional honesty.

During dinner Dorothy began to cry.

"What, she would have preferred the vegetables to the cheese?" said Nanny.

But the girl would not answer. She set both her hands on the scrubbed oaken tabletop, and her shoulders shook with grief. Liir longed to get up and wrap his arms around her. The Witch nodded grimly that he was to stay put. He whacked his milk mug hard on the table, in annoyance.

"It's all very nice," Dorothy said at last, sniffling, "but I am so *worried* for Uncle Henry and Auntie Em. Uncle Henry frets so when I'm just a wee bit late from the schoolhouse, and Auntie Em—well, she can be so cross when she's upset!"

"All Aunties are cross," said Liir.

"Eat up, for who knows when another meal will come your way," said the Witch.

The girl tried to eat, but kept dissolving in tears. Eventually Liir began to tear up, too. The little dog, Toto, begged for scraps, which made the Witch think of her own losses. Killyjoy, who had been with her eight years, a fly-ridden corpse going stiff on the hill among all his progeny. She cared less about the bees and the crows, but Killyjoy was her special pet.

"Well, this is some party," said Nanny. "I wonder if I should have prettied things up with a candle."

"Kindle candle can dull," said Chistery.

Nanny lit a candle and sang "Happy Birthday to You," to make Dorothy feel better, but no one joined in.

Then silence fell. Only Nanny kept eating, finishing the cheese and starting on the candle. Liir was turning white and pink by turns, and Dorothy had begun to stare blankly at a knothole in the polished wood of the trestle table. The Witch scratched her fingers with her knife, and ran the blade along her forefinger softly, as if it were the feather of a pfenix.

"What's going to happen to me," said Dorothy, lapsing into a monotone. "I shouldn't have come here."

"Nanny, Liir," said the Witch, "take yourselves off to the kitchen. Bring the Lion with you."

"Is that old bag talking to me?" Nanny asked Liir. "Why's the little girl crying, our food not good enough for her?"

"I'm not leaving Dorothy's side!" said the Lion.

"Don't I know you?" said the Witch in a low, even voice. "You were the cub they did experiments with in the science lab at Shiz long ago. You were terrified then and I spoke up for you. I'll save you again if you behave."

"I don't want to be saved," said the Lion petulantly.

"I know the feeling," said the Witch. "But you can teach me something about Animals in the wild. Whether they revert, or how much. I take it you were raised in the wild. You can be of service. You can protect me when I go out of here with my Grimmerie, my book of magicks, my Malleus Maleficarum, my mesmerizing incunabulum, my codex of scarabee, fylfot and gammadion, my text thaumaturgical."

The Lion roared, so suddenly they were all jolted in their seats, even Dorothy. "Thunder at night, devil's delight," observed Nanny, glancing out the window. "I better take in the laundry."

"I'm bigger than you," said the Lion to the Witch, "and I'm not letting Dorothy alone with you."

The Witch swooped down and gathered the little dog in her arms. "Chistery, go dump this thing in the fishwell," she said. Chistery looked dubious, but scampered away with Toto under his arm like a yapping furry loaf of bread.

"Oh no, save him, someone!" said Dorothy. The Witch shot out her hand and pinned her to the table, but the Lion had catapulted into the kitchen after the snow monkey and Toto.

"Liir, lock the kitchen door," shouted the Witch. "Bar it so they can't come back."

"No, no," cried Dorothy, "I'll go with you, just don't hurt Toto! He's done nothing to you!" She turned to Liir, and said, "Please don't let that monkey hurt my Toto. The Lion is useless, don't trust him to save my little dog!"

"Do I take it we'll have pudding by the fire?" said Nanny, looking up brightly. "It's *caramel custard*."

The Witch took Dorothy's hand and began to lead her away. Liir suddenly leaped over and took hold of Dorothy's other hand. "You old hag, let her alone," he shouted.

"Liir, really, you pick the most awkward times to develop character," said the Witch wearily, quietly. "Don't embarrass yourself and me with this charade of courage."

"I'll be all right—just take care of Toto," said Dorothy. "Oh Liir, take care of Toto, no matter what—please. He needs a home."

Liir leaned over and kissed Dorothy, who fell against the wall in astonishment.

"Release me," mumbled the Witch. "Whatever my faults, I don't deserve this."

17

She pushed Dorothy ahead of her into the tower room, and locked the door behind her. The long period of sleeplessness was making her head spin. "What have you come for," she said to the girl. "I know why you have tramped all the way from the Emerald City—but go on, tell me to my face! Have you come to murder me, as the rumors say—or do you carry a message from the Wizard, maybe? Is he now willing to bargain the book for Nor? The magic for the child? Tell me! Or—I know—he has instructed you to steal my book! Is it that!"

But the girl only backed away, looking left and right, for an escape. There was no way out except the window, and that was a deadly fall.

"Tell me," said the Witch.

"I am all alone in a strange land, don't make me do this," said the girl.

"You came to kill me and then to steal the Grimmerie!"

"I don't know what you're talking about!"

"First give me the shoes," said the Witch, "for they're mine. Then we'll talk."

"I can't, they won't come off," said the girl, "I think that Glinda put a spell on them. I've been trying to get them off for days. My socks are so sweaty, it's not to be believed."

"Give them me!" snarled the Witch. "If you go back to the Wizard with them, you'll be playing right into his hands!"

"No, look, they're stuck!" shouted the girl. She kicked at one heel with the other toe. "Look, see, I'm trying, I'm trying, they won't come off, honest, promise! I *tried* to give them to the Wizard when he demanded them, but they wouldn't come off! There's something the matter with them, they're too tight or something! Or maybe I'm growing."

"You have no right to those shoes," said the Witch. She circled. The girl backed away, stumbling over furniture, knocking over the beehive, and stepping on the queen bee, who had emerged from the fragments.

"Everything I have, every little thing I have, dies when you come across it," said the Witch. "There's Liir down below, ready to throw me over for the sake of a single kiss. My beasts are dead, my sister is dead, you strew death in your path, and you're just a girl! You remind me of Nor! She thought the world was magic, and look what happened to her!"

"What, what happened?" said Dorothy, pitiably playing for time.

"She found out just how *magic* it was, she was kidnapped, and lives her miserable life as a political prisoner!"

"But so have you kidnapped me, and I asked for none of it, nothing. You must have mercy."

The Witch came near and grabbed the girl by the wrist. "Why do you want to murder me," she said. "Can you really believe the Wizard will do as he says? He doesn't know what truth means, so he does not even know how he lies! And I did not *kidnap* you, you fool! You came here of your own accord, to murder me!"

"I didn't come to murder anyone," said the girl, shrinking back.

"Are you the Adept?" said the Witch suddenly. "Aha! Are you the Third Adept? Is that it? Nessarose, Glinda and you? Did Madame Morrible conscript you for service to the hidden power? You work in collusion: my sister's shoes, my friend's charm, and your innocent strength. Admit it, admit you're the Adept! Admit it!"

"I'm not adept, I'm adopted," said the girl. "I'm sure not adept at anything, can't you tell that?"

"You're my soul come scavenging for me, I can feel it," said the Witch. "I won't have it, I won't have it. I won't have a soul; with a soul there is everlastingness, and life has tortured me enough."

The Witch pulled Dorothy back to the corridor, and stuck the end of her broom in a torch fire. Nanny was hobbling up the stairs leaning on Chistery, who had some dishes of pudding on a tray. "I locked the whole lot of them in the kitchen until they stop their roughhousing," Nanny was muttering. "Such a hubbub, such a racket, such a wild rumpus, Nanny won't have it, Nanny is too old. They're all beasts."

Below, in the dusty recesses of Kiamo Ko, the dog barked once or twice, the Lion roared and pounded against the kitchen door, and Liir shrieked, "Dorothy, we're coming!" But the Witch turned and shot out her foot, and toppled Nanny over. The old woman rolled and slid, *oohing* and *woohing*, down the stairs, Chistery chasing after her in consternation. The kitchen door had burst its hinges, and the Lion and Liir came tumbling out, falling over the big heap of Nanny at the foot of the stairs. "Up, you, up," shouted the Witch, "I'll have done with you before you have done with me!"

Dorothy had wrenched herself free and dashed up the corkscrew stairs of the tower ahead of the Witch. There was only one exit, and that was to the parapet. The Witch followed in good speed, needing to finish the deed before the Lion and Liir arrived. She would get the shoes, she would take the Grimmerie, she would abandon Liir and Nor, and disappear into the wilderness. She would burn the book and the shoes, and then she would bury herself.

Dorothy was a dark shape, huddled over, retching on the stones.

"You haven't answered my question," said the Witch, poking the torch up high, releasing spectres and ghosts among the shadows of the castellations. "You've come hunting me down, and I want to know. Why will you murder me?"

The Witch slammed the door behind her and locked it. All the better.

The girl could only gasp.

"You think they're not telling stories about you all over Oz? You think I don't know the Wizard sent you here to bring back proof that I was dead?"

"Oh, that," said Dorothy, "that is true, but that's not why I came!"

"You can't possibly be a competent liar, not with that face!" The Witch held the broom up at an angle. "Tell me the truth, and when you've finished, then I'll kill you, for in times like these, my little one, you must kill before you are killed."

"I couldn't kill you," said the girl, weeping. "I was horror-struck to have killed your sister. How could I kill you too?"

"Very charming," said the Witch, "very nice, very touching. Then why did you come here?"

"Yes, the Wizard said to murder you," Dorothy said, "but I *never* intended to, and that's not why I came!"

The Witch held the burning broom even higher, closer, to look in the girl's face.

"When they said . . . when they said that it was your sister, and that we had to come here . . . it was like a prison sentence, and I never wanted to . . . but I thought, well, I *would* come, and my friends would come with me to help . . . and I would come . . . and I would say . . ."

"Say what," cried the Witch, on the edge.

"I would say," said the girl, straightening up, gritting her teeth, "I would say to you: Would you ever forgive me for that accident, for the death of your sister; would you ever ever forgive me, for I could never forgive myself!"

The Witch shrieked, in panic, in disbelief. That even now the world should twist so, offending her once again: Elphaba, who had endured Sarima's refusal to forgive, now begged by a gibbering child for the same mercy always denied her? How could you give such a thing out of your own hollowness?

She was caught, twisting, trying, full of will, but toward what? A fragment of the brush of the broom fluttered off, and lit on her skirt, and there was a run of flames in her lap, eating up the dryest tinder in the Vinkus. "Oh, will this nightmare never *end*," screamed Dorothy, and she grabbed at a bucket for collecting rainwater that, in the sudden flare-up of light, had come into view. She said, "I will save you!" and she hurled the water at the Witch.

An instant of sharp pain before the numbness. The world was floods above and fire below. If there was such a thing as a soul, the soul had gambled on a sort of baptism, and had it won?

The body apologizes to the soul for its errors, and the soul asks forgiveness for squatting in the body without invitation.

A ring of expectant faces before the light dims; they move in the shadows like ghouls. There is Mama, playing with her hair; there is Nessarose, stern and bleached as weathered timber. There is Papa, lost in his reflections, looking for himself in the faces of the suspicious heathen. There is Shell, not quite yet himself despite his apparent wholeness.

They become others; they become Nanny in her prime, tart and officious; and Ama Clutch and Ama Vimp and the other Amas, lumped together now in a maternal blur. They become Boq, sweet and lithe and earnest, as yet unbowed; and Crope and Tibbett in their funny, campy anxiety to be liked; and Avaric in his superiority. And Glinda in her gowns, waiting to be good enough to deserve what she gets.

And the ones whose stories are over: Manek and Madame Morrible and Doctor Dillamond and most of all Fiyero, whose blue diamonds are the blues of water and of sulfurous fire both. And the ones whose stories are curiously unfinished—was it to be like this?—the Princess Nastoya of the Scrow, whose help could not arrive in time; and Liir, the mysterious foundling boy, pushing out of his pea pod. Sarima, who in her loving welcome and sisterliness would not forgive, and Sarima's sisters and children and future and past . . .

And the ones who fell to the Wizard, including Killyjoy and the other resident creatures; and behind them the Wizard himself, a failure until he exiled himself from his own land; and behind him Yackle, whoever she was, if anyone, and the anonymous Adepts, if they existed, and the dwarf, who had no name to share.

And the creatures of makeshift lives, the hobbled together, the disenfranchised, and the abused: the Lion, the Scarecrow, the maimed Tin Woodman. Up from the shadows for an instant, up into the light; then back.

The Goddess of Gifts the last, reaching in among flames and water, cradling her, crooning something, but the words remain unclear.

18

Oz stretched out from Kiamo Ko a good several hundred miles to the west and north, and even farther to the east and south. On the night the Wicked Witch of the West died, anyone with the eyes to see so well could have looked out from the parapet. Westward, the moon was rising over the Thousand Year Grasslands. Though the peaceful Yunamata refused to join them, the Arjiki clans and the Scrow were meeting to consider a pact of alliance, given the Wizard's armies massing up in Kumbricia's Pass. The Arjiki chieftain and the Princess Nastoya agreed to send a delegation to the Witch of the West, and ask for guidance and support. As they toasted her and wished her well, not an hour after her death, the messenger crows Elphaba had dispatched for help were swooped upon by nocturnal rocs and devoured.

The moon ran silver up and down the sides of the Great Kells, and silver shadows settled in the valleys of the Lesser Kells. The scorpions of the Sour Sands came out to sting, the skark of the Thursk Desert mated in their nests. At the Kvon Altar practitioners of a sect so obscure that it had no name made their nightly oblations for the souls of the dead, assuming, as most do, that the dead had had souls.

The Quadling Country, a wasteland of mud and frogs, rotted quietly all night, except for an incident in Qhoyre. A Crocodile entered a nursery and chewed up a small baby. The Animal was destroyed, and both corpses were burned, with loud wailing and anger.

In Gillikin, the banks turned over their money to keep it fresh and vibrant, the factories turned over their wares, the merchants turned over their wives, the students in Shiz turned over intellectual propositions, and the tiktok labor force met secretly, in what had used to be the Philosophy Club, to hear the freed and grieving Grommetik talk class revolution. Lady Glinda had a bad night, a night of shakes and regret and pain; she guessed it was the early signs of gout from her rich diet. But she sat up half the night and lit a candle in a window, for reasons she couldn't articulate. The moon passed overhead in its path from the Vinkus, and she felt its accusatory spotlight, and moved back from the tall windows.

Across the low ridge of hills known as the Madeleines, into the Corn Basket, looking into the windows of Colwen Grounds, the moon continued its journey. Frex was asleep, dreaming of Turtle Heart and yes, of Melena, his beautiful Melena, making him breakfast on the day he went in to preach against the evil clock. Melena was a froth of beauty, huge as a world, spinning him courage, daring, love. Frex hardly stirred when Shell tiptoed in, back from some clandestine rendezvous, and came to sit by the side of his bed. Shell wasn't sure he noticed, he wasn't sure his father really woke up. "What I never could understand was the teeth," mumbled Frex, "why the teeth?"

"Who knows why?" said Shell fondly, not understanding the dreamy murmur.

The moon on the Emerald City? It couldn't be seen; lights too bright, energy too high, spirits too wired. No one looked for it. In a room, surprisingly bare and simple for one so powerful and elevated, the sleepless Wizard of Oz wiped his brow, and wondered how long his luck would hold out. He had been wondering the same thing for forty years, and he had hoped that luck would begin to seem habitual, deserved. But he could hear the very mice chewing away at the foundations of his Palace. The arrival of that Dorothy Gale, from Kansas, was a summons, he knew it; he knew it when he saw her face. There was no point in searching after the Grimmerie any longer. His avenging angel had come to call him home. A suicide was waiting for him back in his own world, and by now he ought to have learned enough to get through it successfully.

He had sent Dorothy, locked in those shoes as she was, to kill the Witch. He had sent a girl in to do a man's job. If the Witch was the victor—well, that was the troublesome girl out of the way, then. Perversely, though, in a fatherly way, he half hoped Dorothy would get through her trials all right.

It became a celebrated event, the death of the Wicked Witch of the West. It was hailed as political assassination or a juicy murder. Dorothy's description of what had happened was deemed self-delusion, at best, or a bald-faced lie. Murder or mercy killing or accident, in an indirect way it helped rid the country of its dictator.

Dorothy, more stunned than ever, made her way back to the Emerald City with the Lion, the Tin Woodman, the Scarecrow, and Liir. There Dorothy had her second famous audience with the Wizard. Perhaps he again tried to pry the slippers off her for his own purposes, and perhaps Dorothy outwitted him, spurred by the Witch's warnings. At any rate, she presented him with something from the Witch's house to prove that she *had* been there. The broom had been burnt beyond recognition, and the Grimmerie had seemed too cumbersome to carry, so she brought the green glass bottle that said MIRACLE ELI- on the paper glued to the front.

It may merely be apocryphal that when the Wizard saw the glass bottle he gasped, and clutched his heart. The story is told in so many ways, depending on who is doing the telling, and what needs to be heard at the time. It is a matter of history, however, that shortly thereafter, the Wizard absconded from the Palace. He left in the way he had first arrived—a hot-air balloon—just a few hours before seditious ministers were to lead a Palace revolt and to hold an execution without trial.

A lot of nonsense has been circulated about how Dorothy left Oz. There are some who say that she never did; they say as they said of Ozma before her that she is in hiding, in disguise, patient as a maiden, waiting to come back and show herself again. Others insist she flew up into the sky like a saint ascending to the Other Land, waving her apron giddily and clutching that damn fool dog.

Liir disappeared into the sea of humanity in the Emerald City, to hunt for his half-sister, Nor. He was not heard of again for some time.

Whatever may have happened to the original shoes, everyone remembered them as beautiful, even stunning. Well-fashioned name-brand imitations were always available and never went out of style for very long. The shoes or their replicas, with their suggestion of residual magic, cropped up at so many public ceremonies that, like the relics of saints, they began to multiply to fill the need.

And of the Witch? In the life of a Witch, there is no *after*, in the *ever after* of a Witch, there is no *happily*; in the story of a Witch, there is no afterword. Of that part that is beyond the life story, beyond the story of the life, there is—alas, or perhaps thank mercy—no telling. She was dead, dead and gone, and all that was left of her was the carapace of her reputation for malice.

"And there the wicked old Witch stayed for a good long time."

"And did she ever come out?"

"Not yet."

Son of a Witch

SON

OF A

WITCH

A NOVEL

Gregory Maguire

wm

WILLIAM MORROW
An Imprint of HarperCollins*Publishers*

L. FRANK BAUM's second Oz novel, *The Marvelous Land of Oz* (1904), was dedicated to the actors David C. Montgomery and Fred A. Stone, who performed the roles of the Tin Woodman and the Scarecrow in the first theatrical version of *The Wizard of Oz*.

In that spirit, *Son of a Witch* is dedicated to the cast and creative team of the musical *Wicked,* which opened on Broadway in October 2003—the night before Halloween.

To Winnie Holzman and Stephen Schwartz, foremost and first, for their vision; to Wayne Cilento, Susan Hilferty, Eugene Lee, Joe Mantello, Stephen Oremus, Kenneth Posner, and Marc Platt and his associates, for bringing visions to life; and, among all the capable cast, most especially to Kristin Chenoweth (*Galinda/Glinda*), Joel Grey (*The Wizard*), and Idina Menzel (*Elphaba*), for bringing life to visions.

I HAVE NO FEAR that the poetry of democratic peoples will be found timid or that it will stick too close to the earth. I am much more afraid that it . . . may finish up by describing an entirely fictitious country.

—Alexis de Tocqueville,
Democracy in America, 1835, 1840

ALL COWS were like all other cows, all tigers like all other tigers—what on earth has happened to human beings?

—Harry Mulisch,
Siegfried, 2001

Contents

Under the Jackal Moon

The House
of Saint Glinda

✦ I ✦

SO THE TALK OF RANDOM BRUTALITY wasn't just talk. At noontime they discovered the bodies of three young women, out on some mission of conversion that appeared to have gone awry. The novice maunts had been strangled by their ropes of holy beads, and their faces removed.

Her nerve being shaken at last, Oatsie Manglehand now caved in to the demands of her paying customers. She told the team drivers they'd pause only long enough to dig some shallow graves while the horses slaked their thirst. Then the caravan would press on across the scrubby flats known, for the failed farmsteads abandoned here and there, as the Disappointments.

Moving by night, at least they wouldn't make a sitting target, though they might as easily wander into trouble as sidestep it. Still, Oatsie's party was antsy. Hunker down all night and wait for horse hoofs, spears? Too hard on everyone. Oatsie consoled herself: If the caravan kept moving, she could sit forward with her eyes peeled, out of range of the carping, the second-guessing, the worrying.

With the benefit of height, therefore, Oatsie spotted the gully before anyone else did. The cloudburst at sunset had fed a small trackside rivulet that flowed around a flank of skin, water-lacquered in the new moon-light. An island, she feared, of human flesh.

I ought to turn aside before the others notice, she thought; how much more can they take? There is nothing I can do for that human soul. The digging of another trench would require an hour, minimum. An additional few moments for prayers. The project would only further agitate these clients as they obsess about their own precious mortality.

Upon the knee of the horizon balanced the head of a jackal moon, so-called because, once every generation or so, a smear of celestial flot-sam converged behind the crescent moon of early autumn. The impact was creepy, a look of a brow and a snout. As the moon rounded out over a period of weeks, the starveling would turn into a successful hunter, its cheeks bulging.

Always a fearsome sight, the jackal moon tonight spooked Oatsie Manglehand further. *Don't stop for this next casualty. Get through the Dis-appointments, deliver these paying customers to the gates of the Emerald City.* But she resisted giving in to superstition. Be scared of the real jackals, she reminded herself, not frets and nocturnal portents.

In any case, the light of the constellation alleviated some of the color blindness that sets in at night. The body was pale, almost luminous. Oat-sie might divert the Grasstrail Train and give the corpse a wide berth be-fore anyone else noticed it, but the slope of the person's shoulders, the unnatural twist of legs—the jackal moon made her read the figure too well, as too clearly human, for her to be able to turn aside.

"Nubb," she barked to her second, "rein in. We'll pull into flank for-mation up that rise. There's another fatality, there in the runoff."

Cries of alarm as the news passed back, and another mutter of mutiny: Why should they stop?—were they to bear witness to every fresh atrocity? Oatsie didn't listen. She yanked the reins of her team of horses, to halt them, and she lowered herself gingerly. She stumped, her hand on her sore hip, until she stood a few feet over the body.

Face down and genitals hidden, he appeared to have been a young man. A few scraps of fabric were still knotted about his waist, and a boot some yards distant, but he was otherwise naked, and no sign of his clothes.

Curious: no evidence of the assassins. Neither had there been about the bodies of the maunts, but that was on rockier ground, in a drier hour. Oatsie couldn't see any sign of scuffle here, and in the mud of the gulch one might have expected . . . something. The body wasn't bloody, nor decayed yet; the murder was recent. Perhaps this evening, perhaps only an hour ago.

"Nubb, let's heave him up and see if they've taken his face," she said.

"No blood," said Nubb.

"Blood may have run off in that cloudburst. Steel yourself, now."

They got on either side of the body and bit their lips. She looked at Nubb, meaning: It's only the next thing, it's not the last thing. Let's get through this, fellow.

She jerked her head in the direction of the hoist. One, two, heave.

They got him up. His head had fallen into a natural scoop in the stone, a few inches higher than where the rain had pooled. His face was intact, more or less; that is to say, it was still there, though shattered.

"How did he get here?" said Nubb. "And why didn't they scrape him?"

Oatsie just shook her head. She settled on her haunches. Her travelers had come forward and were congregating on the rise behind her; she could hear them rustling. She suspected that they had gathered stones, and were ready to kill her if she insisted on a burial.

The jackal moon rose a few notches higher, as if trying to see into the gulley. The prurience of the heavens!

"We're not going to dig another grave." That from her noisiest client, a wealthy trader from the northern Vinkus. "Not his, Oatsie Manglehand, and not yours, either. We're not doing it. We leave him unburied and alone, or we leave him unburied with your corpse for company."

"We don't need to do either," said Oatsie. She sighed. "Poor, poor soul, whoever he is. He needs no grave. He isn't dead yet."

· 2 ·

IN TIME, when the travelers had rejoined their cronies and relatives in the Emerald City—in salons, in public houses, in taverns of exchange—they heard more chatter about the hostilities they had managed to side-step. Rumor flourished. Forty, sixty, a hundred deaths resulting from the skirmishes between the Scrow and the Yunamata. Barbarians, the lot of them: They deserved to kill off each other. But not us.

Rumor could be wrong, of course, but it couldn't be uninteresting. Two hundred dead. Twice that. Mass graves, and they would be found *any day.*

But the luxury of safety came later. First, the Grasstrail Train still had to resume its snail's progress through the Disappointments. Geographical variety—the hills, mountains, dales and forests that made the rest of Oz so memorable, such a heartland—was in short supply here. Just flats, shales, more flats, grey as pulped newspapers.

The prospect was dispiriting, and the notion of having to carry an invalid with them didn't improve matters. Oatsie Manglehand's clients had paid good hard cash for her service. Some originating from as far away as Ugabu, and others having joined the group along the eastern foothills of the Great Kells, they considered their own safe travel should be Oatsie's sole concern.

Oatsie reminded them that they didn't have a vote. She'd never rep-resented that her clients would travel unencumbered by waifs and strays. Indeed, by terms of their contracts, she was free of liability should any of the travelers be murdered on the trail by a fellow passenger, a stowaway, a hitchhiker, a native. Oatsie had promised to lead the caravan as safely as she could, relying on her knowledge of the terrain and its populations. That was it. Period. To that end, she'd chosen a new route intended to avoid the current hot spots of intertribal conflict, and so far so good. Right?

The invalid was loaded aboard.

Despite her bravado, Oatsie was indeed sensitive to her clients' fears, and in a way she was glad to have the unconscious young man with them. It distracted the travelers, while he remained oblivious of their resentment.

She bedded him in the third carriage back, requisitioning from her clients the warmest of winter robes. She mounded him into a cocoon. There he languished, day and night, not so much fevered as feverless—an equally worrying condition. After a day of trying, Nubb was able to spoon a few tips of brandy between the lad's lips, and Oatsie fancied she saw his muscles relax in a new way.

She couldn't be certain of this. She was no doctor.

Of one thing she was sure, though. With his arrival, the mood of the Grasstrail Train changed. Why? Perhaps this: If the poor creature had been beaten to within an inch of his life, and lived, there might be hope for all of them. Think about it: *His face hadn't been scraped.* People relaxed. The nasal buzz of prayers around the supper campfire gave way to a quieter mood. Song returned, in time.

We'll make it. We deserve to. The privilege of life has been accorded us, see? We've been saved. Must be for a reason. Spines straightened, eyes grew bright and moist in a rapture of gratitude at the plan of the Unnamed God.

Another week and they had rounded the landmark rocks that marked their U-turn north, and they left behind them in the Disappointments the greatest threat of ambush.

In this month of Summersend, the wind flicked the strands of oakhair in the forest that grew between the lakes. Squirrels spilled nuts on the skarkskin roofs of the wagons. The air was more watery, too, though both lakes were out of sight beyond the miles of woods on either side.

As the oakhair forest thinned and they reached the Shale Shallows, the shady surround and homely walls of an old settlement solidified in the middle of walnut-colored fields. The first stone building they'd seen in six weeks. Despite its steep, aggrieved gables and pinched outbuildings, despite its battlement defenses, nothing—not even the Emerald City—could seem more welcome a sight just then.

"The Cloister of Saint Glinda," they buzzed. "How holy it appears."

The maunts who lived within were divided into ranks. Some took vows of silence and lived cloistered. Others took vows of indulgence.

They indulged in teaching, tending the sick, and operating a hostelry for those traveling between the southern Kells and the Emerald City. So the broad carved doors were swung open when the Grasstrail Train pulled up. The welcoming committee, a band of three middle-aged maunts with well-starched collars and bad teeth, stood at attention.

They greeted Oatsie with frosty politeness. They were suspicious of any unmarried woman who had found a way to live single, apart from female community. Still, they offered her the traditional wipe of the face with sweet rosefern. A fourth maunt, sequestered behind a screen, played a welcoming anthem, poorly. Harp strings snapped, and the sound of a most unmauntish oath issued forth.

The travelers didn't care. They were almost in heaven. To anticipate beds!—and a warm meal!—and wine!—and a captive audience, ready to thrill at the story of their journey!

In this last item, though, the maunts gave bad value for money. At once their attention was riveted by the invalid. They carried him into the loggia and hurried to collect a stretcher so he could be hauled upstairs to the infirmary.

The maunts were beginning to shift the fellow to private quarters when the Superior Maunt wafted by, fresh from her morning devotions. She greeted Oatsie Manglehand with the least of nods, and glanced upon the broken lad for a moment. Then she waved her hands: Remove him.

She said to Oatsie, "We know him. We know this one."

"You do?" said Oatsie.

"If my memory hasn't begun to fail me," the Superior Maunt continued, "you should know him, as well. You took him from us some years ago. Fifteen was it, twenty? At my age I don't apprehend the passage of time as I ought."

"He'd have been a child twenty years ago, an infant," said Oatsie. "I never took an infant from a mauntery."

"Perhaps not an infant. But you took him just the same. He traveled with a disagreeable novice who served for several years in the hospice. You were conveying them to the castle stronghold of the Arjikis. Kiamo Ko."

"He was with Elphaba?"

"Now you remember, I see you do."

"The Wicked Witch of the West . . ."

"As some called her." The Superior Maunt sniffed. "Not I. Her name here was Sister Saint Aelphaba, but I seldom called her anything. She was more or less under a vow of silence—her own. She needed no addressing."

"You recognize him from youth to now?" said Oatsie. "You've seen him since?"

"No. But I do not forget a face."

Oatsie raised her eyebrows.

"I have seen so few faces," explained the Superior Maunt. "We will not talk now. I must have Sister Doctor here to look the boy over."

"What *was* his name?"

The Superior Maunt vanished without answering.

By nightfall, as Oatsie's clients finished their nightcaps, the next generation of rumors was launched. The man-child was the Emperor's confessor. He was a brigand trafficking in the sex trade. He spoke in the voice of a Loon. Except for a single rib, the man-child had broken every bone in his body.

Many of the rumors were contradictory, which in the aggregate made them all more amusing.

◆ 3 ◆

IT WAS A HARD TIME. It had been a hard time, in Oz, for some time (for all time, said world-weary students). The Superior Maunt, too tired for colloquy, removed herself to her chambers and settled in a rocker. Amid trappings more severe than what her younger colleagues could tolerate, she rocked a little and thought, as coherently as she could. (It was a habit of hers, to forestall the onset of vagueness, that she review a strand of history from time to time.)

The Witch—so-called—had lived at the cloistered mauntery a decade and a half ago. One couldn't forget *that*—to the Superior Maunt's knowledge, no one else in Oz had ever been born with skin as green as new lilac leaves. But Elphaba had kept herself to herself, accepting without complaint such assignments as were meted out. She'd lived there for, what, five, six, seven years? And then, the Superior Maunt had hired Oatsie Manglehand to escort the close-lipped novice back into the civilian world. The small boy had tagged along, neither warmly included nor shooed away.

What had his name been, and where had he come from? An urchin left behind by one of the gypsy bands that scavenged for petty mushrooms among the roots of oakhair trees? The Superior Maunt couldn't remember the lad's provenance. Someone younger would know.

Elphaba had gone. Off to Kiamo Ko, there to stew in her own private penance. The Superior Maunt occasionally listened to testimonies of sin confessed by her sisters, but during her tenure as a maunt, Elphaba had never petitioned for an audience. Of this the Superior Maunt was quite sure. Though the nature of Elphaba's sins had been of great interest to the under-entertained sorority, Elphaba had never obliged.

Bit by bit—the news filtered through even to an outpost like this— the maunts learned of the slow evolution of Elphaba into a Witch, by dint of her rash behavior, her unexpected family ties. (She'd been sister to Nessarose, the Wicked Witch of the East, as some said. For the love of the Unnamed God, who could have expected *that*?)

The Superior Maunt sighed, chiding herself for the pleasure she took in remembering her contempt for those days. How she had leapt up from her prayers and clapped her hands, to hear that the long reign of the Wizard of Oz had drawn to a close at last, and the merciless old bastard disappeared into the clouds in a hot-air balloon advertising some obscure commercial tonic. Then the surprise ascendancy to the Palace throne of Lady Chuffrey, née Glinda Arduenna, of the Uplands. A sort of prime minister pro tem, until things could be sorted out. (She'd come out of nowhere, politically speaking: money to burn, and a certain sort of style, but who might have guessed the vacuum left by the Wizard's departure would suck in a society wife with a penchant for glitter gowns?)

"Not a terrible choice." The Superior Maunt began talking aloud, to keep her thoughts straight. "And I say this without need to reflect nicely on our own Saint Glinda, for whom Lady Chuffrey was probably named. Or renamed herself, *Galinda* a rural name, *Glinda* the more so-phisticated: the saint's name. Clever move." No, *Glinda,* as she became known popularly—a single name, like a house pet, like a lapdog!—Glinda managed to run an open court for a while, and much that had gone wrong, at least in that prior atmosphere of Wizardic secrecy, was corrected. There was an inoculation initiative, very thoughtful. Some schools for millworker girls, of all things. Good programs—expensive to run, though. It had seemed generous and intelligent from the perspective of a cloistered spinster—but what kind of perspective was that?

Then Glinda had stepped aside. Ever the dilettante, she'd grown bored with governing, people assumed, and had taken up collecting miniature furniture with a vengeance. Well, to be fair, maybe she'd been pushed out. For a while a puppet government replaced her. A right dolt, calling himself a Scarecrow. Rumors had flown that he was no real Scarecrow, that he wasn't even the Scarecrow associated with the Visitor: Dorothy. He was just some out-of-work bum dressed up to fool the masses. Being paid every weekend at the back door, probably—but by whom? Glinda's people? Her thwarters? The banker barons of industrial Gillikin? Who knew? In due course he was booted out by the latest nuisance, the next hollow man, reeking with glory: the sacred Emperor.

The long years since Elphaba had driven her wild broom across the sky had been quiet—on the surface. Certain atrocities had ceased, and that was good. Other atrocities replaced them. Certain diseases subsided, others had taken grip. Now something was agitating the Scrow and the Yunamata in the West, something so fierce that agents from one or both of the tribes were striking out at neutral parties.

Like the junior maunts sent out on a mission by the toadies helming the motherchapel in the Emerald City. Those sycophantic biddies! They'd cluck themselves to death if their Emperor asked it. Their emis-saries, those innocent young things, had stopped here at the Cloister of Saint Glinda for nourishment and cheer. Where were their faces now, wondered the Superior Maunt. She hoped she'd never see them again, neither in her dreams nor in a parcel in the delivery of post.

She was drifting off to sleep in her rocker. She arose, groaning at the pain in her joints, and tried to pull her shutters tight. One of them stuck and had to stay as it was. She'd meant to have it seen to this afternoon, but with the arrival of the caravan, she'd forgotten.

She visited the toilet reserved for her private use, and dressed in her rough gown for the night. When she settled herself on her horsehair mattress, she hoped she would drift off quickly. It had been a taxing day.

The jackal moon looked in her window at her. The Superior Maunt turned her head so as not to meet its eye, a folk custom with which she'd been raised seven, eight decades earlier, and never shaken.

Her mind went briefly to those days in the Pertha Hills of Gillikin, days sharper and more wonderful in memory than what she could apprehend of current life. The taste of pearlfruit leaves! The water on her father's wagon roof when the rains came. The rains came so much more often in her youth. The snow smelled of things. Everything smelled. Wonderfully or not, it was wonderful that they smelled. Now her nose hardly worked at all.

She said a prayer or two.

Liir. That was his name. Liir.

She prayed to remember it when the time came for her to wake up.

◆ 4 ◆

THE NEXT MORNING, before Oatsie Manglehand gathered her band together for the final push to the Emerald City, she took Nubb to a small plain parlor. There they met with the Superior Maunt, Sister Doctor, and Sister Apothecaire.

When the Superior Maunt sat down, the others sat. Since she abstained from morning tea, the others abstained.

"If we are to help this boy, we must share what we know," began the Superior Maunt. "I've picked up all sorts of hearsay. A report from Sister Doctor, if you please."

Sister Doctor, a beefy woman with questionable credentials but proven expertise in diagnosis, wasn't sanguine about the prospects for the invalid. "He appears to have suffered little from exposure, so he will have been left for dead only shortly before you found him."

Oatsie didn't speak to this. She didn't want to begin by contradicting a professional woman, even if she thought Sister Doctor had to be wrong.

Sister Doctor pressed on. "He is a shattered man, quite literally. It isn't mine to guess how he came to be so wounded, but his state is like nothing I've ever seen. One of his legs is broken in multiple places; both his wrists are sprained. One of his shoulder blades is cracked. Many of his ribs. Four of his fingers. Three of the bones in his left foot. Not a single bone punctured the skin, however. And, apparently, no blood loss."

Not unless the blood ran off in the rain squall, thought Oatsie, but kept still.

Sister Doctor rubbed the back of her neck and grimaced. "I spent so much time setting bones that I could do only a cursory exam of his organs. He is breathing shallowly and with difficulty. The phlegm that runs from his nose is both yellow and bloody. This suggests respiratory troubles. Sister Apothecaire has her own notions about this—"

"To start with the question of the discharge," began Sister Apothecaire, somewhat overenthusiastically, but Sister Doctor spoke over her.

"Sister Apothecaire can speak presently. I utter no opinion about her . . . conjectures."

"The heart?" asked the Superior Maunt, overriding the old tired conflict.

"Working." Sister Doctor grunted as if in disbelief at her own answer.

"The guts?"

"The word might be *wobbly*. I suspect an imploded spleen or the like, and septic poisoning. There's a funny color in the extremities and on certain contusions that I don't care for at all."

"What color is that?" asked the Superior Maunt.

Sister Doctor pursed her lips. "Well, I'm a bit overtired. We worked all night, you know, without resting. But I should have said there's a green tinge to the bruises, ringed with a plum-yellowy margin."

"Suggestive of internal bleeding, you think . . . or a disease? Or maybe something else?"

"He may be comatose or he may be brain-dead. I have no way of knowing. Though his heart is good, his color, as I say, is not, so circulation may be failing. The lungs have been compromised severely—whether by a preexisting condition or by some aspect of his adventures I cannot venture an opinion at this time."

"To conclude—" The Superior Maunt rolled her hand in the air.

"Death by nightfall, maybe tomorrow morning," said Sister Doctor.

"We could pray for a miracle," said Nubb. Oatsie snorted.

"Sister Apothecaire will handle treatment," said Sister Doctor, making it sound as if she thought prayer would be a wiser course.

"*You* could pray for a miracle," said Sister Apothecaire to Nubb. "I have other work to do."

"Sister Apothecaire," said the Superior Maunt. "You have something to add?"

Sister Apothecaire pushed her spectacles down her nose, then removed them, huffed upon them, and wiped them clean on the hem of her apron. She was a Munchkin and exhibited the Munchkin farmwife's passion for hygiene—not a bad attribute for a person in her profession. "It's all puzzling," she agreed. "We have made him as comfortable as we could, and as the mercy of our mission requires. With tape we have bound his limbs to splints and shims. Should he live, he may regain some degree of motor function."

"What does that mean?" asked Oatsie. "Speak clearly to the ignorant. Me."

"He may be able to sit up, to use his hands, if his nerves are not shot to hell. He may be able to walk, in a fashion; that is unlikely, but as I say we aim for the stars. What is more troubling is the discharge from his membranes. The nose, most obviously, but the other orifices as well. Ears, eyes, anus, penis."

"You've had a chance to do some initial work in the laboratory," prompted the Superior Maunt.

"Indeed. Just a start. I've found nothing definitive, nothing I haven't seen before, either in my station here at the mauntery or in my prior position as Matron's Assistant at the Respite of Incurables in the Emerald City."

Sister Doctor rolled her eyes. Sister Apothecaire never lost an opportunity to publish her credentials.

"Can *you* supply us with a hypothesis?" asked the Superior Maunt.

"It would be rash to do so." Even sitting, Sister Apothecaire was shorter than her peers, so her sideways glance at her disapproving colleague required her to poke her chin up, which perhaps gave her a more combative expression than she intended. "Whoever he is, I do wonder if this lad was from high altitudes. The mucous seepage may be due to the systemic collapse of arterial function due to a sudden change in air pressure. I haven't seen such a symptom before, but the Fallows are very low ground indeed compared to the highest peaks of the Great Kells."

The way Sister Doctor murmured "mmmmm" made it plain to all what she thought of her colleague's hypothesis. She straightened her spine as if to say, hurry up; her longer spine gave her height over her colleague, which she liked to use to advantage.

The Superior Maunt intervened. "Do you agree with Sister Doctor that death is imminent?"

Sister Apothecaire sniffed. The two didn't like to agree on anything, but she couldn't help it. She nodded her head. "There may be more to learn," she added. "The longer he hangs on, the more chance I'll have to study his nature."

"You will study nothing in his nature that isn't directly related to the easing of his afflictions," said the Superior Maunt mildly.

"But Mother Maunt! It is in my charge as an apothecaire. The syndrome he dies from may afflict others in time, and this is an opportunity to learn. To turn our noses up at it is to discount revelation."

"I have delivered my opinion on the matter, and I expect it to be observed. Now, to you both: Is there anything we can do for him that we are not doing?"

"Notify the next of kin," said Sister Doctor.

The Superior Maunt nodded and rubbed her eyes. She lifted a saucer of tea to her lips now, and without hesitation the others did the same.

"I propose we get one of the sisters to play music for him, then," she concluded. "If our only contribution is to ease his death, let us do what we can."

"Preferably not the sister who was torturing the harp when we arrived yesterday," muttered Oatsie Manglehand.

"Have you anything to add, Oatsie?" said the Superior Maunt. "I mean aside from your critique of musical performance?"

"Only this," said the caravan guide. I won't bother to apologize for contradicting them, she decided. "Sister Doctor proposes that the boy would have been set upon by brigands and left to die only shortly before we found him. But the terrain out there, my friends, is flat as a rolled-out tart crust."

"I don't follow," said the Superior Maunt.

"The body had to have been lying there for longer than Sister Doctor suggests. I would have seen the marauders in retreat. There was no place for them to hide. There is no tree cover. You know how bright a night it was; I could see for miles."

"Puzzling indeed."

"Do you use magic in your ministrations?"

"Oatsie Manglehand," said the Superior Maunt tiredly, "we are a sorority of unionist maunts. Such a question." She closed her eyes and rubbed her forehead with old, bowed fingers. Over her venerable figure, Sister Doctor and Sister Apothecaire both nodded silently to Oatsie: *Yes. We do. What little we're capable of. When we need to.*

The Superior Maunt continued. "Before resting for the night, I recalled his name. The boy was named Liir. He left the mauntery with Sister Saint Aelphaba—well, Elphaba, I suppose; she never professed her vows. Do you remember the boy at all, Sister Doctor?"

"I had just arrived about the time Elphaba was setting out," said Sister Doctor. "I remember Elphaba Thropp a little. I didn't care for her. Her moods and silences seemed hostile rather than holy. Of the many urchins who are abandoned around here, however, I remember even less. Children don't interest me unless they are gravely ill. Was he gravely ill?"

"He is now," said the Superior Maunt. "And somewhere, if his mind is still able to dream, he is still a child in there, I presume."

"Very sentimental indeed, Mother Maunt," said Sister Doctor.

"I do remember him, now you give his name," said Oatsie Manglehand. "Not well, of course. In the better years I make three or four separate runs, and we're talking twelve, fifteen, eighteen years ago? I have packed more than a few children onto heaps of worldly goods, and buried some by the side of the track as well. But he was a quiet lad, unsure of himself. He shadowed Elphaba as if she were his mother. Was she his mother?"

"Oh, dubious, very dubious," said Sister Doctor.

"There is the green tone to his bruises," Sister Apothecaire reminded them.

"I blush when I'm embarrassed, Sister Apothecaire; this does not relate me to the radish," said the Superior Maunt. "Well, we'll have to ask around. Most of the older sisters who might have remembered Elphaba are dead now, and the others are in their second childhood. But Sister Cook, if she hasn't been guzzling the cooking sherry—or perhaps if she has—she will know something. She always slips food to the children loitering in the kitchen yard, and she may remember where the boy came from.

"Meanwhile"— and the good woman rose, to signal that the meeting was done—"we will do our best with Liir, whether he be witch's spawn or the reject of a gypsy mother. It hardly matters on one's deathbed from whom one has been born, does it? The world is the womb now, and the Afterlife waits for one to be born into it."

She turned rheumy eyes on Oatsie Manglehand. The wagoneer could see that the Superior Maunt was waiting, hopefully, for her own deliverance from this world and delivery unto the next. Oatsie accepted the old woman's cool hands on her forehead, knowing the gesture was intended as a blessing, a forgiveness . . . perhaps a farewell.

"The wind is high," said Oatsie Manglehand. "If we leave now and find the water level low enough at the near ford, we'll make the far bank of the Gillikin by nightfall."

"The Unnamed God speed your progress," murmured the Superior Maunt, though her eyes had shunted inward, as if already on to the next problem. Indeed, she was. Before Oatsie had finished tying the strings of her boots, she heard the Superior Maunt say to her colleagues, "Now you must help me on the stairs, ladies, for I will go to visit our invalid."

"She's a tough old bird," muttered Oatsie to Nubb.

"Let's get out of here," said Nubb. "Don't want to stay under any roofs that house a son of a witch, even if it's holy roofs."

• 5 •

THE MAUNTERY, the oldest bits of which dated back several hundred years, was conventionally arranged around a courtyard. The vernacular of austere Merthic style—flattened stone columns, bricked quoins devoid of plaster or wash—was indicative of the speed with which defensible households had needed to be raised.

Up far too many stairs, the surgery included an office crammed into a closet, where Sister Doctor kept her notes and manuals. In a storage space under some eaves, Sister Apothecaire filled oaken cabinets with her unguents and restoratives, purgatives and negatives. (Small, as many Munchkins still were, she could work upright in a space too cramped for her colleague to stand upright in, so she got the private office. Endless grousing over this.)

The surgery also gave onto two largish dormitories. The right-hand chamber served the poor and ill of the domain. The left chamber was reserved for ailing maunts. Through here, behind a stout door, loomed an odd-shaped space, the finial of a corner tower. Inside, therefore, it was a round room, with narrow slitted windows looking in three directions. The room had no true walls or ceiling, just sloping rafters that met at the top of the conical space. A bedbound patient could stare up and see how the roof planking traversed the ribs. There were bats, but they were cleaner than most of the patients, so they were let be.

It's like nothing so much as being inside a witch's hat, thought the Superior Maunt as she paused to catch her breath. Then she pushed aside the curtain and entered.

Liir—if it was he, and she was rather certain it was—was laid upon the high bed more like a corpse than an invalid. "He's been given no pillow?" asked the Superior Maunt in something of a whisper.

"The neck."

"I see." Well, there wasn't much to see, really. His braced limbs were swathed in wide strips of gauze, his chest bound, his head undressed, and that dark hair cleaned with oil and herbs. His eyes, behind slits in the bandage, were closed. The lashes were long and feathery. "He has not been torrefied, has he? You have tucked him up like a victim of burns."

"The skin needs tending for the sores, so we cannot fully immobilize him."

I suspect not, thought the Superior Maunt.

Her eyes weren't what they had been. She leaned forward and looked closely at the seams where Liir's upper and lower eyelids met.

Then she lifted his left hand and studied his nails. His skin was clammy, like the rind of a valley-skark cheese. The fingernails were crazed.

"Pull back his loincloth."

Sister Doctor and Sister Apothecaire exchanged glances and did as they were bade.

The Superior Maunt had had little reason to become an expert in the male anatomy, but she showed no sign of pleasure or revulsion. She gently shifted the member this way and that, and lifted the testicles. "I ought to have brought my reading spectacles," she murmured.

She needed help straightening up. "Very well, do him up again," she said. Her maunts obliged.

"Sister Doctor," said the Superior Maunt. "Sister Apothecaire. I will not have you loosen his bindings to show me the bruises you report. I rely on your perspicacity. However I make note here, and will do so formally in the Log of the House, that I observe no sign of greenness in his skin. I will tolerate no murmur belowstairs that we are harboring any sort of—aberration. If you have been indiscreet enough to propose such to your sisters, correct the damage at once. Is this understood?"

She didn't wait for an answer, and turned back to the body.

It was hard to take the measure of a man who displayed the flaccid composure of a corpse. No brow is noble when it is dead: It has no need to be. This lad seemed about as close to death as one could be and still harbor hope of recovery, yet the sense she had about him was neither tranquil nor restive.

He was a young man, with youth's agreeable form: That much was apparent despite the bandages. The young suffer and die, too, and sometimes it is merciful, she thought. Then she was filled with an unseemly glee and selfishness that she had lived a long odd life of her own, and it wasn't over yet. She was in better shape than this poor benighted kid.

"Mother Maunt, are you yourself?" asked Sister Doctor.

"A tremor of digestive grief, nothing more."

She couldn't put her finger on it. She turned to go. There was Sister Cook to interview next, and other pressing matters of the day. As Sister Apothecaire fussed with the bedclothes and Sister Doctor dived to confirm the pulse, the Superior Maunt sighed. "We will do our duty, and no more than our duty," she reminded them.

They stood to attention. "Yes, Mother Maunt."

Neither tranquil nor restive, she thought again: It is as if his spirit is not here. His body is not dead, but his spirit is not here. How can this be?

Blasphemy, and bad science besides, she lectured herself, and scooted away as fast as her arthritic limbs could manage.

◆ 6 ◆

THE SUPERIOR MAUNT had long since given up supervising Sister Cook. For one thing, the ancient maunt had little interest in cuisine, her stomach having been soured by too many decades of regrettable food served under bad kitchen government. Those appetites remaining to her, after all these decades, concerned feeding the spirit alone.

So, pausing at the thresholds of the mauntery's kitchens, the Superior Maunt felt a faint queasiness.

Given where the mauntery was situated—on the back route from Quadling Country—the establishment took in its share of Quadling girls deemed too plain or unruly for marriage, or too dull for the mild professions—teacher, governess, nurse. Sometimes their families reclaimed them. More often, the girls ran away, but at least they were older and better fed when they struck out on their own.

Still, while in residence, they were as a population docile enough, and they made good kitchen assistants. Looking for Sister Cook, it occurred to the Superior Maunt that a Quadling girl might sit with the convalescent upstairs.

"Sister Cook?" called the Superior Maunt, but her voice was rusty. "Sister Cook?"

There was no reply. Into the kitchens ventured the Superior Maunt. A few quiet girls worked in a sunny corner, kneading vast tough pillows of bread dough with their bare knees. The peasant practice was generally frowned upon, but the Superior Maunt passed by the novices, pretending not to notice, as she didn't feel up to delivering a chastisement.

Sister Liquor was high on a ladder, giving each purple glass bottle of savorsuckle brandy a quarter turn. She was singing to herself and swaying on her rung.

"Mercy," murmured the Superior Maunt, and kept going.

The pantry offended with the promise of lunch: bread, moldiflower root, rounds of aged skark cheese, and soft blue olives, the kind even donkeys refused to eat. It's not *that* hard to keep your mind on higher things when this is the daily fare, observed the Superior Maunt.

The outside door was open. Beyond the pantry, in the walled orchard, wands of pearlfruit trees twitched and shuddered in the wind. The Superior Maunt went through, as much to catch a breath of fresh air as to see the severe autumn colors of pearlfruit leaves, which shaded from granite pink to a hesitant periwinkle.

In the emerald grass near the well several novices sat on their aprons. They'd taken for a little outing one of the palsied biddies in a wheeled chair and kindly thrown a tartan over her lap. The ancient maunt—older even than the Superior Maunt, by the look of it, or more infirm, anyway—had pulled her shawl over her forehead, to keep the morning sun out of her eyes. Two of the novices were husking pearlfruit pods. A third was fingering some sort of instrument, a kind of zither or dulcimer with lengths of catgut strung along two axes, one set perpendicularly above the other. The effect of her plucking and slithering was more tympanic than melodic. Perhaps the thing was out of tune. Or the player untalented. Or even that it was a foreign way of making music. Still, the other novices seemed not to mind, indeed, even to take pleasure from the droning sounds.

They leaped to their feet at her approach, scattering their work in the grass. They were Quadlings, the younger three of them. "Girls, please," said the Superior Maunt. "To your tasks." Then, deferentially, "Your health, Mother."

The older maunt nodded but didn't look up. Her eyes were on the fingers of the girl playing.

"I was hoping to find Sister Cook," said the Superior Maunt.

"She's in the mushroom cellar, harvesting for a fungal soup. Shall I fetch her?" asked one of them.

"No," said the Superior Maunt, looking one to the other. "Are you all first-years?"

"Shhhh," said the crone.

The Superior Maunt did not like being shhh'd. "Are you professed, the lot of you?"

"Shhhh, he's coming."

"Mother, I have work—" said the Superior Maunt. The sister in the chair raised her wrinkled hand. She had no fingerprints, no lifelines on her right hand—no identity, no history, nothing to read, as if her hand had been burned clean of individuality through some chastening flame.

Only one old biddy had this hand. "What are you on about, Mother Yackle?" asked the Superior Maunt.

The old creature didn't answer, didn't look up, but she did crook one hobbled finger skyward. The Superior Maunt turned. All kinds of romance and lore about visitors from the sky, from sacred scripture to rabble-rousing prophecies. The sky was hard to ignore.

It wasn't the sky, though, that Mother Yackle was indicating, but one of the trees. Out of it fell a ruffling cascade, like a stack of ladies' fans sliding silkily off a credenza. A scatter of brazen feathers, red winking. A gold eye set in a pear-shaped skull.

A crimson pfenix! Male, to judge by the plumage. The species was rumored to have been nearly hunted to extinction. The last known colonies of pfenix lived in the very south of Oz, where the watery acres of marsh began at last to dry out, and a strip of jungle thought to be seven miles wide still defeated travelers to this day. This fellow—blown off course, perhaps, or deranged by disease?

The pfenix landed on the center of the musical instrument that the third girl was playing. She looked up in some alarm; she hadn't been attending anything but her music. The pfenix craned his head and fixed first one, then another golden eye on the Superior Maunt.

"If you're looking for the talented one," said the pfenix—well, the Pfenix, if he spoke—"this is the one for you. I've been watching for an hour, and she takes little notice of anything but her music."

The women said nothing. Talking Birds were not uncommon, but they rarely bothered to speak to human beings. What a specimen this Pfenix was! His rack of tail feathers fanned out laterally, like a turkey's, but a Pfenix just as easily could unfurl his close-coiled camouflage feathers, which spiked globally all about him, affording a sort of private chamber of airy, concealing, fernlike fronds. A mature male Pfenix aloft in full display could look like a shimmering globe in the air.

"Do you know the boy who has been brought here?" asked the Superior Maunt, beginning to govern her own awe.

"I don't know any boys. I don't consort with your kind at all. I am a Red Pfenix," he added, as if they might not have taken it in.

The Superior Maunt disapproved of vainglory in all its forms. She turned to the musician. "What's your name?"

The girl looked up but didn't answer. Her face was not as ruddy as some Quadlings—less red, more umber. Its shape was pleasing, proportioned along the lines of an oakhair nut: broad brow, high cheekbones, sweet swollen cheeks like a toddler's, a small but firm chin. The Superior Maunt, who did not pay much attention to the looks of her novices, was surprised.

She was too beautiful to be a natural maunt, so she must be a moron.

"She doesn't speak much," said one of the novices.

"She's been here three weeks," added the other. "Her whispered prayers are in a dialect we can't decipher. We think she cannot raise her voice."

"The Unnamed God hears anyway. Where do you come from, child?"

"Sister Cook will know," said the first novice.

"Up, girl, up," said the Superior Maunt. "You have been chosen by a Red Pfenix. You don't talk much, but you understand our tongue? Just the one I need." She offered her hand to the musician, who rose, reluctantly. The Red Pfenix nestled in the grass and set to ridding himself of lice.

"Can I send for a bowl of scented water, something? Is there a way we can offer charity to you?" said the Superior Maunt. "We don't have visits from the likes of you often. In fact, I think never."

"I'm only passing through," said the Red Pfenix. "There's a Conference farther west. But the music drew me down."

"You love music?"

"If I loved music I wouldn't have stopped. She doesn't play very well, does she? No, I don't love music; it interferes with my homing devices. I was merely curious to see an instrument like this again. The sound of her playing reminded me of a time I had seen one long ago; I'd quite forgotten. But thank you for your charity. I require nothing but a little rest."

The Red Pfenix looked at the musician, who stood shyly in her pale grey novice's skirts. "She's a puzzle, that one is," said the Red Pfenix.

"Got him!" shouted Sister Cook, coming up from behind with a snare, and indeed she had. The Red Pfenix squawked and thrashed; all the eyes in his plumage contorted. The scream was horrible. "Pfenix steaks!" said Sister Cook. "I have just the recipe!"

"Let him go," said Mother Yackle.

It was not her place to speak next, and the Superior Maunt was irritated. She knew Sister Cook was thinking: Pfenix steaks! With knobs of butter, and tarragon mustard, and small new potatoes roasted in the same pan . . .

"Let him go," said the Superior Maunt, more sternly than Mother Yackle.

"Shoot," said Sister Cook. "I spend fifteen minutes creeping up on this bird, and with my lumbago I actually manage to catch it, and you say 'Let him go'?"

"Do not question my authority."

"I merely question your sense," said Sister Cook heavily. She turned the snare over, and the Red Pfenix exploded away from the orchard, cursing.

"He was on his way to a Conference," said Mother Yackle.

"Enough," said the Superior Maunt. "Enough of this. Sister Cook, who is this novice? Where did she come from?"

Sister Cook was grinding her teeth in annoyance at the missed opportunity. "Candle," she muttered. "Left here by a gypsy cousin for safe-keeping, said he'd be back in a year. Either she'd be mauntified by then or he'd reclaim her, but I said I'd take her on. She causes no trouble because she can't gossip with the other girls, and she knows how to make a mean marrow gravy. I've had her working with Sister Sauce on the feast day roast."

"Can you spare her?"

"Can I spare a Red Pfenix is a better question, and the answer to that one is *no*."

"We don't eat Animals," said the Superior Maunt. "I know times have changed, but it's in our charter. We don't eat anything that can talk back to us, Sister Cook, and if I find you have been butchering behind my back . . ."

"I can hardly spare her," said Sister Cook, looking at the musician. "But if you make her take that unnerving domingon with her, I'll call it even."

"Domingon, is that what it is. I'd read of them, but never seen one. Come, my daughter, domingon and all." The Superior Maunt gestured, with as tender a smile as her crabbed old mouth could assume. The girl rose. She took the Superior Maunt's hand in an easy, unaffected way— the other girls snickered. Yes, she must be simple.

"I had come looking to ask you what you remembered of a novice we once housed—the strange green girl, Elphaba."

"Before my time," snapped Sister Cook, and left.

Mother Yackle scratched her nose and yawned.

The Red Pfenix was still screaming in the sky. He circled the towers of the mauntery, safe now, and recovering the ability to be affronted. He was like a clot of blood swimming above the infirmary.

"Did you say there's a boy in the house?" asked Mother Yackle. She let her shawl slip back, and raised her bleary, milk-clotted eyes toward the Superior Maunt. "Did he bring back the broom?"

· 7 ·

THE SUPERIOR MAUNT was going to need a long rest after lunch, she knew: all these stairs. A certain penance regarding the joints. But she exerted herself, and Candle lent a willing arm without being asked, which was a good sign that the girl wasn't hopelessly slow.

The sun was high enough overhead by now that the room had grown warmer and begun to sink into noon shadow. The young man lay as he had lain, twitchless, blanketed with an unnatural calm. Sister Apothecaire and Sister Doctor had brought their small chores close, so they could be nearby while they worked—Sister Apothecaire, the grinding of herbs in a mortar, and Sister Doctor the annotating of symptoms in a ledger. Sister Doctor sat on one side of the bed, Sister Apothecaire on the other.

"You know this novice?" said the Superior Maunt.

Her colleagues neither admitted familiarity, nor dissented.

"She's a garden girl with an instrument called a domingon. I have heard of these but never see one. Apparently Candle has a small talent at music. Perhaps in the long hours on watch over Liir, she will develop it. Candle, meet Sister Doctor and Sister Apothecaire. You will have seen them at table or in chapel if not elsewhere."

It was not the professional maunts' obligation to bow, but when Candle did not bow either, Sister Apothecaire, out of social anxiety, gave a lurching sort of bob that might have meant any number of things.

To the older women the Superior Maunt said, "There are matters more pressing for you to attend to than the continual observation of our new guest. I have a different assignment for you."

"Mother Maunt!" replied Sister Doctor. "Far be it from me to question your discernment. But I must remind you, in loyal obeisance of course, that while you govern the spirit of this House, I supervise the health of the individual souls within it."

"As to such treatments that may be required," began Sister Apothecaire, but the Superior Maunt held up her hand.

"I will hear no objection. Candle seems a simple soul, but she can sit here and watch the boy. She understands my instructions. If he so much as speaks, she will let someone know. She can practice her scales and perhaps grow in skill. If he is to die, let him be comforted by the peculiar drone of her instrument. This is my wish, and I have made my point."

She cupped her hands before her in an archaic, formal gesture that meant "be it thus" or, depending on the expression of the speaker, "enough out of you, you."

Nevertheless, Sister Apothecaire protested. "I'm well aware of this girl, she doesn't know enough to come in out of the rain. You are making a terrible mistake—"

"In this rare instance Sister Apothecaire is correct," said Sister Doctor. "Should any wound suppurate, or a complication develop—"

"I have other jobs for you two," said the Superior Maunt. "Your insistence at brooking my will convinces me. You two are the ones for the next job at hand."

They paused in their flailing, affronted and curious.

"I haven't yet told you what I recently learned about the three missionary novices from the Emerald City who stopped here some days ago," said the Superior Maunt. "Their small party was ambushed and they were all killed. Scraped, I'm afraid. Someone will need to find out who did the deed, and why."

She turned. "Finish your nostrums and reinforce your binding spells at once, enough to last till dinner anyway, and come with me. I shall nap briefly instead of taking a meal, and we will convene in my sectorium when the lunch prayers are concluded."

She was untrained in their profession. How did she know they'd used several illicit binding spells? This was why she was the Superior Maunt, they guessed. She didn't know medicine but she knew women.

There was nothing for them to do but obey. Walking slightly in advance of them, the Superior Maunt couldn't help but smile faintly to herself. The medical women *were* good, solid folk. They were merely curious, curious as hell, like the rest of the House. And whatever was troubling Liir, inside or out, he would recover or decline more comfortably without being smothered by the attentions of middle-aged maunts.

The Superior Maunt paused to catch her breath. Stairs were the devil. Her two colleagues respectfully froze in place while she wheezed. The willpower of women, she thought. These two, and me besides. I make the awful choice to put them in danger. If anyone can manage the task at hand, they will. Keep them safe, she prayed.

But why do I even have to put my dear sisters in jeopardy? Because my colleagues in the motherchapel dare to send young innocent missionaries into the wild—without so much as a guide. No Oatsie Manglehand for them—just faith, innocence, and courage born of stupidity. Damn the Emerald City for leaning down upon us all. Damn those— those *bath mats* in the motherhouse, for yielding to the influence of the government!

She didn't utter a private apology for the oath. She felt she'd earned the right to swear internally, now and then. When it was warranted.

◆ 8 ◆

CANDLE HARDLY GLANCED at Liir. She sat on a rush-seated chair and rubbed the calloused pads of her right fingers over the upper strings. A faint harmonic vibration buzzed in the lower strings, almost inaudible— a sensation in the air more than a sound.

The light heaved in its uncertain tides, as clouds too thin to see washed across the sky. The room chilled slightly.

Candle let her fingers wander up the frets. She was a skilled musician, more skilled even than the kitchen sisters knew—skilled, and talented besides. This domingon was missing a vital part, and couldn't peal

or chide or keen as she would like to require of it. Still, to keep her fingers alert, from the domingon's double necks Candle drew dull incomplete sentences. They had no power to comfort; this she knew. But she
would tease the lengthy imponderable sounds out into the air anyway.
She had seen the Red Pfenix in the sky. So it was her playing that had
called him down, was it? She could do it again, and more besides.

Abroad

THE DOMINGON PLAYED ON. Unheard by Liir in his state, it had its effect nonetheless.

❖   ❖   ❖

HE WAS LIVING IN THE CASTLE called Kiamo Ko at the time, but he wasn't present at the death of the Witch.

The Witch had locked him in the kitchen with Nanny and that jittery Lion. Showing surprising resourcefulness for one so dotty, Nanny had driven the handle of a one-egg iron skillet into the rotten wood of the doorjamb. Getting the idea, Liir and the Lion gouged at the hinges until the door fell heavily inward.

Chistery, the Witch's Snow Monkey, had skittered ahead of them up the stairs to the Witch's tower-top chambers. But Dorothy was already coming down, her face glutinous with tears, the badly burned broom stinking in her hands. "She's gone," sobbed the girl, and Liir's heart had gone out to her—whose wouldn't? He'd sat on the step and snaked his arm around her shoulders. He was fourteen. First attraction is awkward under any circumstances, he supposed, but this was extreme. It wasn't as if he'd ever seen people being tender. And she was a saint from the Other Land, for pity's sake.

The girl couldn't control her shock, so it took Liir a while to understand what she was blubbering about. The Witch was *gone*. His earliest memory, his bête noire, his Auntie, his jail-keeper, his sage friend—his mother, the others had said, but there'd been no proof of that, and she'd never answered the question when he'd asked her.

Dead, dead and gone, and after her own inspection, Nanny wouldn't let him up to the parapet to see. "The sight would turn the holy blind," she murmured, "so it's a good thing I'm an old sinner. And you, you're just a young fool. Forget it, Liir." She pocketed the key and began to warble in an unfamiliar mode, some dirge from her backwater childhood. "Sweet Lurlina, mother of mercy, shroud of the murdered, shawl of the missing . . ."

Nanny's pagan pieties were somehow unconvincing. But on what basis could he say that? He'd left the unionist mauntery too young to absorb any of the tenets of faith that supported the cloistered way of life. From the distance of a skeptical adolescent, unionism seemed like a thicket of contradictions. Charity to all, but intolerance toward the heathen. Poverty ennobles, but the Bishops had to be richer than everyone else. The Unnamed God made the good world, imprisoning the rebellious human being within it, and taunting humankind with tinderbox sexuality that must be guarded against at all costs.

Lurlinism was no more sensible, to judge by how Nanny spoke of it. Random episodes of mildly erotic dalliance, as Lurlina effectively wooed Oz into being. Privately he thought it was downright stupid, though, being prettier, it was also easier to remember.

Perhaps he just didn't have the feeling for faith. It seemed to be a kind of language, one whose gnarled syntax needed to be heard from birth, or it remained forever unintelligible. But he wished he had a faith now, some scrap of something: for Elphaba was dead, and to act as if the world were no more changed than if some branch of a tree had snapped off—well, it didn't seem right.

She whipped up in his mind, the first brutal memory as sudden and insistent as a bee sting. She was yelling at him. "The Wizard's soldiers kidnapped the whole family and left you behind? Because you were useless? And you followed after them anyway, and they *still* managed to elude you? *Are* you useless?" Even then he had known she was less angry at him than frightened at what had befallen the other residents of the castle while she was away. Even then he had known she was relieved he'd been spared by virtue of being insignificant. Even then he'd smarted at the rebuke of the term. Useless.

"I'll take the broom," said Liir at last. "She can be buried with it."

"I need it, to prove she's dead," said Dorothy. "What else would do?"

"I'll carry it for you then," he said.

"You're coming with me?"

He looked around. The courtyard of the castle was more silent than he'd ever seen it. The Witch's crows were dead, her wolves, her bees. The winged monkeys were huddled on top of the woodshed, paralyzed with grief. With the Arjiki villagers in the settlement of Red Windmill down the slope, or scattered in cottages on the leeward side of the mountain, Liir had had little contact.

So there was nothing to keep him in Kiamo Ko but Nanny. And old as she was, she would soon lapse into her usual fog of deafness and abstraction. In a week she would forget that the Witch had died. Besides, even in her best days she'd never known where Liir had come from. Neither had she seemed to care. So it was no hardship to leave her.

"I'm coming with you," he said. "Yes. And I'll carry the broom."

It was too late to leave now, so they busied themselves instead. Liir fed the monkeys. Dorothy tried to make a meal for Nanny, who wept and said she wasn't hungry and then ate all her portion and the Lion's besides.

After washing up, Dorothy settled cozily in the crook of the Lion's neck, as much to calm him as to take comfort herself. Liir climbed to the Witch's room and looked about. Already it was as if she had never lived there.

He thought of the Grimmerie, that perplexing book of magic. He had never been able to read it. Wherever the Witch had put it last, he let it be. No matter. No Flying Monkey would be able to gibber a spell out of it, and Nanny's eyesight was too poor to decipher its odd scrambling text. It would be too heavy to carry, anyway.

Books have their own life, he thought. Let it take care of itself.

Turning to leave, he caught sight of Elphaba's black cape. A bit worse for wear, its hems threadbare, its collar much sampled by moths. Still, it was thick, and the days would only get colder. He put it over his narrow shoulders. It was far too large for him, so he looped the ends around his forearms. He looked, he supposed, like a small silly bat with an oversize wingspan. He didn't care.

The horizon was frosted with a greenish smear, as if ranks of campfires from distant tribes had divined the news already and were burning an homage to Elphaba before the sun could set on the day of her death.

He could smell her in the collar of the cape, and he wept for the first time.

LIIR DIDN'T BOTHER to say good-bye to Chistery. Let the Witch's most beloved Flying Monkey take care of himself now. Why else had she taught him language, but so that he could keen when she was gone?

On the road, the Lion and that little yapper, Toto, lagged behind with the other two who had been waiting for Dorothy—the Scarecrow, the man of tin—both of whom gave Liir a serious case of the creeps. The wind was brutal and the streaky clouds massed to the east, and if Liir wasn't mistaken, before long rain would fall.

Dorothy asked perfunctory questions, but she was more interested in making sure they didn't lose their way. How would *he* know if they went off course, he asked her—it had been seven or eight years since he'd come from the mauntery with Elphaba, and he'd never left the neighborhood of Kiamo Ko in all the time since. Dorothy had much more recent experience of the greater landscape.

"Yes, well, those Flying Monkeys carried me the last bit," she said nervously, "and I can't claim to have had my wits about me enough to have taken note of landmarks. Still, we're going downslope, and that's got to be right."

"Everything is downslope of Kiamo Ko," Liir told her.

"I like your confidence," she said. "Tell me about yourself, then."

He suspected his memories of young childhood were like anyone else's: imprecise, suggestible, and largely devoid of emotion. He didn't recall defining moments—maybe there weren't any—but he did remember the sensation of things. The shafts of light slanting through the mullioned windows high up in the gallery, pinning silent maunts to their silent shadows on the stone floor. The smell of asparagus cream soup, a little maple syrup drizzled on top. The smell of snow in the air. Liir had been attached to Elphaba, somehow, he remembered that: he'd been allowed to play with his broken wooden ducky in the same room where she sat and spun wool.

"Was she your mother?" asked Dorothy. "I'm terribly sorry to have killed her if she was. I mean I'm sorry anyway, but more so if you were related."

The girl's directness was puzzling, and Liir wasn't used to it. The Witch had never hidden her emotions, but nor had she explained them, and in many ways living with her had been like sharing an apartment with an ill-tempered house pet.

He tried to be honest, but there was so much he didn't know. "I started out with her," he said. "How, as a toddler, I came to be among the maunts, I can't say. No one has ever told me, and the Witch wouldn't talk about it. I remember other women from those times, Sister Cupboard and Sister Orchard, and some of the more playful ones, the novices, who kept their own names, Sister Saint Grayce, and Sister Linnet. But when it came time for Elphaba to leave, they wrapped up my small packet of clothes, too, and I was lifted up to a seat on a wagon, and we joined a party that went through the Kells, stopping here and there until we got to Kiamo Ko."

"It's awfully out of the way," said Dorothy, looking around at the unpeopled slopes of pine and potterpine, and the slides of scree, and the scraggles of mountain lavender going to seed.

"She wanted to be out of the way. And besides, it's where Fiyero had lived."

"Your father?"

Liir was as doubtful of his paternity as he was of his maternity. "He had meant something to her, to the Witch," he pointed out. "But what, I don't know. I never met him. Can you imagine the Witch would sit down and pour out her heart to me?"

"I can't imagine anything about her. Who could?"

He didn't want to talk anymore. The death was too recent, the shock of it was beginning to wear off, and what began to show through was anger. "In a general sense, we're going southwest, and then we'll cut east through Kumbricia's Pass," he said. "I've learned that much by listening to Oatsie Manglehand when she comes through guiding a party. There are tribes around and about."

"We saw no one," said Dorothy, "not for miles."

"They saw you," said Liir. "They had to. That's what they do."

"Not nice, to be spying on us. We're very chummy," she said, putting on an aggressively friendly face. Any party of scouts witnessing it would do well to keep themselves hidden.

Before long the rain came, and he was glad, for it stopped their conversation, which had turned into prattle. A heavy rain, the drops like pebbles. He could see no shepherd's hut out here, not even a clump of mountain arbor to shelter beneath. So rather than sit in the mud and let the rain wick through their undergarments, they trudged on.

Their confidence about their course ebbed, though, what with the shrouding of hilltops—all landmarks wiped out of view.

"Liir, I have no confidence in your sense of direction," said the Tin Woodman, politely.

"Nick Chopper! You're heartless!" said Dorothy.

"Ha bloody ha. And you're an orphan," he replied. "I'll rust in this downpour. Does anyone think of that? No."

"Don't carp. I don't deal well with conflict," said the Lion. "Let's sing a song."

"*No,*" they all chorused.

"What'll you do when you find yourself courageous—assuming the Wizard grants you what you wish?" asked the Scarecrow, to change the subject.

"Invest in the market? Join a troupe of music hall buskers? How the hell do I know?" said the Lion. "Strike out on my own, anyway, and find a better class of associates. More simpatico."

"You?" asked the Scarecrow of the Tin Woodman.

"What will I do if I find myself with a heart?" scoffed the Tin Woodman. "Lose it constantly, I imagine."

They slopped on. Liir didn't think it was his place to continue the conversation, since he hadn't been present at their initial audience with the Wizard. When no one else spoke, though, he said, "Well, Scarecrow, your turn. What'll you do with your brains?"

"I'm thinking about it," he answered, and would not discuss it further.

"Oh, Toto!" shrieked Dorothy suddenly. "Where's Toto?"

"He's wandered off to do his business," said the Lion. "Just between you and me, it's about time he learned to be private about it. I know you dote on him, but there is a limit."

"He'll be lost," she cried. "He couldn't find his way out of a cracker barrel. He's not very bright, you know."

After a respectful pause, the Tin Woodman observed, "I *think* we've all noticed that."

"I hate to be obvious," added the Scarecrow, "but you'd have saved yourself a heap of trouble if you weren't too cheap to invest in a leash, Dorothy."

"There he is," she cried, pitching up a small slope.

The clueless creature was finishing his evacuation at the base of what looked like an ancient traveler's shrine to Lurline. A weathered statue of the pagan goddess gazed blindly out into the storm. The statue was life-size, if you accepted that goddesses have the same stature as humans. Little more than a lean-to for protecting the statue from the elements, the structure could afford no room for the travelers to crawl in out of the downpour. After a while, though, Liir thought of standing on the shoulders of the Lion and slinging the big black cape out over the shrine's roof. Using the scorched remains of the Witch's broom as a pole, he rigged up a black tent under which they could huddle. The Lion's mane reeked, but at least the travelers were protected from the worst of the rain.

"This cape is larger than it looks," said Dorothy. "And the water isn't soaking through."

"Maybe she hexed it waterproof. She didn't like water," said Liir.

"So I've learned," said Dorothy.

"Who does?" added the Tin Woodman, squeaking his joints.

"Tell me more about her," continued Dorothy.

Liir didn't oblige. He found Dorothy congenial enough—but it had been so long since he'd had anything like friends his own age! At Kiamo Ko, when he'd first arrived with Elphaba, Fiyero's three children had allowed him into their small society, but slackly, without much interest. The girl, Nor, had been the only one ever really to play with him. Though he had been little more to Nor than that dog was to Dorothy, a presence to boss around, Nor *had* been kind. That first Lurlinemas, she'd given him the tail of her gingerbread mouse, because no one had thought to make him a gingerbread mouse of his own.

And besides her? No one else to play with, once she and Irji and the rest of the ruling family—Fiyero's survivors—had been kidnapped by the Wizard's forces garrisoned at Red Windmill. Yes, he'd bravely followed, but fecklessly. They'd given him the slip. He had had to return to Kiamo Ko and face the screeching. Then the Witch had prohibited Liir from fraternizing any longer with Commander Cherrystone of the Gale Forcers or from making new friends among the lice-ridden urchins of Red Windmill.

So Liir had lived a lonely life. It could have been worse; he was fed and he was clothed more or less warmly. He had his chores, and the winged monkeys, largely inarticulate, at least didn't go out of their way to move if he sat down nearby. Was there supposed to be more to a childhood? Rehearsing it to tell Dorothy, it seemed a spare, botched thing, and he suppressed most of it.

Of late, the Witch had become more irritable than usual, complaining of sleeping problems. Nanny—her nanny, at one point, and her mother's nanny before that—was well into her eighties and good for little by way of coherent discussion. Liir had been left to talk to himself, and he'd found himself less than stimulating as a conversationalist.

Dorothy's curiosity seemed flat to him, though, perhaps artificial. He wasn't able to tell if she was really curious about his life, about the Witch, or if she was just marking time. Maybe steeling her own nerve by hearing the sound of her voice. He felt leery. Perhaps, the son of the Witch or no, he had inherited from exposure to Elphaba a mild sense of paranoia, as if everyone were after some scrap of vital information that they were unwilling to ask for directly.

He fussed and rolled his eyes and tried to imagine how to change the subject. He didn't want to talk about his toddler days in the mauntery or his boyhood in Kiamo Ko. He was bereft of family, now, something of a hanger-on to Dorothy's party, something of a guide without a clue out here in the cruel terrain. He just wanted to concentrate on the job.

He was glad, therefore, when the Lion started and said, "What's that?"

"It's night coming on," said the Tin Woodman.

"Night coming on makes a sound like the Crack of Doom?" complained the Lion. "Never did before. Shhh, everyone. It wasn't thunder. What was it? Shhh, I tell you."

The Tin Woodman observed, "You're the only one who's talking—"

"*Shhh,* I said!"

They shhhushed.

The downpour made a symphony. An undertone of susurrus—rain at mid-distance—accompanied the solo vocalists rounding vowels of rainwater—*plopp*—*plopp*—or, as Liir thought, of Auntie Witch, Elphaba Thropp—*Thropp*—*Thropp.*

"Did you ever notice how rain sounds like a domingon?" asked the Scarecrow.

The Lion put his paw to his mouth: Shhhh. His grimace was anything but fearsome; he looked like an overgrown child in lion pajamas.

Then they heard what he was hearing, and before they could do anything about it, a stone at the base of the statue of Lurlina was shifted to one side. Up from the earth poked the paw of a creature. A badger, a beaver? Something brown, whiskered, and sensible. A slope grite of some sort, larger than its valley cousin.

"You've some nerve, besmirching the memory of Lurlina with your prattle," said the Mountain Grite. His jowls made a saddlebag flapping noise as he spoke.

"Nerve," said the Lion. "I wish."

"We're merely sheltering from the storm," said Dorothy. "May we have your blessing to stay here?"

The Grite bared an impressive collection of incisors and canines.

"What business is it of yours?" said Liir. "We're not bothering you."

The Grite looked around, as if assessing whether he might take them on all at once and get the better of them. Apparently not. "My digs, if you want to call it that," he said at last, "are directly below. You're a big heavy lot, and you're going to collapse the walls of my lodging."

"A bad place to build," said the Tin Man, for whom the teeth of a Mountain Grite weren't much of a threat. "An insult to Lurlina, actually."

"Maybe, but I dig deep, and if the whole thing gives and you tumble in, you'll starve to death down there. And the stink of your rotting corpses won't appeal to the spirit of Lurlina, however beloved of the natural world she is said to be."

"The storm can't last forever," said Dorothy.

The Grite came forward a little. "Quite possibly I have rabies, you know. Fair warning. I bite first and I don't ask questions."

The Lion sighed and removed himself from the makeshift tent. Out there, the deluge sloped on him like a fountain coursing over a sculptured lion.

"We're not going to let some overgrown rodent chase us into the storm," said Liir. "If you bite me, I'll bite you back, and return your own rabies to you. Go away."

"That's a capable awning you have." The Grite wrinkled his face. "My eyes aren't what they used to be. What is it?"

"It's a cape," said Liir. "What business is it of yours?"

"That's the Witch's cape," said the Grite. "I don't believe it. Where did you get it?"

"I took it," said Liir.

"More fool you. She'll have your head before nightfall."

"She's dead," said Dorothy. Smugly.

The Grite's eyes bulged, and he pushed his face nearer to Dorothy, who flinched and drew back from him: He wasn't an especially handsome specimen of his family. "The Witch is dead? Can it be true?"

They nodded, each one of them.

"Oh, the shock of it." The Grite clutched his paws and worried them back and forth. "The shock of it! The Witch is dead?"

The wind itself answered in a kind of obbligato descant: *The Witch is dead!*

"Get out of here," said the Grite in a colder voice. "Go on."

"I thought you'd be glad," said Dorothy.

The retort was crisp and censorious. "We held her in considerable regard. There have always been some Animals who would have marched at her side, right to the gates of the Emerald City, had she believed in armies, had she ever given the word. You'll find no comfort among us."

"She was my friend," said Liir. "Don't confuse us with assassins."

"You're a fledgling. You could barely manage to befriend her cape, let alone the Witch herself." To Dorothy he added, "Move along, little Miss Thug and accomplices, before I call on reinforcements to deal with you." The Grite sniffed the raw air as if expecting to find proof of their assertions in the smell of the revised world. "The Witch is dead. It can't be. Wait till Princess Nastoya hears. Wait until the Wizard hears."

He was lost to his own ruminations, and turned to look up at the statue of Lurline. "Give us guidance!" he said. "Speak, for once."

The storm thundered very nearby. Everyone shuddered but the Grite. "I mean, speak in a language we can understand," he clarified. But the storm, or Lurline within its might, didn't oblige, and indeed, moments later the worst of the downpour was done, and the thunder shunted elsewhere.

The Grite continued. "I have no reason to give comfort to mine enemy, but there you are. You may be villainous, but you are young, some of you, and perhaps might learn to repent. I'm told that Wizardic battalions are encamped on the banks of the Vinkus River. Find the Wizard's forces and they will protect you. That's my advice to you."

"The Wizard's armies will *protect* us?" snapped Liir. "The Wizard of Oz is a menace!"

"Of course he is. A despot, a suzerain, call it what you will. The boss. And you've abetted him in his campaign to wipe out the western resistance. This news will travel fast, my friends." Every time he said the word *friends,* it sounded less friendly. "But take protection where you can. When the word of the death of Elphaba Thropp spreads through these hills, you'll have a very difficult time of it. I won't answer for what happens next. You've heard my advice. Heed it."

"I'm not giving myself up to any corps of the Wizard's army," said Liir. "If there are forces down the eastern side, we'll keep to our plan to veer west, and take our chances through Kumbricia's Pass. It'll be a longer route but a safer one."

"Perhaps we'd better get going," said Dorothy, nervously.

"You had better go on," agreed the Mountain Grite. "I won't join a posse against you, but nor will I lie to my friends about what I've learned here today. The clouds are passing over. If you've intended to take the hairpin track down the western slope of Knobblehead Pike, you've overshot. You'll have to back up. You won't reach the river valley before dark. Shelter under a black willow; you'll find a stand of them where the track levels out and circles a bit of highland swamp. You'll be safe there."

"Thank you," said Dorothy earnestly.

"Don't be a fool," said Liir. "Thank him for what?"

"You," said the Grite to the Lion, "are a turncoat. You ought to be ashamed of yourself. I'd be especially wary if I were you. Animals don't take lightly to traitors. If you were more of a Lion, you'd know that."

"I did nothing!" said the Lion. "I was locked in the kitchen!" His tail twitched eight or ten times.

THE GRITE KEPT HIS WORD and ratted on them. Before the travelers had finished washing the next morning, a scouting party of Scrow appeared at the edge of the black willow grove. Riding bareback and nearly naked on their purple-white steeds, they looked like wild centaurs in the mist. Without a word but with considerable glower the Scrow contingent circled the grove. There, the travelers were kept loosely penned. Attempts to negotiate were fruitless; they had no language in common.

The languages of Oz. Liir had never thought about them. The father tongue had always seemed universal; even Dorothy spoke without peculiar inflections or special difficulty. True, the dialect of the mountain clans, the Arjikis, was characterized by the growling of syllables halfway down the throat—but the difference had made little impression on Liir. He could still understand the Arjikis.

So why would the isolated Mountain Grite speak the common tongue with clarity and effect, while the Scrow clung to a language only they understood?

Right up to the end, the Witch had kept trying to teach the winged monkeys to speak, as if to be able to testify might save their lives some-day. So much bound up in language ... The language of spells themselves—*spells,* of all things! A way to order sounds to make things shift, reveal what is hidden, conceal what isn't ...

He wished he had a skill for language. He wished he could spell magic as, with effort and increasing control, Elphaba had learned to do. He would bind the Scrow frozen, and he and his companions would walk away safely. But this was beyond him—like everything else.

The Scrow scouts tossed the travelers hanks of repugnant dried meat and smoked corn. It was clear Dorothy and company were to wait here. A day and a half later, the leader of the Scrow arrived, traveling in a slow-moving caravansary that with considerable care negotiated the path to this low-lying western ridge of Knobblehead Pike.

The party included a translator, so Liir found himself requesting an audience with the Highness behind the shabby drapes of the palanquin. He wasn't skilled at bargaining. "The only thing I request is that we, uh, hurry," he said. "My friend Dorothy wants to get safely to the Emerald City; she has an appointment with the Wizard. Then she intends to travel abroad somewhere."

And I with her, he thought to add, but didn't. Would she have me? And if not—what else am I going to do?

The translator was an old, gnarled Scrow gentleman who, despite his tribal appurtenances, had been trained in the university environs of Shiz. "Very well," he said. "I don't see why we should dally. It is in all of our interests, after all. Give her Highness a chance to compose herself, and we shall let you know when she's ready."

Dorothy said, "We don't think much of crowned heads where I come from. Who is this Highness?" The interpreter left without answering.

"How rude," said Dorothy. "Well, who *is* she, this Highness? Might it be the Ozma everybody goes on about?"

Liir explained. "The last Ozma disappeared many years ago, kidnapped as a young girl when the Wizard came to power. Nanny believed the child had been bewitched in a trance, never to grow older by a day until the moment she was released from the charm, like a fairy-tale princess. Then she would rise up and smash the mighty in their comfort, and return the monarchy to its rightful place. But Auntie Witch always pooh-poohed that. She said the child had probably been murdered long ago. The remains of the Ozma Tippetarius would be found deep in the bone bins of the Palace, along with her ancestors, if anyone were allowed to look there."

"I believe in Ozma," said the Scarecrow staunchly.

Mindless fool, thought Liir, but said nothing more.

The court of the Scrow didn't keep them waiting for long. When the sun had reached its zenith, attendants unrolled a green carpet with a puckered selvage. Shapeless pillows, sour with mildew, were placed about. "Stand until her Highness is seated," the translator said, arranging in a kind of lattice pattern the remaining hairs on his pale domed head. "Then you may be seated, too."

She was helped out of her compartment by six retainers. Her muscles were of little use in holding up her bulk, and her large, sagging face twisted into seams of overlapping skin. She grimaced at the pain of every step. An old woman, a monolith of an ancient Scrow matron, easily the size of all her retainers standing together. Like a queen bee among drones.

Her face was scored with green and purple smudges, some sort of ceremonial marking. The waft of vetiver and lily water, pleasant enough, couldn't entirely disguise an animal odor.

"Princess Nastoya," said the translator in comprehensible Ozish, "may I present Dorothy Gale, of parts unknown, and her companions, a Lion, a Scarecrow, a gentleman clad in Tin, and the boy about whom you've been told." He then repeated the lines in Scrow, to indicate how he would go on.

"How do you do?" said Dorothy, curtseying.

Princess Nastoya was lowered to the ground so she could regard them while reclining on her side. Her spine was preternaturally long, as if she possessed extra vertebrae. The servants propped her knees on a yellow cushion, and her elbow on another, and they arranged a small mountain of cushions behind her so she wouldn't roll backward.

The interpreter began a flowery biography, but the Princess cut him off. Her voice was low, tympanic, as if her nasal passages were large enough for the storage of melons.

"I am sore with disbelief," she said, the interpreter translating. "I had only known that the Witch sent out Crows to call for help. Before they could reach me, they were attacked and their flesh devoured by a posse of nocturnal rocs."

"How do you know about the Crows?" asked Liir. "If they were eaten by rocs?"

"Nocturnal rocs are mute beasts," said the Princess, "but the attack was witnessed by a Grey Eagle who keeps an eye on a certain district for me. He drove the rocs away from one Crow, who managed to pass on the message of the Witch's embattlement before dying. The Eagle delivered the message to me as I was closing a convocation with some of the southern Arjiki clans."

"The Witch ought to have been told about that," said Liir. "She considered herself an honorary Arjiki, sort of."

"I won't be lectured on strategy or protocol," replied the Princess. "In any case, I did invite her. But I never knew if my invitation got through. I was told that she was distracted with grief over the death of her sister."

"She was . . . unsteady . . . at the end," admitted Liir. "I'm not sure how much she could have done for you, or if she would have bothered. In truth, she was kind of a hermit. She kept to herself." Even when it came to me, he remembered.

"I'd have put the case forcefully to her, had I gotten her attention," asserted the Princess. "She was no fool. She saw that when the breadbasket of Munchkinland was ruinously taxed by the Emerald City's chancellors, it had to break away and form a Free State. If pressed, we here in the west will do no less than that ourselves. My attempts to build an allegiance with the Yunamata have come to naught, and the Arjikis can enjoy their own insularity, obstinate slope dwellers!—but we Scrow will not stand by and let our Grasslands be plundered. The Wizard is amassing an army on the eastern slope of the Kells. I know how he works, you whippet."

The Princess groaned. "She might have been a help! But it is too late. I hear through the report of a Mountain Grite that the peculiar woman is dead. Elphaba."

The interpreter pronounced it wrong. "EL-phaba," said Liir.

"Is the murderer here among us?" asked the Princess.

"It was an accident," said Dorothy. "I didn't mean it." She put the end of one of her pigtails into her mouth and chewed it.

"The deceased was a curious creature," said the Princess. "I only met her once, but she impressed me with her stamina. She did not seem the type to die."

"Who does?" said Dorothy.

"Speak for yourself," muttered the Lion. "I die a little bit every day, especially if there are unfriendly faces in the room."

Through her factotum, the Princess continued her message. "You are in grave danger. Not least from me. Murder and theft of the Witch's belongings, the way I see it, but even worse: doing so in collusion with the Wizard."

Liir protested, sputtering. "Not in collusion with the Wizard!"

"Well, the Wizard of Oz *did* ask me to kill her," admitted Dorothy. "No use crying over *that* spilt milk. He did, and I won't lie about it. But I didn't intend to do it. I just wanted her forgiveness for the accidental death of her sister. And then there was the bucket of water. And how was I to know? I mean, we don't have witches back home in Kansas. We wouldn't hear of it."

"You've got it all wrong," interrupted Liir. "Listen, Princess Nastoya, please. I lived with the Witch all my life. There's no question of theft. I am the next of kin."

"How so?"

He couldn't answer. The Princess pressed her point.

"Can you prove it?"

He shrugged. His skin was neither green, like Elphaba's, nor musky ocher, like Fiyero's children and widow. Liir was rather pasty, in fact; not a convincing specimen of anything, when you got right down to it.

"It is no matter," said the Princess. "I would not kill you. Oh no, I would not. But others might, and I wonder if I could prevent them. We have no sway with the Arjikis, as the collapse of my recent campaign shows."

"Why would the Wizard's armies bother to raise a hand against us?" asked Liir. "The Witch is dead, and the ruling family of the Arjikis—the house and line of Fiyero—has been obliterated."

"Even the daughter?" asked the Princess.

Liir's mouth dropped. "Do you mean Nor? Have you heard otherwise about her? What can you tell me of her?"

"I have capable ears," she answered, but continued. "Can you prove the Witch is dead?"

"You want us to bring her back to life?" Liir scoffed. "You might as well kill us now, if that's your demand."

The Princess indicated that she wanted to stand. "It's the neck, it creaks under the weight of too much heavy thinking," she said. It took nine men to cantilever her to her feet, and then they brought her a pair of jeweled canes as thick as newel posts. She leaned forward and fixed Liir in the eye.

"You would be of no help at treaties, you boy-calf," she said. "But you wonder what *do* I want of you."

She let her mirrored shawl slip off her shoulders, and three black ivory combs clattered to the ground from her knotted hedge of thick white hair. The air grew very still, and clammy; there was a sense of Presence. The Princess closed her eyes and droned, and her hair seemed to pick at itself, and then to gather into a sleek sliding thing, and it ran off her back into a white coil on the ground. The shapeless gown of cotton geppling shifted on her hips, appeared to draw itself up into a peplum or a bustle, and then it snaked off.

Liir had never seen an unclothed woman before, old or young—only little Nor on washday, lithe in the copper tub, when she'd been a girl of four or five. The effect of a naked Princess was startling, the print of silvery hair at the groin, the pockets of flesh folding one over the other, the bosom flattened by age and gravity. Dorothy murmured "Goodness!" as if she thought she must be witnessing exactly the opposite.

If this was magic, it was still spelling time. The Princess's nose was lengthening, uncoiling, and the skin on her cement-colored cheeks stretched and thickened epibolically. Her eyes, which had been little more than slits in the folds of her face, lost their ovoid shape, rounded into marbles. A net of fine hairs sprouted on her brow and pate, her cheeks and chin and dramatically hostile nose. And ears:—yes, they were capable and then some.

More or less like an Elephant head, though not planted on an Elephant body.

"Perhaps I ought to have given you more warning," she said. "It seems I've upset the girl." Dorothy was retching into her apron, and her dog appeared to have had a nervous fit and passed out. "I have little use for niceties at this stage in my life, though."

Liir didn't trust himself to speak.

"I am an Elephant," said the Princess Nastoya. "From the Wizard's pogroms against the Animals, I have been in hiding as a human all these long years. I'm admired by the Scrow for my longevity and what passes for my wisdom. In exchange for their protection, for a home in the Thousand Year Grasslands, I have performed my duty as a leader. But of late, young boy-thing, I am unable to shuck off my disguise with the ease I once had. Though Elephants pretend to immortality, I believe I am dying. I must not be allowed to die in this half-form. I will die as an Elephant. But I need help."

"How can I be of service?" asked Liir. As if I could do anything, he added to himself.

"I don't know," said the Princess Nastoya. "I once told Elphaba Thropp that if she needed help, she was only to send word, and I would put all my resources under her command. I never thought that the reverse would happen. That the time would come for me to apply to her for her knowledge of Animals, her native skill at spells and charms. But I have started too late, I see, for your companion has murdered my only hope."

"Dorothy was not to know," said Liir.

"Any murder at all, of any sort, is a murder of hope, too."

"It's disgusting, actually," whispered the Lion to the Tin Woodman. "Do you know, my stomach is turning as we speak."

"I don't have a talent at spells," said Liir. "If that's what you're asking."

"How do you know?" asked the Princess. "Have you tried? Have you studied?"

"I'm not a good student, and furthermore I'm not much interested."

The huge proboscis whipped up from nowhere. Her nose-digits grabbed his chin. She would crush his skull, chin-first. "Get interested," she said. "Get interested, or get help. If you're not to be murdered for your crimes against Elphaba—and that might yet happen—get yourself enough knowledge from someone, somewhere, to help. Was there a book, a Grimmerie? Did Elphaba have associates? I don't care how long it takes, but come back to me. I can't die like this. I won't. In the end, all disguises must drop."

"You confuse me with someone else," he said. "Someone with competence. Someone I never met."

"This isn't a request," she said. "It's an order. I am a colleague of Elphaba's." She lifted her nasal limb from Liir's chin and blew her own horn in his face. His eyes stewed in his skull, and some of the hair at the front of his scalp was raked bloodily away by the force of the blast. "If you claim to be a relation of the Witch's, you will figure out what to do. She always could."

"Well, not always," Dorothy corrected her helpfully, "as is woefully apparent at this moment in time."

"I will pay you," concluded the Princess, apparently addressing Liir alone. "I will keep my ears to the ground for word of your abducted friend—Fiyero's cub, Nor. Nor, was it? Come back to me with a solution and I will tell you all I've been able to learn in the meantime."

Liir couldn't speak, but he held out his hands, palms up, in a gesture even he couldn't read. Accepting the task? Protesting his inadequacy? Whatever—it didn't matter. The Princess was done with them. She turned her massive Elephant head, wobbling on its all-too-human spine, and a dozen Scrow rushed to hold her up. They cloaked the acreage of her buttocks, as if to protect her from a sort of ignominy that, anyway, could never have attached itself to her. Even a half-thing, trapped in a decaying spell, she was too much herself for shame to apply.

"She didn't keep one of us as a hostage," said the Lion, almost delirious. "I was sure it was going to be me. But I could never have dealt with it."

"She trusted us," said Liir.

They settled into a pattern of traipsing day after day, under skies of broken cloud and brittle light. To avoid the Wizardic armies, they kept to the western base of the Great Kells. In places the upright thrusts of the mountains rose from the grassland floor as cleanly as the front of a corncrib meets a level floor: one could almost mark with a pencil where the plain stopped and the slope began.

They rested where they could. At least it wasn't a bad time of year to be making their way cross-country. They skirted the edge of the Thousand Year Grasslands, ants in single file on the fringe of a carpet of prairie. After several weeks, they reached the verdant apron that rose into the gorge known as Kumbricia's Pass, a high and fertile valley affording the quickest way through the central Kells.

Liir remembered it vaguely from years past. The air was dense and damp, and the ground quilted with decaying vegetation. If Princess Nastoya had not been able to engage the local Yunamata tribes in a treaty against the Wizard, it was likely she hadn't been able to extend her offer of protection through their territory, either. But the Yunamata kept themselves hidden, as was their way.

Beyond, heading downslope toward the Vinkus River and eventually the Emerald City, the world seemed cold and sore. The year was moving on. The occasional foothill farmhouses were crude, almost derelict, roofing thatch thick with mildew, gardens thin on the ground. If bread was offered, it was offered sullenly. No locals would take them in and provide anything like a mattress. The corner of a barn and a blanket crusty with pigeon droppings were the best the travelers could hope for. Still, exhausted with plodding, they slept hard and dreamlessly.

To Liir, it wasn't a question of how many days or weeks it took to reach the Emerald City, but how many hours a day he had to trudge before he could sink back into a safe sleep again. Not sleep, something richer: blissful annihilation. So he could forget the sideways throb of his flattened heart kicking: *You. You. You.* He kept the thought of Elphaba there, unwillingly; it pressed painfully against membranes so interior he had never known their existence before. *I hated you. You left me. So I hate you more than I used to.*

The Kells dwindled, the scrubby flatland spread its wastes in fields of shattered stone. Oakhair forests began first to fringe the horizon, and then to loom with oakhair breath and the sound of wind in their leaves . . . Little of this registered on Liir without his wanting to say, "Look, look—the world you hated so much that you left it behind. It's so weird. I can see why."

He couldn't say this. He could hardly think it, with Dorothy rabbiting on about Auntie Em and Uncle Henry and various forgettable farmhands. *Elphaba*, thought Liir. *Elphaba*, he felt. *Elphaba*. The world without you.

How am I to manage?

THE KELLS HAD LOOKED CLEAN, conceived by a keen architectural eye, and thrown up with confidence. By contrast, the Emerald City, on first sight, seemed organic, a metastasis of competing life-forms. Liir had never seen a settlement larger than a hamlet before, so he was flummoxed at the way the City punched itself against the horizon. Flummoxed, and daunted.

"Don't be scared," said Dorothy, catching his hand. "Think of it as a thousand farmsteads piled on top of one another."

"And *that* isn't a scary notion?"

"I am going to find myself here," declared the Tin Woodman.

"I'm going to lose myself," said the Lion.

"Just try to blend in," said Dorothy. "Act natural."

"Now that *would* be acting," said the Tin Woodman, and barked one calf percussively against the other to underscore his point.

"Come on," said the Scarecrow, "we're in luck." He indicated a motley crew of traveling players advertising a silly new show done mostly with puppets. They were amusing the guards, and in the commotion the Yellow Brick Road Irregulars and Liir managed to sidle undetected through the City's west portal. They debouched into a broad square. Judging from the stink of skark manure, the space served as a holding pen for beasts of transport while cargos were being unloaded and bills of lading composed. Plain granite storehouses faced the yard, and bears—or possibly even Bears, talking beasts, though they weren't talking now—were hauling sacks of grain and crates of produce. "Ho," yelled the overseers. Some were Munchkins, a third the height of their laborers. Their landing whips loosed splatters as of red rain.

"We're meat here, meat," groaned the Lion. "Not that it's all about me, but I feel so *exposed*."

"The Lion's right. Come, let's duck down this alley," said Liir.

"I'd expected a bit more fuss," said Dorothy. "I mean, like it or not, the Witch is dead, and you'd think the word would have gotten out." She held her own nose with one hand and Toto's nose with the other. "Kansas boasts henhouses sweeter than this."

They wandered through commercial districts, crossing wide boulevards lined with dying cypress trees. Some were splintered in half, pulled down for such tinder as they might provide. Many open spaces, around fountains memorializing successful military campaigns, were filled in with makeshift homes, some cardboard, or oilcloth stretched over chicken wire. Cooking pots stank of dinner. The broken spout from a fountain still trickled a little: a common toilet. "Ugh," said Dorothy. "My earlier visit didn't take me through this neighborhood."

"You had civic guides," guessed Liir. She nodded.

The people of the boulevards ducked behind the shawls tacked up as curtain-doors, or hid their faces in sheets of old newsprint when the travelers passed. "You'd think we were leprous," said Liir.

"Perhaps we're too clean," said Dorothy. "We shame them."

Liir didn't think Dorothy was as clean as all that, but her eyes were bright and her step sure, and perhaps that counted more than cleanliness. "Maybe they're used to police action against them, and they just don't know which side we represent," said Liir.

"Oh, really," said the Tin Woodman. "Look at us: a man of straw, a man of tin, a Lion with a bow in his hair like a lapdog! A girl, a boy, a surly little dog. How could we possibly be authorities? We're too—"

"Unique?" asked Dorothy.

"Lacking in camouflage?" asked the Lion.

"Fabulous?" proposed the Tin Woodman.

"Ridiculous?" asked Liir.

"All of the above," decided the Scarecrow. But the indigent seemed not to be convinced and avoided the peculiar travelers.

WHEN THEY REACHED the great piazza before the Palace of the Wizard, Liir wanted to hang back. The Witch had despised the ruler of Oz; how could Liir show his face? "Don't be a sissy," said the Lion, "I've got that covered for us all."

"It's not fear," said Liir, though it was, in part. It was also anger, he realized. How capable, how flexible anger was: he could feel it for the Witch, who had gone and died on him, and for the Wizard, the orchestrator of her murder, both at once. Then why, for Dorothy, did Liir feel nothing but an increasing exhaustion? Perhaps he harbored a zesty secret anger toward her, too, but if so it kept itself in disguise. If Liir lashed out at Dorothy—well, what would he have left in the world? Who? Pretty nearly nothing. Just about nothing at all.

"Well, we can't wait while you dither," said Dorothy. "You'd be a fool to pass up this chance. The Wizard can give you your heart's desire, after all. He's good at that."

He remembered a conversation with Elphaba, suddenly.

What do you want, Liir, if the Wizard could give you anything?
A father.

"He's like Santa Claus." Dorothy's eyes were button bright with apostolic zeal.

"Don't know what you mean."

"*Santa Claus?* Jolly old elf! Magic as anything. At Christmas every year he comes to your home and leaves you treats, if you're good. Or if you're not, coal in your stocking. We don't always have extra coal in Kansas so once he filled my stocking full of manure. I cried like the dickens but Uncle Henry said it was punishment for me singing too brightly in the hog pen. I was scaring the pigs shitless, he said, and here was the proof."

"The Wizard of Oz puts manure in your socks?"

"No! Listen and stop being an idiot. I just mean the Wizard is *like* Santa Claus: he's a charitable sort. Come and get what you need. What's to stop you? What do you have better to do?"

He wobbled. If the Wizard was handing out rewards, why shouldn't Liir deserve one? He was an orphan now. He didn't need to say who he was, did he?—or where he came from?

"He owes you lots." Dorothy was solemn with assurance. "Without your help, we wouldn't have gotten back alive. The creepy Yunamuffins hiding on the trail, that repulsive Elephant monster, queen of the Scrow-folk. I had jeebies crawling all over my heebies."

"Maybe I will," said Liir.

What do you want, Liir, if the Wizard could give you anything?
A father.

The Wizard couldn't give him a father or a mother, but maybe he could give him some news of Nor. Now that the Princess Nastoya had awakened a hope that Nor might still be alive. Or maybe the Wizard had gotten hold of the missing Grimmerie, somehow. With it, Liir might fig-ure out how to help the Princess shuck off her disguise. In any event, even to approach someone as mighty as the wonderful Wizard of Oz would be, for Liir, both a novelty and an accomplishment: he was hardly more than spinster spawn, and had seen little of the world of men.

"Well, come if you're coming; we're off," said Dorothy, so Liir hid the Witch's cape beneath an ornamental flowerpot in a corner of the deserted café where they had been sitting, and went with them.

Dorothy's strategy for getting the attention of the proper officials at the Palace doors was simple. "I'm Dorothy," she said, "you know. *The* Dorothy."

The guards gawked. Ministers were summoned, and arrangements made for an interview almost at once. "You're not allowed," said the Secretary of Audiences to Liir. "You aren't part of the original contract."

"But I'm here to ask the Wizard for help," said Liir.

"Piss off."

Dorothy shrugged, grinned too broadly, and straightened her apron. "Don't fret, Liir. We shouldn't be more than an hour. All we have to do is show up, and I'm sure the Wizard will grant our requests. We'll meet back at that café tonight and decide what to do to celebrate before I leave."

"Are you sure you want to leave?" asked Liir.

"Of course I'm leaving," she snapped. "This is my exit interview. Why do you think I put myself through this indignity? I didn't ask to kill the Witch, but having done it, I'm going to collect my reward if I can possibly manage it."

He bit his lip. "Then may I come with you?"

"You wouldn't feel at home in Kansas. Few do. Besides, you're supposed to be un-bewitching that old freak elephant noggin. Are my pigtails even?"

She kissed him in a bruisingly incidental manner. Full of stupid trust, she turned and hurried after her friends. The ceremonial doors banged behind them.

Liir went back to the café. Using up almost all the coin he had, he waited with mounting horror and then failing hopes. She never returned. He never saw her again.

She hadn't been much, that Dorothy. Priggish, in a way, proud of her wide-eyed charity. Her kindness, at first magnificent, had come to seem a bit—well, cheap. After all, she'd also oiled the Tin Woodman, and soothed the timorous Lion, and discussed differences between the gold and silver standards of foreign currency with the Scarecrow, who seemed for all his brainlessness to be following the whole discussion. She'd cuddled that rank little dog of hers. In light of all that, her solicitousness to Liir seemed nothing more than the Next Good Deed.

Nonetheless, she had been brave, one foot in front of the other, all the way to the Vinkus, all the way back. When the bells began to toll throughout the City, and Liir finally worked up the nerve to ask someone why, Dorothy wasn't mentioned at all. "The Wizard is deposed," they said. "The Wicked Witch is dead, but the Wizard is deposed anyway. Some other good witch has been hired to oversee Oz in the interim."

"Dorothy?" he asked. "What about Dorothy?"

"Dorothy who?" they replied. The cult of Dorothy had yet to take hold.

ONCE, YEARS BACK, in one of the barns at Kiamo Ko, Liir had been horsing about with Nor and her brothers. The children of Fiyero and his wife, Sarima, were high-tempered, and they had persuaded Liir to sit on one end of a timber that they intended to pivot out over a pile of hay below. He could jump to his safety! It would be fun, they said. And so it would have been, had not one of them—Manek, probably—leaped off the balanced end before Liir was fully positioned. Afraid of smashing himself on the stone floor of the barn, Liir had lurched to safety across the edge of a cart. The falling beam failed to kill him.

However, he knocked the wind out of his chest, and for a minute or two he was unable to breathe. He could feel his lungs kicking, and his heart kicking back, but he thought he was dying. The faces of Irji and Nor peered down over the edge of the loft at him. Lying on his back, stretching in vain to open his windpipe, he looked up at their faces contorting with laughter and mild concern.

What Liir remembered, in as near to extremis as he had experienced in his short life, was how embroidered these last few impressions of the world seemed. How the light breaking over the crowns of Irji's and Nor's heads seemed shaped like segments of overlapping fins, tying the bright expressions of his friends to the rafters, the cobwebs, the knotholes, the looped ropes, the stray feathers. All of a piece, all of a piece, he thought: why did I never see it before, and now I will die and never see it again.

Then he didn't die, but lived. His breath punched itself back into place, and he wailed and his torso hurt and everything splintered into disjointed elements. As angry as he felt at Manek for making him the butt of a well-planned prank, he was distressed at the loss of his fine moment of apprehension: The world belonged together like this. The pieces related to each other. There was no contradiction, deepest down. Complexity, yes, but not contradiction. Only connection.

Now, hunched beneath the doorway of a shuttered butchery in the Emerald City, with Dorothy so newly met, and just as quickly vanished, he remembered the incident in the barn at Kiamo Ko. There is no resolving a good mess, he thought. Every breath one takes is a waking up into disjointedness, over and over.

He rocked hard enough to build plum-colored bruises on his shoulders. They hurt when he prodded them, and he prodded them to make them hurt.

He had nowhere to go, nothing to do. By day and night he meandered like the other bits of human trash that drifted up and down the boulevards. Filching from merchants, begging for pennies, relieving themselves in public without concern for decency or hygiene.

Nightly he returned to the café, in case his sense of dread had been for naught, and Dorothy might still make good on her promise and come back for him, at least to say good-bye. A lucky thing, too, for on the fifth day Liir was turning over newspapers looking for scrag-ends of butter pastry when he was tapped on the shoulder. He turned, half expecting that the café owner had summoned the police as he'd been threatening. Instead, Liir found the Scarecrow.

"You're still here," said the Scarecrow. "Somehow, I thought you would be."

"Where is she?"

"She's gone, you know that." The Scarecrow sighed. "You knew she would go. She was a Visitor, not of our kind; that kind can't stay, you know."

"How do you know? Maybe you just need to invite them."

The Scarecrow affected a superior attitude, and that was his only answer. "A lot is going to change in a very short time," he said. "I hope it's
for the best, but it could get ugly in the interim. I thought it smartest to
let you know. If I were you I would get out of town."

"No one wants me," said Liir, scoffing. "No one cares to come
looking for *me*! No one knows who I am, not even myself. Do you mean
that because someone tittered that the Witch was my mother, I'm in
danger?"

"I don't mean that," said the Scarecrow. "I don't know if anyone
here knows or cares whether the Witch had children, or who they might
be. I just mean there's talk of a cleanup of this neighborhood." He
straightened up—he'd been limping, an odd thing for a Scarecrow—and
cast his clumsy gloved hand down Dirt Boulevard, where the denizens of
the evening were in their cups. A small crowd had gathered around a
couple of half-naked teens making dirty right there on the ground. The
tatterdemalions were pelting them with bits of food and egging them
on. Elsewhere, bottles emptied of their beer smashed on paving stones. A
baby cried piteously.

"What is happening?" said Liir.

"The Wizard has left, and Dorothy is gone, and Lady Glinda Chuffrey, née Arduenna of the Uplands, has been importuned to supervise a
government until something more permanent can be arranged."

"Glinda! I heard of her. The Witch used to talk about her sometimes. Well, she'll do some good, won't she?"

"Doing good, cleaning house, takes a mighty strong broom," said the
Scarecrow. "Speaking of which . . ."

The Scarecrow looked this way and that. The kids on the ground,
wheezing and humping in their throes of lust, had secured the crowd's
full attention. The Scarecrow reached into his waistband and, hand over
hand, drew out a stake. No, a pole—the handle of the broom. The
Witch's broom. Aha. Hence the limp.

He gave it to Liir. "No one wanted it," he said. "No one needed it
for anything. It served its purpose and was going to be thrown out."

Liir accepted it with resignation; one more thing to carry back to the home he no longer had. "What do you mean, things are going to get ugly? Seems to me they're pretty ugly around here already."

"Well, I mean, for the ceremony of Glinda's elevation, they'll have to relocate the urban poor. For one thing. Glinda's quite tidy and likes things just so."

"You seem to know a lot all of a sudden. The brains are working?"

"There's talk that Lady Glinda will eventually yield, and put a wise Scarecrow on the throne," the Scarecrow said, pride—or derision—making his voice sound odd. "After she cleans up the Wizard's affairs. And there are those who think that the charmed child Ozma will be located in some cave almost at once, now that the Wizard's gone. Sounds cynical and desperate to me, but what do I know of government? I've had more access to information the last few days than the rest of my life put together."

"A wise Scarecrow on the throne? *You?*" said Liir, incredulous. "Sorry, I don't mean to imply—"

"I," said the Scarecrow, "or someone like me. Frankly, to human beings, all Scarecrows look the same, which is odd, since we seem to be much more individual than humans. But we're made in their image and likeness, so all they see in us is themselves, and one mirror is as good as another, I guess."

"Do you want to be king? Now that you're so smart?"

"Now that I'm so smart, I know enough not to let on what I want," said the Scarecrow. "We should move away from here, you know."

Liir roped the heavy cape around his arms and took the scorched broom. "Any ideas?"

"Just—away. This is all so unseemly." The Scarecrow indicated the throng. "You're very young for all this."

"You're younger than I," said Liir.

"I was born old," said the Scarecrow. "That's how I was made."

"I don't know how I was made," said the boy. "That's part of my problem."

They crossed a small canal into a quieter street and came to rest on a fundament to which ranks of small private barges and blunt-boats were tied up for the night. The smoke of cooking fires, the smell of boiled beans and potato stew hung in the air.

"I miss Dorothy," he said.

The Scarecrow replied, "It's the Witch you miss, isn't it?"

"I hated her too much to miss her."

"That's what you think."

"You think your own thoughts, and leave me mine." He was outraged at the presumption. "What did you know of the Witch? Auntie Witch? Elphaba Thropp? She was my . . . she was my witch!"

The Scarecrow paid no attention. "It's starting, listen," he said. He held up his hand. The sounds from Dirt Boulevard had altered; a percussion of horses' hoofs, hundreds of them, came thrumming forward, a scatter of shouts turning into screams. "I waited too long," the Scarecrow said. He bundled Liir onto the nearest canal boat. A bearded old coot with a sawed-off hand turned and raised a hot skillet at the Scarecrow, but the Scarecrow deflected it with his gloved fist, and the man tumbled into the filthy water. "Loosen the mooring, push away," said the Scarecrow, "the neighborhood will be in flames by dessert time."

✦ 2 ✦

CANDLE PUT DOWN the domingon to rest. Her fingers were swollen with long red welts. She'd been working hard. The young man—they called him Liir, was it?—breathed shallowly, but regularly. And he hadn't twitched a muscle in the hours since Candle had started playing to him.

At the sound in the doorway, she turned. She expected the Superior Maunt, but it was her grouchy kitchen boss, Sister Cook.

"*Someone* landed a cushy job where she can sit all day," said Sister Cook, without real resentment, but she had eyes only for the victim. Hardly nightfall the first day, and the maunts in the cloister of Saint Glinda couldn't curb their curiosity. "He's not much to look at, is he?"

Candle made a soft sound in her throat, a kind of purr. A demur?

Sister Cook wasn't sure. She knew Candle to be capable of following instructions, so whatever the girl's limitations were, they didn't include deafness or lack of language understanding. She just didn't speak up; with her it was mostly glottal molasses.

Sister Cook wrinkled her nose, as if considering the merits of a joint selected for the holiday roast. A gauze sheet, nearly transparent, casting lavender shadows on the lad's near naked form. The coverlet was woven tightly, affording warmth, and was light enough to be whisked away when medical attention was required. As the evening came in, the blood blisters under the skin on this face looked like medallions of honor—or maybe the sites of subcutaneous leech colonies.

"I came to make sure you were all right," said Sister Cook at last, having taken her fill. She turned back to Candle. "Here. We all must do our part."

She pulled from her apron pocket a long red frond, fringed with airy, asparagus-fern stamens. Candle started, and the sound in her throat was clearly revulsion.

"Not to worry, it was a willing sacrifice," said Sister Cook. "I was alone in the yard mincing the cord onions when that Red Pfenix appeared again. He was distraught. He'd been attacked and wounded by something; he was bleeding from the throat and couldn't speak."

Candle shrugged and hit her chest with her hand, turning it outward.

"Sister Doctor and Sister Apothecaire hate to administer to Animals, you know that," said Sister Cook. "But it doesn't matter. They couldn't even if directed to. The Superior Maunt sent them away after lunch. Off on some investigative mission about those Emerald City novices who had their faces scraped. So what was I to do?"

Candle reached out and touched the Pfenix feather.

Sister Cook said, "Nearly shorn of life, he came back here. He pulled out his axial feather himself and walked up to me with it in his beak. Swans sing when they die; Pfenix do, too, but he couldn't. So you make music for him, please. Out of respect; we're having Pfenix breast tonight."

Sister Cook shoved both her hands in her apron pockets. "Pfenix

breast, though I've diced them small and disguised them as chicken fin-
gerlings so our dear old Mother Rush-to-Judgment doesn't have a conniption stroke. Don't forget to come down when you hear the dinner
bell; we don't get Pfenix around here very often, Animal or otherwise."

She lingered a moment longer and watched Candle hold the red
feather. It was almost two feet long and still retained some of its vital
elasticity. "Well?" said Sister Cook. "I can't stand here forever. Play a
dirge for the Pfenix, who never made it to his Convention or his class
reunion or wherever he was going. He was interested in your playing, I
saw. Honor him by accepting his gift."

Candle tried to remember what she had seen of the domingon
when it was played by its maker. She had swooned, for music or love or
both, and in her exhilaration, maybe she'd overlooked an aspect of the
instrument's construction. Maybe it had had a pfenix feather, and the
master had removed it—pfenix feathers weren't easy to come by. And a
Pfenix feather, freely given besides! What she might learn to play now.

She leaned down and laid the quill end of the feather against the
empty notch at one end of the domingon's lower soundboard. It settled
in perfectly, as if the domingon had been built to accommodate this exact feather. Then Candle gently coaxed the feather flat. There was a
hasp at the soundboard's far edge, a leather tooth on a sprung hinge
that clamped down hard to hold the pinion end of the tailfeather in
place.

Candle turned the pegs, listening to calibrations of tuning too precise for Sister Cook to appreciate. Then Candle flung out both her hands
at Sister Cook: Go! Go!

"Ungrateful, the both of you," said Sister Cook. As she descended
the stairs, she heard the first few notes of an exquisite instrument being
played by an expert. So suddenly it took her back to school days—when
she was a nervous slip of a thing at Madame Teastane's Female Academy,
not the cow she'd become—that she had to steady herself against the
wall. She was thirteen, and suffering her first menses. Coming back from
a dawn visit to the cold lavatories on the third floor, she'd spotted a red
pfenix on the roof of the Master's lodge. The trees had been airy, just

budding, struck with first light, and the bird had looked like red cloi-sonné set in warm stone. A stab of loveliness unmerited, unexpected. It had cheered her then. She continued down the stairs back to the maun-tery's kitchens, cheered again at the long-forgotten thought, though per-haps she was also happy to anticipate a fine, fine meal that night.

Southstairs

THE SUPERIOR MAUNT made it her business to get to the infirmary on a daily basis. She didn't like what she saw. The young fellow made no discernible progress; indeed, a yellowish sweat rolled off him, hinting of turps. His skin was cold to the touch. He was still breathing, however.

"You may wipe him down when he becomes too clammy," she said to Candle, and showed her how. The girl seemed reluctant to touch her charge, but did as she was bade.

Holy intuition, the Superior Maunt felt, did not figure among her own administrative talents. She was a common-sensist. She thought the Unnamed God had given her a brain to use, not to ignore as a snare of the devil. She had tried to lift herself up by clear thinking, and others, too, when she could.

Nonetheless, it was intuition as much as charity that had inspired her to call for a musician. This Candle seemed perfect: demure, even of temper, and increasingly proficient at her instrument.

The Superior Maunt wasn't overly worried that whatever had befallen Liir—whatever it was, those bruises, those broken bones!—would afflict her pair of investigators. The young missionaries from the moth-erchapel in the Emerald City, whose faces had been scraped—the boy himself—were possessed of the loveliness of youth, youth's fine igno-rance of its own fleeting grace. The same couldn't be said of Sister Doc-tor and Sister Apothecaire. Through long years of dedication and hard work, they had grown wizened and doughy, respectively. They would be safe from the attention of those who wanted to despoil the innocently beautiful. And their training in medicine had fostered keen observational skills; they could protect themselves, if anyone could.

The Maunt Superior noted that though her hearing wasn't good anymore, the music of the repaired domingon had a way of traveling. The entire mauntery was filled with its soft phrases. Sister Linenflaxen said it was elegiac, damn it, Candle was wooing the lad to his final sleep. She should play something peppier. Everyone else said *shhhh*. The whole place had fallen under a sort of spell. They were waiting to see what would happen, but the music made them patient.

Sister Graveside ironed a fresh winding cloth and refilled the corked jug with anointing oil, to be ready.

CANDLE WAS MORE OBSERVANT than the Superior Maunt credited, though. She could see that Liir's respiration responded to her choice of music. He went through periods of rhythmic breathing, like someone sleeping peacefully enough, followed by patterns of shallow flutterbreath.

Restored to glory by the feather of the Pfenix, the domingon had become responsive: the harmonic overtones hung in the air and comple-mented one another. When the invalid seemed too agitated, she would bring him back with long furling phrases. But too many of those and she was afraid he would deliver his last, deep outgo and breathe in no more: and then he would be dead. So she would agitate him with pizzicato comments and thumb-struck flat-tone responses, to alert his lungs and stimulate his heart.

She was guiding him. She knew it. She just didn't know where he was.

* * *

LIIR WAS IN THE STOLEN BLUNT-BOAT with the Scarecrow, heading along one of the waterways of the Emerald City. It was a week or two after the Witch had died. There was trouble behind, and darkness ahead, but the windows of the town mansions that lined the canal—one flight above street level, above the barricaded stables and stout front gates— threw trapezoids of gold light onto the stinking canal water. Liir and the Scarecrow passed in and out of one another's view.

"What *will* you do?" asked the Scarecrow. "Where will you go?"

"I have no place to go," said Liir. "I'm not going back to Kiamo Ko. Why should I? Only old Nanny there."

"Have you no obligation to her?"

"*Now* you ask me? In a word, no. Chistery will mind her well enough."

"The Snow Monkey? Yes, I suppose he will. Well, the story of Dorothy is done. We won't see her like again."

"And a good thing, too," said Liir. "Off and away with the fairies, just like that, and not so much as a decent good-bye!"

"Her departure was precipitous," agreed the Scarecrow. "Glinda made the arrangements in something of a hurry."

The light from a party, candles laid out on a balustrade. The music wafting out open doors: agitated phrases, comments and responses, from some instrument with multiple voices, or many instruments playing very close together. Haunting!

The Scarecrow said, "Don't fasten on Dorothy. Only unanswerable longing lies down that road. Gone is gone."

"How wise you are, now that you're packed with brains. Everyone got some party favor from the Wizard except me. Everyone's got some-where to go."

"Don't look to me for a map, Liir. Figure it out for yourself. What about your friend, Nor? That Princess Nastoya seemed to think she might still be alive. Maybe you could find her."

"First I better learn a trade and find a way to support myself. Or watch how the pickpockets practice their trade. Sure, I would like to find Nor, but I'd like to fly, too. Not bloody likely without some help."

"I can't be much help."

"Too highly connected now, I'm sure. Too chummy with the chief cheeses."

"I have my own plans. Appointments to keep. I'm out of here as soon as I can."

"I thought that Glinda person had singled you out for a lead position in the government. That's what they're saying on the streets, where I pick up my news and other garbage."

"Lady Glinda doesn't confide in me. I've heard she intends to rule for six months or so, and then abdicate in favor of a straw man. Who?— well, as I've admitted, one scarecrow is as good as another. Do you think anyone would notice the difference? When a scarecrow blows apart in a gale wind, the farmer just props up another one. It's the job to be done that's important, not who does it."

"That's what they used to say at the mauntery," said Liir. "If a maunt dies and goes to the Afterlife, another maunt comes to take her place. Like replacing a pane of glass. It's the work that's important, not the individual who does it."

"Well, I'm keeping my own counsel about my plans," said the Scarecrow, "and I'm not long for the Emerald City, I'll tell you that much. One day you're a celebrity, the next day you're hauled off to jail."

They contemplated this as they came upon a weir. From here, a system of locks stepped the water level down steeply until it disappeared into a fortified grate. Above, armed members of the Emerald City Guard were having a smoke around a brazier. "Better not get their attention," said the Scarecrow.

"What's over there, that the canal is guarded?" whispered Liir as they regarded their situation.

"Not sure. Couldn't say. But it might be Southstairs."

"Southstairs? What's that?"

The Scarecrow made a face in the gloom. "The high-security prison for the heartland. Don't you know anything? I've only been here a week and I know that."

"Why would they be guarding the canal grate?"

"Who knows? Maybe they're afraid there'll be a move to liberate Southstairs. I'm told a lot of professional Animals ended up there over the decades, cheek by jowl with murderers, pedophiles. Rapists. Political pamphleteers."

"The Wizard's gone. Why aren't they just throwing the gates open?"

"You want the murderers and rapists back in the neighborhood?"

"Well—no. No, but for the dissenters."

The Scarecrow frowned. "Dream on. Who's going to take it upon themselves to decide which is which at this point? The job of personal fiscal betterment is far more urgent."

"Hard to argue with that. And I bet the suppressed Animals agree with you. Are they on the move, do you know? Or hanging low until they see what develops?"

"Look, I got you safely away from Dirt Boulevard before you were swept up in a purge. I'm not going to deliver you to Southstairs so you can check on the Animals there. Let's turn about."

The Scarecrow piloted the blunt-boat backward until there was room enough to swing it around. Their route took them back under the balustrades where the fancy-dress ball was in progress. The laughter was more unguarded, even strident, the music brassier. "Lots to celebrate these days, for those of the right station," said the Scarecrow. "Good news indeed. Could be another Victory Gala."

"Celebrating the Wizard's departure?"

"Celebrating the Witch's death," said the Scarecrow. His face was impassive. "Oh, sweet Oz, it's Glinda's house!" He tucked his head down. "Liir!"

"She doesn't know me," said Liir. He scrambled backward along the boat to its squared-off stern, a small elevated platform for the loading of goods. Craning, he could see a woman leaning her hips against the carved stone balustrades of the balcony. The light from the ballroom fell on her golden hair, which was swept up on her head in a bubbly mass of curls hooped by a diamond tiara. He couldn't see how old she was, nor her expression, for her face was turned away. She was trim and fit, though her shoulders were slumped—grief, or despair? Or boredom? She dabbed a handkerchief at her nose.

Liir didn't speak, he didn't call out—what did he care for Lady Glinda Chuffrey? Auntie Witch had mentioned her only in passing. Sometimes with grudging respect, more often with disapproval. As he watched her, something echoed along the waters of the canal, a sound—as if a private, smoky slide of music accompanied their blunt-boat, counterpoint to the party pandemonium.

Lady Glinda turned, and gripped the rail with both hands, and leaned over as their vessel was slipping beneath a pedestrian bridge. "Shit!" hissed the Scarecrow, and stayed the boat in the shadows by throwing his weight against the pole. "She's seen us!"

"Who is it?" called Glinda. "Who's there?—I almost thought—"

Liir wanted to speak up. The Scarecrow clapped a gloved hand against his mouth tightly. Liir struggled, elbowed the Scarecrow, but he wasn't strong enough to break free before Glinda shook her head as if in disbelief, straightened the epaulets on her ball gown, and returned to her affair.

"What's the matter with you?" railed Liir, when the Scarecrow had let him go.

"What's the matter with *you*?" said the Scarecrow. "I'm trying to keep a low profile in order to help you, and you have to go and signal the heads of state and alert them about it?"

"I didn't signal her!"

"Well, she must have a sixth sense then, for she turned, and she saw you."

"She doesn't know who I am. She doesn't know I exist!"

"And let's keep it that way."

+ 2 +

THE ANIMOSITY THAT OBTAINED between Sisters Doctor and Apothe-caire subsided once dusk fell on their first evening away from the Maun-tery of Saint Glinda. The women erected the frame of thin skark ribs and fixed the waterproof awning to it. Then they huddled together un-der a blanket. When the wolves of the oakhair forest howled their mid-night requiem, the Sisters mangled their devotions into such a gabble of syllables and sobs that, had the Unnamed God been condescending to listen, it could only have concluded that its two emissaries were afflicted with sudden-onset glossolalia.

"The Superior Maunt thought it safe to send us out on an ex-ploratory mission even though the faces of those three young missionar-ies had so recently been scraped," said Sister Apothecaire the following morning, which dawned damp and windless. "I trust her in every partic-ular," she added fiercely, unconvincingly.

"Our charge is clear," said Sister Doctor, "safety or no. We are to make an effort to address the tribal Scrow, if we can locate them, and cer-tainly the Yunamata. We must enquire about the disaster that struck those missionaries. With the conviction of our faith in the Unnamed God, no harm will befall us."

"Do you propose the missionaries were in greater danger because their faith was weak?" asked Sister Apothecaire.

Sister Doctor's lips became thinner as she folded the awning away. "Cowardice, said the Superior Maunt, will not serve us in this task."

Sister Apothecaire relented. "Cowardice is a dubious attribute. Yet I possess it in spades, so I hope on this venture to learn how to use it to my advantage if I must. All gifts come from the Unnamed God, including cowardice, and self-repugnance."

The mules dropped their heavy hoofs on the path, picking a way be-tween ranks of thin trees with branches nearly empty of leaves. Little cover.

"Perhaps," said Sister Doctor, "the Superior Maunt sent *us* out be-cause we would be better able to tend to each other, medically, were we attacked."

"If we survived. Well, I've no doubt that our skills here in the wilderness will prove useful. After all, I do speak a dialect of West Yumish."

"When you've had a bit too much seasonal sherry."

They laughed at that and proceeded in companionable silence until Sister Apothecaire couldn't stand it. "Now Liir is Candle's responsibility. Funny little thing. What can she bring to Liir that we can't?"

"Don't be stupid. She can bring youth and charm, if she can get his attention. She can give him a reason to survive. This is something neither you nor I could do. If he opened up his eyes after a long coma and saw either of us right off, he'd probably kick the bucket in a nonce."

Sister Apothecaire did not murmur assent. She was rather proud of her looks. Well, her face, anyway; her figure was regrettably lumpy. "Perhaps," she said distractingly, "Candle has a natural talent that the Superior Maunt can sense."

"What sort of talent?" Sister Doctor shifted in her saddle and turned to peer at her colleague. "You don't mean a talent for magic? That's distinctly forbidden in the order."

"Come come. You know perfectly well we resort to it when we must. Not that we're very good at it. I need hardly remind you that these are dangerous times. Perhaps the Superior Maunt thinks that in the rehabilitation of the boy, such a talent is called for."

By the straightening of her spine Sister Doctor signaled that she did not intend to second-guess the Superior Maunt's motives. Sister Apothecaire regretted having brought it up. "Well," she continued, falsely jolly, "I don't have much of a sense of Candle one way or the other. If she's got common magic or common sense, it's news to me either way."

"She certainly has no talent for music." Sister Doctor sniffed. "I do remember the day she arrived, though. I happened to be suturing one of the novices in the kitchen. I turned to ask kindly for water, and there was that Candle, her rickety domingon slung over one shoulder like a crossbow. Mad old Mother Yackle had her by the hand, as if she'd just created her out of calves' foot jelly. 'The gypsy Quadling, her uncle leaves her to us,' said Mother Yackle."

"Mother Yackle doesn't speak and hasn't in years."

"That's why I remember the event so distinctly."

"Did you see the Quadling uncle?"

"I went to the window, and he was making his way rather hurriedly through the kitchen garden. I called out to him, for there are procedures for the introduction of a novice, and this wasn't one of them. But he wouldn't be stopped, merely called over his shoulder that he would be back in a year if he was still alive. It's rare to see Quadlings this far north these days. I imagine the poor girl is quite lonely."

"Well, yes. No one speaks Quaddle."

"I believe the term is Qua'ati. So is Candle mute or is it that she just hasn't anyone to speak her native tongue with?"

"I don't know."

Perhaps it was Candle's silence and self-control that had inspired the Superior Maunt to choose her for keeping vigil over Liir. The maunts began to regret their tendencies to bark and spark at each other. Thinking on their noisy failings, they fell into a silence now.

IN THE FOLLOWING FEW DAYS, they came across their share of blue squirrels, bald egrets, and disagreeable emmets. The egrets kept to the ground cover, rarely taking wing; the emmets preferred the bedding. It wasn't until near dusk on the fourth day that the maunts came across an Animal, a lone and pagan Water Buffalo in the shallows of a cove of Restwater, Oz's biggest lake.

"Oh, oh," moaned the Water Buffalo at their approach, "not the missionary voice traveling in twos! Not again! I bury my own waste, I only speak when spoken to, I lick my knees fifty times a night before I sleep—what more am I to do to appease the fates? I don't want to be converted! Don't you understand? Oh, all right, get it over with. I'll lapse before nightfall, I promise you. I can't help myself. Perhaps I'm too far gone for you to bother with me?" He peered, both gloomily and hopefully, at them.

"We're not converters," said Sister Apothecaire. "We haven't the time."

"And who cares about you? You can go to hell," said Sister Doctor, meaning to be cheerful. This was the right note, as it happened; the Water Buffalo began to smile.

"Scarcely see a soul coming from your direction who doesn't have designs on my immortal soul," said the Water Buffalo. "It used to be I was worried about my hide. I always thought a soul was private, but it appears it can be colonized against your will if you don't watch out."

"Well, we *are* maunts," admitted Sister Apothecaire.

The Water Buffalo winced. "*No.* Say it ain't so. You're plates of glamour and glasses of fashion, as anyone who rests a sore eye upon you would have to agree."

"Don't be mincing," snapped Sister Doctor. "These are perfectly respectable clothes for traveling in."

"Depends on where you want to get to," intoned the Water Buffalo.

"Look, we can evangelize like the best of them, if that's what it's going to take—"

"Sorry, sorry!" said the Water Buffalo. "I'll be good. What's your game?"

They told him. He knew nothing of the attacks on the young maunts and their scrapings, nor had he ever heard of Liir or his misadventure. But he had seen airborne battalions of trained creatures flying so high that he couldn't make them out. "Something's amiss," he said. "I know there's been an attempt to call a Congress of Birds out in the west, but lately I've seen few Birds brave enough to fly at anything like a decent height."

"We can't patrol the skies right now," said Sister Doctor. "It's the Scrow or the Yunamata we need to find."

"The Scrow rarely venture this far east. However, you may come across a small band of Yunamata, if they haven't moved off yet. They're down from Kumbricia's Pass. I came across them bathing this morning. We all minded our own business. They don't have anything to do with the Unnamed God, so they don't bother me, and I don't bother them. They rinsed their totems and washed their hair, and one of them gave birth to a baby underwater. They're rather froggy folk when it comes to birthing. They circulated a birth pipe around, passed out in the sun for an hour or so, and then gathered their things and left. They seemed to be heading southwest. Several dozen of them, no more."

"If you see them, tell them we're coming," said Sister Doctor.

"Jubilation, they'll be over the moon," drawled the Water Buffalo. "If you want to meet up with them, better *not* tell them you're coming, honeys."

The sisters moved on, but before they had lost sight of the Water Buffalo, Sister Apothecaire thought to turn and call, "We forgot to ask your name!"

"Only the chattering classes of Animal have names!" the Water Buffalo replied cheerily. "And there hasn't been a professional Animal the length and breadth of Oz for thirty years. If I don't have a name, I can't be targeted as a potential convert, can I?"

A moment later, when he was out of sight, his voice rang toward them thinly: "Though if you had to locate me, I suppose I'd answer to Buff . . ."

"Weird creature," said Sister Apothecaire a while later.

"He'd survived, a talking Animal in the wild," Sister Doctor reminded her. "It can't have been easy. After the Wizard's banishment, the Animals didn't rush for reassimilation. Who could blame them, with all they'd been through."

"Sounds as if the creature's been dogged by zealots, though."

"Indeed. Well, the Emperor is a devout man, and wants all his subjects to enjoy the benefits of faith, I suppose."

ANOTHER NIGHT, and the wolves howled more fiercely than ever. The dawn seemed full of its own arcane purpose, a pale light leaching through grey cloud-hemp. The maunts ventured out across the Disappointments. Then, easy as playing at knackers, they came upon a group of Yunamata doing winter rush-work.

"Hail," said Sister Apothecaire in Yumish, "or have I said *hell* by mistake? Hello? Yoo hoo Yunamata? We come in peace."

"What are you saying?" said Sister Doctor. "They look mystified."

"I'm addressing their tribal gods," said Sister Apothecaire, and in Yumish, "I. Good. Good one. Good human person woman being. I. Good thing. Where is the library?" In her anxiety it was all she could remember.

"They look amused," said Sister Doctor.

"That's respect," said Sister Apothecaire. But amusement was better than hostility, so she began to relax, and more of the plain tongue began to return to her.

The Yunamata were known for keeping to themselves. Nomadic, but not a horse culture like the Scrow, this Vinkus tribe was fleet of foot and economical of domestic impedimenta, needing only a few pack animals to carry their belongings. Generally they sheltered in Kumbricia's Pass or the forested slopes of the Kells south of there. What were they doing out in open country?

Sister Doctor, who never liked to go slumming as a veterinarian, felt she could sniff out an Animal tendency: the Yunamata looked as if they might all have one giant, docile Frog among their ancestors. Way, way back. Nothing like webbing between their digits, no long flickering tongues, no, no; they were human through and through. But an amphibian sort of human, with leathery skin, narrow ridiculous limbs, and thin lips that seemed partly withdrawn into their mouths.

One could laugh at the silliness of them. Laugh—and then be carved to shreds, for when aroused they could be a formidable enemy. The Yunamata had skill with knives. Mostly they used their serrated tools—lethal curved blades set in handles of the hardest mahogany—for aid in the construction of their tree nests, where they harbored at night. Those same knives could carve a pig or eviscerate a minor canon with equal efficiency.

Sister Apothecaire set out to convince the Yunamata that the maunts were abroad neither to betray the clan nor to convert them. Just in case, like the Water Buffalo, they'd previously been targeted as a population ripe for conversion. As a group, they listened, promoting no spokesperson among them. By turns they mouthed small neat phrases. Sister Apothecaire took pains to translate these remarks to her colleague carefully, and to question her own understanding if she had any doubt. She didn't want to assent to human martyrdom merely because she'd forgotten some nicety of Yumish grammar. *Was* there a retractional pluperfect subjunctive in Yumish?

"You are going on quite a while," said Sister Doctor after an hour or so.

"I am doing my job and trying to see if we're going to be invited to stay for supper," said Sister Apothecaire. "Leave me be."

"I hope they aren't teetotalers. I think I'm getting a sniffle."

When the conversation had concluded at last, and the Yunamata retreated to prepare a meal, Sister Doctor said, "Well? Well? I deduce from your smug expression that they're not about to sharpen their blades to scrape our faces from us. Though I'd like to hear it put directly, to ease my mind."

"They speak by indirection. They know about the scrapings. They have seen evidence of it. They say it must be the Scrow. The Scrow have a tradition of royalty, and their queen is an old woman named Nastoya who has been in declining health for a decade. Were we to fulfill the mission assigned us, we would next have to hunt for this Princess Nastoya and reprove her about these infractions. The Yunamata insist that the Scrow must be in allegiance with the Emperor."

"Ridiculous. If the Scrow were in allegiance with the Emperor, would they be scraping his emissaries? Or are the Yunamata lying?"

"Look at them. Could they lie?"

"Don't be soft. Of course they could. The most purring of cats can still kill a bird within half a purr."

"I suppose I believe them," said Sister Apothecaire, "because they *admit* to their capacity for vengeance. But they also have told me that this is the season of the jackal, and out of wariness of the moon's opinion, they take a vow of gentility. Babies born under the jackal moon are considered lucky. Babies born in Restwater are luckier still."

"Are you sure you've understood correctly? Throughout Oz the season of the jackal is considered dangerous."

"Perhaps it's a kind of propitiation," said Sister Apothecaire. "They mentioned the Old Dowager, a kind of deity who harvests souls. She sounded a bit like Kumbricia. Do you remember Kumbricia, from your schoolgirl lessons in antique lore? Kumbricia, the oldest witch from the time of creation? Source of all venom and malice?"

"I turned my back on such things when I entered a unionist maun-tery," said Sister Doctor. "I'm surprised you remember such poppyde-gook."

"I don't know if we're getting a meal," said Sister Apothecaire, ges-turing, "but look, it appears we're getting a pipe of some sort." A dele-gation of Yunamata was approaching with a communal smoke.

"A vile habit," snarled Sister Doctor, but she determined to do her best at being sociable, and stomach such barbaric customs as courtesy required.

• 3 •

No one at the Mauntery, Candle included, knew enough about mu-sical instruments to appreciate the domingon she arrived with. It was made of seasoned wrenwood by a master from the Quadling Kells, and Candle had first heard it played at a summer festival. The master himself performed, using his fingers as well as a fiddle bow and a glass emulant that he kept tucked under his bearded chin when not required. Now Candle recalled that the domingon *had* been fitted out with a feather, though at the time Candle had thought it merely ornamentation—and a sexy fillip at that.

She had thought she was in love with him, and had slept with him before dusk, but a few days later she realized it was the music she had loved. What she heard in its music: a coaxing, an invitation to remember, to disclose. Perhaps because her voice was small and high, she couldn't project, and she imagined it would be more gratifying to play music than to speak. Mercilessly she pestered her uncle to circle back and buy her the domingon; she'd been surprised when he obliged.

Candle was not simple, not in the least, but her debility had made her a still person. She listened to church bells, when they pealed, trying to translate; she watched the way the paper husks of an onion fell on a table, and examined the rings of dirt that onion mites had left in parallel rows on the glossy wet inside. Everything said something, and it wasn't her job to consider the merit or even the meaning of the message: just to witness the fact of the message.

She was therefore a calmer person than most, for there seemed no dearth of messages from the world to itself. She merely listened in.

For a week now she'd been playing the domingon until her fingers ached, watching and listening for the language of Liir's recovery. It wasn't unusual that she had had experience with men; Quadlings were a casual sort in matters of sexual prudence. The carnal experience had neither scarred her nor much interested her. Through it, at best, she had learned something of the human body, its hesitations and reservations as well as the surge of its desires.

In the infirmary, as her eyes moved from the instrument to the invalid, she felt she was picking up some news. Was it some minor language of olfactory signals, an arcane pattern of eye twitches, a hieroglyph etched in the beads of his sweat? She didn't know. She was sure of this, though: Liir's body seemed the same in temperature, comportment, and color. But he was going through a phase of crisis, and would either awaken for sure or die at once: no middle ground.

She didn't know if she should go get the Superior Maunt or if she should stay at her post. She was afraid if she left, if she dropped the domingon on the floor even for the twenty minutes it might take to find the Superior Maunt and get counsel, she would lose Liir for good. Wherever he was, he was lost, and the music of her instrument was his only hope back.

So Candle stayed seated and played till her own fingers bled, in ripples of waltz, as if nothing were wrong. The blue of the sky thinned till it was pierced with star prickers, and then the jackal moon rose and slowly lumbered over till it could look in the window and watch for itself. Watch, and listen, as Candle played Liir through his memories.

❖   ❖   ❖

"She'll be there," said Liir.

"Who? Where? Are you talking about Elphaba?" said the Scarecrow.

"Of course not. I'm talking about Nor. The girl I knew. Maybe my half-sister, if the Witch really was my mother and Fiyero my father, as some have guessed."

"In Southstairs? A girl?"

"Can you tell me why not?"

The Scarecrow didn't answer. Liir thought: Maybe he imagines that someone as insignificant to the mighty Wizard of Oz—a mere girl, no less—hardly merited imprisonment. Maybe he thinks she might as easily have been murdered, or tossed onto the streets to drift and starve. How long had it been anyway since she had been taken from Kiamo Ko? Two years? Three? But then Princess Nastoya had implied that Nor might have survived . . .

They had circled the canals a bit longer and found a place to berth underneath some rotting trees by the side of a pub. "I can't stay with you for much longer, you know," said the Scarecrow. "I only came to give you the Witch's broom, and to wish you well, and to protect you from the clearing of Dirt Boulevard. I have my own path to follow. I would see you safely to the other side of the gates of this troubled city if I could. If you would let me."

"I'm not going," said Liir. "Not without Nor. Or not without finding out what has happened to her."

At a crossroads, unwilling to move, they sat disconsolate.

"Look," said Liir, at graffiti dashed sharply and sloppily on the pub's side wall. It said HAPPY ENDINGS ARE STILL ENDINGS. "You've done your work, you've kept your word to Dorothy. I have the broom. But I won't be ushered out of harm's way. What's the point? I have no happy ending—cripes, I've had no happy beginning, either. The Witch is dead, and Dorothy is gone, and that old Princess Nastoya has asked us for help. As if I could! Just because Elphaba would have!"

"You needn't fulfill some promise Elphaba made. If you're not her son, you have no obligation there."

"Well, there's Nor, too. Call it a promise to myself."

The Scarecrow held his head in his hands. "The Tin Woodman has left to cultivate the art of caring. He has his work cut out for him, poor sod. The Lion is suffering severe depression; his cowardice was his sole identifying trait, and now he's pitiably normal. Neither of them can help you much, I'm afraid. You should get yourself out of here while you can. Start over."

"Start over? I never started the first time. Besides, it's not getting out that I need to do. It's getting in."

The Scarecrow pushed a hand against his heart and shook his head.

"Into Southstairs," said Liir.

"I know what you meant," said the Scarecrow. "I'm not stupid. Now."

"You're the one I need to keep on my side—"

The Scarecrow interrupted with a brusqueness that might have been meant kindly. "Don't bother to look for me. You won't find me. Save yourself for someone you might recognize. I'm not in your story, Liir. Not after this."

So they took their leave, with little fanfare or fuss. The friendship between them was no larger or more hopeful than the shape of a scorched broom, which Liir waved halfheartedly as the Scarecrow loped out of sight, once and for all.

The boy sat in the bobbing blunt-boat and listened to the sound of laughter spilling out the open windows of the pub. The smell was of beer and vomit, and old urine splashed against the wall. The moon was invisible behind the clouds. The sound of a tentative waltz, beguiling and minor, hung over the stinking waters of the canal and the desolate boy there.

THE NEXT MORNING, Liir presented himself at the servants' entrance of the town house he'd passed the night before.

"We don't give handouts and we don't need another coal shoveler, so get yourself out of here before I assist you with a boot in your behind," said the houseboy.

"If you please, I'm not looking for food or work. Sir."

The houseboy smirked. "Toadying bastard. Call me *sir* again, and I'll beat the crap out of you."

Liir couldn't follow. "I meant no disrespect. I just want to know how I can get an audience with Lady Glinda."

The houseboy's sneer needed rearranging with a good swift kick, Liir decided, but when the houseboy guffawed, his voice was less hostile. "Oh, a simpleton. Pardon me, I didn't realize. Listen, the very Margreave of Tenmeadows, Lord Avaric himself, hasn't been able to get her lady-ship's attention. She's got her hands full, what with the goings-on in the Wizard's Palace. The people's Palace now. Or should be. Or will be. What, you want to fling yourself in her lap and call her *mother*? More urchins have tried that already than you could fit on a barge and drown in Kellswater. Now get off with you."

"Whatever mother I don't have, it certainly isn't *her*." He held up the broom and shook it in the houseboy's face.

"What's that then?"

Liir said, "You tell Lady Glinda that a boy at the back gate has the Witch's broom. Tell her Dorothy gave it me. I don't care how long you take, I'll wait."

"That thing? That's a corpse of a broom. Not fit for kindling."

"It's been through a lot. That's how you know it's the real thing."

"You're a stubborn bugger. I can't be standing here chewing the fat all day. Tell you what. Do me some magic with that broom and I'll see what I can do for you."

"I can't do magic. And the broom isn't a magic wand. It's a broom. It sweeps."

"Sweep a floor with that thing, you'll leave char marks, and I'll be the one cleaning up after you. Get out of here, now. Go on."

Liir raised the broom again and tilted it forward. The houseboy shrank back, as if afraid flecks of scorch would fall on his livery. Notic-ing this, Liir decided it would be worth his while to wait around and see what happened.

His instincts proved sound. The houseboy wasn't able to resist gos-siping about his conversation with Liir. Just before noon, a housekeeper came out, tucking her apron strings in and wiping crumbs from her lips. "Love a grouse, you're still here, and that's a good thing!" she gabbled. "The houseboy's been docked a month's pay for being silly-headed! Get over here, Her Haughtiness wants to see you at once! You reek, haven't you washed? The pump, there, boy, scrub your grubby armpits and wipe that smirk off your face. This is Lady Glinda that lives here, not some cow-mistress. And hop smart, you. She's waiting."

HE WAS BROUGHT TO a lady's parlor and told to behave and touch nothing.

He could look, though, and he did. He had never seen an upholstered chair before. He'd never seen one chair face another chair that looked identical. Cushions everywhere, fresh flowers, and gleaming crystal bubbles set on little stands. A collection of commemorative baubles, he guessed. To what end?

A fire of aromatic woods burned in the dainty hearth. Why a daytime fire in such a well-built mansion, when the citizens outside couldn't get close enough to a brazier to warm their hands, let alone soften their supper bricks of congealed molasses?

He wandered to the window to open it, let in some air. It looked out over the canal where he and the Scarecrow had drifted the night before. From this height, he could see the rooflines of the fancy houses. Palaces, almost, or palaces-in-training. Beyond the chimney pots, beyond the roof gardens, the cupolas and spires and domes, two more massive buildings rose: the domed Palace of the Wizard, in the dead center of the City, and off to the right, the steep bluestone ramparts of the prison known as Southstairs.

It was like looking at a picture in a book—not that he'd seen all that many books. Only the Grimmerie, and that only from a distance. Here, the etched rooflines seemed like a hundred man-made hills. Set here and there to delight the eye with infinite variety in depth and perspective.

Under every roof, a story, just as behind every brow, a history.

He hardly believed he had summoned the nerve to come here. But it was all he could think of to do. The Princess Nastoya had promised, in exchange for his helping her, to listen for news of Nor. But why work backward? The Princess would have to be scrubbing the news of the Emerald City to learn about Nor. Whereas now—he was here already—

so let Princess Nastoya work out her troubles for herself. Liir had all the City before him. He would be forthright and claim what he wanted for himself. On his own terms.

"The Lady Glinda," announced a man's voice. When Liir turned, the door was already being drawn closed behind her, and Lady Glinda came near.

It was like being approached by a decorated holiday tree tiptoeing in jeweled slippers. Lady Glinda was the most exceedingly dressed person Liir had ever seen. He almost flinched, but knowing that Lady Glinda had been a friend of Elphaba's stiffened his nerve. "How do you do," she was saying, in a voice like a piccolo blowing soapsuds. She tilted her head. Was it an upperclass gesture, like a genuflection? Ought he pivot his head in reply? He remained upright. "Liir, is it?"

"Yes, ma'am."

He had never called anyone "ma'am" in his life. Where had *that* come from?

"They said it was Liir. I thought I might have misheard. Please, won't you sit—" She took a better look at the state of his clothes and changed her mind. "Would you permit me to take a seat? I'm not resting well these days, and it's a strain."

"Of course." He realized he was to remain standing, though he drew a little nearer. Settling gingerly on a chaise longue upholstered in peppermint stripes, she arranged a bolster at the small of her back, and then reclined, lifting one ankle up from time to time. Maybe she had a twitch.

"I'm told you have something to show me, a talisman of some sort. You've got it wrapped in that shroud. A broom, a witch's broom. *The broom?* The broom of the Wicked Witch of the West?"

"I didn't call her that," he said.

"How did you come by it? Last I heard of it, that Dorothy Gale was humping it around the Palace like some sort of a trophy, brandishing it for all to see."

"I'm told she's gone," said Liir.

"She is." The tone of authority was convincing. Tired, regretful, convincing.

"Gone the way old Ozma is gone? Disappeared? Done in?"

"Gone is gone," said Glinda. "Who knows, maybe Ozma herself will be back someday. I wouldn't hold my breath."

"And maybe Dorothy, too? Or is she gone too far to come back?"

"You ask bold questions of a lady you've just met," said Glinda, and she looked at him sharply. "And you haven't answered mine. How did you come by Elpha—I mean the Witch's broom?"

"You can say Elphaba to me." Liir unwrapped the broom and held it up for Glinda to see.

Glinda didn't look at the broom. She was staring at the Witch's cape. She hoisted herself to her feet and reached to touch its hem. "I'd know this anywhere. This is Elphaba's cape. How did you come by it? Answer me, thug—thief—or I'll have you thrown in Southstairs."

"Fair enough, I'm headed there anyway. Yes, it's her cape. Why wouldn't it be? I took it when I left her castle. I'm her—"

He couldn't say *son*. He didn't know. "I'm her helper. I came from the castle with Dorothy. When the Witch melted, all that was left was the broom. The Scarecrow brought it back to me after Dorothy vanished. No one else wanted it."

"It's a burned stick. Throw it on the fire."

"No."

Glinda reached out a hand, and Liir took it. She wanted help getting up. "Let me look you in the eye, young man. Who are you? How did you come to be at Kiamo Ko?"

"I don't know, and that's the truth. But I served the Witch and saw Dorothy safely to the Emerald City, and I need your help."

"You need *my* help? What for? Bread, cash, a false identity to help you slip sideways through the cracks? Tell me what you need, tell me why I should help, and I'll see what I can do. In memory of Elphaba. You knew her." Her head tilted again, but up, this time, and it was to keep the sudden wetness from spilling into her carefully colored false eyelashes. "You knew my Elphie!"

He would not indulge in cheap grief. "I want to find out what happened to a girl kidnapped by the Wizard's men a few years back. She lived at Kiamo Ko when we got there."

"We?"

"The Witch and I . . ."

"The Witch and you." Her hands reached out hungrily for the cape and rubbed its hem, as if it were leaves of thyme or hyssop. "What girl might that be?"

"Her name is Nor. She is the daughter of Fiyero, one-time prince of the Arjikis, and his wife, Sarima, also kidnapped that very day. You knew Fiyero."

"I knew Fiyero." It was clear Glinda did not want to speak about him. "Why should I bother with you?"

"Nor was his daughter. She was my—" Again, he couldn't say *half-sister*. He didn't know. "My friend."

Glinda reached out and took the charred broomstick and cradled it. "I know about friends."

"Friends have children," Liir said carefully. "If you can't help your friends, you can help their children. Do you have children?"

"I do not. Lord Chuffrey was not so inclined." She reconsidered. "I mean to say, he is so very old. Old and wealthy. His interests lie else-where."

She drifted among the occasional tables. "I don't know why this girl you mention was taken away, or, if she proved that much of a worry, why she should still be alive."

"Everyone knows the Wizard is gone. Surely his enemies don't need to stay imprisoned? If she's alive, why shouldn't she be released?"

A rustling of stiffened tulle sounded in her underskirts. "How do I know you are telling the truth?" she said at last. "These are such treacherous days. I've spent my adult life up till now in salons and theater boxes, not in closed assembly with grasping, pinching . . . *ministers*." She spat out the word. "Insects. And I thought girls at school were devious. Here, every impassive expression hides a bloated ambition for—for dominance, I suppose. And any one of my so-called loyal cabinet could be sending you in here with a tale designed to catch at my throat. I must have more proof you are who you profess to be. This may not be El-phie's cape you're sporting. Maybe my sorrow tempts me into seeing what I would love to see. This may not be her broom. Tell me more, you Liir. How did her broom come to be so burnt?"

"I'm not sure. In truth, I didn't see her die, I only heard what Nanny and Dorothy and the others said. I was locked downstairs. But the broom burnt, that's all I know."

"Anyone could tell a lie!" cried Glinda. "Anyone could burn a broom and make up a story about it!" She beat herself on the breastplate with a clenched fist, and suddenly rushed across the room, overturning a small table and shattering some china dolls. She flung the broom in the fire. "Look, I could do it, too. There's nothing to it."

"Take the broom, burn it," he replied. "Take the cape and burn it, too, or sew it into a hairshirt and wear it under your fancy ball gowns. It doesn't matter. Give me a way to get to Nor, and to get her out; you can have whatever you want. I will come back and serve you as I served the Witch. I have no other plan for my days alive once I answer the question about Nor."

Glinda collapsed on the nearest stool and wept. She needed a man to come and take her in his arms, to give her a shoulder. Liir wasn't a man, nor was his shoulder made for a highborn lady to weep upon. He stood foolishly by, twisting his hands, averting his eyes here, there.

"Look. Glinda, look." In his excitement he forgot to use her title.

She raised her eyes and turned to where he was pointing.

The fire still danced and hissed. Some trick of physics caused the flue to hum faintly like an old folk melody, as if someone were on the rooftop playing an instrument. The music was not merely consoling— and it was that—but commanding: look, it said, look. The broom lay on the back of a log that seethed with flames of pumpkin and pale white. The broom was untouched.

"Sweet Oz . . . ," said Glinda. "Liir, take it. Take it back."

"I'll burn my hands!"

"You won't." Glinda chortled a few syllables in a language Liir couldn't understand. "This is one of the few spells I could ever really master; it came in handy when my husband required me to hand him the burnt toast on the mornings I thought it my wifely duty to prepare his breakfast. Go on. Grasp it and bring it back."

He did, and Glinda was right: the broom had not only neglected to ignite further—but it also wasn't even warm to the touch.

"A burnt broom that has had enough, and refuses to burn further . . . Keep that with you," said Glinda. "I was wrong to doubt you. Whoever you are, however you came by it, this is the Witch's broom. And so I must trust you to be telling me the truth."

She shrugged and tried to smile, and almost began to blubber. "Elphie would know what to do!"

"Tell me what *you* know," he said, as softly as he could.

"I don't have access to the register of prisoners in Southstairs Academy, which is the place your—Nor—is most likely to be if she wasn't murdered long ago. I'm not even sure a register is kept. But I know someone could get you in, at least. Whether you could find Nor or get her out, or yourself either, I can't guess. But I can make introductions for you; in memory of Elphaba, I will do that much."

"Who would help me? A friend of yours?"

"No friend of mine, but a bereaved member of her family. Next of kin to the dearly departed Elphaba Thropp, the Wicked Witch of the West . . ."

"But I thought Elphaba's sister was dead!" said Liir. "Wasn't Nessarose—killed by Dorothy's clumsy house?"

"Yes, she was. But didn't you know? Didn't Elphaba tell you? She had a brother, too. A younger brother named Shell."

◆ 4 ◆

IN COMING TO THEIR SENSES, Sister Doctor and Sister Apothecaire were gratified to find they still possessed their faces. The pack mules were nowhere to be seen though, nor their food supplies, nor their hosts.

"What is that engine in my brain?" said Sister Doctor, after she'd vomited into some ferns.

"I feel as if the jackal moon had been down here snouting around in an unseemly manner." Sister Apothecaire adjusted her garments. "It must be the effects of the ceremonial pipe."

"And that's why the Yunamata never built a city nor invented alge-brarish nor bowed to the Wizard."

"With a smoke that kicks like that, who needs a city or an Emperor?"

They ambled in oppressive daylight. "I suppose we should think about what we're doing," said Sister Doctor.

"Yes. If the Yunamata are right, then the Scrow must be responsible for the scrapings. So we're liable to wander into hotter water if we are able to find them."

"I think that's our calling, isn't it?"

"Hmmm." They had a choice: to venture farther into the foothills of the Kells, and make their presence known to the Scrow—or to go back and claim they'd failed. Without discussing it further, they pressed on. Duty weighed more heavily than dread.

THE MAUNTS KNEW that their professional skills—to be loving, to be de-vout, to be local in their attentions and spiritual in their desires—had not prepared them to be government envoys. Still, since their mauntery served as a way station for those who acted upon the stage of the world, the good sisters considered themselves at least as broad-minded as any other cloistered soul.

Sister Doctor and Sister Apothecaire, nonetheless, were unprepared for the breadth of the Scrow camp when they came upon it. More than a thousand clanfolk, they estimated, maybe fifteen hundred, and a virtual zoography of physical types. The nomads tented in patterns that fol-lowed their occupations.

Some castes managed the animals, primarily a huge herd of sheep collected from fell-swards to be penned for a late winter lambing. Other castes specialized in creating sumptuous hangings and carpets from the wool of those same sheep. A contingent of fierce-browed young men with slender, tapering dark beards seemed to be a kind of clerks' collec-tive, running here and there with instructions, corrections, assessments, revisions. Older men and women—some much older—managed the care of children with surprising mildness and efficacy.

At the center of the hubbub rose a tented pagoda. Around it, a good many brass urns issued an aroma of raspberry and heart-of-musk. It didn't take the maunts long to realize that the incense wasn't devotional, but hospitable: the smell from the Princess's pagoda was, well, a stench.

First fed on a peppery broth that seemed to clear both their sinuses and their brains, the maunts were then allowed a chance to pray and compose themselves. It was almost dusk when they were brought into a tent to meet an ambassador of some sort.

"Please, sit," he told them, and sat as well. He was a portly man on the threshold of old age. One eye wandered as if bedeviled by an interior vision it didn't appreciate. His skin was the color of fine whisky. "We hope you have been made comfortable. Or comfortable enough."

The maunts nodded. Their approach had been greeted without apparent alarm, and they'd been welcomed respectfully.

"Very good, very good," he said. "Even in these uncongenial times, with the Emperor cudgeling us heathen into conversion through the force of his holy mace, we pride ourselves on clinging to our customs. Charity to visitors ranks high among our traditions. My name is Shem Ottokos."

"Lord Ottokos, you speak very well," ventured Sister Doctor.

"For a Scrow, you mean," he said, taking no offense. "I had a university degree at Shiz, back in the days when there was more collegiality at college. I studied the languages, ancient and modern."

"You had a notion to be a translator?"

"My notions are insignificant. I am the chief interpreter for her Highness now. I assume you have ventured into our tribal lands to gain an audience with the Princess?"

Though the maunts believed the native land of the Scrow to be significantly farther west, on the other side of the Great Kells, theirs wasn't to quibble. "Yes," said Sister Doctor. "We have work to complete. We are investigating the cause and agency of the recent spate of scrapings. If it would suit the Princess to grant us an audience, we should be able to clear up our concerns and be on our way almost at once. Is the Princess up to seeing us?"

Without answering, he stood and flicked both his hands, which the maunts took to mean: *Come.* They followed him from his tent and toward the royal pavilion in the center of the camp.

"She has not been well for more years than anyone can remember," said Lord Ottokos as they walked. "She has little energy for idle chat and I will not bother to translate anything that would upset her. I would suggest you contain your remarks to ten minutes, no more. When I get up to leave, so shall you."

"We might have brought tribute . . . ," murmured Sister Apothecaire.

"*Sister!*" said Sister Doctor sharply. "We are maunts of the House of Saint Glinda! We do not bring tribute to a foreign princess!"

"I meant a cake, or a witty novel," she explained unhappily.

"She has no need of cakes or novels," said Lord Ottokos. "Meaning no disrespect to our Princess, I would recommend that you breathe through your mouths. It is not considered impertinent to hold your sleeve in front of your nose. Try not to gag, though; it upsets her Highness."

The maunts exchanged glances.

The interior of the pavilion was dark and dank. Even chilly, come to that. Eight or ten heavy stone caskets with perforated lids slowly exhaled sheets of moisture that hung, nearly visible, in the air. Ice, thought Sister Doctor. They've carried ice down from the higher Kells, where it lasts all year long. And the cold serves to tamp down the smell of rot. Now that's a labor, for ice is heavy, and the higher Kells are not convenient . . . Perhaps that's why they're so far from their normal territory at this time of year, for easier access to the ice pack up the eastern, more gradual slope of the Kells . . .

Sister Apothecaire, whose eyes had adjusted more quickly to the gloom, pinched Sister Doctor's elbow and indicated a massive mound of reeking laundry on a low table. It was rolling on its side and opening its eyes.

"Your Highness, may I present Sisters Lowly and Lower-even-than-that," said Lord Ottokos, before he remembered to speak in his own tongue. "Ladies, the Princess Nastoya acknowledges your presence."

She had done nothing of the sort. She had not spoken nor even so much as blinked.

Lord Ottokos continued. "The Princess enquires after your health, assumes it is sufficiently robust or you wouldn't be here, and compliments you on your courage. Have you news of Liir?"

The maunts turned to each other, but in the darkness of the pavilion they could scarcely read each other's expressions. "Liir?" said Sister Apothecaire faintly. She was beginning to need her sleeve, as had been proposed.

"The boy who denied he was Elphaba's son. Is that not why you came to us? To tell us of him? Where is Liir?"

Sister Apothecaire began, "Why, that's uncanny, I never—"

But Sister Doctor cut her off, saying "We came to discover why the Scrow are scraping the faces of unarmed travelers."

Lord Ottokos made his mouth into a pucker—amused, distressed, it was hard to tell. "I repeat, have you news of Liir?" he said.

"If you're not interpreting our comments to your senior, need we have this conversation here?" said Sister Doctor.

"My good Sister," said Lord Ottokos, closing his eyes briefly, as if experiencing a spasm, "the Princess Nastoya entertains visitors only once every several weeks. Do not waste her time. She is waiting to learn what you have to say."

"We *have* seen Liir, we have!" said Sister Apothecaire, unable to govern herself any longer. "He was found not all that far from here some days ago, and brought to our mauntery for recovery, if he can be recovered."

"Sister!" barked Sister Doctor.

Sister Apothecaire shot her colleague a look that seemed, vaguely, to imply: *Give it a rest.*

Lord Ottokos turned and spoke to Princess Nastoya. For the first time, she stirred; that is, her face stirred. Beneath its greasy robes her body had kept up a constant slow stretching, twitching, creaking. Her eyes widened, and globes of ink-colored tears collected in the folds beside her nose. She was a woman in mighty distress. When she spoke, the voice was deep and plain, a laundry mistress's voice, no sonority to it. She said only a few syllables, but the language of the Scrow must have allowed for much meaning in enunciation and pronunciation.

"Forgive my not getting up," began Lord Ottokos's translation. "I am stricken, a creature severed unnaturally in two by decisions made long ago, when the Wizard of Oz set public policy against thinking Animals. Now, one part of my nature is nearly dead and the other clings to life waiting help."

"I have training in surgery, and my colleague in applications—"

Lord Ottokos spoke over Sister Doctor. "I have entrusted the boy Liir with a task, and I have been waiting his return these ten years. Ten years is a decade to a woman, marking the difference between maiden and matron, matron and crone, crone and harpy—but to an Elephant it is only a breath. A long, foul breath, but only a breath. I know the loyalty of Animals, I know the fickle allegiances of men. Because Liir was possibly a flitch of Elphaba, I had placed my trust in him all these years. I have hoped he might discover or invent a solution for my dilemma. And I have been patient—an Elephant is patient. And you come to tell me you have found him. Bless you, my daughters. Is he coming back to me at last?"

"He is not well," said Sister Doctor.

"He *was* not well," corrected Sister Apothecaire. "Perhaps he's improving. We've been traveling, so we can't report developments in his state."

"Why does he not arrive?"

"Something happened to him," said Sister Doctor. "We don't know what. Perhaps what attacked our sister maunts attacked him, too. He is sunk in a strange sleep from which he may not awake. If we knew what had attacked him, we might better invent how to treat him. Lord Ottokos, *ask her my question!*" she said suddenly. "It is pertinent!"

Lord Ottokos obliged this time, and muttered something to Princess Nastoya.

The reply. "We do not scrape the faces of maunts, nor of mice, nor sheep. We do not treat others as we have been treated. You must hunt the barbaric Yunamata and find out from them why they have taken against travelers."

"It isn't the Yunamata," said Sister Doctor, and in making the remark out loud she suddenly felt certain about this for the first time; she had been dubious up until now. "They wouldn't do such a thing. Can you be sure your people are not forgetting their traditions under the burden of sorrow they feel at your condition?"

"My people, as you call them, are not even my people," said Princess Nastoya. "They honored me years ago and made me their princess, and even in my decay they will not allow me to abdicate. They are a nation that has elevated charity beyond what is possible even in the precincts of your religious order. If out of fealty to me they would rather be governed by a Princess who is partly a corpse, how could they raise a hand against defenseless travelers?"

"The young maunts who ventured this way were intent on conversion," admitted Sister Doctor. "They were sent by the Emperor himself, we hear."

"None of us admires the Emperor's zealotry. But intention to convert is hardly a reason to kill people and defile their bodies. The murderers you seek aren't among the Scrow. Don't waste your time considering the matter. It is the Yunamata or it is someone else. Or something else. Perhaps they had a disease."

"No disease makes one's face fall off," said Sister Apothecaire firmly.

"If you know so much, what is my disease?" said Princess Nastoya.

"We should have to examine Your Highness," said Sister Doctor.

"Enough," interrupted Lord Ottokos. "I won't translate such a barbaric notion. The Princess has dismissed you. You may leave."

But the Princess spoke over her interpreter, and he was bound to listen. He bowed his head and continued, "She says again—and she has too few words left to spend in life to say it a third time—where is the boy Liir?"

"But he is not a boy any longer. We have told you what we know." Sister Doctor put her sleeve to her nose; in her line of work she knew the smell of putrescence all too well. "He is in a comatose state not six or eight days' journey from here, though perhaps nearer to the Emerald City than you would like to venture."

Lord Ottokos snapped, "We are not imbeciles. We know where his body is. You have told us. That is not the question."

The maunts blinked at him.

"Where is he?" Lord Ottokos repeated. "Where is *he*?"

"We don't know where he is," said Sister Apothecaire. "Our talents are not that fine."

Princess Nastoya shivered. Handmaidens came forward to withdraw shawls drenched with sweat and other seepage. "Let me help," said Sister Apothecaire suddenly.

"Don't you dare," said Lord Ottokos.

"I do dare. What are you going to do, have me scraped? Sister Doctor, a vessel of water and some essence of citron—lemons, limoncelli, parsleyfruit, anything. And some vinegar reduced to the usual."

Princess Nastoya began to weep then, full tears of a nasty vintage. They fell on Sister Apothecaire's bare hands and burned them; she was not halted in her work. "What has she said just then, in that low murmur?" she asked Lord Ottokos, who stood sputtering and clutching his beard in rage and disbelief.

Finally he submitted to this dotty, disobedient woman. "She said she wishes she could be scraped," he finally allowed.

"We can't do that," said Sister Apothecaire. "Vows of gentility and all that. But she can be made more comfortable. Sister Doctor, that pillow. The head. Watch the neck. What a weight upon this spine! Where *is* the dratted vinegar reduction?"

• 5 •

FOR A MOMENT, TO REST HER HANDS, Candle set the domingon down. The sound box thunked with a hollow expression. Its cavity was a kind of womb, she thought; how ineffable the secrets born there.

She wasn't given to reflection herself, but she was tired. For a moment she allowed herself to remember her arrival here a month or so before. The one called Mother Yackle had been dozing on a bench in the sunlight; she'd looked up with a start at Candle's approach. She had stretched out a wilted hand, peering with an expression canny, severe, and resigned. Resigned: that was much the way Candle had felt at that moment. Her uncle had tricked her here; he hadn't wanted to keep her any longer. "The way you're going, you'll be pregnant soon enough, if you're not already—and I can't take a child and a child's newborn with me on the road." It seemed he'd bought the domingon from its maker as a way to bargain with her. Go into the mauntery for a year, and the instrument is yours. Do with it what you will, and I'll be back to get you in good time. There's not much left for us in our home marshes, but you'd be ruined in the north. They'd spit at you, your easy ways; they'd laugh, your little voice. Stay here, and remember me wherever I am.

That kind of remembering was another skill, but now she was attending someone else, and her uncle meant little to her.

Candle took Liir's hand in her own. A clamminess. Was his color fading? Or was it just that the sun was setting, and the jackal moon was rising later than it had? The shadows lengthened and browned. By comparison his skin was bleached like an old, sun-whitened bone.

She took up her instrument again and leaned the edge of the minor bridge right on the edge of his bed. Her fingers running into the treble range, they danced in contrapuntal jiggery at the top register, not six inches from his right ear.

Where *was* he?

◆   ◆   ◆

LADY GLINDA SAID TO LIIR, "I can tell you have no intention of leaving that charred broomstick behind, but if you try to walk into a public space carrying it over your shoulder like a blunderbuss you'll be taken for a fool, or at any rate noticed. I think what you are after is something a little more like camouflage."

She paused to regard herself in a convenient looking glass in the stairwell. Adjusting her everyday tiara, she conceded, "It must be said that camouflage is not an effect I have ever strived to master. Still, we'll do what we can."

Liir followed her down the marble steps of the central staircase. The place had gone quiet. "Goodness, everyone takes off for a smoke the minute my back is turned," she said. "Where are the kitchens, anyway? Through here?"

She stumbled into a cloakroom, and then opened the door to a closet where two of the belowstairs staff were involved in recreational exercises. "I beg your pardon," she said, and shut the door, and then locked it.

"Eventually they'll have to thump to be released, and one of them is bound to be cheating. Heaps of fun. But where's the kitchen?"

"Have you just moved here?" asked Liir.

"Don't be silly. Lord Chuffrey had this place long before we married. But I don't cook for myself, if that's what you mean. Nothing other than the toast that I mentioned earlier, and that's done in the breakfast hall. Ah, here we are."

A half-flight of stone steps descended into a cavernous whitewashed kitchen. A dozen members of the staff were sitting about the table so deep in conversation that they didn't hear her coming. "Lady Glinda," said a bootblack, and they all leaped up with guilty looks.

"Glad to be recognized in my own home," said Glinda. "I hate to interrupt what are probably well-intentioned plans to kill us all in our beds, but if you don't mind? A minor request for whichever of you has just a moment to spare?"

They melted away, all but the housekeeper and the houseboy.

"He's about the same size as the bootblack," said Glinda, pointing to Liir. "Suit him up in House of Chuffrey colors and find some decent shoes, and get him a leather satchel on a sling. You know, that long cylindrical thingy that Lord Chuffrey's guests use to carry their arrows when they go hunting in the country. That ought to accommodate the filthy old broom, I think."

"Asking your pardon, Lady Glinda," said the houseboy. "We've no such satchels on the town premises. They're all down to Mockbeggar Hall."

"Do I have to think of everything? Haven't we friends? Haven't we neighbors to borrow from? Aren't there shops still serving the public? Need I go tramping to the marketplace myself with a sack of coins between my teeth?"

The houseboy fled. The housekeeper pursed her lips editorially.

"Don't speak. Don't. It's only a temporary appointment," said Lady Glinda. "Just for the day, in fact. Now feed up this boy; he hasn't had a square meal for weeks, I can tell. And when he's equipped as I require, return him to the Yellow Parlor."

Lady Glinda climbed the stairs, muttering "Kitchens!" in disbelief, leaving Liir behind.

"Well, peel off those beggar's weeds and wash in the cauldron room, just there; I won't have you staining her fancyfart's good livery with your dirty limbs," said the housekeeper. "I'll put out some food, and you be grateful for it, for it's out of our own downstairs supply, and we don't take kindly to ravenous upstarts here in Lord Chuffrey's establishment."

"WHERE ARE WE GOING?" He peered out the window of the carriage.

"Put your head back. Servants don't gawp out of carriage windows."

How odd to be five feet higher than the street. It was not an experience to which he was accustomed. The carriage lurched under arched spans of stone, stopped for a squadron of uniformed cavalry on display, sidelined along a merchants' parade, and picked up speed along Dirt Boulevard. Cleared of its village of indigents, the roadway showed signs of its original elegance, though its parallel rows of trees were in bad shape. It looked as if the grounds were being used for military drills.

Where had all the itinerants gone? "Where *are* we going?"

"To the Palace," Glinda said. "Where you'll keep your head down and your mouth closed. Are you scared?"

It seemed too personal a question for a woman to ask a boy. Perhaps she realized this. She continued, "I was, the first time I came here. It was with Elphaba. We were older than you are now, but only by a few years. And in many ways we were more naive. Well, I was, anyway. And I was terrified. The wonderful Wizard of Oz! My stomach just about dissolved in its own acids."

"What happened?"

"What happened?" She turned the question to herself, examining it. "History happened, I suppose. We saw the Wizard, and we parted ways—Elphaba went underground, as it were, and . . . in time, I hugged the limelight." She sighed. "With the best of intentions, and with limited success."

"And now?" he said, not because he was interested, but because he didn't want any more attention on himself.

"Now, I hold the key," she said. "Now, for the time being, I am intended to stand in for the mighty on their thrones. It's all I'm good for."

"Are the mighty deserving of thrones?"

"That's an Elphaba question, and out of your youthful pouting mouth it sounds preposterous. Like most of her superior cavils, it has no easy answer. How could I know?"

She sighed. "Sit *back,* I said. Yes, I'm nervous. You'll find in time most people are. They simply learn better how to disguise it, and sometimes, if they're wise, how to use their anxiety to serve the public good. Perhaps being jittery helps me pay closer attention. You know, I didn't want the hard work of government. They all say I need to clean house. Clean house! That presumes I've cleaned a house before. I say, hey, what are the servants for? Decoration?"

She was speaking to herself, in a way, but she was also trying to cheer him up. He turned his head, confused by her kindness, and busied himself from watching, at an acceptable angle, as the buildings nearer the Palace hove into view. One mammoth ministry was strapped with bas-relief marble panels depicting various historic Ozmas in characteristic poses. They looked at once venerable and ludicrous, and the pigeons of the Emerald City paid them no high compliment.

"But why are we going to the Wizard's Palace?"

"The people's Palace, now," said Glinda derisively. "Though what the people are going to do with their own palace I have no earthly idea." She chewed on a nail. "There's a clandestine entrance to Southstairs from the Palace. Of course there had to be, a means of instantly spiriting away any treasonous Palace upstart sniffed out in the court. Though the common criminal condemned to serve time is more publicly lowered in a cage into the pit that drops down inside those bulwarky ramparts. You see, it's mostly underground, Southstairs. It's the most impregnable prison in Oz. Nobody who goes in via the cage comes out that way."

"How do they come out?"

"In pine coffins."

SHE DABBED A SACHET doused with oil of clove and root-of-persimmon behind her ears. By the time the door to her carriage was opened by a staff member of the Palace, Lady Glinda had become more regal. Her chin went up, a jeweled scepter was provided for her right hand. Her eye flashed with a steeliness Liir had not noted earlier.

"Lady Glinda," they murmured. She deigned to supply the briefest of nods, as an indication that she was not deaf, and walked by.

Liir followed in something closer to terror than he had ever experienced before. He expected to be rushed away and beaten before he could even begin to protest. But Lady Glinda's penumbra of influence extended eight feet behind her, it seemed, for his progress was unquestioned, and he gained the threshold of the Palace without anyone's objecting.

The place was a maze, and he lost his bearings almost at once. Accompanied by a Palace flunky, Glinda and Liir swept up grand staircases, along arched corridors, past ceremonial chambers and receiving parlors. Another staircase or two, another corridor or three, and at length they traversed a long dingy room, where dozens of staff members were perched on high stools above ledgers. They splashed ink in their nervous abjection, though not on Glinda in her celestial blue gown.

Behind a wall with an interior window, the better for supervising workers, stood an office with a desk and some chairs. An elegant man absorbed in a newssheet was tipped back on the hind legs of his chair, his ceremonial boots propped on the desk and his saber stuck in the soil of a potted fern. "Commander," said Lady Glinda, "we're here. Show some respect, or pretend to anyway."

He leaped to his feet with ostentatious speed. Liir blinked and gaped. "Commander Cherrystone!" he said.

"You've met?" said Glinda. "How droll."

"I'm drawing a blank," said the Commander, wrinkling a brow.

"At Kiamo Ko," said Liir. "You were head of the Gale Forcers at Red Windmill. It was your men that kidnapped Fiyero's widow, Sarima, and her sisters and her children."

Commander Cherrystone smiled deferentially and offered Liir a hand. "Kidnapped? We took them into protective custody for their own good. How were they to know the depravity of the Witch they were harboring?"

"And how well did you protect them?" said Liir.

"Ooh, the boy has spit, has he," said Commander Cherrystone, wiping his sleeve. "I like that, son, but please. This is my best dress uniform." He was equable and seemed to take no offense.

Liir glared at Glinda. "You've taken me here, to him—betrayed me to the very man responsible for Nor's abduction?"

"Recriminations, they get us nowhere," said Lady Glinda. "And how was I to know? Consider it poetic justice: Now he must help you. Because I say so." She turned to Cherrystone. "Look, Commander, I've laid it all out. You got my note? The boy wants to see Fiyero's daughter, if she's still alive. As an officer and a governor of the prison, you can make the arrangements, can't you?"

"It's an institution with its own appetite, is a prison," said Commander Cherrystone. Rather approvingly, thought Liir. "I can't say I remember you, lad, but my work involves many postings. And in none of them have I ever before met a soul who wanted to enter Southstairs voluntarily. You understand: No promises that you will leave it. Either dead or alive. It might be your tomb."

"My name is Liir," he said. He tried to lift his chin as he had seen Glinda do. "We *have* met. I liked you. You seemed decent."

"I tried to be decent, within reason," he replied. "Anyway, I had little choice if I wanted to gain the trust of that knotty little clan in Kiamo Ko."

"What happened to Sarima?" asked Liir. "Fiyero's widow."

"Everyone dies. It's a question of where and how, that's all."

"Oh, bandying, bandying, please, my head," said Glinda. "I feel I'm back at Shiz. The Debating Tourneys: what a migraine. I need a tonic. Are you going to do this for me, Commander?"

"I wouldn't be here if you didn't require it," he answered. "Ready, lad?"

"I'm ready," Liir answered. He turned to Glinda. "Ought I take off these silly clothes?"

"What, and go naked into Southstairs? I wouldn't recommend it," said Commander Cherrystone. Glinda waved dismissively. Then she tucked her hand against her mouth and bit her knuckles. It was hard to know if her pretty ways were studied or innate.

"Oh, oh," she managed, "I don't know that I'll see you again . . . and you remind me so of her."

"I haven't Elphaba's talent," said Liir simply. "I'm not worth mourning, believe me."

"Her power was only part of it," said Glinda. "She was brave, and so are you."

"Bravery can be learned," he said, trying to be consoling.

"Bravery can be stupid," said Commander Cherrystone. "Believe me."

The boy didn't move forward to touch her or kiss her. In Kiamo Ko, only Nanny had been the kissing type, and Liir hadn't figured much in her affections. So he merely said, "Well, good-bye, then. And don't worry. I'll take care."

They looked at one another. In a moment Liir would lose heart; he would do the shaming thing that the houseboy had predicted. He would let Nor's life reach its destiny without intervening—in exchange for having someone stand in as a mother. Lord knows Elphaba hardly had!—and here was Glinda, blinking back tears or something.

She looked at him almost as if thinking the same thing. The moment passed, though. "You do your work," Lady Glinda told him. "Oz-speed. And don't forget your broom."

"Her broom," said Liir.

"Your broom," she corrected him.

◆ 6 ◆

THE ROOM GREW SUDDENLY COLDER. Night was drawing in, and the rump flank of the wind hinted at the winter to come. Candle rose to draw the shutters closed. The jackal moon was at its most self-satisfied; soon the constellation would wane and its elements return to their ordinary, lonelier orbits.

She shuttered most of the windows for the first time, but she couldn't fix one shutter securely; a rope of ivy with a stem stout as a forearm had grown across a corner. Candle took an extra sheet and hung it as best she could against the chill.

When she came back to Liir, she became alarmed. She felt his brow. His skin was colder still, and his blood pressure seemed to be dropping.

She wasn't suited for work of this seriousness. She laid down her instrument on the floor, determined to run and get Sister Cook or the Superior Maunt. She found her way blocked.

The figure stood in the doorway, veil drawn to cloak the features. Candle reared back, startled.

The veil dropped. It was only the addled elderly maunt, the senior biddy in the place, the one known as Mother Yackle. What was she doing here?

"You can't leave," said Mother Yackle. "There's no one else here to do what needs to be done."

Candle picked up her domingon and raised it threateningly. Quicker than could have been imagined, Mother Yackle slid back into the shadows, and closed the door behind her, and locked it.

Candle thumped against the door, and threw her shoulder against it, but the heavy thing was quarter-sawn oakhair wood, and cross-built. She couldn't waste her time clawing at it with her fingernails. Liir was failing.

She turned her attentions to the rest of the room. Not raised in the arts of medicine, she didn't recognize much of what she found in the cupboard. A large mortar and pestle for the grinding of herbs. Several fresh-nibbed pens, with sheets of paper and a stoppered jug of ink, for the making of notes. Unguents of disagreeable viscosities. The body of a mouse on the bottom shelf. A few old keys—none of which fit the room's only keyhole.

She sat down and played a few rapid runnels, in mischief mode, to concentrate her apprehensions. She felt for his pulse again, and brushed his hair away from his forehead. Even his scalp was cold.

She took off her tunic and tried to wave it from the window. Though she couldn't attract attention by yelling, maybe someone in the kitchen garden would see her signal. But a wind came up and took the tunic away, and that was that.

At length she relied on what fate had provided her. She took the cleanest of the pen nibs and sharpened it further by training it along the stone windowsill. Releasing Liir's left arm from its splint, she propped it up against a transept of the domingon, so his hand was raised in the air, a salute. To the extent that she prayed—which wasn't much, even in these environs, even at this drastic juncture—she begged for her hands to be steady. Then she tried to play Liir's bicep as she might her domingon, running her hands in light, feathery scales along the skin. She settled on a place near the inside of the elbow, and using the nib as a lancet, made a neat incision.

She caught his blood in the mortar, and when she'd filled it she rushed to the window and dumped it out. There, jackal moon, you want your blood offering, there it is. She collected a second portion, then a third, and she took off her habit to bind Liir's arm and stop the flow.

In only her broadcloth shift she shivered, and her fingers trembled. Nonetheless she returned to her instrument. Her musical figures went wobbly, but she kept on.

✦   ✦   ✦

AFTER GLINDA HAD GONE, Commander Cherrystone took no more notice of Liir than he might a napping dog. He disappeared behind his newspapers, humming to himself. Liir sat on a stool, waiting; something had to happen sooner or later. He watched the Commander's well-trimmed nails hold the page, listened to various admonitory hums and clicks and editorial *humphs* breathed nasally. The career soldier was a fit man, a calm one, and his lack of attention to Liir seemed suitable. What was hard to fathom was the Commander's composure. It was under his command that Nor and her family had been abducted, yet he seemed so oblivious to Liir's contempt that Liir began to doubt himself. Maybe there was more to the ruling family of Kiamo Ko than he had known.

Not until the business day in the Palace came to an end, and the dozens of civil servants left their desks for home, did the Commander sit up. "Your guide will be along presently—ah, there he is."

A handsome younger man with a keen, guarded expression blustered into the room. "Can't have kept you waiting more than a tockety-tick, have I? Witches' britches, the Palace staff gives you the once-over!

Thought things would loosen up once the Wizard abdicated." He shucked a jacket from his shoulders and slung it across the desk. "You notice. Nice, eh? A clothier in Brickle Lane. Yes, it's black-market Munchkinsheep wool, I'd have nothing else. Feel that weight."

"You've a prettier penny to spend than a military man does," observed the Commander dryly.

"She is not that young and I am not that choosy: conditions for a bargain. Bartered it mostly. Fuck, I'm hungry. This is the boy, then. Got a crumpet or a butter roll anywhere, Cherryvery?"

"This is Liir. You're to take him below and help him as best you can. I know you've your mind on other matters, so I don't pretend to expect you will be thorough in your assistance. But do try. He seems a good sort."

The young man shot Liir a glance. "He looks too wet to be after what I'm after down there."

"I suspect he is," said Commander Cherrystone, "but all good things come to those who wait, and he may grow into a sexual nature before he emerges, if he ever does. Liir, this is Shell."

"The Witch's brother?" Liir felt he had to check.

"The same," said Shell, flexing his fingers. Liir wasn't sure that he could see a resemblance, but Shell looked capable and cunning both. "Are you ready?"

Does he know who I am, wondered Liir. Has Shell ever heard of a Liir? A boy who might be his nephew?

"I'm ready."

Commander Cherrystone flicked a speck of dust off his dress weskit. "The usual arrangements about your return, Shell. Liir—I wish you luck."

He left, locking them into the office. Shell looked at Liir more closely, and his nose twitched as if on the scent of something. Then he shrugged and said, "I'm ready for an ale. You ready for Southstairs?" Liir nodded.

Shell went to an installation of cubbies for the sorting of interoffice mail. Liir couldn't see how his fingers fussed, nor at what, but in a moment the whole wooden unit slid aside on a secret track. Behind, a plain door, and Shell had the key for it.

"Is this where Southstairs got its name?" asked Liir, pointing to the flight of timber steps that descended treacherously, without benefit of railings, into the gloom.

"Dunno. Never thought about it. Let's go. I hope your thighs are good. Watch your step."

"Was your sister a martyr?" asked Liir, innocently as he could.

"Which sister?" he answered, but before Liir could reply, he continued. "Martyrdom implies a religious faith, and Nessarose had so much faith that no one else in the family could breathe. Elphaba affected a salty agnosticism; I never knew whether it was genuine or not. For me to consider them martyrs, I'd have to have faith, and I don't—not in unionism, the faith of my father; nor in the other varieties that clot the calendar with their hobbledehoy feast days. It took all the fancy dancing I could do not to be tarred as a traitor-by-family-association. Luckily, I have little interest in government, and I'm rather good at dancing, as it happens. Look . . . Liir, is it . . . I prefer to save my breath. Shall we not chatter like choirgirls on an outing? That okay with you?"

Liir didn't answer. The wind siphoning through the slitted windows above made a sound almost like a spiral of music. He wanted to ask Shell if he could hear the strange effect, but he kept his own counsel.

They grew colder and colder as they descended. Soon Liir had to put out a hand, not just to feel his way in the gloom, but also because his legs threatened to buckle beneath him. The wall was damp, here and there soft with wet clinging growth.

Eventually the sound of their steps began to echo, and then it was clear a light was burning below. At last they reached a stone floor from which several dark corridors led.

"Here I usually stretch," said Shell, and showed Liir how. Liir rubbed his muscles as directed. When they were ready, Shell took a club from a pile on the floor and lit it from the torch affixed to the wall. "Do the same; we won't spend the rest of eternity together, you know," he said. "Light is helpful. These are limbs of irongrowth stock, so they burn a good long time."

"If we're not going to stick together, how will I find my way out?"

"I don't know. I assume you're clever, though." Shell's nonchalance was cruel. "Very few emerge from here. Only the guards."

Liir tried to memorize all of everything, just in case—but he intended to stick with his guide no matter what Shell might think about it.

The way was dank and sour, sometimes cut with a sulfurous gust. The torchlight made a tidal rush against flattened arches of milk grey stone. Parts of the walls were bricked, though the work was ancient and the brick face crumbling.

As they walked along the crushed cement and scattered rubble, and Liir got his breath back, he tried to think of how to speak to Shell. The man was in his late twenties, maybe early thirties, and a certain class of fop; even Liir, knowing himself a rube and a naïf, could see that. But Shell's eye was keen and his manner, variously courtly or casual, always suave. He was taller than Elphaba had been, sleek where she had been spiky.

As it happened, Liir had no time to ask questions. The path ended in a flight of shallow steps leading farther down. They were reaching the outskirts of Southstairs—not so much a prison as an underground city. The sounds of carts, and a murmur of voices. Somewhere, someone was playing a stringed instrument, far away; somewhere, someone must be cooking, for there was a grievous smell of rendered bacon fat on a hot griddle.

"The cowhand of mercy prepares his rounds." Shell swept off his hat and left it on a ledge; a curl of yellow plume bobbed in the gloom.

"Will you lead me to Nor?"

"I've promised to take you to the central registrar, but I've a few stops to make first." Shell patted the satchel on his shoulder. "Some folks need my attention, and it would be unthinkable to postpone their medications to rush you by first. You don't mind?"

Liir did. "No, of course not."

Around another corner, down a few more steps, and they came to a greasy waterway, not unlike the canals above in the Emerald City. "Come on then, if you're coming," said Shell, leaping aboard an abandoned canal dory. He seemed to be growing cheerier by the moment.

At length, the narrow waterway ran into a wider channel that curved beneath a high ceiling of rock face supported here and there with beams and buttresses. On either side of the channel, padlocked doors were set flush into the stone walls. Sometimes the doors gave out onto ledges or a path between cells; more often, just onto the water.

The stench and the noise grew. Before long Liir and Shell passed grey-clothed laborers hauling buckets of supper one way, buckets of feces back.

"Didn't think a country kid would wrinkle his nose at a rural perfume," observed Shell, berthing the canal dory. "You'll stay and guard this; more than once I've had my vessel nabbed while I was at my errand of mercy." He opened the flap of his satchel and removed a small glass syringe filled with a urine-colored solution. He wiped the needle with a clean cloth and then tapped the plunger once to make sure it worked. "Ripe and ready, she is," he murmured. He looked sideways at Liir. "It's humbling to be able to help those who suffer."

With a practiced hand, he quickly undid the lock on a door and slid through, closing it behind him.

Despite his intentions to cling to Shell like a burr, Liir didn't have the nerve to follow, nor was he tall enough to peer through the small window high in the door. But there was a gap at the bottom between the door and its sill. By sinking to the floor of the dory, Liir could make out the movement of figures inside. Apparently Shell had set his torch in a wall stanchion. His voice sounded soothing, even hypnotic, but the prisoner crouching against a back wall scooched her bare feet underneath her skirts. Shell's boots drew near until he was standing flush against her. She moaned or whimpered, and her feet curled the farther under her skirts. Mercy was hard to accept, Liir guessed. Shell's feet rocked from toe to heel, with a comforting rhythm, and his heels began to lift from the floor.

At the sound of someone approaching, Liir turned.

"You, what're you lying there for?" A portly Ape with a ring of keys, dragging his knuckles on the ground. He was wreathed in his own weather of cheap cologne, protection against the smells, and he wore a collar made of mangy ocelot fur.

"I'm visiting," said Liir. "With permission of Lady Glinda. I'm ac-companying a man named Shell, who is inside tending to the needs of the sick."

"I'll say he is, and he's sicker than most," said the Ape. "But what Lady Glinda dictates means nothing down here; we're our own society. Have you a writ of passage from the Under-mayor?"

"We're on our way to get one. But Shell needed to stop first."

"He sees to his needs. I'll see to yours. Come with me."

"I don't think I'd better."

The Ape insisted, and Liir called out repeatedly for Shell, who emerged, cross and agitated. "What're you bothering my boy for?"

"Oh, he's your *boy*?" asked the Ape. "Ever the surprise, Shell."

"He's under my care for the moment. Leave him be, Tunkle."

"You give our Miss Serenity her weekly jab?" asked Tunkle, jingling the keys.

Shell replaced the syringe. "You interrupted me. I'll go on to the next."

"He's a one-man festival of fun," said Tunkle. "I wouldn't get too close if I were you. He gets fairly hot and bothered over all these errands of mercy."

Shell showed no sign of taking offense. "Clear off, Tunkle. We know the ropes. We're on our way to the Under-mayor. We'll just take our time, that's all. You want a lift?"

"Not on your life. I go upside once a month and I can find my own fun, Master Shell; I don't need your fancy imported sort." The Ape spit in the waterway and let them go by. "Watch your back, lad."

Making no effort to lower his tone, Shell remarked to Liir, "Tunkle. A collaborationist. Saved his own hide, during the Wizard's campaigns, by signing on to bully his own." Still, his tone was neutral, as if this seemed a reasonable enough strategy.

Liir asked softly, "How far are we from the Under-mayor's office?"

"A stop or two, or three," said Shell. "There's more than one would like my attentions, but I pick and choose, trying to be fair. I can't be all things to all people, now, can I?" He brushed his lapel and made ready to continue his missionary work.

LIIR DIDN'T KNOW how much time had passed before they finally reached the Under-mayor's quarters, but Southstairs grew progressively warmer, stinkier, noisier, brighter the farther in they floated. Shell made two or three more stops, always, it seemed, to tend to young women— Liir could hear their voices, supplicating, sometimes weeping, once cursing Shell. But Liir couldn't see them, nor did he want to.

Shell became more distracted as the hour passed, his bespoke clothes more disheveled. At length, however, they reached their destination. A foreman's cabin stood freely beneath the lofty ceiling from which, in the stronger light, Liir could make out rock structures, strange candelabras of dripped stone frozen in place.

The prison Under-mayor was a sallow man, skin soft and pale as bleached linen. He looked as if he hadn't seen the sun in many years. Multiple rings on every finger, even his thumbs: like a fence for stolen jewels. His name was Chyde. "You're raising someone up in the paths of righteousness, I see," he said, cheerily enough, to Shell. "I'm not used to thinking of you as concerned about the morals of the young."

"One does what one can," said Shell.

"I thought your motto was one does whom one can. But never mind that. You bring news of the starlight goddess?"

"Glinda's all right. She's coping. The City's a mess up there, but you'll have heard all about it."

"You always have a special slant, though." Chyde located some beer and a few stale rings of fried castipod. Liir declined, but Shell tucked in.

"Well, after all these years, it's a right rich stew up there, that's for sure," Shell conceded through a mouthful of flaky breading. "The Wizard's departure was weirdly unexpected, given he's been in power for so long. Still, with so many having schemed behind the scenes to oust him, you'd think they'd have gotten their signals straight about what ought to happen next. Lady Glinda is looking in, a glamorous figurehead, and no one knows if she's got a scrap of brain in her noggin. The trade unions should be rising any day, but the municipal militia wasn't quite prepared to recognize a socialite for a queen. Hence, in loyal support of *course,* the guard has been on the offensive, clearing out the neighborhoods where the rabble is more likely to rouse. Glinda thinks it's urban revitalization. So it's an interesting time, a sweep of forces with everyone assessing the power of the other. Heads will roll, of course. It's merely a question of in what sequence: who gets to laugh first, and who next, and whose laugh is cut off by the guillotine blade."

"And you'll be stealing in and out of the bedchambers of the wenches and the wives and the widows . . ."

"The wives laugh neither first nor last, but they do laugh best!"

"I live a quiet life down here," said Under-mayor Chyde to Liir. "It's part of your dad's program of good works to fill me in on the local gossip. I could go northstairs if I could trust a soul, but I don't trust a soul. And the minute the selfish bastards up there remember their relatives down here, if they ever do, I'll be hamstrung before morning and bled by noontime. I've never felt I could leave my post, but especially not now. Not if I want to survive through these interesting times."

"He's not my father," said Liir coldly.

"Oh? I thought I caught a resemblance," said Under-mayor Chyde. "Well, more's the pity. You're training an apprentice, are you, Shell?"

Shell yawned and drained his beer. "No. I promised Lady Glinda I'd deliver this spawnling to you. He's searching for a prisoner."

"We're all searching for someone," said Under-mayor Chyde in a drawl. "People pay me well to begin searches I can't somehow ever manage to complete." He flashed his jeweled hands. "Care to make a contribution to the exhibit, lad?"

"He's not buying your silence or your service," snapped Shell. "Get on with it, Chyde-ey, or I'll report your side business to the authorities. Lady Glinda has an interest in jewels herself, as it happens. A more seemly interest. She might not like to hear—"

"Name?" interrupted Chyde.

"Her name was Nor," said Liir. "Is Nor. About, oh, sixteen? She was abducted by the Gale Forcers at the castle of Kiamo Ko, out west. In the Vinkus."

"I can't say the name sounds familiar, but we house an exclusive clientele, some of whom like to keep a low profile. We respect their wishes, of course."

"Her father was the prince of the Arjikis."

"A crowned head? Well, if she's here, she must have one of the private suites. You haven't been to offer her your particular brand of solace, Shell?" Under-mayor Chyde snapped his fingers with a clink and said, "Jibbidee, bring me the two green ledgers. No, sorry, the ocher ones, if she's a Winkie."

"She'd be young still," said Shell. "Or young-ish. I do have some standards, Chyde."

An elf with ears in an advanced state of decomposition appeared from a cupboard and scrambled about a rickety bookshelf. "Thank you, Jibbidee," said Chyde, without inflection, and the elf returned to his cupboard and shut the door behind him when his job was done.

"You might remember the circumstances of her registering," said Shell. "It was the same castle where my sister lived until recently."

"Oh, *that* Kiamo Ko. How could I be so slow?" Chyde slid a pair of spectacles off his pate and down to his nose, and squinted. "My former wife, save her blessed hide, always said that I'm such a big-hearted guy, you know, everyone's story gets to me, and so I can't keep them straight. My heart bleeds for all. One and all." *Harumph.* "Part of our marital problems, but so be it."

He glanced up over the top of his lenses and fastened on Shell for the first time. "I am sorry about your sisters, though, Shell. Both of them meeting their ends within such a short time. It can't be easy."

"We weren't close," said Shell, studying his nails.

"Munchkinland's in revolt, now that Nessarose is dead. It has to be said she ruled with an iron fist, for all her piety."

"Spare us the civics class. I'm in a hurry, Chyde," said Shell. "Can I leave the boy here for you to finish with?"

"Some poor widowling just aching for your attention, I know, I know . . ."

Liir put it together at last. What a dolt am I! "Are you sleeping with your patients?" he blurted out. "I mean—you know—"

"Patients," mused Chyde. "Nice touch."

"I am seeing to their needs," said Shell, without apology or shame. He patted the satchel. "The comfort I supply is greatly appreciated. And of course they want to show their gratitude. What else does a lady in chains have to offer? She couldn't accept charity. It isn't done in polite circles. So she pays as she can. I'm not so cold as to deny them the chance to show their appreciation. It seems a fair exchange to me."

I'm not sticking with him even if he is my maybe-uncle. Forget it. New plan needed. I'll improvise. "You're disgusting," said Liir. "I mean, really. That's disgusting. You're disgusting. I can't believe it. It's—it's monstrous."

"Oh, I'd need to be a good sight more ambitious to make it to monstrous." Shell laughed. "Chyde? Sometime this week would be nice."

"Might as well leave him." Chyde turned to another volume. "Nothing is coming to light. Are you sure she's here?"

"I'm not sure of anything, but this is the natural first place to start, I suppose," said Shell. He stood and smoothed down his clothes, and offered his hand to Liir. "So we take our parting now, comrade. I hope the rest of your day is as amusing."

Liir thought about biting the hand, but Shell would only make another joke. So the boy tucked his own hands high up in his armpits. "We'll meet again," said Shell. "Likely it'll be down here, since it isn't easy to obtain an exit visa. Sweet dreams, Liir-boy."

He spun on his heel and disappeared almost at a run.

"Oh, the energy of the young," said Chyde, sighing and continuing to flip pages. "You know, I'm not coming up with anything so far. What did you say her name was again?"

· 7 ·

IN THE WESTERN DISAPPOINTMENTS, on the last evening of this jackal moon, the Scrow herders sent their dogs out to round up the sheep earlier than usual. Other workers erected a double row of pliant, bindweed fencing around the far edge of the fold's perimeter. Unless cloud cover prevented it, the celestial beast would brighten the night more brilliantly than at any other time in a generation. It would make a good night for scavengers.

Sister Doctor and Sister Apothecaire had done what they could. They had provided comfort to the old Princess that her own staff could not. She was happier, though the mood in her tent, when she was asleep, was ugly. The Scrow were a proud people—well, what people weren't?—and they were suspicious of foreign clinical practices.

The interpreter put it to the women as gently as he could.

"You should move on," said Lord Shem Ottokos. "We have told you what you came to learn—that we know nothing of the scrapings of those colleagues of yours. If your profession is the extension of charity, you have performed your mission. You've benefited Princess Nastoya mightily. There is no reason to linger, and danger to you if you do."

"We're told you are hospitable to strangers," Sister Doctor reminded him.

"Strangers, yes; that is the way of the Scrow," said Ottokos. "After several days, you are less strange than you once were. You become familiar, and therefore, like family, less agreeable. I'll be happy to provide you with a supply of food, but I recommend that you start home this very evening and take advantage of this unusually bright night."

Sister Doctor said, "In the question of scrapings, we haven't convinced you that the Yunamata are blameless. So why would you send us into danger?"

"You've been so good; we'll provide what we can manage by way of an escort," said Lord Ottokos, and left.

"The nerve!" said Sister Apothecaire. "We're being disinvited. I believe I'm offended."

"Are you going native?" Sister Doctor asked her Munchkin colleague. The tone verged on the cruel.

"They're adorable heathen," said Sister Apothecaire, somewhat wildly.

"Yes. Well, they'll seem less adorable if they conquer their aversion to scraping the faces of their visitors. After all, when you were a child you were an adorable heathen, too, but you got over it."

"I don't appreciate your wit, Sister Doctor."

It began to seem for a short while as if the maunts might disobey the instructions of their superior and split up. However, the Princess Nastoya requested a final interview with them, and she felt well enough to sit up on her pallet.

"Have you taken the full measure of my ailment?" she said, through Shem Ottokos. "To avoid the pogroms of the Wizard against the Animals, I went deeply underground many years ago, accepting a witch's charm as a way to hide myself. I am an Elephant, and want to go to my death as an Elephant, but I am cursed to remain in this human body. I used to be able to change for a brief time, but infirmity and age have eroded those talents, and now I am trapped. I fear the Elephant within me has been dying for some time, and may be in part dead already; but I would join it, if I could only have help. Ten years ago I asked the Witch's boy for help, but he disappeared. Now through your exotic skills you have helped me rally, and so I must press this request. Please return to your hive and collect the boy, the man, Liir. Bring him here or send him here; get him here safely. He may not be able to help me, but even the most blessed of witchcraft has gone underground in these trying times, and he is the only one I know who might be able to help."

"Do you really think he is Elphaba's son?" asked Sister Doctor.

"He had her cape, he had her broom," said Princess Nastoya. "Maybe he wasn't her son, but he cared about her life, and he may have learned something anyway. What other course can I take?"

"We've never even seen him awake," admitted Sister Apothecaire. "It would be hard to promise we could persuade him when we don't know what he's really like. Yet."

"In return for his help, I'd promised him something in exchange." She began to wheeze a bit, and Ottokos collected her phrases haltingly. "I want—to tell him what I've heard—about—the word on the street in the Emerald City."

"I'm sure he'll be fascinated," said Sister Doctor. "If he ever wakes up."

"The threat to Animals during the Wizard's reign crowded me—humanward—and I have been safer than many. Now, as our violently holy Emperor demands all our souls, I want to go to my death as an Animal: proud, isolate, unconsecrated. Find him for me. Hurry. I will give you—two rare male skarks to ride—and a panther to travel by your side as far as the forest. You will travel faster on the backs of those beasts than you did on foot or on mules. If you aren't ambushed by soldiers or wolves or any other enemy, you may make it by sunrise. At the edge of the forest the panther will turn back, but the skark will keep on, and by then the worst of the jackal moonlight will be spent."

The maunts nodded their heads and rose to take their leave. They didn't expect to see Princess Nastoya again, dead or alive, an Elephant or a human. They didn't want to tire her with further discussion. But it was she who raised the last point, when they were almost beyond addressing.

"My friends," she said. They turned. "You have been kind to me, and good to each other. I am not so far dead that I haven't seen this. How can you perform such works in the name of the Unnamed God, whose agents belittle us so?"

"The Unnamed God does not descend from the Emperor," explained Sister Doctor. She was afraid that an obscure point of contemporary unionist theology might be lost on a pagan, but she was reluctant to treat the Princess like a fool. "The Unnamed God, whatever they may say in the Emerald City these days, is still in its essence unnamed. We have as much a right to work in its name as anyone else."

"Hardly seems worth the bother to believe," murmured Princess Nastoya. "Still, life itself seems more than patently fantastic, and we believe in life, so I'll let the matter drop."

THE RIDE WOULD BE SWIFT but rollicking. These skarks were large of pelvis, supported by longer back legs than other skark varieties. Around their legs circled the panther like an eddy of black oil, constantly swishing by.

Lord Shem Ottokos escorted them safely out of the camp. Sister Apothecaire was disappointed that there were so few Scrow to wave good-bye to them. "You'll have noticed the creatures circling," said Ottokos. The maunts looked uneasily at each other. "In the sky, I mean."

"Vultures?" said Sister Apothecaire. "Sensing the carrion of Princess Nastoya? She would supply a healthy portion of carrion to a bevy of vultures."

"They are higher up than vultures, I think," said Ottokos. "So, according to the laws of perception, they must be larger than vultures. Besides, vultures wait for the body to die before approaching. I fear they are a squadron of attack creatures who don't wait until the meat is dead. Perhaps—well, I hardly dare say it. Dragons."

"Dragons are rare in the first place, and in any case docile," snapped Sister Doctor. "Menacing dragons are only mythology."

"Myth has a way of coming true," said Ottokos. "I'm merely saying *Be careful*."

"How kind to set our minds at ease, just as we depart from your protection." Sister Doctor looked livid.

"You have the panther. Nothing will get by her."

"Good-bye, then," said Sister Doctor. "I hope you have learned something from us."

Sister Apothecaire sniffled into a souvenir shawl that she'd bought at an inflated price from a Scrow weaver.

Shem Ottokos watched them leave. He did wish them well, at least as far as the maunter, and the completion of their task for his Princess. Beyond that, he wished them nothing at all: Let their Unnamed God go on unnaming their lives for them.

THE SNOUT OF THE JACKAL moon poked over the line of the trees.

Liir was nearly grey. The bleeding was staunched, but his heart was lurching. Candle worked at her throat, trying to scream for help, but she could not make that strong a sound.

No, she thought, the poor cold boy, no. Not this.

She put her domingon down and rubbed his shoulders. Then she removed his splints and braces and massaged his arms and legs. The air was turning from chilly to icy, and the extra blankets were in the hallway, beyond the locked door. She felt something lurch in him—he, who had been absent for so long—something kicked and resisted the death that seemed to be settling upon him. His breath was halting. A long moment without a breath; another.

She leaned over his brow from above, and held his newly bearding cheeks in both hands, and laid her nose next to his, and breathed into him, and kissed him besides.

✦   ✦   ✦

"WELL, *THERE'S* SOMETHING FOR YOU, NOW," said Chyde. "It never hurts to read the small print, my lad. Jibbidee, my walking stick? And it's not even that far, though in a quarter I rarely get to visit myself. Let's go."

The elf came forward with a walking stick, and Chyde stood erect, or as erect as he could. Long years of desk work had crushed his hips cruelly, and his posture was poor. Still, at a new angle, he was able to look Liir over a bit more thoroughly than he'd yet managed.

"You hadn't ought to have arrived with a firearm," he said with sudden harshness. "You'll leave that with Jibbidee at once, my lad-ee-oh."

"It's no firearm. It's a broom."

"Show it me."

Liir opened the satchel and displayed the top end of the charred broom-pole.

"Let me see the length of it, to be sure it's not a blunder-bulleter in disguise."

The broom was withdrawn and Liir handed it over. "A right wreck of a thing, but for the new growth," said Chyde, handing it back.

"What?"

Liir didn't ask again, but felt it. The broom handle was notched with young nubs, and two of them had split, revealing modest embellishments of pale green leaf, like tiny rare broaches pinned to an old bit of scrap wood.

"It can't grow!" said Liir in amazement. "It can't do that."

"Put it away," said Chyde. "Some folks haven't seen a green leaf growing in twenty years. You don't want to get them all weepy now, do you? Mercy is the name of the game in this trade." He kissed a vulgar emerald on the knuckle of his own middle finger, paying obeisance.

They set off, not in the direction of the waterway, but along a broad passage that served as a commercial parade for the underground settlement. More humans in evidence now, part of the vast employment network that kept Southstairs running, though the shops and stalls were largely staffed by elves who seemed to have raised obsequiousness to an art form. Here and there, the nice contrast of a grumpy dwarf. The noise was ordinary chatter and gossip, and it was some time before Liir realized what made it seem strange. For once, there was no little strain of music playing off to one side. Well, who would play music in a prison, after all?

The roofs of the cavern rose higher overhead, passing out of view into darkness. More of the structures were freestanding, supplied with their own tiled roofs, like buildings on any aboveground street. It felt like a city of the dead. Eventually Liir could see why: this must be the oldest district in Southstairs. It certainly seemed the most decrepit, so far. Above it, all at once, the claustrophobic blackness of cave-dark gave way to the blackness of a different sort: a moonless night, with scratchy scarves of cloud being drawn by the wind across ancient, disaffected stars. It was the middle of Southstairs, the original geologic bucket that must have suggested itself as a natural prison to the first settlers of the Emerald City.

"Stars, they give me the creeps," said Chyde. "I hate to come this way."

They found a set of steps leading farther down. Chyde asked for directions once or twice, and sent Jibbidee scampering to check the marks on buildings. "This'll be it, I guess," he said. "It's an Animal district, so you'll forgive the stench. Hygiene isn't their strong suit, as you know."

The air was so cold, though, with a wind whipping in from above, that the smell seemed negligible. At any rate, Liir was too excited to care. He found himself bobbing up and down, and once he nearly grabbed Chyde's hand to squeeze it. So what that Shell was a bounder, that Lady Glinda was a glamorous airhead! They'd done something good; he'd gotten here. He'd find her, his only peer and friendmate, his half-sister if that version of history was true—the girl who befriended mice, and shared her gingerbread, and who had giggled at bedtime, even when threatened by a spanking. He would liberate Nor, and then—and then—

He couldn't think beyond that. Just to see her, someone he had known once, back when the world had been something other than tragic, back when Elphaba had been stalking about the castle out west in her robes and rages! Back when home was still home!

Jibbidee skittered forward, back, anxious and irritable. "What, what's the matter, thingy?" asked Chyde. "Cat got your tongue? Ha-ha." He turned to Liir. "It did, you know. That's why he can't talk. It'll grow back in time, but at the moment it's a bloody little stump."

They pressed into a building, more a pen than a set of salons. A Sow was lying in straw trying to warm some Piglets, most of whom looked to be dead. Improbably, the runt had survived, but it was not long for this world.

Chyde voiced what Liir was himself wondering. "An odd place to put a girl child. What was I thinking of? You. Sow. We're looking for a girl, a human girl child. Name of Nor. The register puts her in this unlikely spot."

"She had some developmental problems," explained the Sow without opening her eyes. "Some lodgings coordinator decided that, among the likes of me and mine, she wouldn't seem as offensive."

"Where is she?"

"I would construct a good story if I had the strength," said the Sow, "but I'm conserving what energy I have left for my litter. In fact, the girl's own story is good enough. Do you remember when the butchers came through a week or ten days ago to cull the crop because a roast of loin was required? Some celebration Upside. It was the Wizard's deposal, wasn't it?"

Chyde looked slantwise at Liir. "We don't sacrifice Animals for ceremonial meals, don't be silly," he said hastily. "You're talking through your postdelivery deliriums, Sow." He twisted rings on his fingers, turning some jewels palmward, other jewels out.

"Whatever," she said. "My deliriums remind me about a couple of

Horned Hogs, long in the tooth if they'd still had teeth, who were going to make better rump roasts this year than next, I'll tell you. They knew their days were numbered. One of them had broken off a horn trying to escape, and the bone spur was sharp and useful. Didn't you read the report on this?"

"I've fallen behind. Terrible workload, and no one to pick up the slack. Jibbidee's next to useless. Where is the girl, that's what I want to know."

"I'm telling you. The Hogs entered a kind of suicide pact, and the bull killed the bitch and then himself. They arranged it to be done on the same slab of old door on which they'd have been carried out for slaughtering anyway. A kind of final comment on the quality of life at Southstairs."

"Only the best is good enough," said Chyde.

"So they let themselves putrefy, and we neighbors left them to it for as long as we could stand it. It bought us all some time. But you know as well as I that the entrails of Horned Hogs breed a kind of maggot that likes to burrow into human orifices, especially the airless ones—"

"Stop . . ."

"And there's little less airless than Southstairs—"

"I don't want to hear about it—"

"So your colleagues had to cart the carcasses Upside. They had no choice."

Chyde said softly, "You'll get a huge extra bucket of slops for this. Keep on."

"I had no way of suspecting that the poor suckling Nor had a functioning brain left in her skull," said the Sow. "But apparently she did. She climbed onto the door-slab and pulled the Hog carcasses over her. I certainly hope for her sake she plugged all her valves. I saw her chewing candlewax once, so maybe she was softening it for just such a purpose. Anyway, hidden by corpses, she was carried away a few days ago, though what happened to her once she left our happy home I can't say."

"The very least of my concerns," said Chyde. He glanced at Liir, who was tremblingly pale and gulping for air. "You take it so hard, lad? Why is that? Sounds like she got out—something you'd never have persuaded me into allowing. Don't weep, silly boy." Then he said, "Jibbidee. The runt."

"Oh no you don't," said the Sow, struggling to her feet. The elf was defter, though, and he had scrabbled over the boards and across the straw, and snatched the Piglet before the Sow could position herself in full defense. "You bastard!" she cried.

"I've been remiss; I haven't noticed. Poor Sow: You've far too much on your mind. This should relieve you of distractions." Chyde grabbed the squealing Piglet from the elf and hurled it against a beam. His aim was true; the blood spattered and the body fell with a thud into the slop trough.

In shock Liir fell against the fence, and the maddened Sow went for him, but Chyde, laughing, pulled the boy away in time. "You should've let someone know these shenanigans were going on," he said to the Sow. "Being a squealer isn't such a bad thing in a Pig. And we all have to do our duty—you, me, and the least little daisy in the field. Eh? Eh?"

✦ 8 ✦

THE PANTHER HAD GONE as far as she would go, and turned back. Now the canopy of oakhair limbs formed over their heads. In the short time that they'd been away from the mauntery, however, the wind had scoured the trees of their last leaves. The jackal moon, though sinking toward the horizon, still watched Sister Doctor and Sister Apothecaire as their high-rumped skarks fleet-footed it through the forest. The unnamed creatures still circled overhead, following their progress.

"I could use a moment to pee," called Sister Apothecaire at one point. "A Munchkin woman doesn't have as large a bladder as some others."

"Winter wolves come out at dawn," Sister Doctor replied, "so shut up and hold your bladder if you can, or pee in your saddle."

✦ 9 ✦

CANDLE HAD SEEN ENOUGH OF DEATH to know that Liir was about to die. She was breathing him and kissing him as best she could, rubbing his limbs to encourage what warmth remained. His scalp was like ice. She took off her underskirts and tried to wrap them like a turban around his head, to keep his brain alive. From time to time she went and kicked against the door, hoping to arouse some maunt doing midnight devotions, but she couldn't keep up the effort. She couldn't stay away from him. As he grew more distant and colder, she grew warmer in her panic, and climbed atop him and tried to rescue him with her own warmth. She kissed him and licked his eyelids as a cat might, trying to open them. She didn't know what his eyes looked like, even, and she was stretched naked upon him like a wife.

✦ ✦ ✦

LIIR BROKE AWAY FROM CHYDE, stumbling, his eyes shut against the tears and the memory of the blameless Piglet. Just like that, without cause! What then, thinking they had some cause, might they have done to Nor?

"Be it on your own head if you get lost down here," called Chyde, not much alarmed. "You won't get far, and there's none to help. Come back to headquarters when you've had enough wheeling about and I'll get you a hot meal. There's no reason for me to be inhospitable, you being a guest of Lady Glinda and all. I'm not unreasonable. I live to serve, as my dear former wife always knew me to say."

Liir lurched, first running, then sinking almost to his knees and catching himself, then running again. He didn't know how to find the waterway on which he and Shell had arrived. He threw down his torch, hoping it would catch something on fire and turn the place into the hell it seemed, but the torch only rolled once or twice and then dropped into a canal. There it sizzled out, and the stick bobbed like a hard new turd.

The dark was less intense, though, than he'd reckoned on, and in a moment he thought to look around. He was in a small square of faceless buildings, just a few bolted doors, possibly a warehouse district. It was empty of pedestrians and fairly quiet, too, as this place went, and above him was a scatter of starry deep.

His only thought was that there was nothing left, nothing to live for, nothing to wait for, nothing to remember. The stars were cold and he couldn't leap to grasp them, to pass fist over fist along their lofty network of knobs, arrive someplace new, and, if not safe, at least less heinous. They merely mocked, as stars were created to do.

He hugged himself, for here the wind swept in without interference. He pulled the cape like a blanket about him, and clutched the broom as if it were the Piglet, and he could will it back to life. His tears came hot and desperate, the only warmth in the universe.

The broom twitched once or twice, and he took it out of the satchel. It shook itself slightly, and seemed firmer in his grasp. The old dusty straws at the back end, bound in a bristly fagot for sweeping so long ago, were freshened with green—even in this starry half-light he could see the color. Cattails, or grass tips in seed, something like that. He didn't know the plant.

He threw his leg over the broom without thinking and he held on tight, and he rode it up the draft from hell, and into the night.

✦ 10 ✦

WHEN SHE HEARD THE KEY IN THE DOOR OPEN, she came to her senses, and collected her hair from where it had spilled across his face, and climbed down.

Mother Yackle was smiling almost as if she had a sensible thought in her head, though according to the other novices Mother Yackle had been senile for as long as anyone could remember. The old crippled creature pulled the door aside and dropped her head, as if affording Candle some privacy as she composed herself.

Liir stirred, and sighed. Though his eyes remained closed, the lids both twitched, just faintly. One hand clenched, then released.

By the time the jackal moon was gone for another generation, and the Superior Maunt and her returning agents, Sisters Doctor and Apothecaire, had made it up the steps to the infirmary, Liir and Candle were gone, too.

The Service

NOTION OF CHARACTER, not so much discredited as simply forgotten, once held that people only came into themselvés partway through their lives. They woke up, were they lucky enough to have consciousness, in the act of doing something they already knew how to do: feeding themselves with currants. Walking the dog. Knotting up a broken bootlace. Singing antiphonally in the choir. Suddenly: This is I, I am the girl singing this alto line off-key, I am the boy loping after the dog, and I can see myself doing it as, presumably, the dog cannot see itself. How peculiar! I lift on my toes at the end of the dock, to dive into the lake because I am hot, and while isolated like a specimen in the glassy slide of summer, the notions of *hot* and *lake* and *I* converge into a consciousness of consciousness—in an instant, in between launch and landing, even before I cannonball into the lake, shattering both my reflection and my old notion of myself.

That was what was once believed. Now, it seems hardly to matter when and how we become ourselves—or even what we become. Theory chases theory about how we are composed. The only constant: the abjuration of personal responsibility.

We are the next thing the Time Dragon is dreaming, and nothing to be done about it.

We are the fanciful sketch of wry Lurline, we are droll and ornamental, and no more culpable than a sprig of lavender or a sprig of lightning, and nothing to be done about it.

We are an experiment in situation ethics set by the Unnamed God, which in keeping its identity secret also cloaks the scope of the experiment and our chances of success or failure at it—and nothing to be done about it.

We are loping sequences of chemical conversions, acting ourselves converted. We are twists of genes acting ourselves twisted; we are wicks of burning neuroses acting ourselves wicked. And nothing to be done about it. And nothing to be done about it.

IN SOME MORE HUMBLE QUARTERS of Oz, gossip had long held that Elphaba Thropp, the Wicked Witch of the West, had been born a wise soul, already formed, somehow conscious. Why else the mouthful of sharp choppers, not so much baby pearls as python's teeth, which some folk insisted she'd sported at birth? She came into the world with advance knowledge of its corruption, and in the womb she had prepared for it as best she could, by growing those teeth.

That was what was said, anyway.

Not everyone is born a witch or a saint. Not everyone is born talented, or crooked, or blessed; some are born definite in no particular at all. We are a fountain of shimmering contradictions, most of us. Beautiful in the concept, if we're lucky, but frequently tedious or regrettable as we flesh ourselves out.

The governesses of the monied classes often held that a child ought to be kept from witnessing cruelty and ugliness, the better to preserve some ounce of innocence. Rural grannies and spinster aunts—like the Nanny who had helped raise Elphaba—neither mollied nor coddled. They believed it was better for a child to know what befalls a chicken when the feast of Lurlinemas rolls around. Better to learn—from a distance—the tricks perpetrated on the weak, the distractible, the unlucky.

Both pedagogical stances, however, relied on a common assumption. Growth and change were viewed as a reaction to conditions met. One might as easily argue, however, that it is the world's obligation to re spond to children. By force of personality, by dint of their vicious beauty and untamed ways, children tromp into the world ready to disfigure it. Children surrender nothing when faced with the world: it is the world that gives up, over and over again. By so giving up, of course, it renews itself—that is the secret. Dying in order to live, that sort of thing.

You could catalog the thousand ways people shrink from life, as if chance and change are by their nature toxic, disfiguring. Elphaba, with her sympathies far more substantial than her luck, had at least wrestled with the questions. She'd shoved, and barked, and made herself a right nuisance.

By contrast, the Quadling girl, Candle, was an interpreter savant, translating the text of a world whose fundamental nature she hadn't yet grasped, and maybe never would. Did the difference between an Elphaba and a Candle come down merely to a question of focal depth: the big picture versus the little picture?

For his part, Liir had not been a bright child. Even on the edge of puberty he had given little thought to the paradoxes of his existence. He had imagined himself to be more like Chistery, the chief Snow Monkey, than like Nor and her brothers, Irji and Manek. Chistery had a slipsy-doodle sense of language, but he tended toward steadiness. He did his chores without complaining or forgetting, and asked for nothing beyond his basic needs. Even at fourteen, Liir hadn't been much more demanding than Chistery.

But Liir remembered that Nor had addressed the stars, had sung harmony with mountain streams, had loved all creatures whether their initial letters were written Great or small—Animal or animal. She was nuts as a nut tree in a nut forest, of course: that was what he had thought without realizing he was thinking anything at all. That silly Nor was a creature apart. Not just as a girl—though that, too, of course—but as a fragment of human possibility. She had had a sympathetic imagination, and Liir?—he could barely count.

Children often define themselves in relation to their parents: emulating them or working hard as possible to avoid resembling them in any way. Since the identity of both his parents was in doubt, Liir couldn't see himself as taking after anyone for sure. Certainly not Elphaba. In her final months, stooped, crabbed, scrabbling from desk to podium to window ledge, she was more like a quivering scorpion than a woman. At rest her fingers tended to curl up like a claw, or like the petals of a flower gone a bit blowsy: her hand was always out, always open, ready to take what found its way there and seize it. Not at all like Liir, who cowered.

Among the human kind, thought even the most jaded and bitter of Animals, there are many ways to be wrong, but there are only a relatively few ways to be young. In their generous apprehension of the world, for their insatiable appetite for the world, the young are to be forgiven.

SOMEWHERE IN THE SULFUROUS UPDRAFT above the great maw of Southstairs, Liir was born out of a dark vile womb and thrown into the night. He came into himself perched on a broomstick dozens of yards above the highest watchtower. Here was a cushion of wind, billowing him almost onto his side, causing his shins to tighten automatically against each other, his arms instinctively to wrap the broomstick harder. It was Liir and wind and height and stars, it was alone and alone and alone; the understandings were distinct and differentiated, and then suddenly annealed by a process he couldn't name. Maybe fear of heights! His *Liirness* applied, suddenly, applied to himself and no one else.

He didn't know what *Liirness* might mean, and he was sorry Elphaba wasn't around to raise a mocking eyebrow and sling a caustic remark. He might have been hurt by her sly digs, but he could have relished that hurt, too—he saw now. Survived it? Transformed it.

A hurting Liir was a real Liir.

However he'd come to be here—settling on an unstable bolster of thermal, learning to slide up the banister of the night—there was no else doing it but Liir.

The Emerald City gaped at him, but it didn't understand what it saw. He was just a touch of ash from a hearty fire, a scrap of tinder tossed in the winds. Winds that were damned strong; they snatched at the hem of his cape and unrolled it off his shoulders until it trailed behind him, a stain.

For his part, he saw the City the way few others had. Well, Elphaba

must have! And anyone lucky enough to harness a Pfenix, that rare creature. The view was like a model of a city made with an impossibly deft
hand—hundreds and hundreds of buildings, grand and humble, glazed
with tile and black with soot. A city built on a gentle rise, he could now
see: long slicing boulevards and curving promenades, a honeycomb of
streets and canals, parks and squares, a thousand mews, ten thousand alleys, a hundred thousand windows blinking bronzely. A glowing organ,
like the illuminated heart of Oz itself pushed through the flesh of the
land, pulsing with its own life, tricked out with monuments, defaced
with the graffiti of broken trees, the Palace of the Wizard a cancer upon
the landscape, the dead center of it all.

In his grief at having missed a chance to save Nor, and his shock of
the unanticipated flight, and the confusion about what to do next, he was
more successively Liir with every breath.

He circled the Emerald City, afraid if he landed he would return to
being slightly dead. How could anyone live without flying?

So the boyhood of Liir began—began in a new way, as if all that had
gone before had happened to someone else.

But it seemed amazing to him that he'd had the courage to set out
cross-country with that Dorothy. Was it courage? Perhaps it had only
been sheer ignorance of the breadth and treachery of the world.

The broom brought him to ground on the cobblestoned quay near
one of the smaller canals. The wind was strong, so itinerants were huddled face-front around brazier fires made of scrap wood and boards
ripped from fences. No one saw him land.

Bravado was not what he felt; but he felt something, and that was
rare enough. A cold sense of thrill: absorbing the news of Nor's escape,
her being alive. Wounded, cursed, embattled—alive nonetheless.

He walked for a while along the quay but realized it was colder
there, and ducked into an alley. The broom on his shoulder bounced as
he walked and looked for a place to doss down. It bounced harder, as if
thwacking him with congratulations, but this was silly: he was walking
with a spring in his step.

After a while he just jumped, six, eight times in a row, in glee, like a kid playing Hoptoad Hoptoad Call My Hoptoad. He'd look a right idiot to anyone peering out a window, but he didn't care.

A GOOD NIGHT'S sleep under a rubble of marketplace hay neither dampened his spirits nor inspired him with a plan. Eventually he made it back to Lady Glinda's town house in Mennipin Square. Perhaps she could arrange another meeting with Commander Cherrystone, who might be able to find out what had happened when Nor had had herself secreted upstairs. Or maybe Lady Glinda had an opening for a bootblack or a son.

The houseboy who had first talked to Liir reported that Lady Glinda had repaired to Mockbeggar Hall, the Chuffrey country pile near Restwater, there to do good works among the rural poor. It pleased her to dispense largesse from time to time. It calmed her nerves and made her happier with her marriage. She'd brought her cabinet with her, hoping that some grouse hunting of a sunny afternoon would breed camaraderie and unity of purpose, or if not, that one or two of the more difficult ministers might be shot accidentally in a convenient hunting accident. More than one kind of grouse needs bringing down!

That was how the houseboy put it, anyway—with high knowingness. No, there was no way to say when Her Ladyship might return. In her absence, the household was investing in a pack of howling Bratweilers, which as a breed was not known for its docile disposition. And take off that suit of livery, by the by, lest the house of Chuffrey be besmirched by whatever smut you're about to get up to.

Liir was happy to oblige. His old garments, which had been placed in a bin for disposal, were dug out and tossed at him. Wriggling into them, Liir noticed an unfamiliar snugness. As if his limbs were lengthening after just one flight.

The rest of his life, and all its possibilities, were spread like a landscape before him, and he couldn't help taking in three or four breaths, keenly and quickly, to sample the day. The air was bracing and his blood quickened. He felt as lithe and full of ginger as that cunning Shell had seemed. Liir could commit a crime, or . . . or banter with fellows on the street . . . or wink at a girl and cadge a kiss. That's what people did. He could do that.

Soon. First he answered the summons of a carillon and presented himself on the broad steps of a church. He had a dim memory of mauntish prayers, but not of services, and this morning he felt worthy enough to feel humble. He would prostrate himself before whatever-it-was-in-there, and thank the Unnamed God for having brought him that close to Nor. And ask what next.

The doors were flung open and the service just starting. Was it a holiday, and he hadn't known? Or were churches in the Emerald City always this thronged? Peering between the unstooped shoulders of gentlemen standing in the vestibule, Liir caught sight of the wide, bright room, a preacher of some sort declaiming from a plinth to a sea of faces varnished with rapture or, at any rate, close attention.

"I'm sure our Unnamed God requires of us conviction and perseverance. I'm sure our Unnamed God grants us the privilege of obedience. In the face of uncertainty, the one thing we can be sure of is the value of certainty. And the Unnamed God bestows upon us the balm of certainty."

He's sure of a lot, thought Liir; how consoling to stand within the sound of such confidence. And the way he rolls "our Unnamed God" off his tongue—the *our* might as well be *my,* he's that well placed. People say "my God!" all the time, but usually they mean "oh shit." He means something better.

Liir stood on his toes. The homilist was an affable older man, neither handsome nor plain—rather forgettable, but radiant with the effort of explaining the Unnamed God to all these devout, and devoutly interested, people. He looked a bit like an animated puppet, tufts of hair behind his ears taking a red tint from the colored windows behind him. "Let us continue this celebration of Thanksgiving for our deliverance from the Witch. Our independence from the Wizard and our relief from the Witch bring all of Oz to a new chance for greatness. Miss Grayling will lead us in Anthem Eleven: 'One Truth, One Truth Alone.'"

He wasn't sure he'd heard correctly. The room was so very crowded, and now skirts rustled and scratched, boots scuffled, as people rose to sing. He didn't know the anthem but the refrain was simple enough.

"One truth alone we hear:
Your secret holy plan.
With so much yet to fear,
We trust what truth we can."

The choir sang an unintelligible verse and the chorus began again, and this time Liir tried to join in, but an usher grabbed him by the collar and sidled him backward over the threshold.

"I know what you're after," said the usher. "Any cash in these pockets goes into the collection plate."

"I'm not a pickpocket," said Liir.

"Oh? You didn't exactly dress for the service." The usher had a point. Compared to the pious at noisy prayer, Liir looked like a peasant. "Catch you inside again, I'll alert the constable, who's sitting in the back row on the ready."

"Sorry," said Liir. But he found he could listen from the top step almost as well, and the air was nicer outside anyway—not so clotted with perfume and incense.

At the base of the wide stairs loitered a group of urchins, the oldest at least four or five years younger than Liir. They looked up at him as if he were one of them. "You don't go in either?" he asked them.

"Never had a chance," said one; "Never wanted a chance," added another.

"What're you doing here?"

"Charity pennies when the service lets out, stupid."

"Oh. Right. Don't you get cold?"

"No," said a small girl missing some front teeth. "We fights a lot to keep warm."

"It's a good song," said Liir. "Can you hear it from down there?"

"Don't know hymny-singing."

He began to hum the melody and came down a few steps. "One

truth alone we hear," he said with bright enunciation, "your secret holy plan."

They liked the sound of a secret holy plan. "What is it?" said the gap-toothed girl.

"It's secret, stupid," said the older boy.

"Shut up," said Liir, happy to be bringing joy and religion to the masses. "Your secret holy plan . . . get it? Da da da something, we trust what truth we can. Now there'll be another verse and they'll start over. Everyone ready?"

"You're a ragamuffin cleric," said an older girl, but she sang when the chorus came around again, and the others chimed in with more gusto than grace until the usher came out with the constable, and they all had to scatter.

"Thanks," said the urchin leader, "now we got a song, but we got no breakfasts. Come on, looters; we'll go steal bread from the pigeons near the Ozma Fountains."

"Surely there'll be more food to go around," said Liir. "I mean now the Wizard is deposed."

The kids ran and laughed, as all kids can, even malnourished urchins. "What, because he's not around to eat his own portion? We'll see about that!"

Undaunted, Liir wandered about until he came to a small hostelry. A sign read SURGERY FOR THE SENSELESS, and beneath that hung a wooden image of scissors in the act of snipping off the heads of a bunch of daisies.

This time he knew enough not to go in the front door but to wander the alley behind till he found another entrance. A graceful young woman in a dotted purple cloak came to the door when he knocked. "I'm looking for an Arjiki girl, about sixteen, newly sprung from prison, and possibly in poor health. Would she have come here?"

"We tend the wrinklies here."

"Well, then," he ventured, "I'm here to offer my services."

"We have no budget for a houseboy."

"I don't need funds. Just a place to sleep and something to eat from time to time. I can help take care of the senseless. I had an old Nanny who needed all kinds of assistance, and I know how. I don't mind."

"When we're through with them, they don't need much help," said the woman. "They don't care so much what goes right or wrong for them anymore, and that's a blessing, don't you think?"

"I suppose so. I'm merely looking to be of service," he explained. *My life started today*, he wanted to add, but she looked too cross to take it all in.

"I wouldn't be surprised if the solicitor sent you to spy on us," she replied. "We doctor the patients, not their last wills and testaments. We've been cleared of suspicion any number of times. Why are you tormenting us? Isn't there supposed to be some relief of oppression now that the Wizardic administration has left the Palace?"

"I'm not from the Palace," he said, affronted partly, but also impressed: could he seem that old and competent already?

"If you don't go away I'll set the cat on you." She pulled down her sleeve; her left arm was raw with swellings and scabs. "Unlike some, he's not very nice since he's been neutered," she said ominously. Liir had the feeling that if there was a cat in the house, it was really a Cat. He backed off.

"I couldn't just come in and get warm?" he began, but she had shut the door.

DAYS WENT BY, and he was glad to have learned about the stale bread fed to the pigeons at the Ozma Fountains. He kept body and soul together there. Scrambling for food, he wasn't as nimble as some of the street dodgers, but his legs were longer, so he made out all right. At night he had the benefit of the cape as a blanket, so he was warmer than some.

He asked about Nor, but the City was filled with itinerant children, and to the good burghers of Oz, tinker children were anonymous when they weren't invisible. No one had noticed an Arjiki girl on her own, and push off, you, before we call the authorities.

He thought about Princess Nastoya, but what could he do? The famous Wizard of Oz, granter of wishes, wasn't going to stage a comeback just so Liir could beg for help for that old She-Elephant. And there was no one else to ask.

Determined not to be cowed, Liir took to hanging around the army barracks just inside the south gate, known as Munchkin Mousehole, a reference to the diminutive stature of Munchkinlanders. The Emerald City Home Guard was better fed than the poor under the bridges, that much was obvious. After a while Liir decided that membership in the Home Guard would relieve his hunger while he tried to decide what to do next. And maybe he'd find that devoting his life to service paid dividends.

Stuffing the old cape in a sack, pressing it as compacted as he could manage, Liir joined the throng of roughhouse boys on the parade grounds—the boys who played gooseball with soldiers at free exercise. The lads hoped to merit the gift of a cracker or a coin or a plug of tobacco, but Liir wanted more. He bade his time and steeled his nerve.

One afternoon a sudden hailstorm blew in from the Kells. Everyone scattered for cover. Liir ducked into a narrow archway hardly large enough to protect one. The soldier already there couldn't be more than a year or two older than Liir, and so they fell into conversation as they waited out the storm.

The soldier, proud of his stature as Petty Fife in the Guard's musical corps, told Liir where and how to apply, and what to say that would amuse the conscripting officers. "Don't tell them you don't know who your parents are," he advised. "The officers are a high-strung bunch. They think that all the orphans who apply are really sent there by their parents, infiltrating the Guard for an eventual insurrection. If you're really an orphan, lie. Tell them your folks can't keep from screwing and they just had their twelfth baby, and you were kicked out of the family sty. That they'd understand; they're screw-starved here, a lot of them."

In time, Liir followed the advice, and learned it was sound. Though eight other gaunt-cheeked boys presented themselves in the same audience, only Liir answered smartly enough to be signed up. He was given a number, a cot, a cabin, a chit for meals, a key, a position title—Second Scrub—and a job, doing just that: potatoes in the commissary kitchen, morning, noon, and evening. The Home Guard ate little but potatoes, it seemed.

Still, there he was! Here he was! It seemed too good to be true. A smart uniform—someone else's before it was his, for a few old stains hadn't entirely washed out, and one sleeve had been replaced with a new one cut from a cheaper weight of broadcloth—but smart just the same. It came with a cap sporting a stiff silly brim in front, and a cocky periwinkle-colored tuft up top. The outfiteer also located a pair of boots, down at the heel and splayed at the toe, but serviceable enough, for they were conveniently overlarge and could take an extra pair of socks in the toe, which kept out the cold.

Once in a while Liir caught sight of the chatty fellow who had befriended him in the archway, but that soldier was assigned to a different division. In any case, Liir was determined to maintain a comfortable anonymity, so he didn't go chasing for friends, neither in his own division nor beyond it.

One morning in the yard, when Liir was hauling sacks of potatoes from a delivery cart, he spotted Commander Cherrystone arriving in a brougham. The man appeared weary. Liir hung back and kept silent, but he invented reasons to linger in the area. He watched as the Commander spoke with a sergeant at arms. The Commander took a cup of coffee in a china cup and reviewed a construction site marked out for a new latrine or barracks or something. He then disappeared into a foreman's shed with a roll of schemes under his arm.

An hour or so later he emerged, a cigarette between his gloved fingers. Liir approached Commander Cherrystone and reintroduced himself, a new politeness and reserve hiding what remained of his disapproval. Cherrystone might still be helpful.

"Yes, yes," said the Commander, distracted. Liir wasn't even sure Cherrystone remembered him, but the commander listened politely and said he would try to find out what he could about the details of carcass removal at Southstairs. "You mustn't hold your breath though," he said. "I've a lot on my plate. There is much to be done for the defense of our city."

"There is? But we're not at war? I thought peace was at hand."

"Your highborn champion, Lady Glinda, thinks all is peaches and cream. She'd like it to be. But given the uncertainty of the political situation, the economy needs stimulus, and the threat of war is a great incentive to spend. Fiscal frottage."

Liir didn't know what this meant. But things did seem to be happening. For weeks, and then for months, he fed potatoes to the burly soldiers who dug and hauled the earth away from the building site, and eventually began the even harder work of setting colossal foundation stones in place. Liir was glad he was a slender thing, for he was better suited to kitchen work than transporting boulders. But slowly he deduced that, despite his nothing childhood in the nowhere mountains, he wasn't quite as obtuse as he'd imagined.

He had no reason for smugness about it, to be sure. He was a bumpkin when it came to national affairs. He'd had little schooling and less practice at rhetoric. He didn't venture an opinion about current affairs, for he hardly knew what they were. No one bothered to circulate news broadsides in the barracks, and the banter at mealtime boasted about whores and sores. Period.

What Liir discovered, rather, was that merely by hanging around in the company of Elphaba he had picked up—something. Not power, not intuition, which she seemed to have down to her very eyelash. Not understanding. But something else—a good ear, anyway. Would he could find a way to perform a spell! That was the ultimate competence with language, a skill Elphaba had had in spades, and that she used rarely and reluctantly. What is a spell after all but a way of coaxing syllables together so persuasively that some new word is spelled . . . some imprecision clarified, some name Named . . . and some change managed.

Despite his flight on the broom, Liir was sure he had no instinct for magic. It was the broom that had managed that feat: he'd gone for the ride, nothing more. If he'd ever felt the slightest tremor of intuition or capacity, he'd have pounced on it like a cat on a rat. No, he was duller than the other kitchen lads even about basic things. He couldn't even predict when he was going to need to use the latrine.

But he found himself rounding syllables like stones in his mouth, silently. He knew he was shy, and thought to be stupid; he was beginning to suspect, though, that he wasn't stupid. Perhaps not even slow. Merely uneducated. But not, he hoped, uneducable.

COMMANDER CHERRYSTONE DIDN'T COME seeking out Liir to answer his question about Nor. When several more weeks had passed and there was no sign of the Commander again, and no message passed on by his aide-de-camp, Liir began to press the issue to others in the Home Guard. Cautiously he started to circulate a scrap of gossip he had invented. A pair of Horned Hogs was slain in Southstairs—*because the Hogs were magic*. Their carcasses were removed before they could contaminate the other inmates with sorceric powers. Could it be? The kitchen boys, hungry for tales of enchantment, took up the story as if it were gospel. Liir hoped his invention would trip a rebuttal, turning up some useful information about the actual disposition of the Hogs—and by extension, suggest Nor's next whereabouts. But revelation was slow in coming.

The winter crashed in with icy spite. His hands turned red and chilblained from the water into which the potatoes dropped. At least he wasn't freezing or starving to death outside; snow was felling dozens. He bade his time. He was glad he got to feed the fellows who worked at the construction. They had finished shunting boulders onto the site, but even in this cold they were required to lift and set, plumb and point. They got little relief from the cold.

The Home Guard guessed they were building yet larger barracks, as if the numbers of the force might swell sometime soon. Or perhaps warehouses for the defensive artillery supposedly under development. During a thaw, a steep roof was framed and shingled; when the snows returned, the interior was roughed in at a rapid rate. Before long a unionist cleric, his ceremonial garments hidden beneath heavy fur robes, appeared on its steps. With smoking urns and hallowed gestures he signaled the Unnamed God, and the unfinished place was consecrated as a basilica.

The basilica was more or less functional by Lurlinemas. True, the pagan cult of Lurline, the sprite said by some to have founded Oz, was out of favor; few but illiterate country folk paid obeisance to Lurline anymore. But the celebration of that old holiday was still popular. Lurlinism had been quietly absorbed into the common culture, not least because the cash tills splashed with money during the festive season.

Lurlinemas made a welcome distraction from the anxiety about leadership that seemed still to grip Oz, even though the Wizard was now gone half a year. Holiday presents came in on all sides for everyone but Liir. He had prepared a story about his parents' fierce devotion to unionism and their rejection of the heathen custom, but he didn't need to lie: no one asked him about the absence of gifts by his bunk. His mates received parcels in gilt paper, silly trinkets, useful clothes, small wallets of cash scented with cloves. He remembered the time Nor had given him the tail of her gingerbread mouse, and his mouth watered, but he swallowed it down.

The basilica was large enough to hold nearly a thousand at a time, so everyone got to attend the strictly unionist service on Lurlinemas. Liir saw Commander Cherrystone in the front.

A visiting chaplain with an ungainly flapping lip pulled himself into the pulpit and intoned the beginning of a homily. The sung petition petered out into a tirade against the loose morals of the day. Most of the soldiers went instantly to sleep, propping one another up on the benches, but Liir still had had so little exposure to homiletics that he sat straight up and listened. The preacher, perhaps sensing that someone midway down the room on the left was actually paying attention, began to improve.

The minister gripped the edges of the lectern and swayed sideways. "At every stage, even in the decorous and seemly home that the army provides you here, weird rumors of magical uprisings spring up! Like weevils in the wheat, like maggots in the rump roast!" Either his raised voice or the mention of magic stirred the morning crowd awake.

In order to challenge the blasphemous apocrypha, the minister repeated some stories being told and retold about town. "Magic's appeal is sheer pfaithism: the pleasure faith that attracts by the glitter of its surface," he railed. "Change a fish into a farthingale? Or a feather duster? All distraction! All sleight of skin! But change a fish into a fish fillet and feed your hungry mother: now, that's a magic we can applaud: the magic of human charity!"

Liir *was* ready to applaud. Who wouldn't? But no one else stirred, so he settled his hands back in his lap.

"Urban legends; they spring up when times are grim," continued the homilist. "That Ozma will return to govern the humble! That little toast roundlets spread with herbed goat cheese will fall in the desert and feed the starving! That Horned Hogs, in sacrificing themselves, will confer a magical immunity to residents of Southstairs and help them to survive their confinement!!"

Liir nearly jumped out of his seat.

"No, no," continued the minister. "The Ozma kidnapped years ago is dead in an unmarked grave, and her bones are halfway to dust. Toast roundlets don't fall in the desert unless you're in the final delirium of starvation, and they don't taste of much even then. Horned Hogs, when they die in Southstairs, are carted to Paupers' Field, and their corpses burned. Nothing of them remains, not a jot of magical comfort for any of the denizens of Southstairs. Better that prisoners should turn their wretched hearts to the Unnamed God, and beg forgiveness for even imagining such a farrago of faith!"

Paupers' Field, then. Liir committed it to memory. But he listened to the minister's address to the end, in case there was more to learn. The words rolled on, sonorously and as buoying, in their way, as the winds had been, the one night that Liir had ventured on the broomstick.

At the close of the service, Liir bravely pushed forward and touched the minister on the sleeve. The man—older than he'd appeared from below—turned wearily to look at Liir.

They exchanged a few words. Liir asked for instruction in unionism. He'd been moved by the remarks. He wondered aloud if escaping Kiamo Ko the way he did, even at the cost of Elphaba's death, had been the Unnamed God's way of getting Liir's attention. But the minister said, a bit too sharply, "Why? Have you seen or do you know of magic being done? Here? On the premises perhaps? Are you being tempted by the wrong forces? Explain, boy!" Liir was alarmed and shrank back. Foolish to have identified himself so! Shaking his head, he excused himself from the conversation and left.

It was too cold to venture out of the Guard yard. But the weeks would pass, the sun would wheel. When the worst of the season had slunk by, he would think up an excuse to skulk out to Paupers' Field. Learn what he could.

THE DAY DID COME, though not soon enough, and Liir made the trip swiftly, and only a little illegally. (Initially he had invented an ailing mother and a crippled father, and after he'd been in the Home Guard six months, he was given leave to carry them a few coins and a loaf of bread.) Apparently, though, his invention of the story of magic Horned Hogs had worked too well. The legend had spread through the urban population like news of a scandal, and pilgrims had begun to mass at the pyre of the Horned Hogs. The crematorium at Paupers' Field had had to be abandoned and demolished. The squatters whose tents had sprung up on the dreadful spot knew little of what had recently gone on there, and nothing of Horned Hogs, or if an escaped convict from Southstairs had been discovered.

Still, returning to base, Liir found himself less than distraught. If Nor had really had the invention and courage, even after those years, to secret herself out of Southstairs sandwiched between two slaughtered Hogs, she'd have managed somehow to find a warm place for the winter. Their reunion was ahead somewhere, waiting for them.

He would have faith in the Unnamed God, who even now was probably ordaining the right time and place in some secret holy plan. All Liir had to do was bide his time, do his work, peel his potatoes, keep his nose clean and his eyes open, and the UG, as Liir's barracks mates termed it, would tell him what to do next, and when to do it.

As to his hopes for helping Princess Nastoya—it wasn't going to happen. You didn't learn magic in the army. He had nothing to say to her, no way to give comfort. Probably she was dead already, anyway.

THERE WERE NEW HABITS to examine in the privacy of his bunk. Self amusement was the least of it: operating solo beneath the rough sheets was risky business in a dormitory setting, and his mates were always alert to the cues that one of their number was finding himself hot and bothered, and doing something about it.

No, his secret distractions were acts of memory, flights of doubt, even at times a feeble attempt at prayer. (He wondered why the chaplain spent so much time discoursing on the value of prayer to the enlisted man, yet never gave instruction in how prayer ought to be conducted.)

Deep in the funk given off by a dozen young men dozing in nearby bunks, Liir itemized his attributes, and considered how they were being heightened and strengthened by life in the barracks.

Rectitude, for one. Propriety. Custody of the senses!—that was how he (mostly) resisted masturbation.

Also, Liir found he was developing a capacity for respect. The mark of a soldier, of course. Back at Kiamo Ko, he hadn't been respectful—he'd been ignorant and scared. There was a difference.

The army thrived on its *regulae*. Precision, obedience, and rightness of thinking. Had Elphaba possessed any of those virtues? When she'd been sloppy with emotion, vivid with rage or grief—which was most of the time—she hadn't kept to a schedule. Coffee at midnight, waking up the others by slamming the larder door looking for cream! Lunch at sunset, bread crumbs on the harpsiclavier keys. Pelting through the gates of the castle, in any weather, at any hour, no matter if Liir had just laid out a couple of coddled eggs for her. Studying the night through, getting excited, reading things from that—that *book* of hers—out loud, to hear how they went, to hear how they sounded. Waking Chistery on his perch at the top of the wardrobe. Impetuous and selfish, totally selfish. How had he not seen it?

She was obedient—yes—to herself. Though what good had that done her—or anyone else? So far as he could remember—and he spent some wakeful nights examining his recollections carefully—she had rarely asked anything of Liir except that he keep himself safe.

And certainly she'd never asked him to be obedient. How was one to learn obedience unless one was thwacked into line? He'd been left alone, to roam the dusty corridors with Nor and her brothers. He'd picked up reading almost by accident. He'd been clothed by Sarima's sisters, that clot of spinsters who had nothing better to do but brood and bitch. Now, *there* was a group of responsible adults, he thought, though he found he couldn't actually remember their faces.

Still, he reminded himself, stiffly, to be kind. What did Elphaba know of child rearing? When he listened to his companions gossiping about their mothers—those cozy, pincushiony mamas, who never cuffed a child without a follow-up cuddle—he knew that nothing about Elphaba smacked of the maternal. Maybe this was all the proof he needed that she wasn't his mother, couldn't have been. She had had lots of power, in her own way, but she had no more motherly instinct than a berserk rhino.

Even a berserk rhino can bear a child, his deeper voice reminded him, till he told it to shut up.

MONTH AFTER MONTH, his days were spent in drilling. In learning to shoot. How to run holding a rifle without tripping on it and spearing himself. How to march in formation. (He didn't learn horsemanship, as the only soldiers permitted to ride were those who had brought their own mounts with them when they enlisted.)

How to wear his hair saucily, to thrill the maidens on the pavement.

How and when to salute, though not, precisely, why.

How to peel potatoes faster.

What was curiously obscure, Liir thought, was the nature of the menace that the Home Guard was formed to protect against. The commanding officers didn't reveal much about possible threats. When at ease in their dormitories or in the canteen, the enlisted men discussed the question.

Some felt the Home Guard existed to provide mortal comfort to the citizens of the Emerald City. Should the rabble ever rise up, should the denizens of Southstairs break free—hell, should a mighty comet thud into the Palace and burn it to blazes—the Home Guard would be right there, ready to restore order.

Others argued that the Home Guard wasn't a municipal police force but a defensive army. Before the Wizard's departure from the Palace, the province of Munchkinland had declared its autonomy as a Free State. Since the Emerald City's main water supply, Restwater, fell wholly within Munchkinland's borders—to say nothing of the great arable reaches that fed the capital of Oz—hostilities were conducted primarily on the diplomatic level. It was inconceivable that the EC would retaliate against the upstart government in Center Munch; a full-scale civil war in Oz would imperil both the water and food supplies of the capital.

But what if Munchkinland raised an army? If such an army invaded the Emerald City, the Home Guard had to be ready to toss them out on their asses. So the drills were constant, the defenses shored up, and it was said that spies were kept busy trying to find out just what Munchkinlanders were up to.

"Spies," said Liir. It sounded lovely and sexy and dangerous.

Still, he supposed that it was good policy for the enlisted men not to know the precise reasons for their constant drilling. The information belonged to those wise enough to interpret it, and Liir knew this didn't include him.

HE LEARNED A LITTLE MORE when he and five others were singled out of a lineup one morning and told to wash and clothe themselves in their dress uniforms. "Palace detail," said the commanding officer.

Palace detail! How smart! He *was* moving up. Nose to the grindstone, eyes on the prize: it worked.

When Liir and his mates reported for duty, he realized why he'd been chosen. The detail involved six trim young men of identical height and build: two blond heads, two chestnut, two charcoal. Liir was one of the charcoals.

They were to accompany Lady Glinda and Lord Chuffrey into the House of Protocol, said the commander. There, the well-placed couple was being inducted in the ceremonial Order of the Right. The Lady Glinda was being thanked for her period of service to the country, and her husband for his own contributions. It was a high honor for the soldiers of the Home Guard to attend this ancient privilege of the just getting their just deserts, said the commander. So smarten up, top form, eyes front, chin high, buttocks in, shoulders back. The usual.

With his riding crop he smacked one of the blond heads. "You think this is the stables, you dolt? Get rid of that chewy pulp or I'll knock your teeth out your behind."

It is something to be charcoal-haired, anyway, thought Liir. Isn't it?

He'd see Lady Glinda again. That much was for sure. If he had no further campaign with her, at least he had a little history. And who knew? As the throne minister of Oz, perhaps she followed all things; maybe she'd remembered his quest for Nor, and had information for him that Cherrystone had never heard.

At the Palace, Commander Cherrystone caught his eye and winked. Liir and his five mates made a sort of human wallpaper, dazzling in their white sartorials and whitened boots, gold plumes splashing from their half-helmets, standing at the head of the aisle.

Lady Glinda walked a step or two ahead of her husband, greeting the cheering crowds with a rolling movement of her scepter. Her skin was firm and her chin up, and her eyes dazzled as they had done the first time Liir had seen her. She wore antique mettanite struts, and a tiara of cobalts and diamonds, and she advanced in her own warm front of orange blossom fog. Her face was trained on the crowd, giving them love, and when her eyes passed over Liir and he gulped and willed her to recognize him, she didn't.

Commander Cherrystone followed, pushing Lord Chuffrey in a wheeled chair. The nobleman's head was fastened peculiarly on his neck, as if it had come unfastened and been reattached by someone inadequate to the task. Chuffrey drooled on his epaulets. Attending like a nursemaid with impeccable references, Commander Cherrystone discreetly wiped away the spittle.

The ceremony was abbreviated due to Lord Chuffrey's obvious ill health. Perhaps he was dying and they were rushing through this convention as a thanks for all the good he and his bride had done the government. Which in Lord Chuffrey's case, if Liir understood the testimonial talks correctly, seemed to be a canny invention in the field of fiscal accounting that had helped the government avoid bankruptcy some years back. In Lady Glinda's case, it was her dazzling throne minister-ship, over all too soon, but the rewards to be reaped for years to come, and so on, and so on.

Glinda seemed to have learned how to control her blushing in public, or perhaps she just wasn't listening to the speeches.

Toward the end, when Liir's green eyes had begun to glaze over a bit, a rustle and hush in the peplums and fozzicles of the gentry caused Liir to turn ever so slightly to a side door. Supported on both sides by a pretty maiden, in came the Scarecrow himself. He looked greatly inebriated, or troubled by muscular atrophy; his limbs were akimbo and his eyes rolled like hard-boiled eggs on the spin.

At first Liir thought it was a joke, like a Fool at a sacred pageant. But the cornets trilled, and the great and good deigned to applaud. The Scarecrow gave a genuflection of such profound clumsiness that several of the Home Guard snorted. The Scarecrow said nothing, just waved, and Lady Glinda curtseyed, a cataract of tulle bunching in front and frothing around to the back.

The Scarecrow retreated. Liir felt cold and mean. The Scarecrow had been an obvious imposter—nothing like the Scarecrow Liir himself had walked with along the roads from Kiamo Ko. Couldn't they see it? Or were they complicit? Or maybe, in their eyes, one Scarecrow *did* look like every other Scarecrow.

The whereabouts of the real Scarecrow hardly bore imagining, now that Liir had seen the depths of Southstairs. Or perhaps, just perhaps, cannier than he'd ever let on, the real Scarecrow had managed to disappear himself somewhere. Good luck to him, in prison or in hiding.

Liir didn't pay attention to current affairs, generally, or not those beyond the intrigues within the barracks; he thought it beneath him to follow the details of how the civilian world amused itself. Was Lady Glinda stepping down willingly or had she been crowded out by some coalition of antagonists? The question occurred to him, but in dismissing it as meaningless, finally, Liir felt the first flush of adult apathy. It was welcome. About time.

At any rate, to be invisible to Lady Glinda and unrecognized by the next hollow head of Oz—it brought back to Liir the truth of his isolation. He wouldn't approach Glinda for news of Nor; he wouldn't stand the insult of having to reintroduce himself.

At length, the soldiers were shown a side room where they could nibble at dry crackers while Lord Chuffrey and Lady Glinda were received at a luncheon. To avoid possible stains on their dress sartorials, the soldiers were forbidden to drink anything but water. Liir was pissed at serving as a pretty accessory for Lady Glinda. He refused even the water.

When they saw the couple back to its carriage, Liir didn't even bother to let his eyes sweep over them. Should her eyes pick him out, now that the job was done, let her address him. But she didn't.

A YEAR PASSED, another. Nothing was the same, year by year, but little was different, either.

He found himself watching how the men consorted together, realizing long after it had begun that this was effectively his first experience of male behavior. Kiamo Ko had been unrelievedly female, at least in the adult generation; the shadowy presence of Fiyero, long lost husband and lover and father, was real but indistinct. Liir had learned nothing of how men speak, or joke, or trust, or fail to trust one another.

In the service, there were games, and Liir played hard and well. Formal clubs and socials, and he attended—stiffly. His work assignments gave order to his days and brought some satisfaction. He became known as a good listener, though this was mostly because he was unwilling to spill the beans about his quirky upbringing, and listening was easier than chatting.

Liir grew accustomed to his privacy. When furloughs were granted, he chose not to take advantage of them. Once he was invited to join a fellow cadet on a trip home to the family farm somewhere north of Shiz, in Gillikin. Liir had been tempted to accept. But the night before they were to leave, the cadet had a few too many. He began to carol about his doddery old daddums and the good little woman who'd married him and on and on and so forth.

"They're so proud of me. It's the best thing anyone in the family has ever done—to be selected a member of the Home Guard!"

Peculiarly undistinguished lot, Liir supposed.

Oh, said the cadet, but his mother's apple trickle could bring tears to the eye! Indeed, it brought tears to his, but Liir's eyes were stones. The next morning he told the headachy cad to go on without him; he'd changed his mind.

"You don't know what you're missing," said the cadet.

"I'd like to keep it that way."

The fellow returned with a sizable chunk of apple trickle wrapped in a checked cloth, and it was good. Too good, in a way; Liir had never tasted anything so wonderful. He resented every tasty crumb.

A few weeks later, when a commander's rifle had gone missing from the rack, Liir made an appointment to see the commander privately. He said he knew that the code of honor required him to speak. Deftly Liir laid suspicion on the shoulders of the Gillikinese cadet. The lad was hauled off into solitary for a few days. When he had not confessed in a week, he was stripped of his uniform and excused from service, dishonorably.

He never made it home, someone said later; he killed himself on the way. Hung himself in someone's back field, strung up on a black-trunk elm.

Nonsense, thought Liir; that's just army gossip. Who would bother to learn such specific details of a suicide of someone so patently soft and regrettable?

He sat in chapel. "Nothing convinces like conviction," thundered the minister, warning against softness, which when you came to think about it seemed like the UG's way of approving of Liir's maneuver. His own lack of remorse about it seemed authoritative in and of itself. When the rifle was found elsewhere, merely misplaced in the wrong locker, the entire company simply avoided the subject. No one came after Liir to ask him to justify his previous statements. It seemed no one wanted to be caught in the wrong.

A capacity for interiority in the growing adult is threatened by the temptation to squander that capacity ruthlessly, to revel in hollowness. The syndrome especially plagues anyone who lives behind a mask. An Elephant in her disguise as a human princess, a Scarecrow with painted features, a glittering tiara under which to glow and glide in anonymous glamour. A witch's hat, a Wizard's showbiz display, a cleric's stole, a scholar's gown, a soldier's dress sartorials. A hundred ways to duck the question: how will I live with myself now that I know what I know?

The next time Lurlinemas rolled around, Liir volunteered for solitary guard duty in the watchtower that capped the great chapel. He wouldn't agree to being spelled so he could spend an hour at the holiday dinner. "I determine my own duty and I perform it," he said to the cadet assigned to replace him. The cadet was only too happy to sidle back to the festivities. Liir took pleasure in dumping out, untasted, the tankard of ale snuck in to thank him.

ANOTHER YEAR, or was it two? At length the day came when Liir's company learned it was shipping out. But to where?

"You don't need to know," said the sergeant from Detail Desk, looking over his notes. "Your mail will be forwarded."

"Is this a . . . military moment?" asked someone, trying to speak stoutly.

"You get a night on the town before you go, six chits each. A court-martial for you and a fine for your family if you don't come back by the morning call of the roll," they were told.

Liir had no family to be fined, and no one to shame with a court-martial, but he was beginning to have enough of a sense of propriety not to want to be ashamed of himself. And since the months had become years, and the Home Guard was an institution that honored tradition and resisted innovation, he had lost sight of how much he had grown up. He was old enough to have a couple of beers, goddamn it. Because who the hell knew what was coming next?

He had to borrow civilian clothes from mates—a pair of leggings, a tunic, a waistcoat—for he'd long outgrown the rags he'd arrived in. He'd outgrown everything but the old cape, in which he had no intention of swanning about, not in front of his mates, nor anyone else.

He kept the broom and cape in a locker, away from prying eyes. He no longer put his face in the musky pleats of the cape's broadcloth, to harvest piercing memories. He didn't want to think of the past. Memories of Nor were pressed flat as envelopes, juiceless, between the folds of the cape, interleaved with memories of Dorothy, Chistery, Nanny—and oldest, Elphaba. They were of no use to him now. Indeed, they were a hindrance. Neither did he dream of his old associates—he could scarcely call them family, or friends—nor of anyone else.

The fellows who made it a habit of jolly-follying knew where to head for a good time. A tavern, they said, in Scrumpet Square: known for cheese-and-bacon temptos and even cheesier women. The floor was sawdusted, the beer was watered, the elf who served the drinks was neutered, and the tone agreeably disreputable. The place proved to be as advertised, and packed to the rafters, as the news of a Mission had spread. Common knowledge held that departing soldiers were good at loosening their wallets, their trousers, and sometimes their tongues, so an assortment of bamboozlers, shady ladies, and spies were fighting the buckos for the attention of the barkeep.

After so long in something like solitary confinement—solitary because he *was* solitary now, by choice and by nature—Liir found the exercise unsettling but not appalling. He tried to relax. He prayed to the UG that the spirit of relaxation should break the yoke of tension that rode across his shoulders here and now and, come to think of it, always.

Everyone wanted to know where they were going, and why. In all the theories that were shouted from table to table, one of them had to be right, but which one? An uprising among what remained of the Quadlings down there in Qhoyre? No—a final decision, and about time too, to invade Munchkinland and reannex it? No, no, nothing so exciting—only a boring public works project, building a dam across one of the vales of the Scalps, to create a reservoir deep enough to supply the Emerald City and decrease its dependence on foreign water. Or yet again no: no: no: no: something more wonderful than that. The cave of Ozma has been discovered, and she is to come back and rule our Oz, and the idiotic Scarecrow can go stuff himself. Hah! Good one: a Scarecrow stuffing himself.

Liir hunched into his borrowed jacket and tried to look as if he was expecting someone. His mates weren't avoiding him, exactly; they knew they'd be stuck with him for some time to come. They were spilling over with chat and banter on all sides, from all comers. Liir watched pockets being picked, groins being stroked, apron strings unraveling, beer spilling, candles guttering, mice cowering in the shadows, and the elf scampering almost weightlessly about with trays of beer glasses.

When he came to whisk away Liir's glass for a refill, he said, "Three Ozpence, guv; and how've you been keeping since Southstairs?"

Liir's head whipped. When Glinda hadn't recognized him for anything but his function, he had hated her for it. Now he hadn't recognized this elf—and he'd only ever seen one before! Or was that a good enough excuse?

He found the name on his tongue. "Jibbidee?"

"The same. Can't stay to chew the fat. Money's sloshing in the till."

"How'd you get out? I thought no one got out—"

"No one? Hah. You did, didn't you? You weren't meant to, I think. And so did that girl you were looking for, if the stories they told were true. Folks gets out, boy-britches. Many different ways. Sneaks out, flies out, folks their way out. Myself, it was bribery. Once upon a time I recognized a ring too unique to have found its way to the Under-mayor legally. Chyde would've slaughtered me, but elves are hard to pin down." He leaped up in the air like a figure filled with helium; it was true. Elves had little weight. It's what made them so easy to kill, if you could catch them. "So now I'm Upside, enslaved here to the shackles of righteous employment, too tired to think straight, and Chyde is free as a bee down Southstairs, out of mortal company, light, and beauty. Which of us wins the liberty sweepstakes?"

He skirled away without waiting for an answer, but when he came back to drop the next beer on the table, he added, "You're not one I'd have spotted for the military, you."

"Hidden depths."

"Hidden shallows, I think." But Jibbidee wasn't being mean. He grinned. Elves were like house cats that knew how to smile; the effect was unnerving. "That beer's on me."

"I inshist—"

"Don't bother. You've got the welfare of the land on your shoulders. All I have to do is keep awake till last call, and then mop up the vomit." He twitched his ears—which looked in considerably better shape than they once had. "I heard about how the girl you were hunting for was said to have escaped, but not how you did. They're still talking about it down there. Confounded 'em all."

Liir scowled; he didn't like to remember flying. The experience had been grand, and a sense of airsickness had obtained only after the fact.

"Did you ever find the girl?"

"I found out how to mind my own business."

The elf didn't take the offense Liir had intended him to. Cheerily enough, he riposted, "You're the rare one, then, who knows so well the line between your business and anyone else's." He bounded off.

Liir drank up and felt the beer rise in him—an agreeable and uncustomary heaviness. He imagined he could sit there all night, shoulders hunched, watching the circus of human life at a high pitch. After a half an hour, though, he had to go piss it out.

On his way back to the table he lurched against a soldier, who turned at the thump. Liir recognized him. It was the guy who had told him how to apply to the Home Guard all that time ago—the fellow on the gooseball pitch who'd sheltered with him during a hailstorm. Imagining Liir had approached him intentionally, the soldier said, "Oh, it's you."

"Well, it is," said Liir. "All these years, and never thanked you for the skinny on how to get in."

"If you're looking for advice on how to get out, I'm afraid it's too late now," said the fellow. He was sleek and rangy both, with hair the color of clarified butter, swept long across the brow and clipped at the nape. Even in this welter and swelter he was wearing officer's code stripes on the shoulders of his smart civilian tightcoat. A Minor Menacier, by the look of it.

"Liir," said Liir.

"Some do. They can't help themselves," said the petty officer. "*Leer,*" he explained. "How much have you had to drink?"

"Not too much enough of."

"You ought to sit down. You don't want to throw up on my threads."

The Menacier commandeered a small table from a couple of floozies. "Trism," he said, by way of introduction. "Trism bon Cavalish."

"Liir." He never said "Liir Thropp," though that was his closest approximation to a real name. Formally he'd enrolled as Liir Ko—taking the second part of Kiamo Ko as his surname. Now, though, he didn't offer even that. The Minor Menacier seemed not to notice, however.

"Do you know where's we're going?"

"I'm staying put. But if I knew where you were going and I told you, that'd be treason." He took a long pull on his beer. "No, I don't know."

They studied the crowd in a complacent silence as if they'd been friends for years. Liir didn't want to ask questions of Trism's origins, lest Trism ask him the same. So he asked Trism what a Minor Menacier's duties consisted of. Maybe he'd one day get to be one. Day. A Minor Menacier. Someday. Pluck a duck, the beer was telling.

"Development of Defense," said Trism. "That I can tell you."

"Which means what? New sword technique?"

"No, no. I'm in husbandry."

Liir didn't know what to say to that; he wasn't sure what husbandry was.

"Animal husbandry," Trism explained, though in the noise of the bar, Liir couldn't tell if he said Animal or animal, the sentient or the nonsentient creature. "Training for military uses," said Trism at last. "Are you slow, or are you falling in love with me?"

"It's the beer," said Jibbidee, swooping down again. "I'm not sure I'd fill him up with any more, begging your pardon, unless you want to husband him home."

"Sorry; it is the beer," said Liir, suddenly queasy. "I think I need some air."

"Can you manage on your own?" By the tone of Trism's voice he certainly hoped so but courteously he helped Liir up and loaned a strong arm. "Make way, make way; hail hail, the prince of ale," he cried. Liir felt like that old weevily Scarecrow he'd seen at the Palace. His legs had contradictory intentions.

More or less tumbling out a side door, they were almost plowed into by a carriage careering down the alley from Scrumpet Square. It pulled up to let out more custom. "Whoa, your country needs you, don't go slipping under the wheels of this fancy rig," said Trism, hauling Liir back and holding him up.

The door flew open and a man in a fashionable dark brocaded vest jacket descended. "All my small life that stays small and separate comes out now's time to see me drunkish," said Liir, "not fair play, that." The smart figure was Shell.

"Oh ho," said Shell, in a merry mood. "I knew you'd turn up one day! So, laddio, you're doing the town? Out soliciting officers, by the look of it? That's my boy."

"I'm a Guardsman," said Liir, straightening up more or less successfully. "Ow."

"Watch your head. You may need it one day. I wondered where you'd gone! Wicked old Chyde was absolutely flummoxed. He'd no idea what happened to you. Assumed you'd slipped and drowned in one of the canals, but then suicides and other such big shit usually silts up against the grates at one end of the line or the other, and you never did. Somebody said you'd melted, and sifted right through the sieve! Ha! That was a good one."

"I was looking for Nor," said Liir, trying to hang on to any small knot of reality he could pinch.

"Sure, and I remember that well. She'd snaked her way out somehow, hadn't she? And then word of her turned up, now where was it—?"

"I shall leave you to your reunion," said Trism, starting to detach himself.

"Oh, I wouldn't dream of parting chums," said Shell. "We're only young once, lads; make the most of it. And tomorrow you go toodle-oo, I hear. No, I can't stay and chatter; I've work to achieve in the next hour, now that lips are oiled enough to speak what I want to hear. But I'm talking strategy to the armed forces: I'll save my breath for kissing, or kissing up. Off you go, boys. If you want to borrow my trap and get home in a hurry, just see it's sent right back. I was young once, I remember. Go ahead."

"Sir!" snapped Trism. "I am an officer of the Home Guard!"

"And I'm the wicked snitch of the west," said Shell. "Oh well, I was trying to be useful. Not my strong suit. Driver, an hour, and don't have too much yourself; I don't want to end up in hospital. I'm to be back at the Palace by midnight for fun and frolic if I can pay with the coin they require."

"Nor!" said Liir. Saying the very word, after all this time, had made him come round. "Where is she?"

"Am I your personal secretary? I don't know. Was it Colwen Grounds in Munchkinland?"

"Couldn't have been; that's a hostile state," intervened Trism, bulking up.

"*You're* in a hostile state, by the look of it. Don't sneer at me, Minor Menacier. I get around; that's my job. But no, it wasn't there. Maybe it was Shiz. Was it Shiz? I can't remember exactly where. Don't pester me, Liir: I can see you're going to pester me. I have to go."

"Shell!" said Liir, but the man was gone in a snap of cloak and a slam of the door.

"Well," said Trism. "I'm not seeing you home, if that's what you're thinking."

"I am thinking no such thing. Though that coach would have been useful right now."

"I wouldn't take the loan of a boot from the likes of him. Bounder. I'll hail a cab or a street chair for you."

They walked to the front of the pub. Scrumpet Square was bright with torchlight. While Trism hailed a driver, and the cab was being brought round, Liir trained his eyes on some scraps of graffiti written with drippy paint on a public wall. He tried to bring them into focus as a way to sober up. In four different hands, applied at four different opportunities, to judge by the aging of the text, the wall read

ELPHIE LIVES!

OZMA LIVES!

THE WIZARD LIVES!

And then

EVERYONE LIVES BUT US.

Trism dumped him in the cab and paid for it, and gave the driver directions. Then Trism disappeared back into the pub before Liir could even thank him. So Liir settled back against the moldy cushions.

Everyone lives but us.

Nor was somewhere in Shiz. Shiz. Where was that?

He would find her. He should find her. He should leap from the cab right now and go find her. He tried to sit up, but the world beyond the isinglass windows was unsettled and rolled about as if on the backs of a school of earthquakes. When he was deposited at the barracks, his feet found their way to his bunk while his head tried not to hurt, and also tried to remember what was so important.

HE WAS HALFWAY PACKED next morning when he recalled Shell's comment about Nor. Through the sawteeth of his headache he grappled with the question. What to do? Packing, he paused over the cape—leave it behind, leave all the past filed in its pleats? He didn't want to deal with that decision now, while his head hurt. Easier to pack the old thing. Easier to bind the broom's head in a cloth so it would look less womanly, and tie the thing to the satchel laces. Postpone chucking these things out for good. Any minute now inspiration would strike. An idea would form, and as if by magic the courage to follow that idea would flare up. If only his head wouldn't pound so!

Now's a good time for an idea, he said, as he joined his mates in formation to receive orders.

Commander Cherrystone had not been informed about his own new assignment, it appeared, until that very dawn; he arrived at the head of the transport column with an unpinned collar and crumbs in his trim, silvering beard. His expression was thunder. He delivered his instructions in a throttled tone. No one dared ask a question. When the chaplain arrived, Commander Cherrystone didn't join in the public atonements delivered under open skies to the Unnamed God, in exchange for the success of their mission. Whatever it might turn out to be.

"We leave in an hour," said the Commander.

So, oh, what next? If only he had more oomph this morning! Or if he had a place to rest his head till the screech of today calmed down.

He finished clearing his trunk. Unlike all the other men, he had no private books, no mezzotints of family grandees, no clutches of letters from admonitory father or teary mother or whispery girl back home. He was bereft of the more traditional impedimenta, and determined to be proud of it.

He waited in the yard beside the basilica. What did he take of his mock parents? If Fiyero had been his dad, really, Liir had got nothing from him but a possible half-sister. No model of comportment, no word of wisdom, no wallet fattened with funds, no blessing.

If Elphaba had been his mother, he got something more—that much was sure. But what? She had acted to pervert fate, to interrupt and bludgeon history into shape—to topple the wonderful Wizard of Oz, no less—and what good had it gotten her? She was fierce and futile at everything she attempted. What kind of a lesson was that?

She hadn't talked to him much. Only in a cast-off manner. One lunchtime she'd seethed, more to herself than to him; "It isn't whether you do it well or ill, it's that you do it all," she'd said, dumping her attempt at poached eggs on the floor and hurrying back to the books and charms in her tower. That was her legacy, and it didn't add up to much.

So perhaps he should consider the absence of good advice a kind of direction from the universe: Follow where you are led, and take it from there. Maybe fate intends to lead you to Nor. It's gotten you this far, hasn't it?

It was easier to be passive, easier on his brain anyway. His cohorts gathered for departure while he congratulated himself for sorting this out.

And it was indisputably thrilling to fall into formation to the punch of snare drums. The men squared their shoulders and became Men. The wind obliged by whipping the banners and emblems: it was all so glorious and immediate.

The four departing companies of the Home Guard were now collo-

quially named the Seventh Spear, after some magic weapon in a children's fable that Liir had never heard told. The convoy marched in formation through the smell of sweet morning loaves, as Emerald City
shopkeepers were unshuttering their windows and washing down the
paving stones.

What a joy there was in movement! Liir hadn't realized how petty
he'd become, worrying daily about the gloss on his boots, the snap in his
retort. The Guard's culture had trained him into thinking that a well-
brushed smile and a groomed chin were somehow vital to the preserva-
tion of the nation.

He saw the Emerald City—perhaps for the last time?—as if for the
first. And how fitting it seemed that the Seventh Spear was shafting its
way through the capital toward Westgate, the portal through which Liir
had first made his approach. They marched past the polished half-domes
and buttresses of the Wizard's Palace—still called that, even now. The
sun came out and glazed the marble; one could hardly look at it. A giant
broody hen. From this angle, a distance north: the grimmer spectacle of
Southstairs, lurking behind the hunched shoulders of its walls.

Everywhere else—on this boulevard, anyway—the allure of healthy
commerce. Cafés catering, at this hour, to merchants on their way to
their warehouses. Stalls of books, pottery, feathery remnants to adorn
hats and hems. A display, arrayed under a bentlebranch arbor, of several
dozen tribal carpets imported from the Vinkus, suggesting that the West
was trading with the capital these days. And floral silks from Gillikinese
artisans, sprays of lavender and lime, to upholster furniture in better parlors. One merchant had hung an entire chandelier, chase-worked mettanite with crystal pendants, from the bicep of a healthy oak, and he had
arranged below it a dining area for eighteen—table, chairs, Dixxi House
porcelain settings and silver service, with linen napkins folded to look
like swans, one at each place setting.

That those who headed the nation could enjoy their meals in such
luxury!—the men marched with firmer step. The vitality of the capital
gave life to their cause.

The Seventh Spear turned a corner, continuing toward Westgate.
Liir recognized the warehouse district through which he'd passed with

Dorothy and her friends. The convoy paused while Commander Cherrystone negotiated some last-minute business with a wine merchant, and the soldiers were allowed to fall out of formation. Bleary from last night's mistakes, Liir wandered to the brighter side of the street. He propped himself against the wall of an abandoned granary of some sort. Putting one heel against the wall, he closed his eyes and lifted his face to get some sun.

The warmth of the walls behind him, the pleasure of being between moments of his own history . . . his skittery mind indulged in a waking dream. His thoughts wandered up the cracked plaster walls of the cornhouse. It was as if he were looking down at himself from the window on the second level. That's me down there, that young soldier, anthracite-haired, trim, smart enough, having his moment of rest . . . How handsome a figure he managed to seem, from this vantage point: shoulders acceptably broad, the windblown hair on his scalp, the knee thrust forward. A soldier doing the work of the empire: a good guy.

Then the focus of his attentions backed up—for that fragment of an instant in which a revery implies eternity—and Liir had the sense that the young soldier at street level was out of sight again, and out of mind; and the two people who might have been looking out at him from some private aerie above had turned their attention back to each other, lovingly.

Must be the sun! Must be the beer! Filthy slutty mind he had, after all.

"Straighten out!" barked Cherrystone, and they did, and he did.

THROUGH WESTGATE, they turned to the south. The lads knew the habits of the sun enough to be able to tell that much. They marched as suited the Commander's whim—more relaxed when in the rural outback, in parade formation when passing through villages. The companies tented at night, found the dried lentils and local celery exotic and filling, alternated hymns of patriotism to Oz with anthems of devotion to the Unnamed God, and didn't bring out the bawdier ditties until Commander Cherrystone had retired for the night.

Fording the Gillikin River, they came to a broad sweep of pebbly waste, marked here and there by stands of scrub maple and pencilnut.

Once they stopped for water at a kind of oasis, a mauntery of some sort, hoping that some novices would come scupper for them—lean down to reach the bucket, and show evidence of some lovely curve beneath their voluminous habits. But the maunts who supplied some succor were desiccated old biddies who had no curves to flaunt.

Liir waited to feel some frisson of recognition—could this have been the place where he and Elphaba originated? He couldn't decide. Maybe one mauntery looked just like another. Certainly one maunt and the next seemed identical twins.

"If we're going south or east again, wouldn't the Yellow Brick Road give us better speed?" some wondered. But perhaps the Free State of Munchkinland hadn't granted the necessary license.

Another opinion held that since most of the Yellow Brick Road leading south and east fell within the boundaries of Munchkinland, perhaps the final destination of the Seventh Spear was the mysterious west—Kumbricia's Pass, or the Thousand Year Grasslands, or Kvon Altar—romantic locales, full of intrigue, exoticism, magic, sex. Everything over the horizon beckoned more temptingly than anything near.

Crossing into the eastern Vinkus, they continued through the oakhair forest between Kellswater and Restwater. Fording the Vinkus River, too, they paused on the escarpment of its southern bank. A dozen miles or more to the southwest, the Great Kells gave off a faint but redolent breath of balsam and fir. Nearer, scatterbirches in the lowland meadows shimmered in their new leaf, like chain mail on skeletons. Several hundred small grey birds flew by, brazenly low, singing their throats sore.

It felt as if the world itself were blessing the endeavor when Commander Cherrystone gave the signal not to head west toward Kumbricia's Pass, the main route to the vastness of the Vinkus, but instead to the southeast. They would skirt the mountains and, rounding them, head south into Quadling Country.

The where, then, but not the why.

Why Quadling Country? When the Seventh Spear paused to make camp, the soldiers shared what they remembered about the southernmost province of Oz. Quadling Country was your basic muckland. An undifferentiated waste of bogs and badlands, once widely populated by the

Squelchfolk, a marsh people known for their ruddy complexion and fishy odor. Hadn't they mostly been eradicated when the Wizard had drained the wetlands in the hunt for swamp rubies? In the Emerald City you could see Quadling families from time to time. They were clanny, silent in public, making little effort to integrate. In the Emerald City they'd cornered the market on trash removal—all the funnier: trash hauling trash.

But the two larger cities of Qhoyre and Ovvels: surely something of them remained? The southern arm of the Yellow Brick Road ended in Qhoyre, and Ovvels was a nearly impassible distance beyond. A town built on stilts, Qhoyre. A town whose streets were silted with mud, Ovvels. No wonder the Seventh Spear's administration had obliged them to include gum-rubber boots in their packs.

WONDERFUL WEATHER, bracing light, cheery companionship. Now and then a free-held farm or some nobleman's country estate would welcome the convoy. A whole stable of milk cows at one, and they had milk to drink, to pour in their coffee, to splash on their faces; they had milk puddings, cheese temptos, creamed curd, lake lobster bisque. Who needed that fancy dining ensemble for sale under the trees in the Emerald City? The soldiers ate like kings and nodded off under the willow fronds, sassy and satisfied.

One day Liir and a couple of pettys were sent to collect fresh water at the foot of a wooded dale. They paused to rest before starting back with the filled jugs yoked to their shoulders. Other topics of conversation having been exhausted, Liir asked his mates, Burny and Ansonby, about the place of husbandry in the development of new defensive systems for the Emerald City.

As it happened, Ansonby and Burny had both flirted briefly with defensive husbandry. Ansonby had worked in the veterinary arts, and Burny had helped copy some legal contracts with farmers outside the Emerald City.

"It's supposed to be hush-hush, but everyone talks about it," said Ansonby.

"Not to me," Liir said pointedly.

"Well, then, I'm not sure it's my place—"

"Dragons," Burny interrupted. "Smallish flying dragons."

"Dragons!" said Liir. "Nonsense. Aren't dragons mythological? The great Time Dragon and all that?"

"Don't know where the stock came from," said Ansonby, "but let me tell you: I've seen 'em with my own eyes. They're about yea big, wingspan the length of a bedspread. Vicious things, and hard to control. There's a team been breeding them for a few years now."

In the course of their military careers, Ansonby and Burny had both come across Minor Menacier Trism bon Cavalish. They had no opinion one way or the other, except that he was remote and a bit uppity. Good at his job, though.

"Which job is that?"

Ansonby said, "He's a kind of—what would you call it? An animal mesmerist, I guess. He's got a silky voice and is real calm. He can woo an agitated dragon into a sort of trance. Then he takes the dragon's head in his palms. This is seriously risky, you know. The notched beak of a dragon can puncture the skin of your forearm, hook your vein, and unspool it out of your arm with a single jerk. I've seen it happen. No, I have. Really. Not to bon Cavalish though; he's smooth. When the dragon's purring, the dragoneer does something suggestible to the beast. I guess it's about overriding the creature's internal gyroscope, or navigational mechanism. Or just being persuasive and chummy with an attack beast. When he's done, the dragon is directable by voice, at least for a while. Like a falcon with its falconer, a sheepdog with its shepherd. Go, come, round, back, stay, up, dive, lift, attack."

"Retreat?"

"Dunno about retreat. They're attack dragons."

Liir closed his eyes. "I can't picture a dragon, try as I might, except for something fanciful in an illustrated magazine, or a stage prop. And a flying dragon!—sounds effective. Also a little scary."

Ansonby remarked, "Trism bon Cavalish thinks that someone came up with the idea after hearing about those flying monkeys organized by old what's-'er-face out west. The witchy witch. What was her name anyway?"

Nobody spoke. The wind soughed and the leaves scratched against one another. "Come on then, better get on," said Liir nonchalantly. "The water's heavy, and it'll be a bitch to haul. We're rested enough."

"Who made you boss?" said the other fellows, without offense. They dusted themselves off and began to press back to camp.

THERE'D BEEN NO SIGHT of settlement nor even of a solitary hermit for days. No border marking, either, but they knew they'd reached Quadling Country by the change in landscape. Little by little the land was sinking, a series of overgrown meadows stretching for days, every few miles another half inch lower. The grasses went from emerald to the yellow of pears, and then to a ghastly sort of white, as if the fields were being tinged with hoarfrost in the height of summer.

At night they slung hammocks in stunted sedge trees, and tried to sleep, though a zillion mosquitoes emerged, and there was little protection against that. Also a soft, thumpy sort of airborne snail would constantly blunder into their faces at night, perhaps drawn by the steamy exhalation of human breath. The camp echoed with a night-long chorus of stifled girlish screeches or curses as the worm-clods landed wetly across noses, cheeks, mouths.

"No wonder this place is uninhabited," said Burny once.

"It didn't used to be. The Quadlings lived here," Liir pointed out.

"It's one huge stinkhouse. Any locals still preferring this to the rest of Oz must be cretinous. Or subhuman. En't our old Wizard done them a favor to clear them out?"

BUT WORM-CLODS AND MOSQUITOES were hardly enemy combatants, and the Seventh Spear knew things could get worse. It *had* to get worse, or why were they being asked to suffer the indignity of this climate?

They gained an uncharacteristic hummock of land, a half mile across, from which the ground water had drained, more or less. Commander Cherrystone gave them permission to peel off their boots and air their feet. Eighty men scratched between their toes, where the itch was most maddening; flakes of wettish skin billowed before being borne away. It almost looked like snow.

Commander Cherrystone spoke about their mission.

"By my reckoning, we aren't far from the outskirts of Qhoyre," he said. "Common talk in the City treats Qhoyre as a provincial backwater, and compared to Oz's capital, it is, of course. But it has a distinguished history of its own, predating annexation by northerners. In the modern times, there's usually been a Viceroy stationed here to oversee. Not now. Were things calmer, we would have expected someone dispatched from Government House to serve as a translator of the native tongue, Qua'ati. We'll do without, I'm afraid. Unless I have a secret linguist among my fine young men?"

No one volunteered.

"As I thought. It's an ugly tongue but not hard to pick up, I'm told, if you work at it. I'm sure some of you will find yourselves fluent in a matter of weeks, and that will come in handy in due course."

The *matter of weeks* stumped them. Also, *in due course*. Was this some sort of permanent billeting? To what end?

Commander Cherrystone explained. It seemed that the Viceroy had been abducted, and his wife had disappeared, too. No one in Qhoyre admitted to knowing who was responsible, but the indifference of the natives to the situation was unsettling to the Scarecrow's cabinet back in the Emerald City. Quite offensively the Quadlings behaved as if life ought to go on much as normal, whether with a Viceroy or without one.

The job of the Seventh Spear was to befriend the locals, keep the public order, and—best-case scenario—identify and punish the perpetrators. If the Viceroy and his wife could be found and rescued, all the better, though he wasn't an indispensable civil servant, apparently—otherwise he'd not have been saddled with such a hardship assignment. In any case, the brief of the Seventh Spear didn't extend to recovery of the Viceroy; showing some muscle, however, was paramount.

"We'll move into the city, reclaim Government House, and restore order," he said. "There may be some bloodshed, men."

They nodded and clutched their weapons.

"Let us bow our heads and put our holy mission of right governance in the sight of the Unnamed God."

This, so far as it could be said for a fact, they did.

DISAPPOINTINGLY, THEIR RECLAIMING of Government House involved no bloodshed at all. The toothless old woman who had set up a loom in the eastern verandah merely handed over a rusty key that had been dangling on a string around her neck. For one so plump and wrinkled, she took off at a jaunty trot. Before nightfall a cohort of youngish teenagers, possibly grandchildren, appeared in the street to haul her loom away. They left a large tray of aromatic rice, still steaming, and they tossed red blossoms on the verandah floor that, in the moonlight, looked like splashed blood.

Thus a military skirmish fizzled into a social call. The establishment of dominance proved all the more elusive because the native culture was one of deference, hospitality, and bonhomie. "This is going to be harder than I thought," said Commander Cherrystone.

Being built large enough to be pretentious and commanding, Government House could just about domicile the entire company of the Seventh Spear. There was a lot of work to be done in terms of general upkeep, however. Cracks in the plaster, mildewing whitewash. The garden had run to seed and was a total embarrassment. How long *had* the Viceroy been gone? Or had he simply been a hapless steward of government property?

For a good price, the locals supplied acres of mosquito netting, which the men slung from hooks in the ceilings in the local fashion, cocooning each small grouping of cots. For extra protection, lengths of netting were nailed up at the windows, and a webbed arcade was erected from the kitchen door to the latrines at the back of the garden. In their smalls the men could walk to relieve themselves at night without fear of being bitten alive.

Some of the soldiers picked up Qua'ati, as Commander Cherrystone had predicted they would.

IT NEVER SNOWED in Quadling Country. The swamp forests held in the heat. Time seemed languorous and unchanging. How many years had they been there? Three? Four? They'd reopened a school and built a kind of surgery to augment the work of the local doctors. Some of the men had moved out of Government House, informally, and were consorting with Quadling women. This was forbidden during a campaign of occupation, but Commander Cherrystone looked the other way, for he had a common-law wife of his own by now and he hardly cared to enforce an inconvenient standard.

Liir worked mornings in Commander Cherrystone's outer office. He copied documents, he filed, he recommended which of his peers needed punishment for various minor infractions. As often as not Commander Cherrystone was absent from the inner office. Liir could go in and smooth down the crinkled months-old newspapers in which the shipments of Gillikinese wine came wrapped. He read about the Scarecrow's unfortunate accident involving that beaker of lighter fluid—what a horrible twist of fate, that it was *right there!*—and the subsequent elevation of the Emperor. "Would've liked to be invited to *that* investiture," said Commander Cherrystone, coming in on Liir as he jerked upright from his perusings.

"Old news is better than no news," Cherrystone remarked ruefully, about once a week. "Still, maybe it's better to be marginalized. You don't get noticed, and there's a liberty in that, eh, son?"

"You'll want a bottle of the Highmeadow blanc in the water well, sir, if you're having guests at table tonight."

"You remember everything. I'd be lost without you. Can you see to it?"

"I will." He already had.

Once a small crate of perguenay cigarettes arrived. "Bless my sweet bankers, I must've made another killing," said the Commander, reading a note. "Those Shizian accountants are wizards; they can make money out of a massacre of mice. Try one, Liir, you won't find better."

"I've no skill at that, sir."

"It's not much fun to smoke alone. Put down those charts till later and join me on the verandah." It sounded like an order, so Liir obeyed, willingly enough.

The smoke of dried perguenay was nutty and gamy both, hardly disagreeable, though taking perfumed heat into his lungs made Liir cough. "Ain't it grand, the life," said Cherrystone, propping his boots on the seat of another chair.

"You could get used to this if you were an ironsmith. Bit roasty for me, though."

"You learn to love it. So. Liir. What do you hear from home?"

Liir was unused to personal conversations with his peers, and this blunt question from his boss unnerved him. He was glad to have smoke in his lungs; he held it there while he thought what to answer. "Precious little."

"Sometimes the less you hear, the more precious it becomes."

Sentimental math problems were beyond Liir. "I follow my work day to day, breakfast to bedtime, sir. That's my life, and it's enough."

"You're a good lad. You're shaping up. Don't think I don't notice." Commander Cherrystone closed his eyes. "I would've been happy for a son like you, but my fond Wendina only gave me girls."

"You must miss them, sir."

"They're girls," he said neutrally, and his point was beyond Liir. *They're girls, so why bother?* Or *They're girls, so of course I miss them, don't be daft.*

"Since we're chatting, I wonder if it's bold to ask a question of you, sir."

"Ask away."

"If you had children, how could you stomach storming the castle of Kiamo Ko and carting off the widow and children of Fiyero?"

"Oh, back to that! Fair enough; you've earned the right. It was another time, another country—perhaps another me, Liir. When you're off on a posting and your family is left behind, they loom in your daily reflections with a . . . a size, a significance . . . and the thought of them gives you courage in times of doubt. I didn't like the maneuvers at Kiamo Ko, I'll have you know that right now. But I like being a man of my word. I like doing my duty. As I see you do, too.

"Besides," he added, "I did my best to delegate."

"Do you remember seeing Nor? The little girl?"

"She wasn't a tyke, she was growing up. I saw her. She was brave, if that's what you're asking. Quite possibly she didn't understand what was going on."

"Quite possibly." What a phrase. Of course she didn't understand it: how could she? She'd been raised on a mountaintop by a widowed mother and a half dozen spinster aunts. What could she know of military maneuvers?

"I see it still gives you pause."

Perhaps less pause than it once had. Waiting for fate to intervene was hardly taxing, Liir realized. "I think of her from time to time."

"You probably harbor a youthful resentment against me. It's all very normal, my lad. You were young at the time, and what could you know of duty and honor?"

"I am not sure, even now, I know what honor is."

The Commander was silent for so long Liir felt perhaps he'd been rude, or that the Commander thought his remark was rhetorical. But finally he opened his eyes and said, "How would it seem to you to be promoted to the rank of a Minor Menacier?"

Liir felt himself blushing. "I don't deserve it."

"You deserve it, son. You deserve the honor of it. I'm not a wordsmith, I can't define the concept of honor. But I know it when I meet it, and I see by the look on your face you do, too." He grinned almost sheepishly at Liir. His teeth were yellowing in this climate.

WORD ARRIVED THAT THE new leadership in the Palace was displeased with laxness at Government House, and requested the prompt execution of the Seventh Spear's original mission.

Commander Cherrystone turned to Liir. Although chilly politeness often still marked their exchanges, there had come to be some measure of regard on both sides. Liir was often disdainful of Commander Cherrystone for his complicated moods—now a front for the Palace, now a critic of the system—but Liir practiced loyalty and obedience, virtues the Seventh Spear espoused and he shared. And he was grateful for the promotion, and the smarter braid on his dress habillard.

Some of the fellows resented the promotion, but they saw the point. Liir was unusually circumspect for a young man. Not in any obvious way a dangerous loner, Liir kept to the margins, befriended other soldiers only so far as was fitting, and he didn't consort with the Quadlings beyond what the work required. He was the model of a military man at the start of his career, so far as anyone could tell. And since he had no social links with Quadling circles, he was a natural to enjoy what confidences might arise working in the Commander's office.

"Sit down and let me rehearse an idea with you," said Cherrystone one afternoon. Liir remained standing.

Bengda was a small community twenty minutes southwest of Qhoyre on the broad flat river known as Waterslip. In the days before the Wizard had mucked up the water table and wreaked havoc with a centuries-old way of life, the Bengda district had thrived in one of the few dry areas, humps of sandy hill on either side of Waterslip. A bridge between the cliffs had spanned the river. Over the years, with the harvesting of trees, the soil eroded, though. The hills lost height and subsided into the muck. Little by little the Bengdani villagers either left or took to the bridge. Now the hamlet of Bengda supported itself by exacting a toll from the ferries and commercial fishing vessels that used Waterslip as a highway between Qhoyre and points south.

"Entirely improper, of course," said Commander Cherrystone.

"Surely they'll stop if you threaten them with a fine?" asked Liir.

"They might and they might not. I hate to give them a chance to knuckle under, for it's worth more to us if they resist. Can you sniff around and find out if they would?"

"I'm not the man for that job," said Liir stiffly. "Begging your pardon, sir, you have more pull in that department than I do."

"If I start talking, I'll plant ideas in their heads." The Commander spoke wearily. "It'll work much better if it happens below ranks. Your expertise is needed, Liir. Can you put it about among the men that this information is of interest to me?"

Liir did, and came back a week later. The residents of Bengda were stroppy, at least by Quadling standards, but they would probably cave if presented with an order of prohibition or a bill of tax.

"That's no good, then." The Commander rubbed his elbows. "What they're effecting is a kind of extortion of river merchants, really. Perhaps I could charge them triple all that they've collected since we've been here. That would beggar them and they'd have to resist. Find out, will you?"

Liir returned and said that, begging the Commander's pardon, he couldn't really learn the answer to so specific a question without tipping the Commander's hand. "Tip, tip, that's the point!" roared the Commander, so Liir tipped.

The reply came back that the extended families of the Bengdanis would manage to come up with the triple penalty and that the bridge dwellers would stop levying the toll.

"Damn," said Commander Cherrystone, and he had Liir send out a formal censure of the Bengda bridge dwellers with a public declamation and a request for a penalty twice what had already been posted as the triple penalty.

Bloody hell no, said the Bengdanis, in Qua'ati, of course. At least not yet.

They paid up what they'd collected and made no promise as to when the exorbitant balance could be expected.

"That's that, then," said the Commander. "Make sure the whole district knows about their resistance, Liir. This has to get back to the City or my reputation is, like everything else in this Quadling quagmire, mud."

Liir did what he could, talking against the Bengdanis at the mess hall, the local gin pavilions, in the latrines even. It was uphill work now, for the Seventh Spear had become lax, and many men tended to think their Commander was getting high and mighty, not to say unreasonable. "He could just fork over a third of his own salary to his concubine, and she could find a way to get it to the Bengdanis," they said. "Why scapegoat those poor buggers? Why make life so miserable?"

"It's not ours to make life miserable nor to avoid misery when it's required of us," said Liir. "Have you whole lot gone to ground here? That says little about the military discipline we learned."

"Lighten up," they answered.

COMMANDER CHERRYSTONE TOOK LIIR under his arm and gave him the assignment to burn the village right into the river. "Tonight," he said.

Liir's face was stony. "Sir," he said, "you know as well as I that it's almost impossible to set anything alight in this climate. The moisture seeps into everything."

"I've sent to the Emerald City for provisions to help," said the Commander. "I've got six buckets of the tar of pulped Gillikinese maya flower, which would burn in a monsoon. Once night falls, you can paint the struts and supports of the bridge with it. Begin with the beams nearest the ends of the bridge, and paint high. Toward the center, paint low, closer to water level. Light the ends first—simultaneously—to create walls of fire on each approach, so the Bengdanis can't escape that way. They'll be crowded toward the center, and there'll be time for them to consider what to do, to call for help, before the lower-lit struts burn up enough to imperil them."

"Who will come to their aid?" said Liir. "They're twenty minutes from Qhoyre."

"In twenty minutes someone will hear them and, just as important, someone will arrive in time to witness their distress. That's the important bit. I'll see to that if we synchronize our timepieces."

"Arrive in time to witness? Not to help?"

"Liir, it's a bridge. They can jump into the water."

"Commander. Begging your pardon. No one swims in Waterslip at night, and rarely during the day, either. There are deadly water eels in the depths, and alligators that feed nocturnally."

"I didn't settle them there," said the Commander. "Do I detect a note of insurrection in your voice, soldier?"

"I don't believe so, sir," said Liir. He was troubled, though, as he turned away.

So that there could be no possibility of a warning leaked to the

Bengdanis, the campaign would have to commence at once. Liir conscripted Ansonby, Burny, and several others. Learning a trick or two from the high command in the Emerald City, Liir didn't tell them the nature of their mission. They were to dress in dark clothes and to wear mosquito-netted caps, to smudge their faces with mud, and to tell no one what they were doing.

"It's about the kidnapped Viceroy, I think," Liir invented, when someone pressed him. "There's been a lead. We're going to smoke out the kidnappers. But we can't give them a lick of warning or they'll scarper."

Sunset, with its usual caramel-orangey smear, was quick. The night creaked in on the wings of countless wakeful insects churring. An audience of billions.

"DETAILS TO FOLLOW, fellows, but first things first: This is a secret mission." Liir and his companions huddled by the flatboats he'd commandeered for the exercise. "You've been chosen because you have girlfriends here. You'll want to get back to them quickly as possible and hop into the sack with them. My advice is to try something new tonight. Make it memorable for you both, so if there's a call for alibis, you'll be prepared."

"But fraternizing is frowned up," said Ansonby.

"I mean if the Quadlings cry for scapegoats, you'll be covered. Anyone needs advice in the sex department, ask Ansonby. Tell them about position six, Ansonby." Liir winked. "It's known as Choking the Mermaid in some quarters."

He wasn't fooling anyone. Liir was suspected of sexual ignorance, and he had a reputation for an old-fashioned reticence about such matters. The fellows looked unhappy.

"If we're supplied with alibis," said Burny after a while, "what about the fellows who en't?"

"Tough luck hits us all," said Liir. "Sooner or later. Maybe they'll duck it this time. Maybe we will, too. Come on, we're moving out."

Once it grew dark, the mosquito problem drove most Quadlings into their stilted huts, though the odd canoe or flatboat sidled along. No one paid much attention. With the sky moonless at this time of the month—no doubt the Commander had already figured on this—visibility was reduced, helpfully.

A half mile north of Bengda, Liir signaled the boats in. He gestured at the rickety community cantilevered over both edges of the bridge, a hive of windowed light and the noise of supper and chatter. Then he explained the mission.

Burny was the first to speak. "Folks might die," he said.

"Not sure on that score, but I believe that's taken into account. Regrettable, but there you are."

"But women and—and children," said Burny. "I mean, what's children got to do with tolls or paying taxes, or refusing to pay them? En't they blameless an' all that?"

"Are children still blameless if they're going to grow up to be the enemy? I'm not going to discuss this. We're not taking a class in moral philosophy. We're soldiers and these are our orders. Ansonby, Somes, Kipper, you do the far end; we rest will start on this side. Here's the supplies—tar, brushes, a flint when you're ready. Knives."

"What're the knives for?" asked Burny.

"Carving your initials in the supports. You moron, what do you think the knives are for? Use them if you need to. Are we ready?"

"I can't do this."

"We'll ask the Unnamed God for the successful completion of our mission." Four seconds of silence. "Let's go."

They poled the flatboats forward and then nudged their way among the villagers' fishing boats, which as usual were tied in a long barricade beneath the bridge to prevent night traffic from sneaking through toll-free. The soldiers got a shock when they roused an old Quadling grandfather from the bottom of his boat, probably avoiding his scold of a wife. They clapped their hands around his head and bound his mouth tightly. Then they tied him in a burlap sack and dumped him into Waterslip.

Commander Cherrystone had chosen the hour perfectly, for the children of the settlement were fed but not bedded down, and as the soldiers set to smearing the tar pitch, they could hear the shrill laughter, the tired crying, the occasional lullaby filtering down through the rush-matted floors above their heads. The noise made a suitable cover, were any needed, for the quiet work of arson.

Their retreat would have to be swift, Liir knew, not only so that they would go unnoticed by fleeing Bengda villagers, but also so that his men would be spared the witnessing of what was bound to be ugly. All tyrants were harsh, but fire was more ungovernable than most.

He mouthed, "Set. Right. Light." With trembling hands both teams reached for the oil-soaked rags, which were balled by net wire. The men impaled the rags on the end of their swords, and struck their quickflints. The length of the sword allowed each soldier to reach high enough to light the tar his mate had already smeared into place.

One team finished faster than the others, since Ansonby in his haste whipped his sword too swiftly around. Perilously, the clot of burning rag dislodged early, but Ansonby ducked, and the rag hissed into the river.

It was neat, a job well done, and both flatboats were eighty feet back before the timbers truly caught and the night became annealed with the light of hell. The river reflected the crackling timbers, the shuddering bridge, which almost at once seemed to be gateposted with pillars of fire thirty feet tall. Good strong stuff, that maya flower tar! Then the screams, the dropping timbers, the burning water.

They were to have been fully away by now, and some other contingent was to come upon the sight, to report it objectively. But the flatboats got snared bankside in the knotted roots formed by ancient, shadowy sedge trees. Besides, the men couldn't stop looking. They could see Bengdanis running from window to window, house to house, and climbing up the mildewy thatch of their roofs. Some threw furniture in the water and tried to leap upon it; a few were successful, though Quadling furniture, mostly woven rush, was known neither for its strength nor its buoyancy.

One clump of thatch fell lazily through the blackness, like a falling star extinguishing itself, or a burning alphabetic vowel swallowed by watery silence, or a firebird plunging into a suicidal dive in a dark nameless lake.

Drunk on metaphor, thought Liir: that means it's time to scamper.

"Guess we better go. We mess up this part of the job, guys, we've messed up the whole thing."

"What *was* the point of this?" asked the one called Kipper.

"Campaigns are devious; that's why they're called campaigns and not ballroom dancing lessons," said Liir, but his voice sounded odd. He leaned his whole weight against the barge pole and began to move out. "The beds of your lady friends are cold tonight without you, lads, and if you're not back in time there'll be someone else to take your place before dawn. You know it better than I. Look sharp—"

He himself looked sharp, casting an eye around to make sure nothing was coming upriver from the Bengda bridge. How could it, unless it was a river monster disturbed by the conflagration and rising in rage? No boat would ever leave from that bridge again, nor be prevented from passing under it, either; it was falling, timber by burning timber, and its population with it, as he watched.

A man and a woman on the near side, which was collapsing haltingly into the burning water, had grabbed a child between them. Her clothes were aflame and the parents or neighbors tore them off. All their mouths were open, though Liir couldn't distinguish one human scream from all the others. Then the parents braced themselves as upright as they could against the sloping structure and began to swing the girl, arms and legs, to fling her free of the burning.

Liir was reminded of a game he'd played when he was what, seven, eight?—when Irji and Manek had swung little Nor like that, and then swung him, too. But it was into a bank of snow in the wintery heights of the Great Kells, at Kiamo Ko; it wasn't to save his life, or hers. It was for fun.

The girl twisted as they let go, and her arms reached back, as if she could will herself to swim through the night air and return to the arms of her parents. The fire behind them caught up with their legs and ran up their backs as she hovered like a naked girl bird, gilded red-bronze in the light. Then she crashed into the water. The efforts of her parents had worked this much: she landed beyond the pools of burning oil in which everyone else had fallen.

Liir leaped from the boat, hissing over his shoulder "Back to base!

That's an order!" He didn't turn to see if he was obeyed. In vain he looked for the girl. He didn't see her. He didn't see if she had swum ashore, or if she had sunk, or if she had swum back into the fiery liquid to join her parents in their immolation.

GOVERNMENT HOUSE WAS LOCKED down with tighter security than he'd ever seen it, but Liir had no trouble signaling to the night watch and getting in. Despite instructions to the contrary, Ansonby and Burny and the others weren't out canoodling with their local girls; they'd taken refuge in the barracks. The company of their mates must seem more consoling. And Liir observed that *no* one was off the premises that night. The other soldiers must have been alerted not to stray. For defense of the post? For their own safety? That meant the guys assigned to the mission would have been the only ones outside of military protection. Liir saw it now. They'd have been sitting ducks, isolated from each other, naked in bed with native women when and if the news spread and a retaliation was launched.

"The hero of the hour! Where've you been?" asked Somes.

Liir started to say something about the girl. He hadn't been able to find her, partly because it had been hard to train his eyes on the scene. It seared too brightly to be able to read.

"We've been fortifying ourselves with whiskey and patting ourselves on the back. The bridge is history! Come in for a rousing welcome."

"History. History. In a flash," said Liir. "Need to get something first."

He ducked along the upper verandah that looked onto the central courtyard, keeping back in the shadows and out of sight of men lounging by the fountain below. It only took him a moment to grab his satchel, the few things he'd stored in his trunk at the foot of his bed. He put his dress boots on the windowsill: a kind of symbol, he supposed, that he'd jumped. Everyday boots would serve well enough. Then, the old, mildewing cape and the broom on his back, a corked flagon of fresh water slung over his shoulder, he made his way lightly down a back staircase and through the dry goods pantry. Then over the wall, literally and figuratively.

WITH THE WITCH'S BROOM, he had the means to travel swiftly, but his heart was so heavy that he couldn't imagine lifting off the ground—or if he did, only to reach a height suitable for throwing himself from his perch.

He walked, and took no pains to conceal his tracks or silence his footfall. North, as far as he could tell. He corrected his trajectory by checking it against the movement of the sun, and if one day he wobbled too much to the west, the next he would likely wobble easterly.

It was early spring when he left Qhoyre—spring by the calendar, not by the growing season, for in the marshlands, rot and flower and fruit and seed and rot happened simultaneously all year. Long ago the climate had become a second skin from which he couldn't extract himself until, weeks on, his path began to climb, and now and then his foot landed on a hillock of dry grass.

He'd expected some crocodile to snap off a limb while he slept, a marsh cat to take a swipe at him, but the only creatures that seemed aware of his presence were the mosquitoes, and he yielded himself to them without complaint. He imagined them bleeding him dead, a thousand bites a day for a thousand days, until from the inside out he would have dried up entirely. Then—another way of flying!—a strong gust might come along and begin to worry a fleck of skin, and his whole being might toss itself like a scatter of midges in the air and disappear.

Weeks of walking, resting, walking. He didn't look for food, but the amoral landscape threw succor in his path. Thrashes of greenberry bush, ground nuts, the occasional swamp apple, porcupine root. He grew leaner than ever, though his diet seemed sufficient, for he suffered neither from dreams nor dysentery.

His sense of the geography of Oz was limited, but its most salient feature was the scimitar-shaped spine of high mountains that curved up from south central Oz to the northwest. He needed to get through the Quadling Kells—either by the Yellow Brick Road or not. Once he was northside of the mountains, he'd turn west and keep them on his left. Sooner or later he'd come to the gorge known as Kumbricia's Pass, the best route to the vast grasslands of the Vinkus. But he'd move on, until the Great Kells raised their ice-sheathed peaks on the west. He'd have to hit the Vinkus River, and he'd follow it north to where it emerged in a dazzling waterfall from a hung valley in the central Kells. Up the side of that waterfall, tracing the banks of the rightmost branch of the higher Vinkus, and still higher up the middle ridge of Knobblehead Pike, and he'd be back.

Not home. There was no place like home. Just back. Back at Ki-amo Ko.

As he walked, he thought of nothing, when he could manage that. The world in its variety had no appeal, and seemed mocking and vain. Clearing the Quadling Kells with relative ease, he'd come out into an easy summer on the northern slopes, wherein fruit trees sported flocked yardage of blossom, and bees sawed the sunny afternoon with their industry. It was not music, but noise. He stole some maple sap from a hermit's storehouse in the woods, not to savor, just to feed the gut.

In time there was evidence of human habitation again—a homestead here or there, a shrine on the road—to Lurline or to the Unnamed God, he couldn't tell and didn't care, and didn't stop to pay homage. He avoided people when he could, and when he could not, he was stone-tongued enough to be alarming. The kinder of the farm folk might offer a scupper of milk or a blanket in the hay loft, but they wouldn't welcome him in to their table. Nor would he have accepted.

Once he came upon an old woman driving a four-horned cow before her with a switch. She was accompanied by a kid, a boy by the looks of it, who seemed frightened of his granny, and shot Liir a desperate, pleading look. The woman turned her switch on the child and hissed, "There's nothing to look at in him, Tip, so mind your eyes or the road'll trip you up, and you're not riding the cow so stop thinking about it. We didn't come all this way for a prize specimen so you could mope and roll your eyes."

"How far is all this way?" asked Liir—not that he cared, but he thought if the woman would talk to him, she'd have less breath for smacking the boy.

"Gillikin, and we aim to get there before the snow flies, but I have my doubts," snapped the woman. "As if it's any of your concern."

"That's a long way to come for a cow," said Liir.

"A four-horned cow gives quality milk, useful for certain recipes," said the woman.

The boy said, "You could sell me to this soldier, and then you could ride the cow home yourself."

"I wouldn't dream of selling a boy as useless as you," she answered, "the good burghers of Gillikin would have my license for passing on damaged goods. Keep your mouth shut, Tip, or you'll regret it."

"I don't buy children," said Liir. He looked the boy in the eye. "I can't save anyone. You have to save yourself."

Tip bit his lower lip, keeping his mouth shut, but his eyes stayed trained on Liir's. The rebuke seemed to Liir to say: *You have to save yourself? And what proof of that are you, soldier?*

"Although if you were to offer that besom of yours," said the woman, "I suppose I might risk my professional reputation. It's a handsome item."

Liir passed on without replying. A mile or two later, he stopped to tighten his bootlace, and in looking back he saw that the woman, the cow, and the child had veered a bit northward across some meadows. The best route to the Emerald City, and Gillikin beyond, led between Kellswater and Restwater, through the oakhair forest, so now he could guess he wasn't far from Kumbricia's Pass. This proved to be true.

High summer, then, on the banks of the Vinkus River. He bathed in it. The mosquito plague was behind him now, kept away by a steady breeze sweeping down off the flanks of the Great Kells, which like transparent slices of melon were beginning to hover insubstantially to his left. The Vinkus River ran broad and shallow here, and icy cold even in the hottest sun, for it was fed by a thousand rills cascading down the piney slopes of the mountains.

Still, no animals. No herds of dancing mountain ponies, no turtles spending a decade or two in the middle of the path, very few birds even, and those too far away to identify. It was as if he gave off such a stink that the animal world was retracting from him as he moved north and west.

One evening he tried to cut his own hair, for it was falling in his eyes. His army-issue knife had become blunt from peeling porcupine root, and his efforts to sharpen it on a stone had come to nothing. He made a pig's breakfast of the haircut, finally dropping the knife and pulling at his hair, yanking it out by the roots till his scalp bled into his eyes. He thought the blood might refresh his broken tear ducts, and for an instant he imagined something like relief—relief—but it did not come. He dried his face and tied his hair back, and endured the sweat and damp of a heavy burden of hair.

The mountains, nearer now, loomed as a kind of oppressive company, their aroma of granite and balsam unmistakable, unlike anything else, and as unconsoling as anything else. Their million years of lifting their own heads was just a million years, nothing more than that. The summer was going, the sun was sinking earlier, he caught the tang of a fox one day on the wind, and felt the bite of an appetite—to see a fox. A simple fox darting past, out on its own business. He saw no fox.

The world seemed punitive in its beauty and reserve. Sometimes, thought Liir—his first thought in weeks and weeks—sometimes I hate this marvelous land of ours. It's so much like home, and then it holds out on you.

THEN HE CAME to a place where the Vinkus ran by a series of small lakes—none more than a mile or two long, and all of them narrow. Clearly they'd been formed by the same compulsion of landscape, for there was a family feel to them. The water was fresh and moving, and though he could see no fish, Liir imagined there were schools out of sight. Larches and birches and the thin growth known as pillwood made a pinkish fringe on the far shores. For the first time since leaving Qhoyre, Liir aborted his slow tromp north. He took a day to look around, for the landscape seemed obscurely pleasing, and he wasn't used to being pleased anymore.

The middle of five lakes was more fan-shaped than the others, and from the pinched point to the south it opened up to a wide vista of low hills—basket-of-eggs country—that caught the light and made patterns of shadow, one hill to the next. He explored the lake's southern shore and found there a smoothly rounded hill not much larger than a pasture or two, overgrown with pillwood trees, and slashed through with horizontal outcroppings of granite or trusset, he couldn't tell which.

The grass beneath the trees was evenly cropped, and pelleted with droppings, so some ruminant herd loitered nearby, keeping the sward neat. This gave the place a domestic look.

Liir sat down with his back to a tree and looked out over the water, which was lipped by the wind coming south, and striped with light catching on the wave tips.

It could make a home, he thought; pretty enough to tolerate, and no one around. The beyond of beyond. Nether How, he named it, *how* being a useful old word for hill. And how pompous that is, to name a place just because you rested your own *nether how* there for a while!

But he closed his eyes and drifted into a sort of waking dream, as he'd done once or twice before. He saw himself sitting there, almost nodding off, more of a man than when he had started out, but still lost, like most young men, and *more* lost than most. With no sense of a trade, no native skill except to make mistakes, no one to learn from, no one to trust, and no innate virtue upon which to rely . . . and no way to see the future.

He rose to the height of the leaves of the pillwood trees, which were beginning to turn amber, a first hint of autumn. He saw himself below, the ill-cut hair—what a botched job!—and the knees, and the feet turned out as if planted there. If he could just stop breathing, he'd become part of Nether How; sink capably into the grass. When his offensive spirit had left his body, the mountain sheep or the lakeland skark or whatever animal fed here would eventually overcome its fear, and nibble the grass right up to his limbs, keeping it shorn around him.

Then his attention turned to another figure, distantly apprehended though near enough. It was a man in a cloak of purple-rose velveteen, holding a staff and a book of some sort. He was emerging in the air as one seen coming through a fog. He seemed to be off balance at first, and tested the ground with his staff until he found his feet. Setting his funny hat straight on his brow, he pulled at his eyebrows as if they bothered him, and he began to look around himself. Liir imagined he was speaking, but there was no sound, just the apparition of a funny old man, sober and crazed at once, making his way along the brow of Nether How.

The old man passed close by the body of dozing Liir, down below—the Liir-shade in the tree branches saw it. The old man, maybe a scholar of some sort, paused as if curious, and looked at the tree against which Liir was leaning. Then he looked up into its branches. But his eyes could not focus on Liir at rest, nor Liir aloft, and he shrugged and began to make his way down the hill.

A good way to avoid company, if I want to avoid it, thought Liir, as his spirit began once again to settle down into his body, or—put another way—as his little dreamlet ended and the sorrier sense of the world, even this pretty corner of it, flooded back in.

He had left Nether How and was well along the lake's rightmost flank, continuing north, when he remembered the revery and saw something in it he hadn't noticed at the time. He had recognized the book that the old fellow was hauling about with him. It was the Grimmerie, the book that the Witch—that Elphaba—had used as her book of spells.

HE HAD LOOKED for the Grimmerie once, hadn't he? But that was before he'd set out from Kiamo Ko with Dorothy. And met up with that old she-Elephant, Princess Noserag or something. Who had promised to try to help find Nor, or to share what she could learn.

Proud and confident as only the truly stupid can be, he'd set out to find Nor on his own. Smart move, Liir, he said to himself. Good one, that. Just look at where you got to by keeping your own counsel.

Well, that was something, though. At least he was talking to himself—instead of giving himself the cold shoulder.

IT TOOK TWO MORE months to finish the journey. He was in no hurry.

Once, as he rejoined the Vinkus River, he spotted a single stag. It stood alert in the middle of a long line of mature beech trees that ran the crest of a ridge, half-lit by an effect of late afternoon sun and cloud. Knee-deep in dried grass, the stag watched him as he passed. It did not flinch or flee. Nor did it attack him.

AT LAST, something familiar: the small settlements that clung to the slopes of the Kells. Arjiki villages, some with names, some not. Fanarra, and Upper Fanarra, and Pumpernickel Rock, and Red Windmill. It was late fall, early winter; the flocks were down from the heights, noisy in their fold; the summer cording was done, and skeins of dyed skark yarn were knotted and hung out to dry on pegs. The smell of vinegar used to set the dye tightened the skin in his nostrils.

The Arjikis regarded his progress along Knobblehead Pike without comment. If some of them recognized him, they didn't let on. It had been almost a decade since he'd left with Dorothy. Everything had changed within him—he'd broken out of his shell to find himself wanting—but the Arjikis looked stolid and eternal.

He recognized none of them, either.

As he walked the last mile, looking up, the old waterworks towered high from the strong thighs of the mountain. It loomed overhead with impossible perspective, and the clouds above it whipped by so quickly that, as he stood with his head thrown back, he became dizzy. To see it again!—the old pile, once the family home of the prince of the Arjikis, then the castle refuge of the Wicked Witch of the West. Kiamo Ko.

Its stones were streaked with the water from snow melting off the battlements. (Harsh weather sometimes hit the higher mountains as early as Summersend.) Its roofs looked to be in a serious state of disrepair. Crows shot from the eaves, and an oriel window seemed to have collapsed, leaving a gaping maw, but smoke was issuing from a chimney, so someone was in residence.

He hadn't spoken a word since meeting the woman on the road, the crone with the four-horned cow and the child. He wasn't sure he could still talk.

The bartizans were deserted, the ceremonial drawbridge of the central gate was up, but the gatehouse door was wide open, and snow drifted within. Security wasn't the top concern of whoever lived here now.

He gripped the broom in his hand, and tightened the Witch's cape around him—he'd worn it several weeks now, glad to have carted it all these seasons, as it was helpful against the chill. Mercy, mercy, he thought, I'm home from the wars, whatever that means. He climbed the steep steps to the gatehouse and went in to the primary courtyard.

At first he saw no change at all; but he was looking through the eyes of memory, and those eyes were blurred with tears. She might have come back here, he thought at last. Have I been hoping this all along, step by step—is this hope what has kept me from dying? If Nor really had survived her abduction, she might have made her way back here as I have. She might even now be slapping a meat pasty into a hot oven and turning at the sound of my foot on the cobbles.

Then he wiped his eyes with the heels of his hands. The place had gone from rack to ruin, and some of the hard edges of its utilitarian design had become softened by neglect. The cobbles were covered in dried leaves, and a dozen or more saplings like party guests stood here and there, human size or even a little taller, twitching their thin limbs in excitement at a new arrival. A shutter banged overhead. Ivy clawed up the side of the chapel. Several windows were broken and more young trees leaned out.

It was silent but not still; everything rustled almost without sound. He could have heard a baby cry in its sleep down in a cradle in Red Windmill, had some baby needed to cry just then.

He turned about slowly, his arms open, pivoting on one heel. Allowed a torrent of emotion to batter him from within.

When he finished his revolution, the monkeys were there under the trees, on the outside steps, peering out through the yellowing foliage in the windows. They had come from nowhere while his eyes were misted. Some of them trembled and held their wingtips; a couple shat themselves. This breed had never taken to personal hygiene with any conviction.

"Liir?" said the nearest one. He had to walk with his knuckles on the ground; had the years of living with heavy wings curved his spine? Or was it merely age?

"Chistery," said Liir, cautiously; he wasn't sure. But Chistery's face had broken into a grin at being recognized.

He came up and took Liir's hand and kissed it with gummy affection.

"Don't do that, don't," said Liir. He and Chistery then walked hand in hand through the warped door into the ominous, plain, high-ceilinged staircase hall, just as they had done fifteen, eighteen years ago, when for the first time they'd arrived together at the castle with Elphaba Thropp.

IT DIDN'T TAKE HIM LONG to figure out that Nor wasn't there. The sudden lurch of thought about her, though, crackled almost aurally through his apprehensions of Kiamo Ko. It was as if he could just about hear her childish squeals and pattering feet.

Still, he couldn't indulge in moodiness even if he wanted. For one thing, the skanky stench of monkey ordure cut through the complicated memories of childhood. He had to watch where he stepped. Public health hazard.

He was hardly surprised to find Nanny still alive. She'd be in her ninetieth year now, or more? Surely. Her olfactory senses had long fled her, so she seemed unbothered by the fumes, and her own bedding and day gown were in a less-than-pristine condition. Sitting bolt upright in bed with a bonnet on her head and a beaded purse clutched between her hands, she greeted him without much surprise, as if he'd only been down in the kitchen this past decade, getting himself a cup of milk.

"It's hizzie, it's whosie, yourself in all your glory, if you can call it that," she said, and offered her cheek, which had sunk dramatically into a hollow of greying crinkles.

"Hello, Nanny. I've come to visit you," said Liir.

"Some does and some doesn't."

"It's Liir."

"Of course it is, dear. Of course." She sat up a little straighter and looked at him. Then she picked up an ear trumpet from her bedside table and shook it. A ham sandwich fell out, the worse for wear. She regarded it with disapproval and took a healthy bite. She put the trumpet back against her head. "Who is the whosie?"

"*Liir,*" he said, "do you remember? The boy with Elphaba?"

"Now that's one as never visits. Up in her tower. Too much studying and you'll chase the boys away, I always said. But she had a mind of her own. Are you going up there? Tell her to show some respect to her elders and bitters."

"Do you remember me?"

"I thought you might be Grim Death, but it's only the haircut."

"Liir, it is. Liir."

"Yes, and whatever happened to the boy? He was a funny noodley one. It took him forever to get trained, as I recall. Still, he'd fit right in now." She rolled her eyes at Chistery, who stood fondly by with his hands folded. "He never writes, you know. That's all right, though, as I can't read anymore."

Liir sat down on a stool and held Nanny's hand for a while. "Chistery, is there anything like sherry around?" he asked suddenly.

"Whatever hasn't evaporated in its bottles. We don't touch the fumey stuff," said Chistery. That's a bit righteous, thought Liir, and realized, too, that Chistery's language had improved hugely. Now that everyone had stopped trying to teach him.

Chistery returned in time with a dusty bottle. It was ancient cooking brandy, and a B grade at that, but Nanny's palate had clearly deteriorated like some of her other talents, and she sipped it happily, goofily.

After a nap that lasted only a few moments, she was awake, and more alert. Her eyes looked as they once had: less swift to track, perhaps, but no less canny.

"You're the boy, grown up some," she said. "Not enough, I see, but there's time."

"Liir," he reminded her. He wanted to work fast while she was attending. "Nanny. Do you remember when we came here? Elphaba and I?"

She screwed up her face and settled on an answer almost at once. "I do not, Liir. Because I came later. You were already here when I got here."

Of course. *He* had forgotten this. "Elphaba was your charge, wasn't she? You were her nanny. She told you everything."

"She hadn't much to tell," said Nanny. "For an interesting life, you wanted to listen to her mother. Melena. Saucy little thing, got around the parish, if you know what I mean. A trial to her husband, Frex. Now *he* was a good man, and like most good men, a crashing bore about it. The hours he spent trying to convert me to unionism! As if the Unnamed God wanted to take an interest in Nanny! Preposterous."

He didn't want to talk about religion. "I want to ask you something directly. If you know the answer, you can tell me. I'm grown up now. Was Elphaba my mother?"

"She didn't know," said Nanny. Her mouth took the shape of an O—*O!*—as if startled all over again by the ridiculous conceit. "She suffered some terrible blow, and lapsed into a dreamless sleep for months on end. Or so she said. When she came to, and was suitably convalesced, she stayed on to work for some maunts. Then she left them to come here, and they gave her you to take along. That's all she ever knew. She supposed she *could* have given birth to you in a coma. It is possible. These things do happen." She rolled her eyes.

"Why didn't she ask about me—and her?"

"I suppose she thought the answer didn't matter. There you were, one way or the other. It hardly signified."

"It matters to me."

"She was a good woman, our Elphie, but she wasn't a saint," said Nanny, both tartly and protectively. "Leave her her failings. Not everyone is cut out to be a warm motherly type."

"If she thought I *might* be her child, wouldn't she have mentioned the possible father?"

"She never did what another person might. You remember that. Now, I *did* know that fellow named Fiyero, once upon a time, and you don't look much like him, if that's your game. Frankly, you could more easily pass for a child of Nessarose. Elphaba's sister, the Wicked Witch of the East as they called her behind her back. If you *were* Elphie's there'd be the green skin, wouldn't there? It's a puzzle. Is there any more of that juice?"

He poured a small sip more. "Did you raise Nessarose, too? And their baby brother? Shell?"

"Their father, Frex, thought I was too pagan to be over involved with *Nessarose*. Me with my devotions to dear Lurline, our fairy mother. Frex wanted a godly child, and it was clear, with her alarming hue, that Elphaba wasn't it. Nessarose was born a martyr—that unfortunate disability! Revolting, really—and she lived and died as a martyr. If she had even a second or two to understand that a house was about to come and sit on her head, I'm sure she died happy."

"I never met her."

"In the Afterlife, my boy, count on it. She'll be waiting there to improve you some more."

"And Shell? I've met Shell once or twice."

"Oh, *that* lad! The high jinks of that one! He was in and out of trouble like tomorrow's stitches in yesterday's britches. He led poor Frex a merry chase! Shell was hopeless at school, a good-joke johnnycake, in trouble with the masters and in the skirts of the misses. And he grew to have a smart mouth for wine, they say. He used to lie to his father so well that you'd've sworn he was born for the stage. Of course in his line of work, later on, all that came very much in handy."

"What work was that? Medicine?"

"Never heard it called that. I think the term is espionage. Snooping, settling scores out of the public eye, selling information, and if the tales have any truth to them, sexing up the ladies from Illswater to Ugabu."

That made some sense, then, of Shell's activities in Southstairs. He was ferreting out information from political prisoners and getting laid in the bargain.

"I know she's dead," said Nanny flatly, looking out the window. "Dead and gone. At least once a day I remember that much. You could be her son. Why don't you just decide you are?"

"I had nothing from Elphaba but misery," he replied. "It was a happy sort of misery, since children know no better. But she left me nothing—nothing but a broom and a cape. She left me no clues. I have no talents. I haven't her capacity for outrage. I haven't her capacity for magic. I haven't her concentration."

"You're young yet, these things take time. I myself couldn't cast off until I was well into my sixties, but then I could do it so enthusiastically I once fell right out of my chair."

"I think you know if you're different," he ventured. "I think you know if you're gifted. How could you not?"

"You know if you feel set apart," said Nanny, "but who doesn't feel that? Maybe we're all gifted. We just don't know it."

"Does no good to have a useless gift."

"Have you tried? Have you even tried to read from her book of spells? From what I remember, Elphaba had to learn. She did go to school, you know. She was a scholarship girl at Shiz."

"Chistery's learned to talk well," he said, after a while.

"My point exactly," she said, draining her glass. "He had to try for years, and it suddenly clicked."

He walked around the room. The windows were shuttered against the early autumn gale—how well he remembered the way it blew up the valleys, sometimes forcing the snow back up into the clouds that had dropped it. "You have a good life?"

"I have *had* a good life," she corrected him. "Chistery comes from time to time, and the filthy peasants bring their filthy food, which I'm expected to eat as my part in community relations. I do as I'm bade."

"Anyone else?"

"Not in a dog's age. Not since that Dorothy. And you and the others. Did Dorothy ever stop whimpering so? She'll grow up to require the convent, mark my words. Or a husband with a good strong backhand. Her fanny wants spanking badly."

"Dorothy came back?"

"She did?" Nanny's clarity was ebbing.

"If I go up to Elphaba's room," said Liir carefully, "and if I find something of hers, may I take it?"

"What, you're looking for precisely what?"

"A book, maybe."

"Not that big thick thing she was always poring through?"

"Yes."

"Much good it would do you even if she would let it out of her sight. She could hardly ever get those recipes to work. I remember once she was trying to work a spell on a pigeon she'd caught. She was trying to teach it to be a homing pigeon. She let it loose from her window. It zipped away from her as fast as it could, but when she called 'Come back now,' the thing turned and dived like a suicidal lover, and impaled itself on the weather vane." The old woman sighed. "Actually it was kind of funny."

"I'll leave you for a while, Nanny, and I'll come back. I promise."

"I never cared for pigeons except in pies. Poor little Nor, though, was heartbroken."

"Nor," said Liir cautiously.

"The little girl who used to live here. You remember. With the others." But Nanny grew vague now and she could be made to say no more about Fiyero's three children.

"What if I find that book?" asked Liir. "If no one has taken it away, may I have it?"

"You'll have to ask Elphaba."

"If she's not there to ask?"

"Where would she be?" said Nanny. "Where would she be? Where is she? Elphie!" she suddenly bellowed. "Why don't you come when I call you? After all I did for you all my life, and your slut of a mother before you! *Elphie!*"

Chistery came flying from the corner of the room where he had been folding a basket of laundry. He made shooing hands to Liir, who backed out of the room, shaken.

LIIR SPENT THE FIRST few weeks helping put Kiamo Ko to rights. He reminded the monkeys about sanitation, first and foremost. Under his help, the monkeys set to work closing up windows that had blown open, and repairing the roof when the wind didn't imperil them. Liir began to weed the forecourt of its convocation of trees, sad as he did so, for even in their autumnal twiggery they provided some semblance of company. But then he decided to prune and thin rather than remove the trees entirely. Under its ivy and moss and tiny domesticated forest, the place might as well succumb to green. It seemed a suitable memorial for Elphaba Thropp.

He couldn't bring himself to go up to her tower rooms, though. He was afraid he might throw himself from the highest window if the grief took him unawares, like a demon lover.

He visited Nanny and made her conditions comfortable and more sanitary. In a sideboard in the dining room he found a magnifying glass and some dusty old novels written decades ago. *The Curse of the Admirable Frock* was one; *A Lady among Heathen,* another. "Trash," decided Nanny at once and set to reading them with gusto. It turned out she had not forgotten the skill; it was merely her eyes giving her trouble, and the lens helped.

He watched the autumn go golden, then spare. He took care not to get too friendly with Chistery and the others. Isolation was one thing, but forming an unseemly attachment to a Flying Monkey might be quite another. The monkeys kept to their quarters—the old stables, the hayloft and granary—and he slept in the room that Nor had used as a little girl. The days darkened earlier, and when he went to bed in the gloom, he hardly knew if he was twelve or twenty-ish.

A few days after the autumn rains began, a Swan was driven into the forecourt, and huddled for four days under a set of steps. He brought her milk and meal, and helped her wash her bloody breast, for she'd been attacked. She couldn't give a name to the predator; she didn't know what it might be called. She lived long enough to say that she had summoned a Conference of Birds to convene in Kumbricia's Pass, but she'd gotten blown off course in some nasty weather.

"What's the Conference about?" asked Liir.

She wasn't accustomed to talking to a human, and resisted saying more. As her death drew nearer, though, she relented. "The rising threat. Can't you see it? Being creatures of the wing, we have largely escaped the harshness that has befallen the creatures of the soil, but now we are paying for our isolation and pride."

Before she died she said more to Chistery, perhaps feeling that as a winged creature he was more deserving of her confidences. Despite a blinding rain, they buried her beautiful downy carcass deep in the orchard. Out of respect Chistery and Liir didn't rake her plumage for feathers to improve the household bedding, though Liir guessed that they both considered it.

SHE HAD BEEN A PRINCESS among the Swans, said Chistery. Her last wish was that, as a Flying Monkey, he should take her place at the Conference and deliver her opening remarks to those assembled.

Chistery said them carefully, trying to remember.

"She said that the danger imperiling members of the Yunamata and the Arjiki clans, the Scrow and Ugabusezi, and the other tribes of the Vinkus, is related to what threatens Munchkinlanders in their fields and Scalp dwellers in their caves—it is a related sorrow, or the same trouble under different names. Trouble, sorrow, danger, peril: the Animals suffer no less than the Quadlings; the Birds are merely the latest, and neither the least nor the last—but only the Birds see everything, and they are coming together to share their information, to tell what they see, and to sound an alarm."

"I can't make out what you mean, Chistery."

He moaned. "I'm trying to say what that Swan Princess said. Don't ask me what it means! My head! She said, 'It isn't a matter of each generation taking care of its own, each species protecting its own young, each tribe its own kind. It is not a matter of that.'" Chistery's head looked as if it were going to explode. These were not matters he was used to discussing. "The parvenu Emperor is the First Spear of God— that's what he calls himself. He aims it against the whole world; no discrimination left. We have no choice but to resist.'"

"Are you going to go to the Conference? Where is it?"

"The eastern mouth of Kumbricia's Pass. No, I'm not going." Chistery spat. "I'm not a Bird, and I'm hardly a Monkey—more a monkey, really. Besides, my wings wouldn't manage that distance anymore. I need a nice perch and a hot cup of cocoa before sleep, and a good private scratch in the morning, or I can't answer for myself. It isn't pretty."

Liir couldn't force Chistery to put himself in danger. He was the chief of his tribe, after all; the others had never advanced in language or understanding quite as he had. Well, he'd had Elphaba's tutelage.

What would the Witch have done? Liir didn't know. He pestered Chistery until the Monkey cried, "Leave me be! How would I know what she'd do?"

"She always liked you better than me," Liir snapped at him.

"Frankly, Liir, I'd rather be cleaning the chamber pots than having this chat." Chistery left. Liir noticed he hadn't contradicted the assertion about the Witch's affections. Weasely beast.

Liir started up the stairs to see if Nanny was in one of her sharper moments. But she was asleep with the port bottle nestled between her fingers, so he kept going, up and up, at last, to the rooms in the southeast tower, the suite that had been the Witch's study, her home and her hermitage.

The place was much as he had left it a decade earlier, though furred with a cold and clammy sort of dust. The one broad bank of windows looking east was shuttered, enshrouding the chamber with shadows. Mouse droppings littered everything, but that was expected in a castle without a cat.

He had to put his weight against the bar that kept the shutters closed, but at length the thing trembled and gave way. He only opened a segment of the window, so that enough light could come in and save him from barking his shins. As it was, he stumbled over a low chest of drawers, shattering a range of baby roc wing bones that the Witch had been drawing shortly before the end.

The room was a wheel, and he imagined it spun around him, but then that was him turning, wasn't it, turning so his eye could fall on everything at once. He had looked unsuccessfully for the Grimmerie once before. Now he was taller, and his eye better trained: perhaps he would make it out lying slumped on some shelf, or stashed on top of a cupboard.

He didn't see it. Maybe he just didn't want to see it, for it would only reinforce the murkiness of his origins. Elphaba had been able to read that book, to decipher its skittering language somehow, but few else had—maybe no one else. He didn't know. He had been good at Qua'ati, but to master a foreign language of magic was another business entirely. Hell, he hadn't even been able to tie his own shoes until he was ten.

Expecting little, he pushed aside furniture, looked under the mildewed cushions of the window seat. The wardrobe was locked, but he found a skeleton key in a chipped teacup and worried the latch open.

Inside hung a few dresses, mostly in the black that the Witch favored. There were no shelves, and no Grimmerie hidden beneath a secret floor. Just a pair of boots. He pulled them out and looked at them.

They were expensively cut and pieced, made of some supple leather that had been well treated. Where the boots had folded a bit, there were only eyelash cracks. A gentleman's boots, Liir realized. Elphaba kept a pair of men's boots under lock and key?

He felt inside them. One was empty. The other yielded a piece of curling paper about eight inches square. He took it to the window and flattened it on his knee so he could make it out.

A sketch of Nor. No mistake about it. The chin was all wrong, and the eyes too close together, but the joyful tilt of the head, the way the hair whipped off the brow—it could be no other. Liir could see the artist's tentative first lines corrected by definitive cross-hatching in a kind of drypoint, with highlights of coffee-colored wash. Maybe the artist had spilled some coffee on purpose and rubbed definitions in with a finger. Elphaba?

He turned the paper over. On the back, in a crude, distinctive hand, was scrawled

Nor by Fiyero.

This is me Nor
by my father F
before he left

So Elphaba had kept it—as another token of Fiyero, maybe, something from his hand. And perhaps also because she had admired Nor a little, in her own way—to the extent Elphaba could admire any child. Nor had had spunk.

He turned his head to avoid any more of that kind of thinking. The light from the window worked a glint upon a kind of bowl of glass. A ball, really. He rubbed the dust from it; it played like a bright spatter of sunlit rain as he cleaned it.

He found a low stool with five legs, each carved with its own representative foot: a dwarf, an elf, a human, a bird, and an elephant. He drew the stool close and sat down with his chin in his hands.

Lifting his chin this way and that, looking at himself slantwise. Did his chin have a sharp line to it, was his nose sloping and stabbing as Elphaba's had been? Was his skin the color of her brother Shell's? Whatever efforts or accidents had brought him into the world—was he worth it? And if so—worth it to whom? He was poised as a girl preparing for her first party, trying to see her own loveliness. He didn't care for loveliness, one way or the other: but he looked for something that might stand in its stead. Something like merit. Capability.

If only she were still alive to tell him something, anything.

A cloud passed before the sun. The room shook a little, adjusting its outlines. The ball darkened and brightened again. He took it in his hands, the old thing, scratched and crazed, and cracked along several seams. It looked as if it had once been a flat bit of glass, and someone had heated it, thinned and curled and patched it into this makeshift gazing ball. A miracle it hadn't fallen apart. The shapes within shifted as he tilted it this way and that, to try to surprise himself by a new aspect. Catch a new angle, learn a new regret. Anything.

He leaned down and breathed against it, and quickly wrote his name with his finger in the condensation. It dissolved into shapes, his reflection no longer sharp-lined, but foggy. Colored blobs like tossing petals. Then they resolved. The lines he saw were not the carved cornices of the wardrobe or the line where the ceiling met the walls. Instead he saw a skylight, and walls of old cracking plaster, and a white cat observing from the top of a crate. A man moved out of the margin of the mirror, turning his tunic inside out in his haste to remove it. He was dark and beautiful; Liir knew enough about the beauty of men to tell this. He circled an arm about a woman and drew her toward the wall, where he leaned down to kiss her. Then the man turned to open a wide double-doored window, and a flood of light that was never seen in the tower at Kiamo Ko burned into the room in the mirror. *(Liir the young soldier was outside, heading for Quadling Country, daydreaming in the sun.)* Their forms were indistinct in the sun flooding around them into the room. The woman pulled back, away from the window frame, and raised her arms around the man. Her face was hidden. Her arms were green.

Liir set the mirror gently down. He turned as if to say to the white cat, *Hush, that's private*—but the white cat was in the mirror, of course.

Elphaba. Elphaba and Fiyero. Elphaba once upon a time, maybe not much older than Liir was now. And Fiyero, Fiyero for sure. In the light of that distant memory, captured somehow in a looking glass, one couldn't mistake the pattern of blue diamonds that had been incised into Fiyero's skin. Liir had envied how Nor had spoken so affectionately of her father's blue-diamonded skin.

Liir didn't want to see more. He was too constricted for prurience of any sort, much less this kind. But he was young and normal—too normal—so of course he had to look again. He was relieved to find that the circumference of the ball was misting up, and in any case the picture was different. It was the Witch now, the woman he had known so well—fiercer, less forgiving, more impatient, more focused. She was slapping the pages of the Grimmerie, looking for something she couldn't find. Then she closed the book with a *whomp* so hard the globe almost rocked on its stand, even now, at the memory of it.

She turned and raised a crooked arm in the air above her, and her mouth was open, but he could hear no sound; and the broom came rushing forward, dragging its hems across the floor. The Witch wrenched it with one strong hand and settled her rump firmly against the tied top of the brush. They rose as a single instrument and left the room through the broad window. The Great Kells—as they were a dozen or so years ago, as they were today—seemed like fans of lavender and ice in the distance, and he could make out her path for a few more seconds, trading on the currents of the wind, after an impossible prize.

HE SAID HIS good-byes to Nanny, though she seemed mercifully vacant this afternoon. "Tell 'em all to go to hell," she advised. "And save me a good seat by the racetrack when they get there."

Chistery saw him out. "You've no need to take this on yourself," he repeated.

"She would," he said.

"You aren't her; you can't be, and shouldn't try."

"Try to be her, or try to be me? There is a difference. Of course there is. But I've got the broom now, haven't I? So who else should do it?"

Chistery shrugged.

"If the Princess of the Swans was presiding over a Conference of the Birds, so that the flying creatures of the world could share what they knew about the trouble ahead, you know who would be there. She would. She flew on a broom. She qualified. So I'll go in her stead. I may not have her blood, but I have her broom. I'm all there is."

"Go with the winds," said Chistery. "Shall I save supper?"

Liir put on Fiyero's boots. Hadn't he earned them?

Or perhaps not. He took them off again and replaced them in the wardrobe. But he did take the drawing of Nor, and fold it up, and tuck it in an inside pocket of the cape, from where it could not blow away.

He climbed to the windowsill in her old study and threw himself out, trusting that the broom would remember its mission. His eyes closed against the fall, and the crows sheltering under the eaves screeched in shock and terror. The broom stumbled and pitched, rolled and yawed, but Liir kept his boots kicked firmly in the straw and his hands iron-tight around the pole. When after the first few seconds he had not yet whumped into the side of Knobblehead Pike, he opened one eye.

The landscape was a broken thing from this high up. The mountains looked like mud, swept into ridges and painted white and brown and grey and green. Thin flat lines of polished silver: rivers threading along the valley floors. Almost as far as the eye could see, the Kells curved north. The horizon beyond them was white as sugar crystal where the sun made some fun of its own.

To the south, Kumbricia's Pass was out of sight, hidden by the shoulders of mountains between, but it wouldn't be hard to find from this height.

He wheeled about, vaguely southward, leaving Kiamo Ko for the second time in his life. He didn't look back, for the whipping black cape would interfere with his view anyway. To the east, invisible still, the Emerald City, and all that went on there. To the south, a flat plate of greenish brown. Maybe Kellswater in the distance already? That would put Nether How beneath him, and the five lakes west of the Vinkus River. He hadn't the nerve to look down, however; looking out and across was just barely tolerable.

He saw the first sign of the moon, and the weird hump of a snout it had. The jackal moon, Nanny had told him; she'd hoped to get another jackal moon in her long life. There it was, his first, or the first he could remember anyway. It lay on the horizon to the southeast like a dog with its nose on the threshold, barely obeying the instruction to stay outside. It had a cold and a personal look to it.

The wind played tricks in his ears: now a soughing like the breath of a man in distress, now an indistinct glissando almost as of fingers on purely tuned strings. From here one could see nothing of the works of man in the world, and it was the more beautiful for it: how odd, then, that the wind should still sound like human music. Or was it that human music sounded more like the wind than people could possibly know?

On his right, coming over the Kells from the west, three or four clots of dark matter, indistinct because of the light and the wispy streakiness of the skies. He paid the flotsam no mind until a skein of cloud parted and they were nearer. Larger than he'd guessed; now he could see they were still rather far off. But gaining in speed; and gaining on him, slicing toward him in a wide curvet like hounds let loose on the side of a meadow, and he the fox already moving broadly down its middle.

He used the force of his thumbs to press the wood of the broom pole down, and as if possessed of a mind, or as if it had become part of his own body, the broom obliged, and he lost altitude in a hurry. The larger creatures would have a hard time adjusting their speed and height, he thought, and he was right; they were less nimble. But the air below was thicker with the water vapor and breath of forest. What they'd lost in maneuverability, the hunting birds made up in greater weight; they plunged toward him.

Farther, and he dropped farther still, each time catching some small advantage, to lose it within a few minutes. The four birds now penned him in the air: two keeping slightly forward and below, one coming on his left. Above—he could feel it with his peripheral judgment rather than see it—the final one. And closing in fast, to judge by the pair of shadows that he could see racing along the flatlands below: his shadow and his pursuer's.

There was nothing to lose by an attempt to buck sideways and zigzag; with luck two of the dedicated missiles might collide, and each one knock the other unconscious. But the broom didn't seem responsive enough. A small amount of jerking up and kicking back made little difference. The farther the drop, the slower the broom's response: the more resistance put up by the moods of the climate.

Now above the horizon the jackal moon was staring. It had risen as Liir had descended, and their relative positions were reversed. It was the head of a predator on the crouch, and he was the prey trying lucklessly to make it to a mouse hole of one sort or another.

The first attack was of talons, so Liir thought, eagles? Massive eagles—and the second attack was by a tooth or a beak, which might have meant anything. It ripped off the cape as if calmly unknotting it. Then Liir turned to beat at the creature with his arms, since encounter was inevitable, and he came face-to-face with a flying dragon. Roughly the size of a horse, with wings of black and gold, and a venomous eye of gold shot through with black where red should be.

The other dragon neared, and the two of them made their nab neatly, tossing Liir between them as his clothes shredded and his voice raveled. Then, having worried him at last from the broom, they let him fall, and retired with their spoils.

The Emperor Apostle

One Plus One Equals Both

HE HAD HAD EVERY INTENTION TO DIE, and music had forbidden it. He'd been netted by melody not so much beguiling as nagging. That's what he thought, when he could think about it. Though it was another few hours or days (he couldn't count either) before even this much came clear to him.

What he remembered from before his fall from the sky was imprecise at best, and its emotional character muted. Panic over the sight of a girl being slung from a burning bridge . . . disgust at realizing what Shell had been up to in those cells at Southstairs. Consolation at seeing a stag at the far side of a field in early autumn. Panic, disgust, consolation—cheap souvenirs from a holiday. Emotions were portable and obvious: small savories of a life, suitable for kicking his mood upswing or down as the moment required. False, somehow.

But he and his memories alike had awakened into a new capacity of pain and grief. He had awakened to find himself alive again, damn it. Couldn't he even fall from a great height and expect the comfort of a quick death? Need Feckless Liir march on yet again?

Though marching was hardly what he was doing, in literal terms, as he tossed, and kicked the sour blankets in this abandoned mill building or industrial outpost, wherever it was she had taken him.

The girl was named Candle, she said. She spoke to him colloquially in Qua'ati.

She brought him water from a well outside. He could hear the squeak of the pulley as the bucket went down, came back. She brought him nuts and moss apples, which gave him a stentorian diarrhea at first, but cleaned him out and started him up again, and before long he was able to sit up. Then get up and piss in a pail. Then walk to the window and rub a shaky hand against the dirt on the glass, and circle a clean space with his palm, and look out.

His resting room was off the kitchen of a small compound: a few stone domestic buildings connected to dependences built at right angles to one another. In the yard he saw the laundry cart to which Candle and that ferociously old maunt had dragged him. Now the donkey was unhitched and was grazing nearby in an overgrown orchard, braying opinions about nothing in particular. Within a couple of days, out on her scouting adventures, Candle had come up with a hen, too, and once the hen grew familiar with her new home, there were eggs in the morning.

"Is it a farmhold?" he asked her.

"It was once," she said in her half-a-voice. "Old apple trees in the woods, and dozens of barrels in a shed. I think it had been a cidery. But it seems to have been fitted out for industry of some sort since. I've found a . . . a heap of machinery standing in the high main barn. It's been hacked with sledgehammers and I can't guess what job it was meant to perform. When you can get around better, you can tell me what you think."

Beyond the orchards and a few overgrown pastures, as far as he could tell, they were surrounded by a forest. By day it was the color of a hundred fawns, every afternoon brighter as more leaves fell and the light sank nearer to the ground. By night, owls hooted, and in the ceaseless wind the branches made sounds like coughing.

He dozed much of the day and lay awake next to her much of the night, when she fell into a sound sleep. She showed no sign of restlessness. But then, he couldn't play an instrument to trouble her dreams. The domingon, if that's what it was called, hung on the wall like an icon.

"Why did you rescue me?" he asked her. She couldn't answer the question; she seemed not to understand the concept of rescue, though the word in Qua'ati could mean nothing else. "Who are you?" he tried, another way of posing the earlier question. The reply, "Candle," nothing else, gave him something close to comfort, but it was not comfort, quite.

Another time he asked, "Why did we flee that place?"

"The old maunt told us to go. She said they would hunt for you sooner or later."

"They? Who?"

"Perhaps I misunderstood. Anyway, she said you were in danger. She had heard tell of this abandoned place and gambled that the donkey would find the way. Indeed, it did."

"I am still in danger? Then I'd have been safer if you'd let me die."

"I didn't cause you to live or die," she said. "Don't give me credit for skills beyond me. I played music; you remembered. Music will do that. What you remembered—that was within you, and nothing to do with me."

But he wondered, as he grew stronger. So many of his memories included an offstage trickle of melody, like marginalia embroidering a page of manuscript. He hardly recognized himself in the glass of the window, when at night he took a candle to the black pane to see who he was now. Gaunt, and stubbled, almost palsied with the weakness of the infirm. Had her playing helped him to remember his life as it had been lived, or had she enchanted him with music and given him a false past?

He could be anyone, this could be anywhere. He might be mad, and not even know it. There might be no Emperor, no dragons, no broom— no castle of Kiamo Ko before that, no Nor abducted from it a half a life-time ago. No occupying force in the provincial capital of Qhoyre. No parents slinging their daughter clear of the burning bridge. Candle might have riveted his comatose mind with a battery of pretend memories so as to distract him from something more important.

Though she spoke Qua'ati, and so did he. She wasn't likely to be that skilled a player that she could have taught him a whole new language in his coma.

◆ 2 ◆

THE FIRST NIGHT HE COULD MANAGE IT, they pulled two chairs into the open doorway to watch the stars come out. "Tell me about yourself," he said.

She lit a candle, charmingly. Even more wonderfully, she pulled a bottle of wine from out of nowhere. "Mother Yackle gave it me, along with a few other things filched from the mauntery's pantry," she admitted. It took some ingenuity to remove the cork, but when they'd succeeded, they sat with their legs entwined, and sipped from old clay mugs with broken handles.

She told of her past. He tried to listen. After a while he realized that he was waiting for clues to prove that he had been comatose for several years, not merely weeks. He wanted her to be the Quadling girl tossed from the bridge at Bengda, grown up and magically restored not just to life but into *his* life. How he wanted to provide for her—to begin the impossible task of reparation.

It was hard to shake off this hope, but in order to hear of Candle's real life, he had to try to still his own rackety guilt.

Candle was raised in Ovvels, in all of Oz the southernmost town of any size. Well, hardly a town, as she described it: a network of cabanas built in the rubbery limbs of suppletrees above the salty damp of flooded groves. As a child she hunted charfish with her spear. Like most of Quadling Country, her settlement had become economically blighted in the decades of the Wizard's ascendancy. She thought prosperity must once have been possible here: great tiers of granite blocks, eighteen feet at their highest, were set together in long broad curves. One could have driven a horse along the top for nearly a mile. Nobody alive could imagine what such massive structures had been used for, nor how they had been erected; there was no granite anywhere nearby. The locals used the place for fixing their marsh nets and for drying fish.

Beyond that, Candle had little else to say. Her father had lit out long ago, her mother being rather wiftier than was useful in a wife. Food had grown scarce, and some of her relatives had set out to try their luck as itinerants. She'd learned to play the domingon while traveling with her uncle.

"But how did you come to stay in a mauntery?" asked Liir. "The Quadlings aren't unionists."

"In general, Quadlings are inexpressive about holy matters," said Candle, "which means they're not easily offended by other traditions. However, you're wrong about southern Quadlings. A whole passel of Quadlings from Ovvels converted to a kind of unionism several generations ago when a missionary and his entourage came through. I heard my great-grandmother speak of it once. A sickly group of do-gooders, prone to being afflicted with mold in our climate. Frankly, it's a wonder they had any effect. But they did. I was raised on a cushiony variety of unionist thought, so I don't mind the chapel and the devotions that the maunts engaged in. Nor the custom of caring for the sick, either. It seems a decent way to spend one's hours."

"You played for me on that—domingon. Where is it from?"

"It was a gift of my uncle," said Candle tersely, and would answer no further questions on the subject of the instrument or her uncle, either.

"You cared beautifully for me." Liir noted the rue in his voice. "I remember what it was like to fall through the air and see the ground rush up with a speed you can't imagine. It was all a brown blur of wind and earth."

"I couldn't have saved you if you had fallen very far," said Candle. "Likely you imagine it worse than it was."

"But my bones are healed. I can move," he said. "I didn't bleed to death."

"The maunts who tended you first were more capable than they let on. In any case, I am still not clear on why you came to be airborne," said Candle.

He ripped the skin off a wild winter orange she had found in the woods somewhere. The pungency stung his nose with eclipsing sweetness. "With all I seemed to relive in my dead sleep, there's a lot I can't remember," he said at last.

"Do you remember what happened to your broom?"

"I suspect it fell to the ground. I'm not sure. Or maybe the dragons took it, though why they'd bother I can't imagine."

She didn't press him further. It was Liir who did the asking. "Why did you take me away from there? Why did that one you called Mother Yackle lock us in the tower together, and release us when she did? What did she say to you about it?"

"Mother Yackle is well known to be wandering in her mind. In the short time since I arrived at the mauntery, I never knew her to cause trouble nor even, often, to speak. Somehow your arrival engaged her, though whether it was into a further madness or a mysterious clarity, I can't say. Perhaps we were locked in so . . ."

"Finish your thought."

She couldn't, or wouldn't. She merely smiled at Liir. "It's nice to speak Qua'ati again. They thought I was simple at the mauntery. I didn't mind that, really; I suppose I am simple. And my small voice doesn't lend itself to public utterance. But I find it is nice to speak with words again, as well as with music."

"How did you learn your skill with music?"

"We all have skills," she said. "I mean the Quadlings from Ovvels do. They emerge in different ways. We can—see things—is that how to put it?"

"Can you see the future?" said Liir. He gripped her hand. "What is our future?"

She blushed a little; he hadn't known a Quadling who could blush. "It isn't like that," she answered. "I can tell you—I suppose—a little bit about the present. It's not the future."

"Tell me about the present," he said.

"I did already." She pouted, a jest only. "I sat by your side for days and days and played the domingon to you. It gave you your present."

"You gave me memory. That's the past."

She corrected him. "Memory is part of the present. It builds us up inside; it knits our bones to our muscles and keeps our heart pumping. It is memory that reminds our bodies to work, and memory that reminds our spirits to work, too: it keeps us who we are. It is the influence that keeps us from flying off into separate pieces like"—she looked around—"like this peel of orange, and that clutch of pips."

"Play for me again."

"I'm tired of playing," she said. "For now, anyway."

Before they went back inside, they explored the high-ceilinged barn. "I'll look again in better light tomorrow," said Liir after poking around a bit. "But I think this was a printing press."

"Out here in an old farmhouse in the middle of nowhere?" said Candle.

"Maybe it printed seditious tracts," said Liir. "Someone didn't like what it was being used for, and expressed that opinion with an ax and a hammer."

"From pressing cider to publishing broadsides."

"Both are presses. This is Apple Press Farm. I'm naming it."

They retired. Candle fell asleep quickly. Liir rolled up against her for warmth. *I am not a soldier any longer,* he said to himself; *this is not my Qua'ati girlfriend.* He stiffened, as a man will, but took pains to govern the appetite. She was his rescuer and not his concubine. He might be infected with something contagious, and he wouldn't endanger her that way.

When it seemed that the sweet lettucey smell of her breathing, the roll of her breast in the moonlight was too much to bear—that he would sink his mouth upon it—he turned onto his side. A minute or two of envisioning the burning bridge at Qhoyre was all it took to restore him to the sadder state in which he'd spent most of his life.

· 3 ·

IN NOON LIGHT, the mess in the main barn proved more severe. Dozens of trays of letters used by compositors in a back room—once a milking stall maybe—were overturned on the floor. The wheels and weights and great drum of the press proper, cabineted in well-oiled oak and well-blackened brackets and footings of iron, had been gashed, and fairly recently, by swords or axes. The metal cuts gleamed with as yet untarnished brilliance.

They saw no sign of blood. Perhaps the obscure printers had gotten wind of an assault and cleared out in time.

Liir poked about in the charred rubble of the barn hearth. He managed to dislodge a few scraps of a broadsheet. He pointed to the words, but Candle said that she couldn't read the script.

"'Pieties of the Apostle,'" Liir told her. "That's the heading. Here, beneath, it says 'The Virtue of the UGLY.'"

"I didn't know the ugly had special virtue," said Candle, "just a sort of misfortune."

The print was small and Liir had to carry it to the open door in order to make it out. "It seems a blameless sort of religious tract, near as I can tell."

"Perhaps the press was used for more incendiary publications, too."

"Maybe." He rubbed away char and declaimed from the parchment: "'The Apostle boasts no special skill. For his humility the Unnamed God has blessed him with the reward of untroubled conviction.'"

"I told you," said Candle, "we're already converted. I don't need a further catechism."

She left to gather firewood, and when she returned a few hours later leading a goat, Liir said, "You are systematically raiding some nearby farm, aren't you? Is that why you have been carrying your domingon with you?"

"There are a few holdings in these hills, farther up," she admitted. "Mostly they're abandoned at that time of the morning, but it's true: the instrument helps lull any resident grandfather into his morning nap."

"I hope you're not beggaring them."

"Should I bring it back?"

Milk. Cheese, in time? "No."

But what were they doing here? Resting up—for what?

"I've been scrutinizing such flecks of pages as I could salvage," he told her. "I've come to think this circular was not a missionary tract. I think it's oppositional. You just don't see it at first—you read some ways down and begin to find resistance to the notions of the Apostle. It's a clever rhetorical device, in its way; it may have fooled some readers, or convinced others to join a resistance to—this Apostle, whoever he is. It's seditious, this paper, that's what it is. And whoever didn't like it traced its origins here, and made their sentiments known."

"I hope they don't come back."

"What're they going to come back for? The goat?"

She rolled her eyes. "Do you know anything about milking goats?"

"I learned to fly on a broom," he said, rolling up his sleeves. "I can learn to milk a goat, I bet." Though flying on a broom proved to be the easier task, he found.

+ 4 +

CANDLE SAID EVENTUALLY, "The weather is steadily chilling. If we're going to be here all winter we're going to need to get in some firewood. Are you feeling well enough to begin to collect some?"

He was, and he did. In finding his way around the browning dales and hollows, he realized that the press had been set up in a farm that most likely had been abandoned a generation ago. Rangy teenager trees were colonizing some of the pastures, and deeper in the woods, the criss-crossing of stone walls suggested that these had been working meadows not all that long ago.

At suppertime he told Candle what he'd seen. "I don't know much about how land is used anywhere but Ovvels," she admitted. "I have seen those walls among the trees, and I thought perhaps they grew there like lichen."

"The influence of pebbles! To grow stone walls. Wouldn't it be nice if you could plant a farm that way! Drop the seeds of a barn here, drip a tincture of millpond in an eyedropper over there. Plant an egg and get a whole henhouse, complete with cockcrow and breakfast omelet."

"What would make a sheepfold?"

"All you need is a lamb's tail."

"How horrible!"

"Not really. To avoid fly strike, shepherds often dock the tails of lambs."

She didn't like this line of play. She got her domingon—Liir guessed as much to change the subject as anything else. He needled her anyway. "To grow a mauntery you'd have to plant a . . . a what?"

She struck up a tonic depressive and then played it backward. "Plant a prayer," she said, despite herself. "To grow an army . . . ?"

"Touché. Well, the story of the Seven Spears says you plant dragons' teeth." He'd heard the folk story eventually, the one that had given the company of the Seventh Spear its name. A bit close for comfort, that. "To grow a melody?"

"You can't grow a melody on purpose," she said, and slyly added, "you have to plant an accidental." This seemed a musical reference, and it went over his head. "To grow a memory. Tell me that one, mister magic farmer."

"To grow a memory. To grow a memory, one must plant . . . I'm not sure. Who wants to grow memories, anyway?"

"I'll make it easier. To grow a good memory. A happy memory."

He shrugged, indicating, Go on.

"It doesn't matter what you plant," she concluded, "but you must plant it with love."

Then she whipped up a scale and finished with some splay-handed chord clusters. The sounds hung in the air like prisms suspended from the trees on invisible strings. The donkey brayed in an altogether more accomplished voice than usual, looking astonished at himself. The goat cocked her head.

Candle added a few grace notes in a complementary modality.

The hen stepped closer as if surprised, at her age and station, to receive an invitation to dance. She let out a squawk that turned into a nightingale's sonnet, line after line after line, though Liir couldn't imagine what it meant.

Candle added a hedge of bass notes, tense as the girders of a bridge.

The goat opened her mouth and provided an alto obbligato line—rather huskier than would work for a paying audience, but entirely serviceable in a barnyard.

Then the Quadling girl sang something in Qua'ati—some rural advice; Liir had to struggle both to hear her and to translate. He guessed she was singing, "No one can sing unless they can remember." The trio of animals attempted a big harmonic finish, but it was beyond them, and the moment passed.

"You can make the animals sing," he said. "You are a wonder."

"I can play a wonderful instrument," she corrected him. "To grow a song, you must plant a note."

THE NEXT DAY he went for more kindling. His strength returning little by little, he scaled another rise, a higher one than before. He saw in the distance a blurred line of tree heads a different shade of brown. The oakhair forest, in that direction, and, when he turned to see, the suggestion of the Kells in the other.

He collected what he could comfortably carry, not yet having regained full strength, and put off what needed to be said another day or two. Before he could bring the matter up, though, Candle got there first.

She said, "It's a month now since we left the mauntery, and you dropped out of the sky perhaps two weeks before that. I've been nursing you as best I could, and I've assumed we'd winter here together. But is that a false premise? You ought to let me know. I must decide if I want to try to stay here alone through the winter, or return to the mauntery."

"Why would I leave?" he asked, looking for a reason.

She tried to lighten the mood. "To grow a man, you must not only plant a child, but harvest it," she said. "You're not done yet. Are you?" When he didn't answer her, she added, "You ask why you would leave. But I ask, why would you stay?"

"I owe you that much."

"You owe me nothing." She looked as if she meant it, seeming neither combative nor proprietary. "I did the job that was set me by the Superior Maunt, that's all. Though maybe in evacuating you from that keep and bringing you here I exceeded my charge, and endangered you the further."

"I can't be in danger here. Look, what? Are the very elm leaves going to wreathe up by magic and smother me?"

"Something attacked you six weeks ago, and for a reason," she reminded him.

"I had a flying broom. Of all things. No reason more than that."

"You had the power to fly on it, too."

"Any ant has the power to wander aboard an eagle."

She demurred, but didn't want to argue. "You were going somewhere. Surely you remember by now?"

"A Conference. A Conference of Birds in the eastern entrance to Kumbricia's Pass. Though I have no way of knowing exactly when it was formally opening, nor how long it would last. It could be over already."

She sat down. "If I understood what I picked up in the mauntery, we aren't that far from the eastern edge of the Kells."

"No. A few hours by broomstick, I guess. A few days, maybe, on foot."

"There's the donkey."

"Two weeks on the singing donkey. He seems very lazy."

"You're still weak. You ought to ride."

"You're pushing me out of the nest?" He was relieved, in a way: someone was making a decision for him. Or perhaps she wanted to hear from his lips that he wouldn't abandon her, he wouldn't consider it.

Her thinking was further along than that. "I don't know if you want to stay with me for a day, or for longer, or at all," she admitted. "But you should choose what you want and not just fall into it. I abducted you, after a fashion. I will not keep you."

"I'll give myself permission to stay here."

"You'll settle your curiosity first," she told him. "You don't know why you were attacked, really. You don't know what the Conference was for, nor what it might mean to the Birds that you didn't arrive. You should find out that before you make any other decisions."

"I'm not that selfless anymore. Anytime I try, I fail. I learned failure early, and mastered it."

"Be selfish then. Ask those Birds if they have seen your friend. That Nor."

He could hardly believe her generosity. He loved Candle already but didn't have the perspective to know if it was as a savior, a woman, a friend, an alternative to loneliness. Or all of those together. Or if any of those were the right reason to love someone. Well, what personal experience of love had he ever had? And what testimony of love had ever been paraded before him? Precious little.

He knew in many ways Candle was right and that, also, she was giving him a way out.

"I need firewood. If you help me with firewood," she said, "I'll stay here the winter and not leave till spring. Between the fruits and mushrooms I've been drying, the potatoes growing wild in the sunny patch yonder, and what the goat and the hen can provide, I won't starve. If I'm turned out by some landlord, or if trouble chases me away, I'll return to the mauntery. I can be found there, by my uncle if he comes to claim me, or by you. Or there I'll stay, maybe; it's as good a life as most, and they're kind women."

He helped with the firewood, redoubling his efforts to build up the stockpile, and in so doing restoring mass to his muscles and strength to his step. By the time the first hard frost came, and the chimney was issuing its thin braid of smoke all hours of the day and night, he was ready to leave.

He wouldn't take the donkey. She might need it.

"For what?" she asked.

"He's better company than the goat," said Liir at last. He took Candle in his arms on the final morning, and kissed her fondly for the first time. "I do not need to hear about goodness from any Apostle," he told her. "You have given me more to admire than almost anyone I have ever met."

"It's very clear you haven't traveled the world," she chided him, almost lovingly. "Be safe, as safe as you can, dear Liir: and be brave."

"Are we a couple?" he asked, bravely enough.

"We are one and one," she said. "In Quadling thinking, one plus one doesn't equal a single unit of two. One plus one equals both."

For a long time, turning back, he could see the soft curl of smoke hovering over where Apple Press Farm must stand in its encroaching forest. The fire's breath hung like a question mark above the place that she had planted herself, already, to wait for his return.

The Conference of the Birds

WHILE THE TREK FROM the farmstead in the woods to the start of Kumbricia's Pass was short, comparatively speaking, every step he took bit at his bones and taxed his joints in a way that none of the long forays across country had seemed to do before.

Well, he was older. Hardly *old* yet—twenty-three, was he, or twenty-four? Something like that. Not old enough to feel like an adult, really, but old enough to look like one, and to know the distinction between being carefree and careless.

So he took care. Any little scatter of stones might shift beneath his weight, any patch of grass might prove more slippery than it ought. He latched his eyes to the ground. Confidence and stamina returned all too slowly.

But return they did. Eventually he was walking two hours at a stretch before pausing to rest. He fixed his gaze to the horizon and willed himself forward by setting himself serial destinations. That tallest blue pine, that nubble of grasses in the upland meadow, that outcrop of granite. Before long, the prospect grew grander, as the Kells swam into clearer focus, and the steep cut between them said KUMBRICIA'S PASS: enter if you dare.

He remembered his childhood journey with Oatsie Manglehand and the Grasstrail Train, and how the travelers had traded tales. Fierce Kumbricia, the witch from the oldest tales of Oz! Kumbricia was so ancient a figure of lore that she seemed freed from the limitations of any particular moral position. She was not exactly the demon crone from hell, intent on the destruction of mortal souls, nor was she the nodding grand-tit of the world, providing succor in times of trial. Or perhaps, more truly said, she was both. One plus one equals both. Like the most insouciant and playful of earthquakes, collapsing villages and crushing populations, Kumbricia's actions followed her own secret intentions. To a human, what might look like luck one minute was disaster the next, but what meant luck to Kumbricia, or disaster either? In the stories she was fierce, amoral, wholly herself. Unvanquishable and incorrigible.

And unknowable, really.

Like the Unnamed God, when you came right down to it.

Occasionally, Nanny had singsonged, as a nursery ditty, something probably derived from the Oziad or some other baroque history-legend.

> *Kumbricia stirs the pot, and licks the ladle,*
> *Sets the table, pours a glass of tears.*
> *Waits beside the ominous vacant cradle.*
> *Waiting still. She can wait for years.*

Yes, just like the Unnamed God.

✦ 2 ✦

THE CLIFFS OPENED BEFORE him and then closed behind him, for the track into Kumbricia's Pass took several quick turns along the valley floor before it began to rise. The ground breathed different vapors here, and the season was delayed: the browning leaves of the trees hadn't fallen yet. Not enough wind could wend through to tear them away.

The brightness of the sky was shattered into glazed mosaic bits by the fretwork of branches and foliage. This high-slung canyon went on for days, didn't it?—wasn't that his recollection? Until it opened on the western slope of the Kells, and the Thousand Year Grasslands spread out as broad as the imaginary sea from children's stories? How would he ever find traces of a convocation of Birds in this secret haven?

But a good place to gather, he had to concede. The mountains served as ramparts, and the ravine was helpfully overgrown. Here the Yunamata made their home most of the year. And here Elphaba and Liir had picked out their way all those ages ago, pressing on toward Kiamo Ko and the hope for sanctuary.

He had all the time for rumination he needed—and then some. What had he understood, then, of Elphaba's drive? Her need? The force that pushed her around? Precious little. But he remembered the day she had saved the infant Snow Monkey, who would become Chistery. Her native—talent? power? skill at concentration?—or maybe, merely, compassion?—had caused a small lake to ice over so she half walked, half slid across it to collect the abandoned, fretting monkey baby.

That's what his memory said. *The very ice formed under her heels. The world conformed itself to suit her needs.* But how could this possibly be true? Perhaps it was the unreliability of memory, the romanticking tendencies of childhood, that made Liir remember it this way. *The lake went ice. The baby monkey was saved.* Maybe, really, she'd waded. Or maybe the lake was already iced over.

Maybe all that really mattered, as to her power, was that *she saved the baby monkey.*

At the shores of a small tarn, he paused, and became aware of a new variety of silence. It was the sound of everything holding its breath.

At the farther side of the tarn was a small island. A spinney of knot-branch trees grew in the center of the island, their five or six tree trunks so close as to resemble the uprights of a series of doors, all leading to the same interior space among the trunks, some dozen feet in diameter. The trees held what was left of the Conference of the Birds, and the Birds were holding their breath.

He stood, not ready to call out, for he didn't want them to scatter. But they were aware of him, he was sure. How many hundred pairs of eyes blinked or unblinked at him from those ring-coiled leaves? They neither approached him in sortie nor twittered in fright. Perhaps, he guessed, they were stupid with fear.

Finally he thrashed about along the bracken and located a fallen tree trunk substantial enough to bear his weight. He hauled it to the water's edge and pushed it in. No conjuring up an ice-walk for him. With the help of a staff, he balanced himself and began to draw his way across the water. He could have swum, he knew, but that would require his undressing either before or after the swim, and it seemed an undignified way to approach a Convention.

The Birds seemed patient, and as he got closer he thought: It's as if they have been waiting for me.

This was so, according to the hunch-hooded Cliff Eagle who bade him welcome.

"You're the boy-broomist," he said. "The fledgling. We knew you'd been downed. A Red Pfenix got far enough through enemy lines to cry out that much information before being wounded and having to turn back. We trusted you would come. You've come."

The Cliff Eagle paused smartly, puffing out his breast feathers.

"I almost didn't," said Liir. "It wasn't even my idea, really."

The Eagle made a mouth gesture as close to a sneer as he could manage. "Humans are fickle. We know. But you're here. The boy-broomist."

"I'm without the broom." Liir put his staff down on the ground so the Birds could see. "I walked. Have you a name, by the way?"

The other Birds hopped a branch or two closer to see if the Cliff Eagle would answer. They were the larger creatures, mostly—a few random Finches and Fitches, some Robins, and a busy preening department of Wrens—but mostly Eagles, Night Rocs, a youngish Pfenix in its glowing halo. Nine Swans still waiting for their Princess. A blind old Heron with a twisted left leg. Others.

"I know what happened to the Princess of the Swans," said Liir, and told them how he had buried her—and, in a dim sense, come in her stead.

The Cliff Eagle took the news unflinchingly, though the Swans bowed their heads until their necks were white hoops, and their wings shuddered with an airy sound, as of an industrial baffle.

"I am the President of the Assembly," said the Cliff Eagle. "Thank you for coming."

Liir had no use for honorifics. "Am I to call you Mister President? Or just Birdy?"

The Cliff Eagle bristled, and then said, "General Kynot is my name, though my name isn't important. And yours isn't either. We're soldiers at strategy, not a military tea."

"Well, I've been a soldier and I'm not going back to it. I'm Liir, for what that's worth, and I use my name. I'm not Broom-boy."

Kynot ducked his head and bit at a nit under his wing. "Sorry, the place is crawling with nits," he said. "Liir." It was a concession, and Liir relaxed. He was about to ask permission to sit down, and then remembered he didn't need it. So he sat, and the Birds came farther down from the branches, and most of them settled on the hardscuffle with the sound of small loaves of bread falling to a floor.

Kynot made quick work of their concerns. The Conference seemed to be comprised of seventy or eighty Birds who were now afraid to leave. They had met to convene about the threat in the skies, but that very threat had cornered them and grounded them. It would take a talent and a cunning greater than any of their skills to make the skies safe for travel.

"You've come to the wrong beak if you want talent or cunning," said Liir.

"Don't be absurd," snapped Kynot, and continued.

He beat out every point of his argument with a hard flap of his wings. *Whereas* conditions of life under the Emperor had become intolerable, *whereas* his airborne army of dragons had systematically disrupted air travel, unsettled populations of Birds and birds, and interfered with the natural rights of flight and migration and convocation, *now therefore* a Congress of the Birds had been summoned, if sadly beleaguered by aforementioned hostile army, and such delegates as had managed to sneak in had concluded *thereby* that they were singly and in unity incapable of combating the enemy fleet. *Therefore* they needed help. Fast.

"I came to tell you of the death of the Princess of the Swans," said Liir, "because it is what Elphaba would have done. Beyond that, I can't be of much use. If I'm the only hope around, you're in a heap of trouble."

"Unlike Animals, we Birds haven't often lived wing by jowl with humans," replied the general. "The human prohibition against eating Animal flesh being subject to abuse, think how much less strict is any taboo against eating the Bird of the air. We must be shot at and brought down before we can be interviewed to learn if we are talking creatures. Few hungry farmers are willing to extend Birds that courtesy, so those of us who talk tend to congregate in areas less frequented by human scum. My apologies, that was crude of me."

"Don't apologize too fast, you don't know me very well," said Liir. "But still, why ask me for help?"

"You have flown, as most humans have not," said Kynot simply. "You have powers unique among the humans we've met . . ."

"I can keep my balance. So what. It's the broom that has powers. Elphaba's broom."

"The wing doesn't work separately from the feather, Liir. They work in tandem."

"Well, I haven't the broom any longer, or haven't you heard? So I can't fly—which means this hardly concerns me."

"You were attacked by the dragons yourself. Weren't you? Or have I been fed misinformation?"

"Well, I was. But that's between me and the dragons. It has nothing to do with you."

"And they call us birdbrains." Kynot was livid. "There is a common cause among our kind and a flying boy, you dodo."

"I object," said a Dodo, just waking up from a nap.

"Sorry, that was uncalled for. Listen. Liir. You must have been intending to help us, or why did you come here at all?"

He thought of Candle. "It was the suggestion of a third party."

"A suggestion of what? That you deliver your tragic news, and then stay to laugh at us in our plight? That you see your fellow creatures chased, tortured, kept from associating freely, just as you were chased, robbed, and nearly killed, and then you—what? Walk home and retail the event for amusing dinnertime conversation?"

"Don't paint me so bleakly. I'm capable of doing that for myself. Look, it's occurring to me that I might ask something of you. On and off over the years, I've been looking for someone. A girl-child. Perhaps you could help. On your various migrations and such."

"We can't fly freely, or haven't I put that clearly enough, you cretin?" Kynot was apoplectic. "How can we serve your private needs when our numbers are being diminished by the day?"

"Well, then." Liir shrugged. "It's a no-go. I guess I didn't really understand much about this skirmish involving the Birds. It's sad, but it hasn't anything to do with me. And even if it did, I'm powerless . . . I'm not Elphaba."

A small Wren hopped forward and said to Kynot, "If you please, begging your pardon, General . . ."

"Do not beg my pardon! Do not *beg* at all! How many times have I to drill this lesson into your brain, Dosey?"

"Sorry, Gen'ral. Begging your pardon for that one, too. It's just that the young man might want to think on this bit somewhat." Dosey turned to Liir and cheeped. "It ain't just us Birdys, mister. Those dragonfings are bad cess for human beings, too. Scraping the faces of defenseless women in the wilderness! Have they no shame? Have you? If you cain't help *us* out of the kindness of your liver, surely you could work to keep such things from happenin' to your own kind?"

"Well said, Dosey." Kynot sounded less apologetic than surprised.

"Those were unionist missionaries, I'm told," said Liir, his shoulders slumping. "It was horrible to hear about. But I'm not a maunt, and I don't even know if I'm a unionist."

"So what next? They'll kill your brother in his stockings, and you'll say, 'He had grey eyes and I have green, so it weren't really about me a'tall'?" asked the Wren. "They already attacked you, duckie, so's I heard. Ain't you rememberin'?"

"Maybe I deserved to be attacked."

"Oh, save us," muttered Kynot. "Somebody save us. But it's not going to be this nutter."

Dosey wasn't ready to give up. "Mebbe you did deserve it," she snapped. "But that's giving those dragons an awful lot of credit for knowing the insides and the sinsides of your soul! So what if they fly out of the stables of the Emperor! They're not Talking Dragons! They're in the pay of the Emperor of the Ugly! And you cain't be sartain those young maunts deserved what they got, can you? Their faces so scraped! It's hideous is what it is!"

"It's not for me to decide whose faces get scraped or not . . ."

"No," said Kynot. He reared up and looked as if he wanted to peck Liir's eyes out. "No. Leave it in the beak of the Unnamed God, or his mortal avatar, the Emperor. Leave it to the agents of the Emperor, who run the Home Guard for the security of the Emerald City at the expense of all others who live in Oz. Or leave it to the underlings who follow the orders of their superiors. Leave it in the beaks of the dragons themselves. Dragons don't kill people, people kill people. They kill themselves by walking unprotected in a world where there are dragons. You make me sick."

"I don't have any idea why the dragons attacked those maunts—"

"It is increasingly obvious that you don't have any ideas at all. The dragons attacked the maunts to stir up trouble between the Yunamata and the Scrow. Those human populations had finally positioned themselves to be ripe for treaty making, after ten hundred generations . . . They had been learning to trust each other. With random attacks on isolated humans, the dragons could keep the tribes suspicious of each other. Tribes are easier to intimidate when they are not united. You said you were in the military: didn't you learn anything about military strategy?"

Liir thought about the burning bridge. He could see again the letter of burning straw, changing shape as it fell, spelling something fiery and illegible into the vanquishing water.

He thought about Candle, waiting for him to return—having done something. Having completed some action. If Liir assumed he wanted Candle, and how could he know that yet?—he couldn't have her. Not until he had an alternative against which to make a choice.

"Look," he said. "Flattering, all this. But I can't fly anymore. My broom is gone. I risked having my face scraped by coming solo across the Disappointments as far as Kumbricia's Pass. I came for the wrong reasons—as usual. There's nothing I can do for you, even if I am a human. I have no talent. My broom had great talent!—if it even was my broom. But it's gone. Either the dragons took it, or it's lost.

"Listen. Keep listening. Wipe that squawky look off your faces. Please. Why don't you band together to fly out of here? A huge clot of you? The dragons couldn't take you all out—some of you would be bound to get through."

"Nice," said a small Barn Owl. "Very nice. I have an irregular left wing and I tend to fly in loops, which slows me down. I'll be one of the first to go. Gladly shall I sacrifice myself for the great Conference of Birds!" He didn't sound as if he meant it.

"While there are grubs to eat here in Kumbricia's Pass, and the dragons can't see into our hideout, we are imprisoned here," said Kynot. "But to leave would be to risk even one of us—and that is a risk we don't take. We won't. The least little Sparrow that falls diminishes us all. I thought you knew all about that."

"Yeah, well, my religious instruction was pretty feeble."

"I wasn't speaking metaphorically, but of military strategy. You could get to the dragons, couldn't you? A witch-boy passing as a soldier? You could see if they had your broom, for one. You could get it back. You could be our voice—our ambassador. Our human representative, our agent, our proxy—"

Liir interrupted. "If I could get my broom—what good could I do? They would just attack me again. Last time they were satisfied with my broom and my cape. Maybe this time they'd scrape my face."

"You just said it's not up to you to decide whose face gets scraped or not," said the Cliff Eagle. "If you believe that, put your face out there and deal with what happens."

"This isn't going to work," said Liir. "I can't do anything for you. I'm not a Bird. I'm not a witch-boy. I don't even have a broom anymore. And even if I had it, maybe I wasn't meant to fly. Maybe I shouldn't even have that liberty."

"Maybe none of us should have the liberties we have. We keep going as we are, we'll find out soon enough. But if you help us squelch the dragon threat, we'll do what you ask. We'll hunt for that human female you're seeking."

The Wren hopped forward again. "You're going to do it," she said to Liir. "You're going to try, ain't you. I kin tell."

"You read the future, Dosey?" said Liir.

"Begging your pardon, sir—"

"Dosey!" interrupted Kynot. "No begging!"

"Ooh, sorry I'm sure," Dosey continued. "No, Mister Broom-boy. You're going to do it for a perfectly selfish reason—our looking for your lost girl-fing—and that's okay. Why not? Long as the job gets done."

The Birds were silent.

"You've had a taste of it," she said in a softer voice. "Not many has, but you has. You've tried flying, ain't you. Now try giving it up."

She came nearer. "Try giving it up," she said. "Begging your pardon, sir, you cain't."

The Birds began to flap their wings and, one by one, to lift up, making their final argument. They swept counterclockwise around the dead little lake, perhaps in deference to the Owl whose wing anomaly made him list in a particular direction. There were more Birds than Liir had first perceived. Several hundred. The more timid ones must have been hiding higher in the branches, but listening intently: all listening. Now they flew, and as they flew, there could be no leader, no follower: they traced the same track in the air, faster and faster. The very force of their rhythmic pumping made the surface of the lake stand up in waves of its own, higher and higher, till wingtips of white froth were beaten up, and then the clots of pale spume lifted and circled beneath the vortex of birds like a second population, like ghost Birds, like the relatives of the Conference who had been slain. But what were ghosts without voices?

The birds were silent—none of them, even the Geese and Ducks, who liked to honk in flight, dared risk attracting attention to their stronghold.

"Stop," cried Liir and held up his hands—not out of pity, nor fear, nor a new moral conviction: simply out of the lack of any further reason to resist.

The blind, gimpy Heron hobbled forward and pecked at Liir's leg to locate him. "I can't fly either, now my sight's gone," the Heron said. "Makes me no less a Bird, though, do it?"

Kumbricia's Cradle

THE WALK BACK WAS FASTER. Now that his bones were knitted, all this trekking was building up muscle again. He hurt, but solidly, recuperatively.

The Disappointments afforded little by way of a blind, so he traveled by night as much as he could, hoping that dragons wouldn't be abroad then. He tried to keep to clearly marked tracks, goat paths, stream sides, where the going was smoother, though the cover less useful.

Arriving back at Apple Press Farm an hour shy of dawn, he was unwilling to frighten Candle by approaching in the dark. He found an old tree on the edge of the orchard still forcing out small, deformed fruit, and he made a breakfast for himself, shivering with his hands in his armpits. He tried to feel the day warm instant by instant as the sun rose over the horizon, but his apparatus for appreciating such subtlety was too crude.

Then the donkey brayed, and a cock cried out his serrated *Confiteor* through the rising mist. Where had Candle got a cock from? She must still be roaming the province, releasing creatures from homesteads with impunity. She was lucky she wasn't caught, as the donkey and the cock weren't exactly keeping their whereabouts secret. The cock sounded like a tenor.

With all that noise, she'd be stirring by now. Still, he waited till he saw the smoke from the kitchen chimney roll up, and he heard a window shutter bark against the stone. He came toward the house ready to call out, but she was standing in the doorway on one foot, the other foot rubbing against the back of her calf. "What have you been waiting for?" she asked, her head tilted forward. "Isn't it cold out there in the orchard?"

"You've been clearing the undergrowth."

"The donkey has. Makes my life easier; he's done enough for a kitchen garden. If we remove a few more trees, we'll have a good open space, and fertile, by the look of it. But we'll need fencing against the donkey and other comers. Why do you loiter, come in, you must be ice."

He was about to say *I was afraid I'd frighten you,* and then he remembered: She possessed some sort of a talent for reading the present. She'd probably known he was there; and indeed, she admitted as much when asked.

His fists clenched and opened at the notion of touching her sleep-warm body, of wrapping his arms around her, diving his cold fingers into the folds of her simple broadcloth sleeping tunic. But she ducked into the shadowy doorway before he could embrace her, as if his time away had made them strangers again.

The place was that much straighter, simpler, more pleasant. She'd been busy. Dried flowers set round in cracked terra-cotta pots. Tassels of herbs drying from strings, spooling their fragrance across the kitchen. In the fire nook, the andirons had been polished, and from the trammel hung a fine bulbous kettle with scented water roiling in it. "How did you know I'd be back today?"

"The cock crowed more self-consciously, so I guessed he must have an audience. Anyway, I sensed it would be you. Or maybe that was just hope, who can tell the difference? You must be weary. Rest your bones, Liir, and I'll fetch some rennety milk pudding from the cold room belowstairs."

"Don't move about so. Just sit—here." He patted a stool near him and smiled. Her hands flexed and met his at the fingertips, and their fingertips bounced gently against one another. Then she took herself off to get the pudding.

"You'll eat first, and then you'll sleep," she said, like a mother, "for I don't need the skills of divination to know you've been walking most of the night."

She would hear of nothing else. He had to content himself with watching her flit across the kitchen, into the sunlight and out of it again. How is it that she is like a bird, too, he thought, and felt he was on to something, but then the food settled him, and Candle had proven right, for his head was nodding on his spine. She helped him to the room where they had so chastely slept, and after she had taken his shirt off and lightly run a damp cloth under his arms and behind the lengthening mane of hair at his nape, she dropped the cloth on the floor and pressed her hands against his bare chest, as if trying to interpret the arcane language of his heartbeat.

"Later," she mouthed at him, and kissed the space where his lips would have been if he hadn't just then begun to keel backward against the pillow.

The sleep was devoid of character. A good sleep.

He awoke well into the heat of the day, such as it was at this time of year. She had set out a tunic and fresh leggings. What a capable scavenger she was. The trousers, cut for a slenderer man, cinched too tightly at his thighs, but they were clean, and the tunic scented of pomander. In new garb he felt a new man, and looked out of the window to find her.

She was hard at work in the patch she'd mentioned. Using a sharp segment of the printing press's broken iron wheel, she was levering aloft a resistant root of apple tree. Smudged now, where he was pristine, she wiped her face with the back of her hand and in vain tried to scatter a late population of midges who found the smell of her sweat enticing. He called to her, and she waved and fell heavily to her knees as the root chose that moment to yield.

"Let me do that," he said.

"Done now. But I'll rest a spell. Come down."

They walked to the edge of the orchard, by turns sipping sweet well water from a single pipkin. "You've done good work here," he told her gravely.

"I've had good reason." With her little finger she picked at a bit of wax in one ear. "You're back, now, and there's one on its way."

He arched an eyebrow, feeling very Commander Cherrystone-ish. "Company's coming?"

"You could put it suchly."

What was she reading out of this sunny hour that he couldn't see— oh, he couldn't, but then he could. "It's not so. You're not old enough."

She said, "Though like you I can't exactly say how old I am, apparently I am old enough, Liir." Her tone was easy and a bit bored, but he thought he knew her well enough by now to suppose that she was at least a little frightened.

Many of the fellows in the unit had talked about this. They'd shared their observations. Women always knew, and a preternatural calm swept all other earthly considerations aside when it happened. But Candle was hardly a woman!—and not inaugurated into those mysteries. Or not by him.

"I've been gone only a few weeks," he said, trying not to sound cold. "Or had you already charmed a local farmer with your domingon even when I was still recuperating inside? Is that how you got the goat, the cock, the hen—a bartering for your farmyard needs with your farmyard skills? Is that why you encouraged me to leave on a wild Bird chase?"

"You needn't fuss so." She bit her lip and looked at him levelly. "It was no other man, Liir."

"It is not by me. Candle!" He slipped out of Qua'ati for a moment, to spew expletives in the orchard air. "I am a fool and a naïf and a monster, all at once, but I am not stupid about how a girl becomes pregnant. It is not by me. Don't embarrass me with a hopeless ruse. Do you think I would abandon you over it?"

"I don't think—"

"Or maybe you want me to? Well, I won't. I haven't that crooked a soul. Just don't lie to me, for that's intolerable. Candle! The whole thing is beyond belief."

"Liir. I ask nothing of you. You're not married to me. You didn't choose me. I didn't choose you."

"You chose to save me," said Liir despondently, "when I might have slipped away, and a good thing, too."

"I chose to try to save someone. Someone sick in an infirmary, that is all. I didn't know who it was. I didn't know it was you. I didn't know you yet. I don't know you yet."

"I am *not* the *father*," he said. "Am I required to remind you how it works? I kept my distance, Candle. I never slept with you; I never buried myself in your trove. I thought about it, yes, but thinking's not doing, and no child is begat by the midnight thoughts of an adult sleeping alone."

"But you did," she said. Her shoulders slumped. "It would be easier to pretend you hadn't, but it doesn't matter one way or the other. The infant grows. I won't turn it out of its nest now."

"I didn't!" he insisted, and then she told him how he had, and when, and why.

A small rain came up over the orchard, and in an eddy of chill, the drops turned to snow. The season turned several more notches in an instant, as can happen.

They made their way inside without further remark, and Candle put herself to kitchen tasks. She measured two handfuls of coarse flour and shook it through a boulter of cloth. The light greyed, and faded, and he pulled the shutters tight, and built up the fire. There were the cock and the hen to bring in, and the donkey to stable, and whatever else he could think of to do, he did: shifting firewood, scattering clean straw for the floor, arranging things on shelves. Things with handles and spouts, items with purposes he couldn't imagine. He couldn't imagine anything.

They ate, and after eating she said softly, "This is a good thing, Liir."

"Then it couldn't have come from me."

As she prodded, and because it made a distraction if nothing else, he told her about the Conference of the Birds and the charge under which he was laboring—or had so labored, up until this morning upon his return—to find his broom.

She had always seemed unshaken by the notion of flying dragons. When he asked why, she told him that she'd heard rumors of such creatures a few years back. They were involved in an action in the provincial capital.

"Qhoyre," he filled in. "It figures."

"If there were going to be troubles, you'd expect them in Qhoyre," she concurred. "It began as a tax revolt or something. The garrison of the Emerald City military was stormed by Quadlings, and more or less annihilated."

"I don't believe you can be more or less annihilated. You either are or you aren't." He thought of the suave, genteel Commander Cherrystone, and hoped that he had been one of the ones who had been killed.

"Don't look to me for accuracy. I'm a simple soul. I'm merely telling you what I heard my uncle say. Some of the reasons we left." Candle continued. It was calming for both of them to avoid the matter of her pregnancy. "He said that the Emerald City flared up in reprisal. Overreacted. A small fleet of flying dragons was unleashed against the Quadlings at Qhoyre. It was pretty terrible. There were only a few survivors, and who could trust what those poor traumatized loons said? Flying *dragons*? Quadlings are so superstitious. No one knew what to believe—so let's get out of here, said my uncle."

She folded her hands in her lap. "So I'm not surprised that it has turned out to have been true."

He put his head in his hands. The other fellows in his squadron. Had any of them survived? Ansonby, Kipper, Somes? Burny, Mibble? The one they called Fathead? Or what about their girlfriends—were they tarred as collaborators?

It wasn't just the girl slung from the burning bridge—it was all of them. Her parents, their neighbors, the countryfolk. The occupying forces, the officers and the infantry, the support teams, the ambassadors. The repercussions seemed endless and only to grow in force and significance, never to recede.

Candle saw his expression. She took his hand, and he had to work hard not to snatch it away.

"Remember why you went to the Conference," she said. "Before you save anyone else, you have to save yourself, Liir. Otherwise you're just a bundle of tics, a stringed puppet manipulated by chance and the insensible wind."

"I will stay here, whether you've been sleeping round the countryside or not. We are called to be as limbs of God," he said.

"That piety curdles on your tongue, and you know it. If you don't rescue yourself, Liir, you might just as easily be a limb of evil."

"One has to admit one's destiny."

"Naming your destiny the will of the Unnamed God doesn't make it so. And self-glorifying, besides."

They lay down in the same bed that they had shared before. Neither of them slept, though not this time from being racked with desire.

♦ 2 ♦

THEY AROSE WHEN IT was still dark, besting the cock at his own business.

Tea in a cup with a crack in the glaze; small beads of tea lined up vertically. He stared at it, wishing to learn a new language.

"Whom will you choose to save?" said Candle, when the sun made an effort to lighten the room. "I am not that girl, you know. That Quadling girl you saw pitched into the burning river. You cannot make me her by beggaring yourself for my needs. You can't choose me in that girl's place."

"Maybe I can't save anyone," he said. "Since Elphaba died, how many times have I set out to try? There was Nor, who was in prison. There was Princess Nastoya, in medical extremis. I make no headway in either direction. Even some miserable boy I saw on a road, whose granny was willing to sell him in exchange for my broom—I just walked on by. Why should I be beholden to those Birds? Find the old broom! Speak out danger to the world! I'm not a spokesperson for myself; how could I be for them?"

"You can do what you choose to do. You're hardly on death's door," she reminded him. "I mean, not anymore."

"And you'd have me believe that I have lost my virginity, and I don't even remember it. Life in a coma. Well, it figures. It's consistent, isn't it? I'll give you credit for that: you've read me correctly."

"You owe me nothing." Candle stood up and put her hands on the small of her back. "There is enough food and firewood here to see me through my months. It'll be spring before the baby comes. The goat will provide backup milk if I run dry. Or I'll take myself back to the maun-tery for the final lying-in. The maunts will know what to do. It's not the first time the maunts have seen such."

"If I owe *you* nothing," he said, "no one owes *anyone* a thing."

"Maybe no one does."

"Except the Unnamed God."

"Maybe we don't owe the Unnamed God anything," she said. "Maybe not allegiance, maybe not gratitude, maybe not praise, maybe not attention. Maybe the Unnamed God owes us."

He sputtered at her impiety, but she looked queasy: a touch of morn-ing sickness upon her, no doubt. She hurried away to take care of it in private. The yard outside the house was rimy with hoarfrost, and the new sun shone upon it harshly. He had to squint to watch her cast herself away from him.

She was shivering. As the winter came in, she'd have to go more slowly to the outhouse, what with ice on the ground, and a weight in her belly. He would try to tie some straw to a pole, leave her a makeshift broom to sweep away the snow, if nothing else.

He gathered the straw and threw it on the floor while he hunted for cord with which to bind it. In the splayed angles in which it fell, it spelled the burning letter again, a letter he couldn't read.

Dragonfings

◆ I ◆

WAS IT THAT he was better traveled now—or just that he was older? Had the Emerald City actually changed, or just his ability to apprehend it?

The Big Itself had never seemed shy of self-regard—Liir remembered that much. Now he became aware of how everything flourished on a hefty scale. Architectural metastasis. The chapels were like churches, the churches like basilicas. The government houses out-bloated the basilicas, with bigger columns, more imposing flights of steps, higher spires. Private homes were nothing shy of palaces-in-training.

In his absence, the Emerald City had undergone a makeover. Oceans of whitewash had been splashed to obliterate the grattifi. Along the canals, trees had been pollarded to force full head, and ringed with liquid lime to prevent disease. The strip he'd called Dirt Boulevard had been replanted and it served again as a promenade, with well-raked tracks for military drill, and meandering paths among bushes and fountains where the plutocrats might see and be seen.

He supposed it came down to this: The Emerald City was no longer the capital of Oz. It *was* Oz. It survived for the sole purpose of insuring its own survival.

Maybe it always had done so, but now there was no pretending otherwise. Were there always so many ministries, or were they simply better marked? The Ministry of Comfort—that was aid for the indigent. The Ministry of the Home Guard. The Ministry of Sincerity (the sign beneath read FORMERLY THE PRESS BUREAU).

The Ministry of Artistic License. Apparently now you had to apply to be an artist.

Obelisks, cenotaphs, marble statues, fluttering banners and pennants. Souvenirs in kiosks: Everything OZ. I love OZ! A keychain, a whistle, a reticule, a letter opener, a lorgnette case: OZ, OZ. A military band every half mile, performing gratis for the residents of the emerald hive. The City seemed to have its own theme song.

But for what, wondered Liir. For background? For show? Everyone seemed in a hurry, more so than he'd remembered. The cafés were thriving, the public trams dripping with riders, the piazzas clotted with tourists, the museums thronged. "Apostle Muscle," an exhibit showing at the Lord Chuffrey Exposition Hall, was advertised in broadsheets plastered on all the public notice boards. The graphic was brilliant, Liir thought: a male foot in an open, leather-strapped sandal stepping out of a cloud. The painted landscape receding to the horizon showed that wherever the Apostle had already set his foot, communities like miniature Emerald Cities sprung up within the precise outline of his footly influence, from the heel to the sprawl of toes.

Liir turned his back on Southstairs, but it wasn't all that hard to do. The Emerald City had grown taller, more prosperous. Southstairs was more hidden now, though some edict or other must be keeping the land around the Palace relatively low built, so its stately domes and minarets could still dominate the City center.

◆ 2 ◆

AS FOR THE citizens of the Emerald City, business seemed to be profiting them very well. Skirts were thicker, hems were longer, fur trimmed everything, from ladies' hats to brougham bedeckings. Men's waistcoats were cut fuller to accommodate bigger bellies. The dry goods used by clothiers looked overdyed: the colors richly saturated, as if intended to be seen from a distance, as on a stage. The effects would have been comic but for a costive sobriety that seemed to have swept the City like an infection.

It'd be comfortable to be here, Liir decided. Everywhere else, ordinary folks laugh so much because they're nervous. Being stationed in Qhoyre, we laughed like morons: it helped us deal. It also made us friends. But perhaps you don't need to laugh if all your deprivations have been alleviated, your anxieties relieved. You can afford to be judicious, keep a civil tongue in your head, and speak in a lower tone of voice.

There were riffraff, as before—and a good thing, too, or he'd have stuck out even more than he did. Not so many Animals, still. A few in the service industry. An aproned old Warthog Governess, pushing a pram, some Rhino security guards.

And kids. Kids looking terribly old. Probably alley-cat thieves among the younger of them. Older kids, sloe-eyed teenagers, who cast him sly looks, trying to make out if he was an easy mark, competition for trade, or a possible ally.

Ruddy Quadlings in their huddles of family, clam-colored Yunamata indigents surviving on handouts and ale. Dwarves looking uppity, and why not?—dwarves looking shifty, and so what. Munchkins, in sizes small, medium, or grande, who'd emigrated from their own Free State. Or maybe they were turfed out for passing secrets or engaging in black trade. Dirty-looking polybloods in tatters of blanket, stepping on hardened bare feet across raked gravel forecourts, holding out their hands until some welcoming committee came out with a cudgel.

Elphaba had come to the Emerald City once, as a young woman. Maybe even his age—he didn't know. She'd never said much about it. "Pimps and Prime Ministers, and you can't tell the difference," she'd growled once. Had she stuck out like a green thumb? Or were people more accepting back then? For better or worse, he was able to pass.

He guessed by the end of the day he might be imprisoned in Southstairs himself. He thought he was ready for it, and perhaps he deserved nothing better. Still, if that were so, why was he taking care not to stand out? Skulking where he needed to skulk, striding confidently when the streetscape required it? A deeper intention at work, he guessed: that old beast-in-the-bear-trap thing that humans did so well? Even the reprobate who knows he's a moral coward wants to keep drawing breath.

Despite the building boom that the new prosperity allowed, the Emerald City remained familiar. Liir found his way more or less correctly to the Arch of the Wizard and along the Ozma Embankment, through the tony district of Goldhaven right to Mennipin Square, at the far end of which the house of Lord Chuffrey presided.

He wasn't exactly sure what he could accomplish, but he had to start somewhere. The Lady Glinda, née Upland, now Chuffrey, was his only contact in the Emerald City. Even retired from public life, surely a former throne minister would have access to the army, yes? To its barracks, its dragon stables, the lot. Could she be convinced to come to his aid again, after a whole decade?

Mennipin Square hadn't suffered any loss of prestige in the years since he'd been here. The house fronts were decorated with swags of green and gold. Lurlinemas was coming, of course. Ceremonial greens and garlands of winter golds were woven through the uprights of the iron fence that surrounded the square's private gardens.

In order to get to the kitchen yard where he had once presented himself, he had to pass the mansion's front entrance and turn a corner. When he reached the approach to the front door, he paused. Beyond the gravel of the carriage drive rose a flight of granite steps. At the landing, in front of the carved double doors, stretched a huge tiger in the act of licking its balls. A chain around its neck locked the tiger to one of the marble pillars supporting the portico, but there appeared enough length in the chain to allow the beast room to stretch and lunge. Sensibly Liir kept his distance. He looked, though. He'd never seen a wild animal chained in such an upper-purse locale.

The creature paused an instant and shifted its eyes without lifting its head, looking out from beneath tiger brows. "What are you looking at?" he growled softly.

A Tiger. A talking Animal, tied up like a farm dog, to scare off intruders.

Liir wanted to rush on, but to ignore the Tiger's belligerent question was to suggest a condescension he didn't feel. And Elphaba would have taken it all in stride. "I'm looking at a whole lot of Tiger," he said at last.

"That's the right answer," purred the Tiger. "You're either smart or lucky."

"I'm just brave," said Liir. "Have to be. I'm coming to see Lady Glinda."

"Well, you're *not* lucky, then," the Animal answered, "because she's not at home."

Liir's shoulders fell.

"She's off at Mockbeggar Hall. The Chuffrey country estate, down Kellswater way. A month in mourning."

"Mourning?"

"You just rolled off the cabbage cart? Looks like it. Her husband died. Didn't you know? Lord Chuffrey. He made a big donation to the Emperor and the banker's cheque had hardly cleared the First Accountant's office when Lord Chuffrey breathed his rummy last. Perhaps he thought he'd never be in as expensive a state of grace again, and might as well take advantage of it. Lady Glinda's bereaved."

"I'm sorry for her," said Liir.

"Don't be. She's not exactly a pauper widow. And she wasn't much more than a paper wife to him, anyway, so I hardly think she's fussed. She'll miss him, no doubt—we all will. He was a good sort in his way. Supports my family upcountry. Or he did."

Liir slumped against the stone gatepost. "Great. So what next?"

"I wouldn't come too close if I were you," said the Tiger. "I may be chatty when I'm bored, but if I chat too much I might work up an appetite." He winked at Liir, who moved back a few feet.

"Why do you stay?"

"Well, it certainly isn't the chains, is it? I sport these for effect," said the Tiger. He tossed his head and his eyes flashed in anger. "I mean, it's a statement of style, isn't it? Or are you *really* only a cabbagehead?" He was on his feet, and he roared. The gate shook on its pins, and Liir was halfway through Mennipin Square before he realized he was running.

So much for his first idea. Well, he'd have to work without the help and blessing of Lady Glinda, Society Goddess. And he'd hoped for a square meal to set himself up for harder campaigns. He had only the small scraps of dried fruit and bread that Candle had forced into his hands before he left.

The last time Liir had been so destitute in the Emerald City, he had gone to work in the Home Guard. Ready to improvise, he headed again to the main barracks campus near Munchkin Mousehole, in the lee of the low hill on which the Palace in its opulence squatted.

Boys, and a few girls, too, were running about the same sward on which he had once played gooseball with the bored soldiers. The grass was brown and flattened, weary of winter even before Lurlinemas Day, but the cries that rang out among the children seemed green enough to him. Unless he should run forward and capture the ball, and impress himself onto a team by dint of his swift responses, he would remain invisible to the children. Why not? He was a tallish, slightly ravaged young man, thinner, more ribby than the sleek soldiers who toyed with the kids.

He saw himself through their eyes: his cord-held hair, his green eyes, his new habit of ducking his head, scratching his elbows. A handsome enough beggar, maybe, but a beggar nonetheless, and too grown up to be thrown a bread roll for charity's sake. If the notion of charity still obtained here. He wasn't yet able to tell if it did.

Still, children at their games! It pleased him to watch. He remembered the children he had sung to, briefly, on the steps of a church when he first came to the Emerald City. He had smiled at them, had felt for them in a general sense, but he hadn't stood solid with them. Each time of life is such a prison, a portable prison. The children here on this fairway, the soldiers messing about with them, were no more like Liir than a Tiger was, or an elf or a—

"Cutting an old chum with impunity, and not blinking an eye. You've considerable nerve, you have."

Liir shook his head to register. A soldier at his left shoulder, breathing hard; he must have been among the fellows playing at gooseball, and come running up behind him. Hah. So much for the more sublime perception of the isolate.

"You don't remember my name any more than I yours." The fellow swept his damp blond hair off his sweaty brow. "What'd you do to deserve early retirement? *Our* tenures have been indefinitely extended with no right to petition otherwise."

Liir shook his head, wondering if he should play dumb, play it as a case of mistaken identity. Play wounded in battle? Play for time anyway. He hadn't worked out any particulars of strategy, just intentions.

"It's bon Cavalish, if you please. Trism, actually. You came into the service from this very field, and I was the one told you how."

Liir wrinkled a smile at him and shrugged. Work with what you have. *Trism.* Yes. A Minor Menacier . . . and in dragon husbandry, if he remembered correctly.

Coolly, Liir said, "That's a good eye you have for a distant acquaintance. I was standing there thinking how blind we all are to each other, and I didn't even recognize you."

"And I got you, but not your name."

"Ko, that's what I go by. Liir, commonly."

"Liir Ko. Right. You went off somewhere a few years back."

"I did indeed," said Liir, "but I don't want to talk about it, certainly not here."

"O ho," said Trism, and then, "O *ho*. A deserter? No."

"You'll get in trouble being seen with me."

"Trouble. That'd be fun." Trism looked this way and that. "Well, unless you're reenlisting voluntarily, you're making a big mistake showing yourself here. Or do you *want* to be caught? Are you spying for one of our enemies?"

"I don't even know who our enemies are," said Liir. "I never have."

"Well, if you've really gone and scampered, you count as one of them, so you better make yourself scarce. However, don't drift too far. The service is a bit more lenient in some matters than it used to be. They had to relax a few rules if they were going to keep us enlisted forever. We get a little city freedom, if you know what I mean. I'm sprung tonight till midnight. Hang about somewhere and we'll have a drink. Don't forget. Don't forget me." He gripped Liir's collar suddenly. "I haven't forgotten you."

• 3 •

TRISM WAS AS GOOD AS HIS WORD and was waiting at a sidewalk place in Burntpork, the low-rent district. "Welcome to the Cherry and Cucumber," he said, handing up a full pint of lager before Liir'd had a chance to take a stool. "They keep their license to serve real beer because they sponsor the annual Holy Action Day festivities."

"The what?"

"You're *way* out of touch. We can change that. Cheers."

The place was too empty at this hour for Liir to bring up the matter most pressing to him. Voices would carry. Scrawled in chalk on a slate above the bartender's station, though, was a message announcing: "Tonight, Fourth Comeback Tour, Sillipede Herself. 9:30. No tomatoes." The notice didn't actually promise a crowd, but Liir could hope. Or they could wander elsewhere.

Liir wasn't inclined to talk about himself much, and found that easy enough to manage. Trism didn't ask. He relaxed almost at once, and chattered at length about the military as if he and Liir had been best of friends back then. This one, that one, regulations by the book, funny pranks on supercilious superiors. "And what's become of Commander Cherrystone?" asked Liir as lightly as he could. He didn't want to be recognized as a deserter by someone with the power to slap him in chains for it.

"Dunno." Trism turned to survey the room, which, as hoped, was filling up with a noisier clientele, some of whom had been drinking before they arrived.

"We're not likely to meet a commanding officer here," said Liir, "I suppose."

"Anything's possible. Tastes vary. Doubt it, though."

On their third round, Liir began. "You were special forces, weren't you? Back then?"

"To the Unnamed God, we're all special," said Trism. Liir was unsure if he heard sarcasm in the rejoinder. "Minor Menacier back then."

"Husbandry, wasn't it?"

"Oh, the lad's sharper than he looks. Yeah, husbandry, for a time."

"Not now?"

"I don't like to talk about my work when I'm out larking."

"But I'm curious. Sounded very important. We dug the foundations for that new building—the stables."

"Basilica."

"That's right. I remember now. No stables below?"

"Look, it's Sillipede. The very one. A living legend. She must be ninety." An extremely odd, angular creature was being hoisted onto a small stage. Behind her, whisking spittle from the mouthpiece of her willow flute, stood a young woman dressed in little more than golden epaulets slapped strategically about her body. A couple of Bears opened their music cases and began to turn pegs to tune up: an Ugabumish guitar, a violinsolo. "So few Animals with real jobs, but if you drummed Animals entirely out of the music business, nobody'd hear a note."

Sillipede began to warble. She was so old that it was impossible to tell if she was a man or a woman, nor if she was trying to make an attempt to imitate either her own or the opposite gender. In the cracked and breathy voice, though, the singer still had considerable power, and the room quieted down somewhat. Liir had to wait for the first number to end before continuing his remarks.

"I mean, specifically, dragons," he said through the applause.

"Hush, you're not being polite," said Trism. "Isn't she something?"

"Something or something else or something else again. Maybe not to my taste. Do we have to stay?"

"And give up our good seats? Have one more beer and let's see the first set through, anyway."

Sillipede bumbled her way through some difficult patches, talking more than she sang. She lit a cigarette halfway through one number and burnt her fingers, and told her backup to can it. "I'm hardly myself tonight," she told the crowd, "what with this dreadful heathen holiday approaching. *Lurlinemas.* Can you believe the Emperor in his goodness allows any reminder of those archaic superstitions? Can you believe that he in his goodness? Can you believe his goodness? I mean, can you? I'm asking you a question here."

The room was silent. Was she spinning out a comic story or was she losing her marbles? She took a drag on her smoke.

"Don't get me wrong," she said. "I can see on the faces of those of you who still *have* faces that you're afraid you've wandered into a conventicle of traitors instead of a comeback concert. Please. Relax. If we get raided and we all end up in Southstairs, I'll lead singalongs on the weekends. I will. That's a promise."

The flautist relieved an itch beneath one of the epaulets.

"I'm not proselytizing. Neither *for* the Unnamed God nor *against* its holy un-name. That would be plain old sedition, and frankly at my age, I'm just not up to it." She made a face. "Sedition is unthinkable. Although to say something is 'unthinkable' is, of course, to have been able to think of it. And I'm at the age where I'm losing language faster than I'm gaining it. I don't know what sedition means anymore. I never said it. I never never said the word *screwy*, did I? Did I say the word *complicity*?"

Someone in the back muttered something a little ugly. Sillipede said, "I can see you back there squirming. You and your sour puss. Don't get out much, do we? You remind me of someone. You remind me of someone that I would find really annoying. What're you getting so feisty about? I'm just taking a cigarette break. Shooting the breeze. If you think I'm being unscrupulous, give me a break: I'm too old to have scruples anymore. Where would I put them?"

"What is she on about?" muttered Liir.

"She's going to end up either in prison or the ward for the incurably old," said Trism. He was red in the face. "Maybe you're right; we better go."

But they couldn't get up while she was in her monologue: that would single them out for her catcalling, draw attention their way. She'd be all over them.

She wandered a bit in the crowd. Now she looked more like an old man in makeup, now like an old woman trying to look young. She looked more human than anything else, though that didn't necessarily mean handsome. Liir prayed she wouldn't come over and start talking to him. He had a strong feeling she would.

Under the table, Trism reached for his hand and squeezed it. He was more nervous than Liir. This place wasn't sanctioned by the Home Guard, Liir guessed, and Trism would be in serious jeopardy if things got any hotter. Liir detached his hand.

"I'm a ditsy old relic, don't mind me," said Sillipede. "You young things take everything so seriously. But you don't remember the bad old days of the Wizard. The drought. How we lived back then. How we laughed! Hah. A lark. And hardly anyone stood up to him. Only some fool witch from the hinterlands. And we all know what happens to witches."

Someone hissed.

"These days are so much better," the creature said. "Ask Sillipede. Sillipede knows. I'm old enough to remember when the Ozma Regent was still the crowned head of the nation, and baby Ozma a little bundle of coos and poos. I'm so old I was already retired when the Wizard arrived and set things to rights. Hard times then! Things are better now, ain't they? Well, depends on your outlook, I guess. If things ain't actually better, they sure are *gooder*.

"These times," she continued, "so righteous! Everyone so much more moral! Put some clothes on your nakedness, girl, or the vice squad'll be down our throats. Or down your throat, anyway, if you look at 'em like that."

The flutist looked as nonplussed as the audience.

"You got to hold on to your values, if you can still reach them," said the chanteuse. "Buy some values, rent 'em, steal 'em if you have to. Sell 'em for a profit when tastes change. Whatever works. Is this a crock, or what?"

She regained the small stage and put her hand to her eyes, shading the flare of the lights. "I can see you. I know you're there," she said. "I know you're in there somewhere. I can wait." She signaled the Bear on bass and said, "A torch song about lost hopes, Skoochums, how 'bout. For old time's sakes. In the key of E, Harrikin. No, not B. I said E—E for Elphaba. One. Two. Three. Whatever."

The Bear lazily thwacked out a bass run, and Sillipede drew a breath, but then spoke again, interrupting the intro. "And that other problem, all that graffiti! I saw it again on my way here, scrawled on some library wall. 'Elphaba lives!' What's that supposed to mean? I ask you. Isn't it just too much? Why don't they keep their sloppy old slogans to themselves? Elphaba lives! As if."

She flicked her cigarette butt into someone's lager. "Now I just feel all riled up and alive. This ain't happened since I left double digits. So I am going to sing a beautiful old hymn to prove it to you. Anyone who's with the Emperor can stand and sing it with me, to show we're not just scratching our balls here, are we, folks?"

The band patched together an intro and Sillipede sauntered into a familiar melody. The patrons of the place were irritated, a bit unnerved by the theatrics, and unsure who was being made fools of: the Emperor, the Unnamed God, Sillipede herself, or them—or anyone idiotic enough to take a position against the Palace. But the song was balm itself— devotional, a bit flowery, familiar. Complexities gave way to the simpler sentiments. People stood and sang in defiance of Sillipede's posturing. In the shadows and shuffling, Liir and Trism escaped. Trism grabbed Liir's hand as if he might try to duck away; Liir couldn't help squeezing back. He was wound up. *E for Elphaba.* It was as if, these years later, he'd finally attended her wake.

✦ 4 ✦

THEY WALKED ALONG a quay in the Lower Quarter. Elsewhere in Oz it was probably snowing, but with the warm smoke of ten thousand coal fires, Liir and Trism felt only a particulate moisture in the air, part rain, part mist. Flames burning in lampposts gave off a pulsing, melon-colored glow.

"Mustn't be late, I assume," said Liir.

"One can hear the bells of the basilica all over the City. These days of the New Piety, they ring on the half hour. We've some time yet."

"That place made you tense. Where're we going?"

"I've been there before, but not on Treason Night."

"You think that was treasonous?" Liir was aghast. "I thought it"—he governed his language—"only stupid."

"She'd do better to keep her opinions to herself. Or organize them first, anyway. I wasn't even sure what she was on about, but it takes something like whiskey courage to pretend that much skepticism about the Apostle Emperor. He's a good fellow. The people love him. I myself feel flattered to have met him personally."

"You have? Really? What's he like?"

Trism shot him a look. "Of course I have. I was with you the first time it happened. The night before you lot shipped out? Remember? He offered us his carriage. He was cynical and louche then, as I remember. A lost soul. His Awakening hadn't happened."

"The Emperor of Oz . . . no. Shell? Shell Go-to-hell Thropp?"

"The First Spear himself. Can you really not have known? Where *have* you been? The moon?"

The very paving stones on the quay seemed more slippery. "I don't get it. Everyone talks about the Emperor's . . . his virtue. Shell was the last person to have any virtue. He was a spy, wasn't he—didn't someone say? Anyway, he used extract of poppyflower to opiate the young women in Southstairs and fuck them silly. I know that for a fact."

"Well, who better to speak for the Unnamed God, then, than one who has sinned so egregiously? Talk about your recoveries . . . the Awakening happened, and he heard the voice of the Unnamed God, telling him to lead. You know his sisters were the two witches? Nessarose and Elphaba Thropp?"

Liir felt ill. "It's just too . . . uncanny. Too unlikely."

"Not as unlikely as all that. Who is exempt from the claw of salvation? The more sinful you are, the more likely salvation can take root. His father was a unionist minister, after all. A missionary, I think."

"He's a charlatan, Shell is."

"May have been once. Don't think so now. He believes he was Awakened in order to lead Oz through this desperate time."

"Are we so desperate that we need the likes of him—"

"Well, you tell me," said Trism. His voice had gone lower, intimate. He leaned in and almost put his chin on Liir's shoulder. "How desperate are any of us at any given moment? Hmmm? Are any of us so desperate that we might, say, attack an unarmed rural settlement at night and burn it into the river?"

Liir pivoted to glare at Trism, who reached out and pinned Liir's right arm behind his back, whispering, "You shitty little creep."

"Let me go. What is this? A one-person tribunal? A vendetta? Let me go. Where are we?" In the mist Liir had lost his bearings. "How do you know anything about me? And what's it to you? I was doing the Emperor's *work,* Trism. Your precious leader. His bidding. Let me go."

"I'm going to beat your head in and then shove your sorry carcass into the water." By now Trism had both of Liir's hands behind his back, and Trism was kicking at cobbles randomly, to find one that was loose and use it for braining.

Liir struggled. Trism, in military trim, was fitter and had had the advantage of surprise. To yell wouldn't help: a police force would side with Trism at once. "Look," Liir said, trying not to sound terrified. "I'm bone tired. What do you care about what happened south of Qhoyre? Aren't you a company man? Head office mastered that situation in a flash, I've heard."

"I heard what *you* did. How could I not? Soldiers gossip worse than housewives. Because of that attack, the Quadlings around Qhoyre struck out at Cherrystone's garrison. You lost some of your buddies, buddy. And then the Emperor called up his brand-new defensive system and deployed it against the natives."

Liir began to get it. "Oh ho. But that was your specialty. Those were your dragons."

"I was one of the team. Prime Menacier of the division. Right. And I'd been told the dragons were to be held in abeyance, paraded for show on Holy Action Day. The annual display of military might and moral purpose. Scare the rabble and comfort the nervous. Nothing like good defenses to allow citizens to sleep well at night."

"And you believed every word of what was told you, and never meant to hurt a fly. I know that story. Let me go, Trism. Come on. You're hurting me."

"I've only started to hurt you. Get used to it. Because of your fucking about, the dragons were called up from their catacombs. And you haven't seen merciless until you've seen those beasts at work."

Liir was near to spitting. "I have seen merciless, Trism. As it happens. I was attacked by your little trained pets."

It was Trism's turn to start, and with the advantage, Liir tried to pull away. He half managed, but they ended up in a tumble on the pavement, fighting. They rolled in puddles and a plod of horse dung, and Trism ended up on top, his knees on Liir's chest.

"I'm going to kill you. I saw you standing there on the playground, and I thought: there *is* an Unnamed God, and it has delivered you to me to kill. Your cruel actions have sentenced me to a life more wretched than anything you have known. Once the military strategists saw what the dragons could do, nothing for it but that they should be used again. Trained more precisely. My life is *chained* to the job of perfecting the killing capacity of those creatures." He was as close to wailing as yelling, and Liir saw now what he hadn't noticed so far: Trism bon Cavalish was a shattered person.

"Kill me then," Liir said. "It'll make you feel a whole lot better, I can just tell. And maybe me, too, the way things are going. But hear me out first. It was the Emperor's word that started this whole thing. He required Cherrystone to invent an incident. Maybe he wanted a reason to launch a dragony attack all along, I don't know. I was doing the bidding of my company commander."

"And that's all I'm doing, and between us there's hundreds and hundreds dead, and more hundreds living in terror, and even more hundreds ready to kill us back, if they could only find a way."

Liir let Trism sob. Well, he didn't have much choice. Trism's nose dripped on Liir's face, but Liir couldn't lift his arms to wipe it off. "We're more or less in the same boat, you know," Liir said in as even a voice as the sentiment allowed, when Trism had regained some composure. "We've both done some serious damage."

Trism took a huge breath, nodded, and then removed his knees from Liir's chest. Liir sat up and, as discreetly as he could, shook the snot off his forehead.

✦ 5 ✦

THEY WALKED ACROSS the Law Courts Bridge and disappeared into the alleys and courtyards of the Lower Quarter. The place teemed with charlatans, addicts, and runaways; it stunk of sizzling night sausage and sewage, and rang with the laughter of the mad. We belong nowhere else, thought Liir; better get accustomed to it.

They could talk, though, without fear of being overheard; and in not looking at each other they could say more.

Trism bon Cavalish was the chief dragon master. He wasn't governor of the dragon stables, but he trained the creatures with a sure hand and a regulating eye. He had the longest tenure on the staff. His work required him to follow the exploits of the dragons and fine-tune their training.

He knew that a pack of dragons from the west had returned with a broom and a cape, though he didn't know where this bounty had come from. Liir, of all places! Trism knew about the scrapings of the missionary maunts, among, it turned out, several dozen others.

"Scrapings," said Liir with a shudder. Candle had mentioned such a thing. "I hardly know what it means . . ."

The claws are sharp as razors, oppositional pinchers like a human thumb and forefinger, Trism explained. A human can build a miniature ship in an empty jeroboam, and a dragon can remove a face with as few as nine incisions.

Trism was curt. "Don't ask me for the rationale. I know one thing: the dragons only go after the young. They're trained that way." He squared his shoulders. "*I* trained them that way. The theory is that when the young are brought down in their prime, it is more—alarming— useful—than if some old codger or crone is bumped off."

Why hadn't the dragons scraped Liir's face? He was young enough. Maybe they thought the broom and cape were all the trove they needed. Or maybe they saw something in Liir that stopped them.

"But maunts!" Liir said. "Young women devoting their lives to the service of the Unnamed God? It doesn't figure."

Trism explained that the old maunteries, with their traditions of independence, didn't suit the leadership style of the Emperor. The Apostle of the Unnamed God—

"What's all this about the Apostle?"

"That's what the Emperor calls himself. The humblest of the humble has been exalted by the Unnamed God. So the Apostle feels obliged to exercise the authority granted him." It seemed that some of the maunteries about Oz were led by older women raised in an archaic scholastic tradition. Some superiors were becoming dangerously out of touch with the needs of the common folk, and fell to asking bothersome questions about the spiritual authority of the Emperor. Such foment could only erode the confidence of the nation.

"Is that it?" asked Liir. "Is this a moment of foment?"

"I'm not privy to the thinking. Information's meted out on a need-to-know basis. But I've heard the western tribes were close to uniting by treaty, to defend against City interests in their land. The dragon attacks could confound the tribes, cause them to mistrust one another, if they didn't know who was behind the attacks.

"The faces of those young missionaries you mention," Trism concluded, working to maintain his composure. "They've been cured and stored. They're going to be taken out at the next Holy Affairs Day and exhibited. A point is going to be made."

There was worse still. The dragons—there were several dozen of them—were fed on the corpses of freshly killed humans. That bloody diet helped stoke the dragons with the strength needed to fly the hundreds of miles to the west. The cadavers were imported directly from a killing chamber in Southstairs, where a fresh supply was always available, thanks to the culling campaigns of the Under-mayor.

"Chyde," intoned Liir. "The guy with the rings."

Trism was nonplussed. "Is Shell the spy, or is it you?"

"I get around. Find the company I deserve. Go on."

"Well, with all that folderdoodle, human corpses freshly bled and rendered into cutlets, do you wonder I am a wreck? The dragons weren't my idea, but I was elevated to the position, and now they're under my supervision."

"Whose idea were they? Shell's not that clever."

Trism cast Liir a dark look. "Who can believe anyone anymore? But I met Shell again—as Emperor I mean, of course—a while ago. I had a private audience, not long after his Elevation to the Imperialcy."

Liir folded his arms and leaned against a parapet. They'd walked on, climbing out of the Lower Quarter as the streets climbed. The lights of the alleys of the Burntpork district burned below the escarpment. "Do tell."

"He was humility personified, Liir. Make that face if you like. You distrust everything. He's a little thicker about the waist, very quick of wit and . . . almost tender, I guess. His Awakening has given him a largesse and a zeal. He talked about it. Why shouldn't he lead? 'Choosing the lowliest among us,' he said, indicating himself. 'A fornicator and a sot.' He seemed pretty shocked. 'What am I but a shell—waiting to be filled with the spirit of the Unnamed God?' "

"What form did his Awakening take, I wonder? I thought people who heard voices were generally considered lunatics."

"Who knows. He grew up in the thick of it, though, didn't he? He'd had those two powerful sisters; next to them he must always have felt like shredded cabbage."

"Are we talking about the same Shell? Come on!"

"Come on yourself. Suppose everyone in your family was thought to be wicked. Even were called *Wicked,* almost as a title—"

But they were, thought Liir; it was my family, too, or as good as.

"—what would you have done in Shell's place—as . . . alleviation? Compensation? Damage control? Shoot, he may have believed the next flying house or flying bucket of water was meant for him. You'd sign on with a Higher Authority if you were he, wouldn't you?"

"Shell was about the last one I'd have fingered for a low self-image. Surprise, surprise. Now he works out his inferiority at the helm of the nation . . ."

"He sees it as destiny. He showed me a page torn out of a book of magic. The Scarecrow found it in the Wizardic apartments after the abdication. It was in an indecipherable script, but it had been laboriously translated. I suppose by the Wizard. 'On the Administration of Dragons' it said."

Liir felt creepy. He knew that the Wizard had wanted Elphaba's Grimmerie. She had sworn it would never happen. This sounded like a bit of it. How had it gotten here?

"He convinced me it was the right thing to do," continued Trism. "I believed him, mostly because he believes himself. He's not lying; he's not the sham that the Wizard was, or misguided like Glinda the Glamorous, establishing libraries wherever she planted her jeweled scepter. Neither was he the ineffectual front man of a cabal of bankers, like the Scarecrow. He's the genuine article."

"The genuine article of what?" It was Liir's turn to scorn. "He convinced you to take part in something so heinous?"

"He asked me. What could I say? It was like the Unnamed God came down—"

"Isn't the Unnamed God actually unnamed so that you can't confuse it with someone named Shell Thropp?"

"I'm just telling you, since you asked. We've all heard that the bankers in Shiz have been withdrawing investments from the Free State of Munchkinland. Lord Chuffrey was the chief architect of that strategy. Sanctions against the Munchkins. They're not small enough already, bring them to their little knees. The exercise of dragon power was billed as a necessary lead-up to an annexation of Restwater in western Munchkinland. Well, the Emerald City needs the water, you know."

"All that bores me. You still knew what you were training dragons to do."

"I did," said Trism. "The dragons were the Second Spear."

If the Seventh Spear could immolate Bengda, what might the Second Spear be capable of? And the Emperor, the First Spear? "Can't you ask for a reassignment?"

"Dragonmaster bon Cavalish? Reassigned? Don't be absurd. They couldn't replace me. I'm too valuable. My assistants are assigned to the stables on a quick rotation so they can't learn too much. There's no replacement trained to take my place. Not yet anyway, it's all too new. In the development and testing stages."

"You could just leave. Scamper, as you put it. The way I did."

"That would make me feel better for about an hour. It would do no good beyond that. The dragons would still be there. Someone else would figure out how to hum them through their assignments. I'm talented, but I'm not a freak; I'm not indispensable. Besides, I have a family. They'd be fatally mortified if I disappeared in disgrace—and singled out for reprisals, like as not."

"A family." Liir whispered the word as if it meant *gelignite*. He felt cold, as if he was offended that his potential murderer no longer thought him worth the effort to kill. Falling from a great height again, and no warning. A *family*.

"What's *that* look for? I mean parents. Citizens of some standing. From good lines. Also a lunk of an older brother, simple in the head. Not such a good iteration of the bloodlines."

And Liir didn't crash-land but was rescued by that answer.

They were walking, circling, in the mist. It was a clammy night to be out on the street, but neither of them wanted to stop in another establishment. The mist thickened to a fog, and bells rang out. Ten-thirty. Someone emptied a chamber pot out an upper window, and the soldiers ducked together into a doorway just in time to escape being wasted. It put Liir in mind of the time they met, huddled in an archway, sheltered from a hailstorm.

For the first time since Quadling Country, Liir felt the appetite for a perguenay cigarette.

They kept on. Dragons. Where had they come from, these creatures of myth and mystery? Had a cluster of eggs been uncovered in some landslide in the Scalps, or in a mud-pocket in the badlands of Quadling Country? Trism wasn't certain.

Liir didn't have to ask about the more basic *why*. Not if the Emperor's aim was to make rural people cower. If a dragon was really a flying lizard, the original lizard of Oz was the Time Dragon. The foundation myth of the nation. In a subterranean cavern, deeper even than Southstairs, sealed over by earthquakes and landslides, the Time Dragon slept. He was dreaming the history of the whole world, instant by instant.

Trism was thinking along the same road. "I can tell you the inspiration," he said, and—a little pompously—recited the words of the anonymous Oziad bard.

> *"Behold the floor of rhymeless rock, where time*
> *Lies sleeping in a cave, a seamless deep*
> *And dreamless sleep, unpatterned dark*
> *Within, without. Time is a reddened dragon.*
>
> > *The claws refuse to clench, though they are made,*
> > *Are always made in readiness to strike*
> > *The rock, and spark the flint. Then to ignite*
> > *The mouth of time that, burning hot*
>
> *And cold in turn, consumes our tattered days . . ."*

"You have it down cold."
"And it goes on

> *". . . then the burst*
> *Of whitened sulfur spark. The fuse is lit.*
> *The dragon's furnace starts to roar and ride*
> *And time, being dreamt within, begins outside."*

Liir was awed. "You've had some schooling before the service."

"We had to memorize great quaffs of *The Oziad* in primary lessons at St. Prowd's," said Trism. "I was a day student on a bursary. Got top honors though."

"Well, it's awfully, uh, grand," said Liir. "The Time Dragon dreams up when we're born, when we're to die, and whether for lunch we'll get the roast pfenix stuffed with creamed oysters at the head table at St. *Prowd's,* or the day-old ploughman's, the roadsweeper's budget lunch?"

"If the unlettered farmers of Munchkinland and the factory workers of Gillikin believe that their fate is being determined by how the Time Dragon dreams them up, they don't need to bother to take responsibility for their actions or for changing their class and station in life."

"You too," said Liir. "You were brought through primary school to the services, and the Time Dragon dreamed you there at the head of this horrible stable. But you don't know what he's going to dream you to do next. Maybe it's scamper and leave those dragons to their fate."

"I said already. The family."

They came to a newsstand shuttered up for the night. ELPHABA LIVES was scratched in char on the boards. The family! Hah. "They think they own her," Liir said, suddenly disgusted. "The Witch would be foaming at the mouth. She was a flaming recluse and a crank." Even the handwriting had an intimate, proprietary look to it somehow.

"What do you care?"

Liir changed the subject. "Maybe it's your job to kill the dragons. Maybe that's why you're there. Maybe that's why our paths crossed again today."

"Are you *insane*? I couldn't do that."

"You could kill me, or at least you told me that you would. And I'm the least little lick of flame in your past. If it wasn't Qhoyre, if that hadn't worked, your superiors would have set up some other straw threat. I was being used no less than you are now. But I left, Trism. I did. You could, too."

"I told you. The parents," he said. "I'm trapped."

"How would it work?" said Liir. "Quick and permanent? Burn the stables down? Slice their heads off?"

Eleven-thirty bell. Time to start back for the barracks.

"Poison?"

"Didn't you hear me?" said Trism. "They'll kill my next of kin."

"Not if you didn't do it," said Liir. "I'll do it. I'll leave a note saying

I did so, and that I kidnapped you as a hostage. You'll be exonerated. They can't kill my next of kin—I don't have any."

He didn't add: Anyway, by some rumors, Shell is my next of kin, our holy Emperor. Let them go after the First Spear, if they must.

◆ 6 ◆

"Tell me," said Liir as they stood outside the sentry gate, screwing up their courage, "how do you mesmerize a dragon?"

"It's not mesmerism, quite. I focus and I—hum—"

Liir raised an eyebrow. "Sweet nothings?"

"Nothing sweet."

"Come on."

Trism balked, but Liir pushed. They were both avoiding the risky moment of trying to get into the base. "Oh, all right," snapped Trism. "Truth is, my family's not all that exalted, despite the fancy 'bon' in my surname. Gentlemen farmers in Gillikin a couple of generations ago, but the gentlemanly part couldn't be afforded during the drought, and they farmed to eat after a while. I won a few hog-calling contests, which brought more shame than glory to the family, and then I did some sheepdog trials, too. I guess I have a knack. Proved there was dirt under the fingernails; it made my folks crazy. They were trying to breed up.

"Goes something like this," he said. "But I'm not telling you the whole whack: I've picked up the benefits of need-to-know. So this is the general stuff. I get up close to a dragon, which is hard work by itself. They're skittish and inbred, given the stocks we have to work with. Takes time. You have to be totally still and selfless as possible, become like a rag doll in their pen, till they relax. When they do, their breathing changes; it slows. I come in close and mount them. No, you can't ride a dragon, I mean I just climb up the pinions of their wings and settle my chest on their long strong neck, and straddle them. I crook my knees around the forward phalange of their wing. I circle the neck with my arms, the way I'd choke a man if I had to, only gently of course. This makes their ears fill with blood and stand up. It's arousal, basically. They're suggestible but also hugely intelligent, and I hum into their ears. Usually the left one, don't know why; it tends to cock backward a little more, I think."

"It *is* sweet nothings!"

"Shut up. I hum, line by line, the shape of the task at hand. If I hum a dragon to sleep, he sleeps—and I could jump up and down on his sensitive wings without waking him. If I hum him to fly, to hide, to hunt, to act alone, to be a team, to unlatch his dangerous claws, to cut, to scrape, to preserve, to return . . ."

"But you didn't hum four dragons to bully a boy-broomist out of the air and confiscate his broom . . ."

"No. And that's the worrying thing. I didn't. How would I know he'd be there? How could I?"

"Well," said Liir, "we're not a moment too soon, are we. But listen: why don't you just hum the dragons into docility? Or make them fly themselves into dead and deadening Kellswater?" Burning letters of thatch drowning in Waterslip.

"I don't think I could. I've always guessed that dragons are, essentially, antagonists. They take to attack more easily than to, say, flying in military formation."

"You could try."

"Not now. Not tonight." Trism cast a sideways glance at Liir. "I wouldn't trust myself to be able to concentrate so intently. One lapse of focus and I'm the midnight snack."

"No, don't try tonight," agreed Liir hurriedly.

Trism threw his military cloak around Liir's shoulders to finish what camouflage they could manage. "On we go, then, and see what happens."

THE SENTRY WAS yawning and ready for his relief to arrive. He was nodding over a pamphlet that looked suspiciously like "The Pieties of the Apostle," the tract printed at Apple Press Farm. Anyway, its arguments must have proven leaden and soporific; he waved Liir and Trism through the guardhouse without a second glance.

At this hour, the yard was largely deserted. Without opposition Liir and Trism circled about to the basilica with the stables beneath.

Since the dragons needed to be stabled, and yet their claws kept honed for precise military use, the stalls wanted constant cleaning. Dragon fewmets tended to corrode dragon claws. But some months before, Trism explained, sloppy stablehands had left behind a bucket of cleansing solvent helpful in disinfecting the floors of their stone stalls. A dragon had lapped up a quart and died in its sleep an hour later.

Several kegs of the germicide, already tapped and ready for dispersal, stood in the cleaning shed. Trism had keys.

Liir didn't want to look at the dragons. The coma he'd been in had blunted the memory of their attack, and that was fine with him. Still, out of his peripheral vision he allowed himself to take in the golden blur, the furnace heat, the sharp ammonia pong of breath and semen-sweet skin, the sound of deep-throated dragon purring.

But the first dragon turned its nose up at the bucket of risk.

"Not thirsty?" whispered Liir, when hearing Trism's report.

"Dragons are smart," said Trism. "That's why they're so trainable. They learn fast and they remember. This dragon may have seen the other die, or smelled his death and associated it with the smell of the cleanser. Maybe if we disguise it somehow."

The first bell after midnight. They had to work fast in order to have time to get away.

"If they won't drink, maybe they'll eat," said Trism at last. "Come on, the provisions cellar is down this way."

Into a chilly storeroom they tumbled. Bricks of ice laid out on slate stones kept the meat cold. At least it was bundled in old newsfolds and tied with string, so they didn't have to look at it closely. The parcels were sloppy, more mounded than squared off, about the size of saddlebags.

"Stop, don't retch," said Trism roughly. "The dragons will smell your stink and be put off their supper. Don't think of this as human flesh. It's the delivery of a necessary medicine, that's all. And may the Unnamed God have mercy on these poor quartered souls, and on ours."

"And the dragons'," added Liir, but now he wanted to see them, wanted to remember that attack, their canny strength. He needed to block out the thought of what they were carrying, armload by armload, up the stairs, but when he could no longer do that—peppery tears an inch thick in his eyes, all of an instant—he steadied himself:

You poor corpse, you thought you had died in vain, selected for slaughter by Chyde. You didn't. You're bringing down the House of Shell. In the most ungodly way, you're doing good. Bless you.

They doused the parcels with the poisonous decoction. As if they were tossing lighted coals into pools of flammable fluid, Liir and Trism dashed up and down the central corridor of the dragon stables, and along the several transepts, and lobbed the midnight snacks over the stout stone-ribbed doors. Those dragons who dozed woke up and ripped the packets open with their teeth. They ate so vigorously that small glistening gobbets of flesh spun in the air.

Only when the last one was done did Liir allow himself to climb up on a bench and look down into a stall.

The dragon faintly gave off its own coppery light. It was working at its meal without hesitation, snuffling with greed. The forearms twisted with a terrifying capacity for grace. The claws retracted, clicked, leaned against one another in efficient opposition, and gleamed a horny blue-silver. Then the creature turned and looked at Liir. Slobber fell from the back of its jaw as it slowed its eating. The intelligent eye—he could only see one—was gold and black, and its iris, shaped more like a peapod than a marble, rotated from a horizontal to a vertical slit, and widened.

He'd been recognized. This was one of the very beasts that had attacked him.

The creature reared up and slapped its heavy wings forward so that its body arced backward, slamming against the rear wall of the chamber. The snout raised and the mouth opened, and bloody teeth moved into position, and a sound issued that was not a bellow nor a snort, but the beginning of a dragon trumpet volley.

"Shit, that's not good," said Trism, grabbing him by the shoulder. "Let's get out of here."

"They're raising an alarm," said Liir.

"They're dying, and they know it, and at least one of them knows why."

⋆ 7 ⋆

Trism and Liir stopped at the top of the landing. In one direction, the stairs continued farther up, to the vaulted basilica proper. The door to the outside, through which they'd come, stood ajar. There was no sound of anyone dashing about to see what, if anything, was wrong. Maybe dragons snorted and bellowed in their sleep all night long, and this was nothing new.

Liir waited. "What?" said Trism.

"I'm not leaving without the broom. I've promised myself that."

"No reason you shouldn't have it back. But we'll have to hurry." Trism fitted a key into the only other door opening off the landing.

"Wait here," he said. "Inside is the stuff of nightmares."

Liir followed him in regardless. In their treason the two men were bound together, at least for the night, and Liir didn't want to lose sight of his accomplice.

The sloped ceiling suggested the long narrow room was a shed appended to the basilica. Probably built low so as not to interfere with the colored windows giving into the sacred space above, Liir thought. Unheated at this hour, the room reeked with the juices of pickling agents and tanning acids.

Trism used a quickflint to light a portable oil lamp. "Keep your eyes down, if you're going to follow me in here," he muttered, shielding the light from the glass chimney with one hand. "The broom is in the far cupboard, and I'll have to fiddle with the lock." He hurried between tall slanted tables on which some sort of piecework was in progress.

"How much danger are we in?" asked Liir.

"You mean in the next five minutes, or for the rest of our short, sorry lives? The answer's the same: lots."

The small light went with Trism toward the cupboard. In the returning shadows, Liir moved nervously and disturbed a pile of wooden hoops about a foot across. They clattered to the floor. "Shhh, if you possibly can," called Trism in a hoarse whisper.

Picking up the materials, Liir listened to the sounds. The dragons below, snorting and nickering, and their wings like vast bellows pumping. The jangle of Trism's key ring, heavy old iron skeletons throttling against the glassy tinkle of smaller jewel case keys. The snap and thrust of a lock being pulled back, and then the rustle of dried sedge and straw. The broom. Elphie's broom. Again.

He had to see it, as Trism turned; he looked up in something like love. Trism had the Witch's cape looped ungainly over one arm, and the broom under his elbow, as he fiddled to close the closet again and lock its door. Then he turned, and held the light up so he could see his way back to Liir. He was smiling. So, too, in a sense, were the semblance of faces that sprung out of the shadows on the inside wall of the chamber. Ten or twelve or so, plates of face: creepy voodoo stuff, Liir thought at first. The scraped faces, repaired with catgut twine where needed, were strung with rawhide cord inside beech-wood hoops like the ones Liir had upset.

"Shhh, will you shush?" said Trism. "I told you not to look."

✦ 8 ✦

SOME MOMENTS LATER, when at Liir's insistence they had finished removing the dozen remnants of human countenance, and had stored them in two satchels, Trism said, "If you're really serious about leaving a note claiming responsibility, now's the time to do it. Can you manage ink and a pen?"

"I know how to write," said Liir. "I didn't go to St. Prowd's, but I *can* write."

"Shut up. I mean, are your muscles shaking too much to control the nib?"

He had to work at it. The third parchment was good enough to serve.

I abducted your craven dragonmaster and aborted his evil work. He will pay for his offenses against lonely travelers.

Signed, Liir son of Elphaba

"Son of Elphaba?" said Trism. "Not *the* Elphaba?" He looked at Liir with a new respect, or maybe it was outright disbelief. Or dawning horror?

"Probably not," said Liir, "but if no one can prove it so, it's equally hard to disprove, isn't it?"

Trism looked at the note again. "Is *craven* overdoing it a bit?"

"Let's go."

"I hope this is only rhetoric, that I'll pay for my offenses."

"You will pay, Trism. You will. We all do. You'll pay, but you won't pay me." He clutched the broom. "You've already paid me."

As they hurried away, the noise rose. The poisoned dragons were falling into fits, roaring, throwing themselves against the walls of their stables. The basilica above shook with it.

· 9 ·

THEY DIDN'T DARE present themselves at an inn or a hotel at that hour of the night, and all of the gates of the City were closed. After skulking about in the fog, they eventually hopped a fence in one of the City's small private cemeteries, and found a lean-to used for wheelbarrows and digging supplies. The mist turned to a thunderous rain, sheeted with weird winter lightning. There, under the cape, they huddled for warmth, and shuddered. Just before they fell asleep, Liir murmured, "No humming, now."

They rose before dawn. Trism had enough coin in his pocket to buy them milky tea and a few cream biscuits from the first street vendor. They argued about the best way to leave the City without detection, but their bravery had subsided. They chose Shiz Gate because the welfare of the Emerald City and the northern province of Gillikin were the most tightly entwined, and the traffic there the heaviest.

Providence provides: that's why it's called providence. They shambled through Shiz Gate by helping an old merchant whose wagon had suffered a split wheel on the cobbles. The sentries at Shiz Gate paid them little mind, deep in gossip of their own about the attack on the basilica the night before. Word of it was abroad already.

Once through, they abandoned the hapless old man in his search for a wheelwright, and ambled north until they came to a high road looping back. Hatless, in civilian clothes, they meandered westward, the gleaming profile of the Emerald City always at their left shoulders. The sun rose, shone for a while, and then became cloaked in cloud. By nightfall they'd reached the outskirts of Westgate. Liir wanted to keep on toward the Shale Shallows, until he could recognize one of the tracks that led southeast through the oakhair forest, between the great lakes, and back toward Apple Press Farm.

But their limbs, by now, would go no farther, so they counted up their coin. As night fell, colder than the one before, they presented themselves at the door of a ramshackle tavern and inn on the main Kellswater Road. A sign reading WELCOME ARMS dangled on a broken hinge from the lamppost. The Gillikin River ran close by, gurglingly, and bare willows hung over it like ghostly harps.

"Oh, there's not much by way of rooms tonight, only two," said the matron, a tall spindly older woman whose unkempt grey hair spilled from her bonnet. "The locals shivareed a new married couple last night, don't you know, so the best room is a mess. I wouldn't put my own disgusting mother in there. They'll pay, that lot, but meanwhile I'm shy of chambers. I don't want to give you the big room, as I often have a party arriving from the City an hour after the close of gates, don't you know, and they pay government rates. Very nice little sinecure for a widow on her own. But up top a'that there's a space not much used. No fireplace, mind, but I'll gift you with extra blankets. You're young and hot and you won't notice."

She rustled them a supper, buckled mutton with a side of tadmuck, stringy and dried out but warm enough to satisfy. Perhaps a bit lonely, she poured them drinks of yellow wine, and kept them company through the first bottle and the second. But then there were horses in the yard, and she stirred herself to her feet, yawning. "It's the trade I was hoping for, so if it's all the same to you, gentlemen, I'll leave you to a good slumber if you please."

They found their way. The flight of steps led only to their chamber. The small room was an architectural afterthought, the result of a failed attempt at dignity, a mansarded cap on the larger guest dormitory below. Cold, indeed. More a storage space with a feather bed in it than a chamber for guests. A tall round-topped, gabled window was set in the middle of each slanting wall.

Liir sat down, weighted with fatigue and a little tipsy, on the edge of a trunk. The thing was felted with dust. They shouldn't have to pay a penny for this attic.

Trism left to wash in the sink on the landing. Liir stared at shadows, seeing nothing. The smell, the sight, the notion of killing dragons—and what would Elphaba have thought of that?

But he wasn't Elphaba; most days he was barely Liir.

He'd gone to get the broom, only, so he could fly for the Birds, ambassador for them. Then they would pay him by looking for Nor—or so they said. How could he identify her? He didn't even know what she looked like after all this time.

Then, he'd done more. He'd murdered the herd of dragons. The Birds would be able to fly free now. He wouldn't need to fly with them or for them: he'd removed the deterrence.

Trism came back. "Asleep sitting up?" Water slicked down the blond hairs on his thighs. He didn't smell sweet and soapy, just less sour. His green tunic, unbuttoned at the neck and released from the belted leggings, was long enough to preserve modesty and serve as a nightshirt. "I think our dame has got the custom she hoped for, by the sound of it. More bottles opening downstairs. Hope they don't keep us awake; they'll be sleeping right under us."

Ratty brocaded drapes, dating from no later than the days of the Ozma Regent, hung thickly on either side of the windows. Liir regarded the four separate glimpses of night: night north, south, east, and west.

"Come to bed," said Trism. "It's freezing."

Liir didn't answer.

"Come on. Why not?"

"The moonlight," he said at last. "It's so—seeing."

"Well, I'm not going to go to sleep until you lie down. Do you think I'm going to turn my back so you can stick a knife in me? I re-member that line: *he will pay for his offenses.*"

"That was theatrical." Liir shuddered. "It's the moon, I guess," he said.

Trism got up and moved across the floor, huffing in irritation. "Para-noia. Very attractive. No one can see in windows this high, Liir. But we'll block the moon for you, then." The sills of the windows were three feet from the floor, and the columnar bulk of the heavy drapes rose six feet higher than that. Trism said, "Move, you," and nudged Liir off the trunk, which he dragged to the first window. From there Trism climbed to the windowsill, his clean bare feet pawing in the grit and dust for purchase.

He reached up. The curtains hadn't been shifted in decades, and they resisted. He grunted. The light of the moon fell on his ear tips, his lift-ing shoulders as his fingers just grazed the center of the curtain rod and walked their way east and west toward the edges of the drapes.

"Oh, company," he said. "Those horses in the yard—five of them. They've got the Emperor's caparisons. This is a soldiers' sleepery."

"Welcome Arms. I suppose it figures." Liir came up behind to look. As Trism stretched, the shirttail lifted above his shapely rear. Liir reached out and settled his hands there, to support Trism should he fall, for the ledge was shallow and Trism's balance precarious. Trism made a sound in his throat.

He managed to dislodge the first volute of brocade an inch or two, and a colony of blue moths, the size of penny blossoms just going by, is-sued forth and settled upon them both. A thousand pinches without fingers.

The brocade shifted some more. The drapes were cut from an old tapestry design. Once pink and yellow and rose, it was now the color of dirt and ash, but the ravaged faces of society charmers still peered out through threaded expressions. Moths are the death of brocade potentates and hostesses, pavilions and rose arbors and islands in some impossible sea. Moths eat such faces alive. The faces of living humans they merely explore, and the peninsulas of their forearms, and the promontories of their breastbones, and the shallows of their tympanic chests, which when heard close up thunder too loudly for moths to notice.

"Right," whispered Trism hoarsely.

"Come on," Liir answered. "We have to be quiet. Maybe these soldiers aren't looking for us. Maybe she's too drunk to remember we're here. There's no way out, anyway. Not till they're asleep, at least."

"We could jump out the window into the river."

"Too late for that; we've already jumped. Anyway, I'm going to jump you now. Come on, to bed. It's just the next part of history, right? If we're going to be found, we might as well be found out."

✦ 10 ✦

DESPITE THEIR EXHAUSTION, they hardly slept. They clung to each other, making the least possible noise, and when it got too much to bear they buried their faces in pillows. Spent, at least briefly, they dozed, and Liir's last thought was: sleeping with the talent. A dragon mesmerist, of all things—what magic a body is—all that you couldn't know about the world packed up tightly in the flesh lying on your breast.

All the things Ansonby and Burny had known about—not about girls, but about people—how they felt when they were closer than clothes could ever be. How secret, still: how still, and secret. But a connection nonetheless, dared and decided: a new way of knowing, new burning letters falling through the air—and the words that could be spelled weren't all disastrous.

At last, in the deadest part of the night, they crept back into their clothes and braved the staircase. From the larder they nicked a hock of ham, and from the pasture by the river's edge they nicked two horses. Trism's way with dragons, it seemed, had suggested to him a language for comforting horses, too.

They led the horses away by the river's edge, where the noise of the water would afford the best cover. A mile out, Trism showed Liir how to climb into the saddle. Liir had never ridden before. "I'm not sure tonight's the best night for this lesson," he said. "Ow."

"It's the next part of history. Now, where are we going?"

"Are we going together?"

"We seem to be. For now, anyway."

Liir shrugged. "We've got to cross the Gillikin River and keep Kells-water on our right. South through the oakhair forest." As far as Apple Press Farm, he thought, but he didn't want to say that yet.

"I don't know these parts, but if we're crossing the river, let's not wait for a bridge. We'll ford it here where we can, and confound the soldiers if they come looking for their rides."

The moon was nearly down, but there was enough light for the horses to pick their way safely across the water. They gained the far bank, which rose to a prominence. Looking back, the fellows could see the Welcome Arms they'd abandoned. From here, with its smaller second story, it looked like a lopsided old boot.

"The Boot of the Apostle," said Liir.

"The Apostle only wears sandals, to judge by the graphics advertising that exhibit. That Apostle Muscle exhibit."

They rode till dawn, though at a safely slow pace, keeping to well-worn tracks. Gradually the sky lightened, cheerless and without bold character, the look of molasses dissolving in milk. They hoped a wind would arise to shift the scratchy snow and cloak their tracks, but it didn't.

By the time they could see their own breath in the cold dawn, they had reached the edge of the Shale Shallows. They could begin to move faster. They were now apparent to each other again, though in the daylight it was harder to meet one another's eyes. They didn't talk much.

Siege

SISTER APOTHECAIRE WAS drying her hair with a towel when Sister Doctor rushed into the ablutory. "He's back," she said.

Sister Apothecaire did not need to ask who *he* was. "With the girl?"

"No. With a boy. Well, a young man, I mean."

"Do up my veil snap, will you, Sister? I'm *hurrying*."

Along the stairs, they met Sister Cook. "Famished the both, malnourished the one, perhaps, though I'm not a doctor, being only the cook," she reported. "They're both deeply into their third helping of sausage and beans. The Superior Maunt is waiting in her chamber."

Indeed she was. Her hands were composed upon her lap, and her eyes closed in prayer. "Forgive me, sisters," she said when they came forward. "Obligation before devotion, I know. Won't you sit down?"

"We hear that Liir is back," said Sister Doctor. "We should like the chance to see him."

"To inspect him. To meet with him."

The Superior Maunt raised her eyebrows. Sister Apothecaire blushed. "I merely meant that it would be useful in our professional practice to know what the cause of his peculiar ailments actually was.

Likewise we are quite in the dark as to the treatment Candle applied that helped him to recover so."

"Of course," said the Superior Maunt. "And I'm eager to know as well. But I have other responsibilities this morning. The unexpected arrivals are breaking their fast in the refectory, I believe, but I have made an appointment to counsel our other guest in the small chapel. I don't believe I should break my appointment with her. So you will conduct the interview jointly and report to me."

"Yes, Mother."

She dismissed them, but then called after, "Sisters."

They turned.

"In women of your age and station, it is unseemly to pelt so. The young men will not have left."

"Pardon us," said Sister Doctor. "But of course the last time we hoped to find him, he *had* left."

"He hasn't asked as much yet, but I believe he's requesting sanctuary," said the Superior Maunt. "I'm afraid he won't be leaving very soon. You have time. Practice continence in your expression of enthusiasm."

"Yes. Indeed. Quite."

"You may go."

They stood there. "Go!" repeated the Superior Maunt wearily.

She closed her eyes again, but this time not in prayer. The new winter was approaching. Another winter in the mauntery of Saint Glinda. Fires that would not warm her papery skin. Fruit that would grow mealy in the larder. Increased agitation among the maunts, for when there was less work in the gardens there was more gossip and bitchery in the sewing compound. There would be new leaks to repair, and ague would knock a few of the old ones into the grave. She wondered if it would be her turn.

She couldn't hope for this. She didn't hope for it. But the rewards of the winter season seemed richer in her childhood memories, back before she had these tiresome women to govern—the silly affectations of Lurlinemas, which even professed maunts in their strictness remembered with pleasure—the spectacle of sunlight staining birch shadows into the snow like laundry blueing—the way snow fell up as well as down, if the wind had its way—of course, the way birds returned, stitching the spring back into place by virtue of melody.

It was the gardens of her girlhood she remembered most, the earliest blossoms. Jonquils and fillarettes and snowdrops, perfect as the Dixxi House porcelain bibelots that had adorned her mother's dressing table. She had not seen a fillarette in years, except in her mind. How sweet it was to regard!

She prayed for strength to last the winter out. These days, though, she rarely got into the fourth line of a beloved old epiphody before her mind skipped back through some pasture or garden walk of her youth.

Attend, she barked at herself, and stood with difficulty. The cold was already at work in her joints. She creaked as she readied herself for the morning conversation. Noting the raggedness of the face flannel with which she wiped her brow, she hoped that the mauntery's guest might have come to propose a sizeable donation. Or even a little one. But this was beyond what the Superior Maunt thought it was proper to pray for, so she didn't spend her prayer in that direction.

Wisdom is not the understanding of mystery, she said to herself, not for the first time. Wisdom is accepting that mystery is beyond under-standing. That's what *makes* it mystery.

THE FELLOWS WERE NEARLY KEELING OVER into their coffee cups. "You've had no sleep, you've been riding all night," said Sister Doctor, disapprovingly. "It's a dangerous track at best, and foolhardy to venture upon if you don't know your way. Have you come from the Emerald City?"

"We've been round and about," said Liir.

Sister Doctor explained that she and Sister Apothecaire had briefly tended to Liir when he'd been brought in by Oatsie Manglehand, the captain of the Grasstrail Train. "Have you any recollection of that?" she pressed.

"I know very little about anything," he said. "I'm useless, pretty much."

"Any more cheese, d'you think?" asked Trism, draining his noggin of ale.

"You were here for weeks, I'm afraid," Sister Doctor remarked to Liir. "Without the ministrations of our community you should certainly have died."

"Perish the thought. I'm alive, for what it's worth."

"What Sister Doctor is trying to ascertain, in her skittery way, is how Candle did it," interrupted Sister Apothecaire. "She was mute as a lilac, and seemed not overly canny. Yet she managed a miracle with you."

"Professional curiosity requires us to ask how," inserted Sister Doctor.

"Professional jealousy requires it, too," admitted Sister Apothecaire.

"I don't know." The boy had a private look. "In any event, I wasn't consulted."

"Oh, she leached him, she took a lancet and bled him, she sucked his poison out, and a good thing, too," said a biddy on a bench nearby. They hadn't noticed her there.

"Why, Mother Yackle!" bellowed Sister Doctor in a matronizing manner. "Aren't you the chatty one today!" She shared a wrinkled expression with Sister Apothecaire. The dotty old thing. Ought to be in the solarium with the other silly dears.

"She's got a good instinct, that Candle," said Yackle. "The oafs are pleasant enough to bed, in their way, but it takes a daughter of Lurlina to draw out the milk only boys can make . . ."

"Shame and scandal on the house," said Sister Apothecaire. "Gentle-boys, forgive her. You know, their minds wander at that age, and the sense of propriety wobbles ferociously."

Liir turned to look at the woman. Her veil was pulled forward, but the splayed nostrils of her long rude nose showed. "Are you the one who directed us to the farm in the overgrown orchard?" he said.

"She never!" said Sister Apothecaire. "Liir, she's yesterday's potatoes, and mashed at that. Don't pay her any mind."

In a low voice, almost masculine in gruffness, Mother Yackle replied slowly, "I mind *my own business.*"

"Of course you do," said Sister Doctor.

"But if I were you, I'd send those soldiers' horses packing," continued Mother Yackle. "You don't want them found on the premises, I'd warrant."

Liir shrugged, then nodded.

"Look," said Sister Doctor, "this isn't the place to talk. Finish up, lads; we need to have a heart-to-heart."

But Trism had fallen asleep against the back of his chair, and Liir's eyelids were lowering as they watched. There was nothing for the maunts to do but show them to the cots in the guest quarters, and find blankets, and retreat.

• 2 •

LIIR, NEARLY ASLEEP, tossed his body back and forth on the lumpy straw of the bedding. It was as if he had been here before.

Well, he had, but in a feeble enough way. In childhood he'd been more aware of the hems of Elphaba's skirts, of the food in the wooden bowls. An awful lot of oatmeal mush. And more recently, he'd been broken and mindless, wandering his past in a feverish state. Even the night he and Candle had left the mauntery, and she had helped him move, as good as carried him on her back down the stairs, nearly, the halls had been dark. He'd collapsed into the donkey cart and slipped almost immediately into a real sleep, a sleep of fatigue and not one of voyage.

That was his first apprehension of Candle, he remembered. A slip of a thing with the strength and willpower of a pack horse. She'd been mostly naked, and Mother Yackle had thrown a cloak over her shoulders. Here in the mauntery again, Liir tried to lean into that recent memory, the way he had learned to steep himself in other memories. Maybe there was something yet to be understood about whether he'd actually slept with her, impregnated her . . . even more, whether and in what ways he might love her.

Now—a thousand difficult lonely miles away from Trism, who snored a yard to the east—Liir turned over, facing the wall. Candle was a cipher to him, sweet and elusive, and the memory was frail. There was nothing more he could unpack from it, nothing useful. To distract himself, in his heart and memory he walked about and examined the hull of the mauntery, doing a kind of spectral surveillance.

The place betrayed its origins as a gardkeep. It was a fortified house, here on a slight wooded rise, an oasis of trees in the Shale Shallows. The ground floor had no windows, and the front door was reinforced with iron bracing. Behind, the kitchen looked out on a greasy moat crossed by a simple drawbridge. The vegetable plots and cow barn were beyond.

The mauntery would afford little protection in a siege. The place was tall and, at this stage in its history, unsecurable for very long. In any effort to gain unlawful access, a modern police force might be slowed, but it wouldn't be stayed.

Still, at least a few cows could be swept into the parlor, and hay stacked up under the stairs. The fruits of the harvest crowded the shelves and larders, and the garde-manger was bulbous with blood sausage, dried muttock, and nine varieties of salami, to say nothing of cheeses. There was a mushroom cellar and a bin of desiccated fish fragments. And plenty of wine, and that wonderful rarity in a rural establishment, an indoor well.

In his dreams he checked the cupboards for rifles, he blew through each room to look for wardrobes that could be pushed against windows. He did not see the Superior Maunt asking questions of her esteemed guest about the payout schedule of a proposed beneficial annuity. He didn't see Mother Yackle nodding in her own morning nap in the sunlight. He didn't see nor overhear Sister Doctor and Sister Apothecaire squabbling gently in their shared cubicle about how they ought to proceed. The rooms were empty of novices, maunts, guests, spiders, mice, bedbugs, and any presence of the Unnamed God that he could determine.

What he saw, in the topmost room where he had lain, was a figure on a rush-bottomed chair, sitting away from the light, twisting her hands. Her dark hair was looped up on her head with no regard for neatness or propriety, just to get it out of the way. Her eyes were closed, but he didn't think she could be praying. He didn't know what she was doing. At her feet was a largish basket woven of twigs. He didn't look into it; he couldn't. Every now and then her shoeless foot would nip out from beneath the dark hem of her skirt and give the basket a little push, and because of its rounded bottom, the basket rocked for a time. Then the green foot would appear again, and start the rocking over.

HE WOKE WITH A START. It was sharp noon, and the house smelled of warm leek-and-cabbage eggery for lunch. Trism was still asleep, his hair rucked back against the pillow. The sound of cantering horse hoofs grew louder. Liir wanted to kiss Trism awake, but had the notion that the time for that was already over.

He did it anyway. Trism groaned, and made room, and after a while said, "We don't do this sort of thing in our circle."

Did he mean his class at St. Prowd's? His family? The Home Guard? Didn't matter. Liir replied, "Well, your circle seems to have widened, hasn't it."

"Or shrunk," said Trism, reaching for his boots.

◆ 3 ◆

"THEY'RE LOOKING FOR TWO MEN," said Sister Doctor.

"Indeed," said the Superior Maunt.

"One is said to have kidnapped the other."

"Our guests appear to be on a more familiar footing than hostage and abductor, don't you think?"

"Well—yes."

"So tell the soldiers we haven't seen the men they're seeking, and bid them good day."

"The thing is," said Sister Doctor, "they're said to be quite dangerous, these fellows. In an act of desecration, they imploded the Emerald City basilica of the Emperor by causing combustible dragons to—combust."

"How dreadful. I don't think our two look very dangerous, though.

Underfed, if you ask me, and perhaps undecided in their emotions, but not dangerous."

Sister Doctor came back. "I've been told that one of the two they're seeking is named Liir."

"I see. Well, tell them he's not here."

"Mother Maunt. I question your—propriety. Is that not a lie?"

"Well, if one of the two that they seek is named Liir, one is *not* named Liir. So answer in reference to that one, and say he's not here."

"That is devious, Mother Maunt."

"I'm old and muddled. Put it down to that, if you must comfort yourself," she replied sharply. "But I'm still in charge, Sister, so do as I say."

Sister Doctor came back a third time. "They are more explicit. The Commander says that they are seeking Liir Thropp, the son of the Wicked Witch of the West."

"As I live and breathe, Sister Doctor! You extend more respect for my authority than is useful. Need I come up with every rejoinder? Are you never to think for yourself? To the best of my knowledge it hasn't been conclusively determined that Liir is the son of the witch. So, again, since we cannot answer for certain that the person they seek is here, they must conduct their searches elsewhere. Give them my blessing and tell them to hurry, or do I have to come and do it myself?"

Sister Doctor yelled the message out the windows of the scriptorium. The Commander called back, "If you're not harboring felons, why are your doors blocked?"

"Spring cleaning."

"It's early winter, Sister Thudhead."

"We're behind schedule. We've been dreadfully busy."

"Busy harboring criminals?"

"I hate to be rude, but I've work to do. Good-bye."

By late afternoon the thud of stones against the door had become intolerable, and the Superior Maunt herself came to the window. The armed contingent had to interrupt the attack in order to hear her quavery voice.

"It's an inconvenient time to come calling," she said. "For one thing, ladies in community tending to have their menses together, you find an entire household of terribly cross and uncompromising people. We're not up to housing a garrison of soldiers, however rudely they pound on our doors. Please go away at once."

"Mother Maunt," said the Commander. "This household received its original charter from the Palace, and it is with the authority of the Palace that I come and demand access. Your studied resistance proves you are harboring criminals. We know they stayed at an inn last night, and they cannot have come much farther than here today."

"Matters of authority are perplexing, I agree," replied the old woman, "and I would love to stand here in the icy wind and discuss them fully, but my ancient lungs won't stand it. Our original charter, by way of our motherchapel in the Emerald City, does comes from the Palace, I'll concede. But I'll remind you that the Palace in question was the Palace of the crown of Ozma, many generations back, and in any instance we have earned the right to self-governance."

"The Palace of Ozma is long over, and it's the Palace of the Emperor that comes calling now. He is favored by unionist acclaim, and by dint of his apostleship you are under his bidding."

"He is a parvenu Emperor, and he does not speak for the Unnamed God to me," she cried. "And unless he asked for it, no more would I speak of the Unnamed God to him. I reject his expedient and proprietary faith. We stand here on our own chilblained feet, without apology and without genuflection."

"Is this an indication that the Mauntery of Saint Glinda has endorsed and even overseen the publication of recent treasonous broadsheets attacking the spiritual legitimacy of the Emperor?"

The Superior Maunt made a most uncharacteristic gesture.

"That's hardly an answer the courts would recognize. Good Mother Maunt," came the reply, "let us not distract ourselves with the luxury of theology—"

"For me it is no luxury, believe me—"

"I know the boy you are harboring. I met him when he was only a boy, at the castle of Kiamo Ko in the Kells. When fate brought him in my path again, not once but twice, I suspected he had the makings of a firebrand in him. I made it my business to convince him of the rightness of the Emerald City cause. He might have knowledge of Elphaba, or of her missing Grimmerie. I named him my secretary in Qhoyre. I promoted him. I fathered him as best I could. Now listen: he was not Elphaba's match. He could not be her son—too docile and biddable. But he should give himself up regardless. He has kidnapped a soldier of the Emperor and destroyed the basilica of the army."

"Commander," replied the Superior Maunt, "you can save your breath. And you can put down those archaic crossbows or whatever you're readying. We've got company that it would be unseemly for you to disturb."

She turned and beckoned. A figure appeared at the window and lowered a shawl off her forehead. The glitter in the eyebrows stood out in the falling light. Commander Cherrystone made a gesture and the men dropped their weapons as the Superior Maunt intoned, "The widow of Lord Chuffrey, Oz's former throne minister, making a religious retreat to the mauntery that bears the same name that she does. Lady Glinda."

• 4 •

A NOVICE OPENED THE DOOR for Liir and pointed him into the simple paneled parlor, and closed the door behind him without a sound.

"I was told you were in the country," said Liir.

"But I was," answered Glinda. "I am. I had intended to travel from Mockbeggar Hall, our—well, my—country house to come make a bequest to this mauntery. Lord Chuffrey has left me quite wealthy, you know, and I thought it time to help the women in their good works.

"But when my under-butler arrived last night on horseback with news of the attack on the basilica, I decided to change my schedule and come here straightaway. I have a commitment to this house, and I wanted my new bequest registered before there was any move toward disestablishment."

Her glamour was all the more ridiculous and appealing in this setting. "It's good to see a familiar face," said Liir.

"I suppose I shouldn't be surprised to find *you* here. After all, Elphaba was here for a while, you know. It's one of the reasons I like to
support it."

"I know she was."

"She tended the dying."

"And the living," he said, remembering his dream of the basket.
"I'm sorry about your husband."

"Oh, well." She waved her hand dismissively but then dabbed at her
nostril with a scrap of lacy roundel. "We largely went our own ways; it
was that kind of a marriage. Now he's gone his own way for good. I miss
him more than I would ever have let on while he was alive. I suppose I'll
get over it."

She cheered up almost instantly. "Now tell me about you. Last I remember, you were marching off to Southstairs to find some little friend
or other. I lost track of what happened. Well, there was the court to
manage, and various putsches to suppress." She regarded him. "No, I
suppose it was ruthless of me to forget about you as soon as you left. I've
never been good at keeping up with people. I'm sorry."

Liir remembered that he had momentarily hoped for Glinda as a
mother. He pushed the thought aside. "You know the Emperor," he
said. "None other than Shell. Elphaba's younger brother."

"Wouldn't she be surprised to know her brother had succeeded the
Wizard!" She looked rueful.

"Surprised," said Liir. "That's one way to put it."

"Well, yes. She'd be outraged. Piety as the new political aphrodisiac.
I suppose that's what you mean."

He shrugged. "What someone would feel after she's dead—that notion means little to me. She doesn't feel. All that's left of her—shades
and echoes, and fading by the hour."

Glinda closed her breviary with a little slap. She hadn't been attending closely to her devotions anyway. "That pesky slogan you see scrawled
everywhere is right. She does live, you know. She does."

Liir snapped at her. "I have no truck with that kind of sentiment. All butchers and simpletons 'live' in that sense."

Glinda raised her chin. "No, Liir. She lives. People sing of her. You wouldn't guess it, being you—but they do. There's a musical noise around her name; there are things people remember, and pass on."

"People can pass on lies and hopes as well as shards of memory."

"You refuse to be consoled, don't you? Well, that's as much proof as *I* could ever need that you're kin to her. She was the same way. The very same way."

• 5 •

THE SITUATION, the Superior Maunt concluded that evening, was decidedly unsettled. Scouting from the highest windows in all directions, the novices reported that several dozen armed horsemen showed signs of making camp in the Shale Shallows. They'd broken into the kitchen gardens and rooted about in the shed for squashes and such. "It seems unfeeling not to provide them with a meal," said the Superior Maunt, "but I suppose that might give the wrong impression."

Liir and Trism asked for an audience, and she sat with them on a bench at the base of a flight of steps. "We can't have the house put in danger on our behalf," said Liir. "Between Trism and me, while working in the Home Guard, we've been responsible for enough loss of life. We didn't know the dragons would explode. We didn't intend to bring down the basilica. We don't know if there was human death in that catastrophe. We want to do no further damage, if we can help it. We shall give ourselves up to them."

"Since it may ease your minds on that score, I will tell you that I heard of no loss of human life in the collapse of the basilica," said the Superior Maunt. "It was midnight, after all. The place was deserted, even the side sheds and storerooms that escaped being crushed by falling debris. I suspect, however, your foes imagine the basilica was your real target, and the death of the dragons—how do they term it these days?—collateral damage. As to your suggestion that you should turn yourselves in, let me take it up in council before you make your decisions."

"What is council?" asked Trism.

"I don't know. I'm going to find out," she replied.

THEY GATHERED IN THE CHAPEL, the only room in the mauntery large enough to hold all inhabitants and guests. Evening devotions usually occurred on a basis of rotations, some maunts handling kitchen washup or geriatric babysitting while the rest sank into quiet prayer or early nap. Tonight the Superior Maunt requested the attendance of all, even those retired maunts like Mother Yackle who were on the edge of gaga.

Lady Glinda, though a benefactress, refused a seat on the dais up front, and she had removed her trademark diamond strutted collar for a quieter linen ruff. Liir and Trism, unfamiliar with these traditions, stayed standing. The older maunts were escorted in, in wheeled chairs when necessary; the novices took their places on their knees until the Superior Maunt indicated they should sit. "This is not prayer," she said. "Something like it, but not prayer, precisely."

She sat herself down, with difficulty. After a short silence, Sister Hymnody offered a provocatory in plaintone, though her sweet bell-like voice quavered. They were all on edge.

"Sisters, mothers, friends, and family. I shall be brief. Our tradition of charity, reinforced by our vows, brings us this evening into a conflict none of us has anticipated or experienced before. However generous the tithe of Lady Glinda, I doubt it will rebuild this house should the army of the Emperor sack it.

"We are a small house, a mission post on the road halfway between our motherchapel in the Emerald City and the rest of the world. Our isolation has been the cause of loneliness, at times, but also promoted peace and protection. Perhaps even provocation—but I pass over that. Tonight we are neither isolated nor peaceful. It is a truth we must accept.

"I am an old woman. I was raised as a novice in the venerable practice of obedience. Under the rubric of our order I followed instruction, including the one that required me, years ago, to take charge of this mauntery and govern it until death.

"I still believe in obedience. Even while soldiers camp outside our walls, and quite likely call for reinforcements, I must be obedient to the wishes of the powers that placed me here.

"As I speak these words, my dear friends, I hear in them an echo of the Emperor's remarks. He professes subservience to the highest aims and intentions of the Unnamed God. God is the mouthpiece and the Emperor is his striking arm. The First Spear.

"I have not met the Emperor, and I will not. I should decline an invitation were one offered. The Emperor has hijacked the great force of faith and diverted it to further the prosperity and dominance of the City. Who can argue with a man who has the voice of the Unnamed God speaking exclusively in his ear? Not I. I have never heard such a voice. I have only heard the echo that still reverberates, once the Unnamed God stopped speaking and the world took up with itself.

"In our house, we profess to believe that the Unnamed God has made us in its likeness and its image, and this should have enlarged us to be like the Unnamed God. I fear in the Emerald City, they have remade the Unnamed God in their image, and that has belittled and betrayed the deity. Can the Unnamed God be belittled, you ask. No, of course not. But the deity can go unrecognized, and return to mystery."

The sisters shifted. Many of the novices were ignorant of the Emperor's apostasy, and the shoals of theocracy were beyond their ability to navigate. The Superior Maunt noticed.

She stood. "Bring me two other chairs, one at my right and one at my left," she said. This was done.

"The Unnamed God retreats into mystery, and is not especially localized in my heart, my dears. Nor in the Emperor's. The mystery is as equally in your heart as in mine, and in . . . the spirit of the trees and the . . . the music of water. That sort of thing. In the memory of our elders. In the hope for the newborn.

"I break with the tradition of our house tonight, as the decisions now to be made involve your lives as well as mine. I am old; happily I would go to my sweet reward this evening were it provided me by a literal spear of the Emperor. I cannot ask the same of you. Therefore it is my wish that henceforth the mauntery—even if our residency here lasts only till dawn—shall be governed not by a single voice, but by a troika of voices. Were the disagreeables not outside our walls, I should invite your opinions and call for a ballot. Time prevents me from allowing that. In extremis, our family of maunts shall accept the leadership of three. Sister Doctor, will you rise to the chair?"

Sister Doctor gaped. She grasped Sister Apothecaire's hand briefly, and moved forward. Sister Apothecaire trembled and moved to the edge of her seat, perching for approach.

"I shall take the second seat," said the Superior Maunt. "I may be old, but I'm not dead."

The room was so still that the sounds of horses whinnying and stamping outside carried through the cold.

"The third chair I am reserving for the novice known as Candle," declared the Superior Maunt. "I have a notion we shall see her again. For how long, I don't know. But we need the wisdom of age, the strength of the fit, and the initiative of the young. From this moment forward, my absolute command over this establishment is dissolved. I shall enter it so in the Log of the House before I retire. Now, let us see how we get on."

Sister Apothecaire bit her lip and tried to feel more humble than humiliated.

Skirts rustled as the women shifted. Faint whispering, unprecedented in the chapel, sounded, like faraway wind. The Superior Maunt dropped her forehead into her fingers and breathed deeply, feeling that the world had changed utterly, and wondering how quickly she would regret this action.

In the stillness, Lady Glinda stood. Reticence not being her usual thing, she'd had about enough: and anyway, hadn't the Superior Maunt called for a collaborative spirit? "If I may speak," she began, in a tone that implied she knew she could not be denied, "even if the army breaks through the defenses of this mauntery, they cannot do you good women much harm. There will be no bloodshed or rape here. Not while I am in house. Make of it what you will, even though I am retired from what passed for public service, I am still seen as a friend of the government. I have the ear of every society power monger in the country. The army knows well enough they cannot abuse you while I am a witness—and they will not touch me. They daren't."

She added, "I am Lady Glinda," in case some of the younger novices hadn't cottoned on yet.

"It isn't the girls that are wanted," said Sister Doctor. "It is the boys."

"Don't underestimate what people in the throes of passion may do," said the Superior Maunt. "Our rectitude means little to the world beyond our walls, and the commitment of our lives is as cheap as throwaway grain on unuseful margins of field. Still, Sister Doctor, you are right. The army seeks two young men, but they do not know for sure that they are here."

Liir said, "I do not think the broom would carry two, but Trism could climb to the ramparts late at night, and fly to safety. That would leave only me, and whatever fate I have earned, I should face it by myself."

The room grew decidedly chilly. "So the rumors of the broom are true?" said Sister Doctor. The Superior Maunt took in some breath wetly at the corners of her mouth.

Liir shrugged but couldn't deny it. From the side, mad Mother Yackle called, "Of course the rumors are true. The broom came from this very house. I myself gave it to Sister Saint Aelphaba years ago. Am I the only one concentrating enough to know this?"

She might, an hour earlier, have been hushed, and the Superior Maunt began to speak. But Sister Doctor raised her hand and stayed the Mother Maunt's comment, and remarked, "You've been quiet for a decade, Mother Yackle, but of late you've come back to yourself somewhat. Have you anything to add we should know?"

"I don't talk when there's nothing to say," said Mother Yackle. "All I have to add is this: Elphaba should be here to see this hour."

"You have an uncommon association with—the Witch of the West."

"Yes, I do," said Mother Yackle. "I seem to have been placed on the sidelines of her life, as you might say, as a witness. I'm mad as a bedbug, so no one needs to attend, but I've taken some measure of her power. Oh!—but she *should* be here to see this hour."

"Mother Yackle? A guardian angel?" called Sister Apothecaire.

"Well—a guardian twitch, anyway," replied the old woman.

Liir trembled and thought of his lack of power, once again, and of his revery within these walls. Now he remembered what he hadn't seen before: that in the corner of the room where the green-skinned novice had sat rocking the cradle, a broom leaned against a chest of drawers.

"Are there other remarks?" asked Sister Doctor.

Shocked somewhat by the developments, the maunts muttered quietly, but no one else spoke until Sister Apothecaire stood and said, "Mother Maunt, I would like to applaud you for your courage and your wisdom."

Tears ran suddenly from the old maunt's eyes as her house, to a person, stood and paid their respects. Outside, the horses shied and the men started at the sudden rain of noise from the chapel windows.

THE BROOM, THOUGH, wouldn't carry Trism. In his hands it was no more than a broom. "I lack the proper spunk, it seems," he said.

"Maybe it has lost its power," said Liir, but in his own hand the thing leaped to life again, bucking like a colt.

"We might be able to manage a sleight of hand with only one man to hide," said Lady Glinda. "After all, as you pointed out, they are looking for a pair of you. Perhaps Trism could be passed off as my bodyguard. It was unlike me to have ventured here without a bodyguard, after all, though I did. Sometimes I like to confound even myself," she explained. "It isn't difficult."

"If the men who hold us under siege recognize Trism from the barracks at the Emerald City, he will be put under arrest," said Sister Doctor.

"Well, I used to be good at makeovers," said Glinda. "And I could do magic with a blush brush. He's got big shoulders for a maunt, but he's pretty enough, and a little peroxide on the facial hair, which is so conveniently blond—" She tossed her own curls. "Well, I never travel without it."

"I think not," said Trism in a steely voice.

"Then we'll have to take the chance we can pass you off as my servant," said Lady Glinda. "Liir will leave tonight, on the broom, and tomorrow morning I shall ride out with Trism at my side, and make no explanation. If you choose then to open your doors to the soldiers, they will find nothing untoward here. I shall wait outside your gate as an obvious witness until their search is completed. If they are that hungry for blood, they will not dally here but rush on elsewhere."

"But where will you go?" the Superior Maunt asked Trism. By now they had retired to her office, and she was sagging against the worn leather of her chair.

Liir looked at Trism. As much as could pass between them in a look, without words, passed: and another moment of possibility crashed and burned.

"If Trism can get through, he should try to find Apple Press Farm," said Liir. "He might smuggle Candle to safety elsewhere. The Emperor's soldiers are headed vaguely in that direction, and the site has been discovered and ripped up by thugs and vandals at least once already. It seems to have been used as a clandestine press for the printing of antigovernment propaganda."

"Yes," said the Superior Maunt modestly, "so I've been told."

"For you, I would try to find that farm," said Trism. "And I will take the scraped faces, that they not be found here when the army does its ransack."

"As for me," continued Liir, "I've learned something from you." He looked at the Superior Maunt, who was tending to nod. "I promised to try to complete an exercise, and I did this much: I helped rid the skies of the dragons that were attacking travelers and causing fear and suspicion among the outlying tribes. I will finish my work before anything else happens. I should let the Conference of the Birds know that, for now, they are free to gather, to fly, to conduct their lives without that undue threat. With the help of the Witch's broom, and unimpeded by dragonfings, I can manage that shortly.

"Beyond that," he said, "I have other scores to settle. I set out years ago to find Nor, a girl with whom I spent some childhood years."

"But, Liir," said Sister Doctor, "the Princess Nastoya is expecting your return."

Liir started. "I had assumed she'd have died long ago."

"She's been trying to die, and trying not to die, a complicated set of intentions," said Sister Doctor. "She mentioned you, Liir."

"I don't know what I can do for her. I do not have Elphaba's skills, neither by inheritance nor by training."

They sat silently as he worried it out. "In the choice of what to do next, I'm troubled. On the one hand, you say the Princess Nastoya is old and suffering and wants to die."

"Yes," said the Superior Maunt wearily. "I know the feeling."

"On the other hand, Nor is young and has a life ahead of her, and perhaps it is a greater good to help her first, if I can."

They waited; the wind soughed a little in the chimney.

"I will return to Princess Nastoya," he told them. "I know I won't be able to help her to sever her human disguise from her Elephant nature. I'm not a person of talents. But if I can give her the loyalty of friendship, I'll do that."

"You would help an ancient crone over a disappeared girl?" said Sister Doctor. Her sense of medical ethics flared.

"Young Nor found her own way out of Southstairs," said Liir. "Whatever else has been done to her body or her mind, she clearly has spirit and cunning. I shall have to trust that her youth will continue to protect her. And maybe she doesn't need my help now—though I won't rest until I know it for sure. Meanwhile, Sister Doctor, you say that the Princess Nastoya has asked for me. Ten years ago I made a promise to try to help; I owe her my apologies if nothing else. And if I can report conclusively to the Scrow that it was not the Yunamata who were scraping the faces of solitary travelers, I may be able to help effect a treaty of faith between the two peoples."

"Is it hubris to aim for such a large reward?" asked Sister Doctor.

"No," said the Superior Maunt, her eyes now closed.

"No," said Liir. "The Superior Maunt has shown me that tonight. If we share what we know, we may have a fighting chance. This house, as a sanctuary, may survive. The country, and its peoples, may survive."

"The country," said the Superior Maunt. Her mind was sliding sleepward. "Oh, indeed yes, the country of the Unnamed God . . ."

"The country of Oz, be what it may," said Liir.

In a semblance of a toast to hope, they raised imaginary glasses of champagne, as the Superior Maunt began to snore.

SOMETIME LATER THAN MIDNIGHT, Sister Apothecaire showed Liir and Trism to an attic. A window gave out conveniently to a place where two matching peaks of roof on either side sloped together to form a valley between them. Corbelling protected this section of roof from the view of people on the ground.

Sister Apothecaire said, "Sister Doctor mentioned your intentions to me, Liir. I'm glad to have the chance to add what Sister Doctor forgot about. The Princess gave us a message to give you—but of course you had disappeared by the time we got back. She said something about Nor and the word on the street about her. I don't recall precisely, but she has something to say to you."

Liir reached inside the Witch's cape. In the interior pocket, he felt for the folded-up drawing of Nor by her father. He winced at the memory of the childish writing—the chunky downstrokes, the blocky uncials. *Nor by Fiyero.*

Sister Apothecaire wrapped Liir's cape the more tightly around his chest to make sure it wouldn't flap and draw undue attention as he tried to make his escape. She tucked extra loaves of bread and a parcel of nuts into his lapels, and bade him Ozspeed. Then she retreated to give them privacy for their good-byes.

"Neither of us may make it, you know," said Trism. "Before noon tomorrow we may both be dead."

"It's been good to be alive, then," said Liir. "I mean, after a fashion."

"I'm afraid I got you into this," said Trism. "I saw you on the ball pitch and thought I would take my revenge on you. I didn't mean this much revenge—either that you should die, or that we should part like this."

"I was looking for you, too, sort of—you just saw me first," Liir answered. "It might have been the other way round. Anyway, what does it matter? Here we are. Together a moment longer, anyway."

After a while, Trism managed to say, "Are you sure you can fly in this condition?"

"What condition is that? I've been in this condition my whole life," Liir answered. "It's the only condition I know. Bitter love, loneliness, contempt for corruption, blind hope. It's where I live. A permanent state of bereavement. This is nothing new."

They kissed each other a final time, and Liir mounted the broom of the Wicked Witch of the West, and felt it rise beneath him. He did not look back at where Trism stood. He had few talents, did Liir, and while flying a broom was one of them, he wasn't practiced enough to risk breaking his neck.

His other talent, though, was a distillation of memory into something rich and urgent. He guessed, in the hours or years remaining to him, he would remember the effect of Trism clearly, without corruption, as a secret pulse held in a pocket somewhere behind the heart.

The exact look of Trism, though, the scent and heft of him, the feel of him, would probably decay into imprecision, a shadowy form, unseen but imagined. Hardly distinguishable from an extra chimney in a valley formed by pantiled roofs of a mauntery.

The Eye of the Witch

center

◆ I ◆

FLYING AT NIGHT.

He kept low at first, scarcely twice the height of the highest trees. The winds tunneling beneath the cloud cover were ill-tempered, as if out to tumble him. Below, the oakhair forest twitched in the winter gale, looking like the pelt of a great beast lumbering along for midnight rendezvous with sex or supper.

Then the clouds thinned, and the air grew colder still. He remembered more of the attack by dragons than he wanted to—it kicked up a sick feeling. He couldn't manage much more height than he'd achieved so far. Still, with a quick flip of his head left, right, he could make out the southernmost cove of Kellswater and the bay where the Vinkus River debouched into Restwater. From this vantage both lakes looked hard and dead as slate.

He crossed the dark line drawn by the Vinkus River. Now he was halfway to Kumbricia's Pass, which meant that Apple Press Farm was somewhere below. How was Candle faring? He thought of pulling down and seeing.

You could, he said to himself. Now you needn't worry about scaring

center
◆ 293 ◆

her, for if you show up in the middle of the night, she'll be ready: she'll have divined the present and sensed your approach, and prepared the tea for your arrival. And the blankets, and the fire, and the bed, though you're not ready yet to go to her bed again, even chastely.

But no, no, he continued—no. What if she was with someone else? Or what if she'd left? Or what if Commander Cherrystone recognized Trism and arrested him, and tortured him into revealing Liir's hiding place—and thence discovered Candle? And kidnapped *her*—as he had done Nor all those years ago!—as a kind of reprisal against the slaughter of the dragon contingent, the ruin of the basilica?

Liir was learning to think in terms of consequence. He gave due credit to the strategies and devices of the Emperor. In any case, though, concern for Candle would distract Liir from completing his mission, as he had promised her to do. Let Trism get there safely and see to her needs, if he could, if he would. Time enough for me to show my sorry face and find out what's going to happen next.

For now, he would finish what he'd started: at least this much.

He might have caught sight of the farmhouse roof winking, or he might be miles and miles off. He didn't know, and it didn't matter. He kept his eyes trained on the foothills of the Great Kells, which from this height were already beginning to swell, less an actual shape than a shift in the grade of shadow.

The wind strengthened as it rushed down the eastern slopes of Oz's mountainy spine. He lost speed, and it took more effort to keep the broom on course. Like riding a horse in a raging river, he imagined, now that he had some experience of horseback riding under his belt, as it were. Finally he had to come down to earth entirely, from exhaustion. He found a shepherd's summer lean-to, abandoned for the season, and stretched out underneath the cape and fell promptly asleep, the broom between his arms and along his chin like the boniest of lovers.

At dawn, the winds relented, and the mountains burned in pink-ish light. He finished the small meal provided by Sister Apothecaire and pressed on.

Kumbricia's Pass was defined by a color of evergreen specific to the suspended gorge that widened apronlike as it dropped toward the Vinkus River plain. How foreboding the uprights of the cliffs on either side—how much more fortress the landscape provided than Liir had been aware. No wonder the Yunamata, the Scrow, and the Arjiki had never knuckled under to the industrial strength of Gillikin or the military might of the Emerald City. And no wonder the dragons had been an im-portant development—they would have had to work to flap their way along this wind-chased passage, but they would have managed. If the dragon population had expanded, and a whole fleet of them had become available for maneuvers, they could have rained destruction even upon the distant populations of the widespread Vinkus.

And might yet, Liir knew. The strategic knowledge that had devel-oped those dragons into weapons wouldn't have been lost because Trism defected or the basilica collapsed. If nothing else happened, it was only a matter of time before another Trism came along to do the bidding of his superiors and raise up perhaps an even mightier army.

Yet today had dawned, and tomorrow could not be foreseen. No magician in the world had yet mastered the art of prophecy, so far as Liir knew. Not a single venerable bishop with his channels to the divine, nor any tiktok mechanism of subtle apprehension, nor even the best-taught sorcerer with the keenest of inner eyes, had ever accurately foretold so much as whether the rain would hold off for the picnic. It was Time Yet to Come that possessed the strongest force of all, a magic mightier than the Kells themselves, a magic greener than all of green Oz. Inscrutable, terrifying, and exhilarating at once.

♦ ♦ ♦

HE FOUND HE COULD NOT FLY above Kumbricia's Pass. His broom bucked to one side or another, as he'd heard a horse instructed to cross a risky bridge might do. He didn't know whether this was mere exhaustion, a flagging of his will, or some sort of wizardic or magnetic obstruction he didn't understand. He allowed himself to drop, by a series of long, scalloped declines, till at last he found landfall in a clearing, and continued his voyage by foot.

It took time to locate the spot where he had been interviewed by General Kynot, the crusty old Cliff Eagle—the island in the hanging tarn. The place seemed deserted. He could see nothing but random feathers and the inevitable mess of droppings. Maybe they'd moved on to a cleaner lobby somewhere.

On foot he continued west, losing track of time. One of the drawbacks of flying on the broom was that his nose became frozen, and the air at a certain height, while clean of grit, was also curiously scentless. Kumbricia's Pass, by contrast, was a festival of odors.

In the nest of the cape, he settled for an afternoon nap and didn't wake up until dawn . . . and he wasn't even sure it was dawn of the next day, or some day further on.

Nonetheless, he was rested at last, rested in a deep way, and better able to spy winter berries in the thickets, and chichonga pods, and the occasional scatter of walnuts on the ground. Dozens of streams leapt from either side of the great gorge and crisscrossed, occasionally islanding the floor of the pass into hillocks. He didn't go thirsty. He felt that the longer he pressed on, the stronger he became.

At last Kumbricia's Pass made its final abrupt turn before opening out above the beautiful bleak expanse, as far as the eye could see, of the rolling prairie known as the Thousand Year Grasslands. In the shallow caves and along the ledges of the westward face of the Kells, nearly deafened by the constant wind, Liir met up with what remained of the Conference of the Birds.

Their numbers had dwindled in the short time since Liir had left Kumbricia's Pass. When General Kynot spied Liir standing there—so much for the vigilance of their sentries!—he lop-winged over and indicated, with a strict jerk of his head, that they should retreat into the gorge for a bit of a chin-wag.

A few Birds saw the General's intentions, and braved the buffeting winds to join the colloquy. Several dozen gathered, including the Wren named Dosey, who cued in the blind, hobbledy Heron.

"We see you've reclaimed your broom," began the General without formality. "I'm to understand it is not functioning as a vehicle for flight anymore, or you wouldn't have come on foot. And you would have come sooner."

"I came as quickly as I could," said Liir. "What's happened?"

"We've lost half our number," said the General, "or near to it. The Yunamata rushed us, and since we were scared to take high wing, we were caught in a series of nets and traps they'd erected across a narrow part of the Pass. Scarcely a one of us hasn't lost companion or kin."

"That's not like them," said Liir. "Or not like their reputation. They're a peaceable people."

The General glared at Liir. "We've had to leave the Pass, lest it happen again. We're cornered against the sky up here, on display to preying dragons, and without adequate supply of grubs and worms."

Liir said, "I'm sorry about the Yunamata attack. That's the Emperor's strategy—to keep his foes busy nipping at one another. That has to stop. There's no way to survive without our making peace among ourselves."

"Begging your pardon, sir," shrilled the Wren to Liir, and the General was too dispirited to bother correcting her terminology. "One population can't make peace with another by force."

"There are possibilities," said Liir. "The time of the dragons is done, at least for now. You can fly again. *We* can fly again. And before the next threat might come, we have to maneuver ourselves into . . . a coalition. No, not that: a nation."

"Which nation is that?" snapped the General.

"Witch nation!" tittered a Dodo. "I likes that, I do."

"You called a Conference about the raiding skirmishes of dragons," Liir reminded them. "The dragon fleet has been destroyed. But those dragons were a tribe, too: ill-used, malevolent, raised up to strike out, imprisoned by their training. It gave me no joy to poison a dragon, even one that has attacked and killed your kind and mine. Yet the moment is here to fly again. Not just home, not just yet: but fly into the storm. The Emperor has already sent out a guard to hunt me down, and he and his ilk will hardknuckle anyone who gets in his way. No one in the Emerald City can stand up to him, for he claims the divine right of the elect—not elected by people, but by the Unnamed God. Who can dispute that? We are all elect, for here we are, and we must fly for our lives. We must show ourselves to be a company. He sent dragons to scare the skies: we will fly ourselves as a flag right back at him."

General Kynot pretended to peck at his chest for vermin. When he raised his head, his eyes were dry again. "It is not easy to trust the wisdom of a human person," he admitted. "Like so many humans, you could be lying. Leading us into a trap. Promising us freedom, and tricking us into an ambush of yet more dragons. Yet we have so few choices but to trust. After all, you are the son of the Witch."

"Don't base your decision on a false premise," said Liir. "I will never know for sure who my parents were. And even if I did, the son of a witch can be as wrong as anyone else. Let us fly because you are persuaded we should, not because I say so."

"I vote yes," said Dosey.

"So do I," said the Heron, "though I can't fly anymore, of course."

"I didn't *call* for a vote," said Kynot.

"That's why I voted," Dosey replied.

"Witch nation! Witch nation!" said the Dodo.

THEY LAUNCHED AT NOON, maybe ninety Birds, swooping westward into the buffeting winds that ran the span of the prairie to build up enough strength to crash against the Kells.

The venture almost scattered them at once. The Wrens tumbled like husks of dried pinlobble; the Ducks shat themselves silly; the Night Rocs couldn't see in the widest daylight Oz had to offer, and nearly brained themselves by wheeling backward into the peaks.

Liir was giddy and vertiginous. The broom shot out over a rocky sward, so low that he could make out the surprised expressions of wild highland goats. Another instant and he was fifteen times higher than the highest tower of Kiamo Ko, and a silver river winked in the sunlight below him, narrow as a bootlace.

Just fighting to stay together took the better part of an afternoon. When they finally reached air space beyond the forested foothills, above the nearest start of the endless grassland, where the power of the wind diminished, they settled to rest and feed and count their number. Four of their ninety had been lost in the first descent out of Kumbricia's Pass.

But there were grassland grubs and beetles, and the backwash of mountain rills to splash in, so they made their first encampment.

IT TOOK A FEW DAYS of rehearsal for the Night Rocs to learn how to maneuver by daylight, but the Grasslands were forgiving. After hours of uninhibited flight, with no dragons approaching, the Birds grew braver and flew in a looser formation.

For the time being they avoided other populations, though far below them they delighted in the spectacle of wild tsebra wheeling and cantering in their winter migration toward the south, a flurry of black and white markings against the brown ground, an alphabet in the act of writing the story of tsebra migration. Or notes, singing a mythic history.

Draffes, their long tawny necks swaying, saluted them in their high-pitched voices. Liir couldn't hear them, but Kynot said that evening that sentient Draffes were living among draffes, in apparent harmony.

A small band of Vleckmarshes flew up to greet the flying Conference (Kynot would not allow the Birds to call themselves Witch Nation, despite the Dodo's pleading). At the sight of Liir on the broomstick, the Vleckmarshes made common cause with the travelers, and flew alongside.

Then a bounty of Angel Swans, who usually kept to themselves out of pride for the whiteness of their mien, gave wing. So too a noisy clot of Grey Geese, who were wintering together on the banks of a nameless broad winter lake that appeared and disappeared in different places every year, they said.

The Conference flew in waves, the bigger birds working harder, providing a breakfront against the wind, the smaller birds in the slipstream, and lower, in case of attack by air. It was Dosey who spotted the tents of the Scrow, arrayed in the usual geometric precision against the trackless blanket of earth.

Liir did not want to approach the camp, not yet. But General Kynot, agreeing to serve as an emissary, dove out of formation and whipped around the camp until he could decide which tent belonged to the Princess Nastoya.

That night, the Conference having settled under a shelter of windthorn hedge, Kynot reported to Liir.

"I found one who could speak to me, an old scholar named Shem Ottokos," said the General. "I told him you were abroad, but he said he didn't need me to tell him that. He had been able to make you out with his naked eye, because the cape unfurls so blackly against the scrim of the evening. He had the tent lifted for his queen to see, and though she is mostly blind now, she said she could make you out against the sky. He thinks it was the clot of the Conference she was seeing, its whole mass. She wants to see you, said Ottokos. She has something to tell you. Whether you can help her or not."

"If she agreed to meet me later, she can tell me then," said Liir. "Did she?"

"The Scrow rarely travel during this time of year, and they haven't settled any peace with the Yunamata. Ottokos does not know if he can convince the tribal elders to pull up camp and brave Kumbricia's Pass. He doesn't know how to talk to his people about this. But I explained about the extermination of the dragons. Perhaps Ottokos will be persuasive."

"If Princess Nastoya still has time, we have time," said Liir. "It is her time that we need to read, not ours."

NORTHWARD, BEATING AGAINST THE ICY WINTER gusts known in some circles as the Farts of Kumbricia; northward and northward, and the Thousand Year Grasslands went white under drifts of frost. The snow was lipped and patterned by the wind into shapes like the imbricated scales on a fish. Now out of sight of the Kells, now back; now joined by a throng of Snow Geese, five hundred strong, now by a mystic Pale Crane, her partner, and her senile though quite energetic mother.

At last, because the smaller Birds feared freezing to death, and the food stock grew scarce, the Conference wheeled eastward. Kynot had a notion that they could most safely cross the Kells again at the point where the Arjikis had built their mountain villages. If nothing else, there would be the chance of a barn in which to roost, or a bonfire around which to warm themselves. It was rough work, though. Once more suffering the churning of wind against the hard breast of the Kells, the Conference sought a lower altitude, which took more time but afforded quicker shelter should a storm come up.

The weather was with them, at least. Day after day the sky was peerless blue, if pinion-quaking cold. Under snow squalls or rain clouds the Conference would have fumbled. But they always had the chance to move on: this kept the smaller birds brave.

They came at last to the highland valleys and white wastes of the Arjiki stronghold of Kiamo Ko. Liir did not care to alight there, but the nights were drawing in earlier and earlier, and he had no choice but to see it as a blessing.

His rump sore, and almost unable to uncurl his spine from the arched position in which he flew, he landed on the cobbles of the courtyard with 220 of the smaller Birds, while the larger ones waited formally outside for an invitation. The monkeys shrieked, though whether it was out of terror or welcome, Liir couldn't tell. Chistery met him at the top of the steps to the main hall.

"I suppose you've asked me, for old time's sake, to join you," he said. "I'd come if I could. But I don't think my wings are up to it."

"You can't have had news of our intentions," said Liir.

"You're a message, that's all," said Chistery. "No one can watch you raveling and unraveling up the columns of mountain air without knowing you intend to be seen. I'll tell you, my heart was in my throat though, as you came nearer. I thought to myself, It's Elphaba herself."

"No, it's only me," said Liir. "How's Nanny?"

"Past her prime. For the fourth decade in a row, I'd say. She's having a sandwich of egg and dried garmot. Do you want to go up?"

"I suppose I'd better. May we stay here?"

"You needn't ask," said Chistery, slightly hurt. "Until someone else comes to claim it, the house is yours."

Nanny sat up in bed, looking gently at her bread crusts. When she saw Liir, she smiled and patted the bedclothes. "Don't worry, I won't wet," she said. "I've already gone."

"Do you know who I am?" asked Liir.

"Ought I?" She didn't sound worried about it. "Is it Shell?"

"Decidedly not."

"Good. I didn't like Shell very much." She held out the pieces of bread. "I saw the Birds coming, and I saved them something from my lunch."

"That's nice of you."

"Actually, the bread was a bit stale. But maybe they won't notice. It's nice to see you again, whoever you are. Just like old times." She patted his hand. "I never could tell what was going on then, either, but now I don't mind so much."

"Nanny?"

"Hmmmm?" She was beginning to drift off to sleep.

"Did you ever hear of someone named Yackle?"

One eyelid of Nanny's cocked open. "Might have done," she said warily. "Who wants to know?"

"Only me."

"Days a lifetime ago are clearer to me than today. I don't even know what sex I am anymore, and I can remember what I got in my Lurline-mas basket when I was ten. A tin cannikin full of colored beads—"

"Nanny. Yackle."

"I met someone named Yackle once," said Nanny. "I always remembered it because her name reminded me of jackal. Like the jackal moon, you know."

"Where?"

"She had a little commercial enterprise, if you call it that, in the Emerald City. The Lower Quarter, downslope of Southstairs, if you know where that is."

"I do."

"I went in to have my tea leaves read and to ask a question about Melena. Your grandmother."

Liir didn't bother to correct her.

"Yackle was an old crone without much time left, I'd guess. But she still had talent. She gave me a few words of advice, read me the riot act about my petty filching, and told me Elphaba would have a history. Can you believe it!"

"How did she know about Elphaba?"

"Silly. I told her, of course. I told her Melena had given birth to a green daughter. I bought whatever Yackle could provide as a corrective agent to ensure the second child didn't come out green. And she didn't, did Nessarose. Neither did Shell. Only our Elphie. A history! Can you believe that?"

"Must be a common name."

"Yackle, you mean? Don't know about that. Never heard it again. Why do you ask?"

"Do you think Elphaba will have a history?"

"She does already, ninnykins! I just saw her flying up the valley as large as a cloud. Her cape went out behind her, a thousand bits in flight. Nearly touched the peaks to the left and the right. If that's not a history, what is?"

CHISTERY SAW HIM OUT. "You're welcome here anytime," he said. "This is your house."

"She always loved you best, you know," said Liir, grinning as he laced the braces at the clasp of the Witch's cape.

"Considering what she was like, is that a compliment or an insult?" replied the Snow Monkey. "Fly well."

BY THE TIME THEY NEARED the Emerald City, half a month later, the Conference of the Birds was six thousand strong. They'd had to slow down as they grew larger, for fear of midair accidents, but east of the Kells the winds were less harsh. As the Conference crossed the Gillikin River, coming into sight of the smart little villages and spruce knolls and brick factories and millhouses of the rolling Gillikin tableland, its shadow grew more definite by the day.

Liir had no intention of attacking the Emerald City. The Birds were not warriors, and the Conference, or Witch Nation, wasn't military in makeup. Liir didn't want to see Shell, nor the Lady Glinda, assuming she had returned to take up residence in her Mennipin Square town house for the winter season.

He only wanted that they should be seen.

It was nearing evening when they approached the walls of the City from the north. The sun was sagging against a few distant scraggly clouds, heading pinkly for its rest, and then it disappeared behind the horizon. The western sky would remain glassy bright for a half hour yet.

As workers clocked off at the Palace, as the boulevards were thronged with people heading for supper, and as the indigent went to their own work of begging for coin against starvation, the Conference wheeled into place. Anyone looking north at the display of Birds, from the inn called Welcome Arms on the banks of the Gillikin, say, would read only cloud: an invasion, a plague, a disaster. The same impression struck those looking, from the northwest of the city, at the Birds swimming like an ocean away from them.

From the Emerald City, though, from every west-facing window of the Palace, the intention was unmistakable. The Conference of Birds had rehearsed to perfection. They flew in formation for viewing from the east. They were the Witch, hat and cape, skirt and broom, shadowy face tucked down against the wind, but beady-eyed bright. Liir, on his broom, followed General Kynot, whose superior navigational system gave him his location. Liir on his broom played the keen black eye of the Witch.

Was Shell there, wondered Liir, knuckles on some marble windowsill, Lord High Apostle Muscle himself, Shell Go-to-hell Thropp, First Spear, Emperor of Oz, Personal Shell of the Unnamed God? Did he lean forward and squint at the holy ghost of his remonstrating sister, and rub his eyes?

Six thousand strong, they cried in unison, hoping that the echo of their message would be heard in the darkest, most cloistered cell in Southstairs as well as the highest office in the Palace of the Emperor. "Elphaba lives! Elphaba lives! Elphaba lives!"

Raising Voices

◆ I ◆

THE CONFERENCE HAD GROWN too large for a single speaker to address it. On the morning it disbanded, therefore, two delegates from each species met with General Kynot and his loose affiliation of ministers, which included the Wren, the Dodo, and the most aggrandizing of the Grey Geese, a gander who had appointed himself.

Liir was invited, too. He asked the birds to keep an eye out for Nor. "You go everywhere, you see everything," he said.

"We stay clear of humans when we can," replied the Grey Goose, "present company accepted. Pro tem."

"It's probably futile," Liir agreed. "Still." He walked about with the drawing of *Nor by Fiyero*. "She used to look like this. She's older by now, of course."

"All people look alike to me," murmured a Vleckmarsh.

"She's simply beautiful," said the blind Heron.

"Well, thanks just the same," said Liir, tucking the paper away.

The General gave a rambling address that confused everyone, including himself. "To conclude," he conceded, "we go on to new work. The Birds run a risk of reverting to behaviors less than helpful. Now, I don't mean to besmirch the fine Ostriches from the Sour Sands, who because they don't fly were not part of our Conference. But we all know what Ostriches are rumored to do when faced with a crisis. We must not retreat into our claques and clans. Wary of human settlements—yes, who wouldn't be? Let's not be stupid about humans. But wary of one another? A little less so, if we can manage."

"And a little more chatter amongst us," added Dosey the Wren. "In ways we are only beginning to understand, we are the eyes of Oz."

"When can Witch Nation have a reunion?" asked the Dodo. "This was fun."

"The boy-broomist must go and make his own nest. And I?—off and away to my family," said the General. "The wife, you know, and there was a new clutch of eggs last spring. But there are the families of those Birds who were heinously trapped and slain by the Yunamata. Those families should be contacted, if we can figure out how."

"I'll take care of that, sir," said Dosey.

"You take care of yourself, missie."

"Should this be an annual event?" asked the Dodo. "Ought I be taking notes? I mean mental notes, at least?" But the General had lifted himself onto the hump of a sudden, warmer breeze, and whatever he answered over his shoulder could not be heard in the cheer that went up to bid him good-bye.

◆ **2** ◆

Liir didn't ask the Grey Goose for company, but the Goose followed along behind. It was a problem. The Goose was too regal to be servile, and too beautiful; he made Liir feel like a chimney sweep who hadn't seen a bath in a month. The Goose called himself Iskinaary.

They flew from the southern edge of the Emerald City and headed straight out across Restwater, keeping east of the isthmus between the lakes. If the mauntery of Saint Glinda had been torched, Liir didn't want to know about it yet.

Where the Vinkus River seeped along flat-bouldered steps into

Restwater, they stopped to get their breath, and they surprised a fox out of a clump of wrestlebush. The fox dove at Iskinaary and wrenched his wing, but Liir clobbered the fox with the broom, and the fox let go. His wing drenched in blood, Iskinaary shed unashamed tears at his disfigurement. Closer examination proved that the damage was, indeed, slight. Nonetheless, if they were to proceed together, they'd need to go on foot.

"I don't mind a chance to give my legs some exercise," said Liir.

"That's the most disingenuous thing I've ever heard," said Iskinaary. "And it's not as if you have particularly handsome legs."

"They walk faster than yours do, I've noticed."

"If you want to walk faster, you'll have to carry me."

Iskinaary was heavy to carry, and for all his beauty he still smelled very much like a Goose. Still, Liir didn't mind that the trip would take a little longer. So much had happened. A chance for reflection was welcome.

He was returning now, having accomplished something at last—a set of dragon murders, regrettable, but there you go. He was eager to know how his accomplishment would fit in the house. What he and Candle would be like together now. He had no experience of a happy return, ever. He would hardly know what to say, where to smile. He hoped that not knowing might seem wonderful.

He knew more about human warmth, too, from Trism. How that knowledge would translate in the presence of Candle was a puzzle to anticipate with excitement.

When they reached the Disappointments south of the Vinkus River, it was sunset, and the cold dusk made them shiver. But there was evidence of the tiny flower known as Shatter Ice—four little bluets in a nest of the tiniest emerald leaves—which meant the hump of the winter had been passed, and spring, however long it took to arrive, had started on its way.

ISKINAARY'S WING HAD MENDED a bit—not much—by the time they approached the series of wooded knolls in which Apple Press Farm was hidden.

"You're not planning on staying and becoming domesticated, I assume," said Liir. "I mean, it'd be fine to see you, umm, swanning about our meadows, but I can't expect that would give you anything approaching professional satisfaction."

"I have my own ambitions," said Iskinaary. "I'm intelligent as well as gorgeous, you know. Leave it to me."

"To be more specific," said Liir gingerly, "I'm not necessarily inviting you to take up residence with us permanently. No hard feelings."

Iskinaary shrugged, as much as a Grey Goose could shrug. "Makes no difference to me what you say," he replied. "I wasn't waiting for an engraved invitation. I'll follow my own instincts. We Animals still *have* instincts, you know."

"Touché. And your instinct is?"

"To keep my own counsel."

They entered the woods, slopping through mushy hillocks of drifted snow. "And, being instinct rich, Iskinaary, have you any opinion what *my* instincts are?"

"You're not untalented," said Iskinaary, overlooking the slight sarcasm in Liir's tone. "You're even rather smart. For a human. You keep excellent company."

"Yourself."

"Exactly. Furthermore, from what I've observed, you have a talent for reading the past."

"What does that mean?"

Iskinaary honked. "What it sounds. There are very few who can read the future. And you've mentioned this Candle of yours can read the present. But reading the past is a skill in and of itself. It's not just knowing the past. It's feeling it. It's deriving new strength and knowledge from it—learning from it all the time. It's my own guess that this was intended to be the great strength of human beings, when the Unnamed God came up with the notion of you. Sadly, like so many good ideas, it hasn't quite worked out in practice."

"Thank you very much."

"No insult intended."

"I didn't know you believed in the Unnamed God."

"I was speaking metaphorically. I assumed you'd get that. Is this the place you're looking for?"

It was. The low roofs of the dependences, and the main structure of the house itself, and the big barn room in which the broken press presumably still stood. Perhaps it could be made to work again.

They came the long way around, to approach from the open meadow by the front door. There they found that Liir's invitation had been accepted. Nine tents were erected in the meadow, as perfectly aligned as the casual ramble of the fences would allow. Eight subordinate tents made a square, and the Princess Nastoya's tent stood centrally.

With her canny ways, and for all the advance warning of this contingent of Scrow, Candle ought to have known he was coming. Nonetheless, she seemed surprised. Surprised, and flustered, large and slow, even redder of face than her natural coloring suggested was possible. Perhaps blood pressure problems? Or had she been experimenting with native rouges?

He approached her cautiously—as if she were a young novice, not a farm bride. He took her hands and held them, and found out that even now he didn't know how he felt. "I've flown the world," he said.

"Welcome home from the world." Her face was tucked down, as if she were shy. A new shyness.

"Candle," he said, "has the fellow called Trism come here?"

She looked up at him from under a wrinkled brow. "He said you'd ask for him. I couldn't be sure of him; he seemed a soldier of some sort. Well, now you've asked, and right off. Though I'd have thought you'd enquire if I was all right first! All these guests, and me in this state!"

"Of course—of course. But I can see you're all right. And I don't know if Trism survived."

"Well, he did," she said, summarily. "Oh, Liir," she continued, her voice now sounding as if he'd only been gone an hour, and she'd missed him for sixty full minutes, "look what's happened, and I wanted to greet you on our own." She spread her hands at the meadow.

"I know," he said. "I invited them."

"I'm glad you finally arrived to greet them, then. They've been here a week, and my careful larder is just about bare. The one older fellow speaks a rude sort of Qua'ati, but I can't make out a thing from the others."

The Scrow were trying to brew a kind of tea out of the bark of apple trees and such sap as was running in the maples. They wrinkled their noses at it and hardly seemed to notice Liir's arrival.

"In the family way, I note," said Iskinaary pointedly, slipping into Qua'ati effortlessly, "or are you just big-boned, my dear?"

Indicating the Goose, Liir said to Candle, "This is my . . ." He paused; the word *friend* seemed inappropriate.

"Familiar," supplied the Goose.

"Oh, please!" said Liir. "Is *that* what you're on about?"

"Don't mind me, I'll just settle here with the stupid hens," snapped Iskinaary.

"I'm not a witch, nothing near!" said Liir. "You're going on the grossest sort of hearsay."

"Get on with your task, and I'll be the judge," said the Goose. He shifted about three inches to one side and turned elegantly still, which gave him the effect of being statuesque while allowing him to eavesdrop with impunity.

Liir picked up Candle's hands again. He wanted more from her, he willed it so. She let him thumb her palms for a moment, then she pulled her own hands away.

"So Trism got here unharmed?" he said.

"The dragon master? He did," she said, her face turned away again.

"Where is he?"

"He couldn't stay."

Cautious. Gentle step, here. "Why not? Candle?"

She began to lift a huge urn of water from the table in the yard; he took it from her.

"Candle. What happened? Was he all right?" Suddenly Liir had no trust: not in his own apprehensions of Trism, nor of Trism . . . nor even of Candle. Trism, after all, had once wanted to kill him. "Did he treat you poorly?"

"This water needs taking out to the Princess," she answered. "She's being laved round the clock. I've been preparing it with essence of vinegar, as that priestly prince instructed me to do."

"What happened? What passed between you and Trism? Candle!"

"Liir. What could pass between us? He didn't speak Qua'ati. And I could understand what he chose to tell me, but not answer him—I don't speak that bossy a tongue. I have a small voice, a half-voice. As you know."

In succession, Liir thought a half dozen crises. She knows I loved him. That I love him. That he loves me? That he loves her?

That she loves him?

What was this verb *love* anyway, that could work in any direction?

Did he hurt her?

"Candle. I beg of you."

"Don't beg," intoned Iskinaary, standing on one foot. "Remember General Kynot. Don't beg. Never beg."

"We'll talk later," she said. "Now, if you'd take that water to your guest? And then you'd better do what you came here to do."

"I came here to be here! With you."

"And this band of ragamuffins who preceded you? They are, what? The relatives?"

Tears pricked his eyes. "Don't be preposterous, and don't be mean! I've been away, Candle. Doing what you asked. Getting something done. Anything. Learning where I wanted to be."

"I have my bad moments," she admitted, wiping her own face. "It hasn't been easy. Let's not talk. Go straight to work, and help that old sow if you can."

"She's an Elephant."

"Whatever the beast she is."

"Candle!"

"I didn't mean it like that. Liir, you startled me. Carrying this child is hard work. I haven't been myself."

He could see that.

"Did Trism leave parcels for me?"

"Two packets in the press, hanging on strings from the ceiling, to keep the mice from them. The mice are very interested. Are you going to haul this water to the invalid, or shall I? I have other work to do now. Washing. The old woman runs through a dozen towels a day."

She picked up a basket of wet laundry and wobbled outside to an old apple tree, where she began to sling the clothes on drooping branches to dry. She's hurting, he thought: even I, dull as I am, can see that. But from what? My long absence? My affection for Trism? Or is the child inside her making her sick, draining her blood, eating her liver from within, kicking her pelvis sore with its ready heels?

• 3 •

HE WASN'T UP TO DEALING with Princess Nastoya yet, and the Scrow seemed to have settled in nicely. Hell, she'd been dying for a decade, she could die some more for another ten minutes before he finally had his reunion with her.

Stung by Candle's reticence, he wandered into the barn to retrieve the parcels. If Trism had gotten them here safely, then he must have managed to elude Commander Cherrystone. Glinda's glamour had worked once again, and riding at her side as her factotum, Trism had played the shadowy manservant, a known quantity. He'd been smuggled out of the mauntery safely.

But what had happened here? Had he followed Liir's directions and found Candle in residence, beautiful and reticent and large with child? Had Trism resented the notion of a Candle? Had he been stung by the fact that Liir had never mentioned her pregnancy? Had he assumed Liir was the father?

Had Trism been cruel to her?

Liir took down the parcels, struck by the thought that the workings of the human heart could be as various and imperturbable as the workings of human communities. He didn't know enough of love in all its forms to compare, to choose, to sacrifice, to regret. Held in Trism's soldier arms, he'd been strengthened; held in Candle's loving regard, he'd been strengthened, too. Now the only thing holding him was Elphaba's cape. Was her mantle of penitential solitude to be his, too?

He wiped his eyes and opened the parcels. In the slanting light through the barn door, he wheeled out the hoops of face. Now that he knew what they were, they seemed less grotesque—no less terrible than a drawing or a dream of someone. A flat disc not unlike a mirror. They'd had lives, these people, as puzzling as his. No one would ever know what those lives were like, though.

"Well," said Iskinaary, who'd followed him in, "as I live and breathe. Is this what they mean by a human shield?"

"They're the faces of the dead."

"You're in here studying them, when you have a dying woman out there in a tent, waiting for your attention?" Iskinaary was incensed.

Liir looked at them, shaking his head. From the distance he heard the first few notes of a melody. Candle had taken down the domingon again. Whom was she calling with it? The baby within her? Come out, come out? Or Liir himself, stuck in his indecision, his confusion?

"I'm quite an expert at music, as I have perfect pitch. Unusual in a Goose," said Iskinaary. "She's got a way with that instrument. She could play the eggs right out of a mama Goose."

"I heard her encourage the yard animals to sing," said Liir. "I mean really sing, not just bray and cackle."

"Singing lightens the load," said Iskinaary, who looked about ready to deliver an aria himself. He cleared his throat. But Liir suddenly snatched up the hoops from the ground and turned on his heel.

"If she can be persuaded," he said, "maybe she can help the load lighten. She's so weighed down herself—but she's a kind person. What a good idea!"

"Thank you," said Iskinaary, his feathers ruffled. Denied an audience, he hummed to himself in a desultory fashion, but shortly thereafter he followed Liir to find out what his good idea had been.

Liir introduced himself to the man called Lord Ottokos.

"We've met before," said Shem Ottokos, "though since then, you've grown up and I've grown old."

Liir explained what he hoped Candle might do. If she would.

Shem Ottokos seemed to find nothing peculiar in the proposal. "Your wife is very kind, even in her heavy condition, and your husband seemed equally kind."

"She is not my wife, and I have no husband," said Liir. "Indeed, I have no talent except the idea for this. And I do not know if it will work."

"I will tell the Princess Nastoya that you have arrived," said Ottokos. "She is in grave distress, and it is hard for her to talk anymore. But I believe she is still able to hear and understand. I must believe this: it is my job."

Liir took the scraped and treated faces of the dragons' victims into the orchard, faintly budding already, though the ground was still wet with old snow. He hooked the thirteen hoops upon notches of apple tree branch, as near to body height as he could guess each one had required when attached to a living body. The damp sheets and toweling fluttered like liquidy limbs beneath.

✦ 4 ✦

SHE PUT ASIDE her domingon when he approached and asked her for her help. "Don't do it for me," said Liir. "Do it for her."

"I'm already doing laundry for her," said Candle. "I have no more strength."

"You know people and you know kindness. Your music sang me back to life. You have that skill. It's called knowing the present. You could make the barnyard sing. I only ask that you know the present of Princess Nastoya, and play her constituent parts to their own places."

"You think like a witch. I am not a witch, Liir."

"I am not a witch and I am not thinking like one. I am trying to learn from history. I am trying to figure out what happened in the past, and work to use that knowledge again. You played in my past, and brought me my life. Perhaps you can play her death to her."

"I don't feel well." She rubbed her eyes with her forefingers. "Frankly, I haven't been sleeping. I don't know that this pregnancy is going as it should, but there's no one to ask."

"You don't feel as badly as Princess Nastoya does."

"Liir!"

He caught her at the elbow. "Tell me what happened!" he said roughly. "Tell me what happened with Trism!"

"Leave me be, Liir," she said, crying, but when he gripped her arm harder, she said, "He told me to come away with him. He said whoever had followed the two of you so far would not give up that easily. He said the mauntery would be burned, and its members tortured until they disclosed the whereabouts of this satellite operation. Oh, don't look at me like that. Of course the maunts know about this place! Why else would Mother Yackle have sent us here? Or the donkey know the way? Think, Liir!"

"He told you to leave with him?"

"He said I should go with him, for protection: that it is what you would want me to do."

Liir was stunned. "Why didn't you do it, then?"

"I trusted you," she said, a little abrasively, "how do I know whether to trust another soldier? He could have been abducting me to kill me and my child. He could have been lying. He could have been doing it to hurt you. Though now I see he meant more to you than I reckoned."

What he heard mostly was her possessive pronoun: *my child*. Not *ours*.

"And he didn't stay," said Liir, in a voice nearly as small as hers.

"No, he didn't," she answered. "Generally, people don't. They come, they go. He left. The Scrow came. For all I know your Commander Cherrystone will be here in time for tea, and Mother Yackle for the washing up."

· 5 ·

THE SCROW RETINUE carried the Princess into the orchard and set her down on a blanket. She was grey; her legs had swollen like bolsters, her scalp was nearly bald. She'd lost her eyebrows and her eyelashes, which gave her sightless eyes a horrible eggy look. Her chin bristled with enough hair to wipe farm boots clean.

Liir could hardly put this collaboration of bones and muscles and foul odors together with his childhood memories of meeting Nastoya the day or two after Elphaba had died. He didn't try. The Princess was beyond language, groaning and leaning into a screw of physical pain that seemed to implicate the entire orchard. He could never apologize for having abandoned his promise to her for so long. Neither could she speak whatever message she'd had for him. It was too late now.

Lord Ottokos retained his composure. He spoke to her about every shift of limb and placement of pillow. Unsuccessfully he tried to dribble some water into her mouth, but even at this late moment he was afraid he might drown her before she could be divided from her disguise. She would have to go to her death, if this worked, thirsty.

She was prostrate on the ground, her head rolled back, giving her chin some prominence for perhaps the first time in a decade.

"We're ready," said Ottokos. He stood with a gnarled old staff, a bit of sourwood into which iron thorns had been pounded. It looked like a mace of some sort, a scepter, and Lord Ottokos was ready to assume the leadership of the tribe.

Liir nodded at Candle, who had come equipped with an old milking stool. She sat down clumsily. Her legs went wide, but there wasn't enough lap on which to hold her instrument. She had to balance it on an overturned washtub. Still, she looked at Princess Nastoya with a complicated expression, and presently she began to play.

The others in the company had not been invited, but they lined the edge of the orchard, knuckles locked, a Scrow position of reverence. The Goose stood near Liir, a foot or two back, both deferential and significant. It wasn't clear if he was Liir's familiar, or if Liir was his interpreter.

Candle began by dissecting chords and distending them into arpeggios. She chose the lighter modalities at first, but quickly shifted into more subtle variations. The Princess was uncomfortable on the ground, and her blankets were already getting soaked in the snow.

"To grow a death," murmured Liir, holding Candle's shoulders, "you must plant a life."

She shook him off. He began to walk the perimeter of the orchard, trying to see from different angles. Was there something more he could do? He should be doing? Candle was hard at work, and no doubt Princess Nastoya was doing her own, but was more help needed, in this mission of nothing but mercy?

One stretch of the orchard. Another.

"Liir," whispered Candle as he neared her. "I am very uncomfortable here. It is not like six months ago. I can't keep this up for long."

She rotated the instrument a quarter turn and splayed her fingers, cocking them laterally, and she flat-struck the alto quarter, trying a sprigged quadrille, a dance of spring.

The third side of the orchard. Iskinaary wandered over as if at an evening reception honoring the recent work of a well-regarded painter. "You might try concentrating on the past," he said.

"I don't know her past," said Liir. "I don't know a thing about it, except that she knew Elphaba."

"I don't mean her past," said Iskinaary. "She knows her own past well enough, somewhere in there. I mean the others. Even in death, we are a society, after all."

Liir turned and looked at the Scrow, standing a distance away, but then he saw what Iskinaary meant. It wasn't anything the living could do—it was the human dead who were best equipped to call the human disguise off Nastoya. They could beckon it forward, if Candle could play the scraped faces to sing.

But the playing was her talent, and the singing was theirs—it was his job to listen. To witness their histories, and cherish them in memory, his only talent. He had looked into the Witch's crystal ball, after all, and had seen her past, even if it had nothing to do with him. He had stumbled upon his own reveries without benefit of any gazing globe. Maybe his only job was to listen. That much he could do.

✦ **6** ✦

I WAS THE FOURTH OF FIVE CHILDREN, and I loved the way sun warmed stone. Just before lunch, on the flagstones of the terrace, I used to dance barefoot with my mother for she loved it too.

I was happy enough in my marriage, and happier still when I was widowed, though happiness seems incidental to a good life.

I never wanted to take the cane my father gave me, and I picked it up and broke his nose with it, and he laughed so hard he fell into the well.

I made things with colored threads, little birds and such.

I always wanted to go to university at Shiz, as some of my friends would do, but boys like me weren't allowed.

I believed in the Unnamed God and accepted the mission set me because God would take care of everything: the Emperor said so.

I once took off all my clothes and rolled in a field of ferns, and had an experience I never told anyone about.

I was at the ceremony in Center Munch when the cyclone dropped the house on Nessarose, and I saw it with my own eyes, but I lost my ribbon on the way home.

I loved how milk tastes, and the way hills go blue with cloud markings, and my baby sister, her hair black as a beetle brush.

I loved it when I was alive.

I loved it when I was alive, too.

Forget us, forget us all, it makes no difference now, but don't forget that we loved it when we were alive.

LIIR HEARD SOMETHING from each hoop. Every face sang as Candle provided accompaniment. The bud-notched trees shook with the force of their voices, though there were no tongues, and little enough left of lips, and no wind to pass through the aperture and turn their mouths into flutes.

Reminded of human life, the corporeal part of Princess Nastoya melted into the snow. All that was left of her human disguise shook off—a spin of charcoal smoke, smudged in the air like incense. It stood, finding its feet, before it dispersed, and the voices fell silent.

There was nothing left on the blanket but a massive She-Elephant. The Scrow all closed their eyes and began to weep. Her eyes opened and her head rolled back. Her eyes met Liir's for an instant. Her neck snapped.

No Place Like It

AFTER AN HOUR, Lord Ottokos indicated that a surgeon should come forward with a saw. The small bowl-stomached woman went to work at the Elephant's right tusk and removed it in just a few minutes. Then she sawed an inch of disc off the wider end. The tusk being hollow at the wide end, the disc formed a ring with an aperture several fingers wide. The surgeon fitted this on the point of the other end of the tusk, and handed the relic to Ottokos.

He bowed and accepted it. In turn he fastened it to the staff he had prepared. When finished, the staff was a six-foot stake crowned by an arched prong of Elephant tusk, an ivory smile without a face around it.

"I will lead under the influence of Nastoya," he said in a quiet voice, and this calmed the Scrow from their weeping.

What influence is that, thought Liir; a shard of bone, a makeshift totem?

That, and memory. Maybe all the influence needed.

THE SCROW HAD lived so long under the leadership of Princess Nastoya that they hardly knew what to do when she was gone. With effort, everyone tugging at once, they managed to get her body onto the cart that had brought Candle and Liir to Apple Press Farm. Then they began the long trudge back to their tribal homeland. They would burn her on a pyre when they arrived, and the scraped faces besides, and not a moment too soon. Nastoya had never smelled very fine while alive, and now she was a health hazard as well.

Lord Ottokos insisted Liir should accompany them through Kumbricia's Pass in case the Scrow delegation met up with the Yunamata, and trouble flared. "It's the last thing you can do for Princess Nastoya, finishing the task she asked of you back when the Witch first died," he said. "See her bones to safety, anyway."

Liir decided to leave the broom and the cape behind. He wouldn't fly while in the company of the Scrow, and after departing from them, he mightn't be able to fly back, anyway. Kumbricia's Pass had been resistant to his flying above it.

After packing the hooped faces alongside Nastoya's carcass, Liir bade Candle and Iskinaary a quick good-bye. "Mind each other," he said. "Iskinaary, keep watch."

"I can watch over myself," said Candle. "You forget I can read the present."

"Can you read what is in my heart?" he asked. If so, tell me what it is, he continued to himself. Tell me, so I can tell you back.

Candle held his hands but wouldn't meet his eyes. Perhaps, the nearer the baby was to birth, the more she despaired of ever having said it was his. Would he ever be able to map any part of her mystery?

He set out once more, with a sense that his life would be rich in setting outs, and perhaps poorer in homecomings.

THERE PROVED LITTLE DRAMA on the high ground. One evening the Yunamata materialized out of nothing, naked as Birds, painted in tribal markings. They approached the corpse of Princess Nastoya, carrying the lighted roots of hagtooth bush that they used in their own funeral rites. They sang, and melted away again in rather unseemly haste.

At the final gorge, where the Conference of the Birds had departed for its circuit around western Oz, Liir said a quick and perfunctory good-bye to Lord Shem, Prince Ottokos, and turned home with a heavy heart.

The accomplishments of the last six months had been irrelevant, he decided, for all but Nastoya. Was that the only accomplishment that mattered?—that somehow you not bungle your own death? Everything else that had happened in his short adult life had been frothy and mean-ingless, ultimately. Passionate, yes—yes, that, indeed. Passionately felt, but without shapeliness or worthy outcome.

The dragons were dead: some people were still walking about, igno-rant of how their tired lives might otherwise have ended up with a scraping. That much was good. Stack that up against the cursed lives of those Quadlings who daily had to remember their own dead, lost at the burning of the bridge at Bengda. The bit of thatch falling, a letter in the air, flaming and drowning.

And doubtless there were still disconsolate prisoners in Southstairs, and misguided soldiers in barracks, and those abject poor who had sur-vived the cleaning out of Dirt Boulevard. And that kid named Tip, whose granny had probably sold him already for a better brand of cow, a broom, a new pot for the hearth.

To be sure, the airborne Conference of the Birds—a great show, if nothing else. But what did it mean? Where did it get anyone? For all Liir knew, that juvenile spectacle would give the Emperor better leverage to draft additional soldiers, to tax for newer weapons, to dictate for more control over the crown city of Oz. A flying witch made out of birds! In another generation that would have been called pleasure faithism: as if spectacle itself could convince one of anything.

Yet the world was a spectacle, its own old argument for itself. End-lessly expounded with every new articulation of leaf and limb, laugh and lamb, loaf and loam. Surely there was *something* in the world lovely enough to counter the dread of being alone, a solitary figure untroubled by ambition, unfettered by talent, uncertain of a damn thing?

The great force of evil? Shell, Emperor Quake-in-your-Boots, nam-ing himself the Spear of the Unnamed God? Or the next despot, or the one after that?

The colossal might of wickedness, he thought: how we love to locate it massively elsewhere. But so much of it comes down to what each one of us does between breakfast and bedtime.

Remembering Princess Nastoya, he thought: *Sever us from our disguises.* Then he flinched, almost in disgust: was that a prayer?

How he wished the Elephant Princess had been able to deliver whatever message that Sister Apothecaire had advertised she had for him. Another slim hope dashed, so many slim hopes waiting to rise in its wake.

A message about Nor, and the word on the street. Could Princess Nastoya, with her massive ears, actually have learned Nor's whereabouts? Surely she'd have found a way to tell him?

Nor, lovely Nor, wherever she was. He didn't know where, he might never know, except she was in his memory—like everyone else. There, and drawn on the piece of paper secreted into the inner pocket of the Witch's cape. He saw it in his mind's eye, clear as day, the drawing, the coffee-colored wash suggesting the gleaming highlights of preadolescent, perfect skin, the letters written in Nor's peculiar, crabbed printing.

It was as if the burning letter had spelled something, suddenly, just before it was quenched in black water. The thought came like a spasm, and he harvested it before it disappeared. He unpacked the Princess Nastoya's promised gift.

The word on the street. *Elphaba Lives!*

Nor's handwriting.

WHEN HE GOT BACK to the farm a little after dusk, perhaps a week later, he knew at once that it was deserted. One knows those things about an old farmstead. Iskinaary was gone, and the donkey, and the hens had scattered. For a minute he wondered if Trism had come back for Candle, and now—angry at Liir for his quizzical ways, or herself taken with handsome Trism—she'd changed her mind, and cast her lot with him.

Or perhaps Trism's warning had been accurate, and Commander Cherrystone and his band had found Apple Press Farm at last. Found a way to avenge the slaughter of the dragons.

It mattered, and would matter more tomorrow. For now, he was alone, as before. As usual. It was a condition he'd need to get used to, or to tolerate never getting used to—not exactly the same thing, more's the pity.

He walked through the house. Her domingon was gone, which suggested deliberation, but the dishes were unwiped, still crusty with porridge, which suggested haste. Had she taken the broom? No, there it was, put up on the mantelpiece out of harm's way.

He built up a small fire in the kitchen to take the edge off the chill. There was precious little with which to make a meal. As he stood trying to think, though, he heard a barracking in the boggy land some way south of the farm. Thrashing through underbrush, he found the goat hidden in thickets, tied to a tree, sorely in need of milking, and cross as blazes.

He led it back to the barn, and milked it in the shadows of the broken press, glad he had learned one skill at least.

Then, in the dark corner of the stair hall where they left the trash for tipping into the dump beyond the orchard, he nearly tripped over the Witch's cape. He picked it up to shake it out and hang it on a hook, and the lump of dead matter rolled off the hem into the corner.

Oh, oh oh oh. So this was it. The baby had come, come early, he guessed; he didn't know all that much about the calendar as it pertained to babies. It must have come too soon, and it had been dead on arrival, or it had died at once. And Candle had been alone, poor thing—alone but for that vainglorious Goose. How misguided that Liir should have felt the need to honor the corpse of Nastoya and leave Candle to face a possible childbirth or a stillbirth alone, with only a silly Goose to hiss for help.

He had hauled the dead carcass of an Elephant across the mountains on a cart; he had tried to hear the testimonies of people who had had their faces scraped. He had murdered dragons and people. He could bear to touch the small corpse of a human child.

So he picked it up. He held it at a distance. Tears started, though why? He hadn't believed this was his child, and there was no new reason to believe it now. It was just another child, just another inevitable fatality, the next crude accident of the world, and not the last.

He maneuvered its cold form closer. Cold, though not icy; this death had to have just happened. Had the scraped faces sung the fetus to a death, as they'd sung Princess Nastoya?

Maybe the child had been born dead this very morning, as he was making his approach. And a rosy morning it had been, the sun strengthening, and the inane involuntary return of a green blush to the skin of the world. He had even sung a bit of his own. Not his usual way!—he'd yodeled some nonsense syllables, thinking: Maybe it will be all right. Maybe Candle. Maybe Trism. Maybe something will work.

The form was cold. Was it a normal infant size, or smaller? He didn't know human infants. He nestled it against his neck, and thought he felt its mouth move.

Gingerly he stepped from the stair hall into the kitchen. Was it warming up? Or was it just his own heat he felt, reflecting back at him?

In the feeble light of the new fire, he moved it again, shifted it to rest along his forearm. It was a pretty corpse, and now he could see it had been a girl. Its umbilical cord was an unholy mess. Maybe Iskinaary had helped to sever it. It didn't bear thinking about.

The corpse twitched and cried, and stretched a little. He wrapped it from stem to stern, forehead to toes, making sure its dab of a nose had access to air. Then he carried it closer to the fire, in case corpses liked to be a little warm before they were fed milk.

Elphaba had kept a basket rocking at her feet, once: a basket was just the thing. Was there an old onion basket somewhere in the keeping-room belowstairs? He'd find a basket.

He found a basket.

He fed her by dripping goat's milk through a cheesecloth into her pursing mouth. She took the false sucket well enough. She had Candle's Quadling face, already: those beautiful rhomboids that made such splendid cheekbones.

Of course Candle would flee, if she'd given birth to a child and thought it had died. Imagine the panic. Of course she would. Maybe she'd go back to the mauntery, as the Superior Maunt had suspected she would. At least for a time: to recover herself. What an ordeal she'd had. The lonely pregnancy, the lonely delivery, and then—whatever it was that had happened with Trism. And all of Liir's absences. Of course she would flee.

She might come back. She might.

He sat with the infant most of the night. For a while he spread out the cape and even managed to sleep a little—he kept her in the basket, though, so he wouldn't roll over onto her by accident and crush her.

In the first black wash of dawn, he woke up comforted with a different thought. Candle could see the present. Perhaps she'd known he was almost home. What if she had fled—what if a guard of Commander Cherrystone's battalion had indeed found the farm, and she'd led them away, diverted their attention? Drawn them off scent? The mother bird pretends to have a broken wing, to lead predators away from her nestlings in the grass. Candle had as much instinct as a mother bird.

So she knew that Liir would be back in time to rescue the girl, give it a burial if needed, feed it if not. She'd hid the goat for him to find.

She wasn't leading danger away from him, but from the baby. She could take care of herself; they didn't want her, after all. But she was relying on Liir to save her baby, whether he believed it was his or not.

Imagining that, anyway, helped him open his eyes.

There was heavy rain in the morning. The light was greyish and mossy with the low clouds. He had to concede that the baby wasn't a corpse, really. She was alive. Maybe she'd been born stone cold. But she was alive now.

Still smeared with her birth blood, and the watery beginning of her little feces. He took her to the doorway and held her up in the warm rain. She cleaned up green.

A LITTLE PATIENCE, and we shall see the reign of witches pass over, their spells dissolve, and the people, recovering their true spirit, restore their government to its true principles.

–Thomas Jefferson, 1798

M̲y mother was a westerne woman
And learned in gramarye

—K. Estmere, 1470,
collected in *Reliques of Ancient English Poetry,* 1765

✦ ACKNOWLEDGMENTS ✦

T HANKS ARE DUE to the team at ReganBooks, starting with Judith Regan and including Cassie Jones, Paul Olsewski, and Jennifer Suitor.

Thank you to David Groff, Betty Levin, Andy Newman, and William Reiss for commenting on early drafts of *Son of a Witch*.

Thank you to Haven Kimmel and to Eve Ensler, for encouraging words sent at precisely the right moment.

Thank you to Harriet Barlow, Ben Strader, and the company of Blue Mountain Center, New York.

Thank you, again, to Andy Newman, for defending the ramparts as usual, and to Lori Shelly, for able assistance at every wicked little thing.